ALSO BY MELISSA GOOD

Dar and Kerry Series
Tropical Storm
Hurricane Watch
Eye of the Storm
Red Sky At Morning
Thicker Than Water
Terrors of the High Seas
Tropical Convergence
Stormy Waters
Storm Surge: Book One
Storm Surge: Book Two

Partners

Book One

Melissa Good

Silver Dragon Books
by Regal Crest

Texas

ISBN 978-1-61929-118-8

First Printing 2013

9 8 7 6 5 4 3 2 1

Cover design by Donna Palowski

Published by:

Regal Crest Enterprises, LLC
229 Sheridan Loop
Belton, TX 76513

Find us on the World Wide Web at
http://www.regalcrest.biz

Printed in the United States of America

Author's Notes

A lot of people asked me—why sci-fi? And the truth is I have been a fan and reader of science fiction and fantasy since I was old enough to go to the library and bookstore on my own. Science fiction opens the mind to unlimited possibilities. All of that reading led me to science fiction conventions, which was where I was first exposed to the power of community. So gratifying to learn that if you were a nerdy person, who loved science and the stars, and reading, that there were so many others who were just like you.

They say our young girls in this country are sadly lacking in "STEM"—Science, Technology, Engineering and Math. (I think) I got my introduction to three of the four from those books with the little rocket ships on the spine and I took that introduction and it shaped how I thought and what I did to this very day.

~Melissa Good

This book is dedicated to the North Miami Beach public library, which had to deal with my checking out and occasionally returning most of their collection of science fiction books.

Chapter One

HANDS GRABBED HER and she twisted, pulling against straps that kept her flat on her back. She wrenched her arms to pull them free to fight, her jaw clamping down hard. She shook her head violently, pulling it free from fingers digging for her eye sockets.

It was dark. It was loud. She heard screams and explosions. Nearby there was laughter, and then the hot agony as a knife plunged into her back and she arched away from it.

An ankle came free and she twisted more violently, lifting her knee up and kicking out against the hands holding her down.

"Jess!"

She heard her name. She tried to open her mouth to answer but there was a gag in it. She growled in anger and frustration.

"Jess!"

The voice was suddenly louder and she felt a sting on her arm. A breath after that the darkness mottled and faded and the screams muted. She was out of the dream.

It was light, and quiet, and the air was full of the shockingly familiar scent of home.

"Jess."

Hands on her shoulders, shaking her. Her body free. Her back laying on a soft, conforming surface.

She opened her eyes to see a familiar face over her, a medic just behind him, pulling an injector back away from her.

Coiled muscles relaxed and she felt a wash of heat, then chill, across the back of her neck as the tranq kicked in.

The echoes of laughter faded away and the sounds of the citadel surrounded her. She blinked, finding the familiarity of the base on all sides, and no enemies anywhere to be seen. "Sorry, Stephan," she whispered, feeling pain in her throat from what she figured were screams. "Damn it."

"It's okay." Stephan Bock rested his forearms on his knee. "You all right?"

She lifted a hand and rubbed her temples. "Fantastic." She hiked herself up on the bed and peered around, seeing the muted activity of late watch past the open door of her quarters. Slowly the tension left her and she exhaled, willing herself calm.

"You might want to let Dustin here give you a knockout," Stephan said. "Got a while before first watch."

Jess shook her head. "I'm all right. Just another damn stupid ass dream."

"Okay." Stephan stood up. He waved the medic out, then waited for the door to close before he turned back to Jess. "Listen, I know it's tough."

"Yeah. Too bad they don't have a wipe for this that's worth a damn. I'd take it." She sat up and swung her legs over the edge of the bed, resting her elbows on her bare knees.

Stephan sat back down on the padded stool near the bed. "Thought you were against re-patterning," He said. "Weren't you the one who told me only cowards try to deal with their problems that way?"

Jess cleared her throat and looked away from him. "I was. Then I was knifed in the back by my partner and watched my whole team be butchered in front of me. Changes your perspective." Her gaze flicked up to his face, fastened on it. "I know what you're going to tell me, Stephan. Get over it."

He grunted. "You do need to. Not that I don't." He paused. "Jess, I'm not going to sit here and tell you I know how you feel, 'cause I don't. Nothing like that ever happened to me." He shifted. "Hasn't happened to anyone before, that I know of."

"Great. Another first for the Drake family." Jess's face twitched. "Eleven generations in service, always trying to be at the forefront of something." She straightened up and ran her fingers through the dark, straight hair that fell to her shoulders.

"Well, that's the point." Stephan cleared his throat. "As much as we're bred for anything these days, you were bred for this. Just like I was. Just like Mike, Elaine, and Sandy were. You've got a tough mind. You can get past it."

"Sure," Jess said. "Just take a little time."

Stephan nodded. "Good to hear." He stood and patted her on the shoulder. "Get some rest. We'll talk in the morning. I've got some ideas on getting you re-partnered. Maybe it'll help."

Jess merely nodded.

"Okay." Stephan turned and made his way to the door, unlocking it with a palm press and letting it shut behind him.

JESS WAITED UNTIL she was sure the door was going to stay shut. Then she pushed herself to her feet and walked across the soft gray carpet into the sanitary unit, ignoring her too pale reflection in the mirror as she let icy cold water run in the sink and splashed some on her face.

She was tired, but not sleepy, not having any desire to return to the dream world they'd pulled her out of, nor wanting to trigger another visit from the medic. She leaned her hands on the sink and stared at the gray surface, resisting the urge to throw up.

Primitive. She pushed away and went back into the space she'd called home for all the years of her adulthood, a free-form two level room that had her bed and storage space on one side and a curved workspace on the other with a comfortable chair behind it.

On the second level, in the loft, was a small space for relaxing and meditation with cabinets that held her personal gear.

All in shades of gray, blue and sea green, with indirect lighting that lent the space a sense of calm and peace and an almost luxurious feel she was due as the ops agent she was. Jess went to her desk chair and sat down, the surface feeling cool against the back of her thighs and her tank top clad shoulders.

She stared at the door to the left of the exit. It opened into a mirror image of the room she was in, where until her last mission Joshua had lived.

Joshua.

Her outsider partner, with his curly red hair and bright, friendly smile. They'd clicked right off, had the same interests, even liked the same music. Jess often wondered if they'd selected for that when they paired them, but she really hadn't cared. She'd just been glad they'd bonded. And because he'd been carefully selected and undergone the training, she'd trusted him.

Trusted the competence of the board and the professionals whose job it was to carefully pick the teams and vet the outsider applicants. Trusted that when you were on an emplacement, you knew the people at your back were your family and without doubt.

Joshua had fooled everyone. In his tenth emplacement with Jess, he'd turned and literally knifed her, after sounding the alarm and bringing the guards from the detention center they'd penetrated down on top of them.

She'd watched as they cut the rest of the team to pieces. She would have gone the same way, except they misjudged her strength just a fraction. Just a little. Just enough for her to get loose and free a hand, triggering the embedded recall chip just under her breastbone—just enough to get her hands on a gun and let her bone deep training take over.

Then the screams had been theirs. The last being Joshua's as he came into her sights and she blew his brains right out of his head with the heavy projectiles, scattering bone chips and blood all over the room.

She spent a moment reliving it now in her conscious mind. They'd given her a commendation for it, but that hadn't erased the shame and horror, and the sense of deep betrayal she wasn't sure there was any getting over.

There would be no re-partnering for her. No one would live on the other side of that door, standing at her back, ready to put a blade into it.

No way.

"DOCTOR?"

RANDALL DOSS looked up and saw the proctor standing in the doorway. "Yes?"

The tall, brown haired proctor entered. "Here's the report you asked for." He handed over a chip. "And one of the directors of Interforce is here and wishes to speak to you."

"Interforce? What does he want? Is there some problem with the last set we sent them?"

"I don't know, sir," the proctor said. "It's Commander Bricker. He's waiting in your office."

Doss frowned. "Very well." He got up from the tall chair he'd been huddled in, reviewing the digital scoping system. "I'll go talk to him now. I certainly hope there wasn't any mistake." He tugged his work tunic straight and hurried out of the lab, turning right and moving along one of the curving, well lit corridors of the crèche.

He passed through a steady stream of similarly clad men and women, most with digital pads strapped to their arms and comm buds blinking in their ears. They moved in abstract distraction, only honed peripheral vision letting them proceed without collision.

He reached the grav tube and triggered it, waiting for it to open then stepped into the column of gravity, giving the little hop that started him downward along the curve. He turned and looked out as he dropped, admiring for the nth time the curve of the earth below him, and the deliciously crisp blackness of space beyond.

At the bottom level he triggered the exit and pushed himself into the hallway, regaining normal gravity in the faint bunny hop typical to the crèche and the other stations in orbit. Another few minutes walking and he was at his office, giving his attendant a wave as he passed. "Hear I have a visitor, Gigi."

"Sir you do," The pretty young woman behind the console said. She had wavy brown hair and almond colored eyes, along with a delicately circuit traced collar around her neck. "May I bring you tea?"

"Please, and for my guest as well." Doss tugged his tunic straight again and then palmed his door open, revealing his half circle office with it's twin bubble windows giving a gorgeous view of the stars.

A tall man in a formal uniform was standing near the first bubble, looking out.

"Commander...ah...Bricker? They said you wish to see me?" Doss waved the door closed behind him. "What can we do for you?"

Commander Bricker turned to face him. He had iron gray hair, closely cropped to his head, and a neatly trimmed beard and mustache that didn't quite hide a plasma scar across one side of his face. "Doctor." He had a low, burring voice. "I have a problem I need you to solve for me."

"Oh?" Doss felt a little anxiety subside. He went to his desk and sat down behind it. "Anything we can do for Interforce," he said. "Please do sit down. My assistant is bringing us some tea."

Commander Bricker sat down. "You provide us with resources."

Doctor Doss nodded after a pause. "We provide you with biological alternative units. For many purposes. I believe you have our service units and recently we provided you with some higher end samples, for low space jet plane piloting."

"Yes."

There was a small silence. "They have been satisfactory?" Doss finally asked. "There's no trouble with them is there? Our programming schemas are very stringent."

"They're fine." Bricker paused, as the door opened and Gigi entered with a tray. He watched the young woman as she expertly poured the tea and served them. She was wearing a sedate sea green station uniform and space boots, and her well formed body was both graceful and assured as she bowed to him. "Thank you."

"Sir." Gigi straightened and picked up the tray, then left, closing the door behind her.

"New model." Doss indicated the now closed door. "That's a G-G 3200. We're enhancing our basic service module with some entry level tech programming."

Bricker nodded. "So you're experimenting with mixing some of the genotypes. That's good. It bears on the problem we want you to solve for us." He sipped his tea. "To state it plainly, doctor, we need you to develop an advanced design for us, but we don't have time for you to do it from scratch."

"I see."

"I need a bio alt I can put in the field as an operative agent. Military."

Doss straightened up, his eyes wide with surprise.

"I know," Bricker said. "We've told you a dozen times you can't make a model that will have the independent decision making that's required. I still believe that."

"But—"

Bricker lifted his hand to cut him off. "But my problem is this. We had a failure of process. I can't go into the details. But the result is, we don't have confidence in a certain process right now and we have an urgent need for an operative."

Doss stared at him. "Director," he said. "We can do a lot. But this is...these are still biological organisms we're dealing with. They're not machines. They're human beings."

"Legally, no they aren't."

Doss lifted a hand, much as Bricker had done a moment ago. "Legally, no. But from a scientific viewpoint, they are. Regardless of what our society considers them."

"Regardless of how we pretend to ourselves you're not creating slaves, yes," Bricker assented, in a dry tone. "Let's not split hairs."

Doss's shoulders twitched at the blunt rudeness. "In any case, we don't snap our fingers and create a program set just like that," he said. "There are physical, as well as mental structures to consider."

"I know that."

"The models we have in production right now are geared to be assistants, to serve, to provide a helpmate. They're not soldiers. They're certainly not capable of putting on a uniform and going into battle."

"Anyone can be taught to kill," Bricker replied. "You may not believe that, but I've been in this business a very very long time, doctor, and you'll just have to take that on faith from me." He sipped his tea again.

"But as it happens—the operative I need is not required to do that. They need to be a tech, and above all, they need to be absolutely trusted."

"A tech," Doss mused. "Hm."

"Think of it as a possible new line of business," Bricker said with an expressionless face. "If this works out, we could perhaps offer you a deal to supply us with this resource ongoing. It would relieve us of a certain responsibility.

Doss licked his lips. "Well," he murmured. "Certainly we would love to be able to continue our business relationship, enhance it, as it were."

"I have to tell you this is not a popular decision of mine," Bricker said. "Many people think it can't be done."

Doss folded his hands on his desk. "Director, given time, money and talent nothing is impossible." He watched the man smile grimly. "But as it happens, there might be a resource I—well, perhaps we could do some modifications. "

Bricker nodded. "When? The need is urgent, as I said. There is a risk."

Doss was already running the calculations. If it didn't work, he could always say he'd told them so. "Two weeks," he said. "And I'll need to know the exact requirement, including any imprinting."

Bricker's smile widened slightly. "That can be arranged." He lifted his cup. "Got any more of this? We don't get it much downside."

Doss leaned toward his comm unit. "Gigi?"

"Sir."

"First, please bring us some more tea, and then, go to the crèche master and tell him I need to see him. I don't want to disturb him if he's programming by calling."

"Sir."

"Tell him to come to my office when he's available, and to bring the NM-Dev-1 unit with him."

"Yes, sir."

Doss sat back and took a sip of his own tea, swirling the delicate beverage in his mouth before he swallowed it. "The programming could be complex," he said. "We'll have to put a lot of resources into meeting your timeline."

"We'll make it worth your while." Bricker smiled now, with feral completeness. "You can be sure of that, doctor. Cost isn't a concern for us at this moment."

Now Doss smiled, tapping the toes of his space boots together under the desk. "Given that, we'll find the time and talent, director. You know that's how that goes." He lifted his tea cup and Bricker mimicked the motion, as the station rotation moved them into the light and the windows automatically filtered the glare.

"To success, doctor. For both of us."

A SOFT KNOCK came on the top of her helmet. NM-Dev-1 put the program on hold and ducked out from under it, blinking a little to bring her eyes back into normal focus. "Hello, proctor," she said, surprised to see him there.

"Hello, Dev." The proctor sat down next to her. "How are you?"

Dev quickly arranged herself on the bench, sitting up straight and tucking her boots under her. "Doing well, proctor. I finished the first advanced program and I'm looking at the second one now."

"Great." The proctor shifted his body a little and looked at her. "Dev, I came to talk to you because the administrator has asked me to bring you to his office. He wants to speak with you."

She watched his face, seeing the tension there. "Did I do something incorrect?"

"No," he answered immediately. "You didn't do anything wrong, Dev. It's just that some people have come to us and asked us to do a special job for them and the administrator thinks maybe you can do that job."

Dev was momentarily silent. "I'm getting assigned?" She asked, with a small intake of breath. "Really?" Her eyes brightened.

The proctor's brow tensed. "Well." He shifted again, clearly uncomfortable. "These people—they want us to give you some special programs. Then we'll see if you can do what they want."

"Oh," Dev murmured. "Is it hard?"

"It might be. It's not like anything you've done before. But we've tried to give you things that stretch your abilities and this will be something like that again." He watched the young bio alt in front of him, seeing the thoughtful look on her face.

He had his doubts. NM-Dev-1, though an experimental prototype that the name indicated, was not a type he would have ever considered for something as radical as this. She was a little below medium height, and slender, with a pleasant, friendly face and sandy colored hair currently pulled back in a holder.

Though she'd had the usual physical training, she didn't look anything like what he supposed an Interforce soldier should look like, and the idea of her in those stark, gray surroundings made him rather uncomfortable.

He liked Dev. As much as one could like a bio alt. She was good natured and relatively clever, able to hold a conversation and even come up with an idea or two of her own once in a while. She smiled a lot, and was always eager to learn new things.

"Will I go somewhere?" Dev asked, unexpectedly. "I mean, out of the crèche?"

"Yes. You'll need to go downside," the proctor said. "Are you ready to come talk to the administrator? He'll tell you more about what you're going to do." He stood up. "When he's done, I'll take you to the programming center so they can start giving you the programs you'll need."

Dev felt a little apprehensive. "Will you tell me what the programs are?"

The proctor put a hand on her shoulder. "I think it'll be better for you if you just take them, Dev. Not think about it too much before you go." He released her. "Let's go now. The administrator is waiting."

Dev followed along as he turned and started toward the big central grav stack. At this time of the shift it was filling with techs and minders heading to quarters, and at the outside edges, bio alts assigned to the station making their way to the dorms.

Dev really didn't know what was going to happen. The thought of being assigned made her happy, but the look on the proctor's face, and the way he'd spoken made her think there was something wrong with this assignment, at least to him.

They left the tube and walked along the outside corridor of the station, the transparent walls giving a full view of the earth orbit they were in. Dev smiled a little at the stars, and let them distract her as she traced their patterns in their endlessly fascinating variations.

It almost made the walk too short. She followed the proctor, though, as he turned inside a doorway and put his palm to a lock, waiting for the door to slide open then gesturing her inside.

Restricted zone. Dev had never been inside it. At the very end was a taller more impressive door, and that's where the proctor led her.

They stood inside the entrance. "Gigi, can you tell Doctor Doss we're here?"

"Sir." Gigi pressed a button, looking up and exchanging the briefest of nods with Dev.

Dev was familiar with Gigi from the crèche. They were both something of an experimental set, though Dev's programming had started out from the beginning to be advanced while Gigi's added skills had been a recent development.

The door in front of them opened and she followed the proctor in. The administrator's office was very large, and it had pretty white and blue carpet and a lot of clear glass ornaments. Dev turned around and stared at it for a moment, amazed by the tall ceilings, and the sense of light and air.

"Well, hello there NM-Dev-1."

Dev turned and looked at the administrator. "Hello, sir." He still had his lab overlay on, and with his curly hair in constant disarray he never seemed that threatening.

Another man was there, a tall, gray man and he was watching her. She looked at him, and saw the crease in his face, and the uniform. He was looking very intently at her and she felt like moving away from him.

Dev felt a little fear. Was this who she was going to be assigned to?

"This is Commander Bricker, of Interforce," Doctor Doss said. "Do you know what that is, Dev? Have you had that program?"

"Yes, sir, I do."

"Good," he said. "So you know how important Interforce is, right? They protect us from all the people who are trying to hurt us, don't they."

"Yes, sir," Dev said. "They're very brave."

Bricker produced a faint smile.

"That's right," Doss said. "Well, Dev, we have a wonderful opportunity to help Commander Bricker and all those brave people. They have a job, a tech job, and they came to us to see if we could help them, if we had someone who could do that job."

"To go there, sir? To Interforce?"

"Yes," Doss said. "They need our help."

"Sir." Dev felt her breathing go a little faster. She was afraid, and she wasn't. "I don't know how to be brave."

That got another brief smile from Bricker. "We can teach you that," he said, his low, burring voice tickling her ears. "If you have the heart for it."

Dev looked at him and their eyes met. Again, she was afraid—and not—because she could see something real there, something interesting and complex that reminded her a little of some of her history lessons. Some of the people she'd seen there. "Sir."

"We have some programs to give you, Dev, that will help you learn what to do, so you can help Commander Bricker," he said. "I want you to go with the proctor and get started. We don't have a lot of time. They need you very badly."

"Sir," Dev replied. "I'll do the best I can."

Doss smiled at her, a real smile. "I know you will." He gave the proctor a nod. "Robin, you know what to do. Let's get started."

"Right away, sir." The proctor touched Dev's shoulder. "Let's go, Dev. You've got lots to learn." He guided her out of the office and the door slid shut behind them.

DEV SAT IN the programming room, her legs dangling over the side of the body shaped couch. The sensor grid was cocked and in place over the head of it, and across the room the tech was busy setting up the boards.

It was a quiet chamber. The walls were dimly lit and a soft green color, and the light in the room was a soothing light amber. She knew it was designed to make her relax, but even knowing that, she felt her stomach in knots and her mouth dry as a paper.

She'd been in here many times before, of course. Here, or in one of the many chambers like it on this level where she'd gotten her basic, and then advanced skill programming over the years. It was in this chamber, in fact, that she'd gotten her first tech programming skill, waking to a delight of knowledge she'd run right to the sim lab and explored.

This, though, was different.

"Lie down, please," the tech instructed. "The programmer is coming in. "

Dev took a deep breath and swiveled her body, putting her feet up on the gentle slope and her head down under the sensor grid. She watched as it slowly descended, the nodes settling over her head in familiar spots.

She felt the faint twitch as they synced and she took a breath and released it, forcing her hands to relax on the soft surface as the tech came over and adjusted the couch a little.

He had a digital pad on his arm. "Biological Alternative, set 0202-164812, instance NM-Dev-1?"

"Yes," Dev said. "That's me."

The tech nodded. "Okay, just relax for me please. I'm going to test the grid. It might tickle."

Dev closed her eyes and immediately felt the faint twitchy/tickling sensation as the grid came live, sending testing pulses through her head. A flare of colored light behind her eyes, the scent of fruit, the sound of a gong, all without anything audible or truly visible. "Blue, apple, bell," She said, after they'd died down.

"Excellent." The tech patted her arm. Then he wrapped a sensor around her wrist, and gently tapped the center of her forehead. "Go down for me please. Let the system take over. Let go."

And having no choice, Dev did. She felt a weight lift off her chest and she focused on the soft echoes of the gong, still chiming in her mind, the chimes now coming in the pattern of her heartbeat.

Deeper. Slower.

She was down.

The tech consulted a reading, watching the face under the grid of sensors relax and go still, the slim and toned body easing into compliance, hands uncurling, fingers easing out.

He adjusted a few settings, half turning as the door opened behind him. "She's down."

The programmer settled behind the console. "Thanks," he said with a sigh. "Damned last minute admin crap." He settled his hands on the controls and reviewed the display, eyes flicking back and forth in absorption. "Wow," he said, after a minute. "Didn't expect to see this."

The tech trotted around and looked over his shoulder. "That's military," he said, flatly. "I've seen stuff like that in the pilot set."

The programmer nodded. "Yeah, this one's being sent to Interforce." He perked up. "Hey, maybe they're finally figuring out just how useful these guys are to them. Could be a big new contract."

"But on her model?" The tech pointed. "Gonna cute them to death?"

"Tech." The programmer started to work, setting parameters. "All tech side. This is a lot though. Hope she can handle it." He picked up a sensor helmet and put it on, adjusting the leads with expert hands. "Okay, stand by."

The tech went to the monitoring station and settled in, adjusting the monitors to watch the steady biological readouts. "She's good."

Chapter Two

"ARE YOU OUT of your cotton picking mind?" Stephan Bock stared at Commander Bricker seated in the big chair at the head of the table. "John? Are you nuts?"

Bricker let his hands rest on the table, folded together. "You never really lost that archaic language, did you?" He said. "Nuts. Cotton." He flexed his fingers. "I guess hydroponic pod and tartex don't have the same ring."

"John."

Bricker leaned back and studied his old friend. "Stephan, the options here are very limited. We have a problem."

"Yes, we have a problem, but solving a problem with pointless insanity's never been your game play." Bock said. "A bio alt? Why don't you just suggest we put a lab rat in as a field partner. It'd be cuter, and probably have a better chance at making an independent decision."

"You told me you have a trust problem," Bricker said in a calm voice. "You told me you not only have an ops agent refusing to accept a new tech, you have an entire ops group having issues with emplacements since they don't trust the people with them."

"Yes, but— "

"Yes, but nothing." Bricker stood up. "You know how it is with us, Stephan. How small the pool of ops agents is. What do we have, a thousand, tops? In the whole of Atlantia?"

"Nine hundred ninety seven," Bock stated quietly. "That skill set doesn't come up so much anymore."

"Exactly. So—they need to be teamed with a tech skill set, and the only place that comes from is outside," Bricker said. "We take what applicants we have, and we vet them hard."

"Not hard enough." Bock's voice was bitter. "We got lucky nature slaughtered nurture that time."

Bricker sighed. "My point is, we have to take what we can get. You can't force someone into the corps. Much as everyone believes otherwise."

Bock grunted. "Pool's getting shallower," he admitted. "Not enough diversity."

"So, there it is." Bricker stood up and paced. "We have a gene pool that's pathetically restricted, and no resources to support unrestricted breeding. We might even be past the point of no return anyway. We agreed?"

Bock grunted again.

"So." Bricker turned and leaned his knuckles on the table. "We can't afford to lose the agents we do have, Stephan. They have to be able to trust the people at their back if we want to continue this long, painful fight of ours."

"But bio alts?" Stephan said. "John, they're just big collections of cell structures with basic instructions added. How can you seriously think one of them can even be able to do the most mundane tech tasks in the field?"

"The pilots fly."

Bock waved that off with an impatient hand. "Sure," he said. "They fly, they get from point A to point B, they can land and take care of their machines. But if they run into a drone high up in the gray, they freeze. You know it. We've lost a dozen."

"Training's too basic."

"Their brains are plastic bags full of pixie dust."

"Stephan."

"John, they are. Just because I'm ops, doesn't mean I haven't done the research. I took the classes, remember? So I could direct them?" He stood up now and did his own pacing. "Look, I'm not saying bio alts aren't useful. They are. I don't know what we'd do without them, since they take care of pretty much everything in this place except for operational activities. But they just take instructions and carry out the basics. They don't think for themselves."

Bricker sighed and sat down. "I want to try and see if we can make one think."

"John."

"Your ops agent, the one who won't take a partner? What happens if she can't be convinced?"

Bock dropped into his seat with a grunt.

"Worth a try?"

"Jess won't agree to this," Bock said. "She has no use for bio alts, John. She's from Drakes Bay, remember?"

"We have no use for lone ops agents who refuse orders."

Stephan frowned. "John, that's harsh."

"Life is harsh, in case you hadn't noticed," Bricker retorted, dryly. "We're the fine, thin edge trying to prevent complete collapse of our remaining society and frankly, I don't have time for rebels. So either your prima donna decides to help us with this project, or she can go and spend her days harvesting seaweed."

"What if I don't want to help you. You sending me to rake the beds too? What if I think trying to send a bio alt out with Jess is the same thing as putting her up in front of a lead cannon."

Bricker studied him. "Put your jackassery away for a minute and think about one thing. What if it works?"

"It won't."

"What if it does?" Bricker said. "What if we prove we can have bio alts made that can fill those roles, Stephan? If we take them to another level? If we don't have to rely on the recruiters? What if this crazy idea turns out to mean we survive?"

Bock was silent for a few minutes. "You're serious."

"I am," Bricker said quietly. "Look, this first trial, I know it won't probably work. We took an existing model and threw some heavy tech into it. But I want to see the potential, if we can have one made to order, to our spec, you understand?"

Bock grunted.

"If this one even gets a few baby steps, we can see what the long term could be for us."

"And if it doesn't?"

Bricker shrugged. "Then it's just a failed experiment. We send it back and get it wiped, and we look elsewhere. But at least it gives you something to toss at this ops agent of yours. Maybe it'll be a challenge."

Stephan sighed. Then he lifted a hand and let it fall. "What the hell. Sure. Worst can happen is it won't work. I don't think we can put Jess in the field right now anyway. Psych says she's not fit for it."

"That's the spirit, Bricker said. "Did a good clean up job in all that mess I hear."

Bock nodded. "Took out a whole cell. Killed two dozen including the infiltrator and ID'd the locale for the strike team. Made a very big hole in the ground."

"Impressive," Bricker said. "I can see why you want to keep the op around."

"I do, John. I really do."

Bricker studied him. "I'm really not trying to be a dick, Stephan. I just want us to survive. Know what I mean?"

Bock sighed. "I know. It just seems like it gets harder every damn day."

JESS FELT THE steady patter of rain against her skin as she stood in the sentryway, leaning her elbows on the armored rail and looking out.

The sky, as always, was dark gray, filled with layered clouds and allowing only the filtered, muted light to reach the surface that spread out ahead of her.

Gray and black, dark greens and ochres. The cold wind blew against her face, bringing the smell of brine and damp rock to her nose and she exhaled, absorbing the surroundings of home.

The citadel was built into a granite cliff, protected by the hard, basement rock that surrounded it. At the base of the cliff on one side was the endless span of the sea, it's surge flowing through cut tunnels that generated power, and into caverns where they harvested what the tide brought them.

On the other side, rocky ground interspersed with gravel, and the odd patch of lichen spread as far as the eye could see.

There were no trees or plants, though once there had been. There were no people. It had been generations since homes and buildings were seen anywhere and now you had to look hard to even discern the faint outlines of what had been roads, and the odd lumps of rubble that had been civilization.

It was bleak. But it had been this bleak her whole life, and rather than find it depressing Jess always felt a sense of peace looking out over this vastness of solitude, tucked into a fold of what had been called the Appalachian range, in what long ago was called Pennsylvania.

Here at least it was quiet, and safe, their outpost providing defense for the eastern coastline all the way up to where North Base took over near Quebec.

Once upon a time this had been a place of life and plenty. Back in the day when everyone had argued over the impact of humanity on the planet, and how they could somehow fix the effect they were having on it.

Back in the day, when there had been lifestyles, and money, and religion to argue over. Back when they'd thought humanity ruled the world and it was humanity's decisions that would chart the course of the future.

Everyone thought a disaster would come someday. Almost no one predicted that when it did, humanity would have no part in it, and no control over the results.

One after another, six big volcanos erupted along a crack in the planet's crust. It was simply a matter of physics after that. Debris in the air turned into clouds that blocked the sun, and in turn spawned more clouds, acid rain they couldn't escape, or block, or do anything about.

Horrifically, frighteningly fast, how a food chain can collapse. Plants, forests, animals, cultures, and civilization vanished in the blink of a planetary eye, reducing a fertile world to an almost barren bleakness.

Near constant rain. The shifting earth and melting ice making the oceans rise, and coastlines dissolve until the planet was reshaped into a place of restless seas and lifeless rock and vast extinction.

Almost.

The ten percent of humanity that survived had done so because the one great strength of their species was the ability to adapt, and adapt, and adapt again, finding new ways to live, new resources to exploit, and new patterns to fall into.

And so they survived and learned to live again in a hard world where needs were boiled down to stark essentials.

But they were still human, and conflict was so written into the species that even when so few were left, still, there were sides to be taken. Now the conflict wasn't over ideology or trade, it was over raw resources in a world where access to them meant life or death.

Was there a mind on the other side that had data they needed? They'd go take them. An invention they could exploit? Jess, or someone like her, would be assigned to find a way to locate and retrieve it. Was there someone who, though not useful to them, would give the other side an advantage?

Jess had killed her share of them. There was no sentiment. No compassion. Survival was as raw a master as humanity had ever known.

There could be no open warfare. There were't enough of them for that. They just fought step by step, in close rooms, or dark tunnels, infiltrating labs, and invading systems. Their lives depended on the sea, and on the hydroponic stations high above circling the world—havens of technology and relative plenty—far removed from the bleak, cloud covered world below.

Jess licked a bit of the rain off her lips. It had stopped being deadly to them generations back, as their biology adapted to the new conditions and so to her it tasted sweet. It dampened her hair and the workout suit she was wearing, cooling her body down from the gym session she'd just completed.

Thunder rumbled overhead, and she took heed of the warning, ducking back inside the armored door and keying it shut behind her. It closed with a compressed thump and she walked along the corridor toward the rad center.

She passed the occasional steadily moving figure in the hall, giving the brief nod of acknowledgement the contact required. Just past the major corridor that held the dining hall and rec area, she turned into one of many half rounded doorways.

It opened as her presence registered and closed behind her as she entered. The light inside altered from neutral to a soft twilight that outlined her as she stripped off her workout suit and set it on the cleaning shelf.

Naked, she moved into the rad room and it switched on, bathing her in a deep ultraviolet glow. She sprawled on a transparent, webbed chair, letting the artificial sunlight cover her skin. She touched the work pad on the arm of the chair and called up the ops report.

The one thing they hadn't evolved out of, that need for the touch of the sun they no longer saw. Jess rested her elbow on the chair and propped her chin up with it, relaxing in the glow as she caught up on the events of the day.

Her dream of two days past was finally fading. She'd spent a good restful night last night, and was starting to feel almost normal again. The details of the failed raid were fading, along with the scar on her back from the knife.

The trust hadn't returned though, and Jess was silently gratified when the other ops agents had gone to the top and registered big concerns of their own as to how far they could trust the tech partners they'd been given.

She knew Stephan thought she'd egged them on, and she would have, if they hadn't come up with it on their own. If it happened to her, they reasoned, it could happen to any of them.

And that was true. The techs were all very uncomfortable, sitting together in the dining hall as the agents in residence gathered at their own, and getting faintly concerned and maybe a little suspicious looks from the rest of the citadel staff.

Not fair. Jess readily conceded. Joshua was the first turned in as far back as anyone knew, and there was no real reason to suspect any of the other techs, but they were suspected anyway.

Tough luck for them. Tougher luck for Stephan, who was now having to deal with far more than just her problem.

It was time for him, and for his boss, to put the thumb down on the council, since it was their process that screwed up. Someone should pay for it.

But even as she thought it, Jess knew in her guts the finger pointing would eventually deflect fault right back to them, and their group, and her.

Humanity hadn't changed all that much. Crap, still insistently and never-endingly, rolled downhill.

A soft knock sounded at the door, an anachronistic touch that almost made her smile. "Come," she called out, hearing the soft click as the vocal systems analyzed her response and acted on it.

The outer door opened and she saw a shadowy form enter, crossing in front of the dim light long enough for her to recognize Stephan's tall, solid, bulk. "In here."

He crossed into the sun chamber and sat down on the bench. He was dressed in a workout suit much as she'd been, and his hair was plastered to his head with sweat. "You up for dinner?"

"Sure." Jess wondered what the pitch was going to be. "What's up?"

"I've just had a crap filled day and I'd like to sit across a plastic table from a good looking woman and talk about trigger ratios and forget it was a crap filled day," he said, with surprising bluntness. "That's all."

Jess looked up from her pad, watching him. He was sprawled on the bench and she read honest exhaustion in his body set. She knew Bricker had been with him most of the morning, and she knew she was probably one of the subjects of the meeting, but she read no dissembling in his face and that surprised her.

Stephan was a friend. But first and foremost, he was her superior. Even though they'd grown up together, been schooled together, and been in service together for years, she had no illusion of where his loyalties lie.

Ah. There were those trust issues again. She smiled briefly. "Sounds good." She said. "I've got backed up rations, want to share a liter of grog?"

His face creased into a responding smile. "You're starting to sound like your old self."

Jess considered that. "I'm not sure that old self still lives in here. But I got a decent night's sleep last night so who knows."

He nodded. "Know how that feels." He indicated the light. "Mind if I share your glow? Mine's being serviced."

"Feel free." Jess went back to her pad as he stripped out of his suit and went to the transparent lounge, dropping down onto it and stretching out. The floor and walls were reflective, so every inch of them got some of it and though a necessity, she always found it relaxing.

She and Stephan were relatively alike in looks. They were both tall, and they both had spare, well muscled bodies with well developed arms and shoulders and powerful legs. The same training had stamped them, and though the biological differences were still obvious, they didn't obscure the fact that here were two people who had come out of the same mold.

Might even have been sibs, once upon a time.

Jess wondered how long it would take for him to corner her into whatever it was Bricker wanted.

She'd already decided to refuse. What would the threat be? What would the price be?

Did she really even care?

"Anything new on the boards?" Stephan asked, his eyes closed.

"Nothing yet" Jess smiled grimly. "Anything new from the top?"

"Nothing yet."

DEV WOKE TO the soft chime of her scheduler, opening her eyes to find the soft neutral colored interior of her sleeping pod surrounding her. The sedate glow that accompanied the chime intensified a little and she stretched, waiting expectantly until the latch triggered and the pod opened.

She sat up and swung her legs over the side, leaning her hands on the edge and peering out to see the normal, placid activity of the early dayshift in the crèche.

All around there were people emerging from sleep pods, some entering them as well who had worked the night through, groups of her crèche mates briefly chatting nearby. Overhead the walls curved to meet a dome and beams of sunlight arched through to hit solar panels, moving from one to the other in a stately dance as the station that held the crèche rotated.

To either side of her, a line of sleeping pods extended around the curved wall, layered one over the other on sliding tracks that positioned the units for exit at the right time and place. Once a pod was evacuated, it slid up and out of the way, allowing the next one to use the landing space.

And speaking of that, her own pod was gently beeping, warning her of imminent motion.

She stood up on the platform outside, and moved away from the pod, hearing it close behind her as she walked down the sloping ramp and joined a line of bodies heading into the bathing and changing center, all in light sleep-suits, all with bare feet, all with faintly lit collars around their necks.

Like hers. Dev never thought much about it. It was light and fitted very well to her skin, never chafing or causing her any trouble and with the delicate tracery of the electronics on it, she actually found them rather attractive.

Or at least, that's what she told herself.

"Morning , Dev." Aybe 285 was in front of her, flexing his hands and stifling a yawn. There were five or six of his set in front of him, and behind her were some Ceebees, and she spotted Gigi and another of her set as well and gave her a little wave, which she returned.

They all looked alike, of course. But she could pick out the Gigi she knew because the bracelet that let her into admin space set her aside from the rest of her set mates. The Aybes and Ceebees, on the other hand, were indistinguishable from each other.

"Morning," Dev responded automatically. She heard the soft hum of conversation around her, and behind the edge of the crèche she spotted a splash of the sun coursing through the station walls.

She had new skills. She could feel them, a tickly sensation in the back of her skull that almost made her want to scratch her head there as she wondered what the scope of the new knowledge was.

It was tech, that she knew, and a lot of it. She'd spent an evening and the following day in programming, and she'd seen the rings of dark fatigue under the eyes of the programmer when they'd finally let her come up, in a hazy mixture of adrenaline and euphoria that had her breathing hard and shaking.

She was next in line, and went to an open cleaning station, stepping inside and ducking her head a little as the air blasted away the set of paper clothing she'd been wearing to sleep in, the warm pressure feeling good against her skin.

A quick flash of irradiated light cleaned her, and then she was stepping out, turning to the right and going to the line of cabinets that ringed the outer wall. Twenty third in the row to the right of the door, on lower level A, was hers.

She opened the door and stepped inside, waiting for it to close after her. The inside light came on and the sound around her faded and she was in the only piece of privacy she'd ever known, given to her when she'd graduated from basic instruction.

Her crib, as they called it. Barely big enough for her to stretch her arms out twice, it held a cabinet, a padded bench and counter, her workspace, and the narrow, shallow drawer she kept her few personal possessions in.

Not everyone got one. Only those destined for higher skill programs were issued one of the limited cribs and it was a definite mark of status in the crèche along with the ability that went with it to manage the small amount of unregulated time in their day.

She could come here and study, watch a lecture from the library or just sit and think for a few minutes by herself. It was nice to have a place of quiet and peace in the crowded crèche, and the padded bench was even long enough for her to lay down and relax if she wanted to, though she seldom did.

Dev went to the closet and opened it, sliding into an under tunic, then pulling on a snug jumpsuit over that. The fabric was comfortable and a soft blue green in color. The gears patches on either shoulder indicated her assignment to tech and a change for her from the neutral beige of the unassigned.

It felt good. She liked the color. It contrasted with her pale hair much better than the other ones had and it made her feel happy to be getting new skills and the opportunity to be a part of something that the director had told her was so important.

She was still a little apprehensive about the programs, but so far nothing felt strange or out of sorts. She'd had programs that left her sick to her stomach and once had come up with such a headache they'd had to put her back down again and adjust something. Even though these sessions had been very long, she'd come up feeling all right about whatever it was they'd given her.

They were something intended to get her ready, programs that would let her know what to do when she got to wherever they were sending her and give her enough information for her to know the proper way to respond and interact with the people she'd meet there.

It wasn't knowledge, precisely, it wasn't facts she could call up and examine. This was deep stuff. This was the kind of programming they gave the permanently assigned, who were destined to spend all their lives doing certain tasks.

She liked the feeling they gave her.

She picked up her ident badge and clipped it to her front pocket then went to the small mirror and picked up her comb, raking her thick, short hair into some kind of order. She peered at her reflection, nodding a little at it as she put the comb back down.

She checked the chrono over the door, then she pulled back the simple chair in front of the equally spare desk and sat down to review her notes before the time she was due in the lab. After a minute, though, she pushed the monitor pad on it's arm aside and opened the drawer to her right hand, removing a tattered square object and setting in on the desktop.

With a faint smile, she opened the cover of the book and read the first page, as she had so many times before, savoring the images the words brought to her and in the simple luxury of reading—a skill not always programmed in her crèche mates.

It was her first indication that she was going to maybe get to do interesting things. Up until then she'd felt strange in her class, since she was the single member of her set, and unsure of what they intended her to do, unlike the others who had a set history to look at and set their expecations.

But she'd been assigned to the advanced section early and if she had to bear up under the strangeness of being a one off, at least she had that to comfort her.

A teacher had given the book to her when she'd left basic, on the day her birth group had sat in the speaking hall for the last time.

It was an old favorite of his, he'd told her, the book given to him by his grandfather, and passed down through his family. Dev wasn't sure why he'd given it to her, aside from him saying he thought she'd enjoy it, but she was very happy she had it and she often took minutes like this to read a few pages.

She spent a quarter hour immersed in the book, then put it away and headed for the door. The lights dimmed as she left, trading the quiet dimness for the bright lit common space of the crèche and all of it's inhabitants.

The sun speared through the station walls and Dev walked through slices of filtered light, lifting her hand a little to intercept a bit of it and watching as it gilded her skin. It made her smile and she kept smiling as she turned down the hallway and entered the big cross tunnel that led to the tech lab.

The walls slanted into the entrance, which had a bio reader and a screen. Dev stepped up to it and waited for the soft glow to appear overhead. She felt that little tickle on her skin, then the screen lit up.

"Ident." It said, briefly.

"NM-Dev-1."

The door slid open and she continued inside, moving directly across the big entrance to the processing desk that squatted directly in the center. She went to the processing agent and unclipped her badge, handing it to him and waiting as he keyed it in.

He studied the screen, then handed her badge back. "Lab twenty-six, first corridor, third door, eight hours. Reset when done."

"Thank you." Dev clipped her badge back on and then circled the desk and headed for the lab. She didn't pass anyone on the way there, the halls were quieter than usual. Most of the labs were dark and empty, their doors gaping open into the hall.

Lab twenty-six illuminated as she entered and the door closed behind her. Dev paused and looked around, seeing floor to ceiling gray consoles packed into every square inch of the room, leaving only a half octagon desk with a chair behind it.

It smelled just faintly of silicon. She circled the lab first, examining the consoles, but found nothing on them to indicate their purpose, which was intimidating in and of itself. Usually tech rigs had plates and decals, but these were blank and somehow seemed a little scary to her.

Maybe it was the flat gray color.

With a sigh, Dev went to the console and sat down in the chair, feeling the surface of it warm to her body, and conform to her figure a little. She adjusted it to her height, then put her hands down on the tablet surface and heard the almost soundless click and hum of electronics starting up.

A panel slid aside, revealing a headset. Dev took it out and put it on, smelling the newness of the plastic and steel as the contacts settled over her head and she felt the ear piece snuggle into her ear. For another moment here was silence, then the boards all lit up.

She jerked a little, surprised at all the activity. The half octagon suddenly came alive with sensors and readout panels, the banks lining the walls showed a thousand or more systems and she waited, just letting her eyes roam, for the programming to kick in.

It took a little while, sometimes. The instruction sets were all in there, but it was like having a book and it being just out of focus. You knew the words were there, but you couldn't quite see them until you brought them closer or a little further and your mind pulled them into clarity.

Until then, it was just a blast of lights and gauges. She felt a slightly crawling sensation on the back of her neck just before the flickering kaleidoscope abruptly shifted and took on meaning as a blast of comprehension overcame her.

A machine voice started whispering into her ear as she found herself short of breath, her body shaking a little as she tried to sync with the program, let it take over and show her what she needed to know.

She knew what the gauges were now, what that screen was, and this screen was, and why that set of readouts was so important.

A wash of tingling dismay made her lean forward as she took in the whole of it, and understood what the assignment was they had given her. She sucked in a breath hard, her heart beating like thunder as the lights dimmed and went to blue and a scenario started.

The consoles shifted and the two nearest to her changed to show controls her hands jerked back from as the voice whispered about metrics and targets and the three dimensional spatial understanding that now flooded up into her conscious mind.

She felt like throwing up. This was wrong. This was dark and cold and implacable.

But the program had her good and no matter how much she tried to pull her mind back from it, the insidious comprehension pushed aside her doubts, spurring her body to obey the insistently whispered instructions as her hands moved. Her breathing slowly steadied and she lost herself to the rush of it. Lost her grip. Like the knowledge was water, flowing fast as it had in the old story she read, carrying her along to a destination of it's own choosing.

There was no fighting it. The seduction of knowledge pulled her forward after her brief struggle, as she sensed the opening up of corridor after corridor of new skills she knew were waiting for her.

As good as a narcotic to one of her kind. The one thing they all craved, at least those who comprehended that much, was to be given the skills that took them beyond a superficial mediocrity. This was that kind of program, she now understood.

It was tech. Deep tech. Really knowing things that mattered. Knowing people who mattered. Being a part of something truly important with the opportunity to do more than she'd ever dreamed of.

Did it really matter if it was dark? If she sensed it was going to be scary?

The whispered voice wound around her and took hold. She felt her heartbeat settle as her body translated the understanding to a sensual level, as a trigger inside her released a jolt of pleasure into her awareness.

It felt good. The more she relaxed and thought about the skills, the better it felt. The fear faded and the sense of nausea with it, replaced instead with a tingling in her guts and a feeling of anticipation.

She drew in a breath and refocused her eyes on the screens, now nodding just a little as the voice started reporting what she was seeing. Her reflexes woke up, responding to the prompts as the scenario progressed.

She was sure it would turn out all right.

STEPHAN WAITED UNTIL they were halfway through dinner, with a half a liter down before he told her. Public space, he figured, with all the rest of the ops around them would keep her from at least punching him in the face. "So that's the deal."

Jess leaned back and twirled the glass in her fingertips, watching him with an expressionless face. "Let me make sure I understand," she said. "Some idiot decided it was a good idea to try making a bio alt into a tech ops agent?" She had kept her voice down. "Really?"

"Really," Stephan said, encouraged by the calm response. "Frankly, Jess, I told him I thought it was crazy."

"I see."

"It's become really political," Stephan said. "The rest of the ops group lodging protests like that. It got them embarrassed. You know how dangerous that is."

Jess studied the liquid in the glass. "Despite what you think, I didn't kickstart that. Everyone's just watching me and saying that could be them." She looked up at him. "So their answer is to come up with the equivalent of me walking in front of a laser cannon? 'Cause that's what it is. Never mind not trusting it at my back—the poor stupid critter will probably shoot me in it accidentally."

Stephan frowned. "Jess, they said they were programming it to be able to do this."

Jess rolled her eyes.

"Look, what do you want me to tell you? Tell them?"

"That they're liars," Jess said. "Because they are. They're just looking to save face. Put that thing in here, we both get offed, everyone turns around and says, well, I guess the council knew better all the time, and should go on picking the way they always have. But look. We listened to them. We tried!" Her voice dripped with raspy sarcasm. "Rest of the group's just relieved it wasn't them."

Stephan exhaled, an unhappy expression on his face. He'd known Jess for most of the years of his life, had sat across a table from that tall, rangy form with it's dark hair, and those light blue eyes many times, had fought many fights with her. And of all the agents in the group he trusted her the most.

Not because Jess was nice. She wasn't. But she was honest and her focus was true and it killed him that it was her that Joshua had knifed because there were others who deserved it more. "It's a political thing." He repeated. "Not really a whole lot of choice in it, Jess."

"What does that mean?"

They were both keeping their voices down, ostensibly just enjoying dinner together in the uncrowded ops dining hall on level three. There were six other people in the place, three pairs of two at the small tables and everyone else was making a show of pretending to ignore them.

"What does that mean, Stephan?" Jess repeated, slightly louder. "You know I'm not going to agree to this."

He leaned forward. "Not sure you have a choice."

Jess's face went very still.

"Look." He glanced around. "I told you this is political. Bricker has a lot on the line. He has debts to pay to the council. So it's either we cooperate, or— "

"Or?"

"Or he said there's no place in the organization for people who didn't."

Jess's expression got even more still. "So, let me see. Either I agree to walk into fire, or I get booted out into the streets, since I don't have enough years in to retire. Is that right?"

He couldn't even look at her. "It's political," he muttered. "This whole thing got bigger than us."

"Are those my choices, Stephan?"

He finally looked up. "That's what Bricker said. Either you cooperate with the plan, or you're out. But, Jess, listen, give it a chance, for Pete's sake. You don't know, maybe it'll work."

"It won't work," Jess said in a remote tone. "I'm not going to go out on a failure that also kills some poor beast that has no choice in the matter. Tell Bricker he can take his political ass and trash compact himself."

"Jess, think about what you're doing."

Jess put her glass down. "Screw yourself." She stood abruptly. "Process my outpapers. I'll go pack. Not that I've got a lot to." She tossed a chit down on the tray and turned, heading for the door to the hall.

Stephan was far too stunned to react until it was too late and she was gone. He stood up and started after her, aware of all the eyes on his back as he got to the door and went through it, looking quickly right and left.

The hallway beyond was empty however, only two cleaning staff were carefully vacuuming along the wall, their gray coveralls almost blending into it. Of Jess there was no sign, and he debated whether he should go to her quarters.

Go and try to talk her down? Stephan frowned. He started toward the bunkhouse but his comm unit chirped and he stopped as the soft bing and central comm's voice sounded in his ear. "Commander Bock, to central ops, priority."

He paused, then reluctantly headed down a slightly different corridor, a sinking sensation already in his stomach.

JESS KEPT HER pace relaxed until she'd entered her living space, waiting until the door slid shut behind her before she let herself react, spinning her body and slamming her fist into the wall with enough force to dent it.

Then she dropped into one of the chairs and stared at the ceiling, her eyes staring at the Interforce shield above the workspace. "Mother fucking bastards."

Her voice sounded loud in the room. There was no echo. The fabric on the walls absorbed everything, even the crack of her fist against the surface underneath.

Her stomach was in turmoil. The meal she'd just eaten was lodged somewhere up near her breastbone and she suspected it wouldn't be long before she ejected it. "Damn them," she whispered. "Spend your whole life giving it all to them and what does it mean? Jack nothing."

Jack nothing. Jess rested her head against her hand. A hundred emplacements, countless liters of blood shed, more successful missions than any other agent and on top of it, this last damn cluster and what?

Nothing. "What have you done for me lately? Wasn't that the old saying?" Jess felt the anger draining out of her, leaving her mostly just depressed. "Come cover our asses or get lost. Yeah well..." She glanced around. "Guess I'll go get lost."

Literally, she would get nothing. Her last pay transfer, any supply chits she had on record, and a ride out to the nearest shelter. They wouldn't even give her a transfer home.

Not that home had any meaning for her anymore. Jess half closed her eyes. She'd been submitted to the corps when she was old enough to walk, and entered for school and training. The cost was covered by the agency and she was guaranteed a job for life, as long as that life lasted, given what they did.

She'd been back home maybe a half dozen times in all. Strange, awkward visits with her mother and two brothers, the one hardly knowing what to say to her and the two boys resentful they didn't get to go where she had.

No way was she going back there. No way. If her father was alive then maybe it would have been bearable, but without him? No way.

He'd been one of the lucky ones, able to retire to inactive, go civ for a while, get married and have kids and live a kind of life out at the Bay.

But they'd gotten to him in the end. She remembered getting the call at base and the long, somber ride in a transport home surrounded by active members of the force, all in blacks, all grim and angry.

She remembered standing in the cavern and watching his outprocessing, barely exchanging a few words with her blood family as she stood with her service family to say goodbye to a brother.

Ten generations. She was the eleventh. To now find out just what that was worth—it hurt.

Maybe she'd just tear into central command and go after Bricker. They'd gun her down and at least she wouldn't have to suffer living in a crate, scraping seaweed from the rocks downstairs. Be a fast exit, wouldn't it?

She was glad Dad wasn't around to see it. Even more glad he hadn't been around to see Joshua's defection. Close as he'd been to his tech partners, he'd have lost his mind with it.

With a sigh, she pushed herself to her feet and went over to her workspace. She sat down in the big, comfortable chair and keyed in the pad. Would Stephan have already processed her? She waited for a lockout, but the pad logged in and gave her access with no complaints.

She keyed in her own profile and watched it form on the pad, sliding at her command to the section where her service status was and pausing. She reached over to tag herself inactive, when a soft chime indicated some incoming event.

Maybe Stephan was just a step behind her. She keyed over to the input and opened it, finding instead an info packet there.

"That makes no sense." Irritated, she was about to flip back and effectively kill herself in the system when she caught the sending entity and paused, realizing it was from the district assignments group. Reluctantly, she keyed it and watched it open, reading the first few words before she realized this had to be part of the insanity Stephan had told her about.

"Screw that." She closed the file and went back to the status, resetting the field to voluntary dismissal, applying it before she could talk herself out of it and into a compromising honor suck. "Done."

The screen went blank immediately, and she heard a soft whir and clack from upstairs as the weapons locker sealed itself. A glance to the door showed a red light next to it as well and she got up. An irrational sense of loss hit her unexpectedly.

Even though she'd made the choice. Even though she thought it was the right choice, and that it would at the very least save the bio alt they'd picked for a gory, terrifying sacrifice. Knowing she was now no longer a part of this place, of these people, of this world she'd been given to was hard to accept.

Hard to fathom. But she could hear the echo of the weapons lock in her mind and she knew if she tried to go outside she'd be met with an armed guard, denied access to anything except the lockdown if she persisted.

She could stay here until they mustered her out. Then she'd be taken to the service exit and the door would shut behind her, and she would never enter it again.

Done. Over. She doubted any of the others would even come to say goodbye. You didn't, when someone walked out. She certainly had never, though she'd seen a half dozen agents do it, some she'd considered friends.

Quitters. She remembered feeling embarrassed about them, unable to understand why they would just walk out.

Well now she knew.

Jess walked over to the bed and lay down on it, half curling up in a ball and wrapping her arms around the pillow. She felt an odd sensation in her throat, and a tense pain around her heart. She closed her eyes tightly, focusing on letting it all go past her.

Chapter Three

STEPHAN ENTERED CENTRAL comms just as the big screen was fizzling to gray. He walked over to where Bricker was leaning against the main console and looked at him in question.

"Took you long enough," Bricker said in a crisp tone.

"I was in the dining hall."

Bricker turned and put his hands on his hips. "Danao just transmitted a burst report. They got word through some scientist who just transferred up to Garden Station there's been a breakthrough."

"Yes?" Bock tried to focus on it, his mind distracted by recent events.

"Light amplification screen. They got photosynthesis working on a twelve by twelve meter platform," Bricker said. "We need that tech. Council's told me to get that tech." He put a hand on the planning board. "So let's get going on it."

"Commander." One of the ops monitors came over and handed Bock a pad. "This just activated."

Stephan looked at it, and cursed under his breath.

"What?" Bricker said.

"I presented your idea to Jess Drake." He said, handing the pad over. "She elected to muster out instead of going along with it."

Bricker took the pad and stared at it. "Are you kidding me?" He looked up at Bock. "What kind of idiot is this?"

"No kind of idiot, sir," Stephan said, quietly. "Family's been in a long time."

Bricker handed the pad back. "We don't have time for this crap. Agent wants out? Fine. Get someone else to be part of the project. I'm sure you can find someone." He looked at Bock's face. "What's the problem? You need a visit to psych too?"

"Maybe," Stephan said. "Maybe I just got Jess's point."

"What?"

"John, you reminded me how few our resources are. So now you tell me to throw one of them away? We're not machines."

Bricker looked exasperated. "We don't have time for this. Do you not get it? Do you not understand what that breakthrough means? That they've found a way to grow plants again, here, on the surface?"

"I get it," Bock replied. "So now you want me to send people. People, John? Our people? Into enemy space to try and get that technology and bring it back. People who are here, who don't trust us, who don't trust the people that back them now."

"Maybe we should go all bio alt," Bricker said. "At least then they'd do what we told them to do, instead of wringing and crying and being pansy assed pieces of crap. I told you. I don't have time for this. The Council wants a plan, by tonight, to get someone in there."

"I'll see if I can find anyone willing." Bock turned and started to leave.

"If?"

Bock turned. "Unfortunately, sir, until you make good your plan to replace us with biddable robots, we still have a choice. We don't force our people to go. We ask them." He swiveled and left the comms center, heading for his office in the back section of the stronghold.

Word was already spreading. He could see ops agents loitering in the hall, watching his approach, gathered in groups. He remembered being one of them, wondering what 'they' were going to ask now, viewing 'them' as the Brickers of the world who never really cared about what the cost was, only saw results.

Well, he was a them now. Stephan grimaced uncomfortably. At least, that's what his title said.

"Stephan." Jason Anders cut in front of his path, with Elaine Cruz next to him. "Can we speak with you?" Both were experienced agents. Both veterans. Apparently they'd been elected spokespeople and, he abruptly remembered, both were friends of Jess.

Bock regarded them, then sighed. "Sure." He waved a hand toward his door. "C'mon."

"HE DOESN'T GET it," Bricker said to the closed door, and then swiveled around to look at the rest of the people in the comms center.

They were all looking back at him with closed, silent faces. He could sense the anger in the room. "I can replace all of you with them too," he warned. "We have a mission here, people. That's bigger than any of us."

He turned back to the console and started keying in requests.

DEV WAS SEATED on a plastic bench, her elbows braced on her knees, sweat dripping off her as she tried to catch her breath. Her whole body was shaking with her just ended effort, and she blinked salty droplets out of her eyes that landed on the gym floor.

She had never been so tired. She flexed her hands, rough and sore from the climbing system and felt a blister forming just at the pad between her fingers and palms. She was dressed in the light singlet they used in the gym and there were bruises on her knees and arms from all the work.

"NM-Dev-1?"

Dev looked up, to find a phys proctor there. "Yes."

"You have completed group A and group B tasks. Well done," the proctor said. "You are complete for the day." The woman gave her a sympathetic look. "I know it's been a long session."

"Yes," Dev responded, direly grateful for the news.

"The rest of the day is scheduled clear for you to review previous classes. Okay?"

"Yes," Dev said. "Thank you."

"You're welcome." The proctor gave her a smile, then shut her pad down and walked away, leaving Dev alone in the preparation area.

She straightened up and ran her hands through her damp hair, knowing from the ache in her arms she would be experiencing this class for quite some time. At least she had some space to relax now, and a night meal to look forward to.

It was cycle end today. That usually meant the dining hall would give them something a little different, cakes, or maybe even some protein bars and she was glad of it since her body was craving replenishment from the past while.

Footsteps made her look up again, and she blinked as a familiar figure entered the gym and came over to where she was sitting. "Hello, Doctor Dan."

"Hello, Dev." Daniel Kurok took a seat next to her. "How are you?"

"Tired," Dev answered honestly. "It was a very hard gym session."

You could always answer Doctor Dan straight. He was the first doctor she remembered recognizing as a child, and the one who always had the time to talk, and explain things. He was a man of middling height, with straight, blond hair the same shade as hers, and a calm, appealing personality.

She'd always liked him. All the sets did. Doctor Dan was one of the very few who would talk to you as if you were actually a person. Not talk at you like most of the teachers and all of the other administrators tended to.

"I can imagine." Dan's gentle grayish blue eyes regarded her. "I know you've been very busy preparing for your new assignment. Are you excited about it?

Dev thought about that. "I am," she said, eventually. "It's hard, but knowing so much is good."

Doctor Dan smiled at her. "I'm glad to hear that. I came to find you because something has happened and they need you to go to your assignment sooner than we thought. I'd like to talk to you about it before you start getting ready."

"How soon?" Dev asked. "I still have programming to get."

"Tomorrow." Doctor Dan put a hand on her shoulder as she stiffened. "But don't be scared. You have what you need. The rest of the programming is just information, not skills and we'll send it with you." He reassured her. "Can you come with me? We can have dinner and talk."

It was like getting a buzz. Dev wasn't sure what to say. She'd never been invited to go to a meal with anyone except one of her crèche mates. "Yes," she finally answered. "I need to change first."

"No problem." Dan patted her bare shoulder. "Go on. I'll wait for you outside in the lobby." He watched her walk off toward the changing space and sighed, glancing up as someone else walked up. "This makes me very unhappy, Randall."

"I know." Doss sat down on the bench just vacated. "I know you had plans for this one."

"It's not just that." The chief geneticist sighed. "I know you think I'm probably against the assignment, but I'm not. I think it's a damn good idea, matter of fact."

"You do?" Doss seemed astonished.

"Yes, I do."

Doss scratched his head. "So you think this might work?" He asked. "Do you really think one of our products can do this?"

Dan looked at him with an oddly wry expression. "Yes, I do," he repeated. "I just wanted to be prepared for it. Send the right set, properly trained and programmed." He frowned. "Not something jury rigged like this is. I have suspicions about their success motives."

Doss shifted uncomfortably. "What do you mean?"

Kurok stood up. "Never mind. I could be wrong," he said. "But I'll be escorting Dev down there. I have our flight assignments already."

"Oh, but Daniel." Doss said. "You have so much in work here!"

"I know. It will need to wait. I want to find out what this emergency is. My sources in Interforce have told me the situation downside is not good." He frowned. "I don't want us to end up a scapegoat."

"But they wanted us. They came and asked us, Daniel." Doss looked troubled.

"Mm. Yes, they did," Dan frowned. "And you should have brought me in when Bricker was here. I know them better than you do." He turned and headed for the entrance. "You should have known better, Randall."

Doss got up and followed him out the door and into the quiet lobby. "But there wasn't time, really." There were three bio alts sitting on a bench near the door, waiting for their classes to start, but otherwise it was empty. He lowered his voice anyway. "Daniel, please don't cause us trouble. I was hoping this order was the start of something big for the company. A breakthrough."

Kurok looked at him. "I'm afraid you'll just have to trust me, Randall. I'll do what I think is best for all of us," he said. "And if not I'll try to warn you in advance." His face tensed into a faint grin. "But no promises."

"What does that mean, Daniel?"

Kurok put his hands in his lab coat pockets, an anachronism they all kept over their light, pale, one piece jumpsuits. "It means you need to just let me do what I think best. Not that you have a choice."

"Yes, well, all right." Doss sighed. "Please keep me advised on the progress." He hurried off, leaving his colleague to take a seat in the lobby to wait.

Kurok did, dropping into a chair and idly studying the three men seated waiting. Ayebees, he mused, his mind running over the DNA he'd encoded in them, laying down a biological structure suited for the role they were meant to fill.

One of them noticed him, and waved. He waved back, and all three smiled a little, glad to be paid attention to by a doctor they knew held high status in the crèche. "Have a good session, lads."

"Thank you, Doctor Dan." The one who had waved spoke up. He stood then, and led the other two into the gym as the door opened and chimed green, leaving him alone in the hall.

Kurok sighed. Then he caught motion in his peripheral vision and turned to see Dev emerging from the gym, fastening her badge to her coverall pocket. He smiled in reaction, proud of his meticulous work that was so evident in Dev's attractive features and well made body.

He supervised many sets. But Dev was one of his personal efforts. "That was fast." He stood up. "Let's go get something to eat. I bet you're hungry."

Dev smiled bashfully. "They worked me hard in the gym today," she said. "And it's cycle end. I think we're going to get some extra tonight."

"Well, don't worry about it." Kurok led the way through the halls. "We're going to the little place we working scientists eat, so you'll get fed, absolutely, as much as you want." He triggered the door to the grav lift and stepped in, waiting for Dev to join him before he pointed up with his thumb and they both kicked off.

The tubes were pretty empty and they drifted upward through the clear glass, as the station's rotation brought them to aphelion, and they were faced with a vast star field overhead.

Dev enjoyed the sight immensely. She didn't usually get the opportunity, since most of the crèche areas she was accustomed to were down lift. "They're so pretty."

Kurok had been looking up also. "They are, aren't they?" He said. "Savor them, Dev. You won't get to see them downside."

"That's what they said." They reached the top and she followed him through the hatch. They were now in one of the upper residential areas, and she turned her head from side to side looking at the plush carpet, and woven tile walls. "Only clouds."

"Only clouds." Kurok led the way to an entrance where a bio alt was standing, manning a small desk. "Hello, Ceebee 245."

The bio alt, dressed in a black jumper with silver piping, looked up. "Oh! Hello, Doctor Dan." He glanced at Dev, but didn't address her. "Would you like a table?"

"Yes," Kurok said. "For two, please. My friend Dev here is joining me."

Ceebee 245 looked briefly at Dev, then he half bowed and indicated the door behind him. "Of course, Doctor. Please come this way."

Dev felt very out of place. She followed Doctor Dan inside, and found herself in a bubble that held several dozen tables, about a dozen of which were occupied. She knew the people in the room were all looking at her and she had some idea that her kind weren't allowed.

Kurok, though, seemed oblivious to this. He pulled out a chair for her at the table they were led to, and sat down himself. "Ceebee, please bring us two fruit punches to start with."

Ceebee 245 nodded in acknowledgement and disappeared, heading toward the service area.

Kurok leaned on his forearms. "Dev, I know this seems very strange to you. But I'm doing it for a reason."

Dev looked around. "I've never been here before," she said. "It's very pretty."

Kurok smiled. "Yes, it is," he said. "You know, the assignment we're sending you on, I think sometimes you might end up in places like this with your natural born partner. And you might even be wearing clothing that will make people think you're not a biological alternative."

Dev remained silent, listening to him intently. That was all extremely interesting information and she filed it away for study later.

"So I wanted you to just see what this was like before you went downside." He looked at the pad on the table. "But I think I'll order for both of us, if that's okay with you."

"Okay," Dev said. "I don't really know what any of this is." She indicated the ordering pad.

"I know. And for a while you probably won't downside either, but your partner will help you with that."

Dev smiled and nodded.

He keyed in an order, then turned his attention back to her. "They've given you a lot of programming this week, haven't they?"

"Yes." Dev was relieved to be talking about something more familiar to her. "I had two sessions. The first one was very long. It was all tech, really hard. Then I had lab."

"I saw your lab results. You did very well." Kurok said. "The programmers were really pleased with how you took the program, too."

Dev grinned in response. "Thank you."

Kurok smiled. "I've seen the programming. What did they actually tell you about this assignment, Dev? What did they say you were going to do?"

Dev was a little confused. Wouldn't Doctor Dan know that? "Doctor Doss explained there was some problem that they wanted me to try and help with. He took me to meet a man called Bricker, who said I would be working with them to try and solve the problem." She paused. "They didn't say exactly what I would do, but the programming was a lot of tech, so I guessed I would be working with that, and with something to do with security."

Kurok regarded the young, serious face across from him. "Does that worry you?"

Dev considered the question. "I don't know. Should it?"

Kurok waited as two plates were delivered to them, and the server silently left. He watched his dinner companion study the contents, then pick up the implements on one side and put them neatly to use.

That, at least, they'd given her. "They must have told you what Interforce does, didn't they?" He sliced up his protein and took a sip of the fruit juice.

Dev shook her head, chewing thoughtfully and swallowing. "I know what we got from the downside class. That's all."

Figures. "Well, Dev, you're right that you'll be doing something with security." Kurok said. "Interforce sends people to do things that make the lives of people who are on our side better, and prevent people who aren't on our side from hurting us."

Dev thought about that. "That doesn't sound so bad."

"Well, it doesn't, if you just look at the surface of those words," Kurok said. "What that really means, Dev, is that you'll be doing some dangerous things, and it's possible you could get hurt doing them. You could see other people hurt."

"Oh." Somehow, though, Dev had known that. Something in the programming had told her, she reasoned, since she felt no prickle of surprise at the words, nor dread hearing them. "I'll do my best to be safe," she said.

Kurok smiled again. "I know you will," he said. "When I put you together I tried to give you the ability to adapt, and to handle difficult things. This assignment is going to be difficult, but I think you can do it."

Dev produced another tentative smile at the compliment. "Thank you."

"What I am going to warn you about, though, is about how people downside will feel about you, about what you are." His voice gentled. "There are other bio alts in Interforce. But none of them will be doing what you will. Some people might not like it."

Dev nodded. "Like here, when they don't like it when someone else gets higher skills," she said. "They want it too. Or they think they should get it."

Impressed, Kurok regarded this product of his making. The insight was more than he expected, and showed a self awareness he hadn't quite anticipated. "Yes, that's it exactly," he said. "Have you had trouble like that much here?"

Dev shrugged. "A little. I think its also mostly because I'm—" She hesitated. "There's no one else in my set. Everyone else has someone who is just like them, and it makes them stick out less."

"Well, that's true," Dan said. "You're a developmental unit. The other sets know that."

"They do," Dev said. "But it doesn't stop them from wanting the programming too, even if they're not sure what it is."

Kurok put his fork down and touched her hand. "You should have come and talked to me about that, Dev. I could have explained it better for you."

The pale green eyes took on the faintest hint of a twinkle. "It was hard, sometimes," she said. "But...being the only one in my set made me think maybe I would get to do something special. And I guess I will."

Kurok rested his chin on his fist, his face creasing into a grin.

"So even if it turns out to be scary, and maybe really hard and not a lot of fun, I'll still have gotten to do it."

Part of that he'd programmed into her. He'd selected the genes carefully, moving toward a half imagined, not quite all the way designed, different step—maybe forwards, maybe sideways.

A developmental unit. That was what the Dev stood for, but the NM designation also meant new model. His new model. He'd rolled the genetic dice and only now was he getting to see what numbers those dice were returning to him, almost impossible to know before the set reached maturity and a full realization of all the synaptic growth.

Now a thousand questions were poppping up in his head and he felt a sense of regret that his investigation of his project was about to be cut off.

Dev put her fork down and looked earnestly at him. "Doctor Dan, can I ask you for something?"

"Absolutely."

Dev's gaze went to her plate, then lifted up to him. "If it's too hard." She paused. "And it doesn't work out, could you make it so I don't have to forget all this?"

Pinned by that soulful look, Kurok bit the inside of his lip and had to pause to let the tension in his throat relax before he answered. "I promise you, Dev. I'll only let that happen if you ask me to do it."

Dev smiled in relief and returned her attention to her plate. "Thank you. And thank you for letting me come here. This is really good." She indicated the plates rapidly depleting content. "Or maybe I was just really hungry."

Kurok patted her shoulder. "It is good. And it was my pleasure, Dev. I'm glad we got a chance to talk." He put his mind to his plate as well, his thoughts already racing far ahead. "I really am." He glanced back at her. "Would you like another portion?"

Dev's brows hiked up a little and she swallowed hastily. "Yes I would. Is that correct?"

He chuckled. "Sure." He signalled at the Ceebee. "No problem at all."

DEV WAS AWARE of how quiet it was in the crèche when she returned. A proctor caught sight of her and approached, with a pad strapped to her arm. "Hello, proctor."

"NM-Dev-1?"

"Yes."

"You are late back."

Dev regarded the proctor thoughtfully. "Doctor Dan required my presence," she said. "He just sent me back here."

"Doctor Kurok? He didn't log his request with us."

Dev didn't respond to that, having no control over what Doctor Dan did and knowing the proctor knew that.

The proctor tapped on the pad. "We've been told you're being transferred out tomorrow on the first transport, hour ten."

"Yes, they told me."

"You may take one size small pack bag with you. Everything else you need will be provided by your assigned contractor. You have no schedule tomorrow. After breakfast report to the transfer station no later than hour nine. Understood?"

"Yes." Dev hoped the proctor was done. She was tired, and after the evening of being treated to the attention of Doctor Dan, the impersonal and rote instruction felt a little grating.

Just a little.

The proctor nodded. "Very well. The pods are already programmed for this sequence. Since you're late, you'll need to overnight in transit quarters." She consulted the pad. "B32, section 2 in the outer ring has been cleared for you."

"Thank you," Dev said. "Good night."

The proctor glanced up at her in some surprise. She pointed to the outer ring and left, taking her pad with her.

Dev exhaled. Then she headed toward the corridor, glancing back to see the night pods making their slow, gentle transit and realizing she wouldn't be feeling that comforting motion again, at least for a while.

Change was happening. The unknown was pouring down on her far faster than she'd expected. By tomorrow she'd be in her assignment and tonight she stood on the cusp of having her life move to a completely different mold.

Good? Bad?

Or just different?

DEV FELT THE rumble as the transport inserted into the atmosphere and wished they had a view outside. She hitched her body forward a little in it's strapping and looked around, seeing most everyone else sitting with their eyes closed and their bodies pressed back into their seats.

Her heart was racing. She wasn't entirely sure why, since the process they were performing seemed ordinary to the people there. But the stresses around her were changing, and she was starting to feel gravity again, tugs that settled her feet on the ground and as the rumble deepened she imagined the fire outside as the shuttle's shields shed the increasing atmosphere to either side.

It was quiet otherwise in the cabin. There hadn't been much talk during the undock and orbit, the rest of the passengers apparently being used to the travel.

Dev flexed her hands a little as the rumble eased and then they were back in full grav, only it was planet grav, not artificial, and the feeling was curiously different. She couldn't really quantify what the difference was, but shifted in her seat a little, moving around to get used to it.

Kurok opened his eyes and looked over at her. "Feel strange?"

"A little."

"It's more consistent," Kurok said. "On station, the gravity is generated by machine and it's not always exactly the same. You get used to that." He indicated the inside of the cabin. "Downside, it never changes."

"Oh." Dev considered that. "Is that good or bad?"

"Neither," he said. "Just different."

A soft chime sounded. "Atmosphere insertion complete. Please remain in your seats."

Dev settled back in her seat to experience the rest of the trip. She had come to the transport station early and had gotten to see the shuttle dock, watching in fascination as it drifted in, maneuvering jets firing gently as it matched station rotation and locked on.

It had come from a ring of other stations down-orbit from them, and they had been the last stop before it left space and returned planet side to deliver it's cargo and passengers. From the crèche, some bio alts had joined them, Beeaye machine techs and two Kaytee pilots.

No one had spoken, though they'd watched Doctor Dan escort her and she could almost feel them wishing they had his attention too as a physical thing.

Kurok ignored them though, using the time in the vessel to take a nap.

Now they were heading to their destination and she was starting to get nervous. Until they landed, she could just experience everything in sort of a neutral way, as a new thing. Once they got to where they were going it would start to get a lot more real, and the hard part would begin.

She was really glad Doctor Dan was going too. He seemed very relaxed. "Do you go on these very much?" She asked him.

"Oh, I've done my share," he said. "When I was younger, I did a lot of different things. But I haven't in a while. I don't think it's changed much though. There are only so many ways you can enter a planetary atmosphere, you know."

Dev's ears popped and she reached up to rub them.

"Almost there," Kurok said. "Interforce's Base Ten is on the east coast of what was originally referred to as the North American continent."

Dev nodded. "I remember that from basics class," she said. "Now it's just Atlantia." She added. "It's much smaller now too."

"Under water," Kurok said. "Only the highlands survived." He tightened his straps a little. "Okay, Dev, we're gong to land now so sit back."

Dev did and took a breath as she felt the stresses change. The rumble suddenly got a lot louder. The craft altered it's trajectory, and she felt it tipping upward, the vibration of the engines making the cabin shake, jostling it's passengers in their seats.

"Retros." Kurok said, over the noise. "That's normal."

Then the rumbling died down and she felt a thump under them, and they were still.

"Please remain seated." The PA voice came over. "Vessel is being secured. Do not attempt to stand."

Dev could hear bangs and thumps outside. After what seemed a very long time, she heard the clash of locks being released, and a sudden change of pressure that seemed to thrum against her ears.

The inside hatch opened, and one of the flight attendants appeared. "We have arrived. Please prepare to debark," he said, pressing a button on the wall. The straps around them all slacked, and they were free to stand up.

Dev did, as the others did, and she paused to stretch her body out after the ride. Moving felt a little strange and she glanced at Doctor Dan as he likewise manipulated his body. She took a breath and found a strange scent hitting her nose, rough and chemical smelling.

"Ah, the smell of rocket fuel," Kurok muttered. "How I haven't missed that." He indicated the row. "Go on, Dev. Let's get outside."

Dev moved slowly along the seats, watching the rest of the passengers get in line in front of her. She was at the tail end and used the wait to get used to how different the gravity felt. It wasn't bad feeling, just strange, and she flexed her hands as they reached the exit of the craft and she found herself at the top of an outside ramp.

Outside. Dev felt a prickle of shock as a gust of air blew against her. She could taste and smell all kinds of things on it, from machine oil to salt. It felt wet to her and she licked her lips a little as she started down the ramp after the others.

They were in a kind of bay, she realized. Ahead of her was a tall uneven rock wall she remembered from programing and a sealed opening dug into the bottom of it, with some lockers and benches outside and a loading platform full of sealed containers.

Seated on the benches were two people dressed in charcoal jumpsuits and as Dev looked at them, the closer of the two looked up and met her eyes.

It was a woman, with dark hair and a planed, angular face. She looked tired and defeated and sad and Dev's heart gave a thump as she felt a surge of empathy for her without having the least idea why.

Then her foot caught on the ramp and she missed her step and Doctor Dan caught her. When she looked back over, the woman had looked away and it was over.

They were down the ramp and past the benches, and the big door was sliding open to reveal a group of men with weapons, dressed in steel gray armored suits. She had to set aside the strange encounter and focus on this new thing instead.

Everything was strange. The smell of the air was almost overwhelming and she was almost glad when the door behind them slid shut and the movement of it was blocked out. She stood back as three men came forward and took charge of the other bio alts, pointing them toward an orange painted corridor.

They passed through a gateway on the way and she saw the pale blue light as it coursed over each one of them, the gateway softly chiming and data flickering on the console as they passed.

The armed men ignored all of them. Dev wondered what they were there for, then Doctor Dan guided her forward and it was her turn to go through the gate. "What is this?" She asked him softly.

"It records who you are," he said. "Don't worry. They're expecting you. We sent them your scan ahead of time."

Reassured, Dev entered the gateway and felt a sharp tickle against her skin as the beam passed over her. It felt a little bit like being connected to a programming cradle, and it wasn't entirely comfortable. She stepped out of it at the chime and waited for Doctor Dan to join her.

A man in a green jumpsuit approached. "You the new experiment?" he asked Dev.

Kurok quickly came up next to her. "This is NM-Dev-1," he said. "I believe she's expected." He gazed steadily at the men. "Although I probably am not."

The man in green studied something on the pad strapped to his arm, then he looked up sharply at Kurok. "Director Bricker asked me to bring her to the ready center. He didn't say anything about you."

"Well, let's just go ask him, shall we?" Kurok put a hand on Dev's back. "I have the transfer authority for my friend Dev here, so I'm sure Commander Bricker will be happy to talk to me about it."

Dev felt very unsettled. She could sense the hostility all around and the man was looking at Doctor Dan in a very wrong way.

The man in green entered something on the pad. "One minute," he said. "Detail, stand down," he ordered, directing his voice toward the men with the weapons. "The exit event went without issue. Return to barracks."

The soldiers safed their weapons and shouldered them, then started back toward the inside of the building, heading down a blue colored corridor without any comment. That left the man in green alone in the entryway with Dev and Kurok.

"The genetiscan won't positive ident you," the man said to Kurok. "It just passes your scan and given name as secure."

"Mmhm," Kurok said. "That'd be about right."

"Please wait here." The man in green went over to a console on the wall and started typing into it.

Kurok chuckled a little. "Some things never change," he said. "Well, Dev, this is your new home. What do you think about it?"

Dev looked at him in apprehension. "Everyone seems angry here. Or upset," she said. "Doctor Dan, who were those people outside?"

"Which people?"

"The ones on the bench. The ones in dark suits."

"Ah." Kurok cast his memory back a short while, running through their arrival in mental pictorial shorthand. He called up a shot of the wall, and the bench, and two figures—Ah. "Those were enforcement agents, Dev."

"Oh."

He half shut his eyes and focused on one of the two faces, and then his body stiffened a little as he put the presence, and the security troop together.

The man in green returned and gestured toward the furthest corridor, sealed tightly with a metal door. "Please come with me. Commander Bricker asked me to bring you both to the ops center."

Kurok looked at the door, then shook his head and motioned Dev to follow as they left the entrance and headed further into the complex. "Something's not right here. Just hope we find out what it is before it's too late."

Chapter Four

IT WAS STEPHAN who came to escort her.

Jess was sitting in the chair near the door to her quarters, her neatly packed duffel at her feet. The room was bare and clean, the workspace cleared, everything tucked into place ready for whoever was going to live in it next.

She'd come to terms with two things. First, regret for making a snap decision and acting on it before thinking it all the way through. Second, that she was sticking to the decision anyway, even though she knew it was mostly due to ego and not the best choice for her at this stage in her life.

She was stubborn and proud, and she knew it. She knew everyone else knew that also, and given the choice of breaking down and asking for a reneg, or sticking to her pride and doing something stupid, she'd pick doing something stupid every time.

Family trait. Jess was studying the scars on the back of her right hand when the door unlocked and slid open. Stephan walked inside and faced her. "Ready?"

"Yep." Jess stood up and shouldered the duffel. The sudden reality of the moment made her breath catch, but she waited for Stephan to turn and lead the way out, gazing quietly at the floor.

"Jess."

She looked up at him, a little surprised at the expression on his face and the distinct shadows under his eyes. "Yeah?"

Stephan took a breath, and then released it. "Everyone wanted to come with me. Wanted to come see you the past couple days. Bricker blocked it off. Didn't want them getting any ideas."

"Fuck him," Jess said, in a mild tone. "I hope he walks off the edge of that cliff out there and ends up fish food."

Stephan nodded. "I just didn't want you to think no one gave a damn. They did. I do."

Jess wasn't sure if it made it worse or better to hear that. "Let's go," she said. "I'd like to have time to find a place to crash before dark." She appreciated what he'd said, but in her heart she knew if anyone had truly wanted to come and say good bye—they would have.

No one wanted to rock the boat, though. Jess had no illusions about the relationship with the rest of the ops battalion she was leaving. They were colleagues. They occasionally crossed paths during emplacements. They'd step in front of a laser cannon for each other in the field, but there was no one here, save perhaps Stephan, she could have characterized as a true friend.

She'd thought Joshua was a friend. He sure acted like one. She followed Stephan's silent form down the empty hall, memories chasing her footsteps. She remembered the easy companionship, the casual dinners and games of cards in their quarters in the infrequent intervals they'd been in them.

She still wanted to throw up every time she thought about him. With a sigh, she shifted the strap of her duffel on her shoulder as they crossed the central corridor and turned into the series of blast shields that led to the transport entrance.

Doors slid shut after them as they went, each one putting her more on the outside until they got to the last one. She could smell a transport off gassing nearby. Just before the door was a lock clearance, and first Stephan, and then Jess stepped into it, enduring the electric blue tickle of the genetiscan that was the final determination of identity.

Jess heard the soft chimes and burbles. "Ident complete." The calm voice of the system announced. "Final exit confirmed. Do not attempt reentry."

Stephan keyed open the external entrance and the smell of the transport got a lot stronger. He led the way outside onto the landing pad and waited for Jess to join him.

The door slid shut behind her and Jess felt a sudden sense of deep loss that made her jaw clench. Even the sight of the transport, usually an interest of hers, didn't dull it. She moved to one side and sat on the bench to wait, as the big jet's hatch was still sealed shut and the techs were still bringing out umbilicals and cooling to it.

Stephan sat next to her, resting his elbows on his knees, watching the gasses from the jet lifts evaporate. "I'm sorry."

"For what?" Jess leaned back and rested her head against the rock wall. "None of this was your fault, Stephan."

"I know. I'm just sorry. I don't want you to leave. I'll miss you."

Jess was so surprised she nearly fell off the bench. She turned her head and looked at him, but he was staring ahead, his shoulders hunched. "I'll miss you too." She waited for him to look at her and their eyes met. "I'll miss this place. I'll miss the force. It's really the only home I've had."

"Stupid mother fuckers," Stephan said, clipping the words, and clamping his jaw shut. "If Elias was still here—"

"Well, she's not." Jess sighed. "But she would have kicked Bricker's ass, that's true, and put a shut on his damn crazy ideas."

The transport door opened and moved down to form a ramp. After a brief pause, several people came out. Most were in Interforce uniform and didn't really give them a glance on passing. The last two were a man and a woman, both blond and in civ space gear, both looking a bit unsteady under downside grav.

The woman had a bio alt collar, and as she cleared the ramp she looked over and her eyes met Jess's.

It was an almost physical impact. Jess felt her nape hairs lift a little, bringing a chill to the back of her neck as her heart did a funny little thump in her chest. She watched the blonde woman almost trip on the edge of the ramp. She looked away as the man next to her put a hand on her shoulder and urged her toward the entrance.

Jess saw the door close behind them and she jerked her attention back to the transport. Was that Bricker's damn crazy project? "Bricker keeping that bio alt idea going?" She asked, clearing her throat a little as she heard the rasp in her voice.

"Yeah." He stood up. "Told them he wanted to start early, matter of fact." He looked at Jess. "Let's get you settled on board."

It must have been the bio alt. Jess stood up, resisting the urge to look behind her, at the closed door. She'd never seen that set before and she'd come in with what looked like a proctor.

She followed Stephan up the ramp, then exhaled and dismissed the unlikely newcomer, since she was heading in the wrong direction to care. "That's too bad. I was hoping they'd at least kill that idea, and save that poor bastard pain and trouble."

"Yeah, well, we don't have any unpaired agents so I don't know why he wanted them now." Stephan stopped abruptly, almost making Jess crash into him. "Oh." He took a step back. "Sir."

Jess looked up quickly and edged to one side. Standing at the top of the ramp was an older man, with silver white hair and a long, saturnine face. He had a hooked nose and bushy eyebrows, and she felt her own eyes open wide as her brain identified him.

The Old Man. That's what everyone she'd ever known called him, but never to his face, and she was careful to school her tongue not to utter that description rather than his name. Alexander Bain, the man who ran Interforce, though she had no idea what his actual title was, or whether he really did own the vast organization or just operated it for some moneyed consortium.

"Commander, Bock," the man rumbled. "I don't believe we've met."

"No, sir." Stephan inclined his head a little. "It's a great honor."

"Hm," the man mused. "And this is Agent Drake, I assume?"

"No," Jess replied quietly. "Not anymore, sir."

The Old Man studied her, making a little beak with his lips, and knitting his brows. "I see. Well, perhaps you could join me inside for a moment, so we can have a chat. I would hate to lose this opportunity to exchange a few words with someone who has tendered my organization such excellent service."

Jess felt very off balance, and not only because she was standing on a ramp. "Yes, sure." She managed to mutter.

"I didn't know you were arriving, sir," Stephan said, meekly. "We would have made arrangements."

"You didn't know I was arriving because I took some pains to make sure you didn't." Bain said. "What's the fun of being the Old Man if I can't show up unannounced and scare the living daylights out of everyone?"

"Sir," Stephan responded.

"Please go take a seat there, Commander." Bain pointed at the bench.

"Do not contact anyone, do not move until we come back. Understood?"

"Sir."

Bain turned and went back into the transport, clearly expecting Jess to follow him. She did, shifting her duffel a little to allow it to clear the door frame as she went inside, moving off the metal ramp onto the solid steel of the airframe.

They went down the port passageway, past the general seating section with its rows of cramped bucket seats and belt-ins. The lights were dim and there were three bio alts there vacuuming the interior with the intent, single minded purpose of their kind.

Bain led the way through a second passageway, and then down into the aft of the transport, opening a door and passing through into a smaller, more comfortable section.

He took a seat on one of the large, plush chairs and indicated the other with a wave of his hand. "Please sit down."

Jess unloaded her duffel and put it neatly against the wall. Then she sat down in the chair and put her hands on the arms, facing him and waited.

He could be there for many reasons. She wasn't quite vain enough to think she was one of them. Jess knew she could be forgiven if she immediately started explaining her part and viewpoint in the whole situation, but she was savvy enough to know sometimes it was just better to shut your mouth and wait.

So she did.

Bain studied her. "You have a reputation for many things," he said. "For stubbornness and arrogance, for courage and perseverance, for strategic brilliance and occasional criminal insubordination."

Jess pondered that. "That's pretty accurate," she said. "I trust my own judgment and have learned, painfully, not to trust pretty much anyone else's."

"You know, I learned much the same lessons myself," he said. "However, I never quit over any of it."

Jess waited, not really offended by the accusation as it was, in essence, true.

The silence lengthened. Eventually, Bain smiled a trifle. "It occurs to me that perhaps what I was told regarding this entire event was not entirely accurate," he said. "Would you like to enlighten me further?"

Perfect opening. The tantalizingly offered leverage made her tongue itch. Jess watched his body language and evaluated him as she'd had to so many others over the years. "The official report is the official report, Sir. I'm sure Bricker had reason for the report he tendered to you."

Bain steepled his fingers and regarded her. "Come now. I'm sure you have a side to this event to tell. There's always more than one."

"That's true, sir. But my view is my view, not the corps's view. That's what is relevant to you."

Now Bain smiled more easily. "Ah." He leaned back. "Eleven generations, hasn't it been? Given at six, taught and trained by the corps, loyalty bred in the gut for years. Even if the corps just turned its back on you, regardless of your service, at the whim of a single minded chimp with a view so narrow it's a wonder he does not trip over his own jackassery."

Jess remained silent for a few moments as she watched him watch her. Then she exhaled a little, deciding on honesty. "Only home I've ever known," she admitted. "But I'd be damned if I was going to walk the corps into an embarrassing disaster just to serve the purpose of being the scapegoat for the Council."

"Hm," Bain mused. "Is that what you think this is?"

"Don't you?" Jess responded bluntly. "Or why are you here?"

"Why am I here?" He tapped his fingertips together. "Now, that's a very good question, isn't it," he said. "Before I get into that, let me express to you how personally grateful I am that you concluded the ambush you got into the way that you did. I think you must know that the results of that incident turned out badly for the group who planned it on the other side."

Jess wasn't sure how to feel about that. "We lost good people."

"We did," Bain agreed. "But they lost more good people, and it seriously pains me to think our final consequence of that situation will be losing you."

That could only be a compliment. For no apparent reason, Jess suddenly recalled a pair of pale green eyes looking into hers and she let herself have a moment of possibly wondering if there was a way back. "Thank you, sir. It hurts me to separate myself." She paused. "I had hoped by taking myself out of the situation, it might stop Bricker's plans. But it seems not to be so."

"No." Bain shook his head. "But consider this. It might well be the idea of replacing a tech with a bio alt is a pitch to deflect the investigation of the Council."

Jess nodded.

"However, it's equally possible that this idea, as unlikely as it seems to you, might succeed," Bain said. "In which case, almost certainly we will achieve a sea change that might alter the way the corps operates in a good way."

"All due respect, sir, I don't really think so. It takes years to train a tech. They've had only a couple of days to prepare, and even with the knowledge, the instincts aren't there."

"Hm." The Old Man leaned forward. "Jess Drake. Do you truly wish to leave?"

There was a long silence.

"Do you truly wish to become a harvester? Live in a stone box? Sleep on the floor? Scrape moss and seaweed for two meals a day?"

"No," Jess finally admitted. "But I don't want to lose my honor either."

"Ah," Bain said. "That I do understand, as I too put a great stake on my honor." He looked intently at her. "Let me ask you this. Would you put your honor to one side just long enough to accompany me back inside that rock pile? There is something I believe I would like to show you. This might—or might not—allow you to bend your principles enough to consider remaining."

It was so tempting to immediately agree. Jess knew she wanted to. The surge of emotion at the offer was undeniable. Catching Bain's eyes on her, she realized abruptly that he knew that, he was reading her just as clearly as she often read others. She just smiled. "I can do that," she said. "Gladly."

Bain smiled. "I imagined you might say that." He stood up. "Let's go then. Before your Commander Bock cannot sit on his instincts any longer and rushes inside to ruin my surprise." He waited for Jess to get her duffel, then led the way back out.

He paused, just before they were about to exit, and turned. "Drake," he said in a lower, more serious tone. "I do understand what you experienced. I understand why you have lost trust."

Jess studied him. "I'll carry the memory of his laughter as he cut me to my grave," she said. "That takes a lot of getting over. I'm not sure I can."

Bain nodded. "Consider helping me resolve this crisis, as you did the last one, and I will put you in a position that will not require that of you." He watched her eyes intently. "Think on it." He turned and descended the ramp, now in pristine condition from it's cleaning.

Jess took a deep breath and released it. She followed him down the ramp and across the landing pad, seeing a group of bio alts, and several security troops waiting there to board. Stephan saw them and stood up, approaching quickly.

"Bock." The Old Man waved him forward. "Glad you didn't go with your base instincts. Join us."

Stephan just nodded and fell in next to Jess. He raised his eyebrows at her, and she raised her shoulders at him, and they walked on in silence.

The troops braced to attention at Bock's signal. The bio alts just looked confused.

Jess kept her head down as she caught up to Bain at the stronghold entrance, watching him key open the door and step inside. "Sir."

"Hm?" Bain turned and looked at her.

"They'll need to reset my creds." She pointed at the scanner. "I'm not much in the mood to be crisped to death right now."

"Ah." Bain turned and pointed at one of the guards. "Deactivate that." He indicated the scanner, squatting mutely over the entrance.

"Sir, we can't." The guard looked distressed.

"You can," Bain said. "Or did you mean to tell me you don't know how?"

The guard went to the console. "No, sir, I do know, but—"

"Come along, lad," Bain said. "Just tell them I said to do it. I am the last court of appeals. The final judge, as it were." He glanced at Stephan and smiled. "Has a nice ring, doesn't it?"

"Sir," Stephan murmured.

The guard still looked uncertain.

"Or, I could just order Mister Bock here to kill you and do it himself." Bain went on. "Since I am the top sec, as it were, hmm? My name, since you seem unsure, is Alex Bain."

"Sir!" The guard's eyes got as big as clams. "Yes, sir!" He rushed forward to deactivate the sytems.

Jess stood quietly waiting, not exactly sure what emotion it was that was stirring up her guts. As the faint hum ceased, and the light went out over the scanner, she had to force herself to cross under it, wondering if she really hadn't just gone from bad to infinitely worse.

"Well done." Bain started forward with her. "Now don't you worry, Drake. We'll get this all sorted out, tally-ho."

IT WAS A long walk. They followed the guard mostly in silence. Kurok's brow was now creased with worry, and Dev was too busy looking at everything to talk.

It was very, very strange. Dev tilted her head back and looked up at the high ceiling, its irregular surface seeming odd and out of place. She followed the two men through the now open steel door and down a corridor bisected by many other steel doors blocking their way until they were keyed through.

Security? Dev felt the sensation of the space they were in closing in on her, aware suddenly of how much solid material was around them as they moved further inside the facility. There were no other people around until they entered the last door in the corridor, which opened up into a huge central space, with yet more corridors leading off in all directions.

Here, there were people. Lots of them. Dev felt their eyes on her as they passed and she moved closer to Doctor Dan in reflex at the borderline hostility directed at her.

The man in green led them to a door set in stone with a rotating red light over it. He scanned through and then held the door open for them to enter.

"Thank you." Kurok gave him a brief smile, and then he guided Dev inside a round cavern of a room, with consoles around every available edge. Four people were standing in the center of the room next to a table with a big lit screen.

One, she recognized immediately as Commander Bricker. The other three were unknown to her, not even a memory flash indicating they'd been programmed. She followed Doctor Dan down three steps, then across a ramp up to the central table.

Bricker was juggling a light pen. "I thought they were sending her alone," he said. "I don't need anything that needs an escort."

Kurok stepped up onto the platform and took a seat on one of the stools, folding his arms across his chest in a typical pose. "I don't need to turn over one of my projects to ignorant gits," he said. "You cut short the programming cycle. I want to know why."

His voice was casual and unafraid, and Dev felt a certain awe of him. Even though she knew he was important, at least to her kind, she knew from her programming they were in a dangerous space.

The other people in the room were staring at Kurok. Bricker had stopped juggling his pen and was also staring as though unable to believe what he was hearing.

"You have any idea where you are, buddy?" Bricker finally said.

"Yes," Kurok replied. "Station ten, Central Design level four, comm space Alpha, control central, data store prime. Now please answer my question. If you can't, then I'll be more than glad to take my friend Dev here and go back where we came from."

Dev merely stood very still, having no reference at all as to what to do.

"As the chief geneticist of LifeForce on Bio station two, whom you've asked to provide you with this resource, I need to know why you truncated an already insufficient release cycle," Kurok restated his question. "I have no intention of providing you with either a scapegoat or an excuse for failure."

Bricker started juggling his pen again. "So that's who you are. Figures why we didn't have an ident on you. Made sure no one could look at your insides too close. Huh?"

Kurok didn't answer. He merely sat there, head cocked a little to one side, waiting.

Bricker turned to the display table. "Well, you're gonna have to wait, buddy, since I've got an activity in work. If it completes, maybe you can just take this jelly bag with you and go back to that crystal palace you got up there after all."

The door opened behind them, and Bricker glanced over his shoulder as three people entered. "What— " He straightened and started to reach for a pad, then stopped. "Sir."

Alexander Bain strolled up the ramp. "Bricker." He glanced at the rest of them. "I found these two outside. Seems a terrible place to leave agents, seeing as you've lost so many lately."

Dev backed up a little as the two other people emerged from the shadows, revealing the two from the outside bench. Now they looked wary and uncomfortable and she held her breath as they both looked around and she found herself once again meeting the woman's gaze.

Kurok got up off his stool and took a step back, putting himself between Dev and the table as the tension in the room ratcheted up to a higher level. "Well now. This is getting interesting."

Bain's eyes swept over and pinned him, one grizzled gray brow lifting sharply. "You!"

"You asked for a bio alt." Kurok's lips twitched. "I come with the territory, Alex."

"Ah huh," Bain mused, then shook his head. "Bricker, what's going on here?"

Bricker recovered. "Sir, that person requested dismissal. We followed procedure and processed the request." He pointed at Jess. "She was supposed to leave on the shuttle."

"I see." Bain regarded him. "And you allowed this without intervention?"

Bricker shrugged. "I don't need quitters or lone wolves," he said. "I saw no reason to intervene or even ask."

"I see. Hm." Bain half turned and regarded Dev, who was standing as far back as she could on the platform. "And you, my dear?"

"This is Dev," Kurok said. "The resource requested."

"Ah." Bain strolled over and regarded Dev. "What a charming young lady," he said. "My name is Alexander Bain, my dear."

"NM-Dev-1," Dev said quietly, extending a hand in greeting. "It's very nice to meet you."

"And I, you." Bain shook her hand. "Now." He released her and turned back to Bricker. "I received reports your other agents refused assignment. Is that true?"

"They tried," Bricker answered grimly. "I persuaded them otherwise. I have two teams out now, about to make a grab for the new photo synth technology." He tried, somewhat unsuccessfully to keep the triumph out of his voice. He turned and pointed at Jess, who was waiting silently in the shadows. "She tried to make the whole team a bunch of refusers. But I put them against the wall and told them they'd end up in point Alaska without envirosuits if they tried."

Jess took a half step forward and stiffened. Bock put a hand on her arm.

"I see." Bain nodded. "So you felt this was the best way to motivate them?" He tilted his head in a calm, almost quizzical manner.

"It worked." Bricker turned back to the display. "Excuse me. Tac two, report."

One of the techs standing at console spoke up. "Sir, I tracked them. They're in shadow right now, due in position one hundred ninety seconds."

"Sir," Jess said, her low voice echoing softly in the chamber. She fell silent when Bain held a hand up in her direction.

"Commander Bricker, please turn around and face me, "Alexander Bain said.

"Sir, I'm sorry, I'm in the middle of something here." Bricker glanced up. "Can it wait?"

"No, I'm afraid it cannot."

Bricker straightened up and turned. "Yes?"

The room swirled into motion. Bain lifted his hand from his side and there was a weapon in it. Both Stephan and Jess stiffened, then Jess made a sign and they both froze. Kurok spun Dev around and put his body between her and Bain and—

The projectile caught Bricker in the throat and exploded, sending blood and skin out to either side with a splattering sound as it hit the consoles to the right and left of him. His head lolled and dropped off to the floor, and his body collapsed to the ground, thumping and twitching as the techs jumped out of the way.

Absolute shocked silence fell, until Bain replaced the weapon into its hidden holster and dusted his hands off. "I never have approved of shooting anyone in the back," he said. "Now." He turned. "Bock, please take charge, and have this unpleasantness cleaned up."

He looked at all of them. "Any questions for me?" He glanced at Jess. "Drake, I suggest you take a look at what those colleagues of yours are into. I suspect it's not good."

Jess stirred out of her shock and jumped up onto the platform, shoving aside the tech as she stepped over Bricker's body, muttering curses under her breath.

Bain clapped his hands. "Come on, people. We're in some trouble here. Let's think our way out of it, shall we? Start moving."

Bock went to the comms panel and started speaking into it, as the other men on the platform went to consoles, giving Jess an uneasy look.

"Oh." Bain noticed that. "Please don't do anything unpleasant to Agent Drake. She's kindly agreed to rejoin our service and I'm most grateful for that."

The ops staff relaxed and resumed their stations, a few of them giving Jess a nod.

Dev stood as still as she could, her mind on overload trying to absorb all the data she'd just been given. She tried to make sense of it, but found her focus irresistibly turning to the ops console, where the woman Bain had called Drake was sitting, finding it much easier to think about her than about the man she'd just seen made dead.

She no longer looked sad, or depressed. There was energy crackling from every inch of her as her eyes flicked through the screens with intense concentration.

She was so interesting. Dev could see her eyes reflected in the vid screen, surprised at how pale and clear they were, a light crystal blue.

"Dev." Kurok stirred her from her focus. "Are you doing okay?"

Dev started, then looked at him. "I'm all right. I just don't really know what's going on."

Kurok looked around, then shook his head a little. "I'm not really sure either. But we'll find out, don't you worry." He did, in fact, look worried himself. "I won't leave you here otherwise."

Dev nodded. Then she glanced past Doctor Dan to the platform, to find the woman Drake looking back at her, with wary curiosity.

"We'll find out." Kurok patted her shoulder. "Don't worry."

Dev looked down at the ground, surprised to see spatters of blood on the steel only a few inches from her boots. "I'm not worried, Doctor Dan. I'm sure it will be okay."

She looked back up, back at the agent's profile, and wondered.

JESS WAS AWARE of the security team behind her and the medical techs bundling up Bricker's body. She could hear their breathing, a little faster than normal, and sense the insecurity around her as everyone tried to adjust to what had just happened.

She focused past that. She had her elbows on the console and her eyes flicking from status readout to predictors, listening for the incoming bursts from the two teams out there.

Two teams of two people—agent and tech—in armored personnel carriers whose flight characteristics were roughly those of the ancient and mythic sperm whale. Only thing going for them were two engines powerful enough to launch the damn things into space and a lot of strap webbing that kept you from killing yourself inside one.

Jess sighed and flicked a few settings.

Running the boards wasn't her favorite task. She hated being here, and not there, able only to react to what was going on, but she'd done her share of this. Every agent had, in training and in the times they couldn't be out in the field for any number of reasons.

But she was glad she was here now, and able to concentrate on those signals because otherwise she'd have to think about how her life had gone into a radical tailspin in the last hour, and what the hell she was going to do next.

Less time to think about the quiet figure seated near the far wall, hands clasped, eyes absorbing everything around her. NM-Dev-1 wasn't anything like what she'd expected. She'd figured they'd taken one of the pilot duffs, and tweaked him for this gig.

This wasn't a pilot. This wasn't any of the types they'd gotten before. She glanced to one side, watching the bio alt's serious face as she studied the console next to her. This was unknown.

A bleep caught her attention, and she looked back at the screens.

Bricker had screwed it. Jess checked the position of the two teams, seeing them on the very edge of the dark side. "Tac one, Tac two, base," she said into the comms. He'd sent the two in without full intel and they'd gotten their asses chomped by a big armed patrol with long range guns.

There was only crackling for answer. The two teams, in their armored carriers, had gone in over sea and tried to penetrate a small research station. They were caught now on the flats, the edgy cross-lines of laser cannons pinning them down.

"What's the game?" Stephan slid into the seat next to her. "This is crazy."

"I can't get to them." Jess pointed at the scan link. "They're blocking comms. Only thing I can tell is they're intact. I can see the outline."

"Shit."

A blast of antiseptic made them both turn to see a medic with a tank on his back washing down the floor. He glanced at them, then went back to his task.

Jess glanced at Stephan. "Wasn't how I figured this day to go."

Stephan snorted and shook his head. Then he leaned a little closer. "Glad?"

Jess's face tensed into a faint smile.

"All right, people." Alexander Bain came back into the comms center. "Report."

Stephan swiveled in his seat. "No new status, sir. The two carriers are pinned down under tracer fire, no comms."

"Well." Bain strolled over. "Then suppose you go to the briefing center and join me for a strategy meeting. I think we need some strategy. Been sadly lacking here for a while, I believe." He considered. "Drake, please take our new recruit here and have them kit her out. Get her creds. My orders."

Jess stood. "Do I have creds?" She asked. "Hate to walk into security and get shot."

Bain's face shifted into a somewhat piratical smile. "I appreciate a sense of humor, Drake," he said. "I believe my presence has been advertised sufficiently that you should be safe walking the halls. Once that's settled, join us in the briefing center." He glanced at Kurok, then crooked a finger at him. "You come with me."

Kurok regarded him. Then he got up and patted Dev on the shoulder. "Go with the agent, Dev. I'll see you shortly."

They all shifted and moved. Jess walked over to where the bio alt was standing, and gestured. "This way." She waited for the silent figure to join her and they walked down the ramp and out the door.

The halls were very quiet. Jess was glad, not wanting to run into a hundred people all asking her questions. She hadn't decided yet what to tell anyone, so it was good to just walk down the familiar floors passing from the enforcement area into the circling boundaries of security.

She'd passed through the first scan gate before she realized it, her body jerking in reaction at the tickle then relaxing as only a sedate bong reacted to her presence. "Guess he was right," she muttered.

"Pardon?" The bio alt asked.

Jess looked at her. She was relatively short, her head only reaching to Jess's shoulder. She had a slim body presently encased in a standard space jumpsuit. "Talking to myself," she said. "That scanner we just passed could have boiled my brain."

Dev looked behind them, a startled expression on her face. "Oh."

Jess paused as they reached the security center. "Sorry." She eyed the bio alt. "My name's Jess." She extended a hand. "I won't say welcome. You probably don't really want to be here."

Dev reached over and took the offered hand, closing her fingers around Jess's and giving them a firm pressure. "Thank you," she said. "I don't have much say in it. But so far it's been interesting"

Jess cocked her head a little, not expecting so self aware a response. "Right." She turned and keyed the door open. "Let's see how much more interesting it's going to be." She walked inside the center and went to the ops desk. "Jackson."

The security captain had straightened when she entered, and was now waiting for them, his hands resting on the desk. He was big, taller than Jess and about twice her weight, with a very muscular body and the typical security buzz cut. "Drake."

"Bain sent me down," Jess said, briefly. "She needs creds." She indicated Dev. "And I guess I need reissued ones."

"We heard." Jackson said. "He really plug Bricker?"

Jess nodded. "Yup."

"Good. Jackass." Jackson turned and motioned to a sergeant. "Open up Drake's access," he ordered, then turned to Jess. "What level is this one?" He indicated Dev. "Staff? Support?"

"Enforcement ops tech," Jess replied, dryly.

Jackson's jaw dropped a little, and he stared openly at Dev. "Thought that was bullshit rumor."

"Apparently not," Jess said. "Since here she is."

Jackson shook his head. "Jackass," he muttered. "Place is going to hell." He keyed in something, continually shaking his head as he worked. "Go stand in that." He pointed to the genetiscan, waiting for Dev to comply before he continued coding.

Jess didn't respond to the muttering. She nodded at the sergeant when the woman came over to her, running a hand wand over her. She held out her left hand and the wand touched it, making her flinch a little as she felt the chips embedded there react. "Thanks."

"Agent," the sergeant responded. "All clear."

Jess flexed her hand, glancing over to see Dev standing quietly in the scanner, traces blinking in the collar she wore around her neck. Their eyes met and she managed a brief smile she hoped was reassuring.

It was something. The bio alt smiled back.

"They assigned her quarters yet?" Jackson asked. "None coded here."

"Heading to supply next," Jess said. "I guess they'll do that there." She looked up, her face going a little blank. "We've got plenty of space at the moment."

Jackson nodded. "Heard that," he said. "All right, done." He motioned the sergeant forward. "Cred for ops."

The sergeant went over to Dev and scanned her. They were more or less the same height, but the sergeant had the powerful muscularity typical of security and would have had dark red curly hair if it hadn't been shorn close to her skull. "Done." She handed Dev a set of clip on creds. "Wear that for the biology based systems. The mechanicals don't need it."

"Thank you." Dev took the creds and applied them to her jumpsuit.

"Good luck," the woman said unexpectedly, extending a hand. "I'm Boston."

Dev returned the shake. "Thank you."

The sergeant turned and made her way back behind the desk and Jess motioned to the door. "Next." She let Dev go ahead of her, and they exited the security center. "You can expect that kind of reaction," Jess said, after a moment's walking. "Pretty much everyone thinks your being here is asinine."

Dev gave her a sideways look. "Do you?" She asked, in a mild tone.

Jess took a breath to answer, then paused.

"It doesn't offend me." Dev said. "There's not much I can do about it since I'm here and I didn't have a choice about it."

Jess felt very off-balance. This bio alt was turning out to be more of a surprise than she needed at the moment. "I don't know," she finally answered. "I thought it was a bad idea when I heard about it."

"Why?"

Why. Jess was glad to see the supply hallway at her left. She turned and swiped the door controls, leading Dev inside to the big processing center. "Hold that question a minute."

Here there were more bio alts. She watched them catch sight of Dev and react, then go back to their tasks, a little distracted and intrigued by the wary expressions on their faces. She stepped up to the counter, manned by an older man with a scar across his face and one destroyed eye. "Hey Buddy."

The man gazed gravely at her. "Jess. Welcome back," he said. "That was the shortest outprocess in the history of Interforce, I'm guessing. I heard the Old Man himself talked you down, then blew Bricker's head off. Been quite the morning." He glanced to one side. "Who's this?"

"This is Dev," she said. "She's Bricker's experiment. Bain asked me to get her kitted out. He wants to continue it, I guess."

Dev regarded the man and noted he had a somewhat kinder eye than most she'd encountered so far in this new place. She also noted he and her escort called each other by common names, and that Jess also seemed more relaxed here.

The security place had been stern and a little hostile, even though the people there had done what they'd been asked to. "Hello," Dev said.

"Hello, Dev," Buddy replied. "So we need to give you all the crank you need to be a tech, huh?" He keyed in something on the console. "Sure hope they know what they're doing." He looked up. "Plenty of berths available, unfortunately. Preference?" He directed the question at Jess.

Jess took a mental step back and thought about the question. There were a lot of empty berths. Aside from the recent deaths, they'd already been six teams short. Dev could be given any of them, since all of the bunks were more or less the same.

She looked up and found Dev watching her. She knew what Bricker's intent was, and felt the truth in her own rejection of that. Nothing had really changed and yet, in the small space of the morning, everything had changed.

Had she changed? "Put her in Joshua's berth. Bain asked me to get her settled."

Buddy didn't blink an eye. "Done," he said. "I'll have the bulk of it sent there." He glanced at Dev. "Could you please go stand on that other platform there?" He pointed to the outfitting console. "Thanks."

Dev obediently went over and stood in the box, which scanned her with a completely different type of signal. It felt a little warm, not at all tickly, and it took only a moment. Then she stepped out and returned to Jess's side.

Buddy turned and removed a green sack, which he handed over to her. "Basics." He said, as she took it. "Everything else will be sent. Okay?"

Having once again no choice in the matter, Dev nodded.

"Let's go." Jess said. "I'll drop you at your bunk, then go see what the bad news is." She glanced at Buddy. "I guess I need resupply too."

"Already done." Buddy waved her off. "We saw it come active again from security."

"Thanks." Jess led the way again. They went through the doors and turned right. "You got kit on the shuttle?"

Dev touched the small bag hanging at her belt. "Just this," she said. "They told me I would get everything here."

"Well, at least they got something right." Jess produced a brief smile. They continued down the hall and then into the centrum, passing through two scanners, then a third as they entered a blue shaded hallway.

A few turns later and they were at a door. "Scan it." Jess stood back. "Might as well find out if they actually did what they were supposed to do."

Dev put her hand on the keypad and the door slid obediently open. She glanced back at Jess for instruction, then walked inside at the slight gesture she received.

Jess entered behind her. "Listen," she said. "I have no idea how this is going to work out. You could just be in here for an hour, then be packed back upstairs."

Dev nodded. "You don't think I can do what was requested."

Jess let the door shut behind them and then turned, studying the bio alt in silence for a bit. "They train people for years to do this job. You've had a week. So no, I don't think so. Actually I think a lot of people don't want to think so, because if you could—"

"If I could, we could replace you," Dev said. "And we're cheap and expendable. That's what they say." She watched Jess's face, taking a breath as she suddenly saw an intent personality become present there when Jess looked at her, not through her. She saw more intelligence and emotion in that one glance than she'd ever experienced before. "I don't know if I can help either. I just have what programming I have and I'll do the best I can if they want me to try."

Jess exhaled. "Yeah well." She glanced past Dev to the rest of the room. "Lately we've been sort of expendable too." She indicated the room. "Until they figure it all out, you bunk here."

Dev looked around at the space. "By myself?" She asked, in a surprised tone.

Jess twitched a little and looked at her. "What?"

Dev, for the first time, looked a little off balance. "Sorry." She peered around. "It's a big room. It wasn't like this in the crèche."

"No, I guess not." Jess felt faintly amused. "Okay, well, that's the sanitary station." She pointed, then paused. "You know what that is, right?"

"Yes."

"Shower and lav in there, you can put your kit in the cabinet." Jess swiveled around. "Sleep." She pointed at the bed. "Relax." She pointed to the left hand side loft. "And work." She pointed at the right hand side loft. "I'll leave you to explore. We'll call you if we want you to come to the comms center. Otherwise, stick around here. It's easy to get lost in this place."

Dev nodded. "Okay."

Jess turned to go. At the door, she paused and looked back. Then turned and left without speaking.

Dev drew in a deep breath, then she let it out. There was so much to absorb, she was glad she had a few minutes at least to just do that. She set the green bag down, then sat in the chair behind the workspace on the lower level, which was soft and comfortable and reminded her just a little of her sleeping pod back in the crèche.

She sat back and turned it around, regarding this huge space with more than a little bemusement. So here she was. Things were not at all going according to plan, but she'd ended up in this place anyway with all this incredible strangeness around her.

At the very least, she'd have a cycles worth of stories to tell them back in the crèche if they did send her back. Dev pondered that idea, and decided she really hoped they didn't.

JESS DETOURED PASSED the caffeine station on her way back to the strategy center. She put her palm down on the dispenser plate and the system produced a vacuum bottle full of her preference. She uncapped it and took a sip, turning around and leaning against the counter.

She studied the bottle. By this time she should have been in a scavenger station, trading her jumpsuit for an exposure kit, and if she'd been lucky, assigned to a work battalion down in the caverns harvesting seaweed.

And at that she would have been one of the lucky, with basic but functional housing and the promise of a meal so long as the quotas were upheld.

She knew what it was. She had two siblings out there who had done the work. They hadn't qualified for anything better as youngsters but their family's tenure in service guaranteed them at least that.

Those who had neither family connection or needed skills ended up in the out lands, the only shelter there what they built themselves. As for what they lived on? Jess's face tensed into a grimace. They lived on what they could steal, and being caught out in the out lands was as dangerous to someone like her as taking a trip to the other side.

So here she was instead, her whole intent reversed. She'd be lying if she said she was sad about it. It was one thing to stand on your honor. It was another to actually like the consequences of that. Jess was self aware enough to know she'd lead a relatively privileged life and she liked it that way.

It was nice to know she'd likely be lying down in her comfortable bunk tonight rather than on cold stone, or in a rough worn hammock, and she could have caffeine when she wanted and a meal in the ops mess.

She felt a bit guilty over how glad she was Bain had showed up, brought her back in, then blew Bricker away like he'd been no more than a sea rat caught in the storage silo. A bit guilty, but not too much.

She'd thought maybe Bain would come in and take charge, make plans, maybe make some changes. Hell she'd hoped he would do that, but outright kill Bricker?"

Ah, no. More than a little scary. Jess capped her drink and took it with her, heading with no further delay toward the strategy planning center. Outside the door she met up with two of her remaining peers and they all looked at each other in silence for a long moment.

"Jason," Jess murmured. "Glad you two weren't the ones out there."

"Jess," Jason Anders finally said. "What in the hell's going on?" He was a tall man, with thick brown hair and hazel eyes.

"Crap all, from what I hear," the woman next to him said. "Is it true? Bricker's dead?"

"They didn't send a squirt out?" Jess frowned. "Public as it was? Bain splatted him in the middle of central ops for craps sake. In front of some doctor from the bio station on top of it."

"No, nothing." Jason shook his head. "Elaine? You get anything on comms?"

"Not a damn thing." Elaine Cruz shook her head. "I just heard something from one of the med techs they sent in there to clean the mess up." She put her hands on her hips, her rust red hair making her fair skin and green eyes stand out.

Jess glanced at the door. "Well, you got the baseline of it. I was humping up onto the shuttle when I ran into Bain. He knew everything. Asked me to come back with him, and about two minutes after we got to central he pulled a blaster out and took Bricker's head off."

"Damn," Jason said. "Just like that? For nothing?"

"Bain could do it for nothing," Elaine said. "Who'd stop him?"

"I didn't," Jess said. "I got the feeling it wasn't just one thing that caused it." She studied the both of them. "They call you in there?"

Elaine nodded. "Tucker and Brent are in their quarters. Scared to death. Afraid Bain's going to do the same to them."

Jess turned and palmed the door. "Let's find out how screwed we are."

"Jess?" Jason said, just as the door started opening. "Glad you're back."

"Ditto," Elaine said.

The door was open and Jess didn't answer. She led the way into the strategy center, past the outer chamber with it's scattering of austere chairs, to the second portal, which was guarded by two members of the security group.

Jess half expected to be challenged, but the guards merely drew aside and triggered the door for them and the three enforcement agents proceeded inside.

It was quiet. Stephan was seated near one end of the large plotting table and Bain was in the big leader's chair at the very end. The table was lit with statistics, and the curved wall behind the table was brilliant with readouts and scans.

"Ah. There you all are." Bain said. "Did you get your new colleague settled, Drake?"

"Yes." Jess sat down mid table and Elaine and Jason took seats next to her, on the side away from Bain.

"New colleague?" Jason asked, in a low tone. "What's that about?"

"Did you say something, Anders?" Bain asked. "We don't really have time for idle chit chat you know. Not if we're going to find some way of getting those two teams back."

Jason cleared his throat. "Sorry sir. I was just wondering what new colleague we have." He returned Bain's look. "It's been a sore subject here lately."

"So I've heard." Bain stood and leaned on the table. "Perhaps I should explain."

Chapter Five

DEV STUCK HER head into the sanitary facility, entering after a moment and putting her small personal kit down. The space was clean and austere, the stone lined walls with faint flecks of reflectivity in their depths. It was a roughly rectangular space with inset cabinets on both long sides.

A half wall concealed a lavatory. Dev studied it curiously, reaching forward to press one of the buttons on the top and jumping back a little as she was rewarded with a faint roaring sound. She peeked inside the bowl and saw a moving substance, not the vacuum system she was used to. "Ah."

Well, she'd figure that out soon enough.

With a faint shrug, she went on to the counter, which held a neatly folded set of assorted fabric. She touched the surface of one, finding it soft and nubbly. It was too small to wear and she picked one of them up, unfolding it and releasing a faint, unrecognizable scent into the air.

Another puzzle. Dev examined the inset bowl next to them, which had a hole in the bottom and mechanisms at the top. She reached out and touched one and leaped back as something rushed out of the pipe at the top and splashed into the bowl with a thick, almost musical sound.

She searched her programming and found nothing regarding it, but then a deeper memory triggered and she relaxed, recalling something from her basics programming.

She stepped forward again and hesitantly put her hand under the flow, inhaling a little as it chilled her skin. Her other hand joined it and she rubbed them both together, then she touched the mechanism again. She stood with her hands dripping into the sink for a moment, then with a satisfied grunt, she picked up one of the pieces of fabric and used it to dry her hands off. So this was water, freely running water. "Interesting."

She continued her exploration, opening the cabinets and finding more fabric, larger pieces, again neatly folded. At the end of the room was another half wall, and she peeked behind it to find a square space with a drain in the floor. A pipe extruded out with a round, flat head. Curiously, she reached in and touched the controls, letting out a yip of surprise when a blast of water came out of the head and drenched her.

She batted at the controls and turned the water off, then stood, dripping, her arms held out away from her body a little. She blinked and then shook her head, scattering droplets everywhere. "Ah hah." She licked her lips, finding that the water tasted a little sweet. Dev decided staying in the wet jumpsuit in the cool air of the chamber probably wasn't a good idea.

She unbuckled and slipped out of it, laying it across the counter and then turning to the cabinets and removing one of the large, square fabrics. She wrapped it around her as she bent over to unbuckle and remove her boots, setting them down under the counter as well. Going to her small kit, she removed her comb and ran it through her wet hair, setting it to order.

Glad to be free of the cold wetness, she used another fabric to dry herself off, then she went back into the main part of the room. This left her in a quandary though, as she could hardly respond to any of the requests that might be made of her without clothes on. She started toward one of the cabinets in the main part of the room when she heard rumbling behind it. A set of bangs and slams sent her back to the sanitary facility, unsure of what was going on.

A soft chime sounded. "Main stores, provisioning complete."

Dev regarded the speaker, then she glanced at the big cabinet again. The doors, previously solid and dark gray, were now turning translucent, back lit with a gentle golden glow. She approached cautiously, opening the front to find a line of dark jumpsuits hanging there and a set of shelves below. She opened the first one, gratified to find familiar looking underwear there. "At least I know what this is," she muttered. "There's a lot of stuff they forgot to program about this place."

She traded her fabric for the undergarments, which fit neatly, then she removed one of the jumpsuits and slipped it on. It too fit her perfectly, but the fabric was unlike anything she'd ever felt before. It was soft and a little stretchy, conforming to her body and very comfortable.

It had a collar that extended up covering the back of her neck, and was gathered at her wrists and ankles with many pockets and rip strips to hold things.

She liked that. The color was dark green with black trims and it had a deep blue ring around the neckline, but no other insignia to it. Almost the same as the one Jess had been wearing, save hers was all black, except that same blue ring.

She glanced at her reflection in the door mirror, blinking a little at the unexpected outline. She'd pulled the front catch all the way up and the fabric had sealed around her neck, completely covering her collar. A part of her felt a little strange, looking at herself and not seeing that.

She studied herself thoughtfully, wondering how long she would get to wear the new clothes. Then she shrugged, finding several pairs of boots on the floor of the cabinet and selecting one of them to take back with her to the comfortable chair near the desk.

She sat down and set the boots next to her. Then she looked around, wondering if—ah. She got back up and went to the counter on the other side of the sanitary room, where she'd spotted a refrigerated dispenser.

That, in it's essential form, she knew. In the common spaces of the crèche there were always stations you could get a drink from and they looked pretty much like this one.

She opened it and was cheered to find sealed containers of liquid and solids. She removed one of each and brought them back to the desk, feeling a luxury all out of proportion as she opened the liquid, finding it clear, clean and apparently water. She unwrapped the solids to discover crispy little crackers that smelled faintly of brine, and were sprinkled with tiny seeds and salt.

Dev bit into one cautiously. It had an interesting taste and after a few nibbles she decided she liked it.

She sat in her chair, munching her crackers and sipping from the water, looking around at this inconceivably huge space they'd assigned to her. She could see one side of the upper level had consoles and she brightened, realizing she might be able to practice some of her programming. On the other side was a couch, and what appeared to be a big console, with some shelves and mats. Jess had said something about relaxing up there and Dev considered that maybe she could use it like she had her little cubicle back in the crèche—as a place to sit quietly and maybe read some of her book.

Everything was so different here, but different in a way she didn't mind. She finished her crackers and set her water aside, then climbed up to the second level with her book in her hand and sat down on the couch. It had an overhead light and she lay down bathed in it, opening the book and settling herself down to enjoy a page.

After a moment she looked around, then smiled and shook her head.

"ARE YOU KIDDING me?" Jason stared at Jess, aghast. "That's real? They did it? They sent it here? Really?"

Jess glanced across at Bain, who merely tapped his fingers against his lips in silence. "Well." She said. "In that they brought a bio alt here, yes. That part's real."

Jason looked at Bain. "Sir?"

"Yes?"

"Are you advocating this, sir?"

Bain regarded him. "You would not?"

Jason and Elaine exchanged glances. "Sir," he said in a respectful tone. "We..." Then he paused and a frown appeared on his long face.

"Caught in a conundrum?" Bain said. "I believe you were just about to inform me that you have to place great trust in your technical assistants, hmm?" He observed them. "And yet, we do indeed have a trust issue here. You don't trust your colleagues, you don't trust your leadership, and quite likely, you don't trust that I will not blow your heads off as I did Bricker's this morning. Hmm?"

The door slid open and Dan Kurok came in. He gave them all a cursory glance, then took a seat on the opposite side of the table from Jess. "Your central records store is a mess," he told Bain. "I have a query running, but likely it won't turn up much more than a recipe for chocolate cupcakes."

Jess's eyebrows jerked up at his casual address. She was beginning to wonder who this man was, aside from some gene doctor from topside.

"And what do you think, Drake?" Bain turned to her. "Do you still disagree with this experiment of ours, having met it's subject?"

Jess felt all the eyes on her and she hunched her shoulders a bit in reaction. "Why don't we talk about what the plan is before we go into that," she said. "We've got four people out there pinned down and in terminal danger. I think that's more important than how I feel about bio alts."

"And yet," Bain said. "You had her put in quarters adjoining yours. Interesting?"

"Statement stands," Jess responded dryly.

"Very well," Bain said. "As I was discussing with Bock here, it seems the issue was that your colleagues were attempting an insertion here." He pointed at a mapping coordinate. "Where they were expecting to find an exhaust station." He stood and juggled the laser guide in his hand. "What they found were a half dozen armored carriers."

"Trap?" Jason asked.

"Or did they get skunked?" Jess quietly disagreed. "Someone tipped them."

Bain pursed his lips. "I think their plans were known," he said. "As there is indeed an exhaust station at that locale." He brought up another overlay. "Just as the last mission was compromised—but we thought we knew the information vector there."

"They were waiting for us," Jess said. "I heard the hatches clamp just before Joshua turned on me." She studied her hands. "He hadn't had a chance to send comms before we got there. I would have heard it."

Bain nodded. "Someone else within Interforce was compromised."

"Is that why you shot him?" Elaine asked. "Bricker, I mean. Was he the leak?"

"No." Bain regarded her. "I shot him because he was a blithering idiot." He paused. "Although, that could possibly have been the reason for the compromise." He cleared his throat. "The problem is, he was put in place by someone at a high level, who was put in place by someone else at a high level, who was put in place by me."

"Ah." Jess nodded.

"You run out of magnesium slugs after awhile of that," Bain said. "So the truth is, people, we don't know where the hole is."

Kurok snorted softly and shook his head.

Jess looked at her two fellow agents. "So someone is leaking our ops to the other side and it could be all the way up."

"Yes."

"So, Josh was probably turned from the inside," Jason said, slowly. "We've been trying to figure out when he was nicked, and no one could." He looked at Jess. "Maybe he never was. Maybe someone was just talking him into it over dinner, here."

"So we have another quandary," Bain said. "Obviously we need to go and assist the two teams who are now trapped under fire. However, outside this room I cannot tell you that the very plans we make might not be sent ahead."

"Outside this room?" Stephan asked. "So you consider this group secure."

"Yes," Bain said. "Congratulations. No one else is going to die here today."

Everyone flinched a little, except Kurok. He cleared his throat. "So the issue is, you can't trust the outsiders. That includes your techs and most of the staff inside this facility." He looked at Jess. "That was why Bricker came and asked us to design a set that could be programmed for the job. We know what's in their minds. You can't say that about anyone else."

Jess returned his look. "Doesn't do me any good if they can't do the job."

"How do you know Dev can't?" Kurok countered. "Listen, I know you people think what we do is just create amiable rag dolls for slave labor, but I wouldn't be here with her if I didn't think she could be of value to you. Regardless of what Doss promised. He doesn't own me."

Bain chuckled softly. "No one ever did."

Kurok glanced sideways at him, then returned his attention to Jess. "You've met her. You tell me. Mindless?"

Jess was aware of the silence in the room, and very aware of the intent looks focused on her. She thought about her few minutes with Dev, running their conversations back in her mind. "No." She answered, in a somewhat surprised tone. "More complex than I expected, but that doesn't mean she can be a tech."

"Drake." Bain leaned on the table again. "This is the bottom line. For this plan here," he pointed at the screen. "We'll send your colleagues there to stand by, to cover for the two trapped teams. But to get them out, we need to distract. For that we need you, and you need someone with you that you trust, since you'll be putting yourself in the wolves mouth."

"Why me?" Jess asked. "Send someone else."

"Because they want you." Bain said with a thin smile. "You were stabbed and we lost four good teams, all because they were intent on keeping you. And they would have if you hadn't been just that much better than they anticipated."

Jess felt cold. "Me?"

"Crap," Jason muttered.

"You," Bain said. "And before you ask, no, I don't know why. Likely you made some enemy on the other side who has now gained high level there."

"So you're going to throw Jess into the fire?" Elaine asked. "Since you know they want her?"

Bain straightened up and paced around at the head of the table. "Yes. It will provide the distraction we need. When they send all their assets after her, we set the other teams free."

Stephan stood up. "Wait a minute. Sir—"

"Stephan, sit." Jess waved him down. "I'll do it," she said. "We'll give this experiment a try. Worst I can end up is dead." She pointed at the displays. "Send a burst to my account. I want to study the layout. I'll do the setup."

"Jess, c'mon," Stephan said. "I thought you said this was asinine! Isn't this the very same thing you were quitting about this damn morning?"

Jess nodded. "It was. But I didn't have all the intel I needed to make that choice. All I had was your pitch of what Bricker said. Bricker's dead. The story's changed."

Bain gazed at her with surprising fondness. "You are a throwback, aren't you?" He said. "So you will accept Kurok's little project, hmm?"

Jess nodded.

"Jess!"

Was she crazy? Maybe. Jess felt a sudden and surprising shame over walking out and figured maybe this was just her ego's way of erasing that. Right? Wrong? Who the hell knew. She looked up at Kurok, who was studying her with quiet, intent eyes. "Can she drive a carrier?"

"Yes." He said in a quiet tone. "She's been programmed to."

Jess stood. "Give me the dump," she said. "Stephan can you plot the weather? I thought I heard a storm coming in." She glanced around the table. "Are we done here? I've got gear to settle."

"So you don't wish us to go over the plan, Drake?" Bain asked. "All of us together?"

"No." Jess said. "It just became not your plan." She gestured to Jason and Elaine. "We'll meet later. Prep to go less twenty-four."

Silently, the other two agents rose and followed her and she left the conferencing center, the door sliding shut behind them with a soft metallic thump.

"HM." BAIN GRUNTED.

"You wanted her to participate." Kurok leaned back, a faint grin on his face. "Someone used to tell me to be careful what I asked for, as I recall."

Bain gave him a dour look.

Stephan got up. "Would you excuse me, sir? I've got things to do." He waited until Bain nodded, then he turned and left the room from a different door, heading back up the secure hallway to central comms.

Bain sat down and swiveled his seat to face Kurok. "Not a good situation, DJ."

"No." Kurok agreed. "And I'm not sure we're going in the right direction in solving it."

"Hm."

Kurok glanced up at him. "Been a damn long time since I was called that."

Bain smiled briefly. "You may need to get used to hearing it again."

JESS STEERED HER slightly rabid sounding followers into the caffeine station. "Look." She held a hand up. "You're not telling me anything I don't know."

"Jess, how can you even consider going out with one of them?" Elaine asked. "Why not just find a cat outside and let them drive? You're going to get yourself killed. No one wants that."

"Maybe I do."

Utter silence fell for a long and uncomfortable moment. Jess fell back to lean against the wall. She ran her hand through her dark hair, avoiding their eyes. "It'll be fine." She said. "Worse comes to worse I can drive the damn thing."

"What if they catch you?" Jason asked. "You heard what he said, they want you, Jess. Why put yourself in their hands? Tell these guys no. You can. I've heard you."

Jess studied them both. "Because it's not the right thing to do." She said. "We've got four people trapped there— "

"Who could give a crap about you," Elaine said, bluntly.

"Doesn't matter if they give a crap about me," Jess said. "Doesn't even matter if someone dumps the plan. I'm not going to sit here on my ass while four people are out there getting shot. If you two don't want to go out—don't. I'll be the decoy then figure out how to get over to them and get them out."

"Jess."

"So I'm an asshole and it's impossible." She shrugged. "Who cares?" She pushed off the wall. "Now I've got to go prep. Hell if I know what's secure around here. If you're interested, I'll let you know when I'm ready and we can meet in my quarters."

Jason sighed. "Do we bring Tucker and Brent?" He didn't even look at Elaine, sure of her answer. The two had been in training together, were several years older than Jess was, and were frequently paired in the field.

"Do you?" Jess turned the question back at him. "They're your partners."

Elaine went to the dispenser and requested a bottle. "I hate this." She turned around, holding the bottle between both hands as though warming them. "How in hell do we know what's safe and what's not?"

"Tucker and I have worked together for ten years," Jason said. "Brent's been part of the team for twelve."

"And Joshua was for nine." Jess shrugged. "But if what you said in there was right, Jace, and he was turned recently, then time in service doesn't matter."

Jason scratched his scalp at the back of his neck and looked at Jess. "Shit. Maybe your damn bio alt makes sense after all."

Elaine snorted softly. "Until it drives you into a cliff wall." She studied her bottle. "I say you and I meet with Jess, Jace. We can fill them in later. This sounds more like an in and out anyway, no hard tech."

Jess nodded. "Deal." She reached around Elaine and requested her own bottle. "Let's hope the weather clears and we can get this done."

"Let's hope the weather clears regardless." Jason followed them out and down the hallway, heading back toward the residential corridors. "We don't need any more floods."

JESS CLEARED INTO her quarters, glancing around as she entered and spotting the evidence she'd been reprovisioned in her absence. She could see the uniform module in service, and her duffel had been delivered back and was sitting next to her bed.

She dropped into the chair at the workspace and swung the pad around. She reached over to trigger her console, freezing as she heard a slight noise beyond the sliding portal to her left.

For a moment, she'd forgotten. "Ah." She studied the door with a frown. Then she got up and went to the inner door, pressing the annunciator chime and waiting.

After a very long pause, the door opened and she was facing Dev.

Dev had changed, she noted, into the dark green field service kit. "You get settled in?" she asked.

"Yes," Dev said. "They brought everything I needed."

"Good." She held her hand against the door so it wouldn't close. "Um."

Dev tilted her head a little to one side. "Is this where you live?" She pointed behind Jess.

"Ah, yes," she said. "It is." She watched Dev nod thoughtfully. "We're going to have a planning session later on in here. We have to go and get some people out of some trouble."

Dev's body posture altered as she straightened up a little and her chin lifted. "We?"

"That's what you came here for, right?" Jess asked. She looked curiously at Dev. "They did program you to do this, didn't they?"

"Yes," Dev responded. "They did."

"Okay." Jess said. "So I'll call you when we're having the session." She watched the woman nod again. "Did you get a meal?"

Dev turned and pointed at the refrigerator. "They left water and crackers there. I had some."

Jess winced.

"I liked them," Dev said. "Were they not for eating?"

"Let me show you where the mess is," Jess said. "C'mon." She motioned Dev forward. Once Dev cleared the door she let it shut, then she led the way to her own outer door. "You can eat those. Not sure why you'd want to, but they're survival rations."

"Oh."

Jess led the way down the corridor and around the bend toward where the communal area was. She passed a number of people, most of whom did a double take on seeing her, and then a second on seeing her companion.

Mild entertainment. They crossed the large central hall and paused as Stephan caught sight of them and hurried over.

"Jess, here's the weather." Stephan glanced at Dev, then at the film. "Nothing good. Don't think you can."

He stopped talking as Jess put her hands over the report and stared at him. "Thanks," she said. "I appreciate your checking." She folded the film and put it in a pocket. "We're going to the mess."

Stephan glanced again at Dev. "Oh."

Jess circled around him and continued on down the corridor, moving past the operations desk and down the left hand turn that would take them into the operations dining hall. "Only field ops in here." She scanned the door open and motioned for Dev to precede her.

Dev stepped inside and looked around. The room was large, with many different levels to it, the same dark gray as the rest of the facility but with somber splashes of color in the fabric of the chairs arranged around the small tables.

In the back, on the highest platform, there were several large tables arranged near the wall, with seats behind them. They were empty. Two of the smaller tables were occupied and the people at them turned to stare at her and Jess when they entered.

Dev was getting used to being stared at. It didn't bother her. She returned their gaze with a mild neutral expression, waiting for Jess to instruct her further on what they needed to do.

"C'mon." Jess indicated a food line in the back. "We line up for everything but dinner when we come in here. That they serve."

"All right." Dev followed her willingly as they passed through the tables. She watched what the other woman did and picked up a tray, putting it down on the railings as they moved down them. "We had facilities like this in the crèche."

Jess glanced at her. "Did you?" She pointed. "That's lunch."

Dev studied the now incomprehensible things facing her. There were dispensers and trays of what she assumed were edibles, but the smells and sights were completely unfamiliar. "Yes. But there was only one thing. They just gave it to us we didn't have any choice about it." She looked back. "What do you do now?"

"You pick what you want." Jess frowned. "You know how to do that? I didn't figure lunch was a challenge."

Dev's face twitched a little. "I don't know what any of this is," she said. "We had different foods in the creche."

"Ah." Jess rubbed the bridge of her nose. Then she turned and punched in a set of numbers, waiting as the dispenser rumbled and clattered. She opened it to reveal a divided tray of steaming food. She put it down on her own tray, then coded in the same set again. "This has never killed me so it probably won't kill you either." She took the second portion and gave it to Dev.

Dev studied it as she followed Jess down the line, finding a glass of something added to her selection before they picked up the trays and walked over to a small table. She sat down, glad now that Doctor Dan had brought her to the fancy place to prepare her.

People were still staring at her. She retrieved the utensils, reaching over and taking a sip from the glass to give her a moment to study what was on the plate.

The taste in the glass made her pause though and she pulled it back and looked at it. "What is this?"

Jess looked up from cutting her food. "What?"

Dev lifted the glass. "This?"

"Kack," Jess said. "Generic caffeinated grog with vitamins."

It was very odd. Dev took another sip of the dark orange beverage, trying to decide if she liked it or not. It was faintly spicy, and a bit sweet, with a hint of effervescence. She put the glass down and took a bit of one of things on the tray and put it in her mouth.

It had a mildly chewy texture and a nice taste. "And this?" Dev asked. "It's good."

Jess swallowed a mouthful of it. "Fish stew. Most of what we eat here is fish based." She pointed down and to the left. "Locally got."

"Fish." Dev spoke the word thoughtfully. "That is, I believe, an animal that swims in the water."

"Yeah." Jess pointed at the rest of the tray. "That's fish, and this is seaweed, but they make it taste like something." She pointed at the last section. "This is mushroom. They grow it in caverns near the bottom of the cliff."

Dev tasted a bit of the seaweed. It seemed to be in a creamy substance and she found she liked it as well. The mushrooms were dense and rich. They reminded her very faintly of the protein cakes from the crèche.

All good. She dug in with a sense of relief. Doctor Dan had warned her there would be very different things to contend with downside, but she was very glad to see not all of them were different in a bad way.

"That all right for you?" Jess asked, after a moment of silence.

Dev nodded. "It's very good. Thank you."

Jess was silent for a few minutes more, then she looked up again. "What did you have upside?" She asked. "Plastic pellets or something? Must have been if you could eat those crackers."

"Well." Dev took a sip of kack. "Tea mostly, to drink. And they just made a cake for the main thing. I think it had beans or soy, with greens and maybe some fruit. It depended on what the test facility was working on."

"Fruit." Jess said. "Maybe Bain knows what that's like." She went back to her plate. "None of us could afford it."

Dev paused and studied her for a moment. Despite the words, there didn't seem to be any resentment in her voice, just a matter of fact commentary. "You know, only the really important people in the crèche would get to have something like this." She pointed at her plate. "So I guess it's relative?"

Jess glanced up, a look of dark humor in her eyes. "You think?"

Dev wasn't sure how to respond to that. She felt a little bit confused as those pale eyes watched her, almost glad when a throat clearing at her right side made them both look up. A woman was standing there, dressed as Jess was.

"Elaine." Jess half turned. "What's up?"

The woman cocked her head slightly. "You going to introduce me, Jess?"

Jess looked at her, then at Dev. "Sure." Her eyes went to Dev. "What do you want people to call you?"

Dev was caught flatfooted. "Excuse me?"

"You're asking a bio alt what they want?" Elaine's eyebrows hiked. "C'mon, Jess."

Jess glanced at her. "This isn't a pod tech," she said. "I don't invite them to lunch." She turned back around. "What is it you want people here to call you? I know what your label is," she said. "My name is Jesslyn Drake. But people call me Jess." She paused. "When they don't call me bastard, or jackass, or asshole."

Elaine chuckled reflexively.

Dev nodded. "Okay, I get it." She looked up at Elaine. "My designation is Biological Alternative, set 0202-164812, instance NM-Dev-1," she said. "But you can call me Dev."

Elaine stared at her. "That doesn't sound like a regular bio alt set name."

"It isn't," Dev said. "I'm a developmental special set." She blinked placidly at the other woman. "Experimental."

"Oh," Elaine said. "Well, I'm Elaine." She somewhat hesitantly extended a hand in greeting. "I think we'll be working together."

Dev clasped it and released.

"Elaine's an agent, like I am," Jess said. "She works with a tech named Brent. He's over at that table afraid to come here and meet you." She indicated a tall, blond haired man seated nearby.

Elaine frowned. "He's not afraid. He's just not comfortable with all of this. Shit, Jess, don't be more of an ass than you have to be, okay?"

Dev looked at Jess, seeing a clearly defined expression of skepticism there. The man Brent was dressed exactly like she herself was and as she watched he glanced over at them, then looked quickly away.

So was he doing what she would be? Did he think she wasn't capable? Dev thought he probably didn't, for the same reason Jess didn't. She understood that, since she had yet to show any evidence of her skills. It made her a little sad all the same.

"Me being an ass?" Jess said. "You were the one telling me to find a cat." She looked pointedly at Elaine. "Let's just save it for later."

"Fine." Elaine lifted a hand and dropped it, turning and making her way back to the table where the tech was sitting and joining him.

Jess scooped up some of her mushrooms and ate them, then looked over at Dev, who was looking back at her.

They both looked away and Dev picked up her drink and took a long swallow of it.

JESS AND DEV walked back to their quarters through very quiet corridors. "Everyone's keeping their head down," Jess commented.

"I see," Dev said, after a slight pause. "They afraid the man with the gun is going to take them off?"

Muffling a snort, Jess stopped in mid stride and looked at her.

Dev stopped as well and stood there, head tilted slightly in question.

"Did you..." Jess said, then paused, shaping the air with her hands. "Was that a joke?"

"Did you think it was funny?"

"Yes, I did."

"Then it was a joke," Dev said. "If you didn't think so it would still have been a joke, but an unsuccessful one I wouldn't use again."

Jess's lips twitched. "Did they program you for that?" She started walking again. "For jokes?"

"No," Dev replied. "Most of us have a sense of humor." She followed Jess around the corner into the residential hall. "It varies."

"I can see you have the dry variety," Jess said. "Good. So do I. It'll make it easier to work together." She reached up and tightened the knot of hair at the back of her head. "I don't like stand up yuck men."

Dev's ears perked up. She really didn't know what that was, but it sounded like Jess had begun to accept her and that bode well for her not being immediately returned to the crèche. She had no illusions that she wouldn't be eventually, after this experiment was over. But the longer she stayed, the more experience she'd be able to get, and that might mean something later on for her.

If she didn't get hurt doing this, as Doctor Dan had warned. She wondered if Jess had ever gotten hurt doing her job. It sounded dangerous, even more than the tasks she'd been programmed for.

There was a man standing in front of Jess's door, one that she remembered from the communications hall.

"Hey, Jason," Jess said. "Report's not ready yet."

"I guessed." He held his hand up, which had a small, gun like device in it. "Ready for this?"

Jess stopped and looked at him. Dev thought she might be angry and she wasn't sure what was going on. But after a minute Jess relaxed and waved a hand at the plate on her door.

Dev started to go around the corner where her own door was.

"Wait."

Dev turned to find both of them looking at her. "I was going to work on some sims," she said. "I found some in the catalog in that room."

"You can come in this way." Jess indicated her quarters. "I wanted to introduce you to Jason here anyway."

Dev could tell the man didn't like her, but she nodded and followed them inside. She stood quietly as Jess walked over to her workspace chair and then turned, releasing the catches on her jumpsuit and pulling it half down to expose her upper body before she sat down.

Dev blinked a few times as she found herself handling a slew of inputs all at once, some really unexpected. Jess's body was a rich, golden color and she could see a few faint scars, which answered her earlier question.

But the most striking thing was the intricate designs on her arms, starting at the tips of her shoulders and going down. There were black lines and color, and small dots in an uneven pattern between them. She realized one whole limb was complete down to the wrist, the other halfway.

Wow. She had nothing at all in programming for this. What was going on? She knew no one in the crèche had markings like that.

"Jason, this is Dev," Jess said, putting her forearms down on the chair and leaning back. "She's going to drive my bus for me."

Jason looked at Dev. "Yeah?"

"Dev, this is Jason. He's also an agent," Jess said. "He's about to carve me for my last gig."

"Hello. It's nice to meet you."

He stared at her. "Charmed." He turned his attention back to the gun like device, which he triggered, producing a vivid blue light at the tip. "Don't you have some cleaning to do or something?"

Jess abruptly lashed out with one leg, slamming her booted foot against his knee and sending him careening to the floor, juggling the gun frantically as he fell. "Don't be a jackass, Jason. It's not her fault she's here."

"Son of a bitch are you crazy!" Jason managed to get hold of the device and rolled over. "I could have shot the whole fucking room out!"

"We have plenty." Jess didn't look either alarmed or sorry. "Bain wants this project to succeed. I'm not going to be the one who prevents that. If you have a brain cell left in your head, you won't either."

Jason paused in the midst of getting to his knees and stared at her, his eyes narrowing as Jess's brows hiked meaningfully.

Jess waved Dev to one of the chairs near the workspace. "Sit. Not many people get to see one of us get marked."

"Okay." She managed to answer. "What does that mean?" She sat down and tried to assimilate everything that had just happened, but her thoughts wouldn't settle properly and she gave it up after a minute.

It did seem though, that Jess had developed discomfort when the other agent had said something incorrect to her.

Interesting.

Jason got up and pulled a chair over, settling himself next to where Jess was. "I get you." He said, making some adjustments. "It's just really damn hard." He looked over at Dev. "No offense meant, kid," he said. "I've just been at this a long time and I've seen a lot of people kicked downstairs for your kind."

Dev still had no idea what was going on, or what downstairs was. "I'm sorry," she said. "I can tell you none of us wants to harm anyone."

"Of course they don't, Jace. They've got no more choice about being here than you and I did," Jess said. "If you want to be mad, be mad at the bastards at the top. They made the decision." She flexed her arm and turned it slightly. "Put it there."

Jason grunted.

Jess turned to Dev. "They don't let us put patches on these suits anymore like in the old days. You could get a patch or a mark for all your achievements. We can't do that now so we do this." She pointed at her arm. "For every gig, for every mission, we tell the story here."

Dev stared in fascination at the designs.

"Where it was, what it did." A high pitched buzz sounded and Jess licked her lips, setting her feet squarely on the floor as Jason leaned close with the device in his hand. "Who we lost." She took a breath. "Who we killed."

"Ready." Jason braced the hand holding the gun with his other hand. He waited for Jess to nod, then he carefully pulled the trigger and the blue light jumped from the gun to Jess's skin, with a high keening sound and a faint sizzle.

Dev felt a shiver go down her spine. She saw Jess's body stiffen and her eyes closed, though her breathing remained steady.

"Didn't think I was going to get this mark," Jess said after a minute or two.

"Yeah," Jason murmured softly. "Lot of dots for this one."

"Thirteen black. Don't short em," Jess said in a clipped tone. "Twelve of them there and Joshua."

"Hm." Jason grunted.

Dev felt very out of depth. She smelled the faint scent of burned flesh, and saw the muscles in Jess's legs jump. Whatever this was probably hurt a lot. There were a lot of marks on her arms and the whole thing seemed just a little insane.

"Green or no?"

Jess was silent for a while. "Can a complete failure be a green?" She asked. "No. Leave it clear."

"Okay." Jason made another adjustment. "Color," he warned, leaning close again, and the high buzz returned.

"Joshua's the reason you're here." Jess looked over at Dev. "He was my partner. My tech. The other side bought him and he led us into a trap and knifed me in the back."

Dev's eyes widened.

"Bastard," Jason muttered.

"So you're going to be my bus driver," Jess said. "You're never going to be my partner. You understand? No offense. You seem like a nice kid, but I'm not going to trust you at my back." She paused. "Assuming you can actually do the job."

Dev lifted her head a little and their eyes met. "I do understand," she said. "I'm really sorry that happened to you. It must have been terrible." Her eyes never left Jess's and as the silence lengthened, the buzz faded.

Finally Jason cleared his throat. "Sucks it took one of them to say that," he said. "None of us did."

Jess's gaze dropped and she sat there just breathing for a minute. "You done?" she said. "I've got weather to look at."

Jason decommissioned the gun and clipped it to his jumpsuit, getting up from his chair and dusting his hands off. "Yeah. Put some rub on it when you get a chance. I'm going to get some grub." He turned and left and the door slid shut behind him with a faint thump.

It was awkwardly quiet for a minute. "May I look at it?" Dev asked.

"Sure," Jess murmured, sitting still and waiting for the pain to ease.

Dev got up and went to the chair Jason had used, settling down on it and studying the red raw design now carved in Jess's skin. "Wow."

"Stupid tradition." Jess sighed. "But once you start you can't stop it." She looked at her arm, then at Dev. "I always promised myself I'd retire out before I got both sleeves." She pushed herself to her feet. "Now I really do have weather to study." She indicated the inner door between their quarters. "Get some rest. I'll call you in when it's time to talk about the mission."

"Okay." Dev got up and went to the door, then turned. "Thanks for letting me help you," she said. "And thank you for showing me the dining hall."

Jess settled behind her desk and leaned on it, gazing at Dev thoughtfully. "You get it about the driver thing, right? I don't really know what you are. I can't trust that."

Dev nodded. "We're used to being thought of as stupid and sometimes useless," she said. "We always want to do good work, though, and I hope I can for you."

Jess frowned a little. "You're not stupid. Not if you just said that. I just don't want you to be pissed off because I..." She paused. "Anyway. We'll see."

"Yes," Dev said. "We will. I'm going to go run the carrier sims now and be as prepared as I can."

"If nothing else, we'll learn something," Jess said, finally smiling a little. "You're interesting."

Dev paused with her hand on the touch-plate for the door. "I think you're interesting too." She replied, with a faint smile of her own, before she triggered the latch and went through it, letting it close behind her.

Jess sat back in her chair and drummed her fingers lightly on the arms. Then she exhaled and pulled the sheets Stephan had given her over, unfolding them and reaching out to touch the console pad. "Ouch." She grimaced, as she pulled at the newly raw skin on her arm. "Maybe it wasn't smart to do that when we're flying tonight."

She adjusted the light and studied the report, touching a finger on the dotted lines and sweeps, grimacing again as she analyzed the information. "Or maybe not."

DEV STOOD FOR a minute in her chamber, just listening to her own heartbeat slow and settle. Once it had, she went over and got a bottle of liquid from the dispenser, opening it and drinking it down in a draught.

She sat in her chair, trying to decide what to do. Jess told her to get some rest, but Jess also inferred that they might be going out on a mission tonight so her tech skills would be put to a very real test very soon.

She went in the sanitary facility and used it, still bemused by the swirling water. Then she came back into the main part of the chamber and went over to the bed, sitting down on it curiously and then laying down on her back.

Very different from the crèche and it's snug, rotating pods that cradled you and rocked you through the night.

This was cool, though yielding, the surface conforming to her body in a comfortable way, but wide and spacious giving her room to spread out as much as she wanted.

The pillows were also mild and yielding, and they cradled her head, making it easy to relax. She did so for a few minutes, watching the lights adjust themselves as the pressure of the bed was detected and analyzed.

The illumination softened and darkened, and she found herself thinking about everything she'd seen in the long day.

She thought about the design she'd seen cut into Jess's arm, and how sad it seemed to her that these people, these soldiers, seemed to have so hard a life, that they had to carve their accomplishments into their own flesh and get no thanks otherwise.

And what had Jess meant when she said she hadn't had a choice to be here either? Dev looked at the faint glints of mica in the rough cut ceiling. That she didn't really understand, nor what she'd meant when she referred to Elaine's tech as an outsider.

What did that mean, really? And what did Jason mean when he said he'd known people who were kicked downstairs, because of her kind?

Did he mean they'd lost their place here because of bio alts? Dev frowned. What was downstairs? Could it really be that natural born people had been displaced like that? She'd always thought that bio alts did tasks no natural born would want to, and they would have gone on to do something more interesting or rewarding in its place.

Surely that was true. Surely they didn't just throw those natural born out. Dev got up and walked around, feeling a burst of nervous energy. That's how it was in the crèche. The natural born people did the important jobs and the bio alts did the rest.

She climbed up the steps to the training area and seated herself at the console.

She put her hands on the pads and keyed them. But here she was, doing a natural born person's job. This had been Joshua's job.

His job, his rooms and Jess, his partner.

But she wasn't to be Jess's partner. Jess didn't want that. Joshua had betrayed her. She was just here to help.

She wanted to help. She wanted to do well for these people.

She wanted to do her best, certainly, for Jess who had defended her and been nice to her, and who apparently wanted her to succeed.

Who found her interesting. Dev studied her reflection in the console.

Interesting.

JESS TOOK A sip of kack, her eyes flicking from one screen to the other, studying her options. The weather had put a halt on an immediate leave and it looked like she was going to have to wait for daylight to go.

Sucked. She scanned the metrics again. It really was a fairly simple plan. She'd target the laboratory they had the new growth tech in, aiming for a supply station entrance halfway up the hill the place was built into. No doubt she'd draw a crowd.

They'd cut off trying to communicate with the two teams, hopefully giving the impression they considered them destroyed and were no longer interested in them. Wouldn't be the first time. Both sides knew it.

You cut your losses. Made no sense wasting precious resources chasing after a lost cause. Jess knew if she hadn't made her own way out in her last gig, chances were no rescue would have been attempted for her.

She didn't resent that. It was just the way it was. They were valuable resources, sure, but they were, as she'd told Dev, expendable when there were other things at stake.

Her comm buzzed and she tapped it. "Drake."

"We meeting?" Jason asked. "Weather tanked."

"Yeah. Bring Elaine over. We'll be plus eight to go, but might as well go over the outline."

"Be there." Jason cut the comm off.

Jess leaned over and tapped another button. "Dev?" She waited. After a pause, she tapped again. "Dev?"

With a soft crackle the circuit opened "Yes." Dev's voice responded. "My apologies. I was investigating the wet space."

"The what?" Jess stared in puzzlement at the comm.

"There is a space in the sanitary facility with a pipe over it."

"Oh. The shower," Jess said. "You were taking one." She listened to the faint sound of breathing coming over the comm, as her new next door neighbor considered what she'd said. That was one thing she'd noticed about Dev—she waited to talk until she knew what she wanted to say.

"Yes," Dev finally said. "If you mean I went under the pipe and got very wet," she added. "That was unusual."

"You don't have showers upside?" Jess found herself interested by this odd conversation.

"We do," Dev said. "But they don't involve getting wet."

"Oh," Jess said. "Well, dry off and come over. We're going to run the plan."

"All right," Dev replied. "Thank you."

The comm cut off. Jess gazed at it in bemusement for a minute, then she went back to the console screen and started assembling the information she would need to lay out the statistics and the routes to her colleagues.

Two minutes, and a knock on the inner door sounded. Jess pressed the ingress key and the door slid open, revealing Dev's slim figure. her hair was damp, slicked back off her forehead, giving her finely etched features a slightly tougher cast. "So water's a novelty for ya, huh?"

Dev sat down in one of the chairs across from Jess's workspace. "Running water, yes. They made all the water in the crèche. They told us it was expensive. The natural borns had it, I think, in their quarters but we used flash rad to clean our skins."

Jess leaned on her elbows. "Radiation?"

Dev nodded. "It would burn off the first layer or so of skin," she said. "Effective way to get rid of dirt and any bacteria." She inspected her hand. "I think I like water better."

A soft chime came at the outer door. Jess pressed the release button, then sat back as Jason and Elaine entered. "C'mon in." She swiveled both displays around and slid them back so everyone could see them as they approached and took the seats next to Dev.

"Okay." Jess sorted out the sheets. "Weather cranked us."

"Heard that," Jason said. "Shaking the roof upstairs."

Jess nodded. "Big e-stat storm coming overhead. Met figures it'll clear by oh six." She touched a control and displayed a map on the screen. "Here's the frontal boundary."

"Big one," Elaine said. "Wouldn't want to be out in that. Is it going to reach the other side?"

"That's our cover." Jess ran the scan forward. "See that? It's scheduled over the drop site just before twelve hundred. We come in behind it. "

Both Jason and Elaine nodded.

"Then we..." Jess motioned between herself and Dev. "Split off and head for the front door of the lab there." She pointed. "You two come around the side here and tuck in behind the cliffs."

"You're not going to drop in there, Jess," Jason said. "That's suicide."

Jess shook her head. "Not in my plans but I want them to think I am. I'll take out the outer post here." She pointed at a lonely outcropping surrounded by sea. "With the guns and then come in at wave level."

"Freak them out," Elaine said. "And with the chop they can't be sure you're alone."

Jess nodded.

"So we wait for the plugs to rush off to grab you, and we go get Sandy and Mike," Jason said. "We get out. You get out, you join us, we run for home."

Jess nodded again. "Real basic. Nothing fancy. We just want to get them back." She pushed two slips of film at them. "Here's the plotting coordinates. If I were you, I'd wait until we're underway to program 'em in."

Both agents looked very uncomfortable. "Brent's gonna freak."

Jess shrugged. "Fact is, Bain said he thought someone was still talking from inside. You want to risk it?"

"Jess." Elaine leaned back and crossed her legs at the ankles. "I was thinking about that. Doesn't make sense they'd use the same vector twice. They don't, y'know?"

Jess grunted.

"How do we know it's not...I mean, maybe it was Bricker," Jason said. "I remember taking classes with him a year ago. He didn't seem like such a hothead jerk back then. I liked him. So maybe he was turned, and he turned Josh?"

"Jace's right. He has changed,or he did change, anyway," Elaine said. "When he was a group leader, I always thought you could trust him. Hell, he used to play slam ball with us late watch."

It was tempting. Jess studied her colleagues and the silently watching bio alt. Tempting to think it was all Bricker and now that he was dead, they could relax and be safe again. "Josh liked Bricker," Jess said. "He used to have dinner and drinks with him."

Elaine eyed her. "Rumor said more."

Jess put it all aside. "Maybe." She lifted a hand. "But right now we don't have time to look at that. Let's get the teams back, then we can regroup. If we're lucky, you're right and it was him, but if you don't tell your techs and the plan gets spilled, we know two things. One, you were wrong and it wasn't him, and two, there's still someone out there but it's not Brent or Tucker."

"Damn I hope it was," Jason said. "I hate walking around with clouds over my head. And we've got the new group coming in next month on top of it. That's twelve more unknown vectors."

Six new agents, six new techs, fresh from the field school. "I know," Jess said. "But it'll be good to get some of those empty bays back in action. I'm starting to feel like a dying breed here."

They were all silent after that.

"So, flight deck at oh four?" Jason finally said. "I'm going to get some bunk time. My head's exploding." He stood up, stretching his body out. "Meet you all for breakfast?"

Jess and Elaine nodded, and Elaine stood to join him in leaving. They stood in awkward silence, then they turned and went to the door, leaving Jess and Dev alone.

Jess studied the door somberly for a moment, before she turned her attention back to Dev. "You ready to do this?" She asked bluntly.

Dev considered the question. "I have done all the reviews I can on the sims. I am as prepared to execute your request as I can be, given the circumstances."

"Sims aren't the real thing."

"I know," Dev said. "I'll do the best I can."

They were both quiet for a minute. "So you figured out the shower, huh?" Jess said. "I never thought about that whole water thing upside. We have so much of it." She paused. "Want to see a lot more than that shower?"

"Sure."

"C'mon." Jess got up. "It's close to dark, but we can still see it." She led the way out of her quarters and along the corridor, turning left at the central corridor, heading down a dark gray painted hall.

They passed three section scans, then she turned right and went into a longer corridor with low, green tinted lights. It was empty except for the two of them, and as they continued, the air became a little thicker and wetter.

"We can only stay out a few minutes. Storm's coming overhead." Jess turned a final corner and faced a thick metal door with a prominent palm scan. Letters stenciled in black on it were clearly visible.

"External Access. This is an airlock." Dev read them. "What does that mean? In the créche, airlocks were dangerous places."

"Not so bad here." Jess grinned, and keyed the door. It opened with a grinding, sucking sound revealing a square metal box. She stepped inside and waited as Dev joined her with a somewhat cautious look at the stark walls.

Then Jess keyed the outer door and processed the lock. The inner door sealed, and then the outer released, with a pressure change that made their ears pop. At once, the box was filled with the intense smell of salt and a damp wind buffeted them with a roar.

Jess stepped forward onto a small rocky outcropping, and leaned her arms on the rough stone wall. After a moment's hesitation, Dev joined her, their hair lashed back by the ferocious wind.

Dev put her hands on the stone, the surface cold and damp under her touch as the airlock door closed behind them.

It was strange. She was looking out over a wild, white ruffled surface under a cap of solid, multi layered dark and light gray. In the distance she could hear a heavy, almost continuous rumble. "W...what is this?" She asked, raising her voice above the sound.

"It's the ocean," Jess said. "This is what used to be called the Atlantic Ocean." She glanced around at the high cliffs, weather worn and stark. "It's water."

Dev looked out over the wild scene, breathing in the rich, mineral scented air. The water was only about a hundred feet below them, crashing against the wall of rock sending spray up so high it almost reached them.

It was amazing. Dev could only stare at it in wonder, it was so unlike anything she'd ever experienced, or thought she would experience. "It's big."

Jess chuckled. "It's very big. We'll be flying over it tomorrow." She touched the wall. "These cliffs this old place is tunneled into shows two sides. Backside's a wasteland. This side...at least you get the sense the sea's alive."

She looked down at the surging waves. "It's our life now. We generate power by it, take food from it, and it's why you have a water shower. We've got plenty of it. About the only thing in the world we have plenty of."

Dev felt the rumble move through her, and looked out over the surface of the water, seeing a seething motion that seemed never ending. She edged forward and looked down over the wall, seeing the white foam at the base of the cliff washing over the rocks and rushing in and out of holes she caught a brief glimpse of.

They were standing on a small niche, with room for probably a dozen people on it. "What is this for?" She asked Jess. "This little place?"

"Just for us to look," Jess said. "To see storms coming in." She pointed at a line of gray. "That's what's keeping us here tonight instead of going out. See those flashes?"

"Yes."

"Electromagnetic surges. They'll knock a carrier right out of the sky. Shorts the systems out."

"Oh." Dev could see the crackling bolts, and the flashes in the far off clouds. "That sounds difficult."

"We have a cavern downstairs," Jess said. "Sometimes we go down there when it's calmer, and swim."

"Swim?"

"We jump in the water. In the ocean."

Dev looked at her with unabashed wide eyed astonishment.

The rumble got a lot louder and Jess turned and keyed the door. "Time to go in. Storm's too close." She waited for the panel to open, then ducked inside and closed the door as soon as Dev cleared it. When it shut, the sudden lack of sound was almost ear ringing.

Dev ran her fingers through her hair, straightening the wind blown disarray. "That was amazing. Thank you for showing it to me." She licked her lips a little. "It's salty."

"Yes," Jess said. "Ocean's full of salt. We scrub it to make it drinkable and then the salt's used for cooking with the rest of the stuff they scrape out of it."

They walked along in silence for a few minutes. "Do the colors mean something?" Dev asked as they crossed from the gray back into the dark blue, heading for the lighter blue of the residential corridor.

"Sort of. They say they used to all be the same color, and everyone spent all their time getting lost so they changed them up so at least you can see if you're in ops, that's the blue tones, or med, that's white, or security, that's green and so on. There's a chart in the docs in the system. You can look it up."

Dev thought about that. "They did that upside too," she said. "You could tell where you were, what level, and that kind of thing by the walls." She paused. "But it wasn't as big as this and there was nothing like what you just showed me. The only thing a little bit like that was the null grav gym."

Jess keyed her door open. "The what?" She waved Dev forward.

"Null gravity gym. It was a big padded place they turned off grav in, and you got to play catch me, and ball, and do exercises." Dev said. "It was in the top of the crèche, and it had a clear ceiling, You could float for a minute, sometimes, and just watch the stars."

"Stars." Jess paused in the center of her quarters. "I've read about those. They showed us vid in school."

Dev stopped at the internal door between their quarters and looked back. "If you ever come to the crèche, I'll show them to you. I think they're really nice, but not nearly as exciting as the ocean is."

Jess met her eyes, then looked away with the faintest of smiles. "Get some rest. The alarm will go off at 0300. Then we'll get to see if Bricker and Bain were right and you're worth something to the job or not."

Dev nodded, then passed through into her own bunk, letting the door shut behind her.

Jess looked at the door briefly. Then she started toward her workspace, but midway there changed her mind and went back to her bed instead. She lay down on it and put her hands behind her head, looking up at the mica infested ceiling.

"Stars," she murmured.

DEV WENT TO the wardrobe module and examined the drawers again. In the crèche, she'd slept in the soft paper garments they all changed into before getting into the sleep pods, which would be sucked off and recycled the following morning.

Here she wasn't really sure what to do. After a few moments thought, she stripped out of the jumpsuit and hung it up, leaving her in her underwear. Then she put on a light undershirt she'd found on the shelves that came down to her mid thigh.

That seemed all right. She went over and pulled the covers down on the bed, climbing into it and pulling them back over her. The surface of the bed conformed to her at once, and the lights dimmed. Then she felt the covers warm to her skin.

She was tired. With the time alteration and the early start to her day, coupled with the tension and activity, she'd been on edge since they'd left the crèche. Now she was glad to relax her body, and know she had some time to rest before her first big trial.

It was exhausting to be in such a strange place, with all strange people, all disliking her for various reasons.

No one wanted her to be here. She was a little sad about that, because having a placement here had been so exciting for her, despite how hard and strange the programming had been. She'd been looking forward to using that training, and it made her feel bad to know that so many people here were against that.

Only the man with the gun seemed to be for it, and Doctor Dan. The agents didn't seem to trust her, and the other techs definitely didn't want her around.

Then there was Jess.

Dev thought about Jess. She had said that she didn't consider Dev a real part of her team, just a driver.

It seemed quite clear.

But really, Jess was the only one in the place who had a friendly word for her, and who had offered to help her find her way.

Was that because the man with the gun wanted it that way? Dev rolled onto her side and settled her head comfortably on the pillow. If so, she was glad. At least there was someone who was willing to talk to her like she was a real person.

She wanted to do well for Jess. She'd gone through the sim a dozen times, and hoped it would be enough to let her drive the carrier for real.

She trusted her programming. She only hoped Jess would come to trust her.

Chapter Six

THE ALARM BONGED softly at 0300. Jess blinked as the lights inside adjusted and produced a quiet glow that gently illuminated her quarters. With automatic motions, she got out of bed and shook herself, letting the last shreds of sleep fall away.

Wisps of her last dream faded with them and she didn't try to recall what it was. There was an aching tension in her shoulders that meant it was a bad one and she was just glad it hadn't gone on long enough to wake her screaming.

She retrieved a mug of kack from the dispenser and opened it, taking a long swallow as she walked into the sanitary unit as the lights came up inside. She used the facility, then started the shower running, pausing before she entered to go back into the main area and trigger comms to the overhead speaker on listen.

The familiar drone of the ops center filled the air and she listened for a minute, hearing nothing alarming. She took off her sleepwear and stepped into the steaming water.

It felt good and she stood for a bit, letting the water pound against her. She pulled in a breath full of steam, the flat metallic scent of the water so very familiar to her filling her lungs. She took a handful of scrub and burnished her skin with it, then used another handful and washed her hair.

Old custom. Most people in the world now used dry scrub or didn't bother. The rain came every day, and everyone got caught out in it. To deliberately wet yourself was something that had come to be seen as wasteful and strange, but here in the citadel they all did.

Jess rinsed her hair out again, and stood for another moment, letting the hot water relax her muscles. It was also one of the marks of Interforce, that neatly cropped, clean shaven look that was a long ago holdover from the national forces they'd all descended from.

She got out and shut the water down, then toweled herself dry and made her way through the main chamber to the dressing station, popping it open and taking out a set of underwear and putting them on. Then she opened the second part of her cabinet and removed an insertion suit, slipping into it and snapping the catches.

Unlike the jumpsuit they all typically wore in the facility, this was different. It was far heavier and had lightweight body armor built into it, protecting her most vital areas. There were integrated comms and leads for the carrier systems and buckles and clips for her weapons.

She picked up her boots and carried them to the workstation, leaning a finger on the comms. "Dev?"

"Yes."

"Ready?" Jess asked.

"Yes."

"C'mon in here." Jess released the button and sat down to pull her boots on. A moment later the inner door opened and Dev entered. She briefly scanned her slight form, noting she had found and put on the carrier ops rig and was holding her own boots in her hand. "Sit."

Dev did, putting down one boot and putting on the other.

"You sleep okay?" Jess asked. "I can imagine most of this is pretty strange."

Dev glanced up at her. "Really well, thank you," she said. "It's very comfortable." She put on her other boot. "I really like the wet thing. It makes my skin feel good."

"The shower?" Jess smiled briefly. "Yeah, I like it too." She stood up, and after Dev did also, she scrutinized Dev's gear with a critical eye. "They give you programming for this?" She pointed at the suit.

"Yes," Dev said. "But also, there are some things that are left to natural sense. Like putting underwear on and that sort of thing. We don't need programming for that." She paused. "Or sneezing, or using the lavatory."

Jess started chuckling. "You're really different from the rest of the bios we have here," she said. "Are there many like you topside?"

Dev straightened her cuff a little. "I'm the only one they've produced in my set so far, so I guess no."

"Ah." Jess pulled her hair back in a tail and quickly braided it, then tucked it into her collar. "So you're one of a kind, eh?"

"Yes."

Well, that was interesting. Jess climbed the steps up to her weapons locker. "Let me get rigged, and we'll grab some chow." She opened up the case and took out the stun knives, sliding them into their sheaths and added her sidearm into it's holster.

Her heavy weapons were in the carrier, but she took the time to clip on a utility flash and a multi-tool, then trotted down the steps and waved Dev toward the door. "Let's go, kid. Time to make the doughnuts."

Dev followed her willingly, but had a slightly perplexed expression on her face. "What's a doughnut?" She asked. "And how do you make them?"

"They're mythological," Jess said.

"Oh."

"I hear they tasted good though."

DEV HAD TO stop a moment just to stare when they entered the carrier hanger. It was a huge cavern, larger than any space she'd ever seen inside before, and it was full of parked vehicles, most huddling in the dark.

Three were lit, however, and several bio alt mechanics were moving around them with pads and tools. Jess headed toward the one furthest on the left and Dev quickly trotted to catch up with her as Elaine and Jason split off and went to their own crafts.

Overhead were giant panels in the roof that apparently opened to let the carriers out. The whole place smelled of organics and synth oil, and echoed with the sounds of latches engaging and bangs of tools.

Dev's eyes took in the carrier Jess was nearing. Her programming kicked in, and the outline of the squat, powerful vehicle hit familiar chords as information about it poured in. The outside color was mottled gray, except for the identification code stenciled outside the hatch, and Jess's last name printed underneath it.

Jess palmed the hatch lock and ducked inside as it opened. Dev followed her, trying to take everything in as quickly as she could.

Programming gave her the inside before she saw it, and she nodded as she moved past the strapped down bucket seat Jess would ride in and went up into the nose of the carrier, where a second station was waiting for her.

The inside of the carrier was packed with gear. Mostly electronic, monitoring and scanning systems, gyros, and positioning rigs. To one side a rack was lashed that held long muzzled laser rifles and one heavy projectile cannon, and the drop pack with its jet systems.

Dev went to the pilot's seat and settled into it, feeling the gimbals shift as it took her weight. She took a breath and looked around at the console, comforted when a mental image of the sim settled over the reality of the controls and they started making sense to her.

"Run the checklist." Jess's voice was cool and a little distracted. "I assume you know how?"

"Yes." Dev flexed her hands and settled back into the seat, waiting a moment until the programming kicked in and her fingers reached out to start the sequence. "Systems coming live," she said, as the console came to life and in rapid succession, the equipment packs to her right and left followed.

Jess sat down and watched in bemusement as the carrier came alive around her, the slim hand of Dev going through touches and settings as though she'd done it many times before.

Dev activated the leads and hooked them into her suit, sliding the comm rig over her head and tucking the ear cups into place. She flicked her eyes to the registration number and then keyed in a command. "Carrier BR27006 systems check."

"Stand by," a mechanical voice answered. "Stand by BR27006."

"Standing by," Dev said. She looked at the console readouts and pulled a pad over, keying in the various settings and supplies they reported. She saw an incoming request, and reviewed it. "They're asking to setup an intercom."

"Go ahead," Jess said. "That's Jason. It's so we can talk to each other."

"Intercom set to channel 4500, sideband 2." Dev spoke into the comms. "Read back?"

"Confirmed," a male voice answered. "Channel 4500, sideband 2. Brent out."

Jess quickly checked the heavy arms, then reached over and punched the door seal, closing out the sounds of the carrier bay. At once, the internal sounds of the vehicle, the click and whir of the life support, and the low hum of the pre start engines became obvious.

She saw Dev making adjustments, and pulled her own pad over and scanned the system readouts. After a moment, she looked at the back of the pilot's chair and let out a small, surprised breath. "Damn."

"BR27006, systems check complete," a voice called quietly in Dev's ear. "Stand by for switch to internal systems."

"Standing by." Dev watched the readouts as the umbilicals were removed and they were on internal power. She could see the spool ups for the two big engines and the launch jets and she triggered the restraint system that closed around her holding her snugly to her seat.

Her feet in the boots found the side jet controls, the chair gimbals moving to adjust for her height. Now that the internal systems were online, whispered voices started in her ear as systems came up to flight ready and reported to her. "I think we're set," she said. "Everything's online and green."

Jess was seated in her chair, with her arms folded. "You actually know how to do this." Her voice was tinged with disbelief.

Dev turned in her seat and looked back at Jess. "Apparently so."

"Unreal." Jess settled a comm set over her own head and triggered it. "Blue group one, Blue group controller."

"One, Tac one."

"One, Tac two."

The answers came back in clipped tones. "Report ready," Jess said. "We're ready and standing by to launch."

Bare hesitation. "Tac one ready," Jason answered. "Standing by."

"Tac two ready" Elaine said a beat later. "Standing by."

"Ask control to open the gates," Jess told Dev. "We'll launch first, you all follow. When we get to the first set of coordinates, I'll split right you split left. Copy?"

"Understood," Jason reported.

"Gotcha." Elaine said.

Dev spoke into the comms. "Control, this is BR27006. Requesting access for flight please."

Even through the hull of the carrier, they could hear the roof opening, the huge metal panels grinding apart and allowing a thunder of water into the bay, drops falling and slamming into the carrier roof with a muted roar.

Dev settled herself and put her hands on the engine throttle controls, her mind going over her next few steps. She was glad she had the programming so solid for this. Everything seemed familiar to her and the readouts all clicked in her mind.

"BR27006 this is control," the voice said. "Access is granted. Launch when ready."

"Go," Jess said. "Let's get this show on the road."

Dev took a deep breath and let it out, then she thumbed the launch jet controls and felt the carrier shift under her. In the next moment, they were rising past the carriers on either side, and she gently puffed the side jets to position them under the wide opening.

It was like the sim, and not. The rumbling and the sensation was the same, but there was a spatial difference she realized immediately and she gave the launch jets a little more power to get them up and out of the cavern.

Below her she spotted the two other carriers lifting to follow, and then she was above the hatches and into the steady rain still falling around them. She shifted sideways again, and rotated the carrier 360 degrees on the horizon, looking at the endless expanse of craggy lifeless land and then the equally endless expanse of ocean.

The two other carriers emerged from the cavern and hovered, as the big panels slid shut. Dev programmed the coordinates Jess had given her, and then turned. "Ready to fly."

Jess was still watching her with her arms crossed, a bemused smile on her face. "Let's go, then," she said. "So far, you're doing fine."

Dev smiled back, then she turned and settled herself again. She opened the controls for the propulsion engines and triggered them, waiting for them to engage forward motion before she shut down the launch jets and they started forward.

The rumble of the carrier grew and the engines spooled up, increasing their speed as they left the cliffs behind and headed out over open water. It was very dark, but the multi band sensors in her forward display let Dev see in front of her as though it were daylight.

She increased the speed, and then settled down to watch the readouts, tweaking the trim on the carrier until the outer rumble slowed, then faded, as they went through the speed of sound.

"Jess," the intercom crackled.

"Yes, Jason?" Jess leaned back in her chair.

"You driving that thing?"

Jess chuckled. "Nope. I'm sitting in the back, about to start checking my guns."

"Shit."

Dev glanced behind her. "I'm sorry if I'm causing him disturbance." She returned her attention to the readouts, making a slight adjustment to their trim.

"That was a compliment. Don't worry about it," Jess said. "Okay, I'm going to check out the weapons systems. Don't make any loud noise. I've got a jumpy trigger finger and I don't want to shoot Jason's butt from under him."

Dev's eyes widened a little, and she turned around again to look at Jess.

Jess grinned and winked. "Keep your eyes on the road, kid. We're going to have us some fun."

THE LONG TRIP gave Dev ample opportunity to explore all the controls on the carrier and she was now reasonably comfortable with them. She settled back in her chair as the water skimmed under them for mile after mile of ruffled white gray surface.

Jess had tuned the weapons systems that were rooted in her console, laser cannons mounted on all sides of the carrier along with two racks of flash bombs in eject tubes. Now she was working with the pad at her station, keying in trims on the cannons and keeping an eye on their progress.

She hadn't spoken much. Dev occasionally glanced back at her, noting the absorbed expression as she went about her tasks. "Sixty minutes to edge of the storm," she said. Jess looked up and met her eyes.

"Good." Jess said. "Okay, here's the plan." She got up and came over to where Dev was sitting, kneeling at her side with her pad in her hand. "This is the layout of the base." She leaned her forearm on the arm of Dev's chair and indicated a wiremap diagram.

Dev looked at it attentively. There was a triangular block in the center, with a tracing over it outlining entrances and a landing field. "Okay."

"We go past the Gibraltar outpost." Jess pointed at the wedge. "That's where they should pick us up and start chasing us from." She moved the pad image along and pointed at a set of scattered islands. "That's the Spanish Archipelago where most of the experimentation happens, and this is the control center at Andorra." She indicated another large wedge. "That's our target."

Dev nodded.

"The service port those other teams were going for is here." Jess swiped at the pad, enlarging the wedge and pointing out a ruggedly cut square depression just below the summit, obviously a landing pad. "They're pinned down here." She swiveled the diagram and pointed to an uneven overhang in a narrow part of a V shaped crack in the rock.

"Okay," Dev said.

"So the tricky part is, we need to keep this thing in one piece while they chase us," Jess said. "It's got halfway decent shielding but it won't take more than a couple direct hits, and being blown to molecules would ruin my day."

Dev nodded. "Mine too."

"So you need to let them get close enough to think they're going to catch us, but not close enough for them to nail us," Jess said. "You can use these ridges here, and the edge of the cliffs. They have to think we're going for the service port."

"Okay."

"So then we are," Jess said. "You're going to put me down in that entrance and I'm going to leave them a calling card just for what they did to me the last time."

Dev looked at her. "I don't remember you going over that in the plan."

Jess smiled. "What I didn't tell everyone they can't tell anyone else. If Bain's right, and there's another leak inside Interforce, then they'll expect me to just try and draw them off from the others, which means, they won't really chase me. "

Dev nodded slowly. "Okay."

"So then I can get into the service port and give them something to really worry about. That will draw them off."

"But they'll come after you."

"You'll have to draw them off, then come back and pick me up," Jess said. "It'll be tight."

"I'm sorry, you did realize I've never actually done this before," Dev said. "That wasn't anything I ever even sim'd."

Jess studied her face. "So we'll find out for sure if you've got the chops for it. Otherwise, chances are we'll both croak."

Dev frowned. "That seems like a non optimal plan," she said. "Are you sure you want to do it?"

Jess felt a prickle of surprise. One thing Joshua had never done was question her. Techs didn't. They weren't the strategic part of the deal. What did this bio alt know about risk anyway? She looked back at Dev, taking a breath to tell her off when she was caught by the expression on her face.

Serious. Intent. Concerned.

She re-sounded the question in her head. "Why wouldn't I want to do it?" She countered.

"Well." Dev glanced at her consoles, then back at Jess. "If something happens and it doesn't work, then both the other teams, and the two with us, and you and I might not return. Does this achieve your goals?"

Jess revised her anger. "I'm gambling on the fact that they're more interested in me than the others. If I focus them on me, the rest of the teams have a much better chance of getting out of here in one piece."

Dev considered that, and they sat in silence studying each other. "I will do the best I can to do what you ask then," she finally said. "It would be a good thing if we all got out in one piece." She swiveled around and put a hand to one ear. "BR27006."

"Long range scan, one inbound," the soft voice sounded in her ear.

"What is it?" Jess asked, since she'd left her comm set back on her station.

"They're picking up a single signal inbound to us," Dev said. "Directly ahead."

"Interesting." Jess scuttled back to her station and slid into her chair, swinging the comm set up and onto her head. She pulled the pad around and started tapping on it, her eyes flicking to the various screens and readouts on her own console.

Dev focused on the air ahead of them, still full of rain, and wisps of cloud they were traveling through. She adjusted her scans and after a minute, they picked up the inbound signal also, a quick pan showing no identifying squirts that would mark them friend or otherwise.

It was coming fast, though. The comp quickly tabulated a vector and she heard Jess behind her starting to activate the weapons systems.

Her harness snugged down and the inside lights, already fairly dim, went to ice blue. She saw two panels come active and she adjusted the power leads from the engines as they shunted energy to the weapons systems Jess was now spooling up.

Dev took hold of the throttles and keyed off auto gen, holding the course by hand as she adjusted the side jets. The incoming object was heading right for them, and now the scan was warning distance. "Five minutes out."

"Do you have an ident?"

"No." Dev flexed her hands on the throttles. "Do you want me to evade it?"

"Hang on." Jess got her hands into the triggering gloves and activated the targeting system. At once, she had a heads up display of what Dev was seeing through the front windows, and side panels that showed her the sensors on the outside of the carrier." Let it come close enough for visual, then turn to port and come up over it."

"Okay." Dev reviewed what she'd have to do, and nodded to herself. She put the scan up on one monitor and watched it, seeing the blip getting larger and larger on the display.

"Tac one, Tac two." Jess's voice sounded over the intercom. "We're going to engage the incoming. Stand clear of my zenith please."

"Done."

"Clear."

The male voices answering almost sounded alike, except one was a little deeper than the other. Dev had officially met the other two techs at breakfast in the dining hall and their reaction to her had been so unfriendly that Jess had felt she needed to say something to them about it.

Dev wasn't sure that was a good thing. She understood why they felt the way they did. Certainly, she thought the two men and also the other agents had resented Jess's words. But she had to admit to herself she'd gotten a certain odd sensation when it had happened that she still hadn't figured out.

"Okay, here it comes," Jess said. "Get ready."

"Ready," Dev replied. She focused her attention on the forward window, trading the scans for real time. Ahead of her she could see the heavy cloud bank they were flying under and she searched the edges of it for the first sight of the oncoming craft.

A faint flicker, then there it was. "Visual," Dev said. "Evading." She took the craft into a bowing turn to the left, then hit the bottom jets and the starboard side ones, boosting the carrier up and over the intruder.

"Circle back." Jess yelled.

Dev held the turn, then rotated the throttles and blended the jets to bring the carrier around in a tight turn, half on its side. She spotted the craft and dropped down to come alongside it, close enough now to see it clearly. "It's another one of these." She said in surprise.

"Fuckers." Jess slid around in her station. "Tac one, Tac two loose empty, probably rigged. I'm going to take it out clear standby."

"Clear!"

"Clear!"

"Hold her steady," Jess said, as she brought the guns to bear and and fired at point blank range. As a stitching of fire creased the other carrier a bright pinprick of fire erupted near the engines. "Crap! Take her up! Hurry!"

Dev reacted instantly, kicking in the bottom jets and hauling the throttles up at full power, booting the starboard thrusters and peeling the carrier off at a high G arc that took them up into the clouds.

An explosion behind them rocked the air, rumbling through the carrier walls as they punched through the lower cloud layer, and were between that and the upper one. Dev hit the scan and located the other two carriers. She completed the drop, pitching down through the clouds again and sending out a location burst ahead of them on shortwave before she hauled the carrier into a tight turn to bring them back on course.

Her heart was hammering. She was almost at the point where she was overrunning the programming, the sims not quite up to replicating the events she found herself a part of. "Okay."

"Erf."

Dev glanced back over her shoulder, spotting Jess righting herself in her chair. "Are you all right?"

"Peachy." Jess put her comm set back on. "Tac one, Tac two. Stable?"

"Stable, confirmed kill," Jason answered. "Nice. Sent a squirt."

"Stable," Elaine echoed. "Close in scan showed that to be BR24004."

Jess exhaled. "Crap."

"Got that," Jason said. "So we know."

"Damn it," Jess muttered, clicking off comm and staring at the readouts. "Damn it, damn it. They're probably both gone. This is a goose chase. That was one of the two carriers that we're after."

Dev adjusted her controls again and put the carrier back on auto nav. She half turned again in her seat and looked back at Jess. "I'm sorry, but does that mean the people we're going to try and retrieve are not as expected?"

Jess gazed quietly into nothing for a moment. "They're probably either dead or wish they were," she said. "It's hard to get into one of these carriers if the people inside it don't want you to." She glanced at the hatch. "There's an integrity sensor and when it's breached the gun systems implode."

"Oh."

"That carrier looked untouched." Jess felt sad. "So they must have been let in to tamper with it, and given codes."

"Oh." Dev's voice took on a completely different tone. "You're..." She paused. "We're not supposed to do that," she corrected herself. "Programming told me."

"No, Dev. We're not supposed to do that." Jess sighed.

"So are we continuing on this course?" Dev asked after a long moment's silence.

Jess sat back in her seat. "Let me think about that for a bit, kid." She let her head rest against the back of the chair. "Just keep us on track for now."

Dev turned back around and ran her eye over her settings, then she peered out the forward window, seeing the bulky outline of the clouds overhead in the eerie glow of the infrared. She checked the clock, and snugged her straps a bit tighter, wishing she had a drink of water somewhere around.

She heard Jess unstrapping and moving around, but she kept her eyes forward, watching the horizon for the first sign of land, wondering how this latest development was going to change the plan.

After about five minutes, Jess appeared at her elbow, handing over a sealed vacuum container and opening one of her own. "If it were two carriers I just blew up, we'd have turned back already."

Dev examined the container and opened it, finding the cold, slightly fizzy kack beverage inside. She took a sip, wondering if Jess had somehow heard what she was thinking.

"But there's still a team there," Jess said. "I can't just go back and leave them and not know."

"Okay." Dev nodded. "I'm sorry something happened to that other one. I hope it isn't as bad as you think it is." She lifted the container. "Thank you for the drink. I needed one."

Their eyes met briefly. "There's a dispenser there, behind the scan console. It's tucked in back, you can barely see it," Jess said. "Sorry. Should have told you when we came in. It's not standard." She was perched on the edge of the console, running the edge of her finger against the container.

Dev wasn't sure what to do. She sipped her drink, watching her readouts, and from the corner of her eye, watching the silent figure at her left hand side.

"Anyway." Jess straightened abruptly. "So maybe we won't drop. At this point, I don't know what to expect when we get there." She went back to her station and sat down, setting the container in a swinging holder as she went back to looking at scan.

Dev put her own cup down and ran over the engine settings, making sure the power levels were where they needed to be and everything looked normal.

Normal. Dev had to rub the bridge of her nose for a moment. Normal? She had gone from her classes in the crèche to driving a half strange transport into a big fight in just a sun's complete turn. Her life could not possibly have changed more than it had in the last day.

Could not possibly.

"Thirty minutes to the edge of the storm," Dev said.

Jess put her pad away and drained her drink. She got up and went to the drop pack, checking the harness carefully and running the device through its diagnostic checks. Little more than a set of small, tightly controlled air jets it was designed to let a person wearing it fall out of the lower hatch of a carrier and land without killing themselves.

Or that was the theory anyway. Jess had several long healed bone breaks from using the thing, but it was safer and more controlled than either gliders or chutes, and in an area like they were going into, full of cliffs and rocks, at least it would give her a chance at an upright landing.

She opened the harness and got it clipped, ready for her to step into if the time came. Then she set up one of the big laser rifles in its holder on one side, and a grenade launcher on the other, balancing out the weight.

She made sure they were secured, then she sat back down in her seat and powered up the weapons systems again.

So what was the plan now? Jess glanced up at the pilots seat. Joshua would have asked a dozen times already, nervously messing with switches and toggles up there. In contrast, Dev was quietly running her checks, and getting ready to take the ship off auto nav, her eyes never ceasing to move over the readouts, watching them closely.

Very surprisingly competent. Jess was uncomfortably stunned at the level of knowledge the crèche had given this kid in a week, aware of just how long it would have taken a natural born person to get to this level.

On the one hand, at least she knew the kid probably wasn't going to drive the bus into a cliff. At least, not more so than any of the other techs. On the other hand, if they could do this with just one week's lead time...

Holy shit. Maybe that's what Bain really wanted. Get rid of all the troublesome, stubborn artifacts in the company and replace them with cute, competent, smart kids.

Who he could trust.

Who he could order by the dozens if he wanted and not have to pay the family tender rights.

Jess stared at the back of Dev's head. Should she let that happen? "Did you say you were the only one of you?" She asked, suddenly.

Dev turned and looked back. "Yes. I always sort of envied my crèchemates who were part of a set group. They always had people to talk to."

Jess managed a brief smile. No, there would be no instant conversion. Even bio alts took the same years to grow up and mature as natural born did. So even if Dev did work out, it would be... "How old are you?"

Dev's nose wrinkled a little. "Seventeen and a half standard years," she said. "We're not supposed to be assigned before eighteen, but this was a special request."

A kid indeed. Jess did the math. Even if it did work out, she'd be either retired to a watchman's role, or dead by then. So what the hell. "I won't tell anyone," she said. "Let's get in there and see what we see. Play it by ear. I'd like to find out at least what happened to our four."

Dev nodded. "I'll do my best."

"I bet you will."

THEY WERE MOMENTS from the edge of the storm, and Dev throttled back to match the carrier's speed with the energy shot edge of clouds she could now clearly see on the horizon. She checked the positioning estimate and saw the edge of the Gibraltar outpost on the far position on the grid.

That was where Jess said they would start chasing them. She rechecked the sensors, moving from one view to another until she was sure they had a good view all around the shuttle so she could see things coming at them.

The scan would tell her positioning, but she knew enough about the systems to know that sometimes they weren't one hundred percent correct. It was good to be able to see for yourself too. The sims did that. More than once she'd requested a perimeter view and found obstacles, or once even a stalled shuttle that the scan hadn't reported.

So she checked and rechecked, feeling a nervous ball start to form in her stomach as they crept closer.

This was hard. Dev wasn't sure she was up to this task, its demands overrunning the amount of programming she had for it. She knew what to do, but she also knew things would start happening so fast she would have no time to think about it.

Jess exhaled, bringing her systems live. "Okay. Let's get ready to run the gauntlet, kid."

Dev had no idea what a gauntlet was or why they would want to run one, but she settled her hands on the controls, put her boots on the thruster pedals and hit the toggle that would flood her comms with all the inputs of the carrier.

Instantly, the sound of the wind outside trickled in, and she could hear the thunder and crackle of the storm. The screens over her seat came alive with views around the carrier and she focused on the forward screen, where she knew the storm would roll over their target any minute.

Behind it, they were hidden. There was so much disruption in the atmosphere in the leading edge, no scans could see past it. They were coming in hard behind it, the two other carriers to their left and right, a few thousand feet to their rear.

Dev's heart started beating faster. She felt uncomfortable, her mouth was dry and her hands were shaky. Her forward display was showing the nearby flashes and behind her, she heard Jess hitting contacts, making a strange low noise as she did so.

Disconcerting.

"Dev?"

"Yes?"

"Good luck," Jess said, in a quiet tone. "Just go with it."

Dev had no idea what that meant. "Okay," she said. "Storm is over Gibraltar, standby for clearance."

"Here we go." Jess brought the targeting systems online and started hunting. "Tac one, Tac two. Soon as we clear for scan, split left. We meet at the drop zone. Look for the remaining carrier and report."

"Understood," Jason said. "Meet you on the flip side."

"Go," Elaine added. "Luck."

"Thanks," Jess said, clicking off just as the storm cleared the rocky promontory and her scan came alive with signals. "They can see us."

Dev sorted the incoming signals, almost feeling the scans bounce off the hull of the carrier as the storm rolled over the big rock and exposed its raw, rugged flank to them. She could see lights peppered across its surface, and then a beacon flared out, heading toward them.

Instinctively, she pitched the carrier forward and nosed down, and the beacon flashed past them. Lights started to blink on the rock face and the scan told her multiple targets were moving their direction. She hauled the throttles up and hit the engines to full.

Two dart shaped forms came whipping toward them. Dev brought the nose right between the attackers, trying not to flinch as a barrage of laser fire came right at them.

A bare second later, return fire flashed past in her peripheral vision and the two darts split to either side. She arched between them, seeing another line of darts now heading their way.

"Draw them to the right," Jess said. "Get behind the rock then go down to the deck. The waves'll confuse em."

Dev waited for the line to come into range, then she pitched down, then hard right as a hail of hard point missiles rattled against the hull.

"Bastards." Jess twitched her fingers, keeping on scope as the carrier turned half on its side, and the projectiles thumped against the well shielded bottom. The gyros kept pace with the motion though and she let loose a burst of laser pulses that streaked against the gray sky and wrote a stitching of fire across one of the darts.

It blossomed into fire and the machine headed for the water, a small ball heading the other direction marking the pilot's ejection.

Jess tracked the ball and squeezed off a shot just as her world turned upside down as the carrier did. Just as quickly it rolled around right side up and then she was under at least five Gs as they went into a steep climb.

Targets, targets. Warning bells chimed in her ears and she focused on her task, firing long, ripping bursts at the dozens of ships heading toward them.

Laser fire was everywhere, blossoming to the right and to the left, and blanking scan briefly as the carrier dodged the shots.

She was heartened by the reaction. The defenders hadn't been there waiting for her. She'd had a good ten minutes inbound before they reacted. That could only be a good sign. She now capped off the comms, putting the intercom between her and the other two carriers on battle silence, knowing they would be doing the same. "Go go go."

Dev didn't take a second to look back. She was fully engaged in figuring out how to get out of the way of the dozens of ships chasing them, and keeping the carrier in constant erratic motion to dodge the bolts headed their way.

It was scary. She tried to keep them all in view, her heart thumping hard. A group of six heading her way triggered a burst of programming. Something told her about that group, and about that formation. As she pitched away from them she saw them split apart.

She knew, somehow, that they were going to encircle her. She focused on the six, and saw them curving around. Two headed for the waves to cut off an escape. She rolled the carrier and dodged a blinding flash of laser fire then she caught sight of three of the darts closing in on her.

A blast hit them on the left side. She felt the shudder and two red alerts started flashing on the board. Another flash went to port side, and then she twisted the throttles, kicking the side thrusters hard as she slid under one of the darts and the screens momentarily blacked out, as the rumble of counter fire hit at such close quarters it nearly fried the scans.

Another alarm went off as she turned in the other direction, then she pitched the nose down and skimmed past one of the lower guards, so close the dart peeled off and dropped into a spiral to avoid hitting them.

Fire erupted all around them. Dev was totally unsure if it was against them or from them. The flares were so vivid it was causing sparkles in her own eyes. She pushed the throttles forward and dove for the waves, seeing them white and stark against the rock as the gray light grew around them.

She saw one of the darts cross her path, and she turned the carrier onto its side as the dart fired at point blank range, their bottom armor rumbling as it absorbed the energy. The vessel shuddered again as their own guns cut loose.

There was an explosion so close to them they lurched sideways in mid flight. She righted their flying angle and looked frantically around. For a moment, they were in the clear and she saw a ledge projecting out from the big rock and she aimed for it, intending to duck under it and curve along the rock.

She saw a sudden flare of lights along the granite surface, and scan erupted as the darts that had been diving at them diverted and streaked for the wall to get between her and it.

She heard Jess laugh behind her, but she wasn't really sure why. She dodged a spinning dart heading for the waves and reached the ledge moments before the rest of them, turning alongside it and increasing speed as she felt Jess let loose with the guns in a long, continuous, rumbling barrage.

The rumble was replaced with a larger one and all of a sudden the darts were heading away from her and she had a clear shot around the edge of the promontory.

"Faster," Jess said. "Got a boom coming behind us."

A what? Dev obediently pushed the throttles forward and kept as close to the rock as she could, sensing a motion in the air behind them. She checked the rear sensors and her eyes nearly came out of her head when she saw a fireball exploding out from under the ledge.

She hauled up on the controls and shoved the throttles forward again to full speed, hearing the imminent collision alerts and feeling the buffeting as the advance wave of the explosion caught them and she felt the carrier start to tumble.

She went with the motion shoving hard on the side thrusters to keep them away from the rocks as she fought to regain control over the carrier. The two big engines flared, and she was almost deaf from the alarms and the sound of impacts against the hull.

No control. She abruptly cut the engines and felt the carrier drop out of the rampaging explosion and plummet for the surface of the water as the energy flared over their heads.

"Dev?"

"Yes?"

"Didn't mean to show you the ocean this soon." Jess's voice sounded concerned.

"Oh."

Dev was aware of the approaching surface and she flared the side and bottom jets, evening out the flight of the carrier before she cut the mains in again so close to the waves they washed the bottom hull.

Then they were past Gibraltar, and in free air again. Dev gained altitude and started running checks, watching the scan reports for attackers. "Where are they?"

"Keep moving!" Jess called out. "Head for Alterra."

Dev shut off all the emergency alerts, starting some of the programs that would repair what could be repaired in flight. The systems started shunting power, whispers in her ear reporting damage and status.

They had taken damage in the rear shielding, and three of the external sensors were gone, giving her little view on the port side. The forward sensors cleared after a repair, and she looked out to see a gray lit day and a stretch of ruffled white gray water with a few lumps of island rising in the mist.

Her heartbeat settled a little as she realized she'd gotten through her very first air battle. "Wow."

She heard Jess release her harness behind her and after a moment, she felt a hand on her shoulder. With a start, she half turned and looked up, blinking a little sweat out of her eyes. "Yes?"

Jess smiled at her. "Good job."

Dev smiled tentatively back.

Jess reset some triggers and then retrieved another two of the drink containers, handing one over to Dev before she returned to her own chair.

Dev set the container into its swivel and wiped her damp hair back off her brow. She could imagine she still felt the pressure against her shoulder of Jess's fingers and gave herself a moment, just a small one, to savor this bit of accomplishment.

Then she went back to the boards, continuing the process of resetting alarms and assessing damage. They were running at top speed a thousand feet over the waves and she could see fog rising from the water everywhere, swirling behind them as their exhaust stirred it.

It was eerie, and a little beautiful.

"They'll be waiting for us at Alterra," Jess said. "We need to make this fast. I'm feeding you the coordinates to the science center. Head right for it." She keyed something into her pad. "Make em believe we're going to ram this thing right into entrance."

"Okay," Dev said. "Are we actually going to do that?"

"No, Dev. Dying's not on my schedule today." Jess chuckled a little. "Just make them think we are. Then go somewhere else."

Go somewhere else. Dev turned and shook her head a little. She saw the coordinates plot on her navigation grid and she flexed her hands, putting them back on the controls and taking off the auto nav.

At the edge of the grid she could see the Alterra escarpment, and as she did, she saw a set of blinking lights erupt from it. "Is that them?"

"Yes." Jess slammed back into her seat and pulled her controls around. "Looks like they spotted us."

The lights multiplied and doubled, tripled, filling the screen with alerts and causing the scan to erupt. "There's a lot of them."

"Yup."

Dev could see them coming in from all directions. "This is going to be difficult."

"Only hard things are worth doing, kid," Jess said. "Remember that."

Dev stared at the oncoming armada. "Okay." She shifted her hands on the controls. "I will try to remember that."

"Good." Jess tightened her harness and took a deep breath. She got herself set and made live the guns, checking the power reserves and finding them acceptable.

She hoped her diversion would let Elaine and Jason check the place where they'd last seen the other two teams. She had no idea what they would find, given the carrier she'd blown up. But they knew where to look and they knew what to do with what they found.

She checked the time and checked her plan grid. Then she started the targeting systems and let the targets flood her consciousness.

There were a lot. She lined up the first six and launched a blast on alternating forward guns, glad the carrier's weapon systems had a slightly longer range than their enemy's. She could see them forming into attack circles and one of them dove right for them.

In a heartbeat they were in the center of a circle of death. The enemy ships matched sync with them and started firing. Jess fired back, then found herself inverting as the carrier did a barrel roll and the lasers rotated with the ship, nailing at least part of the enemy fighters.

Then they were through that bunch and going nose on to a second, when two of that group dove right at them.

Jess fired the forward guns and as they flashed by she grabbed a breath as she inverted again and went under heavy G as the carrier turned on its tail and her fire went right up the tailpipes of the retreating enemy ships and blew them out of the sky.

Holy crap.

Still upside down, Jess launched a plasma bomb toward a cluster of fighters and then just before she started getting lightheaded they were right way up and she was holding her triggers down on the forward guns as they went full speed through enemy lines.

Dev was concentrating as hard as she could. She was aware of the strain on the engines under her control, but she used all the power she had to keep the carrier on a constantly shifting course as the air around her was filled with enemy fire.

Some were hitting the carrier. She had alarms going off again. The forward screen was almost constantly whitewashed with their own return guns as Jess blasted a path for them through the enemy ships.

The carrier was larger than the defenders, and better armored. The defenders were more agile and faster.

Dev spotted the entrance to the science center, a flat platform halfway up the escarpment with thick barricades in front of it. The door looked like it was big, and metal, and pretty much the same as the ones in the Interforce facility.

She spotted another wheel of figures fit themselves around her and she did another barrel roll, then her eyes widened as she came out of the inversion right into the path of a larger, more well armored craft.

She saw laser cannons on top of it so she sent the carrier almost straight down, flinching a little as two of the enemy crashed into each other over her head. She pulled up in a high G arc with all her engines firing, gritting her teeth against the pressure as she came up just under the bigger craft, hearing Jess let loose with the upper guns on it.

"Nice!" Jess yelled.

Dev managed a brief grin as she dove again, seeing huge breaking waves below her. She could feel the impacts on the hull of fire and a quick glance at the monitors showed a dozen darts coming after her all shooting continuously.

Alarms blared.

Dev aimed right for the sea, hearing the mounting damage in her comm set. She knew she had to get out of range of them before the lasers blew the carrier apart.

Jess was firing the rear guns. "Not much juice left!" She yelled.

Dev pulled the nose up just as they reached sea level and a huge breaker rolled up right into her path. She shot down the center of it, taking the carrier right through the huge phosphorescent tube of water as

Jess let out a shout of surprise.

They shot out the other end of the tube and Dev blinked as the salt wash cleared and they were moments away from the escarpment.

She heard a huge disruption behind her. There was no time to wonder what it was as she fought to control her craft and get the nose up before they went headlong into the rock face.

By a whisper they didn't. She shot up the face of the cliff as Jess launched plasma bombs in a thumping salvo against it. She held the carrier in it's straight up climb until they shot up over the top of it and right into the cloud layer just above.

A blue light flashed hard on the comms console. Dev didn't have time to look at it though. She arched the carrier over as they reached an altitude almost too high for the jets and curved back over into level flight.

Her heart was absolutely racing. Shivers rushed up and down her spine and she was alternately feeling flushed and chilled, panting through her open mouth as she caught her breath.

"Keep going!" Jess yelled. "Go go go! They got them! We did it!"

Dev stared in confusion at the console. "What?"

"The light." Jess pointed. "That's an ultraviolet squirt from Jason. They got them. Get out of here! We did it!"

Dev checked the scan and found only fading targets, blips they were leaving behind as they raced between the cloud layers back in the direction they'd came. "W...why aren't they chasing us," she asked. "Where did they go?"

Jess laughed. "Don't look a gift horse in the ass, Dev. Just fly."

Dev wiped her brow and let out a long exhale, chills still running up and down her spine. "Wow," she said. "That was crazy."

Jess chuckled again.

"But I liked it," Dev said, unexpectedly. "I really did." She half turned in her chair and looked at Jess. "It was fun."

Jess peered at her from behind her targeting console, seeing the intense sparkle in her eyes. "Hm," she said softly. "We may just have to keep you."

"Excuse me?" Dev leaned toward her. "Did you say something?"

Jess smiled. "Take us home, Dev, before this thing falls apart." She leaned back as the battered craft rumbled through the thick, moist air. "There's a lot more work to do."

Chapter Seven

THEY WERE THE last ship back. Dev held the carrier steady, limping in on one engine, as she watched the recovered vessel with its four passengers, and the two that had gone with them, sink through the wide opening into the landing bay.

It was still raining. But it was a steady unrelenting drizzle and the winds had died down, allowing Dev to relax as she waited.

Jess was in her seat, tapping furiously on her consoles and pad, occasionally chuckling to herself. She seemed to be in a very good mood, and Dev cautiously evaluated the idea that she'd done okay in their mission.

Her first one. She had, at least, brought them both back in one piece if the carrier wasn't, and since they'd gotten the other teams back, she figured the whole thing might have been something of a success.

Not too bad for someone who had only driven a sim before now. Dev glanced at her reflection in the curved forward shield, noting her sweat dampened hair. She raked it back and settled her hands on the controls again, the feeling of the throttles against her palms starting to become comfortably familiar.

She moved the carrier forward, tilting the nose down a little with a boost on the landing jets to give her a good view of the bay. She could see clear airspace and leveled the craft, then increased the lower jets and cut off her main engines.

The carrier drifted downward, clearing the bay opening and settling lower and lower into the vast cavern. "BR27006," she said softly into the comms. "Requesting landing pad."

The comm crackled immediately. "BR27006, landing pad eighty-two cleared for your approach."

Dev located the spot, marked with big, easily read numbers and adjusted the side jets to move them over, hovering above the numbers before she cut power to the landing jets and they settled slowly into place.

There was a team waiting. She recognized a group of Ceebees, in pale orange jumpsuits with kits and hoses in their hands. As soon as she cut power to the drive systems, they bolted toward the carrier.

Two sprayed the outside down with something. "What is that?"

"Sealant," Jess said, still slouched in her seat. "In case we popped a line. Don't want to blast anyone with anything." She now had her hands folded over her stomach and was just relaxing. "When they make the hookup, send the logs and the flight recorder detail over to storage."

Dev nodded. She had been waiting, in fact, for specifically that. She saw a light come on midway up the console, and ran her fingers over the keys, accepting the connection and setting up the sync.

Another light, and she shut down internal power. They went into pitch darkness for a few seconds before the external connection kicked in and the lights came back on, along with internal ventilation now being supplied from the dock.

It felt good. The air was cool and fresh and not full of half baked sealant. Dev blinked a little, and unbuckled her harness as she turned her seat around and watched the webbing retract.

"So." Jess regarded her. "NM-Dev-1, you can pilot a carrier."

"Yes." Dev smiled. "Apparently so."

"Where'd you pick up all the upside down stuff?" Jess asked. "I'm betting the other side's never seen one of these do that before, cause I sure haven't."

Upside down? Dev frowned a little and her head tilted to one side. "You mean this?" She lifted one hand and tilted it back and forth.

"I mean when you were flying with the bottom of this thing pointed skyward."

"Oh." Dev nodded. "In space..." She pointed upward. "In the crèche, you get to train in a null grav sim for some of this. It's all...um." She considered. "There's no right or wrong side up in space. You learn in all dimensions."

Jess studied her face intently for a long moment. "Interesting," she said, finally. "Well, I'll tell you what, Dev. You did as well, or better, as anyone I've ever seen driving this bus."

"Are you surprised?"

"Yes."

"Me too," Dev replied, with an almost impish grin. "Sims are one thing, but real is different. This was very difficult. Mostly because I didn't have any programming on what to do. They don't give you programs to know what to do when you're flying at a mountain with twenty planes chasing you and shooting at you."

"Ah," Jess murmured. "So you just did that on instinct."

Dev considered that carefully. "I'm not sure what that means."

"You didn't think about what to do." Jess clarified. "You just reacted. You just did it."

Dev considered again, then nodded. She half turned as the comm crackled, reaching over to accept a key.

"BR27006, you are cleared for exit. Systems stable, please release locks and proceed to debrief," a stolid male voice intoned. "Agent Drake, Mr. Bain's compliments."

"Hah." Jess stood up and stretched. "C'mon. Let's get the brain hosing out of the way and go get a drink. We earned it." She waved Dev forward, and keyed the hatch, waiting a moment as it unsealed and popped outward.

She stepped out and down to the ground, as two bio alt techs edged past her, carrying toolkits. She waited for Dev to follow her, not missing the looks of the other bio alts as she left the carrier past them. Mixture of envy and awe.

Jess was intrigued, but she put it aside as she turned to regard her craft. "Shitcakes."

Dev turned and looked, her eyes getting big and round. "Wow."

Every inch of the craft was scored by fire, its outside a dark and creased dappled gray. One of the external engine pods was sliced through, dripping lurid green fluid on the ground. There was a huge rent right along the side, its end just shy of the curve of the nose where Dev had been seated.

A man came up next to Jess, dressed in a deep orange suit. "Holy shit, Drake. What the hell did you do to that thing?"

Jess glanced at him, bemused. "You should see what the other guy looks like," she said. "Sorry, Clint. Looks like a total overhaul."

The man snorted, then seemed to notice Dev for the first time. "Who's this?"

"This is Dev," Jess said. "She's my p...pilot." She felt her tongue stutter, and felt a pang. "Wait till you see the logs."

Clint regarded Dev thoughtfully. "Oh, yeah. I heard about that. Nice to meet you." He extended a hand. "Hope you don't do this every time. Too much work."

Dev politely shook his hand. "I'll try not to," she said. "They're very sturdy pieces of equipment."

Clint beamed.

Jess sighed. "The way to his heart is through a hydraulic tube, c'mon." She touched Dev's sleeve. "They're waiting for us in debrief."

They walked along the marked floor, as techs and support people swarmed around them, and the other three carriers who had just come in. The rest of the crews had already gone down the tunnel, so Jess wasted no more time and turned off the rocky floor into a tall, scan equipped deep blue hallway.

She felt the tickle as she passed through, and saw Dev blink a little. "You feel that?"

Dev looked at her. "Yes. The scan, you mean?"

Jess nodded. "Yeah. That's all security. You have to be coded to go through. If you're not, you get enough of a blast to take you out when you're inside. Some places, like central command, you get more than that."

"Oh."

"I'll show you the grid when we get back to quarters. We're coded everywhere, but not everyone is. Good to know if you're walking with someone outside ops."

"I see."

Jess led the way toward a closed automatic door, and put her hand on the pad outside it. "Drake, J, and NM-Dev-1 for debrief."

The pad glowed, then the door opened and they went in. "Gotta show you the rec, and your rad area too," Jess said, as they went through another door and into a larger room, this one half full of people. "But we'll get a drink first."

Dev was content to follow along, listening to Jess's ramblings. She considered them, cautiously optimistic that they seemed to be trending toward a tendency to let her stay, at least for a little while.

She recognized Stephan Bock and the four agents they'd gone with. Bain was also there, along with four people she didn't know. She stopped as Jess did, and watched Jess spread her arms out as they all started making noises at her.

Very strange. But Jess looked pleased, so she supposed it was all right. She followed Jess over to two open chairs and they sat down next to each other. She looked over at Bain, surprised to find him smiling at her.

She returned the smile.

Bain leaned back and looked at the people Dev didn't know. "Welcome back, you four. "None the worse for wear I see."

"Was a little tough, sir," Sandy Tucker responded. "Me and Nappy tried to make our own diversion with our boat, but they didn't buy it. We thought we were going to have to try and climb out when all of a sudden they all took off."

"Right," Jason said. "By the time we crested over the ridge just east of them, the guards all hauled ass and it was easy peasy getting to them and getting out. They didn't even leave a comms watch." He glanced at Dev then back at Jess. "What the hell did you do to draw them off?"

"We can roll the flight recorder," Jess said. "Faster that way than for me to tell it." She eyed Sandy. "I guess you know I blew up your boat."

Sandy nodded. She looked at the tall, very muscular man next to her. "Mike figured that might happen. We didn't really have any way of broadcasting it wasn't rigged, or that you'd believe it if we did."

The tall man next to Sandy grunted. "Fuckers. They knew we were coming, Jess." He looked across the table. "We came in polar and had just cleared Gibraltar when they were on us. Chased us to the ridge and we got under cover—blasted the ones who had the guts to come at us, but we were stuck there."

"Saw you on scan," Jason said. "It was a bad plan to start with."

Both Mike and Sandy looked uncomfortable. "Well, you made your view clear," Mike said, stiffly.

Bain cleared his throat. "He was right," he said, in a mild tone. "It was a damn fool idea, and we had to put three teams at risk just to get us back to square one."

Mike looked sullenly at him.

"What about you?" Sandy suddenly asked, looking at Jess. "I thought you were out. Didn't you stand on your pride about that?" She pointed at Dev. "Now you're here? It's here? What's the deal?"

Bain cleared his throat again. "Agent Drake was thoughtful enough to agree to my request that she remain with us," he said. "I'm quite gratified." He looked at Jess. "And how is the experiment going, Agent Drake?"

Jess remained expressionless. "I'll let the flight recorder speak for itself," she said. "But I'll be more than glad to continue with it." She folded her hands on the table. "I like the results so far."

Dev's ears perked. That sounded like a positive thing, since she strongly suspected she was the experiment in question.

"Hmm. Indeed." Bain's eyes twinkled a little. "Then by all means, let's see this recorder." He nodded at Stephan, who was sitting in silence, just watching everyone. "Mr. Bock. Please proceed."

Stephan got up and went to the console, triggering the big display in the back of the room. The panels slid open, and he keyed in the recording that Dev had sent from the carrier. "Here we go, sir."

He sat down as the scene recorder rolled, presenting a view from all the carrier's sensors overlaid to produce an almost three dimensional presentation. On one corner was a mission clock, and on the other a base readout of the carrier's systems.

They heard Dev's voice quietly asking for flight access, then the recorder started forward.

"Go to time lock eleven-forty loc if you want to see the other carrier blown out," Jess said. "And eleven-fifty loc if you want to see the exciting stuff."

Stephan looked at Bain, who nodded. He keyed in the change, and suddenly the carrier was accelerating toward the hulk of Gibraltar and the defender's beacons flared.

Dev was a little surprised at how fast it all went once it started. When she'd been doing it, it seemed a lot longer. She relived the dives and rolls, nodding a little as the carrier wove its way through the enemy, rolling over and over as it darted between defenders and through arcs of fire.

"Holy shit," Sandy said, after a few minutes utter silence.

Jess sat back in her seat and smiled. She could see Bain's face, and even his craggy old eyes were wide and astonished, as they blasted past Gibraltar and she laid a line of fire inside their control center. Then they were past, and she felt her heart accelerating as she relived their one team attack on the heavily defended science center.

"Oh my go...whoa!" Jason yelped, as the carrier dove for the waves.

Diving, diving, the alarms going off, redlining the carrier with all that evident on the screen as they pulled out and into that damn rolling wave at the very last minute, the enemy behind them splashing into the water unable to stop.

Wild.

Then she sat back, remembering the incredible pull of gravity on her body and the ache still in her arms as she kept firing, all the way up the escarpment and over the top into the clouds in one long, screaming, rumbling run that ended in gray silence and the bleeting of overworked systems.

"Holy shit," Sandy said, again.

"That's about it." Jess said, in as normal a voice as she could muster. "The rest you know."

The lights came up a little as Stephan cut the replay off, and they all turned around and stared at the two women seated at the end of the table.

Even Bain, his customary dismissive, offhand facade dropped like a rock off the cliff, his jaw hanging slightly open.

Jess smiled briefly. "Can we get the one by ones done? I owe my pilot here a drink." She jerked her head in Dev's direction. "As a matter of fact, I think you all do too."

Dev was not sure what response would be appropriate, so she decided not to have any at all. She remained silent, her hands folded on the table, a mild look on her face as the rest of the group stared at her.

"Not bad for her first flight, huh?" Jess finally said.

Bain relaxed into his seat, and exhaled. "Indeed."

DEV WAS CONTENT to stick to Jess's side as they all entered a wide, low room with comfortable looking chairs. She took a seat next to Jess and listened to the rest of them chatter, glad to be able to participate in what was evidently a positive experience.

The other agents and techs ignored her. That was all right. She was satisfied that Jess and Bain were happy with her. She was looking forward to the moment when she could go and get in the shower and maybe have a chance to read a page or two of her book.

She wondered if she could find Doctor Dan, and ask him what he thought about the mission. She knew a lot of the programming she'd been given was his, and she was curious if it had turned out as he'd expected.

"Dev?"

Dev looked up. "Yes?" She reached up in reflex and took the glass she was being handed, her eyes darting to Jess's face in question. "Thank you."

"You ever had booze?" Jess asked as she watched her sip at the contents.

Dev blinked and moved the glass away. The drink was a very strange mixture of fruits and something that fizzed and something else that burned as she swallowed. "If that's what this is, then definitely not."

Jess chuckled.

"So, how far are you going to take this thing?" Sandy asked, indicating Dev. "Obviously you're sucking up to Bain, but for how long?"

"Are you really that much of an asshole?" Jess said.

Sandy shrugged. "Takes one to know one."

"Then I'm going to take this all the way." Jess met her gaze. "Dev can go as far as she's able in this place as far as I'm concerned." She leaned back in her chair and extended her long legs out. "And at least I'm not sucking up to someone who got his brains blown out for being a moron, like you were."

"Hey c'mon." Jason gave them both a look. "We just had a successful mission here. Let's not act like jerks."

"That was Bricker's idea!" Mike pointed at Dev.

"She," Jess corrected. "Was Bricker's idea. But no one here can say why." She took a swallow of her drink. "Bain's reason for wanting her here might be a whole other thing."

"Bricker didn't buy into your bullshit mystique," Sandy said. "At least I don't pretend to like you, Jess, or kiss your ass, unlike everyone else apparently."

Dev was listening, her head swiveling to regard each speaker. At this last, she turned and looked at Jess, her brow creased in confusion. "You have a lot of unusual customs." She said. "Programming definitely didn't cover that one."

Jess started laughing, and Jason did too. After a long, frozen moment the rest of them reluctantly started to chuckle.

"Shit." Mike caught Jess's sharp eye. "It— She's got a sense of fucking humor." He grudgingly conceded.

"Look," Jess said. "She's a one off. Just go with the program." She leaned her arm on the chair arm next to Dev's. "So much shit's going down right now, who knows how it's all going to end up.

"One off?" Mike asked warily.

"I'm an experimental set." Dev spoke directly to him. "I don't have crèche mates."

All of the agents in the group seemed to relax just a little.

"There isn't a dozen of her back there waiting to take over," Jess said. "So chill out. Go yell at Bain if you want to for her being here. It's not her fault."

"But you agreed to it," Sandy said. "Talk's cheap, huh? What'd Bain offer you, a roll in the sack?"

Jess stood up abruptly, putting her glass down and freeing her hands.

Jason scrambled to his feet. "Jess, chill."

"Yeah, bring it." Sandy beat him and tossed her glass. "I was damn glad you quit, you little shiftface. Now you come back and bring this with you?" She pointed at Dev. "Fuck you, Drake!"

"Hey!" Mike got up and grabbed her the same time Jason grabbed Jess. "Cut it the fuck out, Sandy!" He shook her. "They just saved our asses. Have some honor."

Sandy glared at him, then she looked at Jess, who was standing absolutely still, her eyes icy and locked onto her. "Honor my ass. You did it to score points."

"No." Jason still had hold of Jess. "We told her you weren't worth risking it for, you sorry piece of shit. But she's a Drake and it didn't matter. So like he said, sit down."

Elaine came up next to Jason. Silent, but explicit in support.

Sandy shook Mike's hands off her and went back to her seat, picking up her glass and ignoring the rest of them.

Jess felt the flashes behind her eyes fade, and she moved back away from Jason, resuming her seat next to Dev. "Fucker."

Jason and Elaine sat back down and picked up their drinks. Jason turned to Elaine. "So, how's the seaweed harvest going?"

Conversation resumed.

The outer door opened and Stephan Bock came in. He stopped to grab a drink from the tray that had been set up near the grouping of chairs they were in, and sat down in an empty one. "So." He looked at them. "You all done sniping at Jess and being rude to her tech?"

"Fuck you, Stephan," Sandy said.

"You want to be put on report for that?" Stephan asked. "I had to put up with your attitude when I was an agent, Sandra. I don't have to now."

"You don't have the balls."

"I do." Stephan clicked his comm set. "Please send a recorder down here from ops. I have a disciplinary action to execute."

Sandy stared at him. "You bastard."

"Guess it's different now that your sugar daddy got his head blown off, huh?" Jason produced a brief smile. "We all know that wasn't his ass you were kissing."

"You all can go to hell." Sandy got up, and her partner, Nappy, did too. He hadn't said a word the entire time they'd been in the room, and followed her in equal silence as she left the lounge.

"We're going to go get cleaned up." Mike stood and motioned to his partner. "C'mon, Chris." He glanced at Jess. "Thanks, Jess. All bullshit aside." He extended his big, muscled hand. "You put it out there for us."

Jess returned the clasp, then released it. "Anytime." She leaned back in her chair and drained her cup, motioning to the bio alt server to replenish it.

Stephan looked tired. He glanced over at Jess, who was sitting next to him. "Bain wants to see you in about an hour," he said. "We've gotten some intelligence he wants to review with you."

Jess nodded. "I'm going to go grab some grub then." She stood up. "Interested, Dev?"

"Yes," Dev responded immediately. "That would be nice." She put her cup down on the tray and stepped aside, as Jess came around her chair and headed for the door.

Jason stood up. "We'll go too. Been a long time since breakfast. Stephan? You up for chow?"

"Sure, why not."

They walked together through the hallways toward the dining hall. Dev stuck close to Jess, but then, out of the corner of her eye she saw Doctor Dan come out of a doorway and spot her.

His eyes lit up. He crossed the hallway and intercepted them, the group slowing as he approached and watching him warily. "Congratulations." He nodded at them, then turned to Dev. "Excuse us a moment. I'd like to speak to Dev."

The group moved on, leaving them behind. Dev did however, catch Jess looking back at her. "I'll be right there." She said, with a little half wave.

Jess waved back, and pointed at the dining hall then ducked inside.

Dev turned back around. "Hello, Doctor Dan."

"Hello, Dev." Kurok leaned forward and gave her a hug. "I just wanted to take a minute to congratulate you for your work today."

Dev smiled. "It was difficult."

"I just bet it was." Kurok chuckled. "I saw the recorder. You did an amazing job for your first flight." He put both hands on her shoulders. "Really good, Dev. Everyone thinks so."

Dev glanced at the now vanished group. "I don't think everyone does, Doctor Dan, but the person I was the pilot for was very pleased with me, I believe."

Kurok's gray eyes warmed as he looked at her. "Jess is very pleased with you," he said. "And she's got a good reason to be. You achieved a very significant thing together." He glanced casually around, but they were alone in the hall. "I'll be going back to the crèche tomorrow, Dev."

"I won't be?" Dev felt a little, excited thump in her chest.

"No, you're staying here." He squeezed her shoulders. "Do your best. You can trust Jess Drake, and you can trust Alex Bain."

Dev nodded. "You trust them."

"I would trust Alex with my life, and have," Kurok said, in a serious tone. "And you can too. But you can also trust Jess, and I hope she comes to trust you."

Dev hesitated, then nodded again. "I hope she does. I want to do good work." She watched Doctor Dan's face, as he smiled gently. "People here sometimes aren't very nice. I think they do not want me to be here."

"I know," Doctor Dan said. "Be strong, Dev. In the end, people who try to hurt people like you, end up only hurting themselves." He let his hands drop. "I have sent my personal comms link to your quarters. Use it if you need to. If you just want to talk or tell me something, do it."

Dev smiled. "I will. Thank you for everything, Doctor Dan. I'll do my best here."

"I know you will." Kurok gave her another hug. "Go get some food. Is that okay for you so far?"

"It's fine," Dev said. "Will you come eat with us?"

He shook his head. "I think I'll make your new colleagues uncomfortable." He patted her back. "I'll be by to say goodbye before I leave. Go on now."

Dev clasped his hand and released it, then turned and headed for the dining hall.

She looked around and spotted Jess, who was standing in the line. She quickly went over to join her, coming to stand next to her in front of the food dispenser.

"Your buddy give you a pat on the back?" Jess asked.

"Doctor Dan? Yes. He's going home tomorrow," Dev said. "He wanted to tell me that, and compliment me on my work."

Jess punched in two sets of codes. "So he was saying goodbye?"

"Something like that, yes." Dev smiled briefly. "So I suppose I'm staying."

"Oh yeah, you're staying." Jess pushed a tray at her. "Later on I'll show you around the place the right way." She picked up the tray and headed for a large table where the others were sitting. She took a seat and Dev took one beside her.

"Lot of people coming in," Jason said, glancing around. "All the prep people for the new class." He forked up some of his fish. "Thought they'd cancel it for a few days."

"Yeah," Elaine said. "Brent, don't you know one of the newbies?"

Brent nodded. "Cousin of mine. I tried to talk him out of it but the jackass didn't listen."

Dev listened politely, as she chewed. The tray held some different things than last time, a crispy cake she liked very much, some chewy protein she guessed was probably fish, and some things in hard shells, which tasted salty.

"So. Um. Dev."

Dev swallowed and looked up at Elaine, with a start of surprise. "Yes?"

Elain leaned against the table. "I've always wanted to ask this. What the hell is the collar for?"

Dev put her fork down. "It's a programming interface," she said. "It gets installed right after you mostly finish growing, when you start to get skills."

"Ah huh," Elaine said. "So, it's a plug?"

"Not really." Dev unsealed the neck of her suit and peeled it down low enough to expose the collar. "There are sockets that the programming system connects to, but then there are leads that go up through the back of your neck here." She touched the back of her head. "And into your cortex."

"They put wires in your brain?" Elaine said, after a pause.

"Yes. It's how they give us programs."

"How do they do that?" Jason asked.

"I don't know. I'm not a programmer." Dev smiled briefly. "It's a special skill. Not many natural born can do it. "

"Natural born." Jess looked at her. "Is that what you call us?"

"Yes."

"Weird." Jason shook his head.

They all went back to eating. Dev closed the collar on her suit and took a sip of the pale fizzy drink, which she was getting to like. She felt okay about getting the questions since at least they were asking and not just talking at her like they were before.

Good sign, she supposed.

"What do you suppose Bain wants?" Jason asked Jess. "That guy scares me. Don't care who knows it."

Jess shrugged. "Can't be too bad. We all made it," she said. "Besides, one of the things I noticed going in was that we surprised them."

Elaine nodded, her mouth full.

"Felt like that to us too," Jason said. "I expected we'd get ambushed.

Hell, I told Elaine we were probably flying into a net coming around the side of that ridge they were hiding under."

"Which is strange." Elaine said. "Because you know we don't usually leave our kind in their clutches if we can help it. If it had been me, I'd have expected us even if we did cut off comms."

Jess grunted. "Point."

"Yeah." Jason frowned. "Hell, though, I'm not going to look a gift horse in the ass."

Dev made a mental note to access her pad when she got back to her quarters and start looking up some of the odd verbal utterances she'd heard so far from Jess and her colleagues. She'd heard that thing about the horse twice now, so she figured it had to mean something pretty important,

"So, who else is coming in the class?" Elaine asked. "Twelve for us and?" She looked at Jess. "Any idea?"

Jess scraped the last of the fish from her plate. "Repair chiefs, some security, and from what I hear, a dozen of the biological guys for downstairs."

"Huh."

"There are some pilots and mechanics coming from the crèche," Dev said. "They were staging them when I left. They were talking about new vehicles."

"Finally!" Jason said. "They've been rebuilding those carriers since I was a baby."

"Last year?" Elaine elbowed him.

Jason elbowed her back. "Shut up."

"Good to see a new bus if it's true," Brent said. "So many things are falling off mine, I was afraid I'd tank someone on the deck when we took off."

"Yeah, if they give them to us, not the newbies." Tucker spoke up for the first time. "'Member what they said the last time, that they had to get the good stuff cause they didn't know better. We could handle all the crap."

Jess rested her elbows on the table and cradled her mug in her hands. "Anyone tries to pull that bullshit line on me, I just point them at her." She pointed at Dev. "They didn't come any newer than she did this morning."

Tucker and Brent gave Dev a grudging nod. "Yeah that's true I guess." Tucker said. "'Sides what your rig looked like when you got back I figure they'd got to build it up from base steel anyhow."

They finished lunch and filtered out the door, most heading for the residential quarters on the next ring of hallways outward. Dev walked at Jess's side, as it got quieter and quieter when the two other teams peeled off to their rooms.

She paused as she went past Jess's door toward her own. She had passed the first test of this new assignment and earned herself a continued presence with the possibility of a longer term stay. But for

How long?

"Hey, Dev?"

Dev turned, to find Jess in her doorway. "Yes?"

"Change then come over. I want you to come see Bain with me."

"Okay," Dev said.

Jess came over and leaned against the wall, folding her arms across her chest. "Don't let the jackassery get to you."

Dev looked at her, blinking a few times. "Is that supposed to refer to the rude attitude?"

Jess nodded. "We're all pretty hard on each other. Sandy and I never got along."

"No problem," Dev said.

"Does it bother you?" Jess asked, in a quiet tone.

"Does it bother you?" Dev returned the question.

Jess studied her in silence for a long moment. "Hmp," she finally grunted. "Damn good question." She turned and headed back to her door. "Very damn good question."

Dev waited until the door closed, then she turned and went to her own quarters, scanning through and letting the heavy panel slide shut behind her. She stopped and looked around, taking in the room with a fresh set of eyes.

On the workspace was a packet, and some covered pads, delivered when she was on the mission. So this, for now, was home. She bypassed the table and headed for the sanitary space, already looking forward to a shower and fresh clothes, and the tour Jess promised her for later.

Today had turned out to be a really, really, really good day.

Chapter Eight

DEV LOOKED UP as she heard a buzz at the door. She got up and went to it, triggering the latch and stepped back as the door slid open and Jess entered. She was dressed in one of the more casual jumpsuits, with fewer pockets and softer fabric.

Dev had realized that there were a few different kinds of garb. One was this type, and she was wearing the same now too, and another was the kind she had worn to pilot the carrier which was a heavier fabric, with clips and embedded links for the carrier's systems to plug into.

"Hello."

"Ready?" Jess's eyes swept briefly over the interior. She spotted the packet on the workspace and walked over to it. "You open this?"

"No," Dev said. "I didn't know what it was."

Jess worked the clamp and opened the padded envelope. "C'mere." She shook out the contents into her hand then turned as Dev approached. "Last bit of archaic crap we use." She reached up and took hold of Dev's jumpsuit collar.

Dev stood stock still, not really sure what was going on. She could feel the warmth of Jess's fingers against her skin, though, and she decided it felt nice.

"There." Jess let her hands fall, producing a brief smile as Dev gave her a questioning look. "It's like the one I have." She touched the insignia on her collar. "Except the bottom enamel strips are green instead of black."

"Oh." Dev reached up to feel the item now fastened to her suit. "Thank you."

"It doesn't mean anything except that you're one of us," Jess said. "I guess when we coded you in as ops tech, it triggered the whole process. That included this." She picked up a few other items that had dropped out of the packet. "This is your chit card."

Dev studied it. "Okay."

"When you go on missions, you get credits," Jess explained. "You can take this and go to the exchange and trade the credits for stuff."

"Stuff?"

"Stuff. You know, like..." Jess paused. "Well, I guess you probably don't know. Never mind, I'll take you there and show you. It's easier than explaining."

"Okay."

"You can also use it at dinner for drinks or extras, which I'll show you today too. And this pad template—you can specify what you want in here and supply will take care of it for you. Like something other than crackers for the dispenser or a different temperature profile."

"Okay."

"You can put the card in your ident pack," Jess said. "Okay? So let's go talk to Bain. I want to get your status clarified before I have to go and have back alley fights with everyone I work with." She turned and led the way to the door.

What did that mean? Dev wondered. She followed Jess through the hallways, passing the ops center and continuing around the curve into a gray shaded hallway she hadn't been in yet. This one had two scans, which she felt as an itchy tingle as they went through.

At the end of the hallway was a shielded door, guarded by two big security officers. They regarded her and Jess as they approached. Only at the very end did they move aside and key the door open.

Jess ignored them. "Thank you," Dev murmured as she went by.

They walked into a small outer office, and the door behind them closed. Jess stood quietly before the inner door, looking around a little as a soft set of bings and clicks sounded, then the inner door opened.

"Ah." Bain was seated behind a big desk, watching as they entered. "Right on time, Drake. And I see you brought your charming companion with you." He got up and came around the desk, extended his hand to Dev. "Hello, my dear. You're very welcome to this meeting."

Dev politely shook his hand. "Thank you, sir."

"You did some excellent work." Bain told her. "Extraordinary, for your first flight, hm?"

"I did the best I could." Dev smiled. "I'm very glad it all worked out correctly."

"Yes." Bain went back behind the desk and gestured for them to sit down in the two chairs in front of it. "Well, Drake, looks like your plan succeeded." He steepled his fingers. "Hm? All of you returned and I've gotten some intelligence here that indicates you left some...hm...consternation shall we say behind you?" He pushed a folder across the desk.

Jess took it and flipped through the plastic like sheets inside. "Ah. So that's what that ledge was."

"Hm. Yes." Bain nodded. "Plasma station. Took out a quarter of the mountain face when it exploded. I daresay you left your mark."

Wow. Jess sounded the word silently in her head. She selected a grainy picture and passed it to Dev. "Big boom."

Dev studied the picture. Suddenly the memory flashes popped in, and she recalled the high speed dive past the cliff. She tried to tie in that memory with the picture, which showed a huge hole where the ledge had been.

"Well done." Bain said. "I would guess you've set them back quite a bit, Drake. Sure you didn't make any more friends on that side though."

"Wasn't the lab they had the new growth experiment in though."

"Ah, no," Bain said. "That's what I wanted to discuss with you. That needs to be addressed. I want you to do it."

Jess closed the folder. "Two days ago I wasn't even cleared for active duty," she said. "One day ago I was being processed out."

"And?" Bain cocked his head at her.

"There's probably a better choice than me to take on a new mission."

Bain shook his head. "I disagree. I realize you were involved in several very stressful incidents, but given the resources we have right now, I cannot recommend another in your place." He watched her expression. "Besides, your wish to leave us was all based around the presence of your new associate here, and I believe you have, as they say, gotten over that."

Jess pondered this. "Yeah, now both her and I are taking crap from every direction because of it."

"Indeed?"

"Indeed," Jess said. "This started off as a hair brained scheme by Bricker. Everyone knew it. Now everyone needs to know what the deal is."

"Hm." Bain tapped his fingertips against his lips. "Yes, it was a hair brained scheme that, unlikely as it was, worked. The people up at LifeSource took him seriously, and gave our friend here what skills they could in so short a time. This morning it was amply demonstrated that their cobbled together effort performed as well as any of our training programs could."

"True," Jess said.

"Hm. Well then," Bain said. "I've decided to inform everyone that Bricker made that request on my orders. I never mind taking credit for someone else's insane ideas, so long as they prove out, hm? So this becomes my idea, and my plan." Bain gave Dev a smile. "Since it has already proven to be a success, we'll instruct LifeSource to continue on developing this program. Hopefully we'll be able to use its results in the future."

Dev shifted a little. "Excuse me, sir," she said. "Is it really a good idea to presume success based on so limited an evidence?"

Both Jess and Bain stared at her.

"Do you doubt your abilities, my young friend?" Bain asked.

"Yes," Dev said. "I haven't seen that much of them. I trust the programming they gave me, but you're risking a lot on untested skills."

Jess half turned in her seat so she was facing Dev. "You don't want to stay here?"

Dev met her eyes. "I do," she said. "But I don't want to disappoint you."

Jess felt the lengthening silence as she studied the young, intense face next to her. Finally she took a breath. "I'll take my chances," she said, shifting to look back at Bain, who was watching them both with an expression of bemused interest. "If you do this, you need to do it all the way. Give her full status. Let everyone know. Then they'll stop taking shots at her."

Bain tapped his fingertips together again. "Agent Drake," he said. "I certainly can send any amount of directives, but I think it will take more than that for your new comrade to be accepted." He gave her a meaningful look, one scrubby gray eyebrow hiking up.

Jess looked away, then back at him. "You do your part, I'll do mine."

Bain smiled. "Deal. Now, about that mission?"

Jess settled back in her seat. "We can't do a frontal assault again. They'll be keyed to it. I'll need to insert."

Bain nodded.

"Send me all the intel," Jess finally said. "I'll work up something."

"Splendid." The old man gave her a fond look. "Now, for a more pleasant subject. In recognition of your performance in this morning's rescue I have added a senior level achievement to your records. In fact, you'll now take the number one agent slot. I hope this doesn't cause you any difficulties."

Jess's eyebrows rose. "Only with everyone else's egos."

He chuckled. "And I have advanced a benefit and comfort package to your colleague." Bain pointed a forefinger at Dev. "Since I know she came from the crèche with very little. Enjoy it, my dear."

Dev had no idea what he was talking about, but it sounded good. "Thank you, sir," she said. "I will continue trying to do my best."

Bain leaned forward, resting his elbows on the desk. "Thank you," he said. "We were in a serious crisis point yesterday. I'm glad we made our way through it, but we're not out of the woods yet. Intelligence showed us that in this case, Agent Drake, there was no leak of information regarding your attack."

"Not that I could tell, no," Jess said. "But does that mean we snuffed the leak, or they're just in hiding, biding their time?"

Bain inclined his head.

"The key is—who turned Joshua," Jess said. "Was it someone on the outside or someone on the inside." She looked Bain in the eye. "I don't think Bricker had the brains for it."

Bain smiled faintly. "He was my nephew."

Only years of field service let Jess remain in her chair and not roll onto the floor. She knew her eyes had widened and she clamped her jaw to keep it from dropping.

"My sister's son," Bain said, in a reflective tone. "She gave him over when he was five. I never thought he had the brains for it either, but he made it through the course," he sniffed. "I agree with you. I don't think he was the leak, and he wasn't the one who turned Joshua."

"So that person's still here, if it was an inside job."

"You think it was."

Jess gazed at him. "I spent almost every waking moment with him for nine years on the outside of this facility. No one outside got close to him."

"Hm."

"But inside?" Jess went on. "That was different."

Bain sighed. "I have security doing an investigation on it. Very low key." He turned to Dev. "You'll let us know, won't you my dear, if anyone asks you to do something against us?"

"Yes," Dev answered immediately. "That's wrong."

"Is that what your programming tells you?" He cocked his head slightly.

Dev thought about that for a minute. "They gave me the rules," she said, after a bit. "But this—I think that's an in here thing." She touched her chest. "It feels wrong."

"Hm." Bain nodded in approval. "Very good." He focused back on Jess. "Be on your way, Drake. I'm sure you have things to settle. I'll have intelligence send you an info pack, and will expect your review in the very near term."

Jess nodded and stood. "Thanks. I'll let you know what I think."

Bain chuckled. "Of that I have no doubt."

HE SAT BACK as they left, resting his elbows on the chair arm and twiddled his thumbs. "DJ?"

Kurok came out from behind the big console behind them and came around to sit in the chair Dev had so recently vacated. "Well?"

"Damn fine job," Bain told him straightforwardly. "Now, tell me the truth. This wasn't a last minute rush thing."

Kurok shook his head. "No. I'd been planning to introduce the idea to you, so I'd done the prep with Dev. The last set of tech skills, yes, that was a rush. We had to write that on the fly, but I had the schema outlines already done."

Bain nodded. "I think she'll do well. She has an interesting mix of intelligence and given knowledge."

"She's a good design," Kurok said. "She won't turn, by the way. They'll have to kill her first. The one thing about the way I engineered her logic structure that wasn't entirely logical."

"You understand that at a gut level." Bain smiled faintly at him.

"Yes." He smiled just as faintly back. "I'll miss Dev. I really enjoyed watching her progress."

"I'm sure she'll be fine with Drake." Bain stood up. "She's already taken up a protective stance over your protégé as well as having been sufficiently distracted to allow her to get past that recent disaster."

"She's good people," Kurok said, as he joined Bain and they both disappeared behind the console, through a hidden door and into a quiet hallway. "I think Dev will do very well with her."

"Hm." Bain eyed him. "Sure you don't want a job?"

Kurok smiled a little. "I have a job."

Bain snorted.

"SO I SUPPOSE I really am staying," Dev said, as they walked along the corridor. "That was a very interesting meeting."

"I told you that you were staying." Jess chuckled. "Yeah, it was. We'll have to go back and see what kind of swag we got. I'm glad he put you in for something." She stepped into the lift, and waited for Dev to join her. "Let's start at the top and work our way down."

"I'm not sure what that means," Dev said. "But it sounds nice."

"Here's the roof." Jess led the way out of the lift to a huge open space, with solid glass covering all of it. Overhead the thick, dark clouds were drifting, and once they'd cleared the lift encasement they could see all around them out to the horizon.

Dev turned around in a circle, looking at the vast, open barrenness on one side, and then out across what was now becoming a familiar venue of open ocean.

"When the new class comes in, we'll all gather here for the induction ceremony," Jess said. "With any luck I'll get you started on the right foot with them and we can work from there."

"It's difficult isn't it?" Dev said.

Jess looked at her. "Would it be easier for you if you stayed down with the rest of the bios?"

Dev put her hands behind her back. "Of course it would."

"Do you want to do that?"

"No," Dev replied without hesitation.

Jess smiled. "Good." She waved her hand. "Let's go. I'll show you the gym and the rad facility, that's on the next floor. Then we can go past the reference center and stop in at the exchange."

"For the stuff?"

"Yeah, we'll get some stuff."

THEY HAD, IN fact, gotten stuff. Dev sat cross legged on her bed, surveying the items around her with a sense of bemusement. She had learned a lot of new concepts including what rad was and why it was important to her, what the concept of luxury was, and the answer to the mystery of what to sleep in.

It was a little overwhelming. Dev looked around her living space. Now not only did she have this place but she had another place, sort of like the little cubicle in the crèche, where she could study and do research while she was getting her required dose of sun replacement.

She had more space to herself here than anyone topside, even the most important people. It was amazing and a little strange, and it felt a little uncomfortable to think about having all this when the rest of her kind didn't.

But she had no intention of trading them for it.

Now, this stuff. Dev sorted among the items. The exchange was full of stuff that Jess had called luxuries. Items that were not given to them, but must be earned. This included stuff from topside, she was surprised to see and she'd gotten a package of the little sweet puffs they'd eaten on rare occasions in the crèche.

You could also get things to wear. Jess told her it was easy to see the most successful agents and techs because they didn't wear jumpsuits in off-time. They wore some of the things you could get in the exchange or—this was very interesting—things they bartered for in the living spaces outside.

For now, Dev had gotten a few pairs of soft short leggings and sleeveless shirts to sleep in, as that's what Jess told her she used. She set those aside and the puffs, and pulled over the box she'd found when she'd gotten back.

Jess had told her it was from Bain. The box was full of things like insulated drink containers and a pack, with compartments, she could take on the carrier with her to carry things in. It had straps and hooks that would fasten to the console near her seat.

It was nice. She liked it. There was also a folding tool she could use to get into hatches, that also had a knife in it—she'd seen Jess carry one—and a thing to wear that was thick and heavy and had a hood that was very warm.

A jacket, Jess called it, for when they were outside and had to leave the carrier.

Very interesting.

Next, she removed a sanitary kit she could take in the carrier also. It had wipes and little bottles of something you could put on your skin, and mouth rinse. Jess told her she could order more when she'd used it all.

Also very interesting.

Dev got up and found places for all her new stuff. Once that was done, she picked up her book from her workspace and climbed up into the relaxing area and sat down on the couch.

She had some time before Jess came back and she settled back in the couch, opening the book and reading from where she'd left off.

JESS FINISHED REQUESTING data, then logged off the intel system and sat down at the small desk, using a stylus to make a few notes on the folder she was carrying. She wrote in silence for a few minutes, then glanced up as the door behind her opened.

Shit. She cursed silently. "Hello, Jared."

The tall, spare medical director came over and sat in the seat next to her. "How long did you figure on ignoring the request to med?"

"I've been busy," Jess said, continuing to scribble. "Besides, what would be the point? Bain put me back into service. He ranks you."

"Yeah, and I heard what he does to people who disagree with him." Jared spared a brief smile. "I wouldn't have said no to him either, but you still have a hold on your chart. Want to spend ten minutes with me and get it cleared legit?"

Jess checked the time on the console. "If it's only ten minutes, sure." She finished writing and stood up. "I've got an appointment to get to."

She followed Jared down the hall, out of the gray section into the white, passing suite after suite of examination and operation rooms. Most fortunately now not in use. She'd spent her time in those rooms, and like any other agent hated the place.

Jared led her into a small exam room, the one she knew was right next to his office. She sealed and put the folder down on the desk and lay down on the exam table, feeling the warmth and tickle of the diagnostic systems.

"You look like you're feeling better," Jared commented, from behind the console. "Your back still giving you problems?"

Jess shook her head. "A little tender, that's all. Still a little heat sensitive."

Jared nodded. "Hold still."

Jess felt the scan focus on her head and she closed her eyes.

"How's your sleeping?"

"Okay the last few days." Jess opened her eyes as the scan faded. "Been too busy to think about it."

"That's what I thought." Jared came from around the console and appeared next to her. "I can still see adherence in there. You could have gotten into trouble going out."

Jess lifted a hand and wiggled its fingers. "The only thing I exercised yesterday were these," She said. "I shot the hell out of everything while sitting on my ass."

Jared snorted, then chuckled a little. "I heard. About that, and about your new pilot." He studied Jess's face. "How's that going?"

"She's fine," Jess said. "Pretty good pilot. Not a bad personality."

"For a bio alt, you mean."

"For anyone. She's a nice kid. We're getting along pretty well. Bain's sending orders down to make her permanent."

"I saw. I got them," Jared said. "I want to see her too, to get a baseline. You think that's going to work? Most people I talked to didn't."

Jess half shrugged. "Most people you've talked to haven't worked with her. They think bios are walking jelly bag brains. Dev isn't. She's not one of us, but she's not one of them either."

"Huh. You sure that's not just wishful thinking?"

"Talk to her and form your own opinion," Jess said. "Done now? I've got places to go and people to see."

Jared leaned against the table. "I'm done. You look like you're finally on the right track again, Jess. You had me worried there for a few weeks. Maybe everything going to shit was good for you."

Jess smiled wryly. "Kicked my head out of my ass, you mean. Yeah, maybe. At least I'm not upchucking all night from nightmares."

"No, you aren't." He turned off the scanner. "Your body weight's stopped dropping. I'm going to release you officially so they don't have to keep overriding me from ops," he said, in a droll tone. "Nice to know just exactly how much authority I really have."

Jess sat up and swung her long legs off the table. "Don't feel bad, Jared. Bain steamrolled over pretty much everything, but then—he's the Old Man."

"Yes, he is," Jared said. "A lot of people got the shit scared out of them by him. No one expected—I mean, you hear the stories and all that, but no one thought he'd just come in here and start shooting."

"No." Jess retrieved her folder. "But he did."

"What I'm wondering now is, will he stay here, or is he going to pick someone to replace Bricker?" Jared watched her face closely. "What do you think?"

Jess shrugged. "I'm just an agent. I try to think as little as possible." She turned and headed for the door.

"Senior agent, now."

Jess looked back over her shoulder and grinned, then she went through the door and was gone.

THE DINING HALL was almost empty when Jess and Dev entered it. None of the other agents or techs were there, just a few console operators from the ops center nearby, and alone in the corner, Stephan Bock.

Jess gave him a casual wave as she took a seat at a small table and motioned Dev to do the same. "So here's how this works," she said. "That screen shows you what's available tonight. You tap on what you want, and they deliver it."

"I see." Dev regarded the screen. "Why do they do that, if they make you go pick it up the rest of the time?"

"Tradition," Jess said. "There are some things we do just because that's the way we've always done them. No one wants to change it because it meant something way back when." She keyed something into the pad. "I'll throw a few credits at this."

Dev studied her choices and made her selection, picking things at random from each section because she still had little knowledge of what the items were. Then she folded her hands on the table and regarded her table mate. "Is it something like these?" She touched the insignia at her neck.

"Something like that," Jess said. "You'll see more of the traditional stuff when we attend the incoming ceremony for the new class." She smiled. "I remember when it was me up there. I'd never seen any place like this before."

Dev pondered that. "I guess it's sort of like that when we graduate from basic learning," she said. "We all come into a big room, and they take record of all our designations and where we would be going for advanced classes."

Jess nodded. "Yeah. I had that in school."

"Then they took us all to medical and had our collars installed." Dev touched her throat. "They said we were all grown up then."

Jess leaned her chin on her fist. "They don't do that special programming with you until you're older?" She looked up as a bio alt wait servant approached with a tray. "Thanks."

The man placed the drink she'd ordered on the table, and then, with the barest hesitation, put a second one in front of Dev.

Dev looked up at him. "Thank you."

The man nodded, then he straightened and went back into the preparation area.

Jess snorted and shook her head. "If he does that again, I'm going to rank him," she muttered.

"That's a Ceebee 245," Dev said. "They do that—the serving thing, up in the crèche too, for the natural borns in the fancy places."

"They do?"

"Yes," Dev said. "They don't give us any programming until we graduate basic. They teach us the regular way before that. Reading and writing, and basic skills."

Jess sipped her drink. "I guess that's not too different from how I grew up. I was in pre school until I was five, and they gave us the aptitude battery. Then they sent me to the academy on my sixth birthday."

Dev took a sip from the glass she'd been given, finding a medium fizzy beverage with a taste that reminded her of the soy nuts that had sometimes been served in the crèche. "What is this?"

"Beer," Jess said. "Like it?"

Dev tasted it again. "I think so," she said, after a pause. "So what did they teach you at the academy? Is that where all of the people here went?"

"What did they teach me." Jess mused. "I hardly remember. Like you said, reading and writing I suppose. Some math, geography. History. How we got to be in the situation we're in, that sort of thing." She paused, as the server came back and put down their plates. "Then at...I guess around age ten they start teaching us the business." She lifted her hand and made a circle over her head, encompassing the structure around them.

"So, you knew you wanted to do this?" Dev cut a bit of the fish on her plate and put it in her mouth.

"Wasn't given a choice."

Dev stopped chewing. "Really?"

Jess looked up at her. "Really. Didn't want a choice, that's what the battery is for. My family's been doing this forever, so when I tested high it was a foregone conclusion that I'd go, and I'd graduate, and I'd come to a place like this and do what we do."

"Wow." Dev took another sip of the fizzy beverage. "So all the other people we work with, the ones we went on the mission with, they all did that too?"

"Not exactly. The agents, me, Elaine, Jason, Sandy...we all did. So did Stephan over there, and the guy who got his head taken off. Anyone who wears the black bars like I do. They do the whole course, from childhood. The techs, like Brent, come in around your age. They get schooled on the outside, and if they pass the tests and the background checks and the psych, they get admitted." She forked up some of the fish and ate it. "Damn, that's good."

Dev was also enjoying the taste. "So that's why I heard someone call them outsiders?"

Jess nodded. "They come to what we call field school. During that, they get matched to an agent, and then sent out as a team, usually with a couple others to someplace like this."

None of this was in the programming, Dev realized. Only the rules and regulations of Interforce, and the technical knowledge she'd need to do the job.

"There are always more techs than agents," Jess said, after a short silence. "We get in the way of blasters more often." She gave Dev a wry wink. "But we can choose to leave. I almost did the other day."

"Yes," Dev murmured. "I'm really glad you didn't."

Jess paused in mid chew, as she met the serious, earnest eyes gazing at her. After a moment she hastily swallowed. "Yeah, I'm kinda glad too. It's gotten a lot more interesting here lately."

Her table mate looked a touch puzzled, but then smiled.

They both looked up, a little startled, as they heard a throat being cleared nearby. Stephan Bock was standing by their table, his hands in the pockets of his jumpsuit.

"Stephan." Jess motioned to a seat. "Join us."

"No, just stopping to offer my congratulations," he said. "I saw your ranking change. Well deserved, Jess."

"Thanks." Jess accepted the words with a brief nod.

Stephan turned to Dev. "And congratulations to you too. The system recorded your permanent assignment here. So welcome."

"Thank you," Dev said, politely. "I'm glad I was able to contribute to good results."

"Well, you did a good job, and I hope we can trust you to keep Jess's ass out of the fire again in the future," Stephan said.

Dev looked at him, then glanced at Jess, as one eyebrow hiked up. "They didn't cover that in the programming either," she said. "I'm not really sure what to do with your ass."

Jess hastily swallowed what was in her mouth and clapped her hand over it, snorting and then dissolving into laughter.

Stephan covered his eyes and abruptly sat down.

Dev regarded them with mild amusement until they recovered their composure. "Sorry about that," she said. "I don't really understand some of the things you say sometimes. I have a few I need to look up in the reference library later on."

Jess cleared her throat and wiped a tear from her eye. "What he meant was he expects you to keep me out of trouble."

Dev pondered that, taking a sip of her beer. "Isn't our job to get into trouble?"

Stephan started chuckling again. "You really do have a sense of humor. But I think Jess would have said, your job is to cause trouble." He rubbed his eyes. "Ah well, it's been a day." He let his hands rest on his knees. "Recap tomorrow, Jess?"

"See you in ops," Jess said, giving him a nod as he got up and headed for the door. After the door closed behind him, she looked back at Dev. "You can just ask if you don't understand what the hell I'm saying, y'know."

Dev smiled as she finished up her meal. "I will next time. Sometimes I can guess what it is by the conversation around it, but all the stuff about horses and asses and things confuses me."

Jess chuckled again. "You're so damn funny."

"Is it? I mean, am I?" Dev put her utensils down. "I wasn't trying to be that time." She paused and looked up as the server came back again, putting down a final set of plates. They contained a square of dark brown substance, which she studied as the man removed the other plates. "Thank you."

"Ahhh." Jess pulled over her own plate. "Now that's a rare treat. I didn't think they were doing these until the induction ceremony."

"They were testing them, ma'am," the server replied quietly. "We were instructed to give them to all the patrons here tonight." He turned and disappeared again.

"Hey, wait." Jess called after him. "Bring us over some kack, then. These don't go with beer." She broke off a corner of the substance and popped it into her mouth. "Mm."

Dev tentatively did the same, mouthing the substance as her eyes opened wide. "Oh." She blinked. "Wow. What is that?"

"It's called a brownie." Jess was busy with her own. "I guess because it's brown." She regarded the item. "One of the very few things from the old times they can still make, though I think they make it now with rice flour from the paddy caverns and gulls eggs." She looked up. "Like it?"

"Yes. It's really nice."

Jess looked up, then looked around carefully. "Want to see if we can steal whatever's left back there?"

Dev looked up from her plate. "I thought I was supposed to keep you out of trouble?"

Jess just grinned at her.

Chapter Nine

DEV CURLED UP on her side, pulling the light cover over her and settling her head onto the cool pillow. She could hear various soft noises, of course, doors opening, and the far off sound of the air circulators and machinery.

Closer at hand, though, now she could hear faint sounds next door, beyond the inner panel that separated her room from Jess's. Motion, as though Jess was pacing. The sound of the dispenser opening and closing.

Voices. Dev listened, and thought she caught Jason's low, male tones, then a definite echo that was Jess's laugh.

She liked that sound. Jess didn't laugh often, but when she did it made her face relax and brighten and her eyes sparkle. Dev was glad to see that because she knew she'd caused it herself a few times and Jess seemed to appreciate the humor when she had.

Very good. Dev stretched and exhaled, finding herself very happy.

It felt good to lie there quietly, after the very long, very active day. Her body was tired but there was so much to think about she didn't really want go to sleep right away.

Jess had shown her where the flight log was in the computer, and she decided she would look over it tomorrow to see what she'd done, and what improvements she could make. Then there was the carrier to go inspect, and Jess said she'd take her to the systems workshop and show her where she could build the modules they would use.

And Jess was working on a new mission for them, so maybe she'd find out about that tomorrow too. And there was the gym to explore, and...

Phew. Dev smiled into the darkness. So busy, but that was good.

She felt sleep slowly coming over her despite her best intentions, and though there was more to think about she let her eyes close.

She was just drifting off when the door buzzer chimed, a soft light coming on next to the inner portal as her eyes popped wide open again.

Quickly, she got out of bed and went over to it, putting her palm against the scan plate and blinking a little as it slid open and the brighter light of Jess's quarters flooded in. "Oh, hello."

"Whoops." Jess was holding something in her hand, her body outlined against the light. "My bad. Didn't know you were sacked out."

"Only just," Dev said. "Is there something wrong? Do we need to do something?"

"No." Jess leaned against the doorway. "I won a flask off Jason on a bet on our rescue. Thought I would share a glass with you since we both were part of it."

"Oh!" Dev smiled and took a step back. "That would be very nice."

Jess took that as an invitation and crossed over to the worktable, taking a seat in one of the chairs and setting what she was carrying on the table. She had two small cups in her other hand and put them down as well, the items softly scraping and clunking against the hard surface.

Dev sat in the other chair and waited, watching her. Jess was wearing the same short outfit she was, and the low lights outlined her tall form with an interesting mix of points and shadows. The red mark, from the burning had gained a black bumpy outline and Dev wondered if there would be one for the thing they'd done that day.

Then she figured she could just ask, and she did.

"Hhm." Jess was pouring a measure of the liquid in the big bottle into the cups. "Not usually for a rescue, no," she said. "That gets a different reward." She indicated the thick jacket hanging outside the gray cabinet. "That, or my promotion, that kind of thing. Missions are planned. They're." She pondered. "Attacks, not defenses."

"I see." Dev took the cup when it was handed to her. "What is this?"

"This comes from topside," Jess said. "Matter of fact, it comes from the other side's topside. It's honey mead." She held it up to the light, displaying a rich, golden color. "From their Ag station. They've still got bees there. We lost all ours."

Dev sniffed it. "How interesting," she said. "We learned about bees in the crèche, but I've never seen them. They used artificial pollination in the gardens there."

"Hold that out," Jess said, and then, when she did, touched her own cup to the one in Dev's hand. "To this experiment, however far it goes." Then she brought the cup to her lips and sipped the contents. "Welcome, Dev."

"Thank you." Dev copied her, finding the liquid thick and rich, and sweet, burning very gently as it went down her throat into her belly. It almost made her shiver. "Wow."

Jess cupped her hands around her glass and smiled. "What do you think of it?"

Dev took another sip, pausing to think. "It's very different. It feels like it's staying on my tongue a long time after I drink it."

"Uh huh." Jess studied her, intrigued and a little surprised at the supple power of her new pilots body, now relatively exposed in the light clothing. Her arms and legs were firm with muscle and she had visible definition under her light golden skin.

Jess hadn't expected that, but then, she had to admit she'd never really thought about it too much before either.

Bio Alts in the citadel were just window dressing. Jess had no idea if any of them even had names. She certainly never bothered to look at them with their clothing off.

But this one, now.

This one interested her. She watched Dev cautiously swallow another mouthful, and after a brief pause, lick her lips, an approving expression on her face. "Like it?"

Those clear, pale eyes lifted and met hers. "It has alcohol in it?"

"Yes." Jess chuckled briefly. "Our one remaining vice."

Dev nodded. "In the crèche, too. Doctor Dan gave me some before I left, but it was really different from this," she said. "I like this, and the stuff we had at dinner."

"Yeah, the beer's not bad." Jess leaned against the workspace table. "You get to taste some really weird stuff on the outside. You'll see."

Dev looked up at that, and grinned. "I'm glad. We heard stories about downside from some of the people who came to the crèche, but it sounded so strange we didn't believe most of it."

Jess grinned back. She was getting used to seeing the collar, the faint glowing traces not really seeming out of place around Dev's neck. The metal itself was very thin and flexed a little as Dev moved and she wondered if it was ever uncomfortable.

What would it feel like? She only just stopped herself from reaching out to touch the thing, and supposed Dev didn't pay much attention to it. Guess you could get used to pretty much anything. "Does that bother you?"

Dev looked around, then at her. "What?"

"The collar." Now, Jess surrendered to curiosity and lifted her hand up, touching it with her fingertips. "Does it pinch, or whatever?" She felt the almost smooth surface shift a little, as Dev swallowed.

"No." Dev cleared her throat, glancing aside with a touch of embarrassment in her expression. "Don't think much about it usually."

Jess lowered her hand. "It feels warm."

"Body heat. When I got it put on at first it used to..." She paused. "I felt it, sometimes. But now I don't." She looked up and met Jess's eyes. "When you get programmed, the sensors come down over your head and clip into the slots here." She touched the collar herself. "Then they tell you to go down, and when you come back up, there's a bunch of new knowledge there."

Jess rested her chin on her hand. "Do you know ahead of time what you're getting?"

"Sometimes."

"Did you ever get something you didn't like?"

Dev considered that. "I don't think so."

Jess grunted softly. "I can remember some classes I wish I hadn't been forced to take. You're lucky."

Dev looked thoughtful for a long moment, then she smiled. "Yes, I am." She glanced away and then back again. "Are we going to go outside soon? For this mission thing?"

"Yes. I just haven't planned out when and where yet. But it'll be soon. They want this taken care of before it can take hold." She added. "So get some rest tonight. We might be on the move after they get me the weather and mechanical status tomorrow. Then the timing and sleep gets pretty random."

Dev nodded. "Night and day didn't mean much in the crèche. At end of schedule, you just reported to your sleep pod, and stayed in it until the cycle completed. She looked around the room. "I like it better here. You don't know what might happen."

"You like that?"

"I think it's really interesting," Dev replied. "Everything's new and different."

Jess studied her cup. "I never thought about it like that. Every day is different here, in a way." She exhaled. "So I better let you get some rest and go sack out myself."

"Thank you for the drink. It was very nice of you."

Jess met her eyes and smiled. "Ah." She stood up. "Dangerous for me to drink it all. I end up walking into walls and singing." She took Dev's cup and the bottle. "I'm glad it worked out this morning, Dev."

"Me too." Dev smiled back, letting her elbow rest on the back of the chair she was sitting in. "You know, it's the one thing we bio alts all really want. To find a place we can belong, and to do good work."

Jess raised the bottle, and then she turned and approached the door. It slid open as she neared, and then closed behind her.

Dev sat there for a while, absorbing the sweet taste on her tongue, and replaying Jess's words in her head. She decided she liked Jess a lot, appreciating her straightforward ways and her quirky sense of humor.

And she had been, except for Doctor Dan, the kindest person Dev had met so far anywhere. Almost treating her just like another natural born sometimes. It was nice, and it made her feel really good and with an abrupt suddenness, she realized no matter what difficulties they would face, she wanted to be here, and not go back to the crèche.

It was good to have interesting people around her, even if some of them were rude. It was good to be able to do hard, and difficult things.

Abruptly, the door between her quarters and Jess's opened, making her blink as the tall, dark haired woman leaned into the opening. "Hello," she murmured, half sitting up and peering through the shadows.

"Door's not locked." Jess outlined the obvious. "So just don't scare yourself if you walk by and it opens." She ducked back away and the door closed again, leaving the room once more in quiet peace.

Dev studied the door, quite surprised. She could see the scan pad light was now a calm green instead of the red it had been before, and she wondered what that was supposed to mean. She diligently searched her programming, but there were no references to anything like that in there.

Figures. Dev got up and went behind her workspace, sitting down and pulling her pad over to her, logging in with a thumb press and calling up the rulebook of the citadel, which had provided her with a lot of useful information so far.

After a few minutes reading, she pushed the pad back, unsatisfied. There was nothing in the book about doors, or quarters, or anything like that. Dev rested her chin on her hand and frowned a little. Then she sighed and got up, returning to her bed and snuggling back under the covers.

Maybe it didn't mean anything. Maybe it was just Jess's way of saying she was happy with having Dev on her team.

Maybe she'd just gotten tired of ringing the bell. Dev wouldn't have thought of going into Jess's quarters on her own. Bio alts were always on the locked side of the door, after all. You found that out pretty fast in the créche.

Dev let her eyes close again, this time fading into sleep before she really had a chance to think about anything else.

JESS SET THE bottle down in her cabinet and put the glasses on the tray underneath. She studied it for a moment, and then she turned and wandered over to her bed, dropping down onto it and looking up at the ceiling.

She was tired. It felt good to be tired, in the way that you got when you'd expended energy in doing something worthwhile.

Body tired, instead of mind tired. She stretched and settled herself, squirming around and getting under the covers as the lights dimmed down around her, as her eyes caught the soft glow of the light across the room.

What, she pondered, would her new pilot think about the door? Would she understand why Jess had turned off the security between them? Probably not. She smiled wryly. Hell, she really didn't understand why she'd done it, except that she'd realized she had found a little bit of sympathy in her for Dev, who had been thrown into her world with only the barest of preparation for it.

She'd always been a sucker for the underdog, and Dev had risen to the challenge, with a calm courage that surprised and charmed her, and made her want to do what she could to keep the kid on the right track.

Everyone had thought Dev was going to be at best an embarrassment and at worst, a mortal danger to the people she was here to work with. It made her feel good to know she'd had a part in having Dev prove otherwise.

Jess wanted her to succeed. She smiled into the darkness. She did. And in the silence of her own conscience she could admit that she did, and it had nothing to do with what Bain wanted either. It felt good to have something to focus on that kept her interested.

Dev interested her. She suspected she would go on interesting her. She also suspected they could achieve good things together, and be successful. Jess rolled over onto her side and wrapped her arms around her pillow.

She felt her body relax, and she spent a few minutes going over the day in her mind, before the pictures slowly faded into her dreams and she was out, her breathing slowing and evening, a smile still on her face.

THE ALARM BROUGHT Dev standing up in an instant, her heart thundering as she looked around her in shocked bewilderment. The lights had snapped on in her quarters, and she heard noises outside, but in this very moment she had no idea what to do.

The alarm was a low, unnerving howl, growing to a climax and then falling again, setting her nape hairs on edge as the screen above her workstation lit up showing a grid of the citadel with lots of flashing red points.

Something was wrong. After a second of indecision, she bolted for the door between her and Jess's quarters reaching it just as it popped open, revealing Jess halfway through getting into her jumpsuit. "Oh!"

"Get kitted up," Jess said. "We're under attack."

Dev scooted over to the dressing case and started getting out of her sleep ware, glad of the clear direction. She hesitated, and then grabbed the suit she used in the carrier, jumping into it and sliding the catches closed with one hand as she grabbed her boots with the other.

"Where are they?" Jess's voice bellowed from the next room. "Airborne?"

Dev got her boots on and grabbed her kit, shaking her head to clear it as she headed again for the door that had stayed wide open.

Jess was fastening her sidearm, her head bent toward the comms unit on her workspace. "The dock? The shuttle dock?"

"That's right!" A voice answered. "Stupid bastards are pounding the landing pad, shuttle's in there—was about to leave!"

"What the hell?" Jess grabbed her heavy rifle. "C'mon, Dev," she said. "Stay close to me out of the way. Not sure if we need to launch or not."

Dev was, again, very glad for the clear direction. "I'm ready."

Jess looked at her, then smiled briefly. "Yes, you are. Good choice on the suit." She turned back toward the door. "Central, live fire in the halls—coming down."

"Watch out! We heard fire in the outer ring! They may have penetrated!" The voice came back. "Ops to all details, stand by! Stand by we may have enemy in the complex!"

"Shit." Jess slammed her comm helmet on her head and headed for the door. "Put your hat on, kid. You see anyone pointing anything at you dive for the floor."

"Yes." Dev put on her own unit, clicking into the comm stream and hearing an eruption of voices as she settled the earpiece in. She got right behind Jess and stuck with her as they went out the door in the front of Jess's quarters.

Lights were flashing a deep, warning red. The entryway to central ops was likewise lit up. Down the curved hall there came the sound of heavy, running footsteps.

"Go in that entryway, put your back to it." Jess stepped out into the hallway and blocked the way into ops, swinging her heavy rifle up and into position as a group of dark clad bodies came barreling around the curve at her.

Dev did as she was told, hitting the wall with her back just as she heard Jess release the safety mechanism on the big weapon she was holding.

Jess let out a powerful bellow. "Halt!"

"Whoa whoa!" The man in the lead put the brakes on and held a hand up. "Security! Hey! We're friendly!"

Dev quickly poked her head out from behind the steel entranceway and saw six men in heavy armor ramble to a halt and duck for cover, despite the fact they were far more heavily armed and outnumbered the lone agent holding the hall against them.

She saw their widened eyes and had to wonder.

Jess kept them hopping for a second, then she shifted the muzzle of the heavy gun. "What's the scoop? Nothing's down here. You guarding ops?"

"Affirm," the man in front said.

"Right." Jess surged into motion. "C'mon, Dev."

Dev followed her down the hall and past the security guards, as they rapidly came past them and took up station at the entrance to the command center. "They were scared of you," she commented to Jess, as they sped through the central hall.

"Sure." Jess was turning her head from side to side, her hands shifting on the gun. "I'm an ops agent. We're nuts and they know it."

"I see."

Jess heard the sound of live fire percussion up ahead and she slowed a little, hugging the wall. "Actually, what they really know is that if I think they've turned, or are working against the best interests of the organization in my estimation I'll blow them apart."

"Oh."

"They have to wait for permission to blow me apart."

"Oh." Dev's vocal inflection changed completely.

"Stay behind me." Jess flattened herself against the wall. She could hear the explosions and she sidled forward and reached the curve, ducking down and snaking her head around the edge to see what lay past it.

The hall, surprisingly, was clear, but she saw flashes past the next set of doors. "Okay, c'mon." She straightened and moved along the hall, coming around the bend and seeing Jason and Brent crouching just out of the line of sight. "Hey."

"Hey." Jason glanced past her, then back down the hall as Jess and Dev joined them. "Fucking mess. I swear this place is going to shit."

"What's up?" Jess touched her ear. "Don't hear crap on comm," she said. "Anyone know what the deal is?"

"Shuttle landed. Next thing we knew we had inbound, and a big bang on the dock," Jason said, in clipped tones. "Heard blaster fire in the out-hall. They blew the cams so no one can see what the hell's going on."

"Let's go. Next door." Jess pointed, then she led the way forward, with Jason right at her side.

Brent and Dev followed along. Dev noticed Brent was also carrying his pilots' gear and he, like her, didn't have a weapon. She hadn't seen any of the techs carry a gun, and she figured that was why she had no programming at all about them.

She knew what they were, of course. She'd seen pictures of them. But she'd never encountered anyone with them in the crèche. Even the security proctors who were in charge of keeping order didn't carry anything more than a shock stick.

The sounds of the explosions got abruptly louder, and then they heard yells.

Jess started running and they came around the corner in time to see the outer doors explode inward, with a percussive shock that nearly knocked them off their feet. "Breach! Breach!" Jess yelled into her comm. "Seal the ring! They blew the outer door!"

Dev heard a deep rumbling sound that rattled her bones and as she glanced behind her she saw huge portals sliding shut, blocking off any escape back down the corridor. As they closed she felt the air compress around her, and then they were in two sets of curved hallway blocked off from anything other than whatever was making so much noise up ahead.

"Down!" Jason bellowed, and they all fell flat on their stomachs as fire came down the hall, slamming into the wall behind where they'd just been standing.

Jason and Jess started firing back, spraying the opening with heavy blasts as they spotted friendly fire from inside the alcove shooting back at the blasted outer door. "We have enemy action on the dock." Jess called into the comm. "We're moving in. Stand by to vent on my mark."

"Standing by. Shuttle crew sealed their flight deck, ops," the comm came back. "They took some heavy damage."

"Roger that." Jess started forward across the ground, firing as she moved. Jason angled after her getting a slightly different line of fire and crossing hers as they covered the opening and prevented anything from emerging from it. "Too bad. They could just lift and end our problem."

Dev clipped her gear to her suit and copied Jess's motions. She tried to keep behind them as best she could, without bumping into the stolidly crawling Brent.

She felt a little helpless, and looking at her fellow tech she thought maybe he did too, since he looked like he was in a very bad mood and he flinched every time the weapons made a loud noise.

He glanced at her. "Don't like being a target," he muttered. "Sucks."

Dev nodded in sympathetic agreement. "It would be better to be flying."

For a moment, Brent stared blankly at her, then faintly, his lips twisted into a reluctant smile. "Yeah."

"Movement!" Jess aimed down a line, and blasted a red flare toward the smoking entrance. "Watch it!"

Jason rolled to one side and took his own aim, hopping sideways at the very last moment as a blue blast scored the ground where he'd just been lying. "Same you!" Jason saw a round blob travel inside and caught it with his blaster, sending a wave of energy through the hall along with a booming roar. "Trigger bomb! Watch your eyes!"

Then all at once a lot of things happened. The opening they were moving toward filled with big, blocky figures and Jess and Jason hauled up onto their knees, blasting away as fast they could as the intruders blasted back at them.

Fire landed all around them and Dev rolled over and hugged the wall, ducking her head as a bolt hit the surface just over her so close she felt the heat against her shoulder blades.

"Duck!" Jess yelled, as she removed something from her belt and threw it, then went flat to the ground and covered her head.

A guttural yell was heard, then a moment later a deep, violet flash flooded the hall, followed by a ripping sound and a huge, ear rending thump.

"Clear!" Jason yelled a half second later, and the two agents scrambled to their feet and bolted forward, with their techs a couple steps behind them. The opening was now empty, and the steel stained a deep, smoky black. They ran through a field of energy that made them all twitch.

It was almost painful. Dev almost cried out. But it faded as they jumped over the still bodies on the ground and were in the outer entry.

It was almost unrecognizable. The door to the shuttle bay had been blown apart, and the console Dev had first seen as she entered was nothing but shards. As they crossed the threshold there was movement to their left and Jess turned and aimed in a motion so fast and smooth it seemed there was no thought at all involved.

Her eyes tracked and targeted the motion and just as quickly, she turned her weapon aside and then turned 360, checking for other intruders as she trusted her senses in marking the threat as a friendly.

The motion continued though, and through the haze and smoke a figure appeared with a blaster in hand and joined them. "Thanks for not blasting me, Drake. Would have been a pity after all that."

"Doctor Dan," Dev blurted, in deep surprise.

"Yes." Kurok tipped the blaster muzzle up and let it rest against his collarbone. "Haven't had to do that in a good long while." He observed the destruction, and the scattered bodies on the outside, as well as the pile of silent figures on the inside. "Nice grenade hit."

"Thanks." Jess regarded him in bemusement. "Was that you laying down fire from the back there?"

"Mmhm." Kurok produced a brief smile. "Certainly got the old blood pumping, I'll admit."

"What the hell happened?" Jason asked, as both he and Brent edged out into the pad, and swept the area. Overhead, the sound of a carrier engine was heard, and they looked up to see four of the big vehicles hovering. "Are we clear?"

"Affirm, ground ops," the comm crackled. "We're clear air side. BR76004, BR76003, remain in formation until released. BR75003, BR74034, return to base."

"BR74034, clear."

"BR75003, clear."

Two of the carriers split off and disappeared, while the remaining started a slow circling patrol over the shuttle bay.

"We're clear ground side," Jess reported. "Six down need a cleanup. Drake eleven on com."

"Affirm, will send. Thanks, Drake."

Brent was kneeling beside one of the intruders and he kicked them over with his boot. "Stormers." He glanced up. "They get dropped? Where's the log?"

Dev slowly looked around at the destruction, and then at Doctor Dan, who was standing easily with the gun resting against his shoulder, as natural with it as Jess had been. He turned and looked back at her, his gentle smile appearing.

"You all right, Dev?" he asked. "Terrible way to wake up, isn't it?"

"Different," Dev said. "I took no harm. Did you?"

Kurok shook his head. "Despite me being far too old to be messing with these things, I managed not to crack anything besides a smile this time."

Jess came back in from the pad, shaking her head. "What the hell was that all about?" She said. "This is the most heavily defended part of the citadel and they know it. What were they after?"

Kurok cleared his throat. "Me, probably...I was scheduled to board the shuttle to leave." He peered outside. "I heard the engines overhead and got back inside just as they came down right on top of the pad."

Jess stared at him. "You?"

"Mm." Kurok thumbed the safety back on the gun in his hand. "Apparently I've made a breakthrough they don't want continued," he said. "Somewhat the same as the vegetation advance you will likely be trying to circumvent on that side, Agent Drake."

"Breakthrough." Jess turned and looked at Dev, then back at Kurok, her eyebrows lifting.

Kurok shrugged modestly. "I was listed on the passenger manifest." He indicated the grounded shuttle. "I should be flattered. They sent a six man team in. I suppose they were supposed to get me between when I left the citadel door and before I cleared the hatch."

"And then what?"'

"Well, either kill me or take me," Kurok said, dryly. "They had their own bio alt program, you know. Never got very far though. They just have some very basic models." He smiled again. "The one thing I suspect they didn't expect is that I'd know who they were and start shooting at them."

"Wouldn't it be easier to wait for you to leave here?" Jason asked.

"Interforce is the last stop on this shuttle run. It goes right up to the station after that. They could try to blow the shuttle out of the sky, but it would go up and into space before they probably caught her," Kurok said. "But it sure was audacious."

"That's damn sure." Jess ran a hand through her hair, and grimaced a trifle. "Well, glad they got skunked anyway."

The room was starting to fill with people. Dev kept to one side, as technicians poured in and Stephan Bock arrived at a run, pulling up to a halt next to their little group. "Came in at sea level," he said. "They were up and over the ridge before the systems caught them." He looked at the bay. "They dropped a team and went topside. Too fast, and too high for us to follow."

"Huh." Jess grunted. "Told you they'd get an advantage going half space with those damn things. We can't chase them."

"Wasn't my decision," Stephan said, shortly. "Everyone clear?"

Jason looked around. "Looks like."

It was then that Bock noticed Kurok standing there. "Mr. Bain was asking for you."

"I bet he was." Kurok handed over his blaster to one of the security men, who took it gingerly. "Well, it appears I'm stuck here for a while longer." He patted Dev on the shoulder. "Let me go see what the Old Man wants."

He turned and left the outer lock, passing through the inner corridors and disappearing as the rest of them watched him go.

"You said he was a scientist?" Jason asked, quizzically.

"He is a scientist," Dev said. "He programmed me," she added, after a brief pause.

Jess's brows twitched. "That might explain a few things."

Jason looked at her. "What?"

"Never mind." Jess exhaled. "Well, they got us good, that's for sure. Never had the guts to go for our bay before."

"You pissed them off."

A cleanup team was removing the enemy bodies, zipping them into bags and latching the bags to the weight carrier they'd brought with them. Technicians were moving aside the destroyed console, and someone else was erecting a set of temporary lights in the corner.

A squad of security showed up, with a portable blast barrier they started to set up to close the gaping hole in the wall

Stephan shook his head. "That was ballsy." He regarded the outer door. "We'll need to keep the inside seal on until they get that rebuilt." He glanced at Jess. "You think it's their way of sending a message back for what you did?"

Jess shrugged. "Stupid if it was. Besides, you heard Kurok. He thinks they were after him. And I wouldn't say he's wrong. C'mon, Dev. Let's go get breakfast now that all the fun's over."

"That was fun?" Dev straightened out her jumpsuit, twisted askew from her crawling on the floor. "I think I liked being chased by all those planes better."

Brent snorted. "Score."

"Yeah, well, let's get chow before the Old Man blows up." Jason joined them "Not gonna be a happy day."

DEV ENTERED HER rad station, her book tucked under her arm as she paused to review the space in front of her.

She liked it. The room was low ceilinged, and cozy, with translucent couches and chairs.

She put her book down on the table and went to the small closet in the wall. She removed her boots and jumpsuit, and put them inside, feeling the faint movement of air against her bare skin as she went to the control panel.

She put her palm on it. After a second, it chimed. "Name." A soft voice asked.

Dev studied it for a minute. "Dev."

"NM-Dev-1?"

"Yes."

"This system will code your presence recording you as—Dev," the voice said. "Stand by for scan please."

Dev waited, and felt the tickle over her skin as the system reviewed her body. "This is my first experience," she said, after a pause.

"Acknowledged," the voice answered. "This session will consist of one standard hour. Advise this system if you experience any difficulty, or if discomfort results."

"Yes," Dev said. "Thank you."

Talking to machines was often easier than talking to people. Dev felt the light change, and she felt faint warmth on her skin as the rad came on and bathed her. There was something in the quality of it that made her smile and she walked into the space with the chairs and picked her book up, sitting down on one of the couches and leaning back.

Jess was working on the mission plan, and she suggested that Dev get her rad in and that she'd come get her when she was ready to go over what they were going to do. That seemed like a good idea to her, and now she was content to relax in the light, enjoying the warmth and the soft sound of the machinery around her.

In the crèche, there never was an issue about getting sunlight. It came and went constantly, and you could always count on catching some in the dining hall, or the gym, or just in the halls while you were waiting for a class.

And, of course, in the sleep pods as they rotated up along the rim of the crèche they were exposed to the sun as the covers turned translucent and so, she'd never had to think about it before.

Here, she did. Dev stretched her legs out on the couch. She wondered what people outside the citadel did, and made a mental note to ask Jess about it later.

She set her book down and folded her hands over her bare stomach, thinking about the attack they'd suffered that morning. It had been scary. She had felt a little like she and Brent were more of a hindrance than a help and it bothered her a lot that there hadn't been anything she could do to assist Jess at all.

If they'd been ordered to launch, there would have been good work for her. But all she and Brent could do was stay on the ground and hope they didn't get blasted.

Brent had even talked to her about it. Commiserated with her. Dev felt good about that, since it was the first time he'd even spoken to her outside ship comm. That was nice. She didn't want the others to feel bad all the time around her. Dev studied the calm, dim room. She would finish her rad, and then go do some work in the gym. Maybe by then, Jess would have her plan all worked out.

Chapter Ten

JESS SLOWLY SAT down at her desk, grimacing a little as her back protested. The spot where she'd been stabbed had slammed against a door handle in all the tumult and she'd felt a sharp spear of pain that, at the time, she'd ignored.

Now, it was throbbing, and the jolts of pain were going up her spine and through her neck and giving her a banging headache.

She should go to med. Jess glowered at the screen in front of her, and rested her forearms on the desk, debating the issue with herself in silence.

If she went to med, she'd be stuck there. They'd ground her again. Jess studied her twined fingers. Before she hadn't really cared that much. After Joshua she'd been more than glad not to be under any pressure to take a new partner on, or go out in the field.

She'd spent her time either curled up in bed convalescing, or out on the ledge, just watching the sea. It had been a long time—hell, it had been since her entrance into field school, since she'd taken a break and just let life run past her for a while.

Now? Jess exhaled slowly. Now, after Bain showed up, and she'd gotten promoted, going off line wasn't really her first option. Bain wanted her to take care of this problem. She had a feeling if she did, there might be more in it for her than he was letting on.

Now things were exciting and good things were happening. Bricker was gone and she saw an opportunity to really get herself ahead.

And then there was Dev. Jess pondered her new pilot. Dev the surprisingly skilled. Dev the surprisingly courageous. If she went off line, Bain would surely put her in team with someone else, so as not to lose those significant skills. And then what?

Would any of the other agents treat Dev the way she did? No one really liked the idea of Dev, especially now that she'd proven herself more than useful. They'd probably find a way to get her into an 'incident'.

She didn't want anything bad to happen to Dev. Jess relaxed a little and felt the pain ease. She wanted to keep on working with Dev and have her be part of the success she could feel out there ahead of them, just outside her reach.

So going to med was out. Jess very slowly sat back. Then she got to her feet and went over to the big cabinet, opening it up and fishing inside her gear pack for one of the packets of analgesic she'd stored in there. She got one out and opened it, swallowing the tabs down with a quick, dry gulp.

"Now what?" She mused. The idea of sitting at her desk made her grimace, so she went over and picked up the info pad, carrying it with her as she slowly climbed the steps up into her relaxation area and adjusted the flexible couch, stretching out on it on her stomach and setting the pad on the shelf at the head of it so she could see the screen.

It wasn't entirely comfortable, but it wasn't entirely uncomfortable and she'd gotten used to the position as her back had started to heal once they'd let her out of the hospital. She settled herself and keyed the pad controls, calling up the mission plan she'd started to work on.

It would be a tough run. She studied the layout of the laboratory. There would be no getting in there any easy way, especially after their attack yesterday. She could see the bounce backs showing multiple layers of scan and figured the lab and all the outer defenses would be on a very heightened alert.

So.

Jess studied the intel report on the lab. Approach from the air wouldn't work. She zoomed in on the facility, realizing after a minute that the latest sim scans were based on digital input that probably came from her carrier.

From their carrier. She watched the replay, remembering that long dive and the feel of heavy Gs on her as Dev made the old bus stand up and really shake its booty.

Jess smiled and then went back to studying the screen.

The lab was buried into granite promontory. The defenses were hardened, and she watched the scan as a transport arrived, going through several layers of security before it was allowed to dock on an isolated landing pad, the muzzles of heavy blasters visible surrounding it.

She watched as guards came out and inspected the transport's manifest Then the pilot was remanded back inside, and a troop of unfriendlies came out to offload whatever the contents or people were.

No easy way in that route.

Jess studied the promontory. If the facility was anything like the one she was in, there were infrastructure components she might be able to take advantage of. She knew they had to generate power and feed themselves not too differently than Interforce did. The granite cliffs likely held caverns full of phosphorescent organisms, the ultraviolet lit growing platforms, the captive fisheries and the rakers of seaweed. Or else some form of equivalent technology to let them feed themselves and create the power needed to run the scientific technology.

She tapped a request into the pad and waited for a response, her body slowly relaxing as the pain medication took effect. As she tapped on the edge of the shelf her mind drifted. She found herself wondering what Dev was up to.

That puzzled her. Why would she care? Why should she care? Jess frowned, but nevertheless, she keyed over to the locater and tapped in Dev's name. After a brief pause, the locater came back with a coordinate, and she grunted, satisfied Dev had taken her advice and gone to rad.

Hm.

The thought of the warm glow suddenly sidetracked her, and after a pause, she got up off the couch and took the pad with her, easing down the steps and crossing over to where she'd left her indoor boots.

Putting them on, she went to the door and through it, heading for the rad area through sparsely populated halls. Why not get a dose of rad herself? It had been several days, after all, and she could just as well go over the plans flat on her stomach in her dose room where at least she'd get something useful out of her time while she waited for the intel to come back.

The drugs made the pain bearable. It remained as a dull throbbing, but at a level where she could put it aside, and it didn't affect her moving and walking. Even her headache had faded a little and she sighed in relief as she passed through the central corridor and turned right down into rec.

A good portion of the citadel was at the attack site, either cleaning up, or taking readings, making reports, developing plans to prevent it from happening again. There was no one there to see her arrive at her door, putting her palm on the lock and passing inside.

Once the door shut, she paused and stood there thinking.

Time was of the essence. Why not get even more done at the same time? She walked over to the com and typed in a code. After she heard a faint buzz, she leaned closer. "Dev?"

There was a brief pause, and then the buzz stopped. "Yes?" Dev's voice came back. "I'm here in the sun space, as you suggested."

Jess nodded to herself. "I'm in mine," she said. "Mind if I join you? I want to go over the plan."

There was another brief pause. "I don't mind," Dev said. "That would be nice. It's sort of making me want to go to sleep in here."

"Yeah. It does that," Jess said. "Be there in a sec." She released the comm and turned, leaving her space and walking the short distance down the corridor to the one assigned to Dev. She put her palm on the lock and the door opened, letting her inside.

She paused in the antechamber, setting her pad down and glanced into the main section. Dev was relaxing on one of the couches and for a moment Jess felt a little lightheaded and short of breath. "Damn drugs," she muttered. "How do you like this?" She added, in a louder voice.

"It feels nice, though it's different than being in the real sun."

"Is it?" Jess stripped out of her jumpsuit and inhaled sharply, as an injudicious motion sent a bolt of pain through her shoulder. She waited for the pain to ease, and then she folded the suit up and put it on a shelf, and added her boots to it. "What's the sun like?"

"Well." Dev turned her head as Jess entered and their eyes met. "It's...um...a lot brighter for one thing," she said, after a pause to clear her throat. "When it comes into the crèche, all the regular lights go off, and it's just...it's different."

"Mm." Jess eased slowly down on the chair next to the lounge Dev was on. "I remember reading that it was yellow."

Dev shook her head briefly. "In space, it's white. It feels good." She looked up at the ceiling. "This feels good too, but not the same way." She looked back over at Jess. "It's too dark to read from." She held up her book.

"What is that?"

"It's a book," Dev said, with a touch of hesitation. "You have them here, right?"

"We have them, but they're on plas." Jess peered at it. "Can I see it?"

Dev passed it over to her. "One of my teachers gave it to me."

Jess put her pad down and touched the book, opening it and running her fingertips over it. The pages were thin and an odd scent came off them as she peered at the writing. It was, as Dev had said, too dim to really read it, but she could make sense of the words if she concentrated on them.

Dev sat quietly, watching her. Jess's head was bent over the book as it was cradled in her hands, one elbow leaning on the chair arm with her legs tucked up half under her.

The brown sigils were very visible on her arms, but now that Dev could see all of her, she saw scars scattered over her skin and thought about how much all of that must have hurt.

There was one long scar from her right knee to her ankle on the inside of her leg that made Dev grimace just to see it.

"I've read it a hundred times," Dev said, into the silence that had built around them. "I find something new every time."

Jess looked up from the book and smiled. "I haven't read one of these since I was very small." She handed the book back. "And I've never read this one." She glanced at the cover. "Lord of the Rings."

"Would you like to borrow it?" Dev asked. "It's really a good story."

"Later," Jess said. "I'd love to." She shifted and reached for the pad, halting in mid motion and closing her eyes, then opening them and exhaling. "Don't think I'm going to get a chance to read it in the next couple days." She lifted the pad and triggered it. "Here's the deal."

Dev put the book down and leaned on the arm of the lounge she was on, studying the pad. After a moment though, she looked up at Jess's face, surprised to see some tension there. One hand was holding her head up, as the other tapped the pad, and there was an awkwardness about her posture.

"So, this is what we're gonna do, if the intel comes back," Jess said. "This is the edge of the Greenland islands. That's where the fishing fleets work out of."

"I see."

"Tough place, but..." Jess tapped the screen. "I've got some remote family here, and we can cross over into enemy territory in this little group where they all trade together."

"How does that assist us?"

"These boats, they trade with the bad guys." Jess drew a line on the screen. "I'm going to get taken on board as a mate, and get into the lab when they go to trade fish to them."

Dev considered that. "I see."

"What I'll need you to do is hide out there and keep comm open, then come get my ass out of there after I finish the job. Got it?"

"What are you going to do?"

"Depends," Jess said. "If I can steal the tech, I will. If not, I'll destroy it." She studied the pad and then looked up at Dev. "I'd rather steal it. Then we get the benefit."

"This sounds difficult," Dev said. "What if they find out who you are? Will they be angry?" She watched Jess shift a little, setting the pad down and leaning back in the chair, as the warm, purple light bathed her.

"Chances are they'll find out, and sure, they'll be angry," Jess said. "That's part of the game." She studied Dev. Dev was stretched out on the couch, but there was a furrow in her brow and she looked a little perturbed. "But the goal is to get this job done. It's important to us, because if they take this technology forward, they could start reclaiming land and that means these skirmishes we do might turn into something a lot bloodier."

Dev's head cocked to one side a bit.

"There aren't enough of us left to have a war, Dev," Jess said, after a long silence between them. "But livable land means more people and more resources. Then they'll have enough bodies to have a war and we won't."

"This is going to sound kind of foolish, or maybe ignorant," Dev said, slowly. "But wouldn't it be more productive to cooperate and assist everyone in making progress?"

Jess smiled faintly. "Yes, it would. But that's not how we're wired, Dev. "

Dev considered the statement. "I will do my best to assist in the plan. I hope you will achieve your goals safely."

Jess sighed. "Yeah, me too." She leaned forward and rested her elbows on her knees. "We'll have to do some trading in the islands and I'll need to put together a cover," she said. "And make sure we can cover up that necklace of yours. That won't work out there."

"Are there bio alts on the outside?" Dev asked.

Jess shook her head. "In the citadels, and in the admin centers, yes. But not in the outlands. They don't even know what a bio alt is. I said cover it so they don't cut your head off and try to steal it."

Dev's pale eyes widened.

Jess chuckled wryly. "Don't worry. They can't break into a carrier. Yet." She leaned back again, the pain having subsided into a mere dull throb again. "I think this is going to work, Dev. We've never hit them this way before, and I've got a lot of chances to back out if it looks like it's going to crash and burn."

"Have you ever done that?"

Jess looked over to find those interesting green eyes watching her, the faintest of smiles on Dev's face. "Done what, back out?"

"Yes."

Jess grinned, rakishly. "No."

"I didn't think so." Dev grinned back. "I'll do my best to take care of your ass, then."

They both chuckled, and their eyes met. After a moment, Jess looked down at her pad and smiled. "I definitely feel safer now." She lifted her hand and rubbed her face. "Rad makes you warm, huh?"

Dev considered that. "Yes, it does, now that you mention it."

Jess looked up again and they studied each other briefly. "Ah, yeah. Okay, so uh..." Jess eased back into her couch. "What was that you said about the book?"

DEV ENTERED THE gym feeling happy. The big facility was nearly empty, and she went over to the changing area, finding the cabinet with her name on it and changing into the short jumper and shoes she found inside.

She wasn't really sure why she was happy, but the rad session had been enjoyable, and she'd appreciated the fact that Jess had stopped to let her see the plan and talk to her about it. It was very different than the rescue, and it had a lot of sneaky bits to it she found really interesting.

Jess had a clever mind. She reminded Dev a little of some of her favorite teachers in the crèche, who always pushed her to look at things from different angles.

Jess seemed to like angles, too, and when she was being extra clever, she tended to smile a lot.

She liked that smile. Dev closed the cabinet and entered the exercise area. The gym was multileveled, and had different sections intended for different purposes, including a climbing obstacle course, a running space, a load bearing area and, to her surprise, since she hadn't seen it when Jess showed her the gym, a huge tank of water.

As she watched, a tall man she didn't know jumped into it, disappearing and then surfacing and starting to move along the top of the water using his arms and legs. "Wow," Dev muttered to herself. "What's that all about?"

"Huh?"

Dev turned to find Brent there, his body covered in sweat and a towel wrapped around his neck. "I've never seen anything like that before." She pointed at the tank.

Brent looked. "Oh. The pool," he said. "Yeah, it's all right. If you like that sorta thing." He regarded the man in the tank. "I'm not much for swimming. I sink like a rock." He glanced at her. "You?"

Dev shook her head. "I've never done anything like that. Water was very precious in the crèche."

"You should ask Jess to teach you. She's a fish. She and some of the others go down into the tunnels and swim in the ocean down there. Crazy nuts."

"I might ask," she said. "I like the shower thing in our quarters. Jess mentioned something about the water in the bottom of the citadel. She took me out to see the ocean and I can't really imagine going into that. It looked dangerous."

Brent snorted. "It is dangerous, but what the hell difference does that make to us?" He said. "Everything we do is dangerous. Hell, Jess threw an antipersonnel mine in the damn hallway this morning. If it'd been keyed wrong, we'd all be dead."

"The purple thing?"

Brent nodded. "Keyed to our scan. But they get it wrong sometimes. That's why it killed those goons. They aren't us."

Us. Dev thought about that word. "Yes," she said. "I'm glad it worked out."

Brent continued on his way to the changing room, and Dev turned and headed into the gym. She was drawn toward the tank, though, and walked over to it, kneeling at the side and putting her hand into the water. The man who had been in it was gone, and now the surface was still, and quiet.

It was pleasant. Neither warm nor cold. She tried to imagine being completely immersed in it.

She couldn't, but she really wanted to, so without any further thought she jumped into the water tank headfirst.

It was, without doubt, the weirdest feeling she'd ever had, as the water closed over her and she was caught in a swirl of it, pushing and bubbling around her as she popped to the surface. Her head broke out of the liquid as she instinctively took a breath.

So weird. So strange. Dev moved her arms as she started sinking, pushing against the water to keep her head up in the air. She could feel the resistance against her motion and cupped her hands, moving her legs as well.

Experimentally, she stopped moving. Sure enough, she immediately sank under the surface, glad she'd taken a breath before her head went under. She opened her eyes, and felt the water sting against them, but also found to her delight that she could see after a fashion.

Then her chest started hurting, so she pushed with her hands again and got back to the surface of the water, spluttering a little and shaking her head as she blinked the water out of her eyes.

"Hey!" Brent rushed over. "Are you nuts?" He went to his knees at the edge of the water tank and held his hand out. "Here! Grab on!"

"I'm all right." Dev waved her hands around to keep afloat. "I just wanted to see what this was like." She pushed the water away from her and moved over to where Brent was kneeling. "It's nice."

"You are crazy," Brent said. "They picked the right one of you to match with Jess. She's crazy too." He sat down on the concrete floor as Dev got close enough to grab the edge of the tank. "You coulda hit your head and drowned."

Dev put both hands on the edge of the tank, holding herself still as her body drifted in the water. It reminded her a little of being in null grav, but it felt completely different and of course it was a lot wetter. "Well, you said it didn't really matter, didn't you?" She said. "That we all do dangerous things all the time?" She looked up at him and grinned.

With a shake of his head, Brent stood up. "Well, be careful. Last thing we need is for one of us to go and get hurt. There aren't many of us left." He studied her for a moment more, and then retreated back toward the dressing room, his head still shaking gently as he walked.

Us. It seemed that Brent, at least, had decided to accept her presence and that felt very nice. She was glad. She released the edge of the tank and moved her hands around again, leaning forward and stroking forward in a somewhat awkward motion.

It did move her, though, and she kept at it for a few minutes, until she became a little more accustomed to it, edging forward not exactly gracefully but at least with some good effect.

The water itself felt wonderful. It smelled like the shower did, rich and wet and interesting. With a good deal of effort, she finally reached the far end of the tank, and discovered it wasn't as deep there and she could actually stand with her feet on the bottom and have her head stick up from the surface.

That was even better. She could fully appreciate the nice way the pressure of the water moved against her without having to worry about inadvertently breathing in the liquid. She knew the man who she'd seen in the tank was doing something different. She decided to look up this whole swimming thing when she got back to her quarters to see if the systems had any information on it.

She bobbed there for a minute or so more, then found the steps that led out of the tank. She felt an immediate chill as the air hit her. She heard footsteps approaching and turned to see Sandy and her partner approaching. "Hello."

Sandy ignored her and just walked past. Nappy gave her a brief nod, lifting one hand in a faint wave as he followed her.

Dev regarded them in mild curiosity.

"Don't pay any attention to her."

Dev turned to find Jason standing there. "Oh, hello," she said. "I wasn't really."

The tall, muscular agent had just finished his exercise, and he, like Brent, was covered in sweat. "Jess around?"

Dev shook her head.

Jason studied her. "What the hell happened to you?"

"I jumped in the tank. I liked it." She ran her fingers through her wet hair. "I think I should probably go put on a dry shirt though and continue my work." She walked around him and headed for the dressing space.

"Hey." Jason jogged after her and caught up. "So what kind of gym work do you do up in space?"

"Well." Dev took a towel from a shelf as they passed and dried her face off. "It's not like this. You do running, walking, jumping, picking things up, things like that, but they adjust the grav so it's harder."

Jason frowned. "What do you mean?"

They were passing the sets of pull up bars and hanging swings and Dev paused, then she went over to the bars and glanced up at them, drying her hands and putting the towel down. "Like this." She jumped a little, and caught the bar, adjusting her hold and then pausing a moment before she pulled herself up so that her chin was even with the bar.

Jason folded his arms and watched her. "Okay, so we do that too."

"Then we do this." Dev hoisted herself, pressing her body up over the bar, and then carefully lifting herself up into a handstand. She held the position briefly, and then let her body fall, swinging under the bar and then releasing it as she came up again, turning in mid air and catching it again and pressing herself back up into a handstand.

"Ah," Jason muttered.

Dev lowered herself until her shoulders touched the bar, then pushed herself back up. Then she fell forward again, releasing the bar and landing neatly with both feet planted. "But they change the grav, so sometimes you're normal, like now, and sometimes you go up to two, three, or when they want to really work you very hard, to four Gs."

Jason stared at her. "Are you kidding me? They work you under four Gs? "

"Not that much, it's too hard," Dev said. "And not what I just did. You can get really hurt. But just walking around, and sometimes carrying things."

"Holy shit."

Dev wasn't sure what to make of that reaction. "Mostly it's two G," she said. "It makes gym shorter too. I'm going to have to work harder here to match what I did in the crèche." She made a little face. "The last gym I did before I came here was the hardest. They had me do a whole round in three Gs and I was really tired when I was finished."

"Holy shit."

Dev managed a brief grin. "Excuse me." She turned and headed into the changing area, going over to her little cubicle and stripping quickly out of the wet exercise suit so she could exchange it for a dry one. She toweled off and changed, then she headed back out into the gym to find some good work to do.

JESS STUDIED THE met data, bracing one arm against the console as she overlaid her situational map over it. Two tightly lined whorls intersected their flight plan and she grimaced, moving the met prediction ahead until they cleared. "Shit."

"What's that, Drake?" The meteorological officer glanced at her.

"Fucking storms biting my ass again." Jess sighed. "Are they getting worse or is it just my natural pessimism rearing its head?"

The met officer came around the desk and studied her plotting. "Has been bad up there this year," he said. "I was just talking to Mort earlier over lunch and he said the same thing you just did. Storms are getting worse and more often."

"Mm." Jess coded the data to her pad and straightened up cautiously. "Well, puts me on ice for a few days. We can't fly into that."

"Yeah? I heard your hotshot new pilot could fly that shuttle to the moon and back," he said. "That's the rumor, anyway, from the mechs."

Jess regarded him. "Yeah?"

"Heard them talking in the mess. They saw the mission logs from your last run and there's a lot of lip flapping on it."

"Dev did a kickass job," Jess said. "Surprised the hell out of me, as much as anyone else."

"That make you nervous?" The met officer asked. "Maybe they can replace you with a sim slot?"

Jess studied him.

"Just a thought."

Jess smiled briefly. "Who knows?" She picked up the pad and gave him a brief wave. "Later."

"Later."

Jess left the met office and walked along the hall, trying not to acknowledge how much a sense of relief she was feeling at having to postpone the mission for a few days. She considered that as she walked, reasoning that it probably was good because it gave her back a chance to heal up a little, and she could make sure all the repairs were done to the shuttle.

Two good reasons. She nodded to herself. Perfectly legit reasons. Nothing to do with any reluctance on her part to go back out in the field in a tricky insertion.

Nothing like that at all. She had no control over the weather, after all, now did she? Besides, it would give her time to work on her cover, and get her plan all nice and settled before she and Dev went haring off into the wild outside.

That was fate talking, she was sure of it. She'd been doing this long enough to know that when all the odds started stacking up against you, the world was warning you that you were pointing in the wrong direction. Ignoring that never led to good things.

Last time she'd done it had been her last mission with Joshua. Her gut instinct had been humming like crazy on that one but she hadn't had the guts to stand up and say so, and scrub the mission. Not with Bricker's strident insistence on the importance of the raid, and her own arrogance and ego shoving aside her doubts.

Very stupid of her. Stupid with a trending to deadly.

"Drake."

Jess turned and waited, as Alexander Bain appeared from nowhere and caught up to her. "Sir." She scanned the area for listening ears. "I was just in met."

"Not good, I take it? Hm?"

"Looks like plus forty-eight to go," Jess said. "There are two tornadic mega storms coming over between now and then." She paused, and waited, watching those cold gray eyes dissect her.

"Hmm. That's bad," Bain said. "However, on the positive side, you'll be present for the incoming ceremony tomorrow night. So not all is negative. I very much wanted you and your new colleague to be there when this new class comes in. This scientific raid can wait the few days. In fact, if it solidifies their findings, better for us."

Jess nodded, feeling a sense of relief shiver through her muscles. "Let them get the bugs out before we steal it," she said.

"Exactly." The old man smiled briefly. "And perhaps it will keep the enemy off our doorstep." He frowned. "Shocking, they made it past all the scans isn't it?" He watched her intently.

"Very shocking." Jess said. "They must have gotten very lucky."

"Hm."

Jess's lips twitched, and she quickly scanned the hallway again, finding it still empty. "Or someone wasn't watching."

"Hm."

"Or someone was deliberately keeping quiet."

Bain leaned against the wall, his spare frame barely seeming to cast a shadow. "Does it seem likely to you that they could have gotten in here with no warning, and no storm to cover their tracks?"

"No."

"And yet it seems that the logs for the hour preceding their arrival have somehow become lost, making it impossible for us to ascertain exactly what we knew, when we knew it."

Jess stared at him, her body stiffening. "That doesn't happen without leaving fingerprints somewhere," she finally said.

"Hm." Bain tilted his head slightly. "Troubling times, Agent Drake." He unfolded his arms and straightened up. "And quite dangerous, perhaps, to those of interest. So keep an eye on your new colleague, hmm? I wouldn't want anything unpleasant to happen to that charming girl."

"I will," Jess said, in a quiet tone. "I don't want anything bad to happen to her either. She's all right."

"Yes." Bains' eyes met hers, and he smiled, just a little. "And I will keep my eye on her creator. Though I'm sure he would be extremely irritated to hear me say that."

"He's a pretty good shot," Jess commented. "He took out two of those guys."

"Dan Kurok has quite a number of unusual skills," Bain said wryly. "Pity we need to get him back to the station before they blow up the citadel trying to find him, hmm?" He pushed off the wall. "A good day to you, Drake."

"Sir."

He glanced back at her. "Do remember to keep your options open."

Jess watched him go, as she replayed his words in her head. Then she frowned, and turned on her heel, heading across the hallway toward the gym.

DEV RUBBED HERSELF dry with the towel, and was headed toward her locker when she heard Jess's voice nearby.

A moment later, Jess stuck her head around the corner of the changing area, and then entered. "There you are," she said. "How'd the gym go?"

"Very nice," Dev said. She removed her jumpsuit from the locker and stepped into it. "The stations are really good, and I jumped into the water tank."

Jess studied her. "You jumped in the pool?"

"Yes." Dev ruffled her hair dry. "I really liked that. But I think I have to work out that whole swimming thing since my head kept going under and it was all a bit difficult.

Jess put her hands on her hips.

Dev stopped her motion, seeing the look on Jess's face. "Is there something incorrect?"

"Ever occur to you that jumping in water and not knowing how to swim is a bad idea?"

Dev considered the question as she put the towel in the container and ran her fingers through her hair to order it. "No," she finally said. "How would I know how if I didn't try it?"

Jess nodded. "Okay. Glad you liked the gym." She exhaled a little. "I have to start getting back in here regularly now that med cleared me." Her voice sounded regretful. "But listen, it looks like we've got a few days break due to met. "

Dev closed her locker. "Okay. Is there something else we need to do?"

"C'mon." Jess started walking toward the door, and Dev followed her unquestioningly. They exited the gym and walked through the central corridor. "Tomorrow night we'll have to go to the induction of the new class."

"Okay."

"And the party afterwards."

Dev walked along at her side in silence for a few strides. "What's a party?"

Jess rubbed the bridge of her nose. "It's when everyone gets together in one room and drink themselves stupid while eating bad seaweed crackers and mushroom dip."

Dev digested this thoughtfully. "Is this a good thing or a bad thing?" She finally asked, as they headed down the long corridor toward the carrier hanger. "You sound like it's a bad thing."

Jess chuckled dryly. "I'm just not a party animal," she said. "You saw the crowd in the bar when we got back from the rescue. More of the same of that." She palmed open the door to the hangar and motioned

Dev to go in.

They walked inside, finding the hangar relatively quiet. "Want to check out the body job," Jess said. "Always pays to put an eyeball on it."

Dev decided just to follow along, since neither remark made any sense to her. She stuck by Jess's side as they walked between the parked vehicles toward the rear where the tech station was. The tall ceiling was shrouded in darkness, the roof overhead firmly shut.

There were a lot of techs moving around. They gave her and Jess brief glances, then went back to their tasks, which made Dev feel pretty good. She liked being treated casually. "Do you have to go to the party?"

Jess sighed. "Yes and no. It's expected. So we go, but..." She paused, and fell silent. "Maybe it was Josh dragging me to all of them I don't know." She led the way around a tool bay and ducked under the fuel piping. "Doesn't matter."

Here, close to where they were rebuilding what was apparently their carrier, the smells were sharp and the mist in the air made Dev's eyes water. She forgot all about the party when she saw the framework of the big craft under the lights, scoured clean of all the battle damage. "Wow."

"Stripped her down to bare," Jess said. "Ugly thing, isn't it?"

"I don't think so, no." Dev edged around to get a better look. Without it's skin on, you could see all the systems and gyros that made the carrier function. She stared in rapt fascination, feeling a strong surge of programming tickling her. "This is very interesting."

A man in a scuffed and stained orange jumpsuit came around the side of the carrier. "What was that?" He sidled over to Dev. "Were you saying you were interested?"

"Very," Dev said.

Jess rolled her eyes. "Oh, no. Now you're in for it."

"Shut up, Drake." The tech motioned Dev closer. "Finally, one of you appreciates my work." He focused his attention on Dev. "My name's Clint," he said. "We almost met the other day when you brought this baby back here."

"Dev." Dev smiled at him, a genuine and appreciative grin. "Are you building it all up from scratch? It looks much better already."

Clint returned the smile. "Let me give you a tour." He steered her toward the stripped down rig. "Beat it, Drake. I know you just think of this as your damned bus."

Jess felt a sudden rush of anger that really surprised her. She surged after them and only just kept herself from slamming Clint in the back. Clint sensed it, and half turned, his eyes going a little wider in alarm.

He looked at her face, and then stepped away from Dev, holding both his hands up, palms outward. "Sorry. Over the top. Didn't mean to piss you off."

Dev had turned too, and she instinctively did the opposite. She moved a little closer and looked up at Jess with a slightly concerned expression, one hand lifting up and touching Jess on the arm. "Is there something wrong?"

Jess felt a flush rising to her face and she was glad of the glaring lights that obscured it. "No," she said. "I just don't appreciate being told off."

Clint let his hands slowly lower. "Sorry, Jess...I really was just razzing you."

Jess felt her body relax, aware that her muscles had tightened into a pre fight posture, her fingers twitching a bit at her sides. "It's okay," she said, briefly. "But you know, maybe I want to see the damn old thing too."

"Hey, no problem!" Clint smiled again. "C'mon." He turned and led them under the carrier, its stark structure now so very evident. "You really torched it this time. We had to rebuild half the front end."

Jess ducked under one of the steel ribs and followed him. After a brief pause, Dev joined her. "Sorry about that," Jess muttered. "He just bites my shorts sometimes."

Dev reached up and pinched the bridge of her nose, giving Jess a sideways glance.

"Just a saying." Jess felt herself relax a little more, appreciating the humor. "He's never been near my shorts."

"So anyway," Clint said, oblivious of the whispers. "Since we had to rebuild this old sucker from the frame, I decided to put in a whole new scan package, and that newfangled targeting system they just released down in the lab."

"Oh, yeah?" Jess investigated the item. "I saw a squirt on that."

Dev poked her head inside the frame and took in the details avidly, setting aside her concern over Jess's reaction a moment ago. Jess seemed to be over the anger, and Dev was glad because she could see that it had frightened Clint.

Just like the security men had been frightened. Dev peeked over and watched Jess as she listened to Clint's explanation of the new targeting system. She was relaxed and interested now, her hands running over the device.

Doctor Dan had told her she could trust Jess. Dev thought about that. She trusted Doctor Dan. So it must be all right. She put a hand on the curved nose, obviously new, and could see through the lines and gears the now empty spot her chair would rest in.

At least for her, it must be all right.

"Dev?"

Dev removed her head from the wiring and moved around the forward struts. "Yes?"

"Here's the mod chamber." Jess pointed to a door behind the dock. "You said you wanted to get some time in there sometime."

"You mod?" Clint kept a wary eye on Jess, but circled back around to where Dev was standing. "You wouldn't be interested in being a part of the assembly would you?"

"Yes," Dev said, instantly. She could feel the programming bubbling up, as she ran her eyes over the internal systems and their schematics flashed behind her eyes. "I would really like that."

"You would?" Jess was watching her in some bemusement.

Dev nodded. "It's in my programming," she said. "How to run all the things inside, and fix them when they break. It would be great to touch and work with them firsthand."

Clint clasped his hands dramatically to his chest. "I'm in love."

Jess rolled her eyes.

Dev grinned, a little uncertainly. "Is that good or bad?"

"Seriously." Clint smiled back at her. "It's really great when one of you all take a true interest in the old buses. We work hard to keep them flying."

"And we take them out and wreck them." But Jess's voice was mild and indulgent. "Be careful, Clint. She kicked my ass as a pilot her first run. She'll take your job away if you don't watch out."

"I didn't kick you," Dev said. "I would never do that."

"I saw the log," Clint said. "So they figured out how to make the real deal, huh? Crazy." He studied Dev with curious eyes. "Oh, well. At least they made her cute."

Dev gave him a slightly startled look.

"Yes, they did." Jess found herself agreeing, somewhat to her own surprise, enhanced when she caught Dev blushing at the words.

That made her blush, the unfamiliar sensation making her swallow. "Hey." She redirected all the attention to the carrier. "So what's the deal with the engines."

Clint hesitated, then he cleared his throat and went with the subject change, moving around to the far side of the carrier where the huge engines were cradled, waiting for installation into the frame. "Y'know I heard rumors we were getting some new gear, but I don't know if the new stuff'll hold up like these babies did."

"They...um..." Dev felt a little confused, and a little lightheaded, but she wasn't sure why. "They had a lot of power. More than the sims. I was surprised."

Clint beamed, fully restored to good humor. "Why thank you, kind lady." He made a half bow. "I tuned them myself. Let me take the cover off the cowling here and show you some of the tunings." He pulled a tool from his coveralls and started wrenching the engine cover, turning his back to them.

Jess tilted her head and regarded her companion. Dev was studying the ground, a faint smile on her face. After a second, she looked up and met Jess's eyes.

For a moment, the hangar faded out a little and then they both looked away. Dev shook her head a little as she stepped forward and joined Clint at the side of the engine.

Jess put her hand on one of the bare struts and stood there watching. She was aware, vaguely, that something a little odd was going on, but she wasn't sure what it was, so she leaned against the carrier and listened to Clint's monologue as Dev circled the engine and peered inside, the bright lights of the work bay gilding her pale hair.

Slowly her mind returned to the plan, and she straightened carefully, moving past the carrier and approaching the engine. "Clint, the Old Man wants me to buzz out probably plus 48. This thing going to be ready?"

Clint looked up at her. "Plus 48?" He exhaled, and looked around. "Crap, Jess. Most of my mechs are working on the retaining wall at the bay. We gotta get that done before tomorrow night."

Jess lifted both hands slightly and let them drop. "Not my schedule."

"No, I know." Clint sighed. "Well, Dev, you up to help out for real? I could use a pair of hands."

"Yes," Dev said. "That would be excellent."

"We'll do our best," Clint said. "But Jess, I'm not guaranteeing anything. You may need to take a loaner if you have to go out plus 48."

Jess frowned. The last thing she wanted to do was go out with a strange vehicle. It wasn't as if Clint's team didn't take equal care of them, but you spent a lot of time learning the quirks of what you were... Her thoughts stopped, and she focused on Dev.

Dev, who had stepped into this carrier for the first time, and flown it with no familiarity at all. "We'll cope," Jess said. "I'd rather have ours, but Dev can handle it."

Dev looked up and grinned at her over the top of the engine, a smudge of silicone grease on her nose. "Thank you," she said. "I am not sure that's really true, but I'm glad you think so."

"Ah, and modest as well." Clint leaned next to her and pointed out a bit of machinery. "See that? Regs say the noz has to be ten inches, but I found a way to put a throttle inside there that really boosts the exhaust."

"Oh yes!" Dev straightened, holding her hands up as though they were around throttles. "I remember that, how much faster it seemed when I was changing direction, and heading up."

"Yeah, I can still feel it." Jess rubbed her shoulder. "Knocked my ass out of my chair twice."

Clint chuckled.

"I did?" Dev seemed amazed. "Really?"

"My fault. Forgot to tighten my harness." Jess eased over and peered inside the engine. The internal mechanics of the technology she'd mastered never really much interested her. She knew how it all worked, of course. Every agent did, it was part of the training. You never knew when you might get caught outside and need to make repairs, for example.

But still. That's what the techs were for, after all, to pilot the carriers, sure, but also to know how they worked, and be up on all the systems so they could keep everything moving at the rate the agents needed to get their goals met.

And Dev, apparently, was going to be one of those kind of techs who slobbered over the gears. Jess gave Dev a tolerant look, as she dug into a gyro.

Without warning, Dev hopped up onto the engine and lowered

herself head down into the inside of the big blast chamber, both arms braced on either side easily bearing her weight.

Clint gave her a surprised look, then cocked his head and glanced over at Jess. "Drake." His face scrunched into a wry grin. "I think you may have gotten more than you bargained for in this new driver of yours."

Jess gave him a wry look of agreement. "Had occurred to me."

"Is that the plasma igniter?" Dev asked, lowering herself a little more. "Wow. I didn't know it looked like that."

Jess walked over and poked her head inside the engine.

"Yes, that's it," Clint said, directing his hand over the object. "It's one of the few things on the old crate that's direct drive. That cabling system routes right into the throttles. Real old school."

"Wow." Dev pulled herself up and sprawled over the top of the engine, flexing her fingers a little. "I didn't know that."

"Wow," Jess echoed. "I didn't know that either."

"Hey, Jess." Clint lowered his voice. "Are you going to trial that new weapons rig? The one they hook up to your head?"

Jess looked quickly around, but they were alone. She gave Clint a warning glare.

He interpreted the look. "Everyone knows. You know how this place is. I heard it in the lunchroom last week."

Jess did know. She exhaled. "Not until they get the bugs out of it," she said. "Since you heard that, you heard about what it did to Don."

Clint frowned, and nodded. Dev remained quiet, looking from one of them to the other.

"Not the way I'd choose to go," Jess said with a note of finality.

"Gotcha," Clint said. "So, anyway, once we get these chambers in here rebuilt, we can remount the engines."

"I would love to help," Dev reiterated. "This is great."

"You want to help too, Jess?" Clint asked.

"No." Jess patted the engine. "I'm going to go run the tactics boards and see what's out there. Catch up with you later, Dev."

"Okay."

Jess gave a light wave, and walked off, wondering why in the world she suddenly had an urge to learn about plasma injection.

And get her hands dirty.

Chapter Eleven

IT WAS LATE by the time Dev got back to her quarters, her head buzzing with all the stimulation from the day and her hands and arms covered in silica gel.

She'd had so much fun with Clint. He had the same enthusiasm for the machinery as she did and it was really enjoyable sharing that while at the same time getting important things done to get their carrier back together.

She'd learned a lot from him, too. Pieces and bits that programming left out, and additional understanding that let her put parts of what she had together better. All good, and they'd made some progress on the engines, too.

She went into the sanitary unit and stripped out of her jumpsuit. Clint had suggested she ask for the kind of work coverall he used, which was a tougher fabric and had more pockets in better places for all the adjustment tools.

Dev flexed her hands, noting she'd gotten a few cuts and scuffs on them from the work, but the discomfort wasn't significant and she divested herself of her underclothes and started the water running.

She had to laugh a bit. Everywhere her jumpsuit wasn't, she was covered in dirt and grunge, and it was very nice to get under the warm water and scrub. She had no idea in the world what she would have done up in the crèche. The amount of rad it would have taken to get this off her skin—boy that would have hurt.

Her stomach growled, and she shut the water off, stepping out and grabbing a towel to dry herself off with. Then she paused and considered how natural it was starting to feel to be here, which in itself didn't seem natural because she'd only been here a few days.

But she did feel that way. She put her suit and underthings into the laundry basket and wrapped the towel around her, walking out into the room and crossing to her uniform case. She opened it and then paused, faced with a small surprise.

Along with the standard jumpsuits and her pilot ones, now there were a few others. One in a deep blue and another in purple that seemed very casual. She pulled aside the regular ones exposing the blue one and touched the fabric, which was very soft.

"Hm." Dev put on a pair of dry underclothes and studied the blue suit, liking the feel against her skin very much. "Wonder where this came from?" Was it another thing from Bain? Or maybe just something that came as part of her job? Maybe it was something she would need on the mission.

Of course. Dev took out one of her regular off duty suits and slipped into it, fastening the catches and transferring her insignia to the collar.

She went back into the sanitary unit and picked up her comb, raking it through her hair to order it.

She was just finishing when she heard the inner door open, feeling a funny little prickle down her spine as she looked in the mirror and Jess appeared in it, leaning against the edge of the entrance. "Hello."

"Finished wrenching for the day?"

Dev turned and put the comb down. "Yes. I really liked it. Is that wrong?" She watched Jess's face, noting anew it's distinctive shape and the piercing quality of her eyes. "I didn't mean to be incorrect."

"You weren't." Jess's eyes shifted and met hers. "You're a tech. Some techs just want to drive and do mods. Some like to wrench. It's all right," she said. "Want to do dinner? I got stuck in comp pulling tracking data. I just got back."

"Me, too," Dev said. "I'd love to go. It's been a long time since breakfast."

"It has. C'mon." Jess turned and led the way through her quarters to the outer door, which she palmed open. "Any good news on the old bus?"

"Yes," Dev said. "I think we did good work today. "

They walked along the corridor, which seemed a lot busier than Dev remembered it. There were a lot of people clustered in groups and passing them.

Jess angled toward the wall to avoid a group of talking men. "Mess is going to be a damn circus."

"What's a circus?" Dev asked. "I've never heard of that."

"What's a circus." Jess mused, as they turned down the hall and paused, spotting a big crowd outside the mess hall. "In the old days, they used to travel around and put up tents, where you could go to see performing animals, and clowns, and trapeze artists." She glanced at Dev, who was staring at her in fascinated incomprehension. "I'll show you on scan later."

They squeezed past the crowd and entered the mess, only to pull up short again. Every table was taken, and more had been shoved in until it was packed with bodies.

Jess turned and went over to the food service area. "I vote we get a bag meal and go sit on the porch."

"Okay." Dev went right along with it, having no real desire to squeeze in with the crowd. She took the wrapped package the Ceebee handed her and followed Jess out the door again, pressing back against the wall as a half dozen men in fancy looking suits pushed past them.

She saw Jess's eyes narrow, but she merely edged past them and headed down to the lifts. Dev kept close after her, and shortly they were going down to the lower corridors. When the lift stopped and they stepped out, they were alone.

"What a nuthouse," Jess grumbled. "I hate these damned ceremonies. Everyone and their mother's asshole shows up for them." She strode down the hall and the air got damp and salty as they made their way to the lock and went inside. "Weather's broken for a while. We can get some air."

Dev waited, holding her package, as the lock cycled and the outer door opened, giving them access to the small platform overlooking the sea.

Unlike the previous time, the winds were quiet and the sea below them was only rustling with a dim roar, not the fierce crashing Dev had heard the last time Jess brought her here. She sat down on the bench next to Jess and unwrapped her meal.

The air smelled wet and salty, but she liked it. She could almost feel the rasp of it against her skin as a physical thing, and as she took in a lungful, it occurred to her that the real thing felt very different than the manufactured air she'd become used to in the crèche.

That never smelled like anything. This she could taste on her tongue and as she took a bite of the roll that was in the package it enhanced the flavor of it. She peered at the item curiously as she chewed. "This is interesting," she said, after a minute.

"Seaweed roll," Jess said, a little indistinctly due to her mouthful. She swallowed and regarded hers. "They take the little stuff they catch in the seine nets—the krill and tiny shrimps and all. Then they mix it with grain and wrap it in leaf weed."

"I like it."

"Me too." Jess smiled briefly. "But you seem to like everything."

Dev leaned back against the wall, extending her legs out and crossing them at the ankles. "Well." She chewed thoughtfully. "Nothing's really been bad yet. I like some things more than other things, but I haven't gotten anything yet that made me just stop."

"Did you up there?" Jess leaned her elbows on her knees, her back too sore to press against the wall.

"Yes," Dev said. "There was a kind of fruit once. I just got a smell of it and it made me sick."

"Huh."

"They stopped making the fruit," Dev continued. "They tried all that stuff on us."

Jess's jaws moved stolidly, ingesting the roll. The pain was killing her appetite but she knew she had to get something inside her before she took more drugs for it. She'd found that out the hard way. And she did like the things, the spicy taste and crunch of the grains appealed to her.

Maybe a good night's sleep would help. She finished the first roll and took out the second one. There were also some rice cakes inside, and a tube of water. At the bottom a piece of sweet dough to finish with.

She'd had many of these meals usually out on assignment, or waiting for insertion, but occasionally in the heat of ops they'd get them delivered to the comm center too. Not fancy, but it kept you going.

She glanced at Dev, who was busy consuming everything in her box with a studious seriousness that almost made Jess laugh. They had both fallen silent, but she was surprised to realize it was a comfortable silence, requiring no chatter between them.

She liked that. Jess herself wasn't much of a talker, and it seemed her new pilot wasn't either which seemed to her to be another good sign. In the dim outside solar powered light that lit the platform, Dev was cast in low color shadows, her pale hair contrasting with the darkness of her suit. She appeared relaxed, looking around as she chewed with a contented expression.

Jess went back to her own meal trying to ignore the once again throbbing ache in her back, trying to remember just how much of the painkiller she had left in her quarters. Maybe she could take some and just sack out—

The touch on her arm nearly made her jump out of her skin. "Urf!"

"Wow. Sorry about that." Dev withdrew her hand. "I didn't mean to alarm you, I just wanted to ask you a question."

Jess turned the seaweed roll around in her fingers for a moment, then glanced sideways at Dev. "Go ahead and ask," she said. "But be careful about grabbing me. Sometimes I don't think first and I could hit you without meaning to."

"Okay." Dev studied her with a serious expression. "Is there something disturbing you?"

Jess was caught by utter surprise at the question. "Me?"

Dev looked around the small platform, then back at her. "Yes."

"Why?" Jess heard a sharp note enter her voice, not entirely intended.

Undisturbed, Dev merely looked at her. "Since this morning, after the attack, it seemed to be you were," she said. "I didn't mean to offend you by asking."

Jess studied those open and guileless eyes, hearing the polite concern in Dev's voice and not detecting any hidden meaning behind the words. "I'm not offended," she said, gruffly. "I said you could ask me things, didn't I?"

"Yes." Dev smiled. "You did."

There was an odd sense of conflict in her. Jess found herself teetering between brushing Dev off, and confiding in her and she wasn't entirely sure why. It was a strange feeling, new and confusing.

Dev spoke up again, a faint hesitance in her voice. "I hope it wasn't something I did that disturbed you."

All at once, Jess decided. "Nah. You've only done good stuff, Dev. I slammed my back against a door handle this morning right where I got hurt last time and it's bothering me, that's all."

Dev looked relieved, and yet, still concerned. "I'm sorry you got hurt. Are you going to med?"

Jess shook her head. "It's not that bad. Just annoying and med tends to make big deals out of nothing."

Dev nodded. "I never liked going either," she said. "You never knew what they'd do to you and then..." She paused. "Well, you never wanted them to think you were really hurt or really sick."

Jess looked at her, head tilted slightly in question.

Dev glanced aside. "Not much use for damaged products."

Jess blinked. "What?"

Dev looked embarrassed. "We're not actually people. Not legally. So if you were really damaged they'd just scratch you and start over." She glanced up at Jess, who was sitting there, roll forgotten in her hand, her jaw a little dropped. "So that's why we like to find a place to do good work," she said softly. "Kind of makes it safer."

Jess reached out and put her hand on Dev's shoulder. "You're as much a person here as I am," she said. "So don't worry about them trying to scratch you as long as I'm around."

It was hard to say, really, which one of them was more surprised to hear her say that. Certainly Jess herself was a little amazed and more than a touch confused as to where it had come from. She barely knew Dev, really.

And yet, it was true. Whether it was that she felt sorry for the kid, or that she felt responsible for her wasn't really important.

"Thank you," Dev said, after a moment. "So that's why I asked if you were upset, and I was hoping it wasn't at me." She studied Jess's face. "And I'm very sorry you don't feel well. I hope it gets better soon."

Jess relaxed. She lowered her hand to her knee and settled slowly back against the wall, not bothering to hide a grimace now. "I'm sure it will be." She sighed. "Never get stabbed in the back, Dev. It takes forever to heal and hurts like hell."

Dev watched the sharp profile across from her, wondering if it was a trick of the half light or if Jess really looked for a moment as sad as those words sounded. Then her companion shifted a little and the impression was gone.

"Okay." Dev went back to scavenging her box. "I'll try to remember that. It's too bad you don't have null grav here. That's where I went when I hurt my leg in training. It made it feel better."

Jess thought about that. "Well." She finished her roll and dug out the sweet cake. "No, we don't have null gravity here, but you know, water's almost as good."

Dev immediately looked interested. "Like the shower?"

"No." Jess shook her head. "The gym pool maybe. It's going to be too rough to go surf the caverns tonight." She glanced up to where clouds were now scudding over them, and the corresponding wind was picking up. "Want to join me later?"

"In the pool?"

Jess nodded. "I forgot the pool's pretty good for therapy. Gets the Gs off you."

"Yes, absolutely." Dev's eyes brightened. "Maybe you can show me how to swim. I didn't have a lot of success with that." She finished her tube of water and folded everything up, putting it back into the container neatly.

"What the hell made you just jump in?" Jess asked.

"I just wanted to feel what it was like. I never had any programming at all about that so I thought the fastest way for me to learn about it was to just do it," she said. "It's like that sometimes for us. You find a hole, and you want to fill it in."

Jess considered that. "Interesting philosophy."

Dev smiled. She set the package down and got up, walking over to the edge of the platform and putting her hands on the railing.

The wind was coming up, and it was a little exciting to her to be facing into it, feeling the pressure of it against her skin as it blew her hair back and made her blink.

"Don't get any ideas." Jess placed her hands on the steel rail next to Dev's. "Jumping in that would be a fast lesson but very very short."

Dev chuckled a little. "We're curious, but not generally self destructive. I know the difference." She studied the view, and exhaled. "This is so amazing though. It's like looking out at the stars in the crèche but better. So unlimited."

Jess leaned on the rail and pondered that, watching Dev out of the corner of her eye as the spray dusted her skin. "Unlimited?"

Dev nodded, pointing out at the horizon. "It goes on a long way but you can tell that. The stars—you can't really tell how far back they go so this gives you a better look at something big. It seems more real."

"It also gets you wet." Jess wiped a bit of spray from her face. "I'm guessing space doesn't do that."

Dev held her hand out and watched her skin get coated. "No. You can't touch space. And it can't touch you. Not like this."

The air of the world filled her lungs, so much thicker and more vibrant than what she'd been used to and she could feel the salt on her lips and smell the pungent scent of the water. "It makes me feel all over."

"You like that."

Dev turned to look at her, with a smile. "Very much. Don't you?"

Jess smiled in return, looking down at her folded hands on the rail. Then she glanced off across the horizon. "I might learn to," she said. "C'mon. Let's go back inside before the storm hits." She turned and picked up her bundle, keying the airlock with her free hand. "See what other trouble we can get into tonight."

SHE WAS GOING to learn how to swim. Dev felt a bit like bouncing around her quarters, as she waited for Jess to finish her discussion outside.

The halls had started to finally empty out as they walked back, but Stephan Bock had caught up with them just outside the operations center and Dev had quickly realized he wanted a private talk with Jess.

In the crèche, she'd gotten that a lot. Proctors and other instructors always wanted to talk outside their earshot, as though bio alts really didn't know what was going on.

Dev found that a little funny. New proctors always acted like they were dumb, and though some sets certainly weren't that sharp, most had average intelligence and knew what was going on around them.

Others, like Dev, were just as intelligent as the teachers instructing them and it was usually a funny moment when the newbies figured it all out.

Like spelling words they didn't think the bio alts would understand. Like they were children or something.

She remembered one of them, a woman who had just come to the crèche from one of the science stations. She was teaching a class in how plants grew, and thought she had to explain to them what a pea was.

Like they didn't live on a biologic test station, and had been fed every single variety of pea the Ag group could come up with in hopes of developing something they could use downside.

Dev had stood up and recited the entire phylum of them, in alphabetical order. She could still hear her class laughing, and see the discomfited look on the teacher's face as she was forced to just stand there and listen.

She chuckled, now, and went over to the dispenser for a bottle of water to sip, but paused when she saw a light sedately flashing on her pad.

Curious, she went over and sat down, pulling the pad over and keying it on. To her bemused surprise, she found she had a message waiting.

A message? Who would be sending her a message? She touched the surface of the pad and the message opened up.

Dev -
Thanks for your help today! I really appreciated the extra hands!
Hope you can come back soon and we can really get into the engines!
Clint

Dev sat back and folded her arms over her chest, rereading the message a few times. It didn't seem to really have a purpose. Clint had said the same thing before she'd left that day, so why had he sent it?

Just to be polite? Dev keyed the screen and the data input came up. She replied to the message, deciding a polite gesture certainly warranted an equally polite response.

Hello Clint -
You are most welcome. I am glad we had good results. I look forward to helping again.
Dev

Dev regarded the message and then sent it, with a little smile. "That's nice," she said. "He's an interesting person."

Another natural born who treated her almost like one of his own kind.

The inner door popped open and Jess trudged in, rolling her eyes and sitting down into one of the chairs near Dev's workspace. "What a shoe box full of buttcracks this is sometimes." She propped her elbow on the chair arm, letting her head rest against her hand.

Dev stopped in mid motion and stared at her, then went back to the pad and started typing on it. She stopped and looked at Jess. "How do you spell that second thing? I think I can guess what a shoe box is."

Jess chuckled wryly. "Stupid. Stephan was trying to convince me to do the intake speech tomorrow night. I told him that was his job. I don't know what got into him."

Dev folded her hands on the desk. "So, he wanted you to talk to everyone?"

Jess nodded.

Dev considered this. "You have a very nice voice. I'm sure the new people would enjoy it."

Jess stared at her with her head cocked just slightly to one side. "What?"

"All of those people who are just getting here," Dev said. "I'm sure it will seem very strange to them, so wouldn't it be great for them to have someone as experienced and nice as you to welcome them?" She watched Jess's eyes open up a little wider. "I would have liked that."

"Rather than having someone beheaded as your welcome? Yeah, I guess," Jess muttered, her brows contracting. "What the hell would I say—wait a minute. Did you call me nice?"

"Yes."

"Me? Nice?" Jess sat up a little.

"Yes." Dev smiled at the look on her face. It was a mixture of embarrassment and uncertainty and she found it sort of intriguing. "You've been very nice to me. I wanted to say thank you for that."

Jess blushed visibly, which was very interesting. "Just trying to help," she muttered, then got up. "Let's do this pool thing." She brusquely indicated the door. "Maybe it'll make my back chill out and I can get a decent night's sleep."

"Okay." Dev got up and joined her and they headed for the door. She was a little puzzled though, since she'd never quite experienced such a discomfited reaction to a compliment before. She reviewed what she'd said, a few times, and decided she couldn't detect any particular reason her words should have caused Jess distress. "I'm sorry if I said something incorrect."

They walked through the central hall, the few people going in the opposite direction mostly ignoring them. Jess glanced to either side as they turned the corner to the rec area, and cleared her throat "Ops agents aren't supposed to be nice."

"Not even to the people they work with?" Dev asked. "Why?"

"Because we're assholes."

Dev frowned. "Here we go with that ass stuff again." She sighed. "I think I have to ask Doctor Dan if he has a translation for all of this. I'm not sure why you all find people's behinds so interesting."

"Heh heh." That put a grudging smile on Jess's face. "We're just typically nasty tempered people," she said. "You saw us in the bar. We'd go at each other's throats every meal if house rules let us."

"Well, okay," Dev said. "But Jess, you have been nice to me. Not nasty at all. You've been nicer to me than anyone else I've ever met."

Jess remained silent as they entered the gym.

At this late hour, it was almost empty. There were a few people in the weight bearing area, and one on a treadmill but the rest of the huge space was quiet, and the lights had been dimmed a bit in response to that.

They walked together into the changing room. Jess went to what was, apparently, her locker and opened it, studying the contents with a dour glare.

Dev decided remaining quiet was probably the best thing to do. She opened her locker, then paused.

After a brief moment, they both looked up at each other at the same time.

Jess came over and sat down on the bench next to Dev's locker, her exercise gear in her hand. "Sorry," she said. "I think we're nasty to each other because we know it's pointless to make friends. You just lose them. After a while of that, you just walk around the pain." She fiddled with her gear, and then shrugged. "Stupid, really."

Dev sat down next to her. "I understand. Sometimes it was like that in the crèche. You never wanted to get too close to anyone because they could get assigned at any time and you'd never see them again."

Jess nodded. "Yeah."

Dev looked down at her hands, clenched a little on her workout suit. "Well," she said. "You know, I'm your pilot, so maybe it'll be that whatever happens will happen to both of us at the same time." She glanced up, getting caught by Jess's intent gaze at close quarters. "So maybe its okay to be nice to me."

Jess frowned a little.

"I thought maybe you were being nice to me because you wanted to please Bain," Dev said, in a quiet tone. "And that's okay too. Nice is nice no matter why—to us at least."

After a brief, still second Jess relaxed a bit, her face easing into a faint smile. "Nah. I'm nice to you because I like you," she said. "I don't like a lot of people."

Dev felt an unusual heat on her skin, and knew it was her turn to blush. "Thanks. I like you too."

Jess's smile became more pronounced. "So let's go swimming," she said, getting up. "Don't pay attention to the crap I say, Dev. Sometimes I just talk out my..." She paused, and laughed. "Sometimes I say things just to hear myself talk."

Somehow, Dev thought, as she changed into her workout suit and followed Jess into the big open space. Somehow, she didn't really think that was true. She thought Jess said exactly what she felt.

At least, she certainly hoped so.

"Okay." Jess led the way around to the shallow end of the pool and stepped into it. The brief exercise clothes just outlined her tall form, and she paused for a minute and let her hand down to test the temperature. "Ah." She sounded surprised.

"What's wrong?" Dev stepped in next to her. "Oh. It's warmer than it was earlier."

"Yeees." Jess seemed pleased. She splashed into the water and then dropped onto her back, making a wave swirl out from her all over the tank. "Oh, I like this."

Dev followed more slowly. She took the time to enjoy the feeling of the water buoying her, it's warmth immediately penetrating her and easing muscles just a little sore from her earlier exercise. "That feels very nice."

Jess had gone to the edge of the pool and was leaning against it, her eyes half closed. "It sure does. Damn, I'd forgotten what that felt like."

Dev made her way through the water over to her side. "Why is it warm now?"

Jess exhaled. "I don't care." She shifted her shoulders and let her head drop back. "Just feels good."

It did. Dev flexed her hands, breathing in the smell of the water.

"Okay." Jess reluctantly opened her eyes. "So here we are, in the pool." She pushed away from the side. "What did you do when you jumped in?"

"Just this." Dev made a paddling motion with her hands.

"Natural instinct." Jess looked approving. "Babies do that when you drop them in the water."

"You drop babies in the water?" Dev's eyebrows went up. "Really?"

"Ahm...well, I've never done it, but that's what they say." Jess launched herself forward. "Watch."

Dev did, avidly. Jess lifted her arms up and put them forward, pulling back against the water and making her go forward. She was also kicking her feet.

"Ow." Jess stopped after a few strokes. "Damn it." She rolled over onto her back and used her legs to move her back to where Dev was, keeping her hands folded on her stomach. "Fucking shoulder."

"It must hurt a lot.

Jess came to a halt next to her. "Driving me crazy," she said. "Okay, now you try."

Dev thought about what she'd just seen and made a picture in her head about it, running through the motions in her imagination before she took a deep breath and presented herself to the water.

At the first stroke, her head went under. Dev only just kept herself from sucking in a breath in surprise, moving her other arm forward and exhaling as her head broke the surface again.

"Whoa whoa..." Jess's voice echoed behind her.

Dev's head went under again, and then she felt hands on her, hauling her up to the surface. She spluttered as she came up again, shaking the hair out of her eyes as Jess came around in front of her and grabbed her other arm just above the elbow. "That didn't work out very well."

Jess was trying not to laugh. "You're sinking like a damned rock."

Dev stopped moving, blinking the water out of her eyes. "That's why I stuck to the paddling," she said. "If I stopped moving I went under." She felt the grip on her, warm and sure, but not uncomfortable.

"So I see." Jess pushed her gently backwards until they were shallow enough for Dev to stand. "Okay." She released Dev, rubbing the tips of her fingers together as she remembered the strength she'd felt under the soft skin.

Interesting.

"You were doing this?" Dev said, and leaned forward a little. She moved her arms in a swimming motion. "Right?" She peered at Jess, droplets of water dripping off the tip of her nose. "It looked so easy when you did it."

"Right." Jess motioned her sideways. "Let me hold on to you and you can practice it here where it's harder to drown." She gave Dev a quick smile. "It looked easy for me because I've been doing it all my life."

"Really?"

"Really. My family lives right on the water and the first thing you get taught is how to swim. Matter of fact, it was so long ago I don't remember learning."

Dev digested this. "Brent said to ask you to teach me to swim. He said you were a fish."

A faint, impish twinkle appeared in Jess's pale eyes. "He said that, huh? Heh. But anyway, c'mere, and lay on my hands, and we'll get you swimming."

That sounded like a very good idea. Dev leaned forward again and Jess moved closer, putting a hand under her belly and another on her thigh. For a moment, Dev completely lost track of what she was doing as her body reacted to the touch, and then the water hit her in the face and she forced her arms into motion.

"That's it," Jess said. "Over your...yeah. Cup your hands, don't slap the water."

Dev did her best with the unfamiliar moves, then as she did as Jess suggested and cupped her hands, she felt the strong pull against the water. Abruptly a sudden tickle of programming clicked in and it went from awkward to familiar in the space of a breath.

Strange, and then not. A familiar sensation to her but usually not this visceral.

She started kicking her feet in the same rhythm, and after a minute of that, she felt Jess's hold shift from her stomach to her back, the long fingers tangling themselves in her light covering and holding her up.

"I'm gonna let you go," Jess said. "Just keep that up...that's right."

Then the grip was gone, and she was moving forward in the water, this time without the odd and jerky lack of coordination that had shoved her head under the surface previously.

"Turn your head on every other stroke and breathe." Jess called out, surprisingly close by. She was swimming alongside her, and every time Dev did turn to that side, she took a breath and saw her companion do the same.

There was a memory there. She realized it wasn't really programming, it was something else. Something dimmer and less certain, a flash of a mental picture that was brighter and colder and had a lot more noise.

A thundering rush, and laughter.

Then it was gone, and it was just her, and Jess, and the big empty space again.

They reached the end of the pool at about the same time, and she grabbed the edge and held on, the bottom far below her feet. "Wow," she spluttered. "I didn't sink."

"Nice," Jess said her. "You keep this up you might not drown if we get dumped out of the carrier one of these trips"

Dev wiped the water out of her eyes with one hand. "Does that happen often?"

"It happens." Jess was also holding on, moving her other arm around carefully. "Huh." She looked a little relieved. "Water's helping loosen it up." She turned around. "Below my shoulder blade, you see any bumps there?"

Dev moved aside the fabric and studied her back. "Here, you mean?" She touched a red, raw looking area.

"Yeah."

Dev gently stroked the area with her fingertips. "I don't...no I think it's just the scar," she said. "No bumps."

Jess was regarding the skin on her arm with a bemused expression. "No bumps, huh?" She turned. "Well, good." She pointed back in the other direction. "Let's try another lap. We'll have you communing with the fishes yet."

"Is that a good thing?"

"Ahheh." Jess chuckled. "We'll have to find out."

JESS SAT DOWN on her bed, the cool air brushing against her bare shoulders. The soft sheets felt good as she slowly lowered herself down onto her back. "Man, I'm tired." She spoke casually to the ceiling. "But that was a pretty damn good time."

It was mid first watch, late and quiet in the citadel and the halls they'd walked back through had been blessedly free of random intruders. Jess exhaled, running her mind over the hours spent in the pool, hearing again the laughter echoing in her ears.

She smiled. Her body was slowly relaxing, and every breath she took made that more profound. She let her eyes close and spread her arms out carefully, feeling a residual ache but nothing like the sharp pain she'd experienced all day. "Ahhh."

Then her comm buzzed. Jess groaned and turned her head toward it, seeing the flashing light that indicated not an internal call, but one from outside. "Huh." She levered herself up and went to the workspace, coming around the table and sitting down in the chair as she touched the console. "Drake."

The screen came on, and after a fuzzy moment, cleared and she was looking into a pair of eyes the same color as hers, framed in a male face with a neatly trimmed dark beard. "Hello, Jess. Sorry. I know it's late there."

Jess leaned forward. "It's all right, Jimmy. What's up?" She said, watching her brother's expression intently. Several years her senior, he'd finally worked his way into a decent position at one of the processing centers and gotten married. Managed to spawn two kids, one little girl and one tow headed boy who was, Jess remembered, around five.

Around five.

"Just wanted to let you know about Tayler," Jimmy said. "He went through the battery last week. They called us today. He's in. They'll take him next month."

"Generation twelve, huh?"

"Yep." Her brother studied her. "The old family tradition."

Jess wasn't really sure how to answer that. She knew she had nothing to do with Tayler's scores, but there was always a bittersweetness to it hearing that another family member had tested in. They'd had at least one and occasionally more in each generation. The one prior to Jess's father's had sent three, and Jess had an uncle serving up in the Arctic somewhere and a cousin out on the west coast.

It was what it was. "If I'm still around when he inducts, I'll keep an eye on him," Jess said. "You can give him my comm if he wants to talk about it, later."

"Thanks." Jimmy managed a brief smile. "At least you know you don't have to donate those eggs to keep the line going, right."

Jess snorted wryly. "Yeah. Like that would need to happen." She glanced to one side, then looked back at the screen. "How's Mari?"

Jim shrugged. "Took it hard. But she knew who she was marrying. At least she knows Jimmy's going to be set and get schooled. More than most do," he said. "Peg's going to be pretty smart, we think. Maybe go into science. She tested that way."

"Good to hear," Jess said. "How's mom?"

"Running for chamber councilor," Jim said, with a wry look. "She's probably going to bunk in with one of those other polits. Said she was tired of looking at pictures on the wall and talking to dad's old boots."

"Don't blame her."

"Me either. Matter of fact, she boxed up a lot of his stuff. "He glanced at Jess, with an apologetic expression. "I told her to send them to you, not dump em. Figured maybe you'd at least like to look through em."

Jess gazed somberly at him. "Thanks, Jimmy. Appreciate the thought. There's still a couple of old goats in service around here who would probably like to take a look too."

Jim smiled. "Anyway, it's late. I'm surprised I caught you there. Things okay?" He asked. "Anything up with you guys?"

"Same as usual," she said. "We've got induction tomorrow night, we're all around."

"That it?" He asked. "Everything okay with you there?"

Jess's brows contracted. "With me?" She asked, wondering if he could have heard about Bricker. "Yeah, matter of fact I got a promotion to senior," she said. "Day or so ago. Booted my allocation up and reg'd me for retirement finally."

"Gotcha." Jimmy nodded. "Hey, congrats. You matched dad." He glanced to one side. "Gotta run. Have a good time at the induction."

Jess grinned. "Thanks. Give my regards to Mari and the kids." Jess leaned back, as she watched him lift his hand in goodbye, and cut the signal off. She pondered the dark screen for a few minutes, thinking.

Jimmy was the only one who took pains to keep in touch. Her other brother, Jake...she wasn't even sure where he was most of the time. Never had any ambition. The last time she'd seen him he was a raker on the coast, and apparently content to stay that way.

When she reached field retirement age, if she did, she'd have the option to take a permanent admin assignment and get married, and have kids.

Jess chuckled wryly at her faint reflection in the screen. She didn't see any of that happening, even if she somehow survived her active phase, but now, with Bain's attention she might possibly end up running something if she did. That would be all right. She could picture herself in Bricker's position, with a lot more savvy and a lot less jackasswardness.

And no Sandy kissing her ass or anything else.

Jess got up and went back to bed, considering her next day's schedule. The halls would be nuts, so maybe she'd show Dev the caverns. Maybe they'd end up in the pool at night again. She got under the covers and stretched out feeling a vague sense of content that was for her quite rare.

She heard the faint sound of movement from next door and turned her head toward the inner portal that separated her quarter's from Dev's, imagining Dev rattling around in the big space, probably settling down in bed much like she was.

She was really starting to like Dev. Aside from her unexpectedly significant skills as a bus driver, she had a gentle and appealing personality that was completely unlike anyone Jess had ever worked with before. Most agents, and even techs, were intolerantly aggressive and ego driven, herself included.

Dev was neither. She had a dry yet pronounced sense of humor, didn't take herself seriously, and her bright and impish smile made it almost impossible to stay in a bad mood around her.

She liked spending time around her. Jess thought about that for a minute. With Joshua, it hadn't quite been like that. It was more like she didn't mind spending time with him. He had been someone she could casually play a board game with, or have a drink while they talked about work.

He hadn't sought out her presence, she hadn't done the same for him. They were compatible in the sense that they could easily mesh on the job and she wasn't irritated by him most of the time. The feeling was completely different than how she felt about Dev.

She wanted to be in Dev's space. She'd almost stopped thinking of her as a bio alt.

Jess studied the ceiling intently. Was she moving toward a place where she might consider trusting Dev? Was the fact that Dev had no choice in any of this making her feel sorry for her? Making her want to protect her? Was Jess's innate sense of honor making a surprising and inconvenient appearance?

"Huh." She let out a small grunt. "Let's just see where it goes." She put the thoughts aside and closed her eyes, rolling over onto her side and tugging the covers snug around her, glad for once to surrender to sleep.

DEV SAT DOWN on the mat in her relaxation area and crossed her legs up under her, leaning her elbows on her knees as she regarded the dimly lit space.

Her body was very tired. After the long session in the gym, and the long session in the pool doing all those unfamiliar things, she felt pleasantly exhausted and she was looking forward to the big comfortable bed downstairs. But first, she wanted to sit and think for a few minutes.

This was something she'd never been able to do. She'd never really had the choice of where to go and what to do, except for those few minutes between class and meals, and lab and sleep.

Now, here in her quarters, she could choose to go downstairs and go to sleep, or sit here and think, or read a page of her book, or even go into the other side of her two level space and run a sim if she wanted to all night long instead of rest.

It was all up to her. The freedom was almost intoxicating.

So though she was tired, she had climbed up into her relaxation area and now she was sitting here on the cushy meditation pad enjoying a bit of peace and quiet just because she could.

She was pretty sure no other bio alts got to do this. The ones in the crèche—certainly not. Dev looked around her space pensively. Here she had the same as any other person in the ops group, an insanity of riches to one of her kind.

So. She figured she had to do a really, really excellent job here at Interforce because she didn't want to go back to being treated like the other bio alts were. Dev felt a little uncomfortable with that, but she also knew it was true.

She'd gotten a taste for what it was like being a natural born, and she liked it. Was that what Doctor Dan was trying to warn her about that night? Maybe it was. But she knew she didn't want to go back to the crèche, or even to be reassigned to a lesser job here.

She wanted this. She wanted to be not only a tech, but the best one here, to do excellent things for Jess, and have Jess come to trust her to do the right thing at the right time and make them both successful. She felt it as a fire in her gut, and it was new and strange, but good.

With a nod, she stretched herself out and lay down on her back, looking up at the rock ceiling with its inset speckles of crystal that were evident in the low, blue light.

They were almost like stars. Dev felt her body relax, and she was able to let go of that determination and think about her day, especially the lessons she'd learned in the pool.

That had been fun. A lot of fun. Not only had she gotten a pretty good idea of how to swim, she'd spent hours with Jess and they chased up and down the pool so many times she could still hear the splash of the water and Jess's low laughter.

When they'd left the gym, it had been completely empty and they'd changed together in a comfortably casual silence before leaving the space and making their way through the quiet halls back to their quarters, but not without a detour to the mess hall for a snack.

Just a fish roll and a cup of kack, but it really hit the spot after all the activity, and especially more so because of the relaxed companionship as they sat in the mess just like any other agent and tech pair. Just like Elaine and Tucker, who gave them a casual wave as they passed through.

Jess. Dev called up a picture in her mind of her next door neighbor. She smiled as she thought about her, aware of a warm, happy emotion that caused. She thought maybe the pool had done Jess's shoulder some good too, because she seemed in less discomfort when they finished, and her mood had improved as the night went on.

All good.

Dev let her thoughts drift a little. Then she sat up, getting to her feet and walking down the steps to the main part of the room. She was already in her sleepwear, and she went to her bed and got under the covers, wondering what the next day would have in store for them.

She only hoped it wouldn't start like the previous day had.

Chapter Twelve

FOR THE FIRST time in a while, Jess woke normally, at her own time. There was no strident alarm, and no soft bong of her timer, just a slow fade from sleep into awareness that left her blinking into the dim light, her body curled into comfort under the covers.

She glanced at the chrono and relaxed, seeing a respectable time that let her stay where she was and enjoy the moment, instead of bouncing out of bed and bolting for the shower as sometimes she had to when she forgot to set the alarm.

She rolled over and stretched her body out, flexing her hands and sighing as she settled into a comfortable position on her back. The room was still mostly dark, the lights embedded in the walls just faintly lit to match what was going on outside.

There was no real beating that circadian rhythm. Jess folded her hands over her stomach. Not that they hadn't tried, and not that she couldn't rig her own for a short while, especially when inserted. But she'd been born in this zone, and given it's preference her body stuck to it.

That turned her mind to Dev. What zone did your body think it was in when you were born on station, whirling around the planet all day long? Did they even have the same rhythms Jess did?

Dev seemed content to wake and sleep when told to, so maybe they'd done something to her that let her adjust without complaint. Or maybe she really did have to adjust, but just didn't bitch about it.

Jess considered that last thought had its merits. Dev wasn't a complainer. Part of that she knew was built in because she was a bio alt, and part she suspected was just how Dev was. At least, she hoped so because it was something she really appreciated in a p...

Jess paused. In a pilot? Sure. She'd told Dev point blank that's all she wanted her to be, just a bus driver. Well that was good. Dev had turned out to be an unexpectedly good bus driver so far, so they both should be very happy.

And yet, there was something in her that didn't like that artificial segregation.

She didn't want a partner. Certainly not a bio alt partner she knew very little about, right? Jess frowned, the words sounding false in her own mental ears because she suspected it wasn't really all that true after the last couple of days.

It just hurt though, thinking of Joshua and that last bitter laughter. She felt embarrassed that she'd been taken like that, even though everyone else had too. She didn't want to risk that happening again, and suffer the shame and the grief of knowing you were so horribly wrong about someone.

It was just too hard. Her stomach felt sick just thinking about it. Wasn't it safer and easier for both her and Dev if she just kept her at arms length? What if Dev flunked out at something, and had to be kicked back to serving bread sticks or washing the floors. Wouldn't it be easier on her if she...

Jess pinched the bridge of her nose. Who in the hell did she think she was fooling? Here she was arguing with her conscience when her ears were already cocked to listen for the first sounds of stirring from beyond that inner door.

A part of her wanted that friendship, no matter what her ego said about it. She wasn't really a natural loner and never had been, enjoying the companionship of first her classmates, and then her fellow agents. Even when she disagreed with them, she liked being part of this closed, eclectic brotherhood.

Jess tapped her navel with the edges of her thumbs. Maybe Dev wasn't structured for that kind of relationship with—what did she call us? Natural borns. She seemed very friendly, but reserved, so maybe she really didn't have a choice after all and she'd have to deal with however Dev was programmed to relate to her.

Jess stretched again, and then pulled the covers aside and got up, passing through her workspace as the lights reacted to her presence and brightened. She keyed the dispenser to provide some kack and touched the ops console comm, nodding a little as the overhead speaker started to echo softly with the current ops chatter.

Nothing sounded out of place. Unlike the previous day, she could only hear standard reports, and the ship comm to two carriers that were on patrol.

Her comm chimed, and she sat down, and keyed it. "Drake."

"Jess, it's Stephan. Listen, I know you really don't want to hear me bugging you again about that speech but I really wish—"

"Okay." Jess propped her chin on her fist. "I'll do it."

"What?" Stephan said. "What did you just say?"

"I said I'll do it. Anything to keep you off my back."

Stephan was silent for a minute. "Really?"

"Really," Jess said. "Anyway, Dev thinks I'm so nice I should greet all the newbies so they feel at home."

Another long moment of silence. "What?" Stephan repeated, more loudly and disbelievingly.

Jess heard a soft tap on her outer door. "Gotta go." She cut the line off and went to the door, checking the sensor, a little surprised to see it was Dev. She palmed it open. "Hey there."

"Hello." Dev had her arms full. "If you thought the mess was crazy last night, you should see it this morning. I grabbed what I could. Want some?"

Jess smiled, and stepped back. "Absolutely. C'mon in." She clapped Dev on the back as she followed her over to her workspace. "Can't think of a better way to start the morning."

Dev looked up from putting down her burden, cocking her head slightly as she regarded Jess with a faintly questioning look.

Jess winked at her and grinned, as she sat down and grabbed a bag meal.

DEV REGARDED HER reflection in the mirror, reaching up to adjust her uniform collar a little. She'd found this new one in her quarters and Jess had told her it was what she was to wear to the induction, and then to the party afterward.

It was more formal looking, and less comfortable. The fabric was heavier, with sedate designs in silver threads along the front of the jacket. She straightened up a little, pulling the sleeves a bit straighter and moving her head as the high collar tickled her neck.

The uniform was a sleeveless jumpsuit and this jacket fit over it. And though it wasn't entirely easy to move around in it, she sort of liked it. She studied her pale hair, caught back in a knot at the back of her head and nodded in satisfaction.

She went over and sat down to pull her boots on. This pair were mid height, and shinier than her regular ones. She fastened them as the inner door slid open.

"Ah." Jess entered, fastening the collar on her own uniform. "I see you're all set."

"Yes." Dev stood up. "That looks really nice on you."

Jess stopped in mid step. "What?" She looked down at herself. "This?"

Dev took a step back and regarded her. "Well, that is what you're wearing. So yes, that." She watched Jess's eyes open wider, unsure of why. The uniform outlined Jess's tall body really well, and her dark hair was loose, framing her face. "Why is my saying that so surprising to you? Is it incorrect?"

Jess's face wrinkled up in sort of a confused grin. "No, it's...um." She let her hands drop. "People don't say stuff like that to me," she said. "Usually." She added in a low mutter.

It was Dev's turn to be confused. "Why not?" She asked. "You're very attractive. Why wouldn't people tell you that?" She cocked her head to one side as she watched Jess blush. "In the crèche, it was always okay to tell others compliments of that kind."

"Um." Jess reached up and rubbed her face. "Thank you," she said. "It's fine. Sorry I'm acting like a nitwit. It's been a long time since..." She paused. "Anyway, if you're ready, let's go. We'll meet the rest of the ops group near the big lift."

"I'm ready," Dev said. "Lead on."

Jess turned and complied. They walked together through her quarters, and out into the hallway, which was now, thankfully, quiet and empty. "Everyone's up there," Jess said. "We're always the last ones to go."

"Why?"

"Tradition mostly, I guess. Everyone goes up in order of their...hm. Well, their ultimate importance to Interforce."

"I see."

"So either we're the most or least important," Jess said, in a droll tone. "I like to flatter myself in thinking the latter."

Dev was pretty sure that was the real truth anyway. She followed Jess as they turned the corner and then crossed the big rotunda. Ahead, she could hear low voices, and as they reached the curve in the hall and went through it, she saw a group of people standing next to one of the big lifts.

It was the other agents and techs, she realized as they got closer. They were standing together and as they approached, the voices stilled. Everyone was dressed like she and Jess were, and there were, she counted, sixteen of them including them both.

"About time," Sandy snarked at Jess. "You stop to blow Bain or something?"

Jess ignored her. "We ready to go up?" She asked Jason. "Someone check in?"

"Almost," Jason said. "They said give it five. Trying to get everyone seated."

A moment later, the light on one side of the lift went on, bathing them in a gentle green glow. "Here we go," Jason said. "Brent, hit the lock, wouldja?"

Brent complied. He stepped back as the big portals opened, revealing a square, utilitarian gray box.

Everyone fell silent. It was awkward, and uncomfortable, and Dev felt like taking a step back from the crowd as they shifted a little. She sensed anger around her, and quite a few of the eyes watching Jess weren't friendly. It was hard to tell though, what exactly the problem was.

After all, Jess was just standing there next to her, with no particular expression on her face, her hands clasped behind her back.

Interesting, but extremely confusing.

Then Jason stepped back and to one side and cocked his head at Jess. "Go on, number one," he said, in an almost anticlimactic way, waving her forward with a casual motion "Clear a path, people."

The discomfort increased, but reluctantly, people moved aside as Jess started forward, some with resigned expressions, some with approving ones, some just angry.

"C'mon." Jess indicated that Dev was to follow.

Dev didn't need to be asked more than once. She stuck to Jess's back as they made their way through the small crowd, and followed her into the lift, their boots making a faintly hollow ring as they crossed the metal floor.

Jess moved to the back, but kept facing the wall. The rest of the group came in after her, filing in with a scuffle of boots and meant to be overheard whispers. She put her hands behind her back again and braced her legs, ignoring it all.

Dev stood quietly next to her, realizing none of the rest of the people in the lift had come even with them. She wasn't entirely sure what was going on, but she could tell there were a lot of mad people, and that something Jess had done had displeased them.

She looked up at Jess's profile, outlined in the harsh white light from the ceiling. There was no emotion there, she merely watched the surface of the wall as they traveled upward. After a moment, Jess looked at her, and winked.

Dev muffled a smile, putting her own hands behind her and waiting in silence.

The elevator reached it's destination, and the doors in front of Jess slowly opened. They now faced into the huge space, which was filled with people, all looking at them, all in the same complete silence.

Dev didn't know where to look first. Near the door they were at were line upon line of bio alts, all in their jumpsuits in various colors. In front of them were natural born, but also in the same kind of jumpsuits. In front of them were techs, and then the admin people.

Near the front she saw Alexander Bain. Standing next to him, to her surprise and pleasure, Doctor Dan. On a low platform at the very end of the space were a big group of people in different clothes.

Some, she recognized. They were from the crèche. Some she didn't, and there were twelve people there in dark gray jumpsuits with either black or green sleeves. She figured those must be the new agents and their techs.

Jess started forward and motioned her to follow.

Dev took a deep breath and did, as they started out and walked down the steps from the lift and into a long, stone aisle that went down the middle of the huge space.

Outside a storm was going on, and there were lightning bursts and thunder, all visible through the transparent walls and roof. It was an eerie counterpoint to the silence of the crowd as they all watched Jess lead the rest of the operations agents and techs through them.

Dev saw the new comers watching them and she straightened up, setting aside her discomfort, and the strangeness of the surroundings. She matched her steps to Jess's as they walked along the aisles, past the bio alts, and the workers, the techs and the administrators as that weird silence beat against them.

Jess walked up the steps to where Bain was standing, coming to a halt next to him and Kurok, as Stephan Bock came up on the other side. She waited for Dev to come up next to her then she turned to face the low platform, letting her arms relax at her sides.

The rest of the ops agents and their partners filed in behind them. As they did, Dev sorted through the positions of the crowd, and the layers of emotion and got a sense of why so many people were glaring at her. She was aware enough of the politics of humanity to understand there was status involved here, and that was always a little uncomfortable.

It had been in the crèche. She'd gone through that sense of discomfort when she'd been singled out in any way for praise, and faced the envy of her crèche mates. There was that sort of thing here. Jess had been singled out, and people were mad because it wasn't them.

Got it. Dev felt a sense of satisfaction, and now she put the issue aside and exhaled in contentment, glad she was standing where she was.

Bain caught her eye and smiled at her. Dev smiled back, then caught Doctor Dan watching her with a proud grin. She wasn't really sure why he was, but it felt good anyway and she stood there quietly at Jess's side, her arms at her sides and her head held high.

Bain waited for a moment more for everything to settle, then he strolled over to the steps and mounted them, arriving at a podium planted on the edge." Well then, people." He rested his hands on the edge of the podium. "Here we are."

He paused, but no one said a word, nor did he seem to expect them to. "I'm quite glad to welcome all of you here." He gestured at the crowd. "And to welcome our newcomers too." He indicated the platform. "I know we've had some difficulties lately, but I think now we're on the right track, and headed in a better direction."

Kurok cleared his throat gently, and visibly suppressed a smile.

Bain raised an eyebrow at him. "At any rate, I'm glad you're all here, and now I'll turn this over to our new senior operations agent, Jess Drake." He stared pointedly at Jess. "Agent Drake?"

Dev felt Jess take a deep breath next to her, and she gave her a smile of encouragement as Jess walked forward and then up the steps to where Bain was standing.

She could see all the newcomers watching her and she suspected if she turned around she would see all the other people watching her too, but Jess merely exchanged nods and places with Bain, leaning against the podium for a long, silent moment.

"So it's a time of new beginnings," Jess said, after that pause. Her voice, low and vibrant, rolled through the chamber and echoed softly. "I've learned the hard way not to live in the past, and you all shouldn't either." She eyed the newcomers. "Don't look back at where you came from, or who you left behind, because every day means something different here."

Bain had stepped to one side, and now he nodded silently.

Jess paused. "If there's anyone here who should be tradition bound, it should be me." She went on. "I'm the eleventh generation of Drakes who've worn this uniform and my brother Jimmy called me last night to tell me my nephew's the twelfth."

The newcomers exchanged glances. "But I figured out recently that tradition buys you nothing," she said. "So do yourselves a favor and keep your eyes open to all the possibilities out there." Briefly, she studied the young faces focused on her. "That's all I have to say. Welcome."

With that, she turned and walked back down to where Dev was, coming to stand next to her and folding her hands in front of her as she stared pointedly at Bain.

"Excellent." Bain didn't miss a beat. "Instead of the long winded blather you'd have gotten from others, we can now perform the induction and start the celebration. Thank you, Drake."

"Sir," Jess said, putting just the slightest drawl on it. She gave Dev a sideways glance, one eyebrow lifting.

Dev grinned at her and carefully imitated her earlier wink.

THE PARTY WAS loud. Dev kept close by Jess's hip as they squeezed their way through the room, toward a place where people were getting drinks. The big space had been rearranged, the podium and platform removed and tables full of food were now appearing on the fringes.

Jess got to the bar and leaned an arm on it. "Gimme a grain straight up and..." She turned to Dev. "What's your poison?"

Dev's brows creased. "No, wait." She held up a hand as Jess started to explain. "Does that mean, what do I want to drink?"

"Yeah."

"Do they have the stuff we had at dinner?"

"And a beer," Jess told the man behind the bar, a bio alt who was staring at Dev intently. "Hey!"

The bio alt jerked and reached for the drinks. "My apologies, agent." He handed Jess a glass and then offered Dev another, taller one.

"Thank you." Dev took the glass. She looked around. "Wow."

"Freaking mess," Jess muttered. "C'mon." She eased past a group of engineers and techs and found an open spot near one wall. "Glad that's over with."

"Are you?" Dev leaned against the wall next to her, watching the crowd go by. "I thought you did great."

Jess half turned and looked at her. "C'mon. Those things are supposed to be an hour long with six pages of notes. I blew them off and everyone knows it."

Dev studied the crowd. "They don't all look unhappy," she said. "And I heard people saying they were really relieved not to have to listen to...um." She paused. "To all the bullshit?" She pronounced the last word carefully. "I think that's what they said."

Jess chuckled wryly. "They did?"

"Yes. What's bullshit?"

"Ah. It's the excrement from a four legged, hoofed cud chewing mammal that no longer exists," she replied. "The male of the species."

Dev looked at her, then she took a sip of her beer and merely shook her head.

"Let's hang out here for a little while," Jess said. "See who comes over and starts trying to suck up to me." She regarded the crowd with an ironic eye. "See if any of the new bios has the guts to come talk to you."

"Agent?" A soft voice interrupted them. "May I take your jacket?"

Jess turned to find a server there, a young bio alt almost her height, with curly red hair. "Sure." She put her drink down on the small table next to them and undid the catches on her jacket, stripping out of it and handing it to him. "Dev?"

Dev had already put her drink down. "Is this usual?" She undid her jacket, as the bio alt patiently waited. "Thank you very much, Ayebee." She handed him the fabric, receiving a real, though brief smile in return. "Have you been downworld long?"

"Six months," Ayebee said. "It's a tough adjustment."

"To some things, yes." Dev picked up her glass. "This." She lifted it.

"Yes." He chuckled. "I will have your garments sent back to your quarters." He gave Jess a nod of respect, then he went on to the next group.

"You know him?" Jess asked, casually.

"That Ayebee?" Dev pondered the question. "I know his set. I trained with a group of them doing rec in the crèche. I don't think I know that specific Ayebee though."

"They all have the same name? I've heard them called all sorts of stuff here."

"They're all Ayebees. A-B." Dev pronounced the letters separately. But they get nicknames sometimes."

"Oh," Jess said. "You don't have that problem."

"No. I'm the only NM-Dev."

"One of a kind."

"Yes," Dev said. "So it seems."

"I like that about you," Jess said, noting the faint blush that was visible despite the low lights. "Do you like it?"

Dev was silent for a while. "I think I'm getting to," she finally said, with a faint grin.

"There you are." Jason appeared next to them, with Brent and Elaine in tow. "Nice speech." He gave Dev a brief smile. "Short and sweet. Half the citadel wants to kill you the other half wants to kiss you."

"Which half are you?" Dev asked, unexpectedly.

Jason paused in mid breath, and stared at her. "What?"

Jess started chuckling. "Which half are you?" She asked Dev, then paused, looking embarrassed.

"Well, I definitely don't want to kill you," Dev said, after just a little too long a pause, as their eyes met.

Jason apparently caught his breath and plowed ahead. "Anyway. Bain's happy. No one else matters." He clapped Jess on the shoulder. "Sandy decided to take a bottle to her quarters and get drunk, so you don't have to worry about her jackass tongue tonight. Ready to dance?"

Jess was still looking at Dev's face. "Sure," she muttered. "I'm ready for anything."

"Great." Jason turned and stood on his toes. "Hey, they finally got the grub out. I'll grab some. Brent, stay here."

Brent took up a spot against the wall next to Dev, folding his muscular arms over his chest and watching the crowd with a skeptical frown.

Dev leaned next to him, sipping her beer. After a minute she turned and looked at Jess, and smiled, getting a smile back as Jess lifted her mug and both eyebrows at her.

"HERE YOU GO." Jess took a seat on the ledge next to Dev, handing her a plate of assorted goodies and then setting her cup down.

Jason and Elaine, and Brent and Tucker were ranged on either side of them, holding an informal court as a long parade of people came up to say hello.

Dev was happy to sit quietly and watch, kept well supplied with treats from Jess's frequent escapes through the crowd. They were on one end of the big room, in the curve, with the transparent panels providing a colorful backdrop as the storm continued to rage.

She had her legs pulled up crossed under her, with a plate balanced on one knee, and was fully occupied in listening to Jess talk to the other agents as she kept an eye on people approaching from her peripheral vision.

There was a lot of conflicting emotion going on. But Jess seemed to be in a pretty good mood, so she supposed the party was going well.

The food was good, and she was enjoying it. She and Brent had traded fish rolls, since he preferred the ones with the crunchy seaweed in them and she liked the other kind, and she had spent some time talking to him about the work she was doing on the carrier.

He liked that sort of thing too, so now he was explaining about how he tweaked the engine torque on his vehicle and she was wondering if she could try doing that on hers. On theirs, she mentally corrected herself, since the carrier really was assigned to Jess.

Jess was sitting side by side with her, and their shoulders were pressed against each other. Since their shoulders were both bare, it was a warm and pleasant sensation she was very much enjoying, just as she had enjoyed their banter earlier.

It made her feel good to think that Jess was beginning to trust her a little, enough to joke around. Dev knew that was rare, both between bio alts and definitely between bios and natural born, but she liked it. She thought about what she'd asked Jason, and then what Jess had asked her, and it made her smile.

She definitely didn't want to kill anyone, but especially not Jess. Bio alts didn't do that. Of course, she really didn't have any idea what kissing her would be like either but since she thought Jess was quite attractive, and she liked her, she supposed it would be an all right thing to do.

"Ah, here they come." Jason nudged Jess. "The kids finally scraped up the guts to come meet you."

"Would you stop it? I've got enough crap to deal with."

"C'mon Jess. Enjoy it for a change." Jason waved the newcomers forward. "You earned the bump. No one gave it to you," he said. "Screw that bitch Sandy and her buddies. They're just farting jealousy in three colors."

Jess regarded the new agents and their partners dourly. They all seemed ridiculously young to her, all slim and leanly muscled, with short cropped hair and cleanshaven faces.

Of the agents, four were men, and two were women. All of the techs were men, but that wasn't unusual. Two of the male agents had dark hair, two had light, and both women had brown hair and looked like each other.

Very average.

The tallest of the men came forward. His name plate said Arias, M and he had a quiet self possession. "Agent Drake, I just wanted to compliment you on your speech."

Jess eyed him wryly. "Yeah? If you blinked, you missed it," she said. "Maybe I'll get lucky and they won't ask me again."

"Remember when Bricker did it last year?" Jason said. "Kept us standing there for an hour and a half. Bastard."

"Well, if that's the case, I'm glad I inducted today." Arias half turned. "This is my partner Chester." He motioned forward a tech standing just behind him. "He's a west coaster."

"Hey there, Chester." Jason lifted his glass. "So am I. Rainer Islander."

Chester produced a grin. "My uncle lives there. He likes it."

"This is Elaine Cruz, and her partner Tucker." Jason went on. "This is my partner, Brent." He paused, then glanced at Jess, raising one eyebrow.

For a moment, Jess stared back at him impassively, then she looked at the new agent. "I guess you already know who I am," she said. "This is my partner, Dev." She tilted her head in Dev's direction. Then she went back to munching on a seaweed fish wrap.

Jason chuckled. "That didn't take long."

"Shut up."

Dev looked over at Jess with a startled expression. Then she recovered, and cleared her throat. "Hello." She greeted the agent. "Nice to meet you. Welcome to the citadel."

"Mike." The agent stuck a hand out and smiled when Dev shook it. Then he turned and motioned the other new agents forward.

Dev took the opportunity of the distraction to look back over at Jess, who, after a moment, lifted her eyes to meet hers. After a brief moment, Jess shrugged a little. "Hell," she said. "I can't go on calling you my bus driver if you keep saying nice things about me, now can I?"

Dev smiled happily as the other new agents came up in front of them. She turned to face them, finding herself looking at one of the new female agents. "Hello."

"You're the bio alt?" The woman asked.

"Yes," Dev said cordially. "NM-Dev-1." She took a quick sideways look as she felt Jess shift, and became aware that her attitude had shifted, from casual to alert, her pale blue eyes fixed on the newcomer. "Is that a good or bad thing for you?"

The woman seemed caught offguard. "Um..." She lifted her hands a bit and let them drop. "I don't know, really. We just heard about it when we were heading out here," she said. "I'm April." She extended her hand. "Did you say... Dev?"

"Yes," Dev said, shaking her hand. "Welcome." She felt Jess relax and turn her attention back to her plate, which was nearly empty.

"So is it true you got all your stuff in a week?" The brown haired man next to her asked. "I'm Doug," he added. "April's mule."

"Doug." The woman gave him a look.

Jess gave them both an approving look, but didn't interrupt.

"That's not exactly true," Dev said. "I had my basic instruction starting when I was five, and went to advanced school when I was twelve. So I've been learning a long time. I did get a big dose of programming before I came here, but that was mostly all the tech stuff I needed to do my job."

"Not so different from us," April said.

"No, not at all," Jess said. "I didn't think a bio alt would work, but Dev proved me wrong," she said, in a matter of fact tone. "Uncomfortable as that is for all of us. It is, what it is."

"I don't think I've proved that yet," Dev said. "I've only done one mission with you."

"Did you know they've been playing the recorder file of that one mission in the rec center for the last two days?" Jess asked, her brows lifting.

Dev blinked. "No, I didn't. Why would they do that?"

"And she's modest too," Jess said to the assembled agents, who chuckled softly. "That's what I meant about going with change. I thought this was going to be crap. I was wrong." She regarded Dev. "Who knows? Maybe we won't need a thirteenth generation of Drakes doing this."

"You really want that?" Mike asked. "It was my ticket to school. Rest of my family harvests grubs, and half of them can't read."

"Mine too," Jess said. "The ones who don't get taken to Interforce, that is. I've got a brother raking weed, and another doing recap for the processing station downhill." She extended her arms, and the light hit them, showing the burned in sigils. "But every dot's a dead body on these."

A silence fell, and the new agents exchanged glances.

Jess turned her arms over, since the sigils went around in a band. "Clear means stalemate. Green means we won. Red means they won." She looked dispassionately at her skin. "Yellow diamond means I ended up in med."

Dev examined her arms intently, since some of this code was new to her.

"Maybe it would be better to have them do it," Jess said, after she let the silence go on for a moment. "Most of us don't survive to forty."

"Wow." Mike finally said.

"Don't tell ya that stuff in field school, huh?" Jason smiled thinly "They didn't when I went through." He hopped off the ledge and stretched his arm out next to Jess's. Despite his greater height, their fingertips matched, though the burned sigils only went halfway down his arms just past his elbows.

Elaine circled to come up on his other side, showing her own. "People will talk crap here." She said to the newcomers. "But this tells the real story."

Dev watched intently, seeing the young faces that surrounded them absorbing the information. She felt that they were a little ambivalent about her, but that was okay. She hadn't gotten the outright antagonism she'd sensed from Sandy and her partner, or the two other older agents she hadn't been introduced to.

She reached over and touched Jess's arm, running her fingers over one of the more intricate sigils, which also had a prominent yellow mark on it. To her surprise, she watched goosebumps rise beneath her fingers and she looked up to find Jess watching her. "Was that a bad trip to med?"

"Broke my back," Jess said. "So yeah." She looked down at the mark, which bore six green roundels. "They kept me in a fuser for a week, and then in a pin rack for two more. I'd rather have died."

Dev grimaced. "Well, I'm glad you didn't."

The sound of clapping drew all of their attention. "Enough war stories, people." Bain was standing nearby. "Go dance and have fun for a change. Tomorrow's soon enough to be serious." He waved them all toward the open area, and as he did, music started playing.

Jess made no move to stand. Jason and Elaine exchanged glances, and then Jason held his hand out. "Shall we? Show the kids how it's done?"

"You're on," Elaine said, and they walked through the crowd as others moved along as well, and the music picked up in both pace and loudness. "C'mon, kids."

The newcomers shuffled, and then trailed after them, as the lights went down to a lower dimness, and that only let the lightning overhead become more prominent.

Jess and Dev were left at the ledge, everyone else obeying Bain's orders.

Jess turned her head and studied her companion. "Do you dance?"

Dev tore her eyes from the dance floor and returned the regard. "I have absolutely no idea what that is," she said. "It looks like they're walking across a very hot floor with no shoes on."

Jess laughed. "Yeah, I'm not much for it either. I'm too self conscious, I think. I'm always aware of how stupid I look flopping around like a fish out of water there."

"Are you a fish out of water here?" Dev asked. "You seem different than the rest of them."

Jess looked up, with a startled expression. "I belong here," she stated flatly. "Are you saying I don't?"

Oh no. Dev felt immediate distress. "I'm sorry," she said. "I didn't mean to be incorrect." She slid off the ledge and faced Jess, her brow creased. "I'm very sorry."

Jess responded to the near panic in her voice, her anger dissolving as she put her hand on Dev's shoulder. "Hey. Take it easy. It was just a weird question, that's all."

Dev studied her with a worried expression. "It's just that you've been so..." She paused, unsure of whether to continue. "I don't want you to be angry. I meant that in a good way."

Jess leaned on her elbows, clasping her hands together. It was almost dark in the room, save the dance lights, and it gave her an illusion of privacy. "Maybe I've always been a little weird," she admitted. "No matter how much history my family has of this."

"You're not weird," Dev said, automatically. "You just see so much more than they do. They're so...um..." She paused again. "Not as deep as you are."

Oh. Jess sorted through that, detecting that it was, in fact, something positive. "Sorry I freaked you out."

"Excuse me?"

Jess chuckled wryly. "You hit a sensitive spot of mine," she said, in a low tone. "I've always been a rebel. They all know it. That's why so many of them are pis...are mad that I got senior."

"Oh." Dev slowly eased herself back up onto the ledge, her heartbeat starting to settle.

"I've never done things the right way," Jess said. "I always did what I thought was best, not what I was told. I've been in trouble more times than..." She sighed. "I embarrassed the hell out of my father. He was such a regulation stickler." She paused. "I wondered if I should change my name so he didn't have to hear it from everyone when I screwed up."

Dev put a hand on her arm. "I'm sorry. I really didn't mean to upset you."

"I know." Jess pulled one long leg up and wrapped her arms around it. "No way for you to know about all that stuff. We've only known each other for what—three days? Four?" She looked sideways at Dev. "It's fine, Dev. It's a good question, and I don't mind talking to you about it."

Dev nodded, and kicked her heels against the ledge a couple times. "To tell the truth," she said, after a long pause. "I think I know I'm different too. "Maybe it's because I'm a dev model. But I was always really aware of being—I think you called it a one off."

"Good or bad?" Jess asked.

Dev thought about that for a long time in silence. "When I became aware of it, I guess I was around ten or so, it was a really lonely thing to think about. None of us has any family. But at least everyone else had their set mates and I remember being at a celebration, sort of like this." She indicated the room. "And I realized I was the only one of my kind there who was alone."

"Mm." Jess grunted softly, deep in her throat.

"It was uncomfortable."

"I bet." Jess looked around the room, watching all the moving bodies and hearing the laughter and music. Then she turned her head back toward Dev. "Wanna go steal a tray of brownies and go for a swim?"

Dev looked back at her and grinned. Then she indicated the room. "This is all a little much for me." She admitted. "I'm not used to it."

"Don't need to tell me twice." Jess slid off the ledge and waited for Dev to join her. Then she put her hand on Dev's back and guided her toward one of the walls. "I know a secret way," she said. "And it passes right by the prep area for the kitchen."

They left the noise and the celebration behind them, as Jess scanned open an unmarked black door and they passed through into a bare, utilitarian hallway. As the door closed, it cut off all the clamor like a knife.

"Oh." Dev looked behind them, as silence took the place of the chaos.

"Soundproof door," Jess said, leading the way to an equally unmarked lift door, which accepted her palm scan without complaint. "Not many people know about this back route." She waited for the lift to open, then stepped inside. After Dev joined her, she keyed a command on the inside panel and the door slid shut.

It opened again, at the lower level, but inside the medical area. Jess strolled through the pristine halls, keeping her eyes forward and not looking into the exam rooms on either side. She debated telling Dev why she knew the back way, then decided against it.

Hopefully, she would never have to witness the situation that elevator was there for.

Chapter Thirteen

THE GYM WAS silent and half dark, and the water was again soothingly warm. Jess carefully spread her arms out along the wall, just relaxing in the liquid and glad of the relative quiet around her.

Relative, because Dev was paddling around idly, practicing her swimming.

Jess watched her unobtrusively. Despite her concentration, she could sense Dev was distracted, the expression on her face thoughtful and somewhat withdrawn. She wondered if Dev was still worried about upsetting her. "Hey."

Dev looked up. "Yes?"

"C'mere." Jess crooked a finger at her.

Obediently, Dev swam in her direction, her body already moving with burgeoning assurance through the water. "Damn." Jess sighed. "I sure wish I could learn that fast."

"What?" Dev reached her and grabbed the edge of the wall, since the bottom was below her reach.

"You're already picking up swimming," Jess said. "I said I wish I could learn like that. And that wasn't anything that was programmed, was it? That's how you learn?"

Dev paused in the water, her eyes going a little unfocused. "I never really thought about that," she said. "But I guess it is. We're conditioned to learn. It's good when you have programming for something, but sometimes you don't and you need to be able to do it anyway."

"Like what you did in the carrier, evading the bad guys."

"Yes."

"I'd say that's a damn good thing," Jess said. She moved along the wall, bumping Dev a little until they were shallow enough for her to stand. "Thanks for indulging me in being an antisocial sourpuss."

That made Dev smile. "The party was okay. But I think it is going to take me a while to get used to things like that. When we had them in the crèche, there weren't any drinks involved and no...uh...dancing."

"Probably why they didn't call it a party."

"Yes, that's true. It was always called a gather, or a gathering. We did get treats sometimes though. Candy balls, or a bit of cake."

"You like that stuff."

Dev nodded, visibly more cheerful. "They told us it wasn't good for us, but yes, I do," she said. "I think you do too."

Jess licked her lips. "The whole tray of brownies clue you in to that?" She laughed. "I'll probably be sick tomorrow from it but I don't care. It was worth it." She paused. "Another one of my faults. I live for the moment." Her eyes went to Dev's face, watching the subtle tension relax.

Ah. That made her feel better. "I think the kids took to you all right," she said. "Better than I thought."

"I don't think they made up their minds yet," Dev said. "They seemed to want to be friendly though."

"They did," Jess said. "Jason was right. I pissed off half the room and at least didn't alienate the other half." She turned and leaned against the wall, stretching her shoulder out. "But at least they got to meet you and interact before some of the other assholes got to them over breakfast."

Dev leaned her back against the wall and folded her arms over her chest. "I don't think Jason was in the part that wanted to kill you, by the way," she said.

Jess half turned and regarded her. "No, and you either apparently."

Dev hesitated, then turned her head and met Jess's eyes, a very faint smile appearing on her face. "You didn't really think I would be, did you?"

"No." Jess managed a small smile of her own. "I'm not the most social person out there but I didn't figure you hated me."

"I don't," Dev said. "I like you very much." She paused and thought. "I did wonder, though, what it would be like to kiss you."

Jess blinked. "You did?"

"Yes."

Live in the moment, isn't that what she said she did? Jess didn't stop to think, even for a second. "Okay." She turned and leaned over, tilting her head slightly to one side and kissing Dev on the lips, completely unprepared for the jolt in her guts and the instant and powerfully sensual wash that sent tingles to every inch of her body.

She meant it to only last a second, but it went on longer than that, until a door slammed in the distance. She drew back to find Dev staring at her, eyes round and astonished. "Uh." Jess croaked out, then fell silent

"That," Dev finally said, on an unsteady breath. "Was not at all what I expected."

Jess was finding it a little hard to catch her own breath. "Me either." She eventually muttered. "What in the hell did I just do?"

"Well if you don't know, I definitely don't." Dev muffled a short laugh. "But wow did that ever surprise me."

Jess folded her arms over her chest and rested her head back against the wall, feeling the unsteady race of her heartbeat thundering in her ears. "Yeah."

They looked at each other. Another door slammed in the distance and Jess looked up, and then back at Dev. "Not sure what's going on. Maybe we should get out."

"Okay," Dev said. "Maybe we should."

They were both silent for a moment more, then Jess started laughing, shaking her head and plowing through the water toward the steps. Dev let herself sink down into the water and swam after her, using the casual motion to give her time to stop...shaking? Her body felt very, very strange.

DEV CLOSED HER locker, aware of Jess's closing presence behind her. She turned just as she arrived and smiled. "That was nice." She said.

"It was," Jess said. "C'mon back to my place. We'll share a cup of mead."

Dev nodded, happy to deposit her damp towel into the dispenser with Jess's and follow along. She found herself still thinking about the kissing thing. That had been—very—interesting. She hadn't expected it to feel like it had and if she concentrated she could still sort of feel how it felt on her lips.

"Dev?"

"Huh?" Dev jerked a little, looking up to find Jess looking at her in bemusement. "Um...sorry."

"You okay?"

Was she? Dev wasn't entirely sure what she was at the moment. "I think so," she said. "Maybe I'm just a little tired. That was a long session in the gym today."

"Yeah, it was," Jess said. "Reminded me again of how little time I've been spending in there lately." She rubbed her bare arms with her hands. "Too much time spent in med instead."

"Is your back all right?" Dev asked.

"Yeah. It's okay." Jess twisted her body cautiously. "Just out of condition a little. Wish they had a pill or an instant program for that, I'll tell ya."

Dev smiled. "Me too. It's a lot of hard work." She looked around at the empty halls. "Is the party still going on?"

Jess had been watching the ground as she walked. "Huh?" She cocked her head. "Oh. Yeah. Right. The party." She pinched the bridge of her nose. "I don't care. Maybe. You want to go back to it?" She looked at Dev who was shaking her head side to side definitively. "Right. I should check met, I guess. See when that window's going to happen. How's the carrier?"

Dev blinked at the onslaught of rambling details. "Ah." She sorted through them. "We did some very good work today and Clint was going to finish the engines tonight. I think it will be ready tomorrow at some time."

"Great." They reached Jess's quarters and she scanned in and they walked inside. Jess halted after a few steps and stood still, her eyes sweeping the room. "Hold it."

Dev stopped and waited.

After a minute, Jess relaxed. "Ah. They just brought the jackets back." She pointed at the chair, where two sets of them were draped. She walked over to them and lifted hers, then handed Dev the other one. "Might as well get out of your monkey suit."

Dev looked at the jacket, then at her.

"Just another saying." Jess tossed her jacket back over the chair back, stepping over to where Dev was standing and reaching out to gently ruffle her hair. "You don't look like a monkey," she said. "Go on and change and then we'll sit down and have a glass of mead together."

She watched Dev smile, then turn and walk over to the door, pausing to let it open and then going through, noting consciously the clean lines of Dev's body and how well proportioned she was. Then she took in a breath and released it, going over to her uniform cabinet and opening it.

Jess put the jacket away and unsealed the catches on her sleeveless jumpsuit, peeling it off her body and setting it onto its holder. Then she paused and regarded her reflection in the mirror mounted in the back of the cabinet, scowling a little at what she saw.

That made her frown, and shake her head. She grabbed a set of shorts and a tank and put them on. What the hell did she care what she looked like? It mattered only in the field sometimes, and then she had her clothes on and looked all right.

Outsiders didn't see the scars. Hell, most insiders never saw them.

She went to the sanitary unit and ran a brush through her hair, which was almost dry after her swim. She met the somber regard of her own eyes in the smaller mirror, her thoughts going back to the pool.

Going back to that kiss.

Damn she'd enjoyed that. Jess stared at her reflection. She closed her eyes as she felt the sensation again, the faint, surprised reaction from Dev, and then, unmistakably, her response. Hard to say really which one of them was more freaked out.

Might have been her. Dev seemed surprised and interested, but that was all. Did bio alts kiss up on station? Or anywhere? Jess was a little bemused to find herself very much wondering about that. Did she want to kiss Dev again?

Hm.

Did Dev want to kiss her again? Probably not. She probably was sitting down in her workspace right now and keying it up on her pad to find out what it all was about.

With a sigh, she turned and went back into her main area, just as the inner door opened and Dev came in, holding a box. "What's that?"

"I was kind of hoping you'd tell me." Dev came over and set the box down. She was also in shorts and a tank, and barefoot. "I found it in my space."

Jess examined it thoughtfully. "It's one of the boxes our nav modules come in," she said. "I'm guessing no one sent you a nav module." She gently opened the box, tipping the top back and exposing the contents. She and Dev peered inside, almost bumping their heads together.

For a moment they regarded the contents in mutual silence. Then Jess reached in and picked up a sample, bringing it out and into the light. "Ah."

"What are those?" Dev asked.

"Seashells," Jess said. She handed over the specimen, an oblong item with a tan and orange pattern on it. "I think you have an admirer." She wasn't sure if she should be amused or pissed off. To have someone send this sort of crap to an ops tech—

"This is interesting." Dev was turning the shell over in her fingers. "What does it mean?"

Well, most techs were men. Jess eyed her new partner. Most of them weren't charming young women. "It means someone likes you, and sent you that because they thought you would like it, and by extension like them. It's a present."

Dev's brow creased. She tilted her head and looked at Jess, visibly confused.

Jess went to her small cabinet and took the mead and glasses out. She crooked a finger at Dev and then went to the steps up to her relaxation area, climbing up them and entering the quiet space.

Dev followed her, carrying the box.

Jess filled the glasses and put the bottle down on the small, low table, then sat down on the comfortable couch and waited for Dev to join her before she handed over her glass. "Here."

"Thank you." Dev leaned back and seemed to relax. "Could you explain this present thing?" She indicated the box. "I don't really understand it."

Jess took a long swallow of her mead, and let it slide down her throat. "Well," she said. "Um..." She looked sideways at Dev. "What do bio alts do when they like someone?"

Dev had to really think about that, so she took her time and did. What was Jess actually asking her? She cast her mind back over her life in the crèche, and tried to imagine just giving something to someone to make them like her. Would she do that? Had she? "What exactly do you mean by like?" She finally asked.

Jess's lips twitched. "Didn't you have any friends up there? People you hung out with? That you wanted to do something for, just because?"

Dev stared into the glass she was holding between her hands, her eyes a little unfocused. Then she took a sip. "I don't think I did," she said, after a long pause. "I had daymeal sometimes with Gigi. We talked about things but I never wanted to do anything for her except maybe hold the disposal door open when she had to put her tray in."

"That's not really what I meant."

"No I didn't think so," Dev said. "Oh, wait. Is it like when I was in the mess this morning, and saw all the people? I thought about how you wouldn't like it so I thought it would be nice if I brought you something?"

"Well..." Jess made a face. "Sort of."

"Is it like this?" Dev held up her glass. "You do nice things for me." She looked up at Jess, with a serious expression. "Do you do that because you like me?"

It was almost a disruptive honesty. Jess bit her tongue as she had the oddest sensation of momentarily losing control over her body, and quite possibly her mind at the same time. "I...um." She felt warmth come over her and realized she was blushing.

What the hell? "Sure. I mean, yes." She regained control over her ability to communicate somewhat. "I think you're...um." Jess found those curious and interested green eyes studying her. "Hey you're my partner. I'm supposed to do stuff for you."

Dev studied her glass again, a faint, wistful smile appearing on her face. "Oh," she murmured. "Well, I'm glad about that. But I was sort of hoping maybe you were being nice just because." She took a sip, holding the snifter between her hands. "That would be an interesting thing to experience."

Jess was caught flatfooted again. She had no idea what to say to that, or what to do about the sort of forlorn expression on Dev's face. It made her stop and think again. "I'm...um...not really..." She paused. "I w...want to be nice to you." She stuttered a bit. "I don't have to be. I don't want you to think I do things because I..." She let the words trail off, not really sure what she was trying to say.

"Because you want me to like you?" Dev offered, softly. "You don't have to. I do like you. I like you just because, and it made me feel good to bring you stuff from the mess. So I think I get that now."

"Oh." Jess felt intense relief. "Good."

"But it really doesn't explain this." Dev put the glass down, and picked up the box of shells. "Why would someone send these to me? I don't know anyone else here but you."

"Oh." Jess set her glass down next to Dev's and took the box. "I think Clint sent these to you," she said. "I think he wants to get to know you better."

"Ah."

Jess was very glad they'd jumped subjects. "Back in the day, when someone was interested in someone else, and wanted to get to know them better, they sent them a nice present. Usually flowers."

"We had those at the crèche," Dev said. "But no one was allowed to send them to anyone."

"These are the new flowers." Jess held up the shell. "So Clint's saying he's interested in getting to know you."

Dev leaned back on the couch and folded her hands in her lap, regarding her companion thoughtfully. "Wouldn't it be more productive for him just to ask me?"

Jess shrugged. "Do you want him to?"

"No."

"Oh." Jess put the box down.

"I think he's pleasant and funny, but I don't want to get to know him any better," Dev said. "I enjoy working with him, but I don't think I would enjoy doing this with him." She picked up her glass and drank from it. "So what do you think I should do about these..." She picked up one of the shells and examined it curiously. "...things?"

"I'll take care of it," Jess said, in a quiet tone. "Don't worry about it, Dev."

"Thanks." Dev smiled at her. "That's very nice of you."

Jess found herself smiling back. She picked her glass up and looked at it. "Do you like doing this?" She indicated it.

"I like spending time with you," Dev said. "You make me feel human."

Disruptive honesty. Jess felt her jaw drop a little, as she tried to process that with sufficient intent to come up with a response that was other than a splutter. She looked at Dev, feeling just a little short of breath, feeling her eyes blink repeatedly.

"Are you all right?" Dev asked, after a long moment. "You seem to be in some discomfort. Was that incorrect for me to say?"

"No." Jess put her glass down and reached over to put her hand on Dev's shoulder. "I think it was a huge damn compliment. Probably more than you know." She felt the weird tension she'd been feeling relax and she smiled. "You make me feel human, too."

Dev studied her for a minute, then smiled back.

"So." Jess released her, and leaned back. "Let's find something less weird to talk about."

"Okay. Could you tell me about this mission thing?" Dev amiably went with the subject change. "Where are we going? What's it going to be like?"

Jess picked up a control on the table and pointed it at a screen embedded in the wall. "Lemme show ya," she said. "I don't usually ask people up here to see my etchings, y'know."

"Oh. Well, thanks." Dev slid a little closer, as the screen lit. "Thats very nice of you."

"When you see how bad I etch, you'll change your mind."

"What exactly is an etching?"

DEV HADN'T CHANGED her mind. She had completely enjoyed seeing Jess's sketches of the places they would be going, and even more, she'd enjoyed hearing Jess talk about them.

Now she was in her bed, curled up under the covers and in a state of almost profound bemusement. She felt strange, and warm, and like she wanted to giggle. She really didn't know why, except that she was having a hard time thinking of anything except Jess.

Well, she supposed that was natural. A lot of things had happened to them today, from their rough and ready meal in the morning, to the ceremony, to the party, to swimming to...well, the whole kissing thing, and then the mead and all that.

Tomorrow night they would finally go on their mission. Jess had told her they would spend several days on it, and might even have to sleep in the carrier while it was going on.

She found that thought very interesting.

Jess had also told her they would pass through at least one of the big strongholds where many people lived, and get a chance to see what that was like, and then go to a very remote place where she would meet with the fishermen she wanted to travel to the bad guys with.

It all sounded good. The mission itself, and the danger she thought Jess was trying to make small, still worried her a lot. But the parts around it were getting her excited, and she had to admit she was looking forward to getting in the carrier and going off to do it.

It would take a lot of hard work to get the carrier ready in time, but she was confident they could do it.

That made her think about Clint. She wondered about the box of shells. It was hard to decide if that was a good thing he'd done or not a good thing, though she thought maybe he thought it was good. He seemed like a nice person, and she didn't think he was trying to get something from her, but Jess seemed to think maybe he was.

She wasn't sure what the something was. Jess had gotten all flustered again when she'd asked, there at the end after they'd found themselves talking about it again so she'd just dropped the subject.

She thought it was really cute when Jess got like that. There was something really sweet and nice about it, since usually Jess was so strong and self possessed. It would be excellent if she knew why simple straightforward questions seemed to evoke that, but she supposed eventually she'd figure it out.

Dev curled her arms around her pillow and exhaled in contentment. It had been such a good day. She was trying to decide which had been the best part of it. Jess saying they were partners, or that kissing thing.

She was so proud about the partner thing. She'd looked the word up when she'd finally left Jess's quarters and found the description to be very good. It said Jess wanted to continue working with her. Maybe it meant Jess was starting to trust her in a way she hadn't expected since she didn't think she'd done much to earn that trust yet.

So that was excellent.

But, now, that kissing thing.

That was pretty interesting too. Dev had, of course, had her basic biology class and she knew all about that. They'd studied the science of reproduction in her advanced level classes, though it wasn't anything any of them would ever expect to know in person since they did things to them to make them not have babies. So there was no point in the rest of it, according to the lessons.

She remembered talking after class, and everyone wondering what the big deal was and why the natural born were so fixated about it.

What she hadn't known was what it would be like, and how interesting it made her body feel. She hadn't felt like that during the class, nor after, but if she closed her eyes and thought about it now, about that touch on her lips, she felt that feeling again, and she really liked it.

She had wanted to ask Jess if they could try that again, but it had gotten late, and she could see Jess was tired. So she saved that for another day, and she figured maybe they could talk about it on the flight.

Jess had said there would be a market in the stronghold they'd visit. Dev closed her eyes and smiled. That would be interesting and she was looking forward to it.

Maybe she'd be able to find Jess a present.

IT TURNED OUT, the next morning, that Dev ended up handling the Clint issue herself. After a very early breakfast she'd gone to the carrier bay, and got to work right off helping get her vehicle ready. She was inside the carrier, lying on the floor with her head inside a console when she heard steps on the ladder and peeked out to see Clint enter.

He came right over and sat down on the floor next to her, crossing his legs and resting his elbows on his knees. "Hi."

"Hello." Dev shifted so her head was in view. "Good morning."

"Listen, I have something to explain to you," Clint said. "I did something but I didn't really think it through, so I wanted to apologize."

Ah. Interesting. "Do you mean the box?" Dev asked.

Clint nodded, blushing a little. "I just thought it would be something you'd like. I didn't think about how new you were, or that... I mean maybe it wasn't something you were used to."

"Because I'm a bio alt?"'

"Uh...something like that."

"I'm not used to it. I had no idea what that was. Jess had to explain it to me." She watched his face tense into a grimace at her partner's name.

Her partner's name. That threw Dev right off her intent and she had to wrestle her attention back with a surprising amount of effort. "I thought the shells were really interesting. I would like to know more about them, but you don't have to send me things to prompt me to talk to you."

Clint blushed a deeper shade of red.

"I'm not really comfortable with all that yet," Dev said in a serious tone. "I got a lot of programming about tech and this." She pointed at the console. "But not very much about how to deal with natural born people."

"Ah." Clint cleared his throat. "Well, sure. That makes a lot of sense. Was Jess pissed off?"

Pissed off. Pissed off. "Was she angry? No, I don't think so." She shook her head. "She didn't sound angry. She said she would talk to you about it."

Clint went a little pale now. "Okay, well, I guess I should get back to work. Anyway...ah, thanks for understanding. Maybe we can just talk sometimes."

"Clint?" Dev edged a little further out. "May I ask you a question?"

"Uh. Sure."

"Why are you so afraid of Jess?"

Clint stared at her for a long, long moment. "Yeah I guess they didn't tell you that much about things, huh?" He said. "Just don't get on her bad side. That's all I'll say." He got up and dusted his coveralls off. "Maybe you should get your...uh...whatever those people are to fill you in a little. "

"You mean a proctor?" Dev asked. "I don't think I can do that but maybe I can ask someone else about it."

Clint froze, then whirled, as a figure entered the carrier. "Hey! Who the hell are you coming in here?" He put himself between the figure and Dev.

"Doctor Dan!" Dev crawled out from her position and sat up. "It's okay, Clint. This is Doctor Dan. He brought me here from the crèche."

"Sorry." Clint edged around the newly installed gunner's couch and got to the door. "Talk to you later, Dev." He scrambled down the steps, leaving them quickly behind.

Dev started to get up, but then sat back down when Doctor Dan waved her back, coming over to sit down on the deck next to her. "Good morning, Dev. Did you like the party last night?"

"It was okay," Dev said. "It was a little strange for me. But it was all right."

"It's a lot to get used to," Kurok said. He was dressed in a plain, dark jumpsuit, with no markings or insignia at all. It contrasted with his pale hair and he seemed comfortable in it. "There were a lot of things going on last night. I wanted to know if you needed me to explain anything to you."

"I think it was okay," Dev said. "But I would like you to explain to me about kissing."

Kurok blinked, his eyes going a little wider. "About what?" He asked, in a very startled tone.

"Kissing." Dev repeated. "I know what we got in school, but I think they left out some details."

Kurok laughed gently, lifting one hand to cover his eyes. "I'm sorry, Dev," he said. "I never anticipated having to discuss this particular subject with one of you." He looked at her. "In fact, a very dear friend of mine would be laughing so hard we couldn't hear ourselves think if he'd been here for it."

"I"m sorry," Dev said. "Was it incorrect to ask?"

"No." Kurok leaned against the console, extending his legs across the carrier deck. "It's never wrong to ask questions, Dev. Even if it's uncomfortable for someone to answer them." He folded his hands together. "Are you asking me this because you want to try it, or because you have?"

"I have," Dev said. "I mean, I did. One time."

"And you want to do it again." This wasn't quite a question, and Doctor Dan was giving her one of his sweet, gentle smiles.

"Yes." Dev smiled back at him. "I really liked it."

Kurok sighed. "Where do I start," he muttered to himself. "I think we need to talk more than once about this, Dev, and I know you have a mission you're going on this afternoon. So let me ask you this first, was it the gentlemen who just left that you kissed?"

"No. It was Jess."

Kurok studied her for a long moment in utter silence. "I see," he finally said. "Did she ask you to do this, Dev?"

Dev shook her head. "No, I asked her. I wondered what it would be like, and said that, and she said okay and kissed me. I liked it." She wasn't really sure how Doctor Dan felt about it all, he was acting a little funny, and now, something else must have happened because he was trying hard not to laugh. "Was it incorrect?"

Kurok rubbed his face. "No," he said. "It's not incorrect. Well, not in that sense, Dev. There are rules...oh, well, not really rules more customs," he said. "That natural born people here know they are not supposed to make biological alternatives do things like that when they don't want to."

"I wanted to."

"Yes, I understand." Kurok's eyes were now gravely twinkling. "You asked her to do that."

"Yes."

He was quiet for a little bit. "It's not unknown, in this service, for people who are working very closely together to want to do things like that," he said. "The most important thing is, that it be something that both people want to do, and not feel like they have to do. You understand me, Dev?"

Dev nodded. "I do. I remember what happened with TeeJay in the crèche."

Kurok's lips compressed, and he nodded. "That's what I mean. I don't want you to get into a situation where something bad happens and you're unhappy."

"Okay," Dev said. "It was only a kiss."

"Yes." Kurok smiled at her again. "But the way it works, Dev, is that you start by kissing, and then that feels good, so you want to do other things."

"What other things?"

"Things like touching, and giving pleasure," he said. "It feels so good you don't want to stop, and it can be very attention consuming and emotional."

"Oh," Dev said. "That's very interesting." She paused thoughtfully. "Does Jess know about all of this? She seemed to know about kissing."

"I'm sure she does. But I think you should wait to talk to her about it until after your mission. I know you'll both be very busy." He glanced up as loud noises started outside the carrier. "And I think there's some work needing to be done here."

"Yes," Dev said. "We have to get the hull sealed. Thank you for explaining that, Doctor Dan." She hesitated. "It's a correct thing, isn't it?"

Kurok looked at that young, innocent face, now smudged a little with silicone grease, and smiled. "To be honest, Dev, if you were in one of the regular bio alt positions, or in the crèche, it would be incorrect," he said, straightforwardly. "Mostly to protect you."

She nodded.

"But you're not. You're in a role that makes you the equal of all the natural born humans around you. I think you know that."

She nodded again.

"So, along with the responsibility of performing that role with excellence, you also have to take on the burden of relating to them as though you were one of them," he said. "That's a difficult thing, because they don't all see it that way."

"No."

"But Jesslyn Drake does," he said. "So no, Dev, it's not incorrect for you in this case. But please be careful. I would hate to see you become unhappy because of all of this."

Dev wasn't sure how kissing could make her unhappy, but she accepted Doctor Dan's words at face value. "I will be careful," she said. "Especially on the mission. Kissing seems to make Jess very distracted. I wouldn't want to do that and end up with less than excellent results."

Kurok started laughing again. "Oh, Dev." He shook his head, still chuckling. "Ah, to be young and facing life for the first time again."

Dev chuckled herself, a little, more because he was than because she understood the joke. "This is such an excellent position. I'm so glad you picked me for it, Doctor Dan."

Kurok let his chuckles wind down, and then he patted her leg. "Go and do well. We can talk more about this when you get back. Okay?"

"Okay." Dev watched him stand up. "Thanks again, Doctor Dan."

He winked at her and then went to the carrier door, giving it an affectionate slap before he disappeared down the stairs leaving Dev alone inside.

Whew. That was a lot to think about. Dev squirmed back under the console and picked up her adjustment tool. In the meantime, there was a lot of work to do, and she decided to set aside the thoughts and get down to it.

Chapter Fourteen

JESS ASSEMBLED HER mission information package and sat down at her workspace to go over it. Met had finally cleared them, and she spread out the maps, laying out the routes she wanted to take and reviewing the contacts.

A small folder was set to one side that had their false credentials in it. Jess paused a moment and opened it, sorting through the scan cards and traveling passports with her and Dev's holos in them.

She studied Dev's. They'd assigned her a fake name of Devlin Marks, using the standard theory that one's own first name should be used whenever possible since it reduced the amount of gotchas in any situation. Her own this time was Jessie Arnula.

Not really one she favored, but what the hell. Jess set the creds aside and poured over the latest intelligence, checking her chrono then reaching over to tap the comms. "Hey Dev?"

After a second and a short crackling noise, Dev answered. "Hello!"

"How's it going?"

"Very well," Dev said. "The interior systems are complete. They're putting the outer skin on presently."

"Great." Jess smiled. "Good job."

Dev's smile could clearly be heard over the comm. "Thank you," she said. "I will be asking for the comp synch soon. And run engine tests."

"Great," Jess repeated. "Keep me looped."

"Okay," Dev said, and signed off.

Jess chuckled and shook her head, going back to studying her metrics. It was a relatively straightforward plan. They'd pull in to Cape Quebec and pick up supplies, then stop at Interforce's North Station and get the latest met as well as any last minute intel.

Then a hop to the outlands. Dev would need to park the bus in an ice cave, and they would have to hike in to the fishing village. "Supply?" Jess pressed a comm button. "Drake," she said, when it answered. "Leaving plus four I need two arctic kits in my bus."

"Got it," a voice responded, and clicked off.

Jess whistled under her breath, then paused, wondering why she was so damned happy. Hadn't she been the one who'd been finding any excuse not to leave just two days ago? Now she felt nothing but anticipation and confidence, and she was human and self knowing enough to stop and wonder why.

Maybe the induction the previous night had helped. Even the grudging acceptance of her new position was bracing, and she'd gone from feeling like something of a failure to being in a place where she was ready to envision success again.

It felt good. She felt good today. She picked up the communications folder and studied the inside of it, seeing the brief acknowledgement from North Station, and the latest overhead sat map of the ice flows.

It would be a cold mission. Jess made a note to get them both some warm undergarments in Cape Quebec, more than the light synth ones they issued here.

A light knock at her door made her look up. "Come."

The door opened, and Alex Bain entered. Jess was caught by surprise, and she half stood as he sauntered over and sat down in one of the chairs across from her desk. "Sir."

"Sit, Drake." He waved at her. "This is an informal meeting."

Jess sat. To have Bain call you in, that they'd come to understand was normal. Even to have him call you to ops command? Normal, though now a bit creepy. To get a visit in your quarters? Way outside. "What can I do for you?"

Bain studied her intently. "I have some information I wanted to pass along to you before you depart," he said. "Where is your charming new colleague?"

"Fixing the bus," Jess said. "At this point it wouldn't surprise me if she could knit one from scratch."

A smile crossed Bain's long, craggy face. "You have developed a...hm, strong appreciation for this bio alt."

Jess hesitated, then she nodded. "She's good."

Bain nodded back. "We have just received confirmation that we still have a leak inside," he said. "That's the main reason I'm here, in your bedroom, telling you and not in the operations center."

"Damn."

"Hm." Bain nodded again. "That's what was behind the attack on Dr. Kurok. Word had gotten to the other side of his success with your new pilot."

"Partner," Jess corrected him quietly.

"Indeed?" Bain's eyes twinkled. "That would dismay our friends all the more, I believe. But it surprises me, hmm? You were so adamantly against it."

Jess looked at her hands, folded together on the table. "It surprises me too. I never got to say it, but thanks." She looked up at him. "Glad I bumped into you on the top of that rampway."

A completely different smile appeared on his face. "It was my great pleasure."

They were both silent for a few moments. "We have to find this person," Bain finally said. "I've had security go over every single record a half dozen times. They have found, nothing."

"We have to trap them," Jess said. "You won't find anything, and the fact that what they sent over was broadly known information should tell you something. Our last run, when no one really knew what the plan was, didn't get leaked."

Bain nodded thoughtfully. "That ah, had occurred to me."

"So," Jess said. "There are two major bits of information I let slide for this mission. One, that I was stopping at Quebec, and two, that I would report in at North before I went on. The rest of the gig, the only person I told that to was Dev."

"I see."

Jess picked up a bit of plasfilm and handed it to him. "That's who I told what. So let's see what happens when I get to both places."

Bain slowly smiled at her.

"Now, they can do one of two things," Jess said. "They can try to stop me before I get there, or they can wait until I get there, and trap me. They tried option two already once. Didn't work out so well for them."

"No it didn't."

"Letting me get close last time didn't work out so well either," Jess said. "So I'm hoping they think I'm dangerous enough to want to stop me ahead of time. If they do, then maybe we'll know who it is."

"Hm." The Old Man grunted. "But you will be careful, won't you, Drake? I would hate for anything permanent to happen to you, or to that charming young lady."

Jess smiled. "Dev is safe with me."

"Hm. And on the mission as well." Bain stood up. "Very well. Keep me advised." He offered his hand. "Good luck, Drake. Glad you rose to the challenge."

Jess shook his hand, and then he was gone, the door sliding shut behind him. She leaned back in her chair and nodded to herself. She figured if she pulled this off, there was a decent chance Bain would kick Stephan into Bricker's job, and her into Stephan's.

She had almost two sleeves. She'd busted her ass. She had more brains than anyone else in the bunch here, and damn it, she'd earned the chance.

Jess gathered her documentation together, and packed it into her flight kit. Then she headed for the door, figuring maybe they could use another set of hands on the carrier to get it flight ready.

She grinned wryly. Or at least, Dev could.

DEV DUCKED BACK into her quarters, half out of breath as she let the door close and took a moment to sit down and think about what she needed to do next.

She'd just taken the carrier through its flight certification, a first for her, and she was very pleased when the checkout pilot had signed her off after a single round of tests.

Very good. Even though the pilot had been grumpy, and seemed not to like her. He'd muttered something about Barbie dolls, which she had no idea of the meaning of, and finally just keyed in his okay and told her to land.

She had, and then gotten Jess's call to get herself ready, and now here she was. The problem was, she really wasn't entirely sure what she was supposed to be doing besides getting into her pilot's jumpsuit and collect her helmet.

A shower seemed appropriate, though, so she hauled herself to her feet and slipped into the wet room, shucking out of her work coverall and into the warm stream of water. Its pulsing pressure felt good against her skin as she washed the dust and grime off it.

She let the hot water pound against her for a minute, then shut it off and shook herself hard sending droplets against the wall with tiny little spitting sounds. "Ahh."

Then she picked up a folded towel and started drying herself off, wrapping the towel around her and tucking the end in as Jess had taught her before she ran her comb through her hair.

"Hey!" Jess's voice echoed as the inner door opened. "Dev?"

"In here." Dev called out. "I was just taking a shower." She was glad she'd finally gotten the word for it in her mental storage, and could now call it by it's proper name. She glanced to her left as Jess poked her head in and gave her a smile. "Hello."

Jess was in the simple undergarment she wore under her heavy jumpsuit. It was a mild gray in color and hugged her body. "We'll have to pack a kit," she said. "A lot more stuff than the last time."

"I just wanted to get clean first."

"So I see." Jess grinned. "Carrier all done?"

"Yes. All ready to go." She followed Jess out into the larger part of her space. "Do you know a person named Davis?"

"Ahhugh." Jess stopped and turned, regarding her wryly. "Johnson Davis? Crotchety old bastard who doesn't have a good word to say for anyone and looks like he sleeps in his clothes?"

"Yes."

"Why?" Jess indicated the pack that had come in the box Bain had sent. "That's what you use for the kit."

"He was the one who did the flight check on the carrier with me. He seemed to be in some kind of discomfort," Dev said. "So I was wondering."

"He's an asshole."

"Um. Okay." Dev got into a pair of under wraps, then a twin of the suit Jess was wearing that felt nice and soft against her skin. "Does he feel uncomfortable about my being a bio alt?"

"No. He just hates women. He probably isn't even aware you're a bio alt," Jess said. "He's the one thing Sandy and I agree on."

"Oh." Dev eyed her. "I see." She paused. "What's a Barbie doll?"

Jess stopped and looked at her. "Did he call you that?"

"No," Dev said. "Well, he might have. He said something about Barbie dolls and it sounded like he might have meant it to apply to me. What is it?"

Jess's eyes narrowed. "If I thought for a minute he meant that and was not just how he felt about women in general I'd go find him and pull his cock off."

Dev blinked in astonishment. "Um...what?"

"I don't care who he thinks he is." Jess avoided the question. "Stupid mindless drunken bastard." She braced her arm against the storage cabinet then peered at Dev, her dark hair dropping across her eyes for a moment. "Sorry," she said, after an awkward pause. "I must sound like an idiot to you."

"Not at all," Dev said. "But I wish I understood what is causing you distress."

Jess straightened and folded her arms. Her face scrunched into an expression of mixed embarassment and irritation. "I don't...we should..." She exhaled. "Never mind, Dev. We can talk about it later. Let's get going on the run."

"Okay."

"So here." Jess pointed. "You'll need the jacket, a couple of extra under suits, and one of those colored jumps like that blue one. We don't wear uniforms in places like Cape Quebec."

"Okay." Dev neatly folded the items and fit them into the pack. "Why not?"

"Hm." Jess held a hand up. "Okay, let's sit down a minute and talk about being outside." She motioned toward the chairs. Dev detoured over to her drink dispenser and got out two containers, then came over and handed Jess one before they both sat down.

"Thanks." Jess studied the container, before she opened it and took a sip. "So you decided you like this stuff?" She held up the kack.

"Yes, it seems so." Dev smiled. "It's a little fizzy, and that's very interesting to my tongue."

"Aha." Jess cleared her throat a little. "Okay, so, the deal is this. When we're here, we're just who we are. You got that right?"

After a brief hesitation, Dev nodded. "I think so."

"When we're out there, most of the time we don't want to be who we really are. It's not always safe."

Dev's eyes lit up a little. "Oh. You mean we'll be undercover." She pronounced the word carefully. "Pretending to be someone else, correct?"

Jess looked surprised. "Right," she said. "Did they give you programming about that?"

"Yes," Dev said. "That came in the job programming. Not specific things, but the need to do that. And how to hide and all that. I know the programmers and Doctor Dan were concerned because we do have this." She touched her neck. "And that's hard to hide."

"Turtlenecks for you." Jess muffled a chuckle at the look of mild bewilderment on her face. "It's a shirt that has a high collar." She explained. "You just have to remember not to take your clothes off outside."

"Okay. I won't." Dev paused. "Well, not unless you tell me to."

Jess shot her a quick look, and swore she saw a twinkle in those green eyes. "Right," she drawled. "I'll have to remember that." She waited, but Dev's expression remained mild and inquisitive. "Anyway, we usually put together a cover before we leave, and we get credentials issued to us that match that. Hang on." She got up and went into her quarters.

"Hang on to what?" Dev wondered to herself. "Hang on to the chair?" She peered around. "To the cup?" She sat back as Jess returned, carrying a folder in her hands. "Hang on to you?"

Jess paused in mid step. "What?"

"Sorry." Dev took a sip from her container. "I was just thinking about something."

Jess sat down, leaning on one arm of the chair. "Okay." She handed Dev a set of cards, and a holder. "This is yours."

Dev accepted them, putting down her container and studying the materials. She blinked, when she realized the first set of cards was a citizen's credentials, with her picture on it and an unfamiliar name. "This is very interesting."

"Yeah, not bad." Jess was sorting through hers. "So, when we go into Quebec let me do the talking," she said. "The names they issued us are close enough to our own that it would be hard to slip up, but think about the name they gave you so you respond to it if anyone asks you about the card."

"Right," Dev said. "What's yours?" She peered at Jess's card. "Oh, okay. I see."

"When we get to the North Station, you just be yourself," Jess said. "But in the outlands, don't let on to anyone that you're not a—what did you call us?"

"Natural born," Dev said. "But they won't call it that will they? So I'll just be a regular person."

Jess smiled a little. "Yes." She paused. "Why natural born?"

"Well, because you are," Dev said. "Born naturally."

Jess considered that. "And you aren't?"

"No. They make us up in test tubes," Dev said, with a brief grin. "The scientists, like Doctor Dan, select the genes and mix us up and then give us a little zap to get the division started. Then they put us in a shell, and once we outgrow that, into an incubator. Then they hatch us."

Jess stared at her, blinking. "Are you messing with me?"

"Messing," Dev mused. "Are you asking me if I'm making a joke?" She watched Jess nod hesitantly. "No, that's really how they do it. So, that's why we call you natural born."

"All righty then." Jess got up. "Let's get packed and get going. We've got a long trip ahead of us." She toasted Dev with her drink. "Stick some of these and some crackers in your kit if you want. Always good to have some extra with us."

"Okay." Dev got up and retrieved her pack, making sure everything was neatly tucked inside it, and taking Jess's suggestion she added a few bottles of kack and several packets of the seaweed crackers. She also tucked a spare pair of under wraps inside, and a set of her sleeping clothes since she remembered Jess saying they would be gone for days.

Then, after a pause, she put her book inside the pack too. She sealed everything up, and went to the cabinet to take down her flight suit and get into it. It made her a little excited, feeling the heavier fabric close around her as she arranged the clips and feeds she would hook into the carrier.

She put her boots on, straightening up just as Jess poked her head in the door, her body encased in its familiar black semi armor. "Ready?" Dev asked.

"Ready," Jess said. "Grab your pack and let's go to the hangar."

Dev emptied her container, then she went back and picked up her pack, slinging it onto her back and adjusting the straps. She ran her fingers through her hair, now mostly dry, and went into Jess's quarters to find her seating her sidearm into it's holster, her hair pulled back into a tail.

Jess shouldered her own pack and they exited their quarters, emerging into the random traffic of the after lunchtime shift change. They didn't stop to talk to anyone, and in a few minutes they were at the hangar, moving across the vast open space toward the landing pad their carrier was sitting on.

There were six or so bio alts scrambling around the outside, and the hatch was open, last minute details being taken care of as their launch time neared.

"Looks good," Jess said. "Nice work."

Dev smiled. "I just did a small part," she demurred. "There were many people working on it."

They cleared around the last work pedestal and approached the pad. "Well." Jess paused, studying the side. "The mech team thought you did a good enough job to put your name on it. Good sign." She pointed at the side of the carrier, where Dev's name had been stenciled right under hers.

"Oh!" Dev's eyes widened. She slowed long enough to study the letters as they walked up the ramp, dodging an exiting bio alt who was carrying a calibration rig. "I didn't expect that."

"I figured once word got around they might." Jess went into the carrier without explaining that cryptic remark, but Dev lingered a moment to let her eyes trace over the blocky, capital letters DEV inked on the metal side. Not her designation, just the short name and she found herself grinning just to see it.

"Looks good huh?" Clint ducked under the engine pod, wiping his hands on a rag. "They just finished. Hope you leave it in one piece long enough for the paint to dry."

Dev made a face. "I'll try," she said. "I know we caused a lot of hard work."

"You did some yourself," Clint said. "Good luck, Dev. Bring her back in one piece and you all in it."

"Thank you." Dev gave him a smile. "I'll do my best." She patted the side of the ship and ducked inside, only just avoiding crashing headlong into Jess. "Oh!"

"Sorry." Jess backed up. "C'mon in. I like the new chair." She let Dev enter then she went over and sealed the hatch. "Once you get everything squared away, let's get clearance and get out of the bathtub."

Dev strapped her pack down next to her station and sat down in the pilot's chair, strenuously resisting asking Jess what a bathtub was. She checked her initial settings, then she started up the comp and began her preflight checks.

Of course, she'd done all that before the certification lift, but her programming told her in no uncertain terms that they had to be done every single time and she could feel the stress on that which indicated to her that this was an important thing.

She listened to Jess rattling around behind her, getting her own pack lashed down, arranging her hold down straps, and checking the weapons and drop kit.

Dev settled the comm set on her head and slipped the earpiece in, hearing the low murmur of ops traffic on the link as she brought the nav comp online. "BR27006, comm check."

"Stand by 27006."

"Standing by." Dev lit up the engine systems board and started running the checks on the new systems, pleased with the response to her test signals.

"27006, Central ops, register comm check, clear channel."

Dev tuned in the channel a little, her sensitive ears hearing the digital shaping as it evened out. "Central ops, BR27006 reads clear channel, good comm check." She locked the signal in and released a test squirt, then studied the engine status and the readouts from the navigation comp. "Systems coming online," she warned Jess.

"I hear 'em," Jess said. "Give me power please."

Dev opened the power channel to the weapons systems, her eyes flicking to her boards as the carrier drew current from their umbilical to soak the batteries. She checked the multiple fuel cells, and nodded at the full charge, reaching over to pre-tune the internal generator that would take over once they were disconnected from the base.

"They asking for a route?" Jess called from the back.

"No, they aren't. Just standing by," Dev said. "Everything's online. Should I ask for flight clearance?"

"Hang on." Jess settled into her bucket seat, locking the restraint straps around her and feeling them gently snug against her body to hold her down. They had a fast release plate positioned over her chest, and a single slap could get her out of them because you just never knew what was going to happen even in flight.

She tested the new chair, feeling it solid and easily swiveled, and she pulled down her targeting comps, pleased with the feel of the new surface under her. The chair was more than decently padded, and she reached behind her back, pushing the supports experimentally. "Hey."

"Yes?" Dev turned around in her seat.

"They put extra pillows in this thing?" Jess watched Dev blush slightly. "Hm?"

"I asked them to add a little bit of support for your back," Dev said. "I thought you would like that."

Jess studied her, caught between embarrassment and pleasure. "Do you have any idea how much crap I'm going to have to take for that from the rest of the agents?"

"No, I don't," Dev said. "I didn't consider them when I asked." She frowned. "Why would they care what your chair was like?"

Jess wriggled a little and felt the comfort of the extra support on either side of her spine, and at the base. It felt good, and she decided she really didn't care if they cared. "I dunno," she said. "It's great, thanks, Dev."

Dev smiled, and turned back around. "All systems are online and ready." She fastened her own restraints, taking a peek at Jess in the small strip of mirror above her console. She could see the little grin on her face as she regarded the chair and she grinned herself, glad she'd asked for that small comfort.

"Okay, tell them to crack open the top," Jess said, as she leaned back in her surprisingly comfortable seat. "Let's get this party started."

"BR27006 to pad support, please undock umbilicals," Dev said into her mic, catching sight of two bio alts ducking under the engine pod in response. She poised her fingers over the power grid, and as they unlocked the port and removed it, she activated the internal power feed and brought them online. "Internal systems green, please clear for lift."

"Pad control, we're clear, BR27006. Good mission."

"Thank you, pad control." Dev changed channels. "Central operations, BR27006 requesting flight access please."

Jess chuckled from behind her.

Overhead, she heard the big doors start to open and a moment later, she heard the clearance come back into her ear. "BR27006 acknowledge. Lifting." Dev spooled up the engines and engaged the bottom jets, taking them up toward the opening roof with steady confidence.

It was a rare moment of no rain. Dev took the carrier up into the clear air, and did a circle, scanning the horizon before she settled with the carrier's nose pointed to the north. She keyed in the coordinates Jess had given her for Quebec City, and checked her consoles one more time. "Ready?"

"Go go gadget," Jess said. "Keep your eyes out for bad guys. I may fall asleep here in my comfy chair."

Dev smiled, and engaged the main engines, heading them off into this new adventure.

CAPE QUEBEC WASN'T that far, Dev discovered. She spotted the cliff face full of lights ahead of them as her nav station beeped, and she adjusted her speed lower. "That's it?"

"That's it," Jess said, putting her hand on the back of Dev's chair and peering through the sectioned windows. "Okay we can't valet park this bus, so you're going to have to land on the plateau there, see the opening?"

"Yes," Dev said. "Go down in there?"

"Yeah." Jess returned to her seat and locked her restraints. "There's an old stairway cut into the rock. It's a hike, but the carrier'll be hidden and they won't see what direction we came from."

It all sounded quite mysterious. Dev angled the carrier toward the cliff wall, and cut the mains, using the landing jets to gently lower the carrier past the crevice. It was all shadows and gray stone, with water drizzling off the edges and making a constant rattle and thunder past them as she found a bit of higher stone and set the vehicle down onto it. "Okay?"

"Great." Jess stood up and hit a set of switches. "We'll blend in here." She started getting out of her armored suit. "Now we need to change into civs."

Dev finished shutting down the engines and as she did, she could hear the rain falling on the carrier's roof, and the drum of the water on the ground outside.

Outside. Aside from her brief movement from the shuttle to the citadel and her visits to the ledge, this would be her first big exposure to outside, and Dev found herself a little unsettled over it. Doctor Dan had talked to her about it. But talking about it and doing it were two very different things.

"You okay?" Jess was apparently watching her.

"Yes." Dev opened her pack and removed the blue jumpsuit, unsnapping the catches on her flight suit. "I was just wondering what it was like to be on the ground outside."

Jess paused as she fastened the neck on her civs. They were rust and gold, flashier than the ones Dev was donning. "Oh that's right. You came from outer space. I forgot."

Dev smiled as she finished fastening her suit. She picked up the jacket Bain had sent her and held it, not entirely sure what should happen next. Jess seemed to be sorting through some things so she put the jacket back down and went to the dispenser and took out a small bottle of water.

"Run an external scan, willya?" Jess asked. "Doesn't pay to take a chance."

Glad of something to do, Dev went back to her station and sat down. She opened the water and took a sip, then put the bottle in its gimbaled holder and activated the scan. She set the routine running, observing the results and glancing outside the carrier window to match the terrain with the scan.

It was rocky outside, and dark with clouds and rain. The carrier was settled between a half dozen large boulders and she had slid it just under a slight ledge which protected it somewhat. The area around them was clear of any life at all. Only rocks and rubble, with some small patches of moss being the only hint of color.

"Clear?"

"Yes," Dev said. "Nothing for 500 meters at least."

"Good." Jess finished tucking various things in her pockets. She walked over and picked up her own jacket. "Okay. Now we climb up the steps to a path I know, and that will take us to one of the outer entrances of the city. You need to stay close with me, and for now, don't talk unless you have to. We're just here to shop. We're a couple of bored techs on a day holiday from the Rocky Mountain generating center. Got it?"

"Got it." Dev rummaged in her memory for details about the generating center, which she'd had some basic programming on. Science and research were done there, she knew, along with its primary responsibility of creating and storing hydro power in massive sealed batteries.

Was it a target, she wondered. Like the facility they themselves were trying to breach?

"C'mon." Jess shrugged into her jacket and fastened a colorful patch on the outside. She waited for Dev to mimic her then attached a similar one on her sleeve. "There. Now you work for Energine." She patted Dev on the shoulder and went to the door. "I'm keying this so only the two of us can get back in. Anyone else tries it'll blow a hole the size of the docking cavern."

"I see," Dev said. "This stop here—it's to obtain supplies?"

Jess hit the door release and the hatch thumped open, admitting a gust of cold, wet air. "Yeah. Some outside gear I need for the ice fields and to get current gossip. The intel we get in the citadel sometimes isn't really current, not to mention it could be planted. I like to listen to what's going on before I do an insertion." Another mistake on her last mission. She'd let Josh talk her into skipping the recon.

She pulled her jacket hood up and fastened the neck cover then eased down the unfolded steel steps and got her boots on the wet rock before she motioned Dev forward. Though her head was well covered by the fabric the half frozen rain pelted her face and she blinked a little at the harshness of it. "Ugh."

Dev spent a moment absorbing the experience. She could feel the half rain, half ice drops pelting the surface of the fabric encasing her, and she made a mental note to go back and thank Alexander Bain for providing the jacket to her. She lifted a hand and pulled the glove off it, feeling the sting of the rain and the chill before she put it back on. "That's interesting."

Jess eyed her. "Not interesting enough to stay out in it. Let's go." She circled the carrier and climbed up a small rise toward the cliff walls, pausing to turn and look back at the vehicle. "Nice," She complimented Dev. "That new mottled skin really works."

Now that the hatch was closed, you'd be hard pressed to identify the carrier against its landscape. The outer shell had taken on the tones of the surrounding rock, blending the metal until it was almost invisible.

"Yes," Dev said. "Clint was really happy with how it turned out. It's a new thing. He said it would help us hide against the clouds, too."

"If we want to hide." Jess turned and started away from the small ledge they'd parked on. "Quebec's a mix these days. Used to just be a supply depot, since they've got a decent harbor, but they finally dug out the cliff and fixed the roofs of all those old buildings, and people drifted in from the outlands."

"I see." Dev was keeping up with her companion's long strides with a bit of difficulty. The uneven ground was new to her, and she was having some trouble keeping her balance on it. "What do they do there?" She asked, more to keep Jess talking since she'd studied the records in comp on the place when Jess had told her they were going there.

"Fish mostly," Jess said. "They've got enough coastline to harvest weed, but they're big on shallow water shellfish too." She licked her lips thoughtfully. "Be glad to introduce you to those. Since they got enough people around, they've got markets and grub too."

Shellfish. Shell, and fish? "Do they have anything to do with that gift from Clint?"

"Well, sort of I guess. They do get tiny crabs out of some of those shells and use 'em in stews. But the ones he sent, those didn't have any crabs in em. They just wash up near the base of our cliff."

"I see." Dev had found her balance now, and was beginning to enjoy the tramp across the rocks. Jess was leading the way across a barren stretch of granite toward a wall. She could see, even through the rain, a narrow uneven set of steps cut into the face of it. It angled up the rock wall to an outcropping above and she couldn't see past that.

It seemed very desolate where they were. She couldn't hear anything besides the far off sound of the surf and the rumble of thunder over their heads and her face was starting to feel very cold where the rain was hitting it.

She blinked a little, as she followed Jess up a slope and across a long stretch of loose, crunchy sounding small rocks that led up to the base of the wall. There were big rocks all around them, and she peered upward as a scattering of tiny stones rattled off the cliff and fell around them. "Did those rocks come from up there?"

"Yeah." Jess wound her way through them. "That's why we park here. People with sense stay far the hell away." She pointed at a long rusted sign tacked to the stone, a pictograph of a crudely drawn slope and what were supposed to be boulders. "It's a rock fall zone."

"I see." Dev regarded the wall. "So one of those could fall down right now?"

"Sure."

"I see."

Jess half turned and grinned at her. "Closer to the cliff you are, safer it is. Don't worry."

"I'm not worried." Dev kept at her heels, as they got to the base of the cliff and started up the stairs. They had been very crudely cut into the rock, and were in some places more suggestions than footholds. "If something unfortunate happens, at least I will have had lots of new experiences."

The steps reminded her of the climbing exercises they'd done in the crèche and she placed her boots with confidence, glad of her gloves as she gripped the rock edge they were climbing up. The coverings were dark gray and made of very tough fabric, thin enough for her to use her fingers well, but thick enough to keep her hands nice and warm.

It was interesting and exciting being here. She felt all sorts of new sensations, the strain on her legs of climbing, the pelting rain, the roughness of the stone under her gloved fingertips. It was all new, and she focused on Jess's tall form, careful to step where she did once she'd moved on.

The rock smelled, she realized. It had a flat, dense scent a little like the walls in the citadel, but different. She could also smell the rain and she experimentally stuck her tongue out, catching some of the icy droplets and tasting them.

Interesting. She saw Jess slow up and halt ahead of her, and she paused, watching her closely. Jess moved again after a moment, but more slowly and she took one hand off the rock and let it rest against the pocket Dev knew she had her weapon in.

She decided to remain quiet, figuring Jess didn't need any distractions if there was something dangerous occurring. They were up near the little ledge, and she watched Jess pause again, one hand resting on the rocks and her head cocked to one side.

After a moment, Jess untied her hood and pushed it down, exposing her head to the rain but also exposing her ears, which were, interestingly to Dev, twitching visibly.

Then, after a moment of silence, Jess pulled her hood back up and continued on, climbing up over the edge of the crevice and then turning, offering Dev her hand.

Dev wasn't sure what that was about, but she reached up and clasped it, a bit surprised to find herself pulled up onto the ledge to stand next to Jess. "Thank you."

"All quiet." Jess moved across the ledge to an uneven square hold in the side of the mountainside. She slipped inside, then activated a hand light and paused before she continued forward. "Let's get outta the damn rain at least."

Dev hadn't entirely minded the experience, but she found the cold a lot less inside the tunnel they were now in, and she pushed her hood back and wiped the rain off her face as she followed Jess in. "Very interesting." She regarded the tunnel, which was as crudely cut as the steps outside, taking off a glove and running her fingertips over the surface.

She could feel chisel marks on the stone. "Did you cut this wall?"

"Me?" Jess chuckled low and deep in her throat. "Hell no. They sent a team out here when Quebec started becoming a population center. Ten guys with plasma cutters. You see all that rubble at the base? That was from them. "

"I see." Dev activated her own hand light, and examined the wall. It had interesting sparkles in it, not that different from the walls in the citadel. The floor was as uneven as the walls, and she focused the light there, avoiding the unexpected angular cracks and bumps as they walked along.

It was out of the wind here too, and warmer because of it. Dev ran her hand through her hair and noticed Jess was having to duck a little as she walked. "Is it a long way in here?"

"No," Jess said. "Couple more minutes."

And in a couple more minutes, in fact, they were moving from the narrow tunnel and squeezing through a crack in the rock so narrow Jess had to take off her coat to fit through, and Dev almost did. Then they were in a more regular hallway, with smooth walls, evenly spaced low lights and a faint look of dusty disuse.

"Emergency tunnel." Jess shrugged back into her jacket and fastened it. "Place for them to run to." She closed her hand light and stuck it in her pocket as she lead the way up a gently sloping floor. "Minute or so, and we'll be in the lower levels."

"Okay." Dev caught up and walked along at her side.

"Whatever you see, just keep your mouth shut," Jess said. "It could be weird for you. There'll be other bio alts here, but it's not like in the citadel."

Now, what did that mean? "Okay." She saw Jess raise a hand a little, and she slowed, keeping behind her as the hallway they were in ended in a big, square opening and a murmur of sound reached her. They crossed another wide hallway that led off into dusty silence in both directions and then they were moving through a wide arched opening into a cavern filled with people.

Jess moderated her pace, turning her purposeful walk into a more casual stroll, sticking her hands in her jacket pockets and letting her head turn from side to side.

Dev copied her, glad she had a chance to absorb what she was seeing. Unlike the uniformity she was used to in both the crèche and the citadel, the people and the sights were far more random here. There were people who looked like workers, but their overalls were patched and so worn and covered in dirt it was impossible to tell what color they were supposed to be.

Then there were other people, in skin tight suits carrying boxes with lights, and other people who were covered in strangely mottled garments and heavy boots.

The smell of the place was past her ability to self describe. It was a mixture of strong scents and musky tones, overlaid with the more familiar intensity of machine oil and salt she was becoming familiar with in her new home. A few people glanced at them, but then moved on, and she followed Jess along the perimeter of the space toward a set of long, shallow stairs.

They passed a pair of men with scrubbers, removing a layer of oil from the floor and Dev felt a jerk of recognition as she took in their visible collars. Effens, her memory supplied, wearing roughly finished gray coveralls with dark maroon sleeves.

They didn't look up as she and Jess went past, their eyes firmly on their task as they patiently scoured the floor. Normal, she thought, having worked with a few of that set in the crèche. They received a lot of programming for cleaning. It's what they did in the crèche, in fact, specialists in maintenance.

Did Jess think she would find that strange? Dev pondered the thought.

They walked up the shallow stairs, moving into a more brightly lit space that suddenly, as they emerged at the top, also became a lot louder. Dev almost stopped walking as they turned a last corner, and she was looking at the inside of a large, high roofed cavern filled with...Well, filled with everything. "Oh."

Jess turned and peered at her, slowing and closing the distance between them. "This is the market," she said. "Remember, we're just techs on holiday, looking to shop."

"Okay." Dev followed Jess's lead and unfastened her jacket, which had started to become very warm. She left it hanging open with its hood pushed back, and followed Jess toward the ball of chaos ahead of them. The rock walls echoed back the sounds of all the people roaming from area to area, voices raised.

After a minute, it sorted itself out and her programming kicked in, and she knew what she was looking at much to her relief. This was a center where people came to offer up things they did and products they made for sale. There were dozens of rows of little rooms, made from what looked like stones cemented together. Each room had some people inside it, and ledges on all four sides where they had things displayed.

And the people. Dev had never seen this many people in one place, not in the crèche, and not in the citadel, including at the party. There seemed an endless sea of them all dressed in widely varied combinations of clothing, strange things on their heads and a mixture of things on their feet that completely escaped any of her programming.

She really couldn't process it all. So she stuck at Jess's side, resisting the urge to latch onto her jacket as they started moving into the market area and into the surge of human traffic. She blinked her eyes a little, finding them watering slightly from the pungent smells.

"Crazy, huh?" Jess said, as she sidestepped two men arguing loudly.

"Yes."

"Everyone around brings their stuff here to sell." Jess confirmed Dev's programming. "You can get some interesting trinkets here, see?" She detoured over to a stone house. She picked up one of the wares, a bit of stone that had been hollowed out to leave a small dish like depression at the bottom. "You put scented oil in here, and light it. Makes a nice smell."

Dev regarded it. Then she looked all around them, and back up at Jess, one of her pale eyebrows lifting a little. "Do they make them any larger?"

Jess grinned, and turned, finding the merchant watching them with wary politeness. "How much?" She indicated the trinket.

"Quarter credit, citizen," the man replied promptly. "Third if you buy two."

Jess dug in her pocket, pulling out a handful of something and singling out two bits of it to drop on the table. "Here." She picked up a second and handed it to Dev. "Keepsake."

The merchant snapped up the glittering bits on the table and gave her a look of much greater respect. "Citizens." He inclined his head in their direction. "Good market to you."

Dev regarded the item with some bemusement.

"We can try it out later." Jess winked at the merchant, then she bumped Dev with her shoulder and led the way further into the melee. "Most of the stuff is pretty useless," she said. "These guys just hope to pick up a credit or two to add to their allotment, maybe afford a bottle of grog once in a while."

"What did you give him?" Dev asked curiously.

"Ah." Jess dug in her pocket again, then held her hand up. "Turn your hand over."

Dev did, only to find a scattering of brightly glinting bits landing in her palm. She studied them, discovering squares of yellow metal with numbers stamped on both sides.

"In places like this you don't have scan cards. People don't like to identify who they are or what they're buying."

"I see."

"So this is hard credit. The biggest one's a full cred, then there's a half, a third and a quarter. It's gold," Jess added. "You know what that is?"

"Yes." Dev looked at the squares in surprise. "I never expected to see it in this form. We used it all the time on logic boards in the crèche."

"Well, here you can trade it for stuff." Jess closed her hand over the credits. "Put 'em in your pocket. Spend 'em if you want." She paused, and her eyes flicked over Dev's shoulder. "But not right now. C'mere." She moved closer and put her arms around Dev, turning her back on the crowd.

Dev hastily put the handful of metal into her pocket and hesitantly returned the contact, feeling the warmth of Jess's body as she pressed against it. She had no idea at all what was going on, but the sensation was very pleasant and she was halfway wishing they could try that kissing thing again after a long moment of it.

"Hold still," Jess whispered into her ear. "Look past my arm and tell me if a tall guy with blond hair and a scar's gone by."

It took a very long moment for Dev to sort that out and figure out what to do about it. She peeked past Jess's elbow, and saw three men strolling by, glancing slowly around them. One was, she noted, tall and scarred. "They're behind us," she murmured back.

She felt Jess breathing against her, and decided it was very nice. "Now they are past us, and going away," she said, after a few more moments. When Jess didn't answer, she looked up, to find Jess looking back at her, with an expression that actually made her heart skip.

It skipped! Dev's eyes widened. What an incredibly odd sensation.

Then Jess sighed and released her. "Okay." She took a step back and turned cautiously, watching the men's backs as they retreated. "I don't think they saw me." She eased out into the stream of people again. "Let's stay behind them, just in case."

Dev's whole body was tingling, and she really didn't much care about the men. However, she followed along obediently. "Who were they?"

Jess chuckled without any real humor. "The bad guys," she said. "Very interesting they ended up here, huh?"

"Very interesting," Dev said, not entirely referring to the men. "Very interesting indeed."

Chapter Fifteen

THEY LOST SIGHT of the men in the crowd a little while later. With so many people and so many distractions it wasn't that out of the question, but Jess was still annoyed with herself that she let them get away. "Damn it."

Dev waited quietly nearby, as Jess quartered around four of the rooms there, letting her own eyes gently move from face to face as the crowd moved past her.

"Hey kid."

It did not occur to Dev that someone was addressing her, until she felt a tug on her sleeve. She looked quickly to her right, to find a stocky man with thick silver hair next to her. "Yes?" She decided no response was probably more dangerous than following Jess's strict order to not speak.

His eyes were dark, and shrewd. "That coat ain't worth nothing. C'mere, lemme show you what I got." He pointed to his little room, which had garments hanging everywhere around it.

Dev scanned the surrounding crowd, finding Jess at the next little room over, picking through some hats while she carefully watched the passers by. Since Jess was so close, she decided it would be all right to look at the garments. She followed the man over and listened to his pitch.

She knew what a pitch was. Her programming had given her enough background on the cities to get by with, and Dev herself wasn't nearly as naive as she apparently appeared. There had been little markets in the crèche, in fact, when they'd gotten a chance to get a few rare treats and she understood the concept of bargaining.

This did not seem the place to engage in that though. Dev studied the clothing, and reached up to touch a piece of it, a jacket made from a smooth, tough substance.

"Ah, like that one, huh? Didn't figure you for shark though." The man came over and lifted it down. "Nice hide."

Shark. Dev glanced over at Jess, who was deep in discussion with the other vendor. With a faint shrug, she took off her issue jacket and tried on this other one, finding it surprisingly comfortable. Shark was a fish, she recalled. It felt very strange to be wearing the skin of an animal, but it felt a bit like heavy fabric and it didn't smell like fish.

"Looks good on you, kid," the man said, watching her shrewdly. "Where ya from?"

Dev removed the jacket and donned her own. "How much cred is this?" She asked, deducing this would distract him from asking her more questions.

"Two cred," the man said. "Don't bother trying to bargain with me, kid. I can see how wet behind the ears you are."

"All right, I won't." Dev handed him back the coat. "Excuse me."

"Wait." The man looked very surprised. "Hold on, you don't want it?"

"Not for that amount." Dev started to move off, angling her steps to end her up in the same room as Jess was. She could see Jess was concluding whatever her business was, and Dev wanted to be close by so they could move off to their next thing. Whatever that was.

"Wait, a cred and a half." The man scurried after her. "C'mon, kid. You know you want it."

Dev turned and faced him. "I have a one cred piece. If you would like that in exchange, that would be good. If not, then I have to be moving on."

"Nah it's worth more than that."

"All right, good bye then." Dev turned and started walking again, seeing Jess putting something in a sack.

"Okay okay." The man got in front of her again, holding the jacket out. "One cred."

The motion caught Jess's eye, and Dev saw her wheel around and start toward them. "Okay." She dug one of the bits of metal from her pocket and inspected it, then took the jacket from him and handed it over. "Thank you."

"Highway robber," the man grumbled, looking at the bit. "Why I should..."

"You should what, Roderick?" Jess had reached them and now she leaned her elbow on Dev's shoulder. "Are you giving my friend a hard time?"

Dev watched his face in fascination as it turned dead white under his beard and he backed away from them with some of the same look of fear as Clint had.

"Not at all, Jess," Dev said. "I was just making a purchase from him."

"No harm, no foul." The man held his hands up. "What brings you here?" He asked, looking around quickly. "Haven't seen you in a while."

"Let's go have a cup of kack and we can talk about it." Jess moved forward, forcing him to retreat. "I had you on my list of people to chat with anyway." She casually looked around. "Business looks slow right now."

Roderick nodded briefly and turned, leading the way back into his room. "Digger, keep a look on the store," he told a younger man standing there. "Me and the ladies have business."

Digger smirked. "Sure." He folded his arms over his faded and patched overalls and watched them go. "No problem."

They followed the merchant into the back of the small room, then down an unexpected set of iron rail lined stairs that went down in a spiral under the floor. The sound from the market dimmed and then cut off, as they reached the bottom, and were inside a cramped, spare dwelling with a low ceiling and rough stone floors.

It was well used, and long lived in. There were shelves made from stones and old boards, and two corridors led off toward the back that were curtained off with carefully opened and cleaned sacks.

Roderick led them into a square common space with a table and four chairs. "Didn't know the kid was a friend of yours, Jess." He pulled a chair back and sat down, placing his elbows on the table and folding his hands.

Jess took the seat facing him. "She's my partner," she said briefly. "Give me the scoop. What's going on here. I saw Red Dog." She glanced at Dev, who took the seat next to her. "I don't think he saw me."

He nodded. "I was surprised to see you. I heard about Wellington."

Jess shrugged.

"There's a price on you," Roderick said, after a bit of silence. "Ten thousand credits. Gold." He cocked his head a little. "I sent that news in to base. So I'm really surprised to see you here. I know you've got brass ones, but that ain't smart."

Jess's face didn't so much as twitch. "I've got a job to do," she said. "That what the Dog's doing here? Looking for me?"

"No." Roderick shook his head. "He and Jersey are looking for dirt on some new project on our side." He glanced around the space. "You hear anything? Some big thing, your way?"

Jess considered the question, giving a side glance at Dev before shaking her head. "Nothing I know of. You?"

Dev's face was a study in wry innocence. "I haven't heard of anything," she said. "But I've only been here a few days."

"Ah, new class. We heard they were in." Roderick exhaled. "Well, I can say you sure pissed off a lot of people, Jess. You get the body count from that last run? Five hundred." He eyed the agent. "Credits or not, if they catch you they're gonna splat you."

"Five hundred for one?" Jess smiled thinly. "Guess the Old Man'll consider it a bargain."

Roderick finally loosened up, chuckling a bit. "Maybe. But be careful. You get caught napping, his ego won't think of it that way. You know how it is." He shifted a bit, tapping his fingertips together. "Anyway, most of what we're hearing is the usual. Seen a few more of them sniffing 'round though."

Jess nodded. Then she turned her head and regarded Dev. "What'd he scalp you for?"

Dev's brow hiked just slightly, as she gazed back at her.

"The jacket." Jess pointed. "What'd it cost ya?"

"Oh." Dev cleared her throat. "A credit."

"Told you she chewed me down," Roderick said. "She's a kid, but not a stupid one. That's one of my best pieces she picked out." He studied Dev. "Where ya from? Waterside I'm guessing since you knew right off the skin."

"She's a west coaster," Jess said. "Monterey headlands. So yeah, she knows the water." She tapped her fingers on the table. "I need some ice boots, two pair. Who has em?"

"I'll send Digger. Petros had about a dozen pair, not sure what's left. He'll steal every last credit of yours if you try it though. He can spot one of us easy as sneezing." Roderick stood up. "Be right back."

Jess waited for him to leave, then she gave Dev a little smile, and pointed at the jacket, making a come hither gesture with her fingers. Once Dev had complied, she studied the garment, her brows lifting a little at the smooth, soft texture and the finely stitched patterns on it. "Nice." She handed it back. "Find me one next?"

"Sure." Dev grinned. "I was actually looking for one for you as I was concluding my deal. I think I saw one on the other side of the little house."

"Sale stall," Jess said. "Rod's one of our outside agents. He gets paid to just sit and sell and watch."

Dev nodded. "I remember from the class." She fell silent as Roderick returned, dusting his hands off as he entered.

"All right, that's set but I gotta go back upstairs. People'll rob me blind otherwise, and we've got Festival coming. My wife wants a few things. Can't afford to lose my stock."

Jess and Dev stood up. "How's Karyn?" Jess asked. "She still working upstairs?"

"Got in with Maersk." Roderick led them back to the stairs and started up them. "Got us a better slot after Festival. Be something moving out of this place."

"Nice." Jess glanced around her as she climbed up the steps. "Maersk, huh? Maybe you'll end up riding one of their super c's. Bet the quarters are nicer than these are."

Roderick chuckled dryly. "We all got our place." He emerged into the store and looked around in a studied, casual way before he moved away from the top of the steps and let Jess come up after him. "So there ya are. See? I made a right bargain." He added loudly, a truculent note now back in his tone.

Jess strolled through the store, examining the wares. "Yah, well, we'll see." She eased between the hanging garments, pausing between two racks to study the crowd. She was aware, suddenly, of a presence at her back, but after the first jolt she realized it was Dev, standing quietly behind her.

Very quietly Jess looked over her shoulder, slightly amazed at the way her new partner blended into her surroundings, standing just so between the haphazardly hung clothing, only her pale eyes moving.

A sudden commotion distracted both of them, and Jess swiveled to face the sound, her hand dropping to her jacket pocket as her body stiffened in reaction. Ahead of them, in the open lane between the stall they were in and the one across, two men had grabbed a tall lanky figure with, she realized, a bio alt collar.

"I told you not to touch me you freak!" One of the men yelled.

The bio alt hunched his shoulders and remained silent, holding his hands up in surrender. "Sir, didn't mean to bump you."

"You did it on purpose!" The man shoved him against the wall. "Probably going after my credits, huh freak?" He lifted a hand and balled it into a fist. "Were you?"

The bio alt cringed. "No sir. I was just walking. I tripped."

"Freak." The man shoved him again, then walked off, shaking his head. "C'mon. Stinks around here. Place is full of freaks these days."

The merchant across the way came out of his stall. "Get out of here." He yelled at the bio alt. "People'll think you belong to me. Move along!"

The bio alt moved away from the wall and hurried away, keeping his head down and by a jog in his stride, missing the kick aimed his way by the irate man. As he passed them he furtively looked their way, jerking his eyes back forward when they met Jess's.

Jess waited a moment, then she turned. Dev was still standing behind her, still with a mild, untroubled look on her face, still completely silent. "It's like that here."

Dev tilted her head slightly. "Like what?"

"What they did," Jess said. "A lot of people who don't have bios don't like them."

"I see." Dev pondered the scene. She saw the man from across the path come over and talk to Roderick, who half shrugged, and lifted his hands in a resigned gesture. "They don't like them, why?"

Jess exhaled. She was saved from an immediate answer by Roderick coming over to them.

"Ladies, you see anything else you want?" He asked, swinging around the shelves and pausing with his hand on one of the racks. "Day's not getting any younger and neither am I."

"What was that all about?" Jess asked, jerking her head toward the spot where the altercation had taken place.

"What?" Roderick frowned. "Oh you mean those guys?" He shrugged. "Usual crap. More of the hooty boys are getting the jelly bag brains and the city's started to put them to work places. Got a lot of old timers who don't like it." He added. "But those guys? They're just a bad fight looking for a place to happen. Wasn't the bio, it woulda been Digger coming back with the boots."

Jess stole a glance at Dev, surprised to find that same mild look on her face. "What do you think?" She found herself asking, her brain momentarily forgetting where she was. She held her breath for a second, wondering what her bio alt partner was going to say about that.

Could almost be anything. She hadn't really dialed in on Dev yet.

"What do I think?" Dev repeated. "I think that one right there would fit you." She pointed at a long coat hanging behind Jess against the wall. "And it matches your eyes."

Roderick chuckled low and deep in his throat. He removed the jacket and took the hanger out, tossing it over to Jess. "Your friend's got some smarts, Jess. Didn't know they were sending them out of school with that these days."

Jess accepted the diversion, shrugging off her jacket and slipping the new one on. She twitched the shoulders straight and found the sleeves long enough for her long arms. "Huh." She fastened it, then turned, raising her arms and holding her hands out. "Not bad."

The coat was actually quite attractive, Dev thought. It was far less bulky than the one they were issued, and the cut of it was flattering to Jess's tall figure. It was made of the same thing the one she'd bought was, and she thought Jess was pleased with it. "It's very nice."

"All right." Jess exchanged coats again. "What are you going to get out of me for it?" She asked Roderick. "You robber baron you."

Roderick chuckled and held a hand up, looking casually all around him before he spoke "I'll bill the old man," he said. "Digger'll drop the rest of it over with Jonton. I assume you're going to go eat there?"

Jess smiled.

"Robber baron? You call me that?" Roderick bawled. "Take it! Get out of here you wanton hussies!" He started forward, waving the hanger the coat had been hanging on. "Get out! Get out! Before I call the guard!"

"Watch it, old man!" Jess yelled back. "Take your threats and shove em! Let's go, Dev." She turned and walked out of the store, heading sharp right and then taking a left as she cleared the next stall over. She paused and got behind a column, leaning against it and looking at the sleeve of the jacket with complete absorption.

Dev stuck right with her, finding something in the booth to look at as Jess watched what was going on around them intently. It was all extremely strange, and she wasn't comfortable at all with what was going on, but she examined the little pouches on display in front of her and kept herself relatively out of view.

"Okay," Jess finally said, turning and putting a hand on her shoulder. "Good job, Dev," she said, in a very low voice. "I know it's crazy here, but you're doing a great."

Dev smiled. "Thanks," she whispered back. "It's very confusing."

"I know." Jess now clapped her on the back. "Let's go get something to eat. I bet you never tried hopping shrimp, now did you?"

Hopping shrimp. Dev had to admit the experience was overwhelming her programming. There were too many new experiences, and too much uncertainty for her to comfortably handle. "No," she said. "I know what a shrimp is. Why does it hop?"

"Ah." Jess put a companionable arm over Dev's shoulder, and guided her along the path, toward another set of long, low steps. "Come with me, my friend. I'll introduce you to my favorite meal and show you why they hop."

"You meet the shrimp before you eat it?"

Jess chuckled. "I'll have to take you shrimping sometime," she said. "Maybe limpet collecting too."

Dev eyed her.

"Maybe we can find some cockle stew."

"I think I'm glad I brought that pack of crackers," Dev commented mournfully. "I wouldn't know what to do with a cockle."

Jess's sudden laughter drew stares, but they were moving up the steps before anyone could get too close a look or stop them and then they were gone, disappearing into the strident chaos of the wet market.

Behind them, a squad of bio alt cleaners tentatively emerged, looking cautiously around before they started sweeping half a day's debris from the floor.

IT TURNED OUT that hopping shrimp were a lot better than they initially sounded. Dev regarded the plate in front of her, a deep blue glazed platter covered in bright orange and pink animals curled in a half circle that smelled really really good.

They had cups of something sweet and fizzy in front of them, and the shrimps, and a flat cake that was rather seaweed like but had a drier, earthier taste.

"Now." Jess picked up a shrimp. "First you rip the head off."

Dev watched her with some bemusement. They were seated in a small alcove at the back of the eating place, amongst a few small alcoves that were tucked away out of sight, with a light gauze curtain around them and artfully placed strong lights on the curtains that made it impossible for anyone to see in, but for them to easily see out.

The man in charge of it knew Jess by sight and had seemed to be expecting her. He'd shuffled them quickly into their little hiding place, and shortly thereafter, the plates had arrived.

"Then you suck their heads out."

Dev jerked, coming rapidly back into focus. "You what?"

Jess applied her lips to the back of the animal's head and inhaled, making an odd whistly sucking sound. "You suck their heads out," she repeated. "Try it."

Obediently, Dev picked up a shrimp and twisted its head off, turning it around and inspecting the interior before she hesitantly put it to her lips and sucked at it. A small mass of spicy goo hit her tongue, and she mouthed it, analyzing the taste before she swallowed it. It was rich and full of flavor and the spices filled her throat in a surprisingly nice way. "Oh."

"Oh good, or oh gross?" Jess asked, in an apparent good mood.

"That's excellent," Dev said. "I've never had anything like that before." She peered inside the head.

"I knew I liked you for a reason." Jess set the head down. "Okay, now on this part, you pull the legs and the shell off, like this." She demonstrated. "And you eat this part inside." She watched Dev, with a complete focus and seriousness that tickled the hell out of her, strip her first shrimp naked and bite into it, chewing it with intense thoughtfulness. "Well?"

Dev swallowed, and stared intently at her plate. "Can I eat this part too?" She picked up the shell.

"No." Jess chuckled. "It's like chewing fingernails. Just eat the inside. So you like it?"

"Yes," Dev said. "Do we ever get this where we live?" She regretfully set the shell down and picked up another animal, ripping its head off with more confidence.

"No. They aren't found around our shoreline, and they won't pay to have them brought in. The idea is we're self sufficient at home." She started in on the rest of her plate. "Damn shame. But it's one of the nice things about going outside."

Dev got through another couple of shrimp before she started conversing again. "You asked me before about the bio alts."

Jess glanced up quickly. "Didn't mean to."

"What were you expecting my reaction to be to that?" Dev asked. "Did you expect me to be upset?"

Jess chewed her shrimp, then took a sip of her drink. "I don't know what I expected. Yeah, maybe. Were you?"

Dev's eyes met hers. "They teach us to expect that," she said mildly. "To expect natural borns to treat us poorly. To make fun of us, to be mean to us, that sort of thing." She sucked another shrimp head, her eyes widening a bit at the odd sound it made. "We know what we are, Jess."

Jess sat quietly a moment, watching her. "Do you?" She said. "I don't think you're like that guy mopping the floor over there." She indicated a lone figure, in the distance.

"I'm exactly like him." Dev didn't sound at all upset about it. "Except I'm a different gene set, and I have different programming." She watched Jess. "Why are you shaking your head?"

"You're not like him," Jess repeated. "I've been working with bios since I got out of field school. I never met any one of them who was anything like you at all." She nibbled a bit of her flat cake. "Is that why you were so surprised when I was...um...nice to you?"

"Yes because you don't have to be," Dev said. "We know that. We just take what we get, you know?"

Jess's face went still and serious for a moment, then she grinned a little. "Well, you got me," she said. "And I don't buy that whole story so you'll have to deal with that." Her eyes dropped to the table and she fiddled with a shrimp, then she looked back up to find Dev looking at her with a gentle, sweet smile on her face.

It made Jess blush. She felt uncharacteristically off balance and she could have sworn all of a sudden her tongue felt fuzzy. "Anyway." Her fingers pried the shrimp apart, and plucked the legs off. Then she looked back up. "Is that why you freaked out when you thought I was mad at you?"

Dev stopped in the act of sucking a head out. She put the item back down. "Yes. We never want to make our assignments mad. It means—they teach us that it means we're not doing a good job."

"That's horsecrap." Jess regained her equilibrium. "People sometimes just get mad. It doesn't mean anything like that, at least not with me." She took a swallow of her drink and glanced past the curtain, studying the passing crowd outside before she returned her attention to Dev. "Okay?"

Dev reached over and touched her hand. "I'm very glad I got you, Jess," she said, simply. "You're really special."

Jess was caught in those eyes again, in the crystal clear warmth of them that made her feel shy and strangely unsure. She'd never really felt like this before and it confused her, a little. Excited her, a little.

Definitely it was distracting her more than a little and she almost missed the subtle shift in the lighting and the sound of approaching footsteps until it all penetrated her senses and she shifted, jerking her head toward the curtain. "Police. Just keep cool."

Dev went back to quietly ingesting her shrimp, producing a mild look of inquiry when the curtain was jerked back, and revealed two men standing there in black suits with shiny black chest plates and helmets.

"ID." The one in front said, extending his hand.

Jess produced hers and handed it over, and a moment later, Dev did the same.

The policeman flicked a scanner over both sets, and studied the results, then handed them back. "What's your business here?"

"Lunch and shopping," Jess said, casually. She held up the neatly tied bundle that she'd made of her jacket, and pointed at the plates.

The man studied her, then studied Dev, who looked back at him with interest.

"Ladies." The man gave them a half wave and moved away. "Enjoy your day."

They went on to the next little alcove, and the curtain swung closed again, obscuring them. Jess waited for them to engage with their neighbors, before she removed a small box from her pocket and keyed it, directing it after the police and tapping a few entries.

Dev heard a very high pitched, very soft whine, and she watched with curiosity as Jess reviewed the results then put the box back into her pocket. "Is that a usual interview?"

"What, the cops?" Jess glanced after them, a faintly disapproving look on her face. "Eh. Looking for non citizens to bust. They attract 'em here, since the weather's such crap. They round them up and toss them back out into the scrub or ship 'em off to the edge to let them go forage there."

Dev looked a bit confused. She picked up one of her few remaining shrimp and worked at it. "What is a non citizen?"

"Well." Jess seemed glad of the distraction. "You get tested, right? Kids do, like I did. Either you get aptituded to a training school, or you test for brains, or some skill, or you don't." She took a long swallow of her drink. "Those that don't can't get citizen status. They get tossed into the outlands, and have to fend for themselves."

"That's very interesting."

"If you can do something, you get cit status. Or..." She lifted a hand. "If your family is in service, like mine is, then everyone gets automatic cit status, and a minimum level job somewhere. Reward, I guess." She picked up her last shrimp, looking regretfully at the plate. "But the non cits try to sneak in anywhere they can, and beg or steal what they can to live off of. You get real tired of scraping lichen to eat and catching water bugs after a while."

Dev tried to imagine that. It was hard for her to fathom, because in the crèche everyone had their purpose. They were made to be useful, weren't they? No one was left out, even if there was an 'out', there was always work, and a function for everyone and they were taken care of, fed, and housed as the valuable resources they knew themselves to be.

"I was glad when I tested in," Jess said. "I didn't want to spend my life hauling nets, or supervising a power station at the waterline."

Dev only just kept herself from reaching out to touch Jess's hand again. "But you do something very difficult."

"I do. We do." Jess smiled at her. "But on the flip side, we live in nice digs, and have creds to spend, and eat well. It's worth it."

Dev looked at her identification, studying the picture, and the name, and the pretty, embossed emblem with a number that marked her as a citizen.

Interesting.

Except she wasn't. She wasn't even a non citizen. Beneath the neck on the rich blue jumpsuit she was wearing she had the same traced collar as the man she could just barely see washing the floor. She knew a moment of deep, disturbing confusion because she wasn't entirely sure of how she should feel about it all.

She was different. She was bio alt. She was hatched and raised in the crèche to serve her assignment.

And yet. She looked up at Jess, who was busily pulling the legs off a shrimp. As if sensing the attention, Jess glanced up and met her eyes, tilting her head a little in question.

And yet.

More footsteps approached and Jess grew wary, her body stiffening up and her balance shifting even in her seat so it was over the balls of her feet. "If I tell you to duck, you duck." She reached out and picked up her glass, casually looking to her right as the curtain stirred and drew aside.

"Ah," she said. "It's you." She relaxed perceptibly.

"It's me, myself." A short, dark haired and bearded man with a thickly muscled body sidled up to the table. "A gift for you, princess." He put a bundle on the padded bench seat next to where Jess was sitting. "And who is your very pretty friend?" He waggled his bushy, thick eyebrows at Dev. "Much improvement over your last one, yes?"

Jess snorted slightly. "This is Dev," she said. "Dev, this is Jonton, more commonly known as the Pirate of Quebec." She gave the man a wry look. "Jonton's something of an old family friend. This is his place, as you probably guessed by the fact his name's on the sign outside."

"Hello," Dev said. "It's very nice to meet you."

The man smiled, showing a mouthful of teeth that were curiously decorated with tiny engravings. "It is my pleasure, Miss Dev." He bowed. "Any friend of my old family friend here, is a friend of mine." He turned back to Jess. "A very great improvement over the last one for sure."

"Definitely," Jess said. "Smarter, has a lot more common sense, a better bus driver and much cuter on top of it." She winked at Dev. "I got damn lucky."

"So I hear." Jonton leaned against the table. "Especially what I've heard lately of your luck." He lowered his voice, touching her arm. "I am pleased to see you here in good health."

Jess grinned briefly. "Thanks." She touched the package. "This the boots? I'm glad they're done. I need to get clear of here. Too many eyes around."

"It is. May you have good wearing of them." He bowed again. "Till next time, princess. And again, so nice to meet you, Miss Dev." He stepped back and then ducked out of the way, leaving the curtains to slowly swing back closed again.

They were both quiet for a moment. Then Dev gently cleared her throat. "What exactly is a pirate?"

Jess chuckled. "I'll tell you later, when we're back on the bus." She studied her plate to make sure she'd consumed everything on it. "We need to get out of here before someone spots me and starts trouble." She looked up at Dev. "You done?"

"Well, since you said not to eat the shells, I suppose I am." Dev gazed mournfully at her plate. "They were excellent. Thank you very much for bringing me here."

"It was my pleasure, Dev," Jess said, her voice taking on a gentle tone. "I remember my first time in this place. My father brought me here after I graduated basic school. I thought the city was the coolest place on earth." She tucked the jacket she'd gotten under her arm, and picked up the boots.

"May I take that?" Dev said, pointing at the boots. "My jacket's smaller."

"Your every thing's smaller." Jess handed the bundle over and they slid out from behind the table, pausing to let Jess study the outside space before she stepped through the curtain and held it for Dev. "To the left there, and down that ramp."

Dev went as directed, and they slipped out of the wet market and started downward. Jonton's place was on the edge of the market, which was now becoming quiet as the merchants started packing up for the day. The market area was high ceilinged, and the sounds echoed, to the counterpoint of thunder rolling overhead.

She stuck close to Jess's side as they passed from the light of the cavern into the darkness of the tunnels, and after a few minutes walk, Jess paused to fasten her jacket.

So Dev did too. She put her bundles down and got herself sealed up, then picked the packages back up as Jess moved on. Neither of them spoke, and Dev could see the tension in Jess's face as she scanned and rescanned the area.

It felt a little dangerous. They walked to the base of the ramp and then Jess turned right and angled over across traffic to a side corridor that led to a set of stone steps. A group of bio alts came past them, easing to one side of the steps to get out of their way.

Dev recognized the set, but dimly, from much earlier memories when groups of bio alts would be loaded on shuttles, all of them happy, waving as they left to what they were sure would be good assignments.

They didn't look very happy now. Dev met the eyes of one of them, and he looked quickly away, hunching his shoulders. A Geebee, she remembered, but this one and his mates had scars on their faces, and threadbare coveralls. One was missing fingers.

Dev exhaled a little, as she followed Jess down the steps and along the right hand side of a busy tunnel. The two of them were mostly ignored, getting only brief, dismissed looks as they made their way downward.

"Here." Jess pointed at a dark offshoot tunnel. She ducked inside and then her hand light appeared to light the way, as they went down a set of crooked steps, and then under a crumbling arch, to another set of steps. These heading up.

The steps were getting narrower, and she shifted the package to her right hand, letting her left one rest against the wall.

The surface was interesting. It felt rough and cold against her skin, and a bit moist. It was irregular, and when she looked down, the steps were too.

They turned a corner and started up a more steep set of stairs, and now Dev felt fresh air coming in and blowing against her face. She could hear the thunder, and was aware of a rich, wet smell. "Is that the rain?"

"Yeah, put your hood up." Jess got hers fastened just as they reached a landing and were faced with a small opening.

Dev fastened the snaps on her hood and followed Jess out into a fierce downpour that pelted hard against her body and nearly knocked her backward. She steadied herself against the rock face and blinked hard as water filled her eyes. "Wow."

Jess turned and gripped her sleeve. "Careful. It's steep here." She slowly worked her way down the rough cut steps they'd climbed up earlier, pressing herself hard against the cliff surface. It occurred to her that staying in the city might have been a wiser choice, but she'd started getting that itch between her shoulder blades and the last thing she wanted was a firefight in the middle of Quebec.

Probably end up with all of them in jail, those that didn't end up dead.

The storm suddenly cracked and thundered right over head, and with a yelp, she ducked as a landslide of sharp stones came cascading down on top of them. "C'mon!"

Dev scampered down after her, feeling sliding under her boots and an unsteadiness in her balance as the rock seemed to shiver under her.

She half slid the last part to the bottom, then she joined Jess in a full out bolt for the carrier as a heavy rumble warned them of trouble coming down.

Rocks started to bounce past her, and she felt an impact on her back as they got to the bottom of the slope and then ran across the boulder strewn area in front of where they'd left the bus.

Jess looked behind her, and her eyes went wide. "Oh crap! Dev! Move it! Get to the bus! Move!"

Dev didn't bother looking. She bolted past her companion and triggered the hatch, ducking inside as Jess caught up to her. She headed for her seat as a sound started coming around them that was louder than anything she'd heard in her life.

She heard the hatch seal behind her and got her harness in place as she was already reaching out to start up the engines and get the power systems up, her hands moving in programming boosted speed and precision she didn't have the luxury to think about.

"Better boost! We're gonna get creamed!" Jess bellowed, thumping into her own seat. "Or there isn't gonna be enough of this damn thing for Clint to...ugh!"

"Hold on!" Dev didn't hesitate an instant. She kicked the landing jets in full force as soon as they spooled and took the carrier straight up for just long enough to clear the boulders before she cut in the mains, boosting clear of the ground as she heard the bump and clang of rocks hitting the outside of the hull.

No time even to put her headset on. She got away from the cliff at full speed for a minute, then she cut in the rear scan and the screens came alive with the sight of the entire face of the cliff sliding down and collapsing in a destructive rush that blasted over the tiny plateau they'd been parked on minutes before.

"Holy shit." Jess stared at the screen.

Another crack of thunder and a blast of lightning rocked the carrier. Dev instinctively ducked and flinched as the forward screens whited out, then she adjusted the tint and cut in comp. "We're getting weather warnings," she said. "Too much interference."

"Find a place to put her down," Jess said. "No one'll be out watching now anyway. Stupid god damned storms." She pushed her hood back and raked the wet hair out of her eyes, as the carrier rocked back and forth between blasts of lightning.

Dev set up comp and searched the map ahead of them, spotting an overhang on the other side of the small valley they were currently coursing through. The carrier flashed over bare rock and dark pools of rain, the coated front window giving her a clear view of the sheets of water slamming against the carrier with intimidating force.

"Get her down," Jess warned, as they both felt the engines hesitate.

Dev did, aiming for the overhang and slamming the landing jets on just as the mains cut out and they dropped hard. Lightning was striking all around them, multiple bolts coming on either side as she got the vehicle under the ledge and cut power just before a bolt hit them full on, making the power blank out completely for a few long seconds.

Then the batts came on and they were safe, the landing feet leveling the carrier as the storm came on in earnest. For a few minutes, the rumble and thump almost deafened them, but after that it steadied down to a dull roar and they both let out a breath of relief at the same time.

Jess let her body relax against her seat. "I'll tell ya, Dev. You really are worth your weight in gold credits."

Dev turned her seat around, glancing down at herself, before she regarded Jess. "I think it's possible I might have to cash that in if I keep almost wrecking this transport." She gave Jess a wry look. "Clint is going to be very disturbed."

Jess started unzipping her jacket. "Probably," she said. "But we made it. Now we just have to wait out the storm and then head off to North Station." She stood up and hung her jacket on one of the hooks near the drop pack. "And hope no one's stupid enough to try and follow us in this."

Dev undid her restraints and stood, getting out of her jacket as well. She hung it up next to Jess's and riffled her damp hair out. "So now we just wait?"

"Now we just wait." Jess leaned against the drop suit, a faint smile appearing on her lips. "Of course, this could be the moment I tell you to take your clothes off."

Dev met her eyes, and smiled. "Because we can wear our uniforms in the North place?"

"Well." Jess pushed off from the suit and started unfastening the wrist catches on her jumpsuit. "That too."

Chapter Sixteen

THE STORM WAS overwhelmingly violent. Dev had perched on the small ledge behind the drop suit, with her back against the dispenser half hidden behind it. Overhead, she could hear the almost continual rumble of thunder, and the lightning strikes were going on around them in an eye blinking barrage of cracks and blasts.

She and Jess were in their gray under suits, the environmental systems in the carrier working well enough to keep the icy chill of the wind and weather from impacting them. It was comfortable and relaxed. Dev was reading a few pages of her book while Jess fiddled with one of the big blaster rifles.

She had halfway wanted Jess to tell her to take her clothes off. For a moment, she'd thought Jess was, but the fury of the storm had distracted both of them and Jess had seemed to turn a bit shy, her face twisting up into a wry grin as she folded her city suit and put it away.

That was all right, Dev decided. There was always time later to investigate the idea.

After a few minutes Jess set the rifle back into it's clamps and stood up, walking over and taking a seat next to her on the ledge. "Crazy outside, huh?" She braced her hands on the edge of the flat surface, her shoulder just brushing Dev's.

"I've never seen anything like this, so yes, I believe it is." Dev was glad to have the solid wall of the carrier behind her, instead of the glass.

Jess hitched herself back and leaned against the wall, folding her hands and letting them rest on her thighs. "Thats right, no storms in space."

"Well." Dev put her book down. "We do have storms, just not water ones. We have sun storms and asteroid storms, and they're both pretty dangerous. I remember one of the asteroid ones when I was little that was so bad it knocked out power and grav."

"Huh."

"It was scary. We were all in class when it happened. All of a sudden we heard a loud noise, then it went dark and we were all floating."

Jess tried to imagine that, and really couldn't. "Wow."

"It was really disconcerting," Dev said. "Even the proctors were scared. You do go through training for emergencies but you don't expect one like that."

Jess considered that in silence. "Space is kinda creepy."

Dev nodded. "It sometimes is. Especially when they show you what explosive decompression does. No one makes airlock jokes after that." She pulled her legs up crossed and leaned on them. "That's what they do to people who die upside."

Jess made a face.

"Well, it's either that or put them in the solar furnace and you know, I think I'd prefer the spacing," Dev said. "I remember in basics class they told us in the long ago past they used to bury bodies in the ground. That sounded pretty crazy."

"It was," Jess admitted. "I guess we don't do any better, processing bodies and just dispersing them into the sea. Gotta do something with all the mass, I guess and I always though it was sorta comforting to know you'd at least give a fish a meal."

"I see." Dev thought about that. "This is quite an unpleasant subject," she said, finally. "Can you talk about fish instead? They live in the ocean?"

"They do. They're the only thing that survived, after it all went bad. They learned to live on the venting algae, and we learned to live on them. That, and we learned to harvest the sea, to use the waves and the tides and the wind for power, and subsist on a lot less than we used to."

Dev nodded. "I learned that in class too," she said. "Except at the crèche we used solar power for everything. They took us when we were kids up to the processing center to see the arrays. They were so pretty, all shining, and moving to follow the sun."

Jess studied her hands. "I'd like to see the sun. Maybe you could show me around up there someday."

Dev made a picture in her head of that. She realized with some internal embarrassment that while she'd love to show Jess the sun, she wasn't really happy about considering going back to the crèche. She tried to imagine returning to her life of classes and sleep pods, and felt an intense sense of discomfort over it.

It was a strange feeling.

"Except I'm pretty sure you don't want to go back there," Jess said after a few moments of silence. "Do ya?"

Dev smiled, and glanced at her. "No. I was just thinking about that." She shifted a little, to face Jess. "I don't want to go back there. I like it here much better." She looked at Jess, watching the interesting shadows the overhead lights were casting on her profile.

They made her a little mysterious looking. There were sharp planes to her face that seemed stark in the half lighting.

Jess reached over and gently touched the exposed collar on Dev's neck. "Do they ever take these off?"

Dev felt the touch, and she swallowed the faint lump in her throat from it. "What do you mean?"

Jess ran her thumb over the metal, and felt the thin, flexible edge. "You said it was for programming. So when they're done with that, do they take them off? When you don't need it anymore?"

Dev remained absolutely still for a moment. "No," she said, resisting the urge to move away from Jess's hand. "Because the other reason we have them is so they can put us down if they need to."

Jess sat up and moved closer. "What?" She said, a sharp note in her voice. "What do you mean, put you down?"

Dev shrugged slightly. "Sometimes things happen. I mean, we are humans, after all. Even bio alts can end up doing bad things and like any other human they can get dangerous." She put her hand out and touched Jess's knee. "It's like those gates in the citadel, isn't it? That's to stop people when they do bad things."

"Yes," Jess said. "It doesn't happen often, but it has happened, when someone just went nuts or..." She shrugged. "I mean, we are dangerous." She indicated herself. "I am. Any of the agents are. Hell, you saw what Bain did."

"So, it's the same for us." Dev said. "They put a code into a system, and it tells the programming interface to send a signal up into our brains and makes us—well, it makes your heart stop. And your breathing." She watched Jess's face, seeing the emotion and tension cross it. "And trying to take it off would do the same thing," she finished quietly.

Jess shifted her fingers from the collar down to Dev's shoulder. "That's why you don't like anyone touching it."

"Yes," Dev said. "But I don't mind if you do."

"Why?"

"I trust you."

Jess looked at her. "Well, NM-Dev-1, I'm sure glad you told me about that damn thing before I tried to get it off you." She patted Dev's cheek. "I'll keep my paws off it though. I don't want to freak you out."

"You won't."

"I won't?"

"No." Dev reached up to touch Jess's hand. "I like when you touch me. It feels good."

Jess felt a curious sensation steal over her and the sound of the storm outside faded as she focused on those pale, gentle eyes facing her. "I'm glad. Feels good to me too," she murmured, letting her hand lay flat against Dev's cheek and feeling the shift under her fingertips as Dev smiled in response.

It did feel good. Seeing that smile felt good, and she felt herself smiling back, her skin feeling warm and sensitized as Dev's thumb gently stroked the back of her hand. "Yeah, I like that." She stroked Dev's cheek. "Glad you do too."

Dev's eyes were twinkling a little. "Oh, I do."

What next? Jess felt a little short of breath. "Um...Want to try that kissing thing again?" She asked hopefully, seeing the instant interest in the pale eyes watching her.

"Yes," Dev responded positively. "I really would."

It was crazy and insane and there was the storm and... Jess leaned over and tilted her head and their lips brushed. And who cared? She made a more solid contact and it grew into something sweet and familiar and she felt herself losing her balance and the next thing she knew they were tumbling together against the back wall of the carrier. "Oof." She grunted, as her head hit the metal surface. "Ouch."

Dev chuckled softly, and righted herself. "That was interesting." She cleared her throat a little. "A bit easier in the water I think." She shifted a little and laid down on her back, folding her hands over her stomach. "I do like it though."

Jess slowly straightened, rolling onto her side and extending her legs out. It put her right next to Dev and she propped her head up on her hand and put her other one on Dev's arm. "Me too. C'mere."

Dev rolled over to face her and they kissed again, this time in a somewhat safer position. She felt the good feeling start up again, and she touched Jess's face, feeling a little heat under her fingertips as Jess's hand came to rest on her hip. When they paused, she was short of breath and so was Jess, and they looked at each other at close distance.

Jess reached up and traced one of her cheekbones. "Ever done this before?"

Dev shook her head.

"They teach you about sex upstairs?"

Dev half shrugged. "They showed us a vid in health class," she said. "It wasn't anything like this. And they didn't say anything about what it would feel like." She felt her heartbeat start to settle. "Maybe they should have." She added, almost as an afterthought.

"Maybe." Jess smiled a little. "Does it bother you?"

Dev sat there quietly for a little while, thinking about the question. "I don't think so," she finally said. "I like how it feels. I just didn't expect it."

"Expect...kissing? Or that you and I would...or..." Jess fished a little. "We do this sometimes. Ops teams, I mean. With each other."

"That's what Doctor Dan said. I asked him after we did it the first time and he told me that sometimes it happened, and about how it wasn't okay with us but that it was okay for me because I was doing this job." She studied Jess thoughtfully. "But even if he hadn't said that, I would still want to do it," she admitted, with an almost bashful look.

Jess looked at her in some mild fascination. "Even if it was...what do you call it, incorrect?"

"Yes." Dev smiled. "I told you that you were really attractive," she said. "You really are, to me."

Jess grinned. "Likewise."

"So I would have broken that rule anyway," Dev said. "Even if I'd known about it before."

"Ahhh...I knew I liked you." Jess's eyes twinkled gravely. "They call me a rogue, y'know. I don't always play by the rules, and that gets me in trouble sometimes." She traced one of Dev's eyebrows. "I knew about the rule regarding bio alts," she said. "But I had no intention of obeying it with you."

Dev's head tilted a little. "Really?"

"Unless you had a problem with it," Jess said. "And I don't think you do." She glanced up as the thunder overhead calmed, and the lightning strikes started to taper off. "We can talk about it when we get back to base. It's more comfortable in bed anyway."

They both sat up and regarded each other. Then Dev hopped off the ledge and shook herself a little, reaching for her flight suit and taking it down off the hook.

Jess reached around her, and then, unexpectedly, ducked her head and gave Dev another kiss. Then she took her own suit and winked, backing up and shaking the suit out in preparation to donning it. "I'm glad you're okay with this. It's been a while for me. Joshua wasn't into girls."

Dev felt quite flushed. It was an interesting feeling. "I see." She got into her flight suit, and went over to the dispenser for a container of water. Her lips were still tingling, and she could taste Jess on them, a little. Also very interesting.

"Are you into boys?" Dev asked, glancing over her shoulder.

Jess blushed visibly. "Are you?" She turned the question back.

"I never really thought about it either way." Dev answered straightforwardly. "Class made sex about as interesting as sweeping out the kitchen, so no one really talked about it much." She hopped into her seat and started bringing systems online. "But I know one thing."

"Yeah?" Jess gave herself a shake, and dropped into her chair.

Dev turned around and looked at her. "No one ever made me want to kiss them like that before." She turned back around and started syncing the comp, slowly bringing the power online and running checks to make sure the lightning strikes hadn't fried anything.

Jess slowly pulled her restraints around her and buckled them, her eyes fixed on the pilot's chair. "Well, we're even," she finally said, as she clicked the catches in place and hit the toggle to retract them. "Because no one's ever made me want to say screw the mission, let's go find a cave somewhere before."

Dev looked over her shoulder again, her pale eyebrows lifting, and then lowering in some confusion.

"Never mind." Jess started laughing. "Boot the engines up."

Dev focused her attention back on her job. The rain had lessened to a degree that she could, with some confidence, activate the landing jets again and ease out from under the ledge. It was hard to concentrate though, and she had to take a few long breaths and release them before she set her hands on the throttles and gently ignited the main engines. She felt them rumble into life, a bit rough as she trimmed the power leads.

She sort of felt like that too, like there were things surging inside her that needed to be trimmed a little. Dev pulled her headset on and settled the ear cups, flicking through the settings and scanning the comp to make sure they hadn't gotten any messages relayed after the storm.

After a moment, her eyes flicked up to the mirror mounted over her position and she found Jess looking back at her in the reflection. Then she had to look forward, and inched the throttles to bring the carrier around the edge of the escarpment and back around in the other direction.

They would pass to the west of Quebec and then up into the northern archipelago to the North Station. Dev had the coordinates locked in, and she let out one final deep breath before she nudged the throttles forward and focused in on her task.

Boy, it was hard. Dev took a drink from her container and put it back in its swinging holder. She studied her consoles a couple of times, until her brain finally lurched out of its bemusement and sharpened as the readings and panel displays triggered her programming in a somewhat belated manner.

She looked out the forward screens, seeing nothing much but gray sky and equally gray land. They were traveling over rock plateaus that were slick and wet with the falling rain, their tops scarred and shaped by the continual impact with the water.

After a few minutes traveling, Dev felt her shoulders relax and she was better able to focus. She ran through her checks and had the systems rescan for damages, her mind running over the readouts as she took in a weather report. The heavy clouds they'd huddled under had passed over, but she could see on the out scan there was another storm moving in.

Dutifully, she reported that to Jess, feeling a prickle between her shoulder blades as she heard the soft click and slither of her partner's restraints coming loose. She flexed her hands a trifle as Jess came to stand next to her, anticipating and getting the friendly pressure of a hand on her shoulder. "There." She pointed at the out scan.

"I see," Jess said. "Damn it." She looked at the powerful lines, the dark reds and oranges telling their own tales of the strong electrical forces buried inside them. "These storms are getting outrageous. We used to have two, three days between them. Now we're lucky if we go twelve or twenty hours."

"Why is that?" Dev asked.

"No one really knows." Jess leaned on the back of her chair. "We've lost so much damn science. Well, we'll have to either make it a very short stop at North or find a place on the ice to hole up if that line comes in fast as it looks like."

Dev's brows hiked up a little. "Hole up on the ice? In the carrier?"

"Sure." Jess glanced back over her shoulder. "I packed cold kits. Includes lined sleeping bags in case we get caught out."

"I see." Dev trimmed the carrier's flight, taking them around a tall peak in a gentle curve, very aware of the hand casually resting on her shoulder as Jess studied the comp.

Ahead of them she saw a long line of craggy bluffs, and the western edges of them had thick gray clouds draped over them. She checked her navigation readouts and let her elbow rest on her chair arm, feeling a bit of warmth through her suit as she pressed against Jess's thigh. "Thirty minutes."

"Mm." Jess gave her shoulder a squeeze, then she retreated back to the back of the carrier, starting to rummage around in the equipment locker. "Once you get within ten, they'll contact you on sideband twelve," she said. "Then ask you to switch to a mainline channel for traffic control."

Dev peered at the empty sky. "Is it a busy place?"

"No," Jess said. "They're just regulation sticklers. Just move to whatever channel they want, and let them call the numbers for you when you go in. They've got a carrier bay like we do, only smaller."

"All right," Dev said. "May I ask you something?"

Jess stopped rummaging. "What makes you think you have to ask permission?"

Dev cleared her throat. "I didn't mean to cause you discomfort," she said. "I was just wondering if the people at the location we're traveling to know I'm a bio alt."

Jess came back up to the front of the carrier. She leaned on the back of Dev's chair. "Why?"

Dev risked a glance up and almost didn't look back down at the console. "I just wondered. It's interesting to see how different people react."

Jess looked thoughtfully through the rain lashed window. Would they know? Dev had only been at the citadel for a few days, and the stations were by tradition autonomous from each other. The less you knew about the structure of the organization, the less you could tell anyone about it.

Only the Old Man knew it all. "Unless Bain messaged them, they probably don't know. But your creds will tell them when you come into the complex. Does it bother you?"

Dev shook her head. "Does it bother you?" She again turned the question on Jess.

"No. But the Norther's are old fashioned. It might damn well bother them." Jess smiled, in a not entirely nice way. "And that could be a lot of fun."

"Fun?" Dev glanced up at her again.

"Fun." Jess gently ruffled her hair, then she went back to her seat and dropped into it, extending her legs out and crossing them at the ankles. "Almost as fun as an ice cave might be."

DEV WONDERED ABOUT the ice cave, as she piloted the carrier along its assigned route toward the North Station escarpment. She could already see it on the horizon, a lonely pinnacle of rock that was an island in the surrounding storm tossed seas. It was stark and forbidding, on the outside not really different from the citadel they'd come from but smaller, and more remote.

A soft chime sounded in her ear cup. "Approaching vehicle, identify," the voice demanded, low, and with an interesting lilt to it.

"BR27006 approaching from the southwest," Dev said. "Requesting entry and landing."

"Stand by."

Dev kept the carrier on course, but slowed her engines a bit as she flicked off the auto nav and took possession of her throttles. She saw the alert on comp as they were scanned, imagining that she could feel the beam as it passed over them. She acknowledged the alert, and keyed in their ident beacon in response that would provide the encrypted codes to the station's comp.

Jess was leaned back in her seat, her hands folded over her stomach and her eyes half closed. "Probably keep us circling out here for an hour."

"Really?"

"Yeah. Just jerks sometimes," Jess said. "They're the furthest on the edge, makes them a little nuts."

"I see." Dev studied the readouts of their own scan, which was picking up transports closer in to the station, and the signatures of turbo generators near the bottom of the cliff. "Do they think we might hurt them?"

Jess shrugged. "Meh." She wriggled into a slightly more comfortable spot on her surprisingly comfortable new seat. "Sometimes between stations there's a lot of ego. You know what that is?"

"Yes," Dev said. She glanced at Jess in the mirror, wondering if it was just the reflection that made it seem that way or if Jess's legs were really that long.

"BR27006, ident confirmed. Please approach and switch comms to channel twenty-three, sideband five."

"Ahahaha. We got lucky," Jess said. "They don't have a prick on duty this time."

Dev couldn't match her programmed definition of prick to anything applicable so she merely settled her ear cup and keyed the mic on. "North station, this is BR27006, acknowledge. Switching channels." She made the adjustment and reacquired the station signal, then saw the landing beacon start to transmit and locked onto it.

So far so good. She ran a set of checks to make sure all the systems she'd need to land the carrier were functioning, and that they hadn't taken any damage during the storm. Everything seemed nominal, so she boosted up the speed a little and headed toward the gaping hole in the side of the pinnacle where the beacon was leading her. "The entrance isn't on top like ours."

"No. No flat surface up there," Jess said. "That's a natural cavern entrance they modified. Smaller, but at least the rain doesn't kick you in the ass when they open the doors like in ours."

Ours.

Dev liked hearing that. Ours. We. Us. She descended to the level of the landing bay opening and centered her approach as the big doors started to open. She could see the pale blue light inside the cavern and she focused on the opening, where a dim blue tracer was indicating an in path.

She cut in the landing jets and put the engines in idle as she came into the cavern, seeing carrier landing pads below her not that different from the citadel's. "North landing control, this is BR27006, requesting pad assignment." She cleared the entrance and let the carrier slide to one side of it, putting solid rock at her back.

"You fly nice," Jess said. "You never bounce my kidneys."

Dev flicked a glance in the mirror. "Thanks," she said. "I think?"

"BR27006. Landing assignment D23." The comm brought her attention back. "Stand by after landing for security scan. Remain sealed until notified."

"Mph," Jess snorted. "Oh look the jerk woke up."

Dev located their assigned pad and gently lowered the carrier onto it, spooling down the main engines and cutting off the landing jets as the bottom skids touched and the carrier came to a halt. She secured the power systems and safed the weapons, glancing outside as she did so. "Oh."

Jess lifted her head and peered out the windows. A ring of security guards were surrounding them, heavy rifles pointed at the carrier. "Ugh. Idiots." She relaxed and let her eyes close again. "Just chill."

"I'm pretty warm, thanks." Dev sat back and loosened the chair restraints. She copied the logs to storage, and did the rest of her shutdown checklist, doing her best to ignore the ring of muzzles facing her outside. She saw a light come on and she studied it. "Jess, they are asking for a comp interface."

"Yeah?" Jess released her restraints and got up, coming forward to lean on Dev's chair and peer at the board. "Anything in comp?"

"No. I hadn't even plotted our next destination. Just this one," Dev said. "Some weather reports, is all."

"You know how to set a trace?"

Dev smiled. "Yes." She touched her keypads in a rapid sequence. "Let them in?"

"Yup." Jess leaned further, watching as Dev set up the connection. She studied the screen as the North systems linked in, watching the request for information intently. "Want to know where we've been eh?" She glanced outside at the security guards. "Good thing we didn't take a joyride into the arctic first."

After a moment, the connection shut down, and the audio came live in Dev's earpiece. "BR27006, you are cleared. Please prepare to egress."

"Aw. Guess we told the truth," Jess, said, with a mock pout. "Next time remind me to slip a trip to space in there, see if they catch it." She pushed herself upright, and went to the weapons rack, sliding her handgun into its holster tucked under her arm and picking up the heavy blaster and seating it into the flexible web system that went down her right leg. "Let's go, partner."

Dev stood and made sure her insignia was straight, then she uncoupled her leads from the carrier and clipped the ends in place as she walked over to join Jess. She paused behind her as Jess also paused, her hands on the hatch controls. "I'm ready."

"Don't let them freak you out," Jess said. "Just ignore what they say if they start talking crap."

Dev nodded, and then she twitched a little as Jess triggered the hatch and it popped outward with a thump and hiss. The ramp extended and they walked down it, just as two jump suited figures appeared from between two other carriers and approached them.

The security guards had withdrawn, save two that were stationed on either side of an inner door. Dev kept Jess's face in her peripheral vision, watching her reaction to gauge what was going on. She seemed relaxed though, so Dev relaxed and waited just behind her as the welcoming party approached.

It was two men, and the one in front was dressed as Jess was, the one behind him was in a standard jumpsuit in a dull orange color. Neither of them looked particularly friendly, but neither of them looked like they were about to start fighting with them either.

"Drake," the man said, as they came up even with them.

"Hello, Sydney," Jess drawled a little. "How are ya?"

"Very busy as always," he said. "What can we do for you?" He glanced past her and looked at Dev, then returned his eyes to Jess's. "We don't have much in the way of spare parts or supplies to offer."

"Just looking for local info," Jess said. "The bus just got overhauled. We don't need anything." She half turned. "This is my new partner, Dev. Dev, this is Sydney Lang. He's the senior agent here at North."

"Like you are in our place?" Dev asked, mildly, not missing the sudden jerk as the North agent focused on her. "How interesting. Nice to meet you." She extended her hand.

Warily he took it and pressed it, then released her, returning his attention to Jess. "Did you get promoted? We hadn't heard." His eyes shifted to her collar insignia. "Oh, yes, I see you have." He extended his hand. "Congrats." He indicated the waiting figure behind him. "Luke Turloute, my chief mechanic. In case you needed anything done to the carrier."

Jess nodded at the man, who nodded back, but said nothing. "Shall we get a cup of kack and chat?" She said. "Don't want to take much of your time. The bus doesn't need anything, does it, Dev?"

"Everything is optimal," Dev said. "We're fine."

"Okay, certainly." Lang's manner had changed completely. "Let's go to my lounge. I'll ask Dom to join us. He was just assembling the daily recap."

He turned and led the way to the inner door. It opened as he approached and Dev felt the familiar tickle of scan across her skin, noting that Jess's hands were clenching slightly at her sides as she passed through it. The hallway they emerged into was familiar looking, granite walls and the smooth cut floors, though a slightly lighter shade of gray.

Jess was on edge, it seemed. Her right hand was gently resting on the stock of the big blaster, a casual grip that wasn't entirely casual.

"So. When did you get promoted?" Sydney asked. "Really strange we didn't hear."

Jess smiled with no humor evident. "Just recently. I did a long run on the dark side and did a bit of damage. Impressed someone I guess."

"Really. Last thing I heard you all were having serious problems there." Lang lead them into a small lounge and the door shut behind them. He gestured to a drink dispenser then took one himself, and sat down in one of the chairs. "That's what I heard, anyway. Matter of fact, I heard you almost got skunked."

Jess took a drink and handed it to Dev, then took one for herself and sat on a second chair. "We're always in some kind of trouble, aren't we?" She asked. "We had some changes up top, and a new class come in. Nothing more than the usual."

Sydney's eyes flicked to Dev, who had seated herself and was merely watching and listening. "I see. So what can I tell you? Nothing new here but more and more storms."

Jess nodded. "We noticed. I was just telling Dev here, that it seems they're coming in every half day. I can't remember a single day lately without one."

"She doesn't know about storms?" He looked intently at her.

"She's spacer born," Jess said, casually. "So, no. But what I was really interested in is any word you have of ice pirates. We got intel they've been infiltrated by the other side."

Dev had to school her face quickly not to react, since certainly that bit of information was as much a surprise to her as it apparently was to Sydney Lang. His eyes opened wide and he put his drink down, straightening up in his chair as he looked at Jess.

"Ice pirates?" He said. "Are you kidding me? Those people haven't been seen in these parts in years. They're all dead, Jess. Where did you get that crazy idea from?"

Jess leaned back against the back of the chair. "Not according to the intel we got. We only thought they were gone. Two fishermen were found dead frozen in a berg with their gear stripped and a head cut in their chests not two weeks gone."

Lang's jaw dropped.

The door opened and another man entered, this one in a tech jumpsuit. "Sydney, you called?" The man glanced warily at Jess and Dev, circling them to come up on the other side of Lang. "Hello, Jess," he said. "Didn't know you were here."

Lang shut his mouth with a click. "Sit down, Dom," he said. "Jess is looking for intel on ice pirates."

Dom chuckled as he sat down. "Want some on Santa Claus too? There are no ice pirates anymore."

Dev studied the two of them. The newcomer was tall and very thin, and had brown hair and eyes, where Lang was more heavily built and shorter, with black hair and gray eyes. They were both older than Jess, and she got the impression that Lang was far from pleased about Jess's promotion.

Jess seemed to find that funny. Dev made a mental note to ask her why later.

"Apparently either that's not true, or someone's imitating them." Lang said. "But that's news to us, isn't it?"

Dom snorted. "I'll say." He folded his arms and looked at Jess. "Where'd you get that wild tale from?"

Jess smiled. "Can't share the source, sorry," she said. "But anyway, me and Dev are going out to do a recon over the ice fields. See how true the story is." She leaned on the arm of her chair. "So I was just wondering if you had any word of them."

Sydney focused suddenly on Dev. "Where in space?" He asked.

Dev studied Jess's face in her peripheral vision, but she seemed both relaxed and inclined to let her answer her own questions. "Biological Station two," she answered promptly. "I've just been downside a week. I'm still learning all the differences."

Dom blinked. "You're the damned bio alt."

Dev nodded. "Yes," she said. "Biological Alternative set 0202-164812, instance NM-Dev-1. But please call me Dev. It's short, and it's what they painted on the carrier."

The two North agents stared at her as though she'd grown another head. "Are you kidding me?" Dom looked at Jess. "You really went along with this?"

"I did." Jess appeared to be enjoying his consternation. "I had my doubts but Dev's grown on me." Her eyes twinkled a little. "She's a kickass bus driver. Matter of fact, she helped put the damn thing back together after we blew apart Gibraltar a couple days back."

Dev produced a mild grin. "It was the least I could do." She said. "Since I banged it up doing that."

"I thought that was just a crazy rumor." Sydney finally spoke up. "Something I heard on the ops report. She's really a bio alt?" He stared openly at Dev. "She doesn't look like one. Not one I've ever seen anyway, and most of the sets cycle through here for ice experience."

"I'm an experimental set," Dev said. "Developmental. That's what the Dev stands for."

Both North agents looked very uncomfortable. "Well," Sydney said. "No telling what comes out of Base Ten." He twitched a little. "I did see the report on Gibraltar. Bet you made some enemies with that one, Jess."

"Bet I did." Jess got up. "But, if you all have nothing to share, we'll be on our way. Can I get the latest met?" She looked at Dev, who had also stood and was watching her. "And you said you had a daily recap?"

Dom got up and went over to a console, sliding behind it and into the chair. "Sure," he said. "We sent a team to do ice measurement a few weeks ago. Looks like some glaciations building up again. Maybe drop the water table a little. Give you guys at ten back your beach."

"That trick at Gibraltar give you your gold bars, Jess?" Sydney asked.

"That and a few other things," Jess smoothly replied. "Bain appreciated the effort."

"Bain?" Sydney and Dom both looked up at her in surprise. "How'd you get involved with him? I thought he was busy in his fortress of solitude at Pichu," Sydney said. "Haven't seen him in these parts in years. Is he at ten? What's up there?"

Jess shrugged. "Who can say what he's up to? He's the Old Man," she said. "You'll have to ask him if you want to know. I'm not gonna speak for him, that's for damn sure." She held her hand out for the films Dom had retrieved. "Who knows? Maybe he'll drop by here next." She winked at Sydney, who managed a sour smile in return. "Thanks. C'mon, Dev."

"Nice to meet you," Dev said to the two men, then she turned and followed Jess out of the room, and back down the hallway toward the carrier bay. "That was interesting."

Jess chuckled. "Yes it was." She guided Dev back through the scan, and ducked past a team of bio alts who were in exposure suits with the helmets removed, their hair damp with sweat. They were standing around a big block of ice, and Jess paused as she was almost passed them and turned back. "Whatcha got there, boys?"

The bio alts looked at her warily. "Agent," one said. "This is an ice sample." He glanced at Dev. "Tech."

Dev cocked her head and studied him. The group of bio alts were older, possibly twice her age, and she wasn't familiar with the set. Apparently, the bio alts weren't familiar with her either. "Hello," she said. "Why were you taking a sample of the ice?"

"We were told to," the man said. "Do you require something?" He looked from one to the other. "We are assigned work."

"Thanks." Jess clapped her hand on Dev's arm. "We were just curious." She nudged Dev ahead of her and they crossed the carrier deck and wound their way between the landing pads. She lowered her voice. "We can talk after takeoff. Not before."

"All right." Dev led the way onto the pad, surprising a bio alt technician who was examining part of their engine pod. "Is there something irregular?" Dev asked him.

He jerked, and turned. "Nothing." He backed away. "Just looking at the new intakes." He pointed at the front of the engine. "Never saw them before." He was an engaging looking man, almost Jess's height with curly red hair and freckles.

"Decco!" A voice rang out. "What are you doing over there? Get back to work!"

The bio alt turned and rambled down the steps, ducking past a re-generator and disappeared into the shadows quickly.

"Hm." Dev reached out and triggered the hatch, the scan tickling her palm. "That was also interesting, but in a different way."

Jess chuckled under her breath. She followed Dev up into the carrier, slapping the door lock and just barely clearing the door before it sealed. She felt better, the moment it had. The itchy spot between her shoulder blades eased, and she felt some of the tension come out of her as she unholstered her guns and put them back in their racks.

"Those men were not...ah." Dev sat down in her seat and started up her checks. "They were in some discomfort with us being there."

"Oh, yes." Jess laughed and dropped into her chair. "Sydney hates my guts. He's at North because of me," she said. "That's a long and sordid story I'll be glad to tell you after we get our asses out of here." She swung her own console around and fed the films into it. "I loved doing that. Stuck up jacktard."

"What's a jacktard?" Dev got her restraints on. "And what are ice pirates?"

"Hehehe. They're an old fisherman's tale, Dev. There's no such thing."

Dev started up the power systems. "But you said there were."

"I lied," Jess said cheerfully. "But I bet they now send out six teams to find the bastards because they think I know something they don't."

Dev turned all the way around in her chair and peered at her. "Excuse me?"

Jess got up and came over, crouching down and resting her hands on Dev's knees. "What I was here for was to find out what they knew, and what they didn't," she said, in a suddenly serious voice. "What I found out was, they don't have an ear inside Base Ten. They didn't know about Bain, and they didn't know he offed Bricker. "

"But they did know about me," Dev said, resisting the urge to get lost in those close by pretty eyes.

"They did know about you," Jess said. "So their latest news is about a week or so back, right? They heard about Gibraltar because everyone on the damn planet's probably heard about that. We blew up half a mountain. But they didn't know the inside stuff they would know if they were in contact with anyone inside our base." She reached up and put her fingertip on Dev's nose. "And that is interesting."

"Hm." Dev thought about that. "Should they know?"

"Something as big as Bain showing up? That's gold plated prime gossip, Dev. The kind of thing the night ops revel in sharing in those little wee hours when it's just them, and the boards. You know what I mean?"

"Sort of. I know what gossip is," Dev said. "We had to be really careful about that. If they caught you telling tales about people, you could get punished." She watched Jess's expressive face react, her eyes narrowing and a bit of chill coming into her gaze. "So we used to find sneaky ways to talk about it that no one would figure out." She smiled. "Some of us, anyway."

"The smart ones," Jess said, resting her elbows on Dev's thighs. "Right?"

Dev hesitated, then she smiled a little wryly. "I think so, yes. There were some of us there that understood more. Like me and Gigi."

"Okay, so it's the same with Interforce," Jess said. "There are some really smart people around there, and some people not so smart. The not so smart ones we can use for our purposes. The smarter ones, it's harder."

"Must be very hard with you then. You're very smart." Dev let her hands drop and rest on Jess's arms. "That man, the other agent, was angry about you being senior. Why?"

"Ah." Jess stood up. "Let's get on track and then we can talk about that." She patted Dev's shoulder and went back to her seat, strapping herself in as she glanced at the console. She scanned the daily report, noting the un-obvious gaps in it and shook her head. "Hope the met data's worth the plastic it was printed on."

Dev settled her comms onto her ears and dialed in the landing channel. "BR270006 to control. Requesting lift." She got her systems ready as she waited for the response to come back. As the silence went on, she glanced outside, half expecting the men with guns to be back surrounding them.

But the carrier bay was empty. "BR27006 to control, are you receiving this? We are requesting lift permission and egress," Dev said, glancing into the reflector and seeing Jess watching her, a quietly alert look on her face.

"Give me juice," Jess said.

"If I activate the weapons systems, they will detect that," Dev said.

"I know."

Dev ran her hands over the controls, bringing up the power to the engines, and then opening the links to the weapons, lights and readouts coming online as she heard the hum rising on either side of her. She looked out the front screen again peering around to see if anyone was going to react to it.

After a moment, a crackle in her ear gave her the answer. "BR27006 you are cleared to lift. Outer doors are open."

Jess chuckled behind her. "Jerks."

"Would you really have shot something?" Dev ignited the landing jets and lifted off the pad.

"Yes, and they know it," Jess said. "Anyway. You have the coordinates up there? Let's get out in the white. With any luck, we'll run headlong into a storm and have to find a place to hide until it passes."

"If we're lucky?" Dev glanced in the mirror, finding Jess smiling at her. "I see." She rotated the carrier and moved toward the outer doors at a stately pace. "This should be interesting."

Chapter Seventeen

THE ICE FIELD astounded her. Dev saw the edge of it approaching as she came in low over the waves, feeling the tug of wind against the carrier's outer shell she had to compensate for. The water seemed very dark here, a deep almost black color under the gray skies that contrasted starkly against where they were heading

She glanced into the mirror. Jess was slumped in her seat, her eyes closed, and her body relaxed and after a moment, she realized her partner was sleeping. She had her hands resting on her thighs, and her chest was moving with a slow and steady motion.

Well, that was curious. Dev returned her attention to the screen, though she had the autonav on. She checked the chrono, and saw they still had two hours of flying left and decided to let Jess get some rest since she always seemed to have that just slightly drawn look Dev always associated to the programmers and the people who worked with Doctor Dan who had too much to do and too little time to do it in.

She focused on the console. The scan had just retrieved some new data and she studied it, noting the meteorological component that seemed to indicate lines of strong thunderheads approaching from the west. That was interesting. She recalled the last couple of days and it seemed to her that storms did tend to approach from the west, and flow east. They'd followed one right into their last mission, in fact.

Why was that? Dev hadn't gotten much instruction on downside weather patterns, and she resolved to find some labs about them when they got back. Jess seemed to be concerned about the storms, so she decided to find out what she could about them so she could maybe provide some helpful information.

She checked the scan, which had come back empty of targets to its terminus. The carrier had far more limited systems than either the station they'd just left, or the citadel they'd come from but still it surprised her to find the scope so empty of anything.

Ah well. She settled down to fly and monitor, letting the time pass as she studied the information the carrier's systems had on their destination. After a time, a very soft chime sounded, and she returned her attention to the screen.

The ice line was approaching, and Dev sat forward a little, looking out at it with great interest as they left the ruffled waters and skimmed over the white surface. It was not as flat as she'd thought from afar. It was full of folds and rises, and as she glanced down between them she saw bits of reflected blue in the hollows, a rich and bold color that surprised her.

It was pretty. It was also bright and she blinked a bit as her eyes refocused after so many hours of going over the dark sea. It reflected some of the wan, gray light up too, and she shaded the screens as she didn't want it to wake up Jess.

A quick glance behind her reassured her it hadn't. She checked her coordinates and resumed looking out the window, fascinated by the beautiful contrast of white, gray and blue. Far ahead of her, she could see a line of mountains, and she knew their course would take them up near them before they turned and went east.

She settled her ear cups on and turned on the outside sensors, sending the output to her panel so it wouldn't hit the inside speakers. At once she could hear wind outside buffeting the carrier, and beyond that, a soft, irregular crackling. It sounded odd and strange, and then a flicker of motion caught her immediate attention and she tracked to it, seeing a moving form cross the ice and disappear behind a big crack.

She inhaled slightly in surprise, not really sure of what she'd seen. It had been small, and fast, and she hoped the scan had caught it so she could show it to Jess later since she was confident Jess could identify it.

The wind started pushing against them a little harder. Dev took the throttles into her hands and curled her legs around the mounts of her chair, requesting another scan and looking to her left, seeing the already tightly clouded sky growing darker in that direction.

Reluctantly, she half turned, then she released the restraints and got up, crossing back into the back of the carrier quietly. "Jess?" She called softly. "Jess?"

Jess's eyes remained closed. Dev eased up next to her chair and put a hand on Jess's shoulder, pressing it lightly. "Jess?"

For a moment there was no response, then she saw Jess's body take on tension and her eyes fluttered open to blink at her with some bewilderment. "The weather's getting worse. I thought you needed to look at it," Dev said, in an apologetic tone. "Sorry about waking you."

Jess raised her hand and rubbed her eyes. "I fell asleep?" She asked, in a disbelieving tone. "Are you kidding me?"

There didn't seem to be a reasonable answer to that, so Dev merely went over to the dispenser and retrieved a container, bringing it back over to her. "I think maybe you were tired?" She handed it over. "Nothing occurred of interest."

Jess looked bemused. "It's not that. There's nothing I like better than a good catnap but I don't usually do it in the middle of a damn mission." She opened the container. "Must be the fault of your extra comfy chair here."

Dev smiled and went back to her seat, resuming her headset.

Jess sipped at her drink and studied the pale head just visible over the seat. She could still feel sleep's hold on her, faint wisps of some formless dream drifting out of her awareness as she took stock of her surroundings. Had she been that tired? She sighed, acknowledging the fact that her body still hadn't truly recovered yet. "How long was I out?"

Dev glanced behind her then looked back at the console. "I didn't notice when you went down," she said. "But at least two hours."

Went down. Jess wrinkled her nose at the statement, not entirely sure it was comfortable. What had been comfortable though, was the fact that she, apparently without much conscious thought about it, had determined that Dev was completely and honestly trustworthy in a way she hadn't really expected.

Maybe that had started when she'd unlocked the portal between their quarters. She'd been trained to such an instinctive degree that the sound of the door opening would wake her, as it always had when Josh had done it. She'd never slept in the carrier with him driving.

Never.

Now, this bio alt had been her bus driver for what—a week? And here she was going completely out without any care in the world on her second flight with Dev. What the hell was that? Was she that convinced Dev was so totally on her side?

Really? What was her subconscious saying there? And more importantly, could she trust that? Could she trust her own judgment when she'd been so damn wrong about Josh? Jess studied the reflection she could see in that mirror up front, the pale eyes watching through the window, so intent, and so serious.

Was she just fooling herself? Or was having her tech be another woman changing the dynamic so much? Less competition? More? Different?

Dev looked up and their eyes met. Jess felt a sense of warmth spread across her chest and the uncertainty faded before the unambiguous steadfastness she saw in that expression. This was not a Josh. Jess smiled and watched Dev smile back. This was a construct that had been designed and developed to be able to be trusted. That's what the difference was. With Josh, they only knew what he decided to reveal to them, and the background they were able to check.

Dev?

There was nothing they didn't know about her. Kurok had handed over her programming to them the day they'd gotten there, and she'd already leafed through it. Jess's shoulders relaxed, and she took a longer sip of the kack. Her falling asleep just proved it. She could think whatever she wanted, but her instincts were bred in and bone deep and if her battered subconscious, which had kept her on a hair trigger since the ambush, allowed her that level of trust then she had little choice but to accept it.

So now that she'd talked herself into believing what she really wanted to believe, it was time to get the hell up and work. She unlocked her restraints and stood, stretching her body out, aware at some level of an ironic understanding that there was something a little out of control going on with her.

It felt good. She'd always been attracted to risk and somehow, this new and uncertain change in her life was flushing out the recent dark memories in a surprising way. If she went back and tried to recapture her gloom of just the week prior, it felt old and faded.

She didn't want to feel old and faded anymore. Life had pitched her out back over the cliff edge. "So what do we have here." Jess went over and leaned against Dev's console, peering not at the readouts but out the window. "Ah." She studied the line of clouds racing toward them. "That's not good."

"No," Dev said. "I didn't think so, but I wanted to see what you said." She trimmed the carrier's flight again, adjusting the side jets to compensate for the stiffening wind. "The autonav's having a problem keeping level."

"Get me a topographical," Jess said. "Can you kick the speed up a little?"

"Yes." Dev keyed the report back to Jess's station, and rocked her head from side to side to release a little of the stiffness from her concentration. She adjusted the throttles and keyed in the change to the autonav, inhaling in surprise when she felt Jess's hands come down on her shoulders and start to squeeze them.

It was a warm and strange feeling and for a moment she went still and wasn't sure what to do.

"I'm not hurting you am I?" Jess asked. "You looked a little stiff."

Dev thought about that. "What are you doing?"

"Giving you a massage," Jess said. "Usually it's supposed to relax you and make you feel better."

"Oh." Dev felt the squeezing pressure intensify and she focused on it, letting her head rest back against the back of her seat. The pressure worked the tension out of her neck, and she found the sensation really very nice. "I like that."

Jess chuckled. "Paybacks for my cushy seat," she said. "Besides you've been working here the whole afternoon while I sacked out." She finished her massage and gave Dev a pat on the shoulder. "Let me go see if I can find a route for us that doesn't involve getting this thing blown ass over teakettle."

Dev would have been content to have the squeezing go on longer, but she shifted a bit in her seat and retracted the restraints, the gimbaled chair moving forward as she reached out to put her hands on the throttles and Jess retreated back to her station.

Of the last statement, she had to regretfully discard understanding most of it. She knew what a teakettle was, but that was about it and she seriously doubted actual tea had anything to do with what Jess was talking about. She considered the context, and decided it probably had something to do with the storm.

"All righty let's see what we got here," Jess said. "Oh, Dev, Dev, Dev. This ain't good." She sighed. "Damn it. I wanted to get past the big wild before we ran into that storm. Son of a bitches in North skewed the data."

"On purpose?" Dev felt a little shocked. "I thought they were on our side?"

Jess snorted. "They wouldn't deliberately send us into hell but if they could screw up my pitch or embarrass us they would. It's not about sides, Dev, it's about status." She scanned the limited met they were getting from the carrier's sensors. "If I had to call for rescue? Get lost? Sure. They'd love it."

"I'm not sure I understand." Dev adjusted the trim again, then took the carrier off autonav as the buffeting became more pronounced. She could feel the engines struggling against the wind, and a fast look at the console made her eyebrows hike up. "We are in force twelve conditions."

"So I feel." Jess tapped at her pad. "Hang on, just keep her steady, Dev."

What, again, was she supposed to hang on to? Dev got her boots settled on the thruster pedals and studied her options, noting the winds were driving the carrier off its course to the east. She altered the angle and tuned the jets, flying the craft off its axis to counter the pressure.

Then something caught her attention. "Jess?"

"Hm?"

"It appears a large cone is coming toward us. It looks like it might b..." Dev stopped talking when Jess hit the back of her chair, thumping her forward and nearly sending her into the console. She worked hard to keep control over the carrier as Jess leaned next to her, looking out the front window. "Yes, there."

Jess stared at the cone, then looked forward. "See those mountains?" She indicated the range they were heading for. "If you don't get to them before that cone catches us we're going to splat." She pointed at the nearest of the cliffs. "If we can duck in there we might be okay."

"I see." Dev uncapped the triggers for the engine afterburners and adjusted the power to send all of it to the drive systems. "You might want to sit down."

"I'm fine, g'wan," Jess said.

Dev threw the throttles forward and hit the burners, dumping everything into the engines as a roar built around them and they slammed ahead at full speed. The force drove her back into her chair and detached Jess from the console, sending her tumbling back in a roll of long arms and legs.

"Okay, so maybe I wasn't." Jess grabbed the base of her chair and hung on as the gravitational force increased against her, flattening her against the deck of the carrier as it picked up speed.

"Sorry about that," Dev said.

"You did tell me to sit my ass down," Jess said mournfully. "Let me know when it's safe to get up."

Dev felt the air changing around them and she focused on the screen, checking the power levels and adding the side jets in a bit as she felt the carrier start to pitch. The outside sensors were bringing her the sound of the wind now and it was a rising roar.

Frightening. Dev saw the fold in the mountain that Jess had pointed out and she laid in a course directly for it, hearing thumps and bangs as debris started hitting the craft and she saw a huge chunk of ice flash past them from behind. "I would stay down there for now." She advised Jess. "I'm not sure we're going to make it in time."

Jess untangled herself from her chair and squirmed around to face forward, moving toward Dev with a powerful, sinuous motion. She ended up next to her boots, and wrapped her arms around Dev's seat base, turning over onto her back so she could watch Dev pilot. "In that case, we'll go to Hell together."

The distraction was almost lethal. Dev yanked the steering back as the carrier almost turned on its side, following her body motion as she found herself attracted to the tall form now practically hugging her feet. "Whoa," she muttered. "What's hell? Is that where we're heading?"

Jess snickered. "In ancient mythology, it was a place you went when you died if you were an amoral bum like me."

Dev focused on holding the carrier steady, feeling it jerk through the air as it was buffeted from behind. "Is that sort of like the incinerator?" She asked, distracted. "Why would it matter—wait, what's a bum?"

Jess patted her calf, not helping matters any. "Relax. We can talk about it later once you make it to that canyon. If we don't, maybe you'll find out the hard way." She took a tighter hold on the chair and relaxed otherwise, crossing her ankles as she looked up past Dev's knee at her face.

What a nice clean profile she had. "C'mon, Dev. I know you can do it." She saw a faint line of color work its way up Dev's neck, and a faint smile appear on her face. She took a hold with her free hand on the catch bar bolted to the console and reveled in the feeling of uncontrolled motion as the carrier was suddenly thrown sideways.

Dev was working hard. She could see the lines of fine tension in her body and the narrowing of her eyes as she leaned forward as if it would help them go faster. She had both throttles gripped in her left hand, and she was trimming the side jets with her right hand, and both boots were controlling the thrusters with a frantic intensity.

Jess could drive the carrier. She'd done it on more than one occasion, for a number of different reasons, but watching Dev, she had to admit this was a kind of skill she really didn't have. Josh had always mocked her a little about that, and she'd always had the sense that he felt himself to be a more complete agent than she was.

"I'm going to have to go high G," Dev said, apologetically. "Really, really hang on."

Jess did, then her eyes nearly came out of her head as the carrier banked hard right and went on its side and the only thing that kept her in place was her dual grip. She muffled a curse as her back protested, her recently healed injury sending a bolt of pain down her spine into her lower thighs.

Then she was slammed back to the ground and the craft arced upward, the G force holding her in place until Dev crested something, then dove down abruptly just as something hit the carrier with tremendous violence from behind. Then they righted just as abruptly, and the speed cut to almost nothing, the roar of the engines reducing to a low rumble.

Jess looked up. "Are we dead?"

Dev looked at her for a brief fraction of a second, then went back to her piloting. "I don't think so, since we're in the canyon," she said. "Unless this is Hell. You'll have to tell me."

Cautiously Jess rolled over and eased up to her knees, peering over the console top. They were between two rock walls, moving at just over idle, over a covering of ice covered in blue streaked crevices. It seemed very cold, and very desolate, but at the same time heartstoppingly welcome in its shelter. "Good job."

"We probably need to look at the back of the carrier," Dev said, with a plaintive sigh. "I'm getting all kinds of damage alerts from there."

"Okay." Jess pointed at a looming darkness ahead and to their left. "We're going to have to squeeze through that pass there between the walls, then scoot into that cave."

Dev regarded the gap. "Is that an ice cave?"

"Real good work, Dev. Not only is that an ice cave, but it's one of our ice caves, and it's safe." Jess paused. "I hope."

"Me too." Dev was nursing the engines. "Please hold on. We need to go sideways to get through there."

Jess felt the craft move and let her body move with it, ending up wedged against Dev's chair with her ear just within reach. She blew in it and heard Dev laugh lightly as she got through the narrow spot and righted the attitude. Then they were sinking down and entering the cavern, a wide, open space that featured a floor of solid ice.

It was dark. Dev switched on the running lights and turned the carrier around in a complete circle to give them a chance to see what else was inside. It seemed to be empty, but she spotted a ledge halfway in that was chipped clear of ice and was ringed with tech casements. "Oh."

"Set 'er down." Jess exhaled in relief, since a glimpse outside had shown her a heavy wall of snow falling. "We made it." She pushed herself to her feet and went back into the back of the carrier, going right for her service locker and opening it. She removed a small bottle of painkillers and shook four of them into her hand, closing the bottle and putting it back.

Back in her seat, she swallowed the pills with a swig from her drink container and waited, feeling the gentle bump as the carrier seated itself on the pad and Dev cut the engines.

Dev was peering outside. "Is there service tech here?"

"Basic," Jess said. "And an emergency stock of food and water. This area isn't really owned by anyone. It's wild, and getting caught out is dangerous. We've got ten or so of these caverns scattered around up in the ice fields just in case." She waited a minute for the pills to start kicking in then got up and went to the equipment locker. "I'm going to check it out. Can't be too careful."

Dev privately didn't think Jess was careful at all, but she nodded and released her straps, glad she'd been able to get them away from the cone. She joined Jess at the locker, and copied her in donning the heavy jacket and gloves. "How long will we stay here?"

"Long as we have to. Storm's got to go past, for one thing and you need to fix your burners, and..." Jess leaned against the locker and regarded her. "We can relax and talk about our plan." She smiled faintly. "Or just talk."

Dev felt a pleasant mixture of anticipation and confusion fill her belly. "Okay. I like talking to you." She leaned next to Jess and looked up at her. "Sorry the ride was so rough. Did it give you any discomfort?" She asked. "I thought I heard you...um..." Yell? Scream? Grunt? "Make a noise before," she said.

Jess's eyes dropped and then lifted again. "Bumped my back. Maybe you can look at it when we get back inside."

"Of course," Dev said gravely. "Maybe you can show me how to do that massage thing."

"Of course." Jess winked. "So let's go and get this over with so we can get all this personal investigation done all the sooner." She turned and keyed the hatch open, nudging it all the way when it was reluctant to fully retract.

A blast of icy cold air hit them, and at once their breath became visible as the environment inside the craft released outside and crystallized on the edge of the door. "Brr." Jess blinked her eyes. "Don't lick your lips, and keep your tongue away from any of the metal."

With a cautious look, she stepped out and down onto the pad, since the small ramp didn't want to extend either. One look at the outside of the carrier explained why. "Wow." She put her hands on her hips. "What the hell hit us?"

Dev hopped out and joined her, eyes going wide at the dent in the side of the craft. "Oh, no," she said. "We just fixed it!"

Jess draped her arm over Dev's shoulders. There was a long crumpled crease in the outer skin and part of the engine guard was completely missing. "Nothing we can't make better," she said. "But it'll take a little while so it looks like we're stuck here for now. Interesting, huh?"

Jess released her and went over to the other side of the pad, down a set of steps that had been chiseled into the rock. She drew her blaster and started around in a circle, searching the shadows cast by the carrier's outside lights.

Dev watched her for a moment, then she stuck her hands in her pockets and wiggled her rapidly chilling nose. "Getting more interesting every minute, actually. But I better close that door or where to put my tongue is going to be a much bigger problem than it is right now."

JESS GOT TO the edge of the cavern in time to see the storm redouble, sending a mixture of heavy snow and ice pellets rattling against the stone all around her. She checked the entrance carefully though, finding nothing much to interest her save the fading light and the worsening weather.

Behind her she could hear the steady, light hammering as Dev banged the creases out of the carrier's alloy skin, and as the snow fell harder, and the wind started to whistle through the ice canyon she fell back, content that no one had used the place at least very recently.

There were a million slot canyons and a million caves and crevices in the wild ice, she knew about this one only because of its mapped coordinates and the chances of someone happening on it by accident were extremely limited. She hadn't told anyone at Base Ten she was intending on landing here, except for Dev, and therefore she hadn't expected the information to have gotten out to anyone else.

It was bone chilling cold. Even with her heavy coat, and the thermal gloves on her hands she could feel herself shivering a little and she pulled her lined hood up, fastening the throat flap. She walked across the ice surface, her boots crunching and the tough steel spikes she'd extended on the bottoms preventing her from slipping.

She detoured around the edge of the cleared platform and unlatched the storage shed, the temperature making any automated system impossible to maintain. Instead, you had to know how to unlatch the catches, a metal puzzle system designed to frustrate anyone who didn't know the sequence to unfasten them.

This was her fifth or sixth time using the ice cave, so Jess was well aware of the puzzles answer. She bumped the door open and pushed her way inside as it scraped over the layer of ice on the floor. Inside were neatly packed and labeled rations, spare parts, ammunition, and other supplies, all quietly waiting for use. She made a mental note of the stock, then she backed out and closed the door, turning as she heard a thump and a latch coming home.

Dev had just re-seated the engine cowling and was stepping back to survey her work. She had her hood up and her collar sealed and now she tucked her hands back inside her gloves then tucked her hands under her arms.

Jess promptly trotted over. "How's it going?"

"I think that's all right now," Dev said, her breath visible in a steady stream. "But I think I need to get warm before I start working on the back. My hands are really cold."

Jess could see the blue tinge on the skin of her face. "More than your hands." She triggered the carrier hatch. "Let's get some hot stuff in us."

They got inside and Jess sealed the hatch, reaching over to her own console to start up the internal environmental systems. "Guess you didn't have cold like that up there, huh?"

Dev kept her arms wrapped around her, her entire body shivering. "Actually, we did," she said, after a moment to make sure her teeth weren't going to chatter. "Space is a lot colder than this, and you could feel it, through the airlock glass sometimes. But never for a long time."

Jess walked over and opened her arms. "C'mere." She folded Dev in them, pulling her close as she felt the shivers working through her body. "Let me give ya a hug. We'll put our thermal under suits on before we go back out there again." She rubbed Dev's back. "But it's getting dark outside, so we should set up camp in here anyway."

Dev was finding this whole hug thing absolutely delightful. She was perfectly content to forgo the thermal under suits, and the outside, and just remain encircled in Jess's arms, her shivers already abating. She felt warm blood surging to pretty much her entire body, as a matter of fact, and after a moment she gave a sigh of relief. "That feels excellent."

It did, didn't it? Jess smiled, as the carrier internal systems warmed up and she had to reluctantly release her hold. She took a step back and unfastened her jacket. She watched Dev take off her gloves and stick them into her jacket pockets, then undo the catches with slightly hesitant fingers.

As if she sensed the attention, Dev looked up. "All this clothing's a little strange," she said. "It's kind of hard to move around in."

"It is." Jess stripped hers off and hung it up, then took Dev's. "It's always a pain in the ass operating up in the white. But here, there's no people to have to worry about watching you and the field's wide open, as they say." She went over to the provision area, aware of Dev trailing along at her back.

She felt stiff from the cold. There was an ache in her bones that bothered her, and she looked forward to the warm beverage and a refresh of her painkillers. She set the dispenser cycling and stood waiting, her arms crossed, thinking over the next step in her plan.

Dev's hand touched her shoulder blade, and the plan evaporated effortlessly. She looked sideways and saw that Dev was watching the dispenser, but after a second, those light, clear eyes turned to her. "Can I interest you in a ration pack, some hot seaweed tea, and a nice bunk made out of survival bags?"

Dev considered that for a bit. "Yes," she finally said. "That would be excellent."

"C'mon." Jess left the tea heating and went over to the storage locker, popping it open and sticking her head inside. As she'd asked, there were two ice kits in there and she turned and hit a latch to one side of the locker releasing a shelf that came down to cover the back section of the carrier.

It hooked into the other set of storage lockers, making a platform that was just large enough for two people to sleep on and it had a few inches of padding on the top. "Not as comfortable as our beds." She turned and removed one of the kits, loosening the velcro straps and opening it up.

Inside was a sleeping bag and survival tent. She left the tent alone and pulled out the bag, turning to spread it out over the platform.

Dev removed the second kit and did likewise, copying her. She smoothed down the surface of the bag and surveyed the platform. The soft plush of the bags and the snug space reminded her a little of her sleep pod in the crèche, and that made her smile. "I like it."

Jess eyed her. "You do?"

"Yes."

"You're weird. I like that about you." Jess went back and retrieved two ration packs, and pulled down another ledge between her seat and the dispenser at knee level to make a small table. She set down the packs, and retrieved the tea, and motioned Dev to join her on the floor.

It wasn't nearly as nice as lunch had been, but they shared the contents of the ration packs, and sipped their tea. Outside, the light faded completely, only the dim emergency LEDs of the carrier casting the faintest of glows against the windows. Jess adjusted the interior lights to match, and she leaned back against the lockers, extending her legs out and crossing them at the ankles. "So."

Dev looked up from nibbling on her crackers. Despite the terrible weather outside, she found their present location actually sort of nice. It was quiet and warm in the carrier, and the cramped surroundings were familiar to her from station, making it seem more homelike than she'd felt in the citadel.

And, of course, it was nice having Jess there without even a hatch to separate them. Dev suspected the night would be interesting, and she was definitely looking forward to it. She took a sip of her seaweed tea, finding the taste mild and astringent and just a bit sweet.

"Not like real tea, huh?" Jess spoke, having been silent for a while apparently deep in thought.

"It's nice. It's like green tea." Dev licked her lips. "It tastes like there's a little bit of honey in it."

Jess smiled. "A little," she said. "Wish I could have brought that bottle of honey mead with us. Should have looked for some in Quebec." She studied her glass. "So, from here we go find the fisherman's village."

"You didn't give me coordinates for that."

"It's on an iceberg," Jess said. "It moves. I know basically where it is but we'll have to land the carrier off one of the ice escarpments on the Greenland cliffs and then hike."

"Hike," Dev said. "That sounds like it might be difficult, if it's as cold as it was here today."

Jess nodded. "We'll take ice axes. It won't be easy, especially for my aching old bones." She looked up as she felt a touch on her knee, and saw a look of concern on Dev's expressive face. "Cold's murder when you've been kicked around as much as I have."

"I think you would like the sun," Dev said. "There was a place in the crèche where the ceiling wasn't all polarized, and you could feel how warm it was when the sun hit your skin. I remember I was up there after gym one day, and my shoulders really hurt. It felt so nice when the sun was on them."

Jess released a sound somewhere between a groan and a sigh. "Warm would feel nice right now," she said. "It's never really warm. Not outside, not up here in the wilds, not in the citadel. Only place I ever get warm is in bed."

A little silence fell. Then Dev looked over at the padded platform, one eyebrow lifting as she turned her gaze back to Jess. "Would you like to get warm?"

The thought of climbing into the survival bag and having Dev next to her put a flush of another type across her skin. But at the same time, she suddenly felt a little shy. "We should get some sleep," Jess said, after a pause. "It was a long day today, and tomorrow'll be worse. Those fishermen—they're long off kin of mine but that doesn't mean they'll cooperate with us."

Dev packed up her rations and took the remains of Jess's. She put them in the trash container strapped to the edge of the carrier frame and turned, offering Jess a hand up. Her palm was gripped and she leaned back to brace herself against her partner's weight, tilting her head back as Jess got to her feet. "If we're staying here until the morning, we have a good length of time to get some rest," she said. "And get warm."

Jess undid the wrist catches on her suit and let them hang open, then loosened the seals at her throat. "I think that's a good idea," she said quietly. "The boats go out at dawn, and come back in at dark. So we should leave before it gets light to catch them. It's not far from here."

Dev tried to make a picture of that in her head, as she took off her outer suit, and it was difficult. There was a very tiny, very cramped sanitary unit in the carrier and she used it, wondering briefly how Jess or the muscular Jason managed. "This is a very restricted facility," she commented when she rejoined Jess.

"Ugh." Jess seemed to relax a little. "One of our biggest gripes about these old model carriers. Most of the guys just open the hatch and go freestyle."

Unfortunately for Dev, she could make a picture of that in her head and she grimaced a little. "Unfortunate for anyone beneath you."

Jess started laughing. "You're probably the only one in the corps right now who can fit in there without bending something. Enjoy it, I guess. The newer model of this bus has a better internal arrangement." She removed her boots. "Let me suffer and get it over with. I end up with a lump on the top of my head or a bruise somewhere whenever I use it."

Dev hopped up onto the sleeping platform and scooted back, laying down flat and evaluating the relative comfort of it. It wasn't, as Jess had said, as comfortable as their beds in the citadel but it wasn't terribly uncomfortable, and she thought they could get a reasonable amount of rest on it.

Jess emerged, rubbing the top of her head and giving Dev a wry look. Then she joined her up on the platform, laying down next to her and dimming the overheads.

They both exhaled a little, and looked at each other.

Jess cleared her throat and pulled a control pad on an arm next to her over to review some information. She keyed in a few things, and then studied the results. "Want to make sure the sensors are reading right.

Storm or no storm, wild or no wild, I want to know if anyone's trying to sneak up on us."

"Sounds like a good idea." Dev regarded her own data pad, which was displaying the technical information about the carrier, and it's internal systems. She could see the skin temperature reading, which made her shiver a little, and she was glad she'd connected the carrier up to the embedded power cell in the pad to make sure their internal heating systems would continue to cycle and not drain off their internal batteries all night.

"Jess?"

"Huh?" Jess jumped a little. "What?"

Dev turned her head, surprised at the reaction. "I just wanted to ask you about the pad. I know we had a power lead, where does it come from?"

"Oh." Jess scratched the bridge of her nose. "Um...let me think here. There's some geothermal activity, I think. They use temperature energy exchange to store in the embedded cells." She clipped her pad to the locker wall and folded her hands over her stomach. "Damn useful."

"Very." Dev clipped her own pad down, then she let her head rest on the built in soft puffy area the survival bag used as a pillow. It was very basic, but she felt her body relax. "Otherwise it would be really cold in here."

"In the old days, they'd have burned trees for warmth." Jess eased over onto her side and propped her head up as she regarded her partner. "I saw that once."

Dev turned her head. "Really?"

"When I was little. They found some old, dried up driftwood on the beach near our house," Jess said. "My father gathered it all up and set it on fire, and we sat around it and grilled some fish over it."

Dev now turned onto her side, her face alight with fascination. "Really?"

Jess held her hand out in front of her. "Yeah. It was..." She rubbed her fingers together in memory. "It was warm and it had a good smell to it. I've always remembered that. It always..." She hesitated. "It was kind of a link back to the past." She let herself call up that image, the cool breeze off the water and the smell of salt and sand and the family all there.

Last time, really. She'd gone to basic camp five or six months later and they'd never managed to all get together again. But for that night, they'd enjoyed the moment and it had left her with a mental picture of melancholy happiness. "We cooked marshmallows."

"What?" Dev reached over and touched her hand, clasping it gently.

"Marshmallows. It was a really old package. I guess my father had been hiding it for a very very long time or maybe..." Jess chuckled. "Maybe he got it from someone but they were these puffy sweet things, like tiny pillows, and when you put them in the fire they got all brown on the outside and soft and gooey on the inside."

Dev wasn't really sure what that would be like, but she could tell by the smile on Jess's face that it must have been good. "I've never had anything at all like that. It does sound interesting."

Jess exhaled. "Anyway. So here's the thing with tomorrow." She was aware of Dev's fingers, lightly clasped around hers. "I was going to leave you with the carrier, but I think it'll be better for me and safer for you if you come with me."

"Okay." Dev looked pleased.

"I just have to figure out what the hell I'm going to tell them you are. Spacer I guess, but why are you here?" Jess pondered.

"Well, you could tell them that I'm a scientist who wants to take sea measurements," Dev said, clearing her throat a little. "Maybe I'm looking for a new kind of fish."

"Hm."

"You could say I was from Bio Station Beta. They do all kinds of experiments there." Dev warmed to her subject. "I remember we had one of the scientists come and give us a speech at the crèche, about how we could be assigned there and help them find new ways to use the ocean, or breed special fish."

"What about me?" Jess asked, an intrigued look on her face.

Dev studied her. "Do these people know who you are?"

"They know who I am, but not what I am. They're cousins of my mother's," Jess said.

"So maybe the station hired you as a guide. They did that when they came downside," Dev said. "I remember Doctor Dan telling me about going downside with some people from the fabrication station and they hired some guides who took them someplace."

Jess smiled. "You know what, Dev?"

"What?"

"I think you've got a talent for fabrication."

Dev considered that. "You mean lying?"

"No." Jess squirmed a little closer, pulling the light cover from the bags over her and tossing the other end of it over Dev. "You make up good stories we can use in the field. That's a big plus," she said. "Not everyone can do that. Josh couldn't. He had the imagination of a rock."

Dev smiled and felt a surge of happiness at the unexpected praise. "Thank you." She squeezed Jess's hand and then released it, as she stretched out her body and put her head down on the raised, pillowish area. She watched Jess do the same, and then reach out and turn down the already dim lighting.

Beneath the light cover she was suddenly aware of the warmth coming from Jess's body and her heart started to beat just a little bit faster. She had never been this close to another person for this length of time before, much less with the prospect of spending the night next to them.

It felt strange. She wondered if it was strange for Jess, but then she figured Jess had probably had many such experiences before.

Hadn't she? Dev had spent her entire life alone. "Jess?"

"Yes."

"Why is everyone so afraid of you? I don't understand."

"I told you. Because I'm crazy."

Dev rolled over and tucked her arm around the pillow area. "I don't think you're crazy. You don't act crazy, at least not like they taught us about."

"No, well. Not crazy. Just..." Jess squirmed a little closer. "I don't have a conscience. I don't...it doesn't matter to me what I do to people." She plucked a bit of the survival bag, making a soft sound. "So people are scared of me, and the other ops agents I guess, because we can, and will, kill people just like that."

Dev reached out again and put her hand on Jess's wrist. "Is that really true?"

"It's true." The quiet response came back. "I've killed thousands of people in my career so far. They were either the enemy, or just people who got in my way when I was on a mission. I didn't care. I don't care. You saw Bain. That guy he blew away was his nephew. He didn't care."

"But even Clint was afraid. He isn't your enemy."

"Ah." Jess smiled and it was audible in her voice. "That's a different thing. He's known me a long time, and he knows I have a wicked temper. He's seen me lose it. I guess he thought I was in that space the other day."

"Were you?"

Long silence, there in the dim light. Then Jess laughed very softly. "Maybe I was. I didn't like him messing with you."

Dev remained quiet for a time absorbing that. "Me?"

"You." Jess gave in to the craving and leaned forward, finding Dev's lips in the darkness without any trouble at all. "You're my partner. He thought I thought he was poaching."

Dev was losing interest in the explanation. She was much more engaged with feeling the electric buzz in her guts at Jess's touch, and the sense of wanting that erupted in her. She felt Jess shift a little closer, and she mirrored the motion, her breathing going unsteady as their bodies pressed together and Jess's hand came to rest against her hip.

Oh. That felt so interesting.

"He thought I might hurt him because of that." Jess broke off for a moment, watching Dev's eyes track to her. "Maybe I would have."

"He didn't do anything besides work on the carrier with me," Dev said. "I don't understand why you would be upset."

The mixture of innocence and desire facing her was making Jess's breath come very short. She kissed Dev again and felt Dev's hand touch her thigh, gently stroking it. That sent a rush of passion through her, and she welcomed the wash of energy, driving back both the aches and her fatigue.

It felt clean, and good.

"I didn't find him attractive at all," Dev said, pausing between kisses. "Not like you."

Not like me. Jess felt a lightness in her heart she hadn't for a very very long time. Dev was so honest and open it made her a little giddy. "I didn't want him to mess with you because I felt the same way," she said. "I think he knew that."

Dev thought so too. But she wasn't very worried about it at the moment. She felt Jess's lips touch her neck, and then nibble softly at her earlobe and she was sure she wasn't worried about Clint, or the citadel, or the mission for that matter.

Doctor Dan had been right, of course. She wanted this feeling, and she wanted it to keep going just like he'd told her she would.

There was, however, one minor issue. "Jess?"

"Hm?" Jess shifted closer and ran her fingers through Dev's hair. "Still got questions?"

"Well, sort of," Dev said. "We just got that one vid. I really don't have any idea what to do next."

Jess's brows drew together and she paused, her thumb brushing Dev's cheekbone. "You're not programmed for this?"

A faint smile appeared on Dev's face. "Jess." She reached over and put her hand on Jess's chest. "They program our heads. They can't program our hearts."

Hearts. Jess felt hers start to pound. "Ah. This is a heart thing."

They both regarded each other.

"I guess they just thought we'd figure it out," Dev said, finally. "But I really don't know where to start."

Jess gently drew Dev closer. "We'll figure it out," she said. Then she looked briefly down at Dev's hand. "And you've already got a pretty good idea where to start."

"Really?"

"Really."

Chapter Eighteen

DEV ALMOST DIDN'T hear the signal. She was very engaged in that kissing thing, with Jess's tongue doing something weird and heart stopping that was making the blood hammer in her ears and it was only on a raggedly indrawn breath that the sound of the alerter penetrated her consciousness.

Alert?

She really wanted to ignore it. Her hands were gently exploring Jess's strong body and she didn't really care much about what the sound was, except that there was a tiny part of her brain that was telling her to pay attention to it. Then Jess's hand brushed her breast and that brought a whole new distraction to her attention.

The alert sounded again. "J...Iess," she managed to stutter.

"S'matter? Am I hurting you?" Jess lifted up a little and focused on her.

"Comms." Dev said. "I can hear it."

"Comms?" Jess's pale eyes stared into hers for a long uncomprehending moment before she cursed and shoved back, slamming her head into the decking covering their bed space. "Ouch. Shit!"

She dropped back down onto the padded surface, but twisted to one side. "Get it!"

Dev squirmed out past her, tumbling out of the alcove and nearly tripping over her partly unfastened undersuit on her way to her console. Her knees felt rubbery and she had to work very hard to get enough coordination in place for her to hit the keys on comp and get an ear cup in place. "BR27006, echo twelve."

She licked her lips, tasting Jess on them, and peered at the console, seeing the comm signal flashing there without really looking at it.

She was sweating and breathing hard, and she blinked a few droplets from her eyes as she waited for the response. The deck felt very cold against her bare feet and she lifted them up, resting them on the thruster pedals as she flexed her toes. The cup returned nothing but a slightly static filled silence, and she rested her head against her hand as she continued to wait.

She felt very shook up, but not in a bad way.

"Who the fuck is calling us on mission?" Jess growled. "Should have shut that stupid thing down." She felt the top of her head gingerly. "Ow. Gonna have a lump from that damn overhead."

"Sorry about that." Dev glanced over her shoulder. "I didn't mean to startle you."

Jess was in her under suit, the top half undone and hanging down at the waist and her hair was in total disarray. With most of her upper body exposed, and the stark overhead lights shining down on her, she was an odd and almost scary figure that Dev found amazingly attractive.

"Glad it didn't break skin." Jess grinned briefly at her. "That'd been an embarrassing scar to explain." Her eyes flicked past Dev. "Call em again."

"Okay." Dev was catching her breath, her heartbeat finally slowing down. "Comms, BR27006 copy," she said into the mic, keying it manually. "Re trans ident please." She was very grateful to her programming now. The codes and processes came to her automatically, undeterred by her internal chaotic state.

A soft crackling echoed into her ear. "BR27006, squirt, endit," a low, mechanical voice sounded, then clicked off.

"Confirm." Dev hit the buttons that would capture the encoded transmission then she eased the ear cup off, glancing down as a gust of chill wind came in through the outer vent and made tiny bumps go across her exposed skin. "It's an automatic broadcast." She fastened the catches on her under suit with one hand, her other still holding the commslink.

"Even worse." Jess poked her head around the edge of Dev's chair. "If that's just a rules squirt or some other piece of shit, I'm going to find and kick whatever automated ass that sent it."

Dev felt that she probably agreed with whatever that was. Her body was wanting very much to go back to exploring this whole sex thing, which had just started to become really, really interesting. "I'll decode it." The carrier's comp ingested the message and chewed over, as Jess leaned against her chair back and watched.

"So whatdja think?"

Dev stared at the comp, then turned her head and regarded Jess in some bewilderment. "It's not done yet. I don't think anything about it."

Jess chuckled, and blew gently into her ear. "I didn't mean the message."

"Oh." Dev blushed, which felt warm and strange. "It was good."

"Good?"

"I really liked it," Dev said, in a soft voice. "Though I really don't know what it's all about yet."

"You will." Jess leaned over and kissed her neck, then gently caught a fold of skin in her teeth. She released her, then tilted her head, watching her with a mischievous look.

"Oh." Dev felt a prickle of desire run up and down her spine, ending up as a teasing ache in her groin. "I really hope so."

Jess chuckled.

The comp finished its run and displayed the message. Dev tore her attention from those twinkling eyes and studied it, letting her mind run over it at least twice before the words made any sense. "It's weather," she said, after a long pause. "But I'm not sure what it means."

Jess obligingly leaned over her to look at the screen. After a moment, she came all the way around the chair and braced her hands against the console as her eyes flicked over the information. "Wow. Storm that came over us is slamming the ice pack. They picked up distress signals from the fishing fleet. Must be driving the seas up."

Dev looked at the wire line map, filled with bumps and arrows. She saw two white crosses on the edge of the map, and they were slowly blinking. She reached out and put her finger on one. "Is that who we were going to see?"

"Maybe," Jess said. "The fleet's pretty big. Might not be the boats we're looking for." She checked the chrono on the console. "They're expecting it to last another twelve hours. We maybe could get out in ten and chase it."

"Like we did on the last mission?"

Jess nodded. "Get behind it and come in as it passes. Might make up some time."

Dev studied the map, seeing the lines of weather clustered close and tightly packed over where they were. "I see," she said. "Will we go help them?"

Jess leaned back against the console. "No. That's not what we do," she said. "We get the squirt so we don't fly into it. Interforce isn't the coast guard. They go help them. That's their job."

"I see." Dev digested that. "So they'll get this information too?"

"Yes," Jess said. "Well, they'll get something like it. Our met tends to be a little better than theirs." Her lips twitched a little. "Not that they'll admit it. They lost a lot when the government collapsed and they had to depend on regional bosses for money."

"I see," Dev said, who really didn't.

"We'll go see what their status is, the ones we're looking for, after the storm passes," Jess went on. "If they can't help us, I'll have to come up with another approach. Happens sometimes." She regarded the report. "On the other hand, if they need help we could use it as leverage to get what we want from them." She looked thoughtful. "They can be hard assed bastards."

"But we can't go until the storm is over?" Dev asked. "It could be too late to help anyway."

"Yeah, we're stuck here." Now Jess turned her entire attention back to Dev. "What a shame, huh?"

Dev managed a mild, rakish grin. Her skin prickled as Jess reached over and removed the ear piece from her head, tracing the edge of her ear with one finger. It made that sense of wanting erupt in her again, and she closed her eyes as the touch continued.

But the message disturbed her a little. She opened her eyes again and glanced at it. "What will happen to them?"

"To who?" Jess tilted her head, then followed Dev's eyes. "The fishermen? I don't know. Depends where they were I guess. Might have gotten caught in a cracked flow and trashed or been washed overboard."

Dev's brow creased. "That will hurt them?"

"Kill 'em, most likely," Jess said, offering her a hand. "C'mon, let's get back to our investigation."

Dev tried to imagine what it might be like for the fishermen, but found she didn't have enough information to even make a picture in her head about it. So, regretfully, she closed the message and stood up. "It's too bad we can't help. I think it would be a good thing for us to do that."

"Why?" Jess asked.

Dev looked at her, but there was honest interest in her expression. That made her stop and think about the question. "They teach us it's good to help people," she finally said. "Everyone does, in the crèche. It makes you feel good."

Jess folded her arms over her chest and regarded her for a minute in silence. "People you know," she clarified. "Not just anyone."

"No, anyone," Dev said. "Even sets we didn't know."

"Huh."

"So I think about those people in the storm and it makes me feel bad we can't do anything to help them," Dev said. "Even though I know we can't, because of the weather." She watched Jess's face intently. "Is that disturbing?"

Jess uncrossed her arms and let them drop. She eased into Dev's chair and hiked one knee up, resting her elbow on it. "I don't know. I never thought about it before." She tentatively did just that, imagining the boats out in the ice, and how cold it would be for them.

She'd spent a few days out there when she was much younger. She remembered the sting of the wind against her face as she'd watched them steer into it and remembered her once removed uncle slitting the throat of the first fish they'd caught and letting the wind take the blood as a superstitious offering to whatever ruled the winds and waves.

Grisly, she supposed. But it hadn't bothered her and now, thinking of them out there possibly being killed by the storm didn't bother her either. The fact that Dev was bothered baffled her. "I'm not sure what the hell that is."

"I didn't mean to cause you discomfort." Dev was at her side, putting a hand on her arm. "I'm sure you know the right thing to do."

"Do I?" Jess mused. "Depends on how you look at it I guess." She sighed. "They don't care about us, so I don't know why you'd care about them. But the weather's the weather so it's a moot point anyway."

"Okay." Dev rubbed her arm gently. "Just my programming I guess."

Jess studied her. "Well." She got up from the chair and put her arm around Dev's shoulders. "Let's get some horizontal time while we can." She guided them both back to the crude sleeping platform and eased onto it, watching the overhead as she scooted back.

Dev hitched herself back, leaning against the wall of the carrier as she lifted her drink canister out of its holder and took a swallow from it. Then she set the canister back and laid down flat again, as Jess adjusted the lights and settled down beside her, not without giving the overhead an evil look. "Did you really hurt your head?" Dev reached over and touched Jess's hair, feeling a faint lump under her fingers. "Oh. You did!"

"My pride more. My head's like a rock," Jess said. "I'm fine. Just not used to having a ledge over my pillow." She slapped the overhead. "Now." She shifted into a more comfortable position. "Where was I?"

She watched Dev turn to look at her, that faint, half embarrassed smile appearing on her face. "Is this freaking you out?"

"No," Dev answered instantly, then she paused. "Well." She made a face. "Yes, but it's okay. I like it."

Jess chuckled. "You're so damn funny."

"I'm not trying to be," Dev said. "There's just so much happening." She relaxed onto the padding, watching the dim lights make shadows over Jess's body. "It's a little confusing."

"Confusing. Well I'll try not to confuse you any more." Jess casually undid the top fastening on Dev's under suit, peeling it back to reveal bare skin. "Want me to stop?" She paused at the second fastening, and raised an eyebrow.

"No." Dev eased over onto her side and leaned forward for a kiss, hearing the soft sound as the second catch was undone and she felt the light puff of air as the suit was gently pulled down off her shoulders. "I don't."

"Good answer." Jess moved closer, keeping her lips engaged as she slipped her hand around Dev's back. She undid the catches on her underwear, feeling them come loose as Dev shyly did the same for hers. She relaxed, as they brushed against each other skin on skin.

Oh that did feel nice. Jess continued her exploration. She found Dev's body sexy and interesting, a mixture of delicacy and power that continually surprised her. Her short stature and relatively slight form were very deceptive, and as she ran her fingers along Dev's side she could feel muscles contracting under her touch.

Nice.

She felt a sudden electric warmth as Dev somewhat hesitantly touched her breasts. She returned the attention, feeling the tiny intake of breath through Dev's lips as she teased her nipples, getting an immediate reaction from them. "Like that?"

"Ah, yes." Dev copied her motion, and seemed a little surprised at the growl of approval Jess uttered. "Is that okay?"

"Very okay." Jess forced herself to go slowly, remembering that Dev had no experience at any of it, not wanting to scare her or creep her out. "If you don't like something say so," she whispered into Dev's ear. "Okay?"

"Y...yes."

Thus encouraged, Jess nudged her over onto her back, rolling over herself and getting her weight up onto one elbow as she started to work her way down Dev's body, nibbling and tasting as she went.

So far, so good. She could feel Dev's breathing increasing as she let her fingers trail down the centerline of her navel, and come to the last set of catches on her under suit.

She undid them, unsurprised when her own came loose around her hips. She could feel a touch at her ribs, and then lower and she went ahead, sure now of her reception. It didn't seem like Dev was going to freak out, and from what she could tell, her partner was enjoying her attentions.

She'd never been anyone's first before. Definitely was an odd sensation. She hoped she'd do right by Dev and she'd come out the other side liking it, because she suspected she was going to enjoy the process and she wanted the first time not to be the last. "Here we go."

Dev hardly knew what to do with herself. She tried to copy what Jess was doing, but what Jess was doing was so distracting it was really hard to concentrate. The gentle touches and snips sent sparks of pleasure up and down her body and as Jess kept up her attentions she had to keep clenching her jaw to keep from crying out.

Her body had never felt like this before. There was a growing craving in her guts that made her want more and more of it, every touch making the sensation deeper and stronger.

She wanted to touch Jess back, and somehow she managed to keep focused long enough to undo the stays on her suit, feeling warm skin under her fingertips and the motion as Jess drew in a deep breath.

A bit of cooler air hit her hips as she felt her under wraps come free. That was replaced by heat as Jess's touch slid over her lower stomach and gently eased between her legs.

It was an explosion of wanting then. Dev forgot completely about where they were and what they were there for, her entire attention focusing on the fingers that touched her and teased her, making her own hands nerveless as they rested against Jess's belly unable to move.

A pressure was growing inside her, an aching, building pressure that made her short of breath and sent pulses of red against the back of her eyelids. She clamped her jaw shut as the sensation got stronger, and then Jess changed the pressure, and did something else that sent her rapidly into a whirl of pleasure, making her hold her breath and open her eyes in surprise as it crashed over her in a long, rolling wave.

It was wonderful, and scary, and overwhelming. Dev could feel sweat dripping off her and her entire body was shaking, her eyes wide and amazed as she stared over Jess's shoulder.

It took at least a minute more, with Jess gently stroking her, for her to be able to catch her breath, her body relaxing back onto the padding with a tiny thump.

For a moment, there was silence. Then Jess cleared her throat softly. "You okay?"

For another moment, Dev stared at her mutely.

"Hello?" Jess reached up and gently tapped her on the forehead. "You there?"

Dev exhaled. "Okay," she said. "I now understand why this is such a big deal to you natural borns. I get it."

Jess started silently laughing.

"But wow, did they ever leave a lot out," Dev said, in mournful tone. "That sure would have made class a lot more interesting."

Jess continued to laugh, rolling over onto her back and holding her stomach.

"Wow."

Dev blew the damp hair out of her eyes and studied the bulkhead over them. Her body was still tingling, and she slowly shook her head back and forth as she went over what had just happened.

It felt amazingly good. Her body felt like it was humming to itself and she now had an insight into why the natural borns were so interested in this. She was glad that Jess seemed to like it too, and now she really wanted to learn what it was that Jess had done, so she could do it back.

The thought of making Jess feel this good was very, very attractive. It was exciting and absorbing, and now she was glad the storm was going to take as long as it was, so she could find out more about this before they had to go off and do their mission.

Doctor Dan had been right. This feeling was rich and overwhelming and it made her want to do it more. Very distracting. "Jess?" She turned her head toward her. "I want to do that to you."

Jess's face broke into a frank, happy grin. "Glad to hear that."

Dev grinned back. "Are you still angry at the weather?"

"Nope. You?" Jess reached over and traced a line down Dev's exposed belly. "Want to start learning now?"

"Yes."

"Don't need a break?"

"No."

Jess chuckled and pulled her closer. "Good answer."

THE SOFT CHIME woke Dev up at once, and she opened her eyes to find herself curled up next to Jess, the taller woman's long arms draped over her, Jess still deep in slumber. After a moment of bemusement she relaxed, remembering what they'd done before going to sleep.

Amazing. She tilted her head a little, looking over to study the tall figure next to her.

Jess had a very interesting face. Asleep, she appeared relaxed and her usual skepticism was smoothed away but the strong lines were still evident, a somewhat squared jaw and high cheekbones, that outlined deep set eyes and spare, yet well shaped lips.

She had a scar under one eye, faint and almost invisible, and another along her jawline. Dev only just restrained herself from reaching out to touch them, settling instead for wrapping a bit of Jess's dark, straight hair round her finger and stroking it with the edge of her thumb.

It was soft. So few things about Jess were. Dev thought about all she'd experienced in such a short time. She had a sense that her life had become so intense and compressed that each minute was packed full of stuff that she had to sort through and ingest and figure out what to do with.

Now this sex thing, for example. Dev felt her face twitch into a grin.

That was an awful lot of intensity to absorb in a short period and she thought perhaps they might take some time when they got back to the citadel and explore it further. Would Jess want to do that? Dev thought she might, since after some trial and error she reasoned she'd done pretty well with her sex lesson and Jess had seemed to enjoy it.

It would take practice, she'd told Dev, but there had been a distinct smirk on her face when she'd said it, just before they dimmed the overhead light completely and fell asleep.

Dev had absolutely enjoyed it. However, she figured they could do that in a spot that was more comfortable and less dangerous to Jess's skull than the alcove.

Their beds back in the citadel for example. They were nice and big and comfortable. But Dev would also keep a kind memory of this little padded alcove because this was where she'd gotten to learn about it for the first time. Right here, in her...in their carrier.

There was something she really liked about that. Though lacking in comfort, it was quiet, and very private in a way she'd never known before. She thought about the fact that she and Jess were probably the only beings for a long way around them and realized this was as alone as she'd ever been in her life.

Very alone. Very private. She looked up at Jess's face. Very personal.

A quick look at the dimly lit chrono told her they still had hours before the end of the storm, and she eased her hand out to shut off the chime before it sounded again.

The motion woke Jess though, and she felt her body shift and take on tension, just as her eyes flickered open and she swept the small alcove in a brief, mild confusion before she focused on Dev. "Ah." Her expression brightened.

"Ah." Dev amiably responded. "Alarm just went off."

Jess's pale eyes lifted to the overhead, then she settled back down on the padding. "So I see. Interesting to dream about something and wake up to..." She paused. "Anyway. Sleep good?"

"Excellent," Dev said.

Jess rested her chin against Dev's head. "We can have some rations, get the bus warmed up, and see if we can get out of here. Get this show on the road," she said. "Sound like a plan?"

"Yes, it does."

"Good."

Dev ingested this. Jess didn't seem to be inclined to immediately put her plan into action, and she found it quite pleasant to remain where she was, enjoying the comforting warmth of the casual embrace they were in. She had never felt anything like it before, this close contact to another being, and she decided she could easily get used to it.

Another new thing to absorb. She studied Jess's arm, her eyes tracing the dark patterning on her skin and thought about the mission they were on. Would Jess get a new mark for it?

Could she get one? Would she be allowed to? Did she want to?

Hm.

Jess finally started moving, rolling over and stretching her body out, then easing forward and standing up to continue the process. Dev followed, adjusting the inside lighting before she set about collecting all the bits and pieces of clothing that were scattered about.

"Messy process huh?" Jess said, in an amused tone. "Hope you had as good a time as I did."

Dev looked up and smiled. "I think so."

Jess squeezed herself into the sanitary unit, chuckling as she did. "Start some kack going, huh?"

"Yes." Dev had gotten her under layer on and was working the dispenser. She felt well rested, and she sidestepped over to her console while the dispenser was churning to key up the carrier's status reports and start them running.

The sensors powered up and started scanning, and the windows de-tinted and showed the dim interior of the ice cave they were parked in. The batteries had recharged, and Dev was very pleased to see that the repair work the carrier had undertaken had completed, so far as it was able.

She still had some work to do on it, but she considered the results and decided the carrier would indeed lift when she asked it to, and she would be able to reasonably steer it.

"Bus not immediately falling apart?" Jess came up behind her and peered down. Then she ducked her head and looked out the window. "I'm going to go out and make sure we're clear."

Dev glanced at her. "Like that?" She frowned. "I should probably turn the outside heaters on then."

Jess looked down at her naked form, then she delivered an extremely droll look at Dev. "Wonder if we paid extra for that sense of humor." She tweaked Dev's nose. "No. I'm not going outside and freezing my nipples solid, no matter how entertaining that would be for you."

The dispenser finished and they got their hot drinks along with a ration pack and sat down to consume it in companionable silence. Jess had thrown her under suit on and she was sitting on the low bench with her long legs splayed out as she chewed the seaweed wrapped roll. "Last time I was in these parts I got to taste bear jerky. That's something different."

Dev studied her. "Bear?"

"Polar bear," Jess said. "Only large land mammal left on the planet and it only survived because it lives off the ocean like we do." She finished her fish roll and tucked the remains of her pack into the compactor. "Let me go make sure we didn't heat up the skids and get us frozen to the deck." She winked at Dev, and went to the slim compartment their over suits were hung in and got into hers.

Dev took the last remains of her own meal over to her console and sat down in her chair, pondering what Jess could have meant about those skids. She set her drink in the holder and paused, remembering blinking sweat out of her eyes the last time she'd sat there.

Then she felt her face warm as she figured it all out. She turned her chair and watched Jess put on her coat. "You don't really think we could have melted the ice down there do you?"

Jess looked up and grinned. Then she put her gloves on. "Be right back." She picked up her big blaster and hit the door controls, ducking out and closing the hatch behind her so quickly only a small blast of frigid air made it's way in.

"Yeesh." Dev rubbed her face, and returned her attention to her console. The scan had picked up a collection of intelligence and she put it on the display, settling into her seat and keying on all her systems. She finished her fish roll and dusted her fingers off, washing the roll down with a sip of her drink before she started bringing everything up live.

She keyed the diagnostic panel for the engines, looking up every few moments to watch Jess making her slow way around the cavern. She had her blaster cradled in her arms and she was turning in circles as she walked, watching everything around her intently.

Her hood surrounded her face with insulation, but as Dev watched, she pushed the hood back and stood still, her head cocking to one side as though she was listening to something.

Dev keyed in the sensors and turned up the gain, hearing a soft crackling and a gentle popping noise she couldn't identify. She could almost hear Jess's breathing, watching the vapor issue from her nose. She tuned the sensor a little higher as she watched Jess's eyes slowly scan and rescan the area, her body still and tense.

Operating on some instinct, Dev started bringing systems online. She ran the external diagnostics and then triggered the unlock for the umbilical that was tying them in to the cave's systems. She heard it retract, the rattle and snap sounding very loud and making Jess turn to look at the carrier.

Then she got up and went to the small closet, getting her flight suit out and getting into it. The fabric constricted around her, and she picked up her boots and went back to her seat to sit down and get into them.

Not without another look out the window, though. For a moment she didn't spot Jess, then she did, finding her over near the platform edge where the carrier was perched, carefully examining everything there. She still had her hood down, and as Dev watched she turned her head and their eyes met through the window.

Oh, that was interesting. Dev felt a jolt of reaction deep inside her. At the same time, a smile appeared on Jess's face, and she turned in a circle then continued her inspection.

Dev got her boots fastened and went back to bringing the carrier into a flight ready state. She hooked up the control leads to the ports on her suit and got her comms set in place, studying the readouts and adjusting levels as everything came online. The carrier started making sounds all around her, leveling a little on the pad and thumping as she turned on the engine heaters.

After a moment she initiated the pre-start. Once the engines reported online she shunted some power to Jess's weapon systems. Their backup boards came up on her station as the hatch popped open and Jess entered. "Are we frozen?"

Jess chuckled, as she shed her outer jacket. "No, but there's something here I don't like. Can't put my finger on it and I want to get out of here so..." She looked around at the interior of the craft and Dev's already suited figure. "So I guess you read my mind and we're about ready, huh?"

"You seemed unsettled," Dev said. "I thought it would be a good idea to get things going."

Jess seated the blaster and went to her own console, shaking her head and chuckling under her breath. "Boy was I wrong." She sighed. "I remember sitting on my ass back on base and saying something stupid like there's no way you could train someone to be a tech in a week."

Dev reviewed her panels, a smile appearing as she absorbed the indirect compliment.

"Not only can you, they give me one that reads minds, wants me to teach them sex, and has already picked up on my field signals without me having to say a word." Jess reviewed her station, pulling her restraints around her and buckling them. "How did you know to bring up my guns?"

Dev buckled her own harness, her smile growing a bit wider. "I thought it would be correct," she said, modestly. "Things seem dangerous in this place, and they did teach us that when things are dangerous, it's best to make sure the weapons are ready."

Jess chuckled audibly. "Well, there's training, and then there's aptitude. I have a feeling you got a big helping of both, my friend." She cracked her knuckles. "Get us out of here, Dev. Something doesn't smell right."

Dev wasn't really sure what that meant, but she pulled her seat forward and locked it into flight mode and got her hands and feet on the engine controls. She peered around through the windows and checked the back scanner and then she ignited the landing jets and felt the carrier shift.

Apparently they weren't really frozen to the pad. Dev smiled a little, as they lifted and she touched the side jets, rotating the carrier in her typical circle to check position and her surroundings before she went further. She touched the carrier's external lighting and the cavern interior came into raw relief as the powerful beams bounced off the inside walls.

"Give me forward view please, Dev," Jess said.

Dev transferred the view back, then she tickled the engines and started them forward, heading for the opening to the cave. The inside of the cave seemed very empty, and she didn't spot anything moving, but there was a certain relief in her gut when they cleared the cave entrance and moved into the crevasse that it was buried in.

Outside, it was gray and still stormy. White snow was scattered all around them, but the winds had dropped and she had no trouble maneuvering. She cautiously lifted up out of the crease in the ice and emerged over it, again turning in a circle to survey the space before checking her coordinates and moving off.

"Who taught you to do that?" Jess asked. "The circle thing? Was that programmed?"

Dev thought about it. "No," she said, after a moment. "I used to watch the mechs who serviced the outside of the station sometimes. They would always do that when they came out of the service bay and I thought it was a good idea, to see what was around you. They wanted to make sure they didn't have any leads or umbilicals hung on them anywhere that could get ripped off."

Jess tilted her head a little. "How would...oh. Everything floats up there, right?"

"Outside the grav field, yes," Dev said. "Everything does." She looked forward and prepared to bring the engines up to full speed, then paused. "Oh! Jess! What's that!"

Jess nearly ejected herself right into the ceiling as she hit the release and leaped up, bounding forward to collide with the back of Dev's seat. "What?"

"There." Dev pointed. "That thing moving there." She slowed the carrier and brought it around in a lazy circle, watching the thing below them race along.

Jess stared in silence for a long moment, blinking. "Oh," she finally said. "I think...yeah, that's a bear." She leaned forward. "I've never seen one alive before. But I've seen pictures. Bigger than I thought it would be."

The thing was big. It was white, and roundish, and it had a black point on it's face and Dev watched it in utter fascination. It was moving fast, using all four of its limbs to run over the white and icy surface. It was completely strange but also, oddly beautiful. "Wow."

"That is pretty cool," Jess admitted. "The ice people hunt them, but they don't find them often." She reluctantly tore her attention away from the bear. "Not sure I would want to be on foot near that thing. They have claws the size of my hand." She held hers up. "And fangs like this." She held her fingers up with her thumb and index ones extended.

The bear disappeared behind some ice hillocks, and Dev returned the carrier to it's course, thinking about the creature. What was it doing out on the ice? Was it a boy or a girl? Did bears have boy and girl or were they just bears?

Jess went back to her seat and resumed her restraints, bringing her console up closer and starting a thorough check of the weapons systems. She was pretty sure she wasn't going to need them until they got a lot closer to the border but it never paid to take a chance out here in the ice wild.

So many things could kill you out here. The weather and the ice, and closer to the edge, the freezing sea spray that could coat the carrier with ice in minutes. Now, she supposed, she also had to add encountering a bear to the list. "That was cool."

"Excuse me?" Dev glanced in the mirror.

"Seeing the bear," Jess said. "Good catch."

Dev settled into her seat, watching the auto nav as she tested the repairs the carrier had made overnight, and finding herself very pleased with both herself, and the way things had gone the past couple of days. Things were going really well, she thought, and now she also had finding a bear to her credit.

Life was pretty amazing at the moment.

With a smile, she studied her readouts, pausing briefly to glance up at the mirror to find Jess's eyes watching her in it. She felt her throat go a little dry and an image of the pleasure they'd shared surfaced, making her want to experience that again. A soft chime distracted her though, and she went back to studying the control sets, picking up her drink and taking a long swallow of it.

After all, it was time to work now. She snuck a glance at the mirror again, though, and saw Jess looking at her own systems, but with a smile on her face that didn't look like it had anything to do with the blaster energy readouts.

Yes, time for work.

Chapter Nineteen

TWO HOURS LATER they were coming up on the storm edge. Dev felt the winds increasing, and she snugged her restraints a little tighter, trimming the engine power to keep them on course.

"Met's getting ugly," Jess said. "Let's slow down. I don't want to run into the back of that line of nasty." She sent the met scan up with the storm line circled in light pen. "Stay clear of that."

"Okay," Dev said. She cut power and took the carrier off autonav, taking the controls and turning the craft into a shallow curve to run parallel to the storm line.

Ahead of her she could see the roiling clouds, and in one spot, one of the big cone spouts they'd run from. It looked big and dangerous, and she could see down at the bottom there was white ice and debris being thrown everywhere. The last time they'd run in behind the storm it had been full dark and she'd seen very little.

This was different. She could see the power of the storm, and it made her think of the people in the boats that maybe were inside it. She remembered what it had been like when the storm had come up over them, and hoped the boat people would end up okay. "Jess?"

"Hm?"

"Is there a place for the people down there to hide like what we found, when the storm comes?"

Jess remained silent for a bit, only the sound of her touching keys and relays echoing softly. "I don't know," she finally said. "Maybe...if they have a sea level cliff, or a pocket in an iceberg or something. Why?"

"I just wondered," Dev said. "I wonder what the bears do."

The clicking stopped, and she looked up in the mirror to see Jess looking back at her, with a puzzled expression. "They're alive too, so I just wondered."

Jess shook her head and went back to her console.

Dev figured bears probably didn't mean much to Jess, even if they were cool to see. Then she remembered that Jess hadn't really much cared about the boat people either, and it reminded her of what Jess had said, that she had—what was it? No moral sense? Did that mean she just really didn't care about anything?

Hm.

She slowed the carrier further, and dipped lower toward the ice, scanning its surface to see if maybe she could see another bear. The ice seemed very disrupted though, there were big chunks scattered everywhere, and as she ran along the storm's edge she started spotting dark lines in it.

The ice seemed to be moving. As she slowed down, she could see it shifting, and then she realized that the dark lines were open water between huge chunks of the ice showing through. As she observed, the chunks moved, and the water splashed up between them, sending a spray high in the air.

"Stay clear of that," Jess said. "The water coming up. It'll coat the outside of the bus."

"Yes, I see." Dev checked the skin temperature of the carrier, which seemed all right for the moment. "How far should I go?"

Jess glanced up. "Go to open ocean. Let's see if we see any debris if those ships got caught."

Dev increased her speed, keying the scan up and checking to see if any other squirts were pending. Comms had been completely silent since the last one though. She tipped the carrier into a little bit of a down nose attitude and waited, as she saw a much darker line coming up on the horizon.

That was open sea, according to scan. She nudged the craft into a bit of an arc, coming up over the line between ice and water and heading out in a shallow circle. The buffeting from the storm was lessening as it moved on ahead of them, and she felt the carrier level and the pressure gradients ease.

Jess came up behind her again, leaning on the back of her seat as she looked out the window. Dev thought that was a just a bit odd, since she got a perfect view from the console display, and in fact, since that was augmented by the forward scan she could see more than just by looking.

Yet, here she was.

Dev concentrated on flying. She watched the scan return, seeing nothing at the moment but ice and water, and the rough and scalloped edge of the storm itself. The sea surface was wild and surging, white waves crashing over the ice and sending up spray almost to where they were.

She turned up the outside sensors, and the carrier was filled with the noise of it, the roar and thunder of the waves, and the snapping and crack of the ice being battered along with the wind's howling. It was very wild and a little bit exciting, but Dev was glad she didn't see anything that might have been the boats in trouble floating around.

"Hey. There," Jess said suddenly, pointing over Dev's shoulder at the edge of a tall iceberg. "Look. See the opening?"

Dev certainly hadn't, and even if she had she suspected she wouldn't have known what she was looking at. "I see it."

"See if you can get down in there. I want to see what's in that crack."

Dev studied the space, then glanced at Jess. Then she shook her head a little and complied, dipping the carrier down and heading for the sea's rough surface. She kicked the engines on and skimmed over the water, weaving in and out of the waves as they exploded up on either side of her.

"Guess we get to see if those heaters work after all." Jess let her elbow rest casually on Dev's shoulder.

"I think we will." Dev felt the spray hit them, and in an instant, the window was covered in ice. She pumped energy to the skin of the carrier and it cleared, only to be washed over again as another wave came from a different angle. "I'm glad comps up." She studied the readout, piloting by it's return and ignoring the visual distraction.

"I'm glad you're driving," Jess said as they skimmed between the ice and the sea and dropped into the crack she'd seen from the outside. The front window cleared again and now that they were in a somewhat protected space, it stayed clear as Dev dropped the craft down toward the opening. "You might want to hold on," she warned. "I think I will need to go sideways."

Jess pulled a standing restraint from its wall pocket and snapped into one of the weapons hard points on her suit. "Go baby go. Let's see what this hunt gets us. "

Dev tilted the carrier nose down and put it on its side, skimming between the two ice walls as she narrowed in on the opening Jess had spotted. She directed the outside lights into the crack, and in a moment they both had a brief sight of a craft, stubby figures, and the glare of a plasma blaster as it opened fire on them. "Oh!"

Dev swiveled the craft on its axis and took the hit on the bottom of the carrier, then she kicked the engines to full power and pointed them back toward the sky, the gravity pressure slamming her hard in her chair and throwing Jess against the bulkhead. "I don't think they wanted us to see them."

"Ya think?" Jess grimaced, as she pulled her head away from a door handle. "Remind me to rig up a rubber padded suit for flying with you."

"Sorry." Dev pulled them out of their steep climb and arced over, going from two gravs to near null and sending Jess floating away from the wall. "Hold on."

"Need a damn bungy suit. Can I hold on to you?"

Dev felt her face heat up, but she got the carrier level without sending Jess flying again. As a reward, Jess leaned over and kissed her, then unclipped from the wall and bounded back to her seat, dropping into it and pulling her full set of restraints around her.

"Now." Jess licked her lips. "Let's try that again, only this time, with me on the forward guns."

"Are you sure you want to do that?" Dev asked.

"Oh, yeah. No one shoots at me and gets away with it. Go baby go."

Dev suspected this might possibly end up to be a very long day.

THEY WERE AT sea level again, coming in hard toward the ice cliff. Dev felt the weapons systems humming around her, and she could see on one of her aux screens that Jess was running targeting projections.

She saw that the crack they'd gone down before had widened a trifle, and she ran a very quick calculation, bouncing a probe off the opening and decided they could go in right way up this time. The hit on the bottom shields had done no damage, and comp was telling her the blaster that they'd hit them with wasn't that powerful.

She wondered what Jess was going to do to them. "Stand by for entry."

Jess was whistling happily under her breath. "All right you piece of shit bastards, let's see how you like these apples." She got her hands on the targeting controllers and slipped her heads up view in place, the glare of the ice replaced with wire line grids showing her the planes and angles instead.

She let off a tiny burst to test the guns, pleased at the response. She unlocked the gimbals on her seat and concentrated, her eyes looking past the crevice Dev was rapidly heading toward, to the potential targets beyond.

A moment later, they were in the fold and coming through a burst of spray that thundered up from below them. The cavern came up quickly on the right hand side and she put her fingertips on the triggers, feeling her breathing slow and her body relax as she waited.

Then they were down and at the opening and she spotted the gun swinging at them and she let off a full power blast, seeing the energy bolts hit the plasma platform inside and blow it up in a whirl of flinging metal.

She could see figures running, and the cavern dock beyond where two big ships were docked. "Slow down."

Dev did.

"Take us in."

Dev looped them in a circle and came back square on to the cavern, slowing as she eased the carrier inside the space. She could see bodies lying on the ice below, and a spatter of red, and figures diving behind ice ledges and away from the big things floating in the water.

Boats? They must be.

"Well." Jess sighed. "This is going to be awkward."

"Excuse me?" Dev didn't want to tear her attention away from the flight controls. There wasn't much space inside the cave and she wasn't sure if there were more guns around.

"I think I just blew up some cousins," Jess said. "But on the other hand, at least they didn't croak in the storm."

"Oh." Dev studied the view. "These are the people we're here to see?"

"Uh huh."

She could see figures now lined up behind the ice ledges, with weapons pointed their way. Dev risked a glance in the mirror and saw a bemused expression on Jess's face. "The ones you wanted to help us?"

"Uh huh."

"I see." Dev held the carrier steady. "Interesting," she said. "What would you like me to do?"

"Take your clothes off."

Dev turned her head and looked at Jess, both her eyebrows hiking up almost to her hairline.

Jess smiled. "Just kidding. Use the shortwave sideband. Scan the channels. See if they're interested in talking to us now that they know who we are."

"They do?"

"They know we're Interforce," Jess said. "These buses are pretty distinctive."

Dev kept one hand on the throttles and keyed comms with the other, switching from the long range system they used to receive messages from base to one that would only be useful at close range. She started a scan, sending out a blip with their generic ident on it to see what would happen.

She jumped a little, as the guns on either side forward of the engines flared a little, and looked back at Jess in question.

"Just want to make sure they know the lights are on," Jess said. "So they don't just start shooting at us with those hand blasters." She exhaled. "Damn it, this'll kill my cover too. Son of a bitch I hate when plans blow up in my face."

Dev concentrated on controlling the carrier, watching the figures facing them down on the ground. After a moment of silence the comms crackled. "Who are you?" A male, rough voice asked.

Dev glanced in the mirror. "Should I answer?"

Jess drummed the edges of her thumbs on her triggers. "Yeah. Give them our designation. Tell them we want to talk to them."

Obediently, Dev keyed the comm. "This is BR27006. Requesting open comms," she said. "Standing by sideband twelve, endit." She looked back, but Jess remained locked into her station, her eyes flicking over the screen with fierce intensity.

It was confusing. She wasn't really sure what Jess was going to do. Adjusting the throttles a little she eased the carrier slightly to one side, giving the forward scan a better look at the inside. It was a lopsided cavern, the water a deep and vibrant green blue and there was just enough water for the two boats to fit inside.

Around where they were docked were narrow ledges of ice, and toward the back, where the ceiling was very low, were piled rocks and dark clothes, evidence of people living there.

The comm crackled again, and a different voice came on. "What do y'want?" A low, male voice issued from the console. "We don't want nothing to do with your lot. Take yourself off."

Dev turned in her seat and looked at Jess in question.

"Gimme comm." Jess waited for the lights to come on her console before she fitted her ear piece in and keyed it open. "Don't be so hasty, Uncle Jacob. You fired on me first. You don't want to end up on the blacklist do ya?" She clicked off, and waited .

Could go either way. The fisher families were fiercely independent, and they didn't generally take any crap from anyone. Not from Interforce, not from the other side, not from any of the regional leaders who cropped up from time to time. Jacob hadn't seen or heard from her for years, might not even remember who she was.

Or he might. Jess thought she'd impressed him, all those years back, with her work on the boat and her resistance to seasickness.

"Jesslyn," the voice returned. "This where you landed up?"

"Yep. Just want to talk. That's all."

The silence now went on for a protracted time. Jess kept her systems up, and kept scanning the area, despite having offered up her identity. You just never knew with people. She had no idea who she'd blasted down there, and the fishermen were known for taking revenge when they could against anyone that hurt them. Jess didn't blame them for that. She respected them in fact.

"All right," the voice came back. "Drop. Quarter hour, that's it. I have fish to catch."

Jess chuckled wryly under her breath. "Endit." She put the comms down and released her harness. "Okay, Dev. I'm going down there." She got up out of her seat and went to the locker. "Keep this thing hovering. I'll signal you for a pickup and when I do just come down and open the hatch and I'll jump in."

Jess could tell now from Dev's careful lack of expression that she really didn't like the plan. There was something a little charming about that. "No, huh?"

"It sounds like it's dangerous," Dev said. "But I will do my best to keep you safe." She adjusted the jets. "Where do you want me to let you off?"

Jess snapped the catches on her suit and seated her guns in their holsters. "Right on that ledge down next to the ships. Turn us around so I can just step out of the hatch. Show off a little."

Show off a little. Dev flexed her hands and lowered the carrier until she heard the faint hiss as they impacted the water. "Ready?"

"As I'll ever be." Jess stepped up to the hatch and waited, pulling her hood up and snugging the neck closure tight. She felt the carrier move and she opened the hatch, grabbing hold of the heavy bars on either side of the opening as the carrier turned on its axis, and at the same time, slid sideways to end up right next to the ledge she'd pointed out, the edge of the craft a bare foot from the ice. "Nice," Jess said. "Be right back."

"Be careful, Jess," Dev called out.

With a smile, Jess stepped out of the hatch and onto the ice, feeling the tiny spikes on the bottom of her boots grab into the surface. She stepped away from the craft and it lifted clear, moving back out over the water and turning again so its nose was facing her.

The forward windows were shielded and mirrored and she couldn't see past them, but she knew Dev was there, watching her, with that adorably serious look on her face.

With a smile, Jess turned and made her way up the icy slope, toward where a small group of people were waiting for her. They were all tall and spare, and though she hadn't seen them for many a year, she recognized her far off kin easily. "Uncle."

Jacob was very tall, and had close cropped gray hair that outlined a square and grizzled skull. He was wearing a thick hide jacket and trousers and boots that came up to his knees. He was weathered and his face was scarred and he didn't look at Jess with any real fondness. "Jesslyn."

He looked past her to the carrier, hovering patiently over the water. "How long you been out of school"

"Ten years," Jess said. "I posted to Base ten."

He nodded. "What do you want?" He glanced to his right and left, where several men were just waiting, hands on long knifes and the big hook poles they carried on the sips. "Only reason I'm talking to you is we did shoot first. Otherwise I'd gut you. No family here."

Jess merely nodded, unsurprised. "Never is, with us," she said. "We got a squirt on a mayday from the fleet. We were in the area, so we thought we'd look for survivors." She let her hand rest on the butt of her heavy blaster. "Didn't expect to get fired on."

Jacob relaxed a little. The men around him also shifted, some glancing back toward the boats. "I heard it," he said. "Figure two, maybe three of Jan Henry's boats got caught in a crush." He gestured to the men. "Go get the ships ready to ride out."

The men turned and left without any comment, heading down the ice slope toward the slips where the fishing boats were waiting. Jacob watched them for a moment, then he turned back to Jess. "Sit." He pointed to an ice ledge covered in a thick fur.

They walked over and sat down and Jess rested her elbows on her knees. "Glad the boats weren't yours," she said. "That was a hell of a storm. It caught us coming over the rim and we nearly ditched."

Jacob glanced at the carrier. "Hunting?"

"Maybe. We saw a bear." Jess grinned briefly.

"Yeah?" Now her once removed Uncle looked interested.

"Big one. On the way out here," Jess said. "Thought we saw other things moving but the storm blocked scan." She looked squarely at Jacob. "So what was that firing all about? You always shoot before you ask around these parts now?"

Jacob studied her face for a long moment. "Been attacked twice," he said finally. "Lost two boats in the last three months."

Jess straightened "What?"

His eyes met hers. "You didn't know," he said. "Been raiding up here a lot. Looks like pirates."

"Pirates," Jess said. "As in, ice pirates the phantom ghouls of the arctic?"

"Lost thirty men to them ghouls," Jacob said. "Don't know if they're the pirates of old, or just new raiders who took on that flag, but that's the answer for the quick trigger. Weren't sure what you were, weren't taking chances."

Huh. Jess was internally startled to find a silly story she'd dredged out to taunt Sydney was now plonked live and real in front of her from the lips of her kin.

Now Jess had to wonder, and maybe doubt a little where she'd gotten it from. Could it have been something in a report she'd read without thinking too much about it? "Haven't been reported around here for a long time," she said. "Same scheme?"

Jacob shrugged. "Sounded like the old tales. Show up either in a hovercraft or ship, pulled you to, wanted your catch or be blasted. Two of my ships resisted, and they blasted."

Now, the unwarranted attack made sense. Jess pondered the information. "Attacks increasing?"

"Yes."

Intel pivot. "So, how about this," Jess said. "How about you let me ride with you, and if they show up, we can do something about it? Worth a shot?"

Jacob stared at her. "You'd come out on the boat?"

She nodded. "If it's pirates, we want to know. If it's the other side, we really want to know. Worth me getting my feet wet and my face slapped with fishtails. What do you think?"

The old fisherman turned his head and stared off at the ships. "Don't know that the crew'll buy that," he said. "Most of 'em don't trust your side any more than the other, but you know that."

Jess nodded. "No offense taken. It is what it is."

Jacob grunted. "Let me see what the weather is." He stood up. "Wait here."

Jess leaned back against the ice seat and spread her arms across the back of it, the thick fur protecting her skin from the hard surface. She extended her legs out and crossed them, regarding the cavern as she listened to the thunder of the waves outside.

With an exhale of mild relief, Jess looked up to see Jacob returning, striding up the slope toward her with a non committal look his face. She kept her relaxed pose though, working hard to make it apparent that she didn't really care one way or the other what his decision would be.

He sat down next to her. "Crew's all for it," he said, sounding as surprised as Jess actually was. "Didn't expect that. Maybe they like the idea of someone with a gun on."

"Huh." Jess grunted. "Could be."

"Need to be fast though," Jacob said. "Going out with the tide." He looked over at the carrier. "And what's with that? You can't leave it here."

"My tech's aboard." Jess got up. "Let me go pack a sack and go over a plan with her."

"Her?" Jacob snorted. "They not getting enough recruits these days?"

Jess looked at him, then down at herself, then back up at him. One of her dark brows lifted.

"You're a generation. You don't count," he said. "Wouldn't have mattered what you were."

Well, that was true enough. "My partner's damn good. Didn't really matter what sex she was either," Jess said. "Corps doesn't care. You should know that."

He shrugged. "Get your kit," he said. "We've no time." He got up and headed back toward the ships, raising his voice and motioning to a group of men standing nearby.

Jess stood up and brushed her hands off. She turned and made her way down toward the edge of the ice, feeling the shift in air pressure as the carrier lowered and swooped over to meet her. She ambled down the slope and continued steadily toward the water, pausing as the craft settled next to the ice and the hatch opened.

She hopped inside, and slapped the door controls. "Well." She quickly unbuckled her overcoat and pushed the hood off her head.

Dev backed the carrier up and lifted it, turning it so they could see the ship harbor. "Did it go well?" She set the auto nav and pushed her comm set back, turning in her seat to look at Jess.

"Better than I figured." Jess came up next to her and leaned against the console, propping her boot up on the base of Dev's seat. "Seems they've been being attacked by pirates."

Dev blinked. "Pirates?"

"Pirates."

The blonde woman pondered that a minute. "You mean, the story you told those people in the other place was true?"

"Apparently."

"Did you know that? I thought you said it was just a story."

Jess shrugged both shoulders and produced a charmingly sheepish smile. "Sometimes I just get lucky." She leaned forward unexpectedly and gave Dev a kiss on the lips. "Like with you." Her eyes twinkled. "Anyway, I janked them into agreeing to let me go with them on the ship so I could protect them against the pirates."

Dev studied her very gravely. Then she cleared her throat a little. "How can I help?" She asked. "It sounds dangerous and I want you to be safe."

Strangely, that touched her. Jess felt an odd warmth fill her belly as she absorbed the look Dev was giving her. "Well," she said. "I'm not looking to get hurt. I got enough of that my last mission." She studied the ground briefly "I know we talked about you coming with me, but it would make more sense for you to take the carrier and shadow us."

She looked up and met Dev's steady gaze.

"Take me with you," Dev said, after a minute of silence.

Jess smiled at her without really knowing why. "You're a little crazy y'know. I like that." She straightened up and gave Dev a pat on her side. "Okay, let's find a place to put the bus down. We'll go fishing together." She went to the locker and pulled out a backpack, setting it on the shelf and starting to sort through supplies to put in it.

Dev turned around and thumped back into her seat, feeling a sense of buoyant happiness that made her smile. She settled her comms more solidly and started to sweep the carrier around, looking carefully at the inside of the cavern.

It wasn't big, and there weren't a lot of places she could pick, but after a few minutes she thought she saw a spot in the back the craft might fit in. She boosted the jets up and got as close to the roof of the cave as she could, then started across the open space over the dock the ships were parked in.

There wouldn't be much clearance. Dev concentrated hard, and handled the throttles delicately, watching the scan as she skimmed over the ships, the tops of them just clearing the bottom of the carrier. Through the sensors, she could hear people yelling, but she ignored the distraction and then started down toward the back section. "Hold on."

She heard Jess grab hold of the locker as she tipped the craft sideways, going down and to her right in a balanced descent that eased between the ships and the descending roof, sliding into the one spot she could park the carrier and still have a chance of getting it back out again.

She extended the skids and settled onto them, checking the scan on all sides before she cut the power to the engines and let them wind down. "There." She glanced up through the window and found a lot of people outside staring at the craft, then she turned around to find Jess leaning against the wall, also watching her. "Was that correct?"

Jess walked over and unlocked her restraints. "C'mere." She gently pulled Dev up and into her arms, spending a very long moment giving her a frankly passionate kiss. "You are the bomb. Let's go kick their asses," she said, when they finally separated. "Let's get your bag packed and we'll go see where this takes us."

Dev felt like she was floating, a well remembered sensation from the crèche now happening to her down planet. She got up and trailed after Jess, happily wondering what pirates were like, and whether she'd get to see live fish.

Or more bears.

Without a doubt, it was going to be very, very interesting. "I wonder what a bomb is?" She muttered, as she pulled her gear out and started packing it. "Hmph."

JESS LED THE way down the dock to where the ships were preparing to depart, her pack on her back fitted neatly over her new jacket. She had a pair of ice gloves tucked into the pockets of it, and she was aware that she and her companion were possibly getting themselves into a good bit of trouble.

Dev didn't seem aware of possible trouble. She was bopping along behind Jess looking at everything with keen interest, unfazed by the slippery walk or the looming fishing vessels.

Jess chuckled softly. She had her jumpsuit on under the jacket, and her weapons seated in the holsters in the hard points, along with a long knife strapped to her forearm. Her heavy blaster was slung over one shoulder, tucked in alongside the pack that held tools and some spare underclothes.

At her tail, Dev ambled along, her slim frame encased in sharkskin, and her profile much narrower than Jess's since it lacked anything in the way of weapons. She also had her pack on her back. It had an extra section on the bottom that held her portable scanner and tools.

"So here's the deal," Jess said, as they reached the dock. "We'll stick with the story about you coming from Bio Station Two, okay? They don't know much about what goes on topside. There aren't any bio alts out here at all." She glanced at the waiting crew. "Some of them, if they've been to Quebec, might know about them, but they won't tie the ones they've seen to you."

"Okay," Dev said. "I guess in this case it's good I was the only one in my set."

"Yep, one of a kind." Jess patted her on the back as they approached the boarding area. "But keep quiet when you can. They'll try to pump you for info."

"Info?"

"About Interforce. How we do things. Why we do things," Jess said. "We're not really friends, and not really enemies."

Dev considered this. "I don't know any of that stuff," she said. "So I can't tell them much, except the color of the walls and how much I like my shower."

Jess muffled a laugh. "Atta girl. If you have to say, tell them you're part of the last class that came in, which is just about true. I'll tell them you're a newbie."

"Also true." Dev craned her neck to observe their destination. "Those are big."

The ship they were approaching was indeed large, at least ten times the length and breadth of the carrier, and solid metal in a green gray color with rust stains everywhere. It had a taller section in front, with glazed windows and the middle and back were full of equipment and nets.

Jacob was standing next to the boarding ramp, with another man next to him. The second man was shorter and wiry, with flaxen hair and piercing blue eyes. He studied them intently as they arrived.

"Uncle," Jess said. "This is my partner, Dev."

Jacob gave her a brief nod. "Tech," he said gruffly, then turned to the blond man. "This is Sigurd Rolafson, captain of the Northern Star."

"Captain." Jess nodded at him.

"Hello," Dev added.

The captain cocked his head at them, heavy blond brows twitching. "Got enough guns there, Agent?" He asked, in a low, almost rough tone. "They'll be welcome if you can hit the broad side of the bastards."

"Do my best," Jess said, mildly. "Glad to have a chance to put them to use on your behalf.

"We'll see." The captain next looked at Dev, and a faint grin appeared. "Where ya from, Tech?"

"Bio Station Two."

"Spacer?" The captain looked surprised.

"Yes."

He chuckled. "Good to know some Viking blood got off the planet after all, eh?" He pointed to the boat. "Let's cast off. Wind's coming down." He rushed up the ramp, clearly expecting them to follow.

"Good luck," Jacob said. "Nice piece of landing there, tech."

"Thank you," Dev said. "It should be fine there. If it starts making odd noises, don't go near it. It's still due some repair after that storm."

Jacob stared at her in bemusement. "Right."

"Thanks," Jess said. "I may need to relay through the carrier from out there. I'll trigger the relay remotely." She started up the ramp, with Dev a step behind her. They crossed onto the deck and as they did, several of the crew pulled the boarding ramp onto the ship and with a loud metal clang, the grapples holding them in place let loose.

Immediately the ship moved, backing away from the pier and swinging around the second ship, which was still grappled at berth.

Jess put a hand on Dev's shoulder and aimed for the spot the captain had headed for. "Hope you don't get seasick. Forgot to ask you about that," she said "You know what that is?"

Dev cleared her throat gently. "I guess it's like being space sick, in null," she said. "It involves a lot of regurgitation. Not something you really want to deal with in zero G."

"Ah. No." Jess made a face.

"You get past it when you're about two. At least I did," she added.

"Good." Jess squeezed her shoulder.

The crew stared at them as they moved across the deck. "Jess?" Dev lowered her voice.

"Mm?" Jess ducked her head a little.

"What did he mean about...vikings?"

"Ah." Jess paused, as the captain did, and turned to face them. "Hang on. Tell ya later."

"So," Rolafson said. "The old man said you'd been out before." He addressed Jess. "True?"

"Short tour," Jess said. "I was a kid."

The captain studied her. He had sharp eyes and a rugged, interesting face. "Drake, eh?"

Jess nodded.

"Service family?"

Jess nodded again.

"Boats my family," the captain said. "S'why I told Jacob I'd let you on. Warn you though, deal with them pirates or I'll throw you overboard. I got no real use for the force."

Jess cleared her throat, but didn't say anything.

The captain smiled. "You're kin to the old man?"

"Something like," Jess said. "Couple times removed. My

grandfather's brother."

Rolafson grunted, then he turned and motioned them to follow. "Get you berthed while we pull out of here." He palmed a hatch and it slid open "Watch your head."

Jess ducked through, and then they were inside the front structure of the ship, as it started moving underneath them. Inside the area was lit by dull green lamps and they moved down a very narrow corridor with hatches on both sides.

Dev looked around, absorbing the motion, the smells and sights with a sense of deep fascination. The hatches and inside passageways reminded her a little of the crèche, but here she could smell fish, and brine, and a heavy scent of machine oil.

It was exciting. She could feel the rumble of engines, and to either side hear people moving around and speaking. As they passed one of the half open hatches she peeked in, blinking as she saw three young children inside, playing with some kind of box.

They were oblivious to her passing, but they were slight in size, and had light blonde hair very much like her own.

That made Dev think again about what the captain had said. Then she had to stop since Jess did, and they were in front of a small hatch that the captain opened.

"Not much. Hope you like sharing," the captain said. "No room to spare on board." He turned and backed away a step so they could enter. "Going to the bridge. We'll be out at sea in a quarter hour, and past the coast on the hour. After that, anything can happen."

He rambled off down the hallway, leaving them alone.

Jess ducked her head and moved inside. "Oh this is gonna be fun."

Dev eased in after her. "Ah," she said. "Very restricted." She put her back to the wall, as she looked at the space they'd been given. It was about the size of her old study space back on station. Just enough room for Jess and her to stand, and two iron bunks with deep lips bolted to the wall.

It was cold, and clammy inside, and it smelled of oil and metal. There were two tables attached to the wall and a single water dispenser to one side. Jess squeezed past her and looked out the hatch, then she pulled her head in and let the metal door swing shut. "Sanitary unit's across."

Jess tossed her pack up onto the top bunk and pushed her hood back. "This is going to be a real picnic, partner. Wish I'd left you back on the bus."

"No." Dev shook her blonde head definitely. She put her pack on the bottom bed and studied the space. "I'm really glad I'm here." She took a seat on the bed and looked around. The floor was metal like everything else, but it had a covering of what appeared to be woven seaweed on it, which was giving up a musty green scent.

"Really?"

Dev turned to her. "Really. It's all new. It's interesting. I've never been in a place like this, or on a boat at all." She reached out and touched the wall as the sound of the engines increased and the motion became more pronounced. "And if we can stop the pirates, that will be excellent, won't it?"

Jess sat down next to her on the bottom bed. "Yes," she said. "It will be excellent, matter of fact." She tapped the lower part of Dev's pack. "Better get settled."

There wasn't much space to get settled into. Dev discovered that there was a small storage space under the bed's padded top and she knelt on the seaweed pad to get her few things arranged in it. Above her, Jess was doing the same, and they worked in companionable silence for a few minutes.

This constricted space was actually a little comforting to her, Dev realized. It was more like what she'd been used to all her life, and this spartan room with its thin mattresses and plain steel surfaces made her think of the crèche. Once she'd gotten her things in place, she took out her portable scan tucked into its pouch and started setting it up.

Programming triggered instantly, and she felt the overlay as she looked at the parts of the unit, and her hands fitted them together. This was one of her first programs. The first set of labs she'd done after coming up after that long, long session.

Portable scanners and electronic scopes, to listen and analyze everything around her. She remembered being curious about the lesson, and now that she was assembling her gear, she sensed more programming surfacing.

Her fingertips moved quickly over the controls and she brought the scanner online, tuning the leads as the device started to listen and probe.

It detected her, of course. She registered her ident and let it continue. Then it picked up Jess, the sensors alarming as they picked up all of the weapons Jess had on her. Dev acknowledged the alerts and registered Jess as friendly, then she let the tuning continue.

Jess was ordering her guns, checking the charges, though she'd done so prior to leaving the carrier. She seated both blasters and then removed the knife from its sheath, sighting down its length with an expert eye. "These people can be rough, Dev."

"I assumed that," Dev said. "The children in that room had knives on their belts."

Jess stopped and looked at her.

Dev sensed it and looked up. "I thought it was interesting," she said. "Did you see them?"

"Went by too fast." Jess sat down on the bed. "Little kids?"

Dev nodded. She adjusted a setting. The scanner had scoped out the inside of the ship and drawn her a wiremap of it, pinpointing human figures and mechanical devices, the probes now working on the electrical components. "Here." She pointed to the room with the children in it, showing three small heat signatures.

"I see it." Jess glanced at the scanner, then at Dev. Then she shook her head. "I remember how long it took me to learn how to use this," she said. "Knowing you picked it up in a few days..." She let the words trail off.

"It's intimidating, I guess," Dev said.

"Yeah."

"It's just how I always learned so it never seemed strange to me," Dev said. "But I guess it is, isn't it?" She looked at Jess. "Can they do that with you?"

Jess remained silent for a long while. "Not..." She hesitated. "If you've been in something bad, really bad, they can do something to kind of...change it. Make you not think about it. I've seen it done to agents once or twice."

"Ah."

"It's scary," Jess admitted. "They wipe parts of your memory out I think. They offered to do that to me after I got back last time. Didn't want it."

Dev reached out and put her hand on Jess's, squeezing it a little. "They can do that to us too," she said. "Sometimes, when bio alts get older, they get—they change. They argue and things like that so they take them and they..." She paused, then looked at Dev. "They come back and they don't argue anymore. I think they're happier."

Jess made a face.

"Yeah." Dev nodded. "We think about that when we go down for programming. They can take stuff, you know? You never know what's going to be there when you come back up."

Jess stopped cold, and thought about that.

"Programming is different," Dev said, after an awkward pause. "It's all skills and knowing things. But this—it changes you. It changes what's in here." She touched her chest.

"I never want to have that happen," Jess said. "To either of us. Someone tries that on you I'll shoot them."

Dev smiled and gave her hand another squeeze. "It takes a registered programmer to do that," she said, matter of factly. "Not just anyone."

Jess leaned against her and returned her attention to the scanner. "So, what...thirty people aboard?"

"Yeah, looks like it." She traced the wire line with one long finger. "That's the engine room."

Dev regarded the heat signature. "Yes," she said. "Most of the people are here." She pointed to one spot. "And the three I saw here." She touched the smaller room. "Everything down below here is empty."

"Fish tanks," Jess said. "When they catch 'em they put them in there until they get to the offloading station. Then whoever they're selling to takes them and processes them. Back in the day they all worked for big processing companies. Now there's much less fish, so they sell direct."

"I see."

"Families are competitive. Each one has a boat, maybe two, and they fight for fish out there," Jess said. "Mostly live on the boat. Not a comfortable life."

Dev looked around. "I can see that." She adjusted a setting. "Should we go get a full scan?"

"Let's." Jess stood up and offered Dev a hand. "We'll go to where everyone is. Chances are, they'll have a hot drink there." She rubbed Dev's back as she stood and headed for the hatch. "Captain's family, way way back, came from Norway," she said. "That's where Vikings came from. They were ancient fighters who went out in boats and conquered places."

"I see."

"Nordies mostly have blonde hair and pale eyes," Jess said. "Kinda like yours."

"Oh." Dev pushed the hatch open and stepped into the hallway. "Really?"

"Really." Jess kept her light hold on Dev as they walked along, feeling the motion of the ship become much more pronounced. "We're out in open water, I think." She could hear voices ahead of them. "So that's the Viking connection. Don't discard it. If they think you're a long lost cousin it could be good for us."

Dev thought about that. "If they start asking me about my ancestors we could be in trouble. All my aunts and uncles are test tubes."

Jess choked off a laugh. "Shh." She pushed the big hatch at the end of the hall and they entered a medium sized room that had a metal table mounted in the center, and built-in cabinets all around. About a dozen people were standing around, and they all looked at them as they came inside .

It was an awkward moment. None of them looked friendly.

"Hi." Jess broke the silence. "My name's Drake and this is my partner, Dev. We're here to put our lives between you and whatever the hell's attacking people, so lay off the screwy eyeballs and just tell me where to get something hot to drink before I risk my ass for you."

Dev worked to keep a startled look off her face. She'd never really heard Jess talk like that, her voice all low and growly and rough. She sounded mean, and the rest of the room reacted to that, taking a step back away from her and looking alarmed. Jess also had her hand resting on her blaster grip and Dev eased back behind her and out of the way.

Most of the people were of middling height, save two men who were around Jess's length. One of them pointed at a rust stained dispenser and actually walked closer to them. "Cups in the top," he said. "We appreciate you being here, agent," he said. "No need to be a jackass."

Jess gave him a droll look. "You mean the bitch you were referring to before I walked in wasn't me?"

The man actually blushed.

"Hello." Dev gently eased from behind Jess. "I don't think Jess wants to be a jackass." She paused. "Whatever that is, but we know we're not really exactly welcome."

The man studied her. "Tech," he said. "We just don't like outsiders on the ship. No offense was intended."

"I'm sure." Dev said. "Could you explain how all this works?"

The man unbent visibly, responding to Dev's gentle inquisitiveness. Jess took a step back and watched Dev work, wondering how much of what she was doing was programming and how much was just her. It made her think again about what they'd talked about in the room, and she felt a sense of discomfort when she thought about someone messing around in Dev's head.

Jess took another step back and leaned against the table, letting Dev become the center of attention as the ship people drifted over. They were all pale haired and Dev fit right in with them, nodding somberly as the tall man pointed out the consoles over the cabinets and explained them.

They seemed to accept her. But every one of them was giving Jess a wary look and she finally found it all just a little bit funny.

The inner door opened and the captain stepped in. He walked over to stand next to Jess, watching the rest of the group around the met scope. "Finding things?"

"Dev's doing a primary sweep," Jess said. "So what's the pattern been? They wait for you to get fishing then hit you?"

The captain chuckled. "Nah. Wait till we're hauling half full at least. Ain't stupid," he said. "Hope your little friend there has a strong stomach. We're heading for storm edge."

"I asked her," Jess said. "She said something about null gravity, and regurgitation and the fact she'd gotten over that at age two. So I suspect she'll be fine."

The captain looked at her, then at Dev. "She's really a spacer?" He asked, his voice rising in surprise. "Born up there?"

Jess nodded.

"What the hell is she doing down here? I heard they got life good up there. Plenty of work."

"She wanted some adventure," Jess said smoothly. "You know how it is. You can have a nice safe, plush life but be bored to death."

The captain snorted. Then he faced Jess. "I told the crew you're here. You can go where you want, but if I were you I'd not go alone, and bring your hardware with you," he said. "Nothing personal, agent. You seem a good sort. But we don't fly either flag, and we've had some of your kind do the same as those pirates."

Jess stiffened. "What?"

"You heard me," Sigurd said. "Now, I know your family name, Drake. You've got history with us. But not all your lot does. I've seen with my own eyes black and greens boarding a ship and taking from it."

Jess stared at him. "I'll shoot them as fast as a pirate."

"Know that. It's why I told Jacob I'd take ya." Sigurd squinted at her, then winked. "All right you lot." He lifted his voice. "Let's get this tub ready to fish!"

The group broke up and headed for the big, sealed doors that led from the housing area to the ship's deck. Dev came over to where Jess was standing and leaned against the table as the room slowly emptied and they were left alone. "You look unsettled."

"I am," Jess said. "Just heard something I didn't really want to." She sighed. "Why in hell did I have to make up those damn ice pirates? Next thing you know we'll find Santa Claus flying over a berg and he'll dump a load on top of us."

Dev eyed her.

Jess sighed. "Let's go out on deck. Might as well get a view while we can." She shoved away from the wall and headed for the hatch, just as the ship pitched to one side and nearly sent her tumbling. She grabbed a rail with one arm and Dev with the other, and waited for the deck to right. "Oh, yeah. Gonna be a picnic."

"What is a picnic?"

"Later."

Chapter Twenty

DEV BRACED HERSELF against part of the ship's metal structure, leaning back as she watched the waves roll toward them and lift the vessel up. The motion was rough and impressive, and she thoroughly enjoyed it. It reminded her of the sim sessions for the carrier she'd run, only this was real and she was getting a faceful of cold wet spray when the ship plunged down into the waves.

Behind her, back past the structure on the flat part of the ship, the rest of the crew were working to get things ready to catch fish. They were preparing cages and nets, but nothing they did triggered any programming in her so she had no idea what it all was for.

Ahead of them, she saw the darker, roiling clouds that were the front of the storm. From what she could tell, the ship was heading right toward it.

Why? She'd heard the captain tell Jess that storms brought the fish up. Interesting. Dev glanced down at her scanner, observing the cluster of returns around her, and then a few much farther out. She looked out over the ship's rail, and squinted, as she thought she saw another profile on the surface heading in the same direction they were.

It matched scan. She extended it and tuned the probes. The wiremap came back almost instantly, showing her a profile that was like, though not exactly the same, as the craft she was on. She heard a door close behind her somewhere, and then a moment later the captain crossed the deck and took hold of the outer wall, peering over it.

Then he turned around and came right over to her. "That thing comp?"

"Portable scan analyzer," Dev said. "Is that another fishing boat out there?"

"That thing say it is?"

Dev obligingly showed him the screen. "It looks like it," she said. "I saw the other ship, and I thought it might be like this one. Scan said it is." She reviewed the results. "Here's a hires." She tapped a control and the wiremap was replaced with a realtime image, bounced to the analyzer from an overhead met sat.

"Ah!" The captain leaned closer. "It's the Seagull." He nodded. "Headed same place we are. Lucky for me we're faster." He winked at Dev and spoke into a comm clipped to his shoulder. "Bridge, put the fire on. Plane up."

A moment later the ship surged forward at a higher rate of speed, and the front part lifted up out of the water.

Dev enjoyed that a lot. "Excellent."

The captain eyed her. "Like that?"

"I do," she said. "It's fast like when I pilot the carrier."

He leaned against the structure next to her, bracing himself against the motion. "Must be real different from up in space," he said. "Been down here long?"

Dev shook her head. "Not that long. Have you always been on this boat?" she asked. "And your family? I thought I saw some children before we left."

"Ah, yes." He smiled. "My little ones. The latest generation in a very long line going back way before the end times. Long before the world took itself back from us. When there were still trees and grass back in the home country." He folded his arms. "But my family's always been on the sea."

"Wow." Dev was impressed. She knew Jess talked about her family's long history but this was something else entirely. There was a sense of independence about the captain that was interesting. "That is a long time."

"What about you?" Sigurd asked. "What does your family do up in space?"

Dev had thought a little about how she would answer that question, since she and Jess both figured it would get asked. It was interesting, in a way, to get a chance to build a history for herself other than her real one. "I grew up on a bio station," she said, since it was the truth. "I don't have a family. I never knew them."

She saw the reaction in his face, a look of near dismay. "Now I"m a tech, so the people around me there are sort of like family, but it's not the same, is it?"

"No," he said. "Not the same at all." He studied her face. "You could be kin of mine, y'know. I got a daughter looks pretty much just like you. I can see it in the bones of your face. We probably share a great great somewhere way back."

Dev smiled a little. "That's nice to think of," she said. "The one thing that really interested me when I came downworld was the water here." She indicated the ocean, which was pitching and rolling around them full of whitecaps. "I thought it was amazing. It was one of the first things Jess showed me and I will never forget it."

"It is amazing." Sigurd smiled. "And that's a sure sign you're one of us." He chuckled, turning slightly as Jess appeared and made her way along the deck to where they were standing. "Looks like we're in a race."

Jess went to the outer wall and put her gloved hands on it. "Another fisherman?"

"Yup. I even know who it is, thanks to your tech here," he said. "Not one of my bigger enemies. We trade met sometimes."

Jess turned and came back over to them, rocking a little with the motion. She took hold of the grab bar Dev was leaning against and regarded the sea. "Aside from the obvious, how do you win the race? What do you do when you get there?"

Sigurd folded his muscular arms. "Thought you were out at sea?"

"Never saw any other boats, and besides I was six. You might have changed your methods since then."

Sigurd laughed. "We'll change our traditions when Interforce does," he said. "It's a stake. You pick your spot in the ocean and you got that, plus the distance a boat can travel at ten knots in ten minutes to fish in." He spoke into the mic again. "Head for the banks. Drill it between the deep reef and marker twelve."

"How do you know where to go?" Dev asked. "To find the fish I mean."

Sigurd winked. "That knowin's been in the bloodline for a good long time. You just know." He pushed away from the wall. "Gotta get ready to work. Stay out of the way. Don't want to explain to Jacob if either of you get nailed by a hook."

He ambled off, his body balanced against the movement in a completely natural way.

Jess waited for him to disappear, then she took up the spot against the wall he'd vacated. "So," she said. "What do you think so far?"

"What do I think about what?" Dev asked. "I think this is amazing." She indicated the ocean. "I really like riding on the boat."

"You do?"

"Yes." Dev showed Jess the scanner. "I showed this picture to him. I hope that was not incorret."

Jess studied the live image, then she shrugged. "They know we bounce off the sats, so don't see much harm in it," she said. "Did he tell you anything interesting?"

Dev keyed off the image and reset the scanner to long range biological. "He does think I'm related to him apparently. Something about sharing an ancestor way back." She pondered that. "He said I looked like an offspring of his."

Jess studied her for a moment, then shifted her gaze to one side. "I can see it," she said. "Might even be true. Do they keep track of that sort of thing up there?"

Dev waited for her scan to parse. "They keep very close track of the genetic arrangements, of course," she said. "They mix and combine them for specific sets. But making that trace back to actual people? I don't think so." She looked up at Jess. "You know all about your family, don't you?"

"Sure," Jess said. "I"ve got a family scrapbook in my quarters at the citadel. I"ll show it to you when we get back. Helps when you're in the out beyond sometimes, if you're from a known family. Like with Sigurd here. He knows my bloodline, so he knows what to expect from me."

Dev pondered that. "Not that different from us then, is it?" she said. "They know what to expect from us, because they know our genetics and programming."

"Sometimes," Jess said. "But not always. They don't program us." But as she said it, she had to wonder. What then was the training she'd gotten since age six if not programming, just in a different way? She pushed the thought aside and bent over the scanner. "Whatcha got?"

"I was looking for bears," Dev said. "But I don't think that's them unless they swim under water." She indicated a mass below the surface ahead of them. "What are those?"

"How did you get it to penetrate the water?" Jess took the device from her. "I've never seen it do that. Usually we just get refraction waves back."

"Oh." Dev cleared her throat. "Well, I was going over the comp from our last mission and I was looking at the intel stream from when we were heading directly at the ocean and—"

"Those are fish." Jess grabbed her arm and started across the deck. "C'mon. We can maybe make some major points with this." She cradled the scanner in one hand and shouldered the door to the interior open. "G'wan with your story."

Her story? "Oh." Dev hurried to catch up. "Anyway, I thought it would be a good idea next time to be able to see where we were going if we were heading for the ocean so I ran the comp through a backscatter decoder and figured out the sine wave differences."

Jess stopped, and looked at her. "This isn't something you were programmed for is it?"

Dev shook her head. "No. That's the genetic part. Doctor Dan told me he equipped me to be able to figure things out by myself. So I made a routine to bend the scan waves to match the ones in the water so we could see under it."

Jess simply stared at her in silence.

"Was it incorrect?" Dev asked, hesitantly, after a long moment.

"You scare the shit out of me sometimes," Jess said, mildly. "No it's not incorrect. C'mon." She started moving again, hauling up as she almost plowed into Sigurd. "Ah. Just the man I was looking for."

"For what?" He said. "I'm busy."

"Want fish?" Jess showed him the display. "Just off your port bow if you slow down long enough to catch em."

Sigurd grabbed the scanner and stared at it. "That's two hundred fathoms down. How in the hell are you seeing them? Nothing we have goes more than fifty anymore and all it can tell is rough relief not identify damn species." He grabbed his comm. "Hold hold hold! Engines full stop get ready to deploy the deep nets! Move it! Move it!"

He tossed the scanner back to them and turned. "We'll see if you're not bullshitting. If you are I hope you like swimming." He slammed back through the inner door and then they felt the radical motion as the ship went from full speed to nothing, and they were thrown roughly against the inner wall.

They heard bells ringing outside, and a thunder and crash of heavy machinery.

"Sure hope that scans right," Jess said. "I do like swimming but not in those waters."

Dev recovered her scanner and adjusted it. The readings came back with the same results and she was relatively sure they were accurate. "Can we go watch them?"

"Sure." Jess moved gingerly through the hall, glad it was narrow since the motion of the vessel was now extreme since they'd stopped their forward motion. She stepped over the threshold of the hatch into the next section, keeping her head down to avoid slamming it into the overhead.

Dev followed closely, slinging the scanner around her neck so she had her hands free to keep her balance.

She stepped over a last divider then followed Jess up a tunnel that brought a blast of fresh, cold air to push back the smell of oil and steel. A moment later and they were outside, on the back part of the ship. Jess pulled her to one side and back against the bulkhead, and they both stood there trying to make sense of what was going on.

The crew on deck were all in motion, dragging bins over to a huge wheel in the center of the deck that was wound around with netting. As they watched, a heavy hatch at the rear of the deck was lowered, and the roiling sea boiled past it and flooded everything.

"Holy crap." Jess grabbed her and hauled her up onto a crate in a smooth motion, just as the backwash from the water thundered against the bulkhead wall, splashing and spraying everything in it's path.

"Go go go!" A man nearby yelled. He was standing on a rotating platform, his legs braced and his hands moving rapidly over a set of controls. "Nets going out!"

The noise was incredible. Dev resisted the urge to cover her ears and watched as the wheel started to turn. As it did, she felt the ship start to move forward, and at the same time, felt Jess's arms close around her to keep her in place.

It seemed to take a long time as they went around in a broad circle but then the loudest of the noise stopped and the boat rocked as they unhitched the end of the net and it went free into the water.

Then it was quiet, save the rumble of the engines and the sounds of the crew securing things on deck. The bell stopped ringing and some of the men started dragging the bins back to the overhang next to the bulkhead, shaking their heads.

The back hatch closed, and the water drained out and they climbed down off the crate and went back to the deck. The crew looked at them, then looked away, ignoring them as they went about their tasks.

Jess led the way cautiously into the open. The back deck of the ship had a low wall on the sides, then the higher gate in the back and the steel deck in between was weathered and beaten and had patch upon patch upon patch welded into it. On either side were huge cranes with grapples on them and in front of the wheel was a huge hatch with doors the crew was fastening the grapples onto.

"Least this'll be fast." One of the men was saying. "No idea what cap'ns doing. Ain't never been no fish here."

"Miss out on our spot near the front." His companion griped. "Crazy ass."

The clouds roiled overhead, and the wind shifted. The men looked up at the sky. "Now what?" The first one said. "Let's go check met. That didn't feel right."

The ship swung around again, making a big circle around the bobbing floats that were tied to the net. "See if they got 'em." Jess nudged Dev. "Before this damn storm screws us up again." She braced her hands on two of the deck supports, blocking the wind and the motion from sending Dev flying.

Dev appreciated that. She was now between a bulkhead and Jess, and she could use both hands to study the scanner, tuning it carefully and starting her program running. For a moment, it just blinked placidly, then the display shivered into a view of what was beneath them, giving a wiremap of the topography and showing a huge white mass just about right under them. Not knowing really what it meant, she showed it to Jess.

Jess chuckled. "If they don't catch 'em they can't blame us." She eased out from under the overhang and looked up. The clouds were getting darker and as she watched, rain started coming down, slapping her with cold, wet drops. She ducked back under cover and tugged her hood up as the wind increased, bringing its chill with it. "Brr."

The man on the platform was watching a gauge, ignoring the rain as it dripped off his oversuit. It was made of some repelling fabric since the water beaded and dropped off it, but his face was exposed and he frequently blinked to shed the rain from his eyelashes.

Pale blonde, like hers. Dev noted. The man was around the same age as Sigurd, she guessed, but he had close cropped facial hair and she wondered if it was because he had to stand outside on the platform all day.

Then the bell started ringing again, and the deck erupted into chaos, men bolting from the forward structure and heading for the big wheel, and the man on the platform working his controls to open the hatch doors.

"What are they doing?" Dev asked.

"Pulling the net in," Jess said. "I think. Got to be honest and tell you I don't remember much from the last time except how cold it was, and how good fresh oysters tasted on the way in."

Dev smiled, moving over just a little and leaning against Jess's tall body. She was holding on to a pole, but a moment later, her free arm draped over Dev's shoulders and there, in that rough and rolling sea in the rain Dev felt a sense of comfort she'd hardly expected. "What are oysters?"

"Shellfish. You get them in the shallows, then you just open them and eat them whole in a swallow."

Dev went still. "While they're still alive?" She asked, her voice rising in surprise.

"Yeah. I guess," Jess said, after a brief pause. "They don't make noise or move around or anything."

Dev looked up at her with a very dubious expression.

Jess laughed. "I think I finally found something that freaks you out in a bad way."

Dev was momentarily quiet. Then she produced a pained grin. "I think you're right. I sure liked the idea of that whole sex thing better," she said in a mournful tone. "I don't think I'd like consuming live animals."

They both turned when loud noise sounded, and got back under cover as the ship churned to a halt again and four men on the back wall started throwing metal hooks into the water, pulling them back at high speed and sending tails of wet rope skittering over the deck.

"Go go go!"

The wheel increased its speed, and the net started coming back onboard the ship, as several more men gathered on either side of the opening with huge, long hooked poles.

A blast of water washed over the deck and picked a man up, throwing him up the flat surface toward the overhang.

"Should we help him?" Dev asked, watching the tumbling body with some concern.

Jess considered in silence, then made a motion that was half shrug and half shake. "Wait here." She jumped down off the crate and bolted across the floor, leaping over the next rolling wave and two bags it brought with it, keeping her balance across the pitching deck seemingly with ease.

She reached the injured crewman and grabbed his arm and his upper leg, hauling him up and onto her shoulders and then bracing her legs as the next wave sought to take them from under her. She waited for the water to roll back then she loped across the deck over to where a platform was bolted on the outside of the deck structure, gently letting the crewman down onto his back on top of it.

The man on the platform turned to watch her, his expression interested. Then he turned back around as the rest of the crew started yelling, and the boat suddenly changed its angle, going down at the aft as the wheel struggled to bring the net onboard. "Whoa!"

A woman came around the corner of the hatch, hopping over bins and hanks of rope as she skidded to a halt at Jess's side. "Svein! What happened to him?" She gave Jess a suspicious look. "What did you do to him?"

"She didn't do anything." Dev had slid across the deck to join Jess. "Jess just got him from the water and brought him here."

Jess eyed her, a faint smile crossing her face. "Don't worry," she said to the woman. "If I wanted to kill him I would have just done it. I don't waste time beating people up." She got up. "You a medic?"

"Yes," the woman said stiffly. "Sorry. No offense."

"None taken. C'mon Dev let's—"

They both grabbed for something as the ship pitched upward violently, and high keening sound broke through all the rumbling of the engines. Jess slid against the bulkhead and grabbed hold of a steel strut, reaching out to grab Dev as she bounced over next to her. "What in the hell?"

The raucous yells of the crew rang out and they ducked their heads around the over hang to see the net being hauled back in, stuffed with brilliant wriggling forms. The draw was so immense it was nearly taking the aft of the ship underwater, and the excitement on deck was palpable.

The deck door opened and Sigurd hopped out, a grin on his face. "C'mon you slugs! Get that damn thing unloaded before it drags us under! Bet we fill the tanks with one damn throw!" He reached out and slapped Jess on the arm. "Lucky little bastard you are, Drake. Haven't seen a haul like this in ten years."

"Captain." Jess's voice cut through all the excitement, and brought him around to face her. She was standing very still, her head cocked a little forward. "Don't hit me again."

Sigurd looked her in the eye in silence for a moment. Then he lifted a hand up, palm outward. "Just treating you like one of the family, Drake. No offense intended," he said, in a quiet, serious tone. "You did me a favor, you and your tech. We appreciate it."

Jess relaxed. "Sorry," she said. "Been in the field a while."

He nodded. "Better warn your tech not to stick so close then." He winked at Dev. "She'd look lousy with bruises." He turned and started across the deck, heading toward the cluster of crew now working feverishly to get the fish out of the net and into the tank before the drag pulled the back of the ship under water.

Jess exhaled, then she turned to regard Dev, who was tucked against her with a puzzled expression on her face. "Don't worry," she said. "You're safe. I only whack people I don't like or don't know." She paused. "Or those who double cross me and nearly get me killed."

Dev pondered that. "I'm really glad you like me then," she finally said. "And I'm glad you helped that man." She blinked against the wind driven rain. "Should we get out of the weather? I'm really getting cold."

Jess relaxed completely, and smiled. "You bet." She undogged the hatch and pushed it open. "We've done our good deeds for the day. Let's get something hot and check our intel so far before we get washed overboard."

"That sure was a lot of fish," Dev said, as she stepped over the threshold.

"Sure was."

Dev paused, as they opened the inner door. "They don't eat them alive, do they, Jess?"

Jess chuckled.

"Do they?"

AS IT TURNED out, they didn't. Dev sat quietly on a low bench against the wall of the common room, cradling a mug of pungent seaweed tea between her hands as she watched the crew stream in and out as they finished their tasks, or started new ones, their high good humor very evident.

The net had hauled in a good catch, and after they cast it out again, they had been happy with the result and ended up with enough to fill up one of the tanks and now they were powering along in the waves heading somewhere else.

It was damp and cool in the common room but still a lot warmer than outside. On one side three women were working on preparing some food for everyone. Unlike in the crèche, or even in the citadel, they were doing this in the open, cutting up some things and putting them in a big container that seemed to be over a heat source.

Whatever it was they were doing smelled good. Dev was just glad there was heat involved, which meant she wasn't going to have to consume something either raw or alive, the thought of which was giving her quite a bit of discomfort.

Across the room Jess was talking to Sigurd, and everyone seemed to be ignoring the motion of the ship, even when the front of it seemed to be smashing into the water every few moments.

The bench she was on had a padded rail behind it, which you could hook an arm around to stay in place, and that was exactly what she had done, wedging herself into a corner to ride out the waves.

She was pleased her scan had resulted in success. It seemed to have broken the ice with the crew, as Jess had hoped it would, and now, though not really friendly to them, she didn't see people glaring at them anymore. That was good. She watched Jess, seeing her reach out to casually grasp a hold bar against the wall as the ship pitched hard to the right.

Then Jess turned her head and their eyes met. Dev found herself smiling for no apparent reason at that, watching a responding smile appear on her partner's face. It was nice to see that, in this cold and strange place. Dev regarded her cup, then looked back up to see Jess lifting a hand briefly to Sigurd and then head her way.

She had good balance, Dev noted. The motion of the ship didn't knock her offstride, and she ended up next to Dev and dropped down onto the bench without missing a step.

"Hey."

"Yes?"

"He wants you to use the scanner again." Jess lowered her voice, though the sound in the common room with all the engines going blocked out most listening ears anyway. "I told him we can't run around catching fish for him."

Dev considered that. "Of course I can do that," she said. "But wouldn't it be better if I looked at their gear, to see if I could get it to do the same thing?"

Jess glanced around quickly. "Can you do that?"

"I don't know. I would need to look at their equipment."

Jess leaned on the back rail. "Interesting bargaining chip," she said. "Keep quiet about that."

"Okay."

"We give that to them, they get a big advantage over the rest of the fleet," Jess said. "We're not supposed to tip their balance."

"I see."

"On the other hand, they'd really owe us one. But I'd wait until we're in more sheltered waters. I don't want you banging your head on their crap trying to rig it."

Dev didn't really have much to say to that, so she remained quiet, sipping at her tea. The brew was strange and unlike anything she'd tasted before. The seaweed it was made from stronger and a soft purple color rather than the green she'd been used to.

Jess peered in the cup. "Sea grape tea. Haven't seen that in a while."

Silently, Dev offered her the cup. Jess took it and sipped from it, rolling the liquid around in her mouth a little before she swallowed it. "Not bad." She handed Dev's cup back. They're making a stew back there. Should be pretty good."

"And it's not alive," Dev said softly.

"We made good progress." Jess lowered her voice again. "Now I've got to convince Sigurd to take this haul and sell it to the other side so I can get this mission moving before we get interrupted by pirates."

"Aren't we supposed to be trying to find the pirates?"

"No. I just want them to think we are," Jess said. "I mean..." She glanced around. "Hell, if we bump into the damn pirates I'll be glad to get in a fistfight with them, but we have to focus on the plan, Dev. I need to get that data. That's the goal. Don't lose sight of it."

"I won't," Dev said. "I'm just trying to keep everything straight in my head. What can I do to help?"

The ship rolled at that moment, sending Jess practically into Dev's lap. "Holy shit." Jess hauled herself upright. "Sorry about that, partner."

"I'm not," Dev replied in a straightforward way. "You can do that at any time." She had moved her cup away and her skin was still tingling with the sudden connection. "It feels excellent."

Jess eyed her, and a rakish smile appeared on her face.

The women finished their work across the room, and they rang a small, yellow metal bell that immediately made everyone else shut up and move toward them.

"We'll wait until they get theirs," Jess said. "Even though we rank them, and don't have to."

Dev cautiously extended her boots and crossed them. She was now relatively warm, and sitting next to Jess was making her feel even warmer.

The crew was watching them. Dev could see them glancing over, then glancing away, as they filed passed the back counter and came away with steaming bowls clutched in their hands. Whatever it was smelled good, and Dev felt her stomach growling in response.

She spotted one of the women approaching and she glanced at Jess. "Are we expected to help?"

Jess laughed. "No." She nodded at the woman, who had brought over two bowls with eating utensils stuck haphazardly in them. She took one and Dev took the other. "Thanks."

The woman didn't say a word to them. She just turned and went back over to the work area.

Dev watched her go. "Did we do something to cause discomfort?"

Jess sniffed her bowl, then picked up the combination spoon and fork and fished out some fish, nibbling it cautiously. "Nah." She licked her lips. "These guys like their women, but they like them quiet and busy cleaning and cooking and taking care of the kids."

Dev took a spoonful of the wet, lumpy substance and found it quite tasty. "I see."

"They're fine with that, but they think we're freaks," Jess said. "I've been called everything from unnatural to a monster up here by the ice." She shrugged. "Even when I was here as a kid, they tried to make me help them. I kicked one of them in the crotch and they left me alone."

"I see."

"That's why they warned us when we came on not to go around the ship alone. Not that it worries me," Jess said. "I've got more firepower strapped to my body than they could buy with a dozen hauls on this thing."

"I'll make sure to stay close by you then," Dev said. "Because I don't have anything dangerous tied to me."

Jess chuckled. "These guys aren't impressed by us being Interforce, but Sigurd knows my rep and if he's got any sense he'll have told his roughnecks to steer clear."

Dev ate what was in the bowl, looking up when she heard footsteps approaching to find Sigurd and another man hunkering down next to them.

"I'm not gonna chase the storm edge," Sigurd said. "I got word we had a big pack ice break northeast of the divide. I'm going to take us out there and you're gonna find me another haul. How about it?"

Jess considered his words as she continued to eat. "Northeast," she said, after a pause. "Sure that's smart?"

Dev blinked, since she'd figured in her head that northeast was exactly where Jess said she wanted to go.

Sigurd gave them both a reckless appearing grin. "Scared? 'Fraid the abominable snowman's gonna getcha?" He looked mockingly at Jess. "I let the crew know you nailed that bait ball we pulled onboard. Now they want to see if it was a fluke."

"Not my job to find fish for you," Jess said. "You want to risk taking this tub into the ice pack? You can drop me off on a berg. Not my idea of fun." She scraped the bottom of the bowl. "What makes you think you'll find any fish there anyway? Maybe you're just looking to embarrass us."

Sigurd laughed. "Maybe I am," he said. "I guess we'll just find out won't we?" He got up and tapped the man with him on the head. "Let's go, Lars. Tell the crew they got till mids, then they need to start cranking."

Jess watched them go, tipping her bowl up to drain the last of the liquid into her mouth. Then she let her elbows rest on her knees and licked her lips. "Nice."

Dev just scratched her nose, having nothing really to add to that. She poked in her bowl and scooped up a bit of fish, chewing it thoughtfully. The meal was mostly that, with thick, well cooked pieces of seaweed in it and it was a little spicy.

From her peripheral vision, she saw the women take away their work materials, moving off through a heavy door set in the center of the common space. "What's in there?" She indicated the door.

Jess glanced at it. "That's where they live. Got some common crew quarters on the outer corridor, where we got put. In there's where the kids usually are, and where they bunk. I was surprised when you said you saw them outside."

"I see." Dev set the bowl down and picked up her scanner, adjusting it and directing the beacon toward the door. The wiremap came back quickly, diagramming a dense, compact space of three levels that had a number of hot targets scattered across the rooms.

Jess peered at it. "Don't let them see you doing that," She said, in a very low tone. "They take their private space very seriously. But get as much detail as you can."

"Okay." Dev tuned the device, aware of Jess's body pressed against hers. After a few minutes, she turned the scanner off and let it hang from the strap around her neck. "What do we do now?"

"Wait." Jess stood up and stretched. "Wait for us to get into this back of beyond spot he's got his eye on. Let's go get some rest, Devvie."

Dev's brows twitched at this morphing of her name, but she got up and followed Jess across the open space, her balance only slightly tested as the ship seemed to have found a less fractious path for a few minutes. She set her bowl in a deep sunken space with the rest of them and tried to ignore the intent stares from the men they were passing.

Jess seemed oblivious. She led them toward the side door in the bulkhead and worked the wheel latch that held it shut. She pulled it open and ducked inside, with Dev right behind her as they moved from the stale, flickering light of the common room to the dim, burnished orange glow of the corridor.

Here, the motion didn't matter as much as the space was barely large enough to admit Jess's shoulders when she was facing forward. The walls were rough and covered in old weld points, and the lights themselves were wrapped in steel and thick gritty glass.

They were alone in the corridor.

"What is this area?" Dev asked, as they went through a slightly wider space.

Jess looked. "Probably was an engineering station," she said. "Most of these old boats are from that last big fight. When humanity realized they were so fucked they couldn't afford open warfare anymore and they abandoned everything."

"Oh." Dev examined the now dark consoles with some interest. "So the fishermen took them over?"

"Some of them, yeah." Jess reached their little space and bumped the door open. "No locks," she said, as she entered, ducking her head to clear the hatch. "There were the very few who could get the creds to run them, since they had fish to trade." She waited for the hatch to shut behind Dev and then she examined the latch, removing her long knife and wedging it in place to keep the mechanism closed.

"I see."

Jess went over to where she'd lashed her pack and stood quietly for a moment, studying it. Then she touched the bio patch on the side and regarded the gentle green light that flashed briefly before she opened it. "Least they've got some brains here."

Dev had done the same to her pack. "Did you expect someone to come in and disturb our things?"

"Never can tell." Jess started divesting herself of her weapons. "More expect the kids to come in looking for swag than anyone else. They're always looking for trade goods." She unfastened and removed her jacket and hung it on one of the two hooks near the hatchway.

Beneath the hooks there was a metal grilled box split in two, and Jess deposited her boots in one side of it. "I remember hearing stories about those times, when this was a fighting ship. Remind me to look 'em up when we get back home."

Home. Dev stood up and took off her outer coat, putting it on the hook next to Jess's and feeling the cool damp of the room penetrate her jumpsuit. She'd never really had much to call her own at the crèche, so the thought of her quiet, spacious quarters in the citadel being home was surprisingly appealing to her. "Okay."

"Cold?" Jess was watching her.

"A little." Dev rubbed her arms. "I'm glad we brought these." She indicated her dark green jumpsuit, which at least covered her pretty much from head to foot. "Jess, you seemed in discomfort when they said where we were going. Didn't you want to go that way?"

Jess unpacked her sleep bag and was spreading it out on the top bunk. She chuckled softly. "I do," she said. "I'm not sure I really want to enter the pack ice, but it's the right direction, and if he gets a good haul chances are he'll want to offload where we need to be."

Dev copied her motions, snapping the hooks at the four edges of her bag to the bed supports. "Okay."

"But I don't want him to know that's what I want," Jess went on. She was now in her black jumpsuit and she boosted herself up onto the upper bunk and sprawled over her sleep bag, exhaling as her body relaxed. "You scanned for comm, right?"

"Yes." Dev was just putting her scanner into its dock. She triggered a download of the scan, taking a seat on her bunk and extending her legs out into the small space of the room. "Most of the tech is in that central area. In this space, there's nothing really except for the lights and a comp in that place I saw the children."

"Library probably," Jess said. "Kids were getting lessons." She stretched and sighed again. "One of the things they trade for in places like Quebec on our side, and Dover on the other side. Comp mods for the kids, and for nav and met."

"It's an old comp." Dev studied the readouts.

"Sure."

"If I could mod our scan to find the fish, I'm not really sure why someone hasn't," Dev said. "We got sine wave mods as basic in school."

Jess didn't answer for a few minutes, then she shifted a little, rolling over onto her stomach and peering down at Dev. "I never did."

Dev looked up in surprise. "You didn't?"

Jess shook her head. "They teach us what we need to know. Sine wave manipulation wasn't on the curriculum for front line soldiers in the cause, back in school." She studied Dev. "There's a feeling too, I think, that old fashioned goons like the ones here don't trust tech."

Dev blinked at her, obviously confused.

"You take tech for granted," Jess said. "So do I, since my family's pretty stocked and I went from home to Interforce and there's plenty of that there. But out here, tech's like your crazy uncle. Know what I mean?"

"Not in the least."

Jess chuckled. "These people rely on themselves. Not on outsiders, or tech, or comp. They use it when they can get it, just like they're using us for their own purposes, but they don't trust it."

"Or us."

"You got it," Jess said. "So they might trade for something that could do something useful, like that scan, if you could set it to just do the fish finding. They'd never waste their time learning the theory behind it. Does that make sense?"

Dev remained quiet for a brief time. "It makes sense as in, I understand what you said, but it doesn't make sense as in, how do they expect to make things better if they don't learn how it all works?" She settled the scanner into its case, making sure the connection to the inductive charging system was solid.

Then she wriggled back and lay down on her bag, watching Jess's face hanging over the top bunk, its dark and shaggy framing outlined in the low, orange light. "Don't they want to improve their future?"

"There is no future here," Jess said. "It's all short term, just like it is for us. You can't really think about what you're going to be doing in a year, or ten years, or even tomorrow, when your focus is on how to survive today." She extended a hand down and smiled when Dev reached up to grasp it. "Let's get some rest while we can."

Dev squeezed her fingers then let her go, squirming around and getting the bag's covering over her, relieved when the light, strong fabric immediately trapped the air around her and warmed it. She wished, briefly, that they were back in the carrier, uncomfortable as that had been, since then at least they'd been able to sleep next to each other.

Warmer. She remembered the feeling she'd had when she'd woken up before, with Jess's arm draped over her. Warmer, and nicer.

She thought about the fishing people, living from day to day.

She thought about school, and all the things she'd learned and never wondered why and about the kids here who were only taught the things they needed to know to do what they did.

She wondered, a moment, about what really the difference was between natural borns and bio alts.

"Hey." Jess's voice interrupted her.

"Yes?"

"Y'know, it's warmer up here."

On the other hand, Dev now found herself appreciating the need to deal with the present. "Is it?"

"C'mon and see."

Well. Keeping warm was important, wasn't it? Dev climbed out of her nest and lifted herself up onto the upper bunk, where Jess was already enfolding her in fabric and a tangle of long arms and legs and, she was glad to note, much warmer air.

Nice.

Chapter Twenty-one

THEY WOKE TO chaos. The lights had gone completely off, and a klaxon blared suddenly, making the walls vibrate as it jerked them both upright.

Dev was glad they hadn't decided to meet up in her bunk on the bottom or else she suspected Jess would have been knocked out cold. She felt Jess shift and she quickly tried to get out of the way, as the sheets pulled tight against her.

"What the fuck?" Jess released the catches on the sleeping bag. "Don't move." She planted her hands on either side of Dev. "Coming over."

Dev pressed flat against the bed, her heart hammering as she felt Jess launch herself over her, landing on the ground with a thump of bare feet against steel. Once she was sure Jess was clear she reached down and grabbed the scanner, turning it on and using the screen to light up the cabin they were in

Jess was halfway into her jumpsuit, now outlined in the blue silver glow. "Thanks," she said. "Let me get this suit on then you grab yours. I want you with me."

Dev had absolutely no argument with that at all. She waited for Jess to move toward her over jacket and then she slipped out of the bag and rooted around for her own clothes. She left the scanner leaning against the bedpost and jumped into her suit, getting the catches closed just as a voice blared on the speaker calling battle stations.

Battle stations?

"Looks like they kept the old comm chips." Jess had her coat on, and was seating her weapons in their holsters. "Once we get out to the deck keep that scan on and recording. If this goes way bad they'll want to pick up the comp."

Dev was pretty sure she didn't really want to know what that meant. She got her jacket on and slipped the scanner around her neck, fastening the outer closures as she reached down for her boots.

The klaxon continued. Jess got her boots on and headed for the hatch. "Stick close." She yanked her knife free and sheathed it, and then worked the latch and shoved the door open, ducking to get through it as she flipped on the light from her kit and slapped it into place along the axis of her blaster.

The hallway beyond was also dark, and the ship was rolling, sending them slamming from side to side as they made their way aft toward the working part of the ship.

Dev heard running feet, and the whine of machinery and the sound of men yelling. Above that though, she heard a roar that didn't seem to be part of the ocean. She put a hand on Jess's hip and stayed close by her, the sound of the klaxon making her grimace as they passed under one of the speakers.

They reached the door and Jess put her shoulder to the hatch and shoved it open, hauling herself back and sweeping Dev behind her as they were hit with a blast of light.

Then the light was gone and Jess surged forward. "I got a bad feeling about this." She hopped out the hatch and onto the deck, and bolted for the bulkhead wall.

It was loud and chaotic. There were crew behind several walls and the pedestal, all yelling, the laser traces of hand blasters blinking in the darkness in multihued flares.

Dev followed, seeing the blast of light cascade across the deck, coming from above. She tipped her head back as she headed for where Jess was flattened, seeing a huge silhouette momentarily outlined in backwash against roiling black skies.

Programming triggered, and she sucked in a shocked breath as she reached Jess's side. "Jess!"

Jess unsafed her heavy blaster. "Yeah?"

"That's a carrier over us."

"You got a look at it?" Jess turned and stared intently at her, going otherwise very still.

"Really fast one," Dev said. "But it matched a pict image." She touched the side of her head. "Older type, BM series, not like ours. Smaller engine cones, bench inside, multiple launch attack model."

Jess sighed. "Fuck." She gently pushed Dev against the wall. "Stand there, poke the scan out that square hole and just get good vid of what I do."

"Okay," Dev said, feeling unhappy and incorrect. "Take care."

Jess smiled briefly. Then she closed her eyes, and took a breath in, letting it out slowly. Dev could see visible tension coming into her body, and when her eyes reopened, there was an intense, cold focus in them that shocked her.

Then Jess simply exploded into motion, coming around the bulkhead and onto the deck just as it lit up with a huge flare of white light, that outlined forms dropping from the sky.

Dev got her scanner in place and triggered the recorder, blinking her eyes rapidly to clear the light flare so she could see. The deck was alive with alighting figures and as they landed and rifles started swinging around, Jess attacked.

It was awful and to her, scary. Jess was moving so fast it was hard to keep sight of her, blaster fire missing her on all sides as she twisted and turned, a dozen figures swiveling to target her as she calmly laid down her own fire.

Rifle tucked against her side, hand gun in her left hand, she was shooting in two directions at once while moving in a third, never pausing in motion for even an instant. She took down one of the enemy, then two, then she leaped up onto the side wall of the ship as it pitched, jumping out and over two others who were rushing toward her.

Dev's jaw dropped a little, as she watched her partner flip over in mid air, shooting down at the two figures and blasting them into pieces just before she landed and turned and let off a barrage in a sweeping motion that took out two more descending figures and sent them spinning off into the ocean.

No hesitation. All smooth and deadly motion.

She was a deadly force, and the men facing off against her knew it. Dev could see their faces in the wash of the light, their eyes wide, pointing, diving for the deck, ducking away from her motion even though they wore the same uniforms and were cut from the same apparent cloth.

Through the roar of the surf and the carrier engines, she heard a wild yell ring out, high and bold that made the hair on the back of her neck lift. She saw one falling figure shift sideways and head right for Jess only to watch in astonishment as her partner took one long step and then crouched, shooting off the deck and colliding with the figure as she swung her free hand out and around and the light caught a thick spray of liquid as the figure seemed to come apart as she hit it.

Jess tumbled in the air and then righted herself and landed, dropping into a crouch as bolts flew over her head and slammed into the outer wall of the ship and ricocheted back almost catching her as she leaped again over them and tumbled lazily into the air before the deck came up to meet her and she landed square, turning in a circle with both guns outstretched.

Men were yelling. The carrier above them suddenly shifted from white to red lights, and a loud horn blared out. Dev had no idea what it all meant, but she kept recording, as Jess closed in on two more of the attackers, now too close to use blasters so it was hand to hand.

She kicked the legs out from one and sent him into the fire of another of the enemy, his body blasting apart into chunks as the plasma bolt touched him. Then she grabbed the second, swinging him around as he aimed the butt of his gun at her head. He missed his target by a fraction, then Jess had her knife out again and slashing, and the red light caught a spray of liquid as the knife cut deep and then flashed free.

Her laughter suddenly rang out over the chaos. She slid sideways and put her back to the ship wall, head swinging around as she looked for her next target.

Hooks suddenly caught the light, and four figures hauled on to them, as the carrier started to lift off. Jess dropped to her knees and braced her rifle, sighting up as the figures lifted clear and the lower guns of the craft activated, and swung around.

"Jess!" Dev let out a yell, as she recognized the configuration. "Guns live!"

"See em!" Jess yelled back, squeezing the trigger and letting off a barrage at the muzzles moving her way. The carrier's shielding took the hit and she knew she was likely about to get blasted along with the rest of the boat, when a fast moving body made her jerk around just as Dev hit the deck next to her, sliding across the icy surface and slamming into her with stunning force.

Her automatic reactions seized up, throwing her body into confusion as the kill instinct was unexpectedly stifled, and she went with the motion as they both ended up behind the big net wheel just as the deck lit up with an overhead barrage and she had to throw her hands over her head to protect her eyes from the flash.

"They're going to shoot you!" Dev yelped. "Get down!"

"They're going to shoot you too now!" Jess yelled back, as a line of blaster fire came right at them, counter to the carrier's motion as it lifted away and headed south. With a curse she grabbed Dev and yanked her out of the way, rolling out of the line of fire as the blast hit the deck again and sent a cascade of energy across it.

The backwash hit them and Dev felt her ears pop and her body arch and cramp, an almost fire burning over her senses before it was gone and over, and the sky was dark again.

Every inch of her was tingling. Dev got her knees under her and straightened, twisting around to find Jess right behind her, gun muzzles still glowing faintly, a light that vanished as the ship recovered and turned on the outside lights on the deck, bathing them in a white orange glow.

The engines rumbled to life. Dev caught her breath, and looked at Jess. "That was interesting. In a bad way."

Jess slowly put her guns down on the deck and sat down next to them, letting her hands rest on her knees, her fingers twitching in a jerky rhythm. Her breathing was coming short and hard, and after a minute, she looked up at Dev with cold, expressionless eyes.

Killer's eyes. Compassionless and remote.

It was stark, and terrorizing, seeing the cold and merciless machine behind those eyes and yet, Dev didn't either think or hesitate before she reached out and clasped her shoulder, far more worried than scared. "Are you all right?" She asked. "You seem in real discomfort."

For a moment Jess kept staring at her, then her eyes blinked, and the muscles under Dev's fingers relaxed and the breath came out of her in a long, trickling sigh. She lifted her hands and rested her head against them, fingers still twitching.

Dev forgot all about the bad guys. She put her back to the chaos on the deck, blocking the view of the crew. "Jess?"

"I'm okay," Jess muttered. "Just coming down. Give me a minute."

Dev wasn't sure what that meant, but she watched the planes of Jess's face ease after a moment, taking on familiar character and leaving behind that cold, hard mask that had put a chill down Dev's spine. "I'm sorry if I was incorrect," she said, in a quiet tone. "You told me to stay behind."

Jess blinked a few more times, then she looked up at Dev with a strangely wry expression. "We'll talk later."

"Hot damn!" Sigurd's voice rang out over the deck. "Get the engines revved! Put us back on course and get this deck ready to fish!"

Jess lifted her head. "Don't..." She scrambled to her feet and sucked in a breath. "Hold it!" She called out in a commanding tone.

Dev got up and stood, uncertainly, at her side. "What's wrong?"

"Go get a scan of the bodies, especially the hands." Jess turned to face her. "Before they throw them over," she added. "Need to know who the hell they are."

Dev studied her for a moment. "Are you sure you're okay?" She asked, lifting the scanner up and keying it.

A very brief smile appeared on Jess's face. "I'm fine." She patted Dev on the arm. "G'wan so they can clean up."

Somewhat reassured, Dev turned and made her way across the slippery deck toward the first of the bodies. The engines had steadied the course of the ship, but they were still plowing through white ruffled seas and she balanced carefully as the crew backed away as she approached.

Strange. She had no idea why they might be wary of her, since all she'd done during the fight was yell and slide across the ice like a crazy person.

She knelt down beside the body and started the scan, glad she'd put on her heavy coat when a blast of ocean spray coated her liberally. The scan chimed softly and she reviewed the results, then she passed it over the hands that were already freezing to the deck.

The body was in a typical black battle suit, the twin to the one Jess was wearing, right down to the blue trim on the collar. She finished the scan and got up, storing the results before she headed to the second, catching sight of Sigurd crossing behind her and heading in Jess's direction.

Dev circled around the body and knelt down, positioning herself so she could keep an eye on her partner. Jess had picked up and holstered her weapons, and was tucking her hands inside her jacket as Sigurd reached her.

She seemed all right, but Dev was still concerned. She set the scan up and reached out to grasp the stiffening shoulder, rolling the body over and straightening it. The fact that the man was dead didn't bother her.

Bio alts were programmed to be very pragmatic about life, and death. Dev herself had seen any number of her kind put down in the crèche, for various reasons, and she felt no emotional charge as she studied the dead man's face. Dev captured the details carefully, then she passed the scan over his hands, waiting to hear the beep as the device picked up the embedded chips under the skin.

The device remained silent. Dev redid the scan, but got the same results. "Hm." She did it a third time, this time recording the result or lack of it and closing the cover. Unexpected. She got up and went to the other casualties and then she headed back to where Jess was still talking to Sigurd.

Six bodies in Interforce uniforms, five of them without the chips Dev knew they all carried, including herself. She'd gotten her set the morning before she'd left the crèche, and she remembered the bone deep tickle as they'd activated the programming for it.

"Jess." She paused, seeing the suddenly intent look from her partner.

"Done?" Jess said.

"Yes."

"So, captain." Jess put a hand on Dev's shoulder. "Did we deliver?"

Sigurd grinned. "Gotta admit, that was pretty slick work," he said. "Bastards came down on top of us before we even caught them on radar. Looked like your side, huh?"

"It was a carrier," Jess acknowledged. "Bet they won't be back though."

"Not today," Sigurd agreed cheerfully. "You done now? I need to clean my deck."

"Done," Jess said, watching him as he walked off, yelling orders at the crew. "Shit." She exhaled. "Wasn't looking to have to report this today."

"Jess." Dev opened the scanner and called up the results. "I found something unusual." She keyed up the second set of comp and showed it to her. "No ident."

Jess took the scanner and peered at it. "None of them?"

"The first one had." Dev reached over and switched the record, displaying it. "The rest didn't. I thought it was a bit unusual."

"A bit?" Jess's voice lifted. "Those are reg uniforms. Here's the scan tag." She pointed. "And that was a carrier, even though it was an older one. No one should be onboard it that isn't one of us."

Us. Dev again felt just the tiniest prickle of pride at that, no matter how inappropriate the time for it. "What does this mean, Jess?" She asked, as her partner slowly started to move across the deck, still studying the scanner. They eased past the crew who were now dragging the bodies to the side, and gained the shelter of the bulkhead.

"Good question," Jess finally said, handing the scanner back. "Let's talk about it later." She folded her arms and regarded the busy deck. The attack didn't seem to have fazed the crew at all, and most were returning arms to an insulated locker before moving out to go back to work.

Sigurd came back over to them, rubbing his hands. "Ready to head into the slot?" He said. "See it? Right there." He pointed up and forward, where the solid inky black of the sea was abruptly bisected by a ghostly gray wall looming up unexpectedly in front of them.

"I see a head on crash," Jess said. "Not much else."

Sigurd chuckled "There." He grabbed a post as the ship veered. "That crack."

Jess squinted, seeing a long, dark line in the gray. "You're taking this thing in there?"

"Scared?"

"Yes."

Sigurd looked at Jess in surprise. "Thought you jiggers didn't admit to that."

"Stupid ones don't." Jess eyed the oncoming wall. The ship lights now bounced off the ice and she could see the separation between the two big sheets, the waves rushing up against it and bouncing back. Her breathing was returning to normal, and the energy that had been making her muscles jerk was easing.

She was out of the need to be zoned. The harsh black and white flatness had eased from her vision, and she felt the bowed tension in her back releasing as she leaned against the wall of the ship.

Had she freaked Dev out? She watched her grip the rail to keep herself steady, her head turning a little as she watched everything. It didn't seem like it. "Dev?"

"Yes?"

Jess hesitated. "Never mind. We'll talk later." She turned to Sigurd. "Why there?" She asked, walking over to the side of the ship and peering over the rail. "What do you think you'll find in there?"

"You tell me," Sigurd said. "How about it, tech? Wanna give that thing a whirl?" He came over next to Jess. "We know schools tend to hide up in the crevasse. Give's 'em shelter from the big current they're just a little tricky to set the nets into."

"Why at night?" Dev asked.

"That's when they're there." Sigurd grinned at her. "They sleep at night. Get it?"

The alarm went off. "Standing by to move forward, cap'n!" A voice rumbled over the hailer. "Have clearance."

"C'mon." Sigurd motioned them forward. "See it for yourself. You'll only get the one chance." He rambled toward the side of the ship, clearly expecting them to follow, and they did.

The walls of ice towered over them, and Jess tipped her head back, feeling a blast of cold air hit her, along with a wash of icy spray. She refastened her neck cover a little more firmly and felt her eyes widen a little as the brash lights of the ship hit the ice and sent a dozen jolts of color through the surface.

She felt like they were entering a cave. The dark clouds over head were formless and impenetrable, and as they slipped between the walls the thunder of the waves nearly deafened her, thrumming against her ears with an uncomfortable vibration.

She lifted one hand and covered her right ear, wincing.

Through the thickness of her jacket she felt Dev's touch on her, the heat of a grip on her elbow and then the press of Dev's shoulder against hers as they were surrounded by rumbling echoes.

"Loud huh?" Sigured yelled.

The noise was pounding in her head and Jess felt suddenly sick.

"Drop the net!" Sigurd bawled into the loudspeaker. "Drop! Drop!"

Dev saw the real discomfort on Jess's face. She looked around at all the activity, then she carefully gripped Jess's arm and tugged her toward the hatch that would block some of the sound that was bombarding them from all directions.

It wasn't terribly comfortable for Dev. The discordant waves were making her head ache and she was glad to get the hatch open, and then closed after her and Jess, the seal thumping into place and dropping the noise level by three quarters.

It was a physical relief. "Ah." Jess leaned against the wall, rubbing her ear and wincing. "Thanks."

Dev shook her head rapidly to clear it. She could still feel the ship moving but the roar of the waves and the echoes had faded to almost irrelevancy. They were alone in the mostly dark corridor, in relative safety.

Jess exhaled, flexing her hands. "Let's go look at that scan," she finally said. "Something's not adding up. What was that ambush all about?"

"They wanted the fish?" Dev hazarded a guess.

"Why drop a full on assault team to the deck in that case? Why not just put the guns on them and threaten them? Were they after fish, Dev, or were they after something else." She slowly turned her head and looked around. "Like this ship instead?"

Dev picked a spot on the wall next to her and leaned on it. "Why would they want this ship?"

"Why would they want an old carrier?" Jess countered "How many of them didn't have tags? They weren't Interforce, Dev. You were right about that. Those weren't agents." She exhaled reflectively. "If they were I'd be dead."

"I see," Dev said, then paused. "I think."

"We all get the same training. Some of us are better at some things than others, but we can all do a first class job of kicking ass. Those guys could no more kick my ass than they could flap their arms and fly."

"You seemed very successful."

Jess stared quietly at the opposite wall for a few moments. "I'm very good at killing people," she said. "You shouldn't have come that close to me while I'm like that. I don't always know the difference between friends and enemies when that old fog of war descends."

"In the big pl...in the citadel, when those people attacked us, you knew Doctor Dan wasn't a bad guy."

Jess half shrugged. "Yea, but you can't always depend on that," she said. "Don't take chances with me. Last thing I want to do is screw up and pop you one."

Dev remembered that laugh. She thought about what she'd done, and that run across the deck and the irresistible need that had driven her. "I didn't think about what I was doing," she said. "I just did it."

Jess nodded. "Let's go back to our digs." She draped her arm over Dev's shoulders and pulled her close. Then she turned fully and wrapped her arms around Dev and hugged her.

Dev smiled, returning the hug with a sense of wholesale relief. Things might be getting confusing, but this, at least, certainly wasn't.

JESS WAS VERY glad to get back into their little scrap of a cabin, away from the sounds and the wary eyes of the crew. She felt raw, and it occurred to her it was the first time she'd been in the zone since Josh's betrayal. She hadn't thought about going into that space before she'd done it, and now that she'd come out of it she wondered why she'd felt so nervous back in the citadel.

She remembered being nervous, and that sick, roiling feeling in her guts as she'd imagined going back into action, but when the time came, she hadn't even thought about it.

She hadn't thought about killing, Dev hadn't thought about saving her own ass. What did that say about both of them?

She looked up at the ceiling, flat on her back on her upper bunk as Dev worked to consolidate the scan files and parse the data inside.

Dev.

Dev had done good. She'd done just what a tech was supposed to do right up until she'd broken orders and bolted across the deck, more concerned about Jess being in trouble than her job. Even though that was against regs, and wrong from an ops perspective, Jess was smiling at the ceiling because every agent she'd ever known always wished for a tech who would do exactly what Dev had done.

You wanted to trust. You wanted to know someone really, honestly, had your back.

Jess thought about what Dev's body coming apart in a blast meant for her, and she closed her eyes, because it did hurt. A fierce pain gripped her chest and she reached up to rub the spot, shaking her head a little at the discomfort. She flushed the image and after a moment the pain faded, and she could breathe again.

"Jess?" Dev came over and stood next to her head, her blonde hair gently reflecting the dull light in the cabin. "Here's an ops recap. Do you want to review it?" She leaned her arms on the bed frame and turned the scanner so Jess could look at it.

Jess found herself unable to focus on the screen. She looked at Dev's profile instead, watching the faint twitches along her smooth skin and admiring the nice shape to her face. After a moment of silence, Dev looked over at her, head tilting just a little in question.

What amazing eyes she had.

"Jess?" Dev asked, after another long, silent moment. "Are you all right?"

Jess grinned briefly. "Yeah," she said. "Sorry. I'm still buzzed from the fight. Takes me a while to come all the way down." She focused with some effort on the screen. "Roll it. Let me see if you got my good side."

Dev complied, glad that the ship had mostly stopped tossing around. She held the scanner steady and watched Jess watch it.

"That is an old carrier," Jess said, after a pause. "They were current when I was in field school. I trained on them." She studied the text scroll. "Look at those guys." She leaned closer and pointed at the figures dropping from the carrier. "Lines."

"Not the jet pack we have?"

"No. They'd be idiots to use that in the weather we were in anyway, but this is old style. We used to rappel before they stabilized the packs so—" She watched the scanner print the ident details on the still moving figures. "Nice job of integrating the scan, by the way."

Dev smiled, and her eyes twinkled a little. "Thank you."

"This guy." Jess pointed at the screen. "He was chipped." She studied the readouts. "We won't know who he is until you squirt that back home, but he was one of us." She watched the man move. "See that? That's field school training." She watched him swing clear of the deck obstacles and release at just the right time to drop him behind a barrel for shielding. "He went faster, and got behind something. Not an idiot."

Dev nodded. "Those people didn't." She watched three others drop. "But they're all in our uniforms."

Jess nodded. "They make a good show, but one thing's for sure, they don't have current comp because if they scanned us before they put a move on us they missed picking up on me." She flexed her hand. "They didn't know I was here."

"No, I don't think they did," Dev said, as she watched the recording. "You can see this person here, that one you said was real? He saw you, and look." She pointed. "See his face?"

Jess smiled ferociously. "Know what that is?" She said. "That's an 'oh shit' face." She could, in fact, see the expression and the widened eyes as her own figure flickered past, arms outstretched, guns firing. It always made her twitch, watching herself on the comp, always thinking of what she could have done better or different, always finding some fault with her body position or aim or...

Anyway.

"You move so fast," Dev said. "It's amazing."

Jess eyed her. "You think so?"

"Yes."

Jess watched the scan play out, until the lights blared on and she saw the carrier start a recovery phase, and the picture suddenly got out of sync and lost focus. The pickup caught some low voice and then Dev's yell to her warning of the carrier gun shift. "Did you curse?"

Dev pondered that. "I think so. When I realized they were going to try and shoot you."

Jess reached over and patted her on the cheek. "Good girl. You learn fast."

Then scan cut out, the playback ending as Dev had shut down prior to her bolt across the deck. The scan screen went dim, and Dev shut it down. "Do you want me to send it?"

"You think you can get a signal out?" Jess asked. "No, wait, tell you what. If you can get sig, then just squirt the bio idents we pulled off. Let's see what that gets us. I'm not..." She paused. "I'm not really sure where the vector is on this, Dev. It could be tied in with the leak."

Dev nodded. "Okay, I'll see what I can do." She turned and sat down on her bunk, then she squiggled back and leaned against the pillow, raising up one knee to brace the scanner against as she worked.

Jess folded her hands over her stomach and studied the ceiling again. There was so much to think about. Who were the impostors? Why were they attacking ships dressed as Interforce agents? Were the interesting little golden sparkles in Dev's eyes something that happened naturally, or were they engineered that way?

She let out a slow breath. Now, where did that thought come from? Why should she care either way about those sparkles? "Hey Dev?"

"Yes?"

"When they make you," she said. "Do they pick stuff like what color hair you have, or is it just skill sets?"

Dev didn't answer for a little while. "I'm not really sure." She finally said. "I never heard Doctor Dan say anything like that. About what we look like, I mean." She paused. "It's more about what you do, than what you look like I think."

"Huh."

"Why did you ask me that?"

"Just wondered," Jess said. "Just was curious if he did it on purpose or not."

"Do what?"

"Made you so damn cute."

Dev swiveled and stuck her head out from under the top bunk, peering at Jess with a puzzled expression. "Am I?"

Jess rolled over onto her stomach and peered over the edge of the sleep bag. "I think so. I really like looking at you."

Dev blushed a little, but grinned. "I'm glad."

They remained in place, studying each other. "You think I'm cute?" Jess finally asked, resting her chin on her wrist.

"I think you're beautiful," Dev answered readily. "And also cute," she added, when she saw the surprising blush darken Jess's skin. "I've never seen anyone as pretty as you are."

"Okay, got it." Jess felt lightheaded from the blood rushing to her head. "Thanks."

Dev pulled her head back in and extended her body out on the bed, resting her head on the pillow area of her bag. That had been interesting, if a bit confusing. She was glad Jess liked how she looked since she didn't have any choices in that area.

It did make her wonder though, about whether they made bio alts look a certain way or if they left it to chance like the natural born did. That made her think about what Sigurd had told her, about family, and how he thought he could see something in her face that he recognized.

Was that true? She flipped through the vid in the scanner until she picked up an image of him and she studied it briefly. Was there something familiar there?

She really didn't know. But then the image shifted and Sigurd glanced at the record sensor with a certain look and Dev realized there was something she recognized there but not from her mirror. There was something in that look, in the half humorous expression that reminded her very strongly of Doctor Dan.

Ah. She nodded to herself. Maybe that was why she felt like she knew him. That idea made sense to her, more so than some story of ancient connections between them. Feeling more settled, she set up the transfer for the squirt and started parsing for signal, narrowing the range and tuning out the discord of the metal interference around them.

She could feel the ship moving under her, pitching back and forth but the motion was far more gentle and it came across as almost soothing. The scanner meeped at her, and she regarded the tuning, shaping the signal and altering the waves to lock on to a master sync passing overhead.

From the met sat, she registered the channel and riffled through the interconnects to find one for her relay. There were two, and she picked the strongest, encapsulating the squirt and sending it through. A full second later she got the relay confirmation and then she severed the connection, backing out of the sat and closing down the channel.

She set a timer to go back for retrieval, since the scanner was a send and reply system only not consistently online like the carrier was. "Jess, the ident has been sent and accepted."

"Good," Jess said. "Sigurd said the carrier was on top of them before they realized what the signature was on their radar. Too much EMF. Not surprised they didn't see it."

Dev was studying the scanner, keying through its comp. "We didn't see it either," she said.

"What?"

"I left the scanner on low band," Dev said. "While we were resting. It didn't pick up anything either."

"Really?" Jess swung her head over the bunk edge again. "Nothing?"

Dev slid out of bed and set the scanner on Jess's bunk again, displaying the screen. "Just the systems onboard. Even the met scan, I see the storm edge here, but nothing else." She ran the comp back several hours, flickering across the screen. "See?" She leaned her elbows on the bunk, her head nearly touching Jess's.

Jess ignored the screen, and leaned closer, grabbing Dev's earlobe in her teeth and gently nibbling it. She heard the hastily stifled laugh from her partner, and then she released her and refocused on the scanner. "Sorry. What were you saying?"

"Um." Dev studied the screen. "No scan. No sign of the carrier before it attacked us." She ran the comp again. "I didn't try to scan them as they left, though."

"You were busy protecting my ass," Jess said. "So." She studied the data. "Either the trash in the sky obscured them or they obscured themselves. Found a way to block the scan spectrum."

"Is that possible?"

"Used to be. We used to know how to build stuff that could hide from anything. Now?" Jess shook her head. "Why bother? We can use storm fronts and vectors to slip in undetected. Stealth is expensive." She pondered the thought. "Though it sure gave them the advantage tonight, didn't it?"

"Did it?" Dev asked. "What would have happened if Sigurd had seen them coming?" She set the scanner down and studied Jess instead. "Could he have hid this ship somewhere?"

"Granted, not many places to duck behind on the sea, but Sigurd's been sailing these waters since the dawn of time. He could have avoided them I bet."

"Hm." Dev put her chin down on her forearm. "Do you think these guys were the pirates?"

Jess shook her head. "Other side."

"Even though that one person had a chip?"

"Even though." Jess sighed. "A few have changed sides, over the years. I didn't recognize him though. Not someone I knew. Could have been from another base. I'm thinking they wanted the ship to help them infiltrate one of our centers. Maybe even Base Ten."

Dev propped her head up against her hand. "So. They were trying to do the same thing we are?"

Jess chuckled wryly. "More or less, yeah."

"I see." Dev straightened up. "Would you like some hot tea? I will go get some from the big room." She shut down the scanner and put it back in its cradle. "I think we're still in the ice thing."

"Sure," Jess said. "Just be careful. After tonight I don't think any of them would put a finger on you, but watch out."

Dev shrugged into her jacket and closed the fastenings, tugging the hood up into place before she went through the hatch and stepped into the hallway. Mindful of Jess's warning, she looked in both directions, but the hallway was empty and she turned and proceeded down it toward the common room with almost silent steps.

Far off, she could hear the sounds of the crew working, and below, the grind of the engines and gears. It was quiet as she emerged into the central corridor and then made her way to the inner hatch, pushing it open and going inside cautiously.

The room was mostly empty as well, only the two women were inside, working at the rear of the room. They turned and looked as she entered, but then went back to what they were doing without speaking.

That was okay by Dev. She went to the dispenser and took out two cups, studying the choices. After a moment's pause, she decided on seaweed tea and requested two portions, waiting as they brewed and emitted a gentle cloud of spicy sweet steam into the air.

The inner door to the room opened, and a set of piping voices emerged. Dev turned to see two of the children come in, their tow heads and small bodies attracting her attention. A little boy, and little girl. They clamored around the two women asking for a snack, their tousled hair and hide singlets contrasting with the steel deck and dull gray paint in odd counterpoint.

One of the women turned and caught Dev watching. "What are you looking at?"

"The children," Dev answered readily.

The two had spotted her now and they focused on her. "Who're you?" The boy asked, tipping his head back to look up.

"Dev."

"Keep clear of her, Edguard." The woman said. "Her kind's not safe for the likes of you."

Dev regarded herself, then she looked at the woman in question, cocking her head to one side. "My kind?"

"Those that do nothing but kill and maim, and take," the woman said. "Like those who attacked us. You're one of them, no matter you don't carry the guns openly."

Dev capped the now finished cups. "We defended you against them," she said, after a pause. "Does that make us the same?" She studied the women. "We mean you no harm."

"Don't you?" The woman herded the children back into the inner sanctum, leaving the other woman to finish the work.

The second woman waited for the door to close, then she turned and regarded Dev. "Don't mind Eva. She hates everyone." She came over, a small case in her hands. "Some of us know the difference between techs and agents, and between you lot, and pirates. Really."

Dev produced a mild grin. "Jess doesn't think the people who attacked you before were Interforce."

"Of course she'd say that." But the woman smiled back, offering the box. "Have a cake. I bear no ill will to you. If they were, or weren't, you fought on our side tonight so all's fair for now." She studied Dev's face. "They said you were a spacer."

"Yes." Dev took one of the wrapped items in the box. "I was born in space, on a bio station." She examined the item, then put it with the cups. "Thank you."

"My name is Hilda," the woman said, and offered the box again. "Take one for your...ah...whatever it is you call each other."

Dev did. "Jess is my partner," she said, unable to repress a tickle of pride at the words. "I'm sure she'll appreciate it, so thank you." She put the cake with the other one and picked up both cups, grasping the handles in one hand. "Please excuse me now. The tea will get cold."

Dev ducked through the hatch and re-entered the corridor, now spotting two dimly lit figures making their way toward her. The ships roll had almost ceased now, and she was able to keep a steady balance as she approached the men.

Would they cause her trouble? Dev kept her expression mild, as she came within the nearest pool of light and they spotted her. But the two men paused as they recognized her, and both moved back flat against the wall to let her pass.

"Tech." One said, in a respectful tone. "Can I get the hatch for ya?"

Ah. "Yes, thank you. It's that one there." Dev waited for him to undo the latch and open it for her. "I appreciate that very much." She smiled at the crewman.

The man touched his head with one hand, and then they went past, continuing down the hallway toward the commons. Dev stepped through the hatch and leaned against it to close it behind her, her eyes flicking to the inside of the room to find Jess near the far wall, her suit stripped down off one arm. "Hello."

"Hey." Jess turned to face her, one hand holding a pad against the front of her shoulder. "Give me a hand with this, wouldja?"

Dev put the cups and the cakes down and went over to her. "What's wrong?" She stripped off her jacket and put it on the hanger.

Jess removed the pad, exposing a puncture wound halfway between her neck and shoulder. "Pain finally kicked in. Just need you to clean this out and pack it." She regarded her arm dourly. "When I'm fighting I never feel it." She looked past Dev. "Whatcha got there?"

"Some tea, and some little cakes the woman called Hilda gave me," Dev said, absently. She focused on Jess's shoulder and nodded a little at the burst of programming that told her what to do with it. This had come in the second round of deep time, and she'd woken with an almost discomfiting understanding of critical aid.

She retrieved the small aid kit from their pack and took out the cleaner, as Jess edged around her and investigated the cakes. "I got to see the children. They seemed to be afraid we would damage them."

Jess snorted, as she unwrapped the cake and sniffed it. She took an experimental nibble as Dev cleaned her shoulder, making a pleased, grunting noise at the taste. "Not bad."

"How did you get this?" Dev asked, ignoring the edible commentary. "I thought they had energy weapons with them. This seems to be a sharp implement that hit you." She could see whatever it was had a jagged point, and it had gone almost the length of her finger joint into Jess's body. But the bleeding had already mostly stopped.

"My own clumsiness. I threw myself against the wall where the harpoons are." Jess finished the cake and took a sip of the hot tea. "Anyone give you any trouble on the way there and back?" She asked. "Seems pretty quiet."

"No, everyone was correct." Dev applied salve to the wound, and sealed it with a breathable skin bandage. "I heard a crewman say they would remain here in the ice space until dawn."

"Good." Jess reached up and cupped the back of Dev's neck, tilting her head to one side and gently kissing her on the lips. "Tomorrow we need to get Sigurd to sell his fish to the bad guys. But between now and then I think we should work on keeping each other warm, don't you?"

Dev was surprised. They were in a strange ship, where lots of unusual things were happening, and Jess wanted to spend time practicing sex?

Jess's lips touched hers again, and her body reacted, her hands reaching out to caress the smooth, bare skin she'd only so recently been working on. "Sounds like a great idea," she heard herself say, as she savored the rich burn in her guts.

"Thought you'd agree."

She did agree. She didn't really understand, but as her body pressed against Jess's, and the sensation built she decided she really didn't need to understand it.

She just needed to enjoy it.

Chapter Twenty-two

JESS OPENED HER eyes into darkness, her time sense telling her it was still before dawn outside. The ship around her was very quiet, and just gently moving under her, a bobbing motion that was almost soothing.

Not nearly as soothing as the solid warmth of Dev's body pressed up against hers though. Jess found herself quite surprised at that, since it had never been her habit to remain in bed with anyone past having sex.

She could have told Dev to go back to her own bunk. The small space was hardly big enough for Jess's tall form, and it was nothing less than squishy with the two of them there together, but after they'd finished it had just seemed easier to stay where they were.

Besides, she'd said they had to work to keep each other warm, right? It certainly was warmer together under the covering than it would have been apart, and she'd noticed that Dev seemed to get cold a lot faster than she did.

Maybe it was her having been born in space, under all that atmo control. Jess felt the gentle movement as Dev drew in a slightly deeper breath and then found herself wondering if her new partner dreamed.

She hadn't, this sleep. It had been a restful few hours, matter of fact, and her body appreciated that. Especially after all the energy she'd expended in the fight.

Ah, the fight. Now, Jess could smile about it and she did. Even though the attackers hadn't been Interforce, it had felt curiously good to wreak havoc again and she didn't mind admitting that to herself as she lay here in the dark, her arm tucked around Dev's middle.

She'd noticed that Dev hadn't seemed to mind the bloody splattering and the bodies. She'd rolled them over to scan with no emotional charge at all. That was a good sign. It had taken Josh a half a year to be able to handle that.

Good sign.

Dev seemed to be nearly perfect, in fact. Aside from her knowledge, and her driving skills, and her willingness to sleep with Jess, she seemed to have all the right stuff anyone would expect in a good tech.

Jess let her eyes close again, as she the gentle rocking lulled her. She had at least two hours before dawn, and she figured getting as much rest as she could before they entered the other side was a very good idea. She felt Dev take another deeper breath and then they both jerked as the comp fastened to Dev's bunk chimed softly.

"Comms," Dev said, her voice soft and husky.

"The long arm of the nerdy." Jess reluctantly released her, unsealing the sleep sack and letting a rush of cold, damp air in. "Brr."

"Brr," Dev repeated, grimacing a little as her bare feet hit the deck.

She sat down on the lower bunk and pulled her legs up crossed under her, opening the device and triggering the comms module. She started to shiver, and she rubbed her arms a little as she waited for the connection to clear.

"Hell of a way to wake up, huh?" Jess had her head over the edge of the bunk and was watching her

"Not exactly pleasing," Dev said. She focused on the screen and studied the readout, watching the scan lines flutter. "Squirt."

"Figures."

"They sent ident on the scan," Dev said. "Ruthgart Chambers."

Jess pondered that. "Doesn't mean a damn thing to me. Anything else? Any data?"

Dev stifled a yawn. "He was assigned to Virginia Bluffs. They lost contact with him two standard years ago," she said. "They're asking for confirmation of death."

Jess chuckled.

Dev continued studying the screen.

"Cold?" Jess suddenly asked.

"Well." Dev sorted through the requests. "Having no clothes on is probably inhibiting my ability to hold this still enough to read, if that's what you mean."

Jess bounded out of her bunk and removed the over sheet from her bed sack, ducking her head and taking a seat next to Dev and wrapping the fabric around both of them. She peered over Dev's shoulder, feeling Dev's shivering abate after a moment. "Tell them I confirm the ident."

Dev had to read the letters several times before they made sense to her, the sudden warmth around her distracting her completely. "Okay," she finally said, tapping in the code. "Should I send the vid now?"

Jess considered the question. "No. Let's hold off on that until later." She fell silent for a bit. "Something's still not right back there. I don't want to give them too much information."

"Okay." Dev shut down the connection and hung the comp on its strap back on the bunk support. "What do we do now?"

"We can get more rest. Got a few hours to dawn yet," Jess said. "We're still in that ice split, no sense in wandering around the ship in the dark." She looked around the cabin, lit only by the faint line of emergency illumination along the floor. "Glad we brought a couple flashes"

Dev considered the gloom, all the more gloomy since she'd shut down the comp. "Why is it so dark?"

"Saving power," Jess said. "They're lucky this thing runs on a converted ion generator. They suck in sea water and make ergs using chemical reaction, but getting parts for the damn thing's a bitch. They turn it off when they can."

"I see."

"Got a point. If they don't have to move and everyone's sleeping, no sense in running the batts," Jess added, after a brief pause. "Hate to see what would happen if they had to get moving fast, though." She rested her elbows on her knees.

Dev cleared her throat a little. "Should we lay back down?"

"Sure." Jess unlatched the sleep sack on the lower bunk and squirmed into it, waiting for Dev to join her before she sealed it back up. Now, with the coversheet from her bunk, and the full sack on this one, it got nice and warm rather quickly. "Ah. That's better."

She felt Dev relax, then she let her eyes close, only to open them a moment later when she heard soft footsteps coming down the hall outside.

Stealthy footsteps. Jess had heard them often enough to know. "Someone's coming," she whispered into Dev's ear. "Shh. Stay still."

Dev pressed herself against the bunk as she felt Jess ease herself over her, unfolding her long frame and ending up standing at the foot of the bunks. She waited for Jess to clear the edge of the mattress then sat up silently, reaching out to find her jumpsuit and slipping into it.

Once she'd sealed the catches around her throat she lay back down, aware of Jess's tense figure still locked in place. She couldn't hear anything, but she trusted that Jess heard what she had heard and was preparing to do something about it. That something might possibly mean light, and Dev wasn't sure their reluctant hosts were ready to find a bio alt in their midst.

Jess moved silently, and there was a very faint sound as she drew her blaster from its holster and put the holster back down on the small shelf. There was a brief flicker of red as she activated the weapon, then she put her back against the wall and got in position.

Dev heard the sound of metal cushioned in grease moving, the tiniest suggestion of a echo that stopped at once, and went silent.

Everything went silent. Then there was a rush of motion on the other side of the hatch and then a booming, solid thump hit the surface, making Dev jump before she flattened herself back down on the bed. But the hatch stayed shut, and a faint, soft curse echoed through the steel, before she heard the distinct sound of someone walking rapidly down the hall away from them in bare feet.

Silence came back, then Jess exhaled, and chuckled very softly. "Forgot I jammed my dagger in the lock," she said. "Poor bastard probably knocked himself silly."

"Who was it?" Dev whispered.

"Someone looking either for trade stuff or a roll in the hay." Jess reholstered her blaster and put it on the shelf. "Morons. Probably one of the kids taking a dare."

"Taking a dare?" Dev squirmed to the back of the bunk as Jess climbed back up into hers. "In hay? What is that?"

Jess chuckled. "I'll tell you later." She stretched out on her back. "Sleep if you can. If I get what I want and we end up in the other side's clutches, there won't be much time for rest."

Now what did Jess mean by that? Dev settled back down anyway, composing herself to stillness. When you were in the crèche, you learned how to put yourself down when it was time for it and she did, taking in a lungful of air and releasing it as she let her body go slack and felt her breathing slow.

Who had been at the hatch? What was Jess going to do? Where were they going to go, and if she was with Jess, who'd fly in and help them get out?

How did she feel about going with Jess into that kind of danger?

All questions for later.

She let go. The darkness around her and the relatively soft, gentle motion reminded her strongly of the crèche, and her sleep pod and she went deeper and deeper into the rocking motion and drifted free.

And then, seemingly just a moment later there was a touch on her arm and she opened her eyes to the same darkness, but with a sense of Jess next to her. "Hello?"

"Near dawn," Jess said. "Let's get up and see what we can see."

Obligingly, Dev sat up and swung her legs over the side of the bed, as the room was suddenly lit with the warm glow from Jess's suit light. She looked up to see her partner's body outlined against it, and that made her smile as she stood up and retrieved her sanitary pack from her gear bag. "I don't think we've moved."

"Me either." Jess pulled her jumpsuit on over her shoulders. "Ow."

Dev paused in her motion toward the hatch. "Are you in discomfort?"

"Stupid shoulder," Jess muttered. "G'wan. We can look at it later."

Uncertainly, Dev nodded and then she went to the hatch, carefully untwisting the heavy dagger from the lock. She examined the weapon briefly. Despite the impact against it, the metal was unmarred, and it had a dark patina to it that barely reflected any of the glow from inside the room.

"Like it?"

Dev turned to find Jess watching her, with a hint of amusement in her expression. She walked back and handed the knife over. "It's interesting," she said. "I hadn't held one before. It's heavier than I expected." She waited for Jess to take it, then she went back and opened the hatch, pausing to listen before she went through it.

Jess slid the knife back into its holster. "Yeah, I guess they don't have those up there, huh," she muttered to herself, grimacing as her shoulder wound protested. "How stupid was that? I'm surprised I didn't gut myself with a fishhook." She turned the light a bit higher and finished fastening the wrist catches on her suit, feeling the ship move a little under her.

Aside from the shoulder though, she felt pretty good. There was a residual ache in her back from the old injury, but the stiffness she'd felt the night before had eased and she counted herself ready to face the day.

A minute later the hatch opened again and Dev slipped inside. "It seems very quiet," she said. "Do you want me to run a scan?"

"Sure." Jess shrugged into her weapons harness, the sound of the catches loud and solid in the room. "Let me take a peek." She went to the hatch and emerged into the hallway, also lit only by the emergency lighting along the ground. Jess straightened up and peered around, blinking as her eyes adjusted to the gloom.

The shadows faded into silver and gray and she studied the hall, now understanding what Dev had meant. There was a silence around her that set her senses on edge and she turned and ducked back inside the hatch. "Anything?"

Dev was standing near the bunks, her elbow resting on the top one as she studied her scanner, its light outlining her features in a mix of pale blue and green. After a moment she looked up. "I'm not getting any returns, except for the animals in the bottom of the ship."

Jess's nape hairs prickled immediately. "No other life?"

"No."

"Let's go." She went to the locker next to the bed and picked up her heavy blaster, seating it into the side holster and pulling her jacket on. "Let's go see what the hell happened."

"Okay." Dev set the comp down and put her jacket on, snapping the catches and then slinging the scanner over her shoulder. She followed Jess out of the room and into the silent hall, hoping her comp had got it wrong since the results seemed to have caused Jess serious distress.

They walked through the silent darkness and Jess paused before the big hatch at the end, drawing out her light blaster and flipping off the safety before she worked the lock. "Ready?"

"Yes," Dev said, not entirely sure what she was ready for.

But Jess nodded, and paused a second, before she gently booted the hatch open and moved sinuously through it in a continuous motion. She cleared the space then paused again. "C'mon."

Dev poked her head through and followed, finding the space beyond empty. She walked behind Jess as they crossed the common room, where only a safety light shone over the space the women had been fixing the meal on. Everything was locked down and put away, with bars holding the containers and cabinets closed.

Jess turned gracefully in a full circle, then continued on to the center, inner doorway. "Scan it," she said softly, turning and making her way over to the porthole to look outside.

It was dark. She could see the outline of the ice around them, a ghostly gray surface that continued to where the crack they had entered through split into a much darker outline. After a moment, Jess turned and looked at Dev, who was studying her comp. "Anything?"

"No." Dev joined her, turning the scan to show her the screen.

"Okay." Jess led her to the hatch to the outside and carefully worked the lock, bumping the heavy metal door open with her shoulder as she peered out onto the deck. A cold blast of air hit her and she blinked, before she emerged into the inner deck area.

Still, all silent. The working gear was all put away, lashed against the deck, and only the soft clank of the anchor chain echoed softly in gloom. Jess walked across the open platform, turning as she did to take in the entire area as she crossed toward the big wheel in the back.

Dev continued to scan. She could see the motion below the deck where the fish were, the bio sensors detecting them without any trouble at all. But if she turned around and pointed the scan at the rest of the boat, all it showed was the electronics that controlled it, and the outline of its structure.

No bio signs. Dev wondered if perhaps they'd found a way to shield against the scan, remembering what Jess had said about them not liking intrusion. Curious, she tuned the comp, bringing up her matrix and shaping the waves as she probed the internal structure.

The sine waves rippled, and then she turned, as she picked up something off to the right of where the boat was. "Jess," she called softly.

Instantly, Jess was at her shoulder, peering over it. "What?"

"Trace echoes," Dev said. "From over there." She pointed off to one side, and they both walked over to the railing to peer over it.

The front of the boat was moored into a chunk of ice, the long heavy chain disappearing into the white solid surface. From where the chain emerged was a roughly chopped path, visible now as it moved off into the distance, between two up thrust ice peaks and, just visible, disappearing into an unevenly shaped hole in the ice wall.

"Huh," Jess said. "They all got off?"

"It seems so," Dev said. "That explains why they turned everything off. They didn't need it."

"And left us there." Jess's eyes narrowed. "Nice."

"I don't think they really trust us," Dev said. "Even though we helped them."

Jess holstered her blaster and put her hands on her hips. "Wonder if this is one of their hidden hole ups," she said. "I've heard about them, but no one ever really found one. Makes sense they'd put it in a place like this. Only an idiot would risk entering the ice like this."

Dev regarded the path, then she turned and looked at the anchorage. "Why is this a bad thing?"

"Because the ice can shift and close this gap," Jess said. "Being crushed to death ain't my idea of fun. I've seen the bodies it spits out."

"Oh." Dev now felt a bit nervous. "Does that happen often?"

"Hm." Jess grinned suddenly. "Let's go see if they left the keys in the ignition." She started across the deck heading for the control room. "Bet you could drive this if they did."

Drive this? Dev felt her jaw drop a little. Wait, what? "I don't think I know how to do that." She chased after Jess, who was already halfway up the ladder that led to the control house. "We didn't have any sims for boats."

"Ah, can't be that different than the bus." Jess found the door locked. "Stand back." She took a step back and drew her gun out, pointing it at the lock and triggering the weapon. A bolt of energy smacked into the metal, turning it bright red, and producing an odd, spicy hot smell.

It clicked, and she kicked it, shoving the hatch inward and stepping over the verge. "C'mon."

Dev followed, finding herself in a space that held control surfaces on every inch, reminding her suddenly of the crèche's sim lab.

Her eyes went to the controls and much to her surprise, she felt programming kick in.

"Let's see." Jess went over to the main console. "Wonder if we can turn the juice back on. At least we could go down and steal breakfast."

"Not there." Dev went to a side panel. "Here." She ran her fingers over the controls and then, after a moment, she nodded and started pressing them as a programming overlay made the shapes and positions make sense to her. "I think, yes." She flipped a cover off and pressed a button, and the deck started faintly vibrating. "Yes."

She turned to find Jess looking at her.

"I guess you do know how to do this," Jess said, dryly. "Got any other surprises?"

Dev let her hand fall to her side. "I don't know," she said. "They are surprises to me sometimes too."

Jess nodded. "Okay." She gestured to the controls. "Get this thing powered up and see if you can retract the anchor." She went to stand near the front of the bridge. "Let's get out of here and do some of our own hunting."

"Those people will be in great discomfort if we do that."

"Yes, they will." Jess smiled. "Hope they've got supplies."

With a soft grunt, Dev went to the main console and sat down, letting her eyes scan the surface before she started triggering things and bringing up power. "This should be interesting."

Jess chuckled.

IT WAS INTERESTING, and also hard. Dev flexed her hands, glad at least the control center was closed, and warm. She checked the power settings, hesitating a little before she engaged the heater that would warm the anchor line and get it to release. "Is this correct?" she asked Jess.

"Is what correct?" Jess was examining one of the old style comp readouts.

"Taking this ship?"

Jess glanced over her shoulder. "Was it correct for them to leave us here alone on it? Don't get sentimental because that old salt liked you."

Dev thought about that for a minute. She checked the readings, then triggered the anchor chain retraction, hearing the rumble as it engaged. "We don't know why they left us," she said, after a long pause. "They might not have meant to cause us discomfort."

Jess snorted. "Just get us out of here," she said. "I don't like that ice."

Dev settled into the operator's chair. They could always bring the boat back, after all. If the fisher folks had been somewhere off in the ice all this time, they were probably okay. She confirmed that the anchor was seated back on the boat, and then she engaged the engines, her hands moving the throttles with uncertain motions.

She glanced at scan, surprised that the noise of the boat coming active hadn't attracted any attention. "I would have thought they'd come if we were leaving with it," she said.

Jess leaned against the console and regarded the ice. "Yeah, you'd think."

They were drifting away from the ice wall now, and Dev turned on the sonar, seeing the faint return from the ice all around her. She looked over at the uneven opening in the wall again, expecting to see at least Sigurd come running, but the opening stayed stubbornly empty and she frowned, still not feeling right about all of it. "Jess..."

Jess's hand came down on hers. "Sh."

Dev closed her mouth, and waited. She watched Jess's face, which was tense and twitching a little. She had turned her head to one side, and Dev could see the muscles around her ears moving.

For a minute, they were both silent. Then Jess drew in a breath and straightened. "Get us out of here," she said. "Fast."

Dev shunted aside all her questions and responded to the urgency in her partner's voice. She laid her hands on the throttles and moved them forward, aiming the front of the boat for the opening in the ice.

"Faster," Jess said. "Hurry!"

Dev had no idea what the problem was, but obeyed, moving closer to the console and standing up, leaning against steel and adding power to the engines. The boat surged forward, and as it did, she squinted at the opening. "Is that getting smaller?"

"Yes." Jess bolted for the other side of the control space. "Hurry!"

Now the urgency made sense. "Hold on." Dev braced herself and shoved the throttles full forward. The boat responded immediately and lunged toward the crack, not feeling at all like a carrier or anything else she'd ever sim'd. This was new, and strange, and she fought the controls to keep the boat straight as she felt the water crashing against the hull.

The walls were moving closer. Dev's eyes widened. She wasn't sure what exactly was happening but a very quick look to her right showed her Jess's face looking as alarmed as she felt. She pushed the throttles forward as much as she could, and heard a crash and heavy, scary crunching noise as a huge chunk of ice tumbled past her and thumped into the water next to them.

The boat rocked, but she kept it under control. Another chunk of ice struck the bow, but bounced off and then they were at the wall and rocketing between the edges of the opening which was closing against them as they squirted through. Then they were outside, and in higher surf, and she was grabbing everything she could to keep the boat on course as it bounced across the waves.

Dawn had broken, and the sea was alive with white froth, with a mist gray sky glowering overhead. Waves were crashing up against the ice and sending spray high up in the air.

"Whoa!" Jess grabbed the console and thumped into the wall as she stretched to look behind them. "Nice driving, Devvie!"

Dev got the boat under control, panting a little. "Thank you." She moved them away from the ice wall, turning the bow around so she could see the crack. "Are the..." She paused, looking at the now solid wall behind them, the only sign of an opening the newly floating bergs of ice bobbing near the center. "Oh."

"Yeah." Jess moved behind her and put both hands on the control chair to hold herself steady. "That would'a been ugly. I'm not much for being squash frozen."

Dev stared at the wall. "Did you know that was going to happen?" she asked. "Did they?"

Jess drummed her thumbs against the chair back. "Good question," she said. "Did I know? I had a gut feeling something was wrong," she admitted. "Did they know? Who knows?"

An iceberg floated past, its white and gray exterior bobbing in the deep green blue ocean. "Are they dead now?" Dev asked, after a moment of silence.

"Don't know, don't care." Jess slapped her on the shoulder. "Let's get moving toward the bad guys. This makes it easier for me, anyway. Don't have to screw around talking Sigurd into taking us there. And we've got a ride back."

Dev settled into the chair and hooked her boots on the foot rest of it. She studied the controls, then she keyed up the navigation comp. "Do you have coordinates? To where you want to go?"

Thinking about the fishermen bothered her. She wasn't sure she was sentimental about it. Actually she wasn't really sure what sentimental was, but Sigurd had been friendly to her, and it disturbed her to imagine him and his family crushed to death in the ice behind them.

Especially the little children.

"Ah, yeah, let me get 'em." Jess was busy at the navigation comp. "Basically east, then southeast from here. Gimme a minute."

Jess wasn't disturbed at all about them. Was that what she'd meant when she said she had no conscience? That she really didn't care if other people died? But she'd helped that fisherman, hadn't she?

"Okay, here." Jess was at her side, with a tablet. "There." She pointed at a set of coordinates. "That's their deep sea fishery. We can pull in there."

Dev plotted the course, hesitating a little over the unfamiliar, then familiar comp. "Won't they recognize you?" She asked, after she finished. "You said a scan would find you."

"Not the fishery," Jess said, with a note of quiet confidence. "Or, if they do, I'm not sure they'd care. What they want is the fish. Takes a lot of 'em to feed everyone."

"I see."

"Then we'll take the credits we get for the fish, and pick up luxuries in the black market there." Jess rested her arm on Dev's shoulder. "And that, my friend, is what will get us into the science compound. No one likes fancies like eggheads do."

Dev turned and looked at her.

Jess patted her on the back. "It's all good, Dev. We're back on track." She paused. "So, you said you didn't know how to drive this thing, then you did. What's the deal?"

"I didn't think I did." Dev put aside her disturbing thoughts with some effort. "I don't know why they would give me that, but when I saw the controls, I felt it kick in. It wasn't something I sim'd or anything. They must have given it to me on the second long session."

"So you don't know all of what they put in your head?"

"No. Not until I need it. I really didn't expect to need this." She set the course and activated it, feeling the keel come around as the engines engaged and they started off toward the east. She waited for the boat to settle into its motion before she turned again to Jess. "Does it bother you?"

Jess studied her. "Every time I think I've got you squared, you change it up. I'm not sure how the Hell I should feel about that."

Dev was briefly silent. "I'm sorry," she finally said. "I don't think there's anything I can do about it." Her brow creased in a worried little expression.

"No, me either," Jess said. "But at least all the surprises have been pleasant ones so far." She grinned a bit rakishly. "Time it would have taken me to figure this thing out we'd be bloody popsicles right now."

"That doesn't sound good."

"No." Jess leaned against the chair. "Would have been a painful way to die." She peered through the heavy leaded glass over Dev's shoulder. "Looks like the weather settled."

Dev had to take her word for that. The overcast clouds, and the fractious seas looked the same to her, except that the water washing over the control center was splashing from the waves, not rain from the sky. Now that the boat was at speed though, it plowed through the surf stolidly, and she started to relax a little.

"Power on downstairs?" Jess asked. "I could use a cup of something hot. You?"

Dev glanced at her, and smiled. "That would be very nice, yes."

Jess winked. "Be right back." She went to the door and slipped through it, turning to climb down the ladder to the deck.

The engine roar was subdued and far off, the bulk of the ship blocking out most of the sound. Dev took a deep breath and released it, relaxing into the chair as she studied the controls.

It was a relatively cramped space, with consoles on three sides, the chair in the middle, and lockers behind her. On one side of the workspace was a big book, and she turned her chair to get closer to it, opening it up and peering inside curiously. There were many pages, and a lot of scribbled lines and it took her quite some minutes until her eyes were able to translate the squiggles into actual letters.

It still didn't let her read it though. The letters made words, but the words were unknown to her and she decided they were in some kind of code. That she had programming for, but only very basic kinds, and she closed the book and left it for later perusal.

So. Dev put her elbows on the chair arms and settled back. They were on their way again. She left the whole subject of the fisher people alone for now, and focused on the mission, as she knew Jess was.

The door bumped open and Jess entered, carrying a box tucked under one arm leaving her other free to help her climb up the ladder. She closed the door behind her, locking the chill outside and set the box down on the side console. "Found some wraps too." She opened the box and started sorting things out. "Damn good thing, because I have no idea how to use that food machinery downstairs."

Dev kept her eyes on the seas, and her hands on the controls. "I don't think I do either."

"You said that about this boat."

Dev chuckled softly. "Yes I know I did, but I really don't think I have any programming at all about food. Everything in the crèche was constructed by the processors. We never even really looked at what was on our trays."

Jess brought over a cup and a roll, and handed it over. "Well, I've got something on ya then but not with machines," she said. "One of the things we used to do in the citadel when we went swimming is bring up some grub. I can actually make that taste like something."

"Really?"

"Really," Jess said, seemingly in a good mood. "The Drakes have lived in a stone house by the sea for a lot of generations. I got my share of fresh seafood." She paused. "Well, six years of it anyway." She glanced out the window. "After that, it was spotty, in school."

Dev took a sip of the seaweed tea, once again enjoying the taste. "Did it bother you to leave your family and go away?" she asked. "One of the proctors in the crèche did that. Left their family behind and came up to station."

Jess went and got her own meal and took a seat on one of the stools. "It was a really long time ago. I don't think I remember how I felt."

Which was a lie, she realized, even as she said it. She did remember, being that five year old child and coming back into the house soaking wet, to see mom and dad standing there watching her with that strange, stomach twisting look.

She remembered her mother turning away, and her father taking a deep breath, and kneeling down to talk to her, telling her she'd done so well on the tests that she'd earned her place at the school.

At his school, the one daddy had gone to. He'd seemed so proud, but so sad.

She remembered the transport picking her up, and that sudden spurt of fear as she waved goodbye, not truly understanding that home, and life, and family would all change its meaning for her as fast as it had.

"Jess?" Dev touched her arm.

She looked up to find Dev studying her with a quiet, serious expression. "It was fun at school," she said. "I met a lot of other kids there and we had a pretty good time." Her pale eyes shifted, then went back to Dev's face. "Until they start teaching you the business." She smiled briefly. "You know, how to break necks and use blasters."

Dev sucked in a tiny breath. "That's something they didn't program me for."

"Sure?"

"Yes." Dev glanced at her. "I knew that when I saw you do it. When I saw Bain do it." She paused thoughtfully. "I think they wanted to, but we ran out of time."

Jess nodded. "It wasn't in your script. I looked through it," she said, in a casual voice. "You know they teach us. They make us kill a seal first. They take us out on the ice, up in the back of beyond in the north and they find one, and you have to slit its throat."

Dev frowned. "But it didn't do anything to you. Why did they make you do that?"

"That's the point. Sometimes you kill things just because." Jess leaned her elbows on the console. "They're sort of cute, seals. They have pointy faces and whiskers, and big dark eyes."

Dev adjusted the throttles a little, turning the bow so they were cutting through the waves. "I see."

"Mm." Jess picked up her roll and took a bite of it. "I killed the instructor instead." She munched the fish and seaweed inside. "I should go find that seal. He owes me one."

Dev had gone quite still, and now she turned her head to stare at Jess.

"Completely stupid. Got me tossed in lockup for two months." Jess took a swallow of tea to wash the mouthful down. "Everyone thought I was on the crazy side after that. Not sure if it helped my career or hurt it."

"Why did you do that?" Dev finally asked.

Jess pondered briefly, using the time to ingest more of her roll. "I liked the seal more than the teacher," she finally said. "Guy was ugly as hell and he'd tried to bugger me in the shower. I figured he had it coming anyway."

"Well." Dev turned her eyes back to the console. "I'm really glad you like me then."

Jess chuckled. "That seal would have been stew if it'd been him or you. You know, I did miss my family. I missed home. I think we all did for a long time. Just no one said anything because you weren't supposed to. They didn't like it when kids acted like kids."

"I don't think I know what that's like."

"No loss to ya," Jess said. "Just makes your guts hurt. Not worth it."

Looking at Jess's face, though, made Dev think that wasn't entirely the truth. There was a sadness there that she could see plainly, a look of melancholy that was really very unlike her. She reached out and touched her arm again, closing her fingers around it and gently squeezing.

She didn't know what to say so she didn't say anything.

Jess looked up at her, her eyes half hidden by thick, dark hair.

For a moment, she felt a pang in her chest, odd and strange and discomfiting.

Then Jess winked, and bumped her. "Let's stop being sad sacks," she said. "Past's the past. Can't change it." She straightened up and started eating again. "This thing going what, ten knots?"

Dev put her hands back on the controls. "Twelve," she said "A lot slower than the carrier. This will take us a long time to get to those coordinates."

"We can trade off driving," Jess said. "Doesn't look that hard. Got most of it on auto, right?"

"Right," Dev said. "It's a lot simpler than the carrier. Just these engine controls, and this one, that steers." She indicated the rudder control. "You have excellent reflexes. I'm sure you could easily handle this."

Jess smiled at her. "You sweet talker, you."

"Excuse me?"

"Thank you for the compliment," Jess said. "Especially since I've been known to drive a carrier right into an iceberg."

"Really?"

"Really."

Dev picked up the roll and took a bite. The knots in her stomach relaxed, and she settled back in the big chair, wondering a little at all the strange feelings she'd had over the last little while. She wasn't sure about a lot of them, but one she knew she liked.

And it was strange, because there was nothing to like about what Jess had told her. She thought again about that seal, and felt herself smiling all over again. Was it strange? She thought maybe it was terrible that she was glad the animal had lived and the human had died, but really she didn't feel like it was terrible.

She was glad. She was very glad Jess had disobeyed her orders, and saved the seal. She wasn't even really sure why she felt that way, but in her head, she had a picture of this animal, and its eyes looking at Jess, and Jess deciding not to hurt it, but to hurt the one who'd ordered her to kill it instead.

"Jess?" She looked at her. "Can we see a seal? Are they out here somewhere?"

Jess grinned at her. "After we find the bear?"

Dev smiled back. "I'd like to see one of those too," she said. "The scan got some pictures of the one we saw before. I didn't have a chance to look at them though."

"Tell you what," Jess said. "You keep driving, and I'll hang out on the rail and see if I spot any seals. Or bears. Or whales."

"Whales?"

"C'mon, Devvie. You'll be surprised what we can find out here." Jess ruffled her hair, and then she picked up her cup and returned it to the box. "Let's try to enjoy the trip." She tugged her jacket up and ducked back out the door, moving to the outer railing and shading her eyes.

Dev watched her. Then she sighed. "I would like to see a bear." She snapped a few switches, and then wondered if the portable scanner could help Jess look.

And, after all, they could go back when they were done and find out about the fishermen, maybe even rescue them and give them back their boat.

Dev nodded in satisfaction. It would all work out.

Chapter Twenty-three

JESS LEANED HER elbows on the rail and watched the sea go by, very content with how her plan was progressing. Like most of her schemes, it had no real structure, and left a lot of things up to chance, but she had a clear place to start, and a goal, and everything in between would usually fall into place.

Stealing the boat was a good example. It wasn't part of the plan, but as soon as she'd realized what Dev's scan had found, she wanted to do it. It gave them a transport, and a way in to the other side, and took away all the fishermen impediments all in one fell swoop.

She'd just been lucky that she'd heard the ice creaking, and that Dev had known how to drive the thing. But her luck was like that. When it was good, it was really good, and when it was bad, she usually courted death with it.

Now she just had to find Dev a seal. Or a bear. She scanned the ice pack, just off their port bow and watched for either the telltale blow holes, or something white moving on white. There was plenty of time to look. She figured they'd be two days to the fishery.

Jess smiled, and swung her head from side to side, watching the passing water and ice intently. The one downside was that they'd have to take turns sleeping, and that meant they wouldn't be sleeping with each other during the ride.

Jess sighed. Oh well. On the other hand, they did have a tank full of fish, and if she caught one, and she could figure out how to turn the heating apparatus on in the prep area, she could treat Dev to fresh broiled fillets and toasted sea grapes. She licked her lips, tasting it in her memories.

A flicker of motion caught her eye, and she turned her head, shading her eyes as she searched for what had alerted her. It was waterside, and she peered eagerly ahead, hoping it was a whale, and not too disappointed when she caught sight of the sleek, surfing forms of dolphins.

"Hot damn." Jess reached over and tapped the glass, looking inside to see Dev watching her alertly. She pointed ahead of the boat to the motion ahead of them, and waited until she saw Dev jerk and then peer over the bow. She circled the control center and stuck her head in the hatch. "Slow down! You see them? They're dolphins!"

Dev immediately slowed the engines down and put them in idle, setting them to rocking glide in the waves as she engaged the auto pilot. "What are they?"

"C'mon." Jess guided her out to the bow and pointed. "See there? They're jumping. They're coming this way."

Dev glued herself to the chilly rail and watched as the motion resolved itself into moving animals, gliding through the water in a rhythmic way. She could see puffs of water coming out over their heads, and now that they were closer, she saw the sharp fin on the tops of them, and the rounded heads. "Are they fish?"

"Matter of fact, no." Jess leaned on the rail next to her, thoroughly enjoying herself. "They breathe air."

"They do?" Dev's eyes opened wide as one of them came right up out of the water and splashed back into it. "Wow!"

"Be right back." Jess loped off toward the fishing deck. "I'll get some bait for em."

Dev frowned. "Bait? We're not going to try and catch them are we?" The animals came even closer, and as she looked at them, they seemed to see her, and veered right toward the boat's hull. Her eyes got bigger and bigger as they slowed and cruised past, apparently watching her out of one round, dark eye. "Hello," she called out.

Jess returned, with a pail. "They here? Oh, yeah." She pulled something out of the pail and tossed it in the water. The closest porpoise immediately chased it down, grabbing it in its mouth and swallowing it. It then opened its mouth and made a sound at them, an odd, discordant chittering.

Dev's jaw dropped and she stared at it in delight. "Is it laughing? Wow!"

Jess chuckled. "Sure sounds like it." She tossed another piece of bait at them. "Look at those suckers. They're huge!"

Dev leaned against the rail and felt the cold wind against her skin, blowing her hair back as she avidly watched their visitors. "You said they were dolphins? And they breathe air?"

Jess nodded. "I went swimming with them once. Really cool." She leaned closer. "Look at the hole on their head, see that? That's how they breathe."

"No way."

"Yes way."

Impossible to really imagine that. "Can I give them some?" Dev edged over next to her, taking a chunk of bait from the bucket when Jess offered it to her. She tossed it gingerly into the water, delighted when one of the smaller animals retrieved it and flipped it in the air, bolting it down when it fell into its mouth.

It watched her hopefully with its round eye, nodding its head up and down as if encouraging her to throw some more.

So she did.

She could see them blowing air out of the hole, and she leaned over further, watching them in utter fascination. "That's amazing."

Jess grinned wholeheartedly and tossed more bait in the water. She was very glad she'd found the dolphins, and even more glad that they'd come over to the boat and showed the intermittent curiosity she'd seen from time to time from them. "Hey buddy!" She stuck her arm over the side of the boat with a big chunk of fish in it. "C'mere."

"Jess!" Dev's eyes widened as one of the dolphins swam away, then back at the boat, moving faster and then leaping up out of the water to grab the fish right out of her Jess's hand. "Oh!"

"Hah." Jess chuckled. "Did you see that? Jumped right up here."

The dolphins chittered at them, and Jess gave them the rest of the bait before turning to Dev with a regretful smile. "Gotta get going."

Dev leaned on the rail and watched the dolphins swim off, admiring the bow of their bodies, and the sinuous movement. "That was awesome. Thank you, Jess."

"Anytime."

Dev headed around the deck to the hatch to the control center and ducked back inside, still thinking about the dolphins. Just looking at their faces had been interesting, and she wished she'd taken her scanner outside to record them so she could look at them again later.

Oh, well. Maybe they'd see more of them later on. Dev took her seat and picked up the remainder of her roll, nibbling on it as she checked the controls and started them off toward the east again. The boat came up to speed and she settled back against the cushion, watching Jess from the corner of her eye as she roamed around behind her. "Tell me about the swimming thing."

"With the dolphins?" Jess sat down on the stool and hooked her feet up on the rungs. "Ah. Well, yeah. I was goofing around near the citadel one morning, just collecting some shells on the beach, that sort of thing. We had some time off and it wasn't raining. Anyway..."

Dev smiled, adjusting a throttle with a tentative nudge.

"They dared me to dive off one of the ledges—almost underwater now but then it was pretty high—and I climbed up there and did. Midway down I saw the water start moving and freaked out."

"Oh."

"Yeah, thought they were sharks," Jess said. "I flipped around and got myself in a ball so when I hit the water nothing was sticking out. Next thing I knew they were bopping me around like I was a toy and making that chittering noise."

"Did they hurt you?"

"Nah." Jess smiled in memory. "Made me laugh. I uncurled and they swam around me, bumping me with their noses. I touched one of them. Their skin's softer than I thought it would be."

"Wow." Dev sighed. "That would be so interesting."

"Next time." Jess patted her knee. "I'm going to go exploring. See if there's anything we can use on this crate and get our sleeping bags." She got up and went out the hatch, leaving Dev alone with her controls and the white ruffled sea they were cruising through.

Jess whistled as she went down the steps and through the hatch into the common chamber, closing it behind her to keep the cold wind out. She crossed the floor and went to the inner door, not surprised when the hatch didn't open to her touch. She looked around for something to pry with, and then, finding nothing, shrugged and drew her blaster and aimed.

The bolt touched the latch and the very next moment her own reflexes reacted without her conscious thought as she threw herself across the room and behind the table just as a loud blast rocked the boat. Jess ducked her head behind the table base and heard metal shrapnel rattling against the other side of it just as the boat's engines cut off and she heard a slam outside.

Jess surged up and over the table just as the hatch flew inward and she caught Dev just as she came inside and pushed them both back against the wall.

Dev's eyes were wide "What was that?"

"Just me blowing up things," Jess said, peering cautiously around the still open hatch door to look at the one she'd blasted. "Your six times removed fourth cousin Sig apparently figured he'd made sure his family jewels were safe and put an explosive trap on the hatch to his digs."

Dev absorbed that. "I see." She peered around the door. "Is it safe now?"

"Probably."

"Would you like to let me go?"

"Nope." Jess had her arms wrapped around Dev and she felt Dev's body relax against her as Dev tilted her head back and looked up at her with a wry grin. "Thanks for coming to my rescue."

Dev blushed visibly. "I wasn't sure what was going on. I heard a loud noise."

Jess gave her a brief hug then released her. "Yeah, bombs are loud. G'wan back up and get the bus moving."

Dev hesitated. "Are you sure there aren't more bombs? It would cause me great discomfort if you got damaged by one."

Jess studied her for a moment in curious silence. "Would it?"

"Yes," Dev said, after a pause. Then she ducked out the door and trotted along the deck back to the ladder.

Jess closed the hatch, a thoughtful look on her face. She picked her way through the debris of the door and paused, drawing her blaster again before she entered the family quarters, this time with very cautious motions.

She felt the engines start up again and braced herself as they moved, slowly letting her eyes roam around the space, a faint smile still tugging at her lips. "Now would it, Devvie?" she murmured. "Sure damn would discomfort me to see you get squashed, that's for sure."

That was odd, and new. While she had always been expected to work together with her tech, and keep their skins whole, she never, ever felt like this before about one. Not even Josh, who'd been what she'd considered a friend.

It was really kind of shocking, how fast she'd become comfortable with Dev, and Dev apparently returned the liking.

Was it the same thing? She'd never heard of bio alts having relationships of any kind, though she had heard more than once of them being used for pleasure.

Was that what she was doing? Jess felt an uncomfortable twist in her guts thinking that. Was she just taking advantage of Dev because Dev thought she couldn't say no?

Or did she realize she could say no?

Did Jess want her to realize?

"Peh. Later." She gave her body a little shake and continued her exploration.

The inside of the family quarters was full of odd things. Jess suspected they were family heirlooms, and remembered a couple of counters in her own home that had something of the same. Old pics and holos, bits of carved white substance she thought might have been bone, old spears, a few stuffed big fish on the wall.

She liked it. She moved carefully from room to room, not letting her nostalgia get in the way of looking for more booby traps. The beds were thick and looked comfortable, and the kids' rooms had hammocks in them, the sight of which made her smile.

To one side there was a storage bin. She nudged it open and looked inside, making a soft chuckling sound under her breath as she spotted the packaged rations they probably used when the seas were too rough for them to cook.

Another storage bin coughed up two spare hammocks and thickly woven blankets, and she happily shouldered them along with the hooks the hammocks hung on.

After another sweep, she backed out of the space, gently booting the hatch closed on its broken and twisted hinge. "Waste of metal." She sighed, as she holstered her gun. She went over and collected a thermal carafe full of the tea she'd brewed, and headed for the hatch with her burden, whistling softly under her breath.

Dev was occupying her time looking at the log book she couldn't read. She leafed through it, looking up when the hatch opened again and Jess reappeared. "Did you find anything?"

"Nah." Jess set the tea down and then put down her armful of hammocks. "Just stuff to make us more comfortable." She examined the hooks, prowling around the command chamber looking for places to hang them. "They use these things down at the kelp factories."

"What things?" Dev divided her attention between the control console, and Jess, though they were on a reasonable course and there was nothing in front of them but water.

"These." Jess pointed at the hammocks. "Hanging beds."

"Really?"

"Uh huh." Jess found an eye bolt in the wall and slid one of the hooks through it, then she went over to the right angled wall and found another one at just the right length. She put the other hook up and then went back to get the hammock, stringing it up between the two hooks before she stepped back to examine her handiwork. "What do you think?"

Dev half turned to look. "Oh," she said. "That's sort of like what we use when we have to sleep in null."

Jess sat down on the hammock then rolled into it, stretching her body out and putting her hands behind her head. She rocked back and forth with the ship's motion, and grinned in satisfaction. "Almost as comfortable as our beds back at base. Since we're gonna trade off driving, I figured it made sense to bunk out up here."

"Excellent," Dev said "I think that would be the safest thing too, especially if there are bombs on board."

Jess rolled out of the hammock and wandered over next to her, taking a seat on the stool again. "Whatcha looking at?"

Dev showed her the book. "I was seeing if there were any dolphins or whales in the pictures. I can't read the words. Can you?"

Jess studied them. "No. I think it's his language."

"His language?"

"Yeah." Jess propped her head up on one fist as she idly thumbed the pages. "They didn't teach you about languages?"

Dev considered the question. "I know machine programming languages. Is that the same thing?"

"No." Jess chuckled. "Believe it or not, before the whole world went to crap there were enough of us human bastards around to have each bunch of us talk a different way. A different code, I guess."

"How did you understand each other then?"

"We didn't."

"I see."

"They still speak some different stuff on the other side. But there were so few of us left when it all went down, they picked the easiest and most bastardized language, which was what used to be called English, and pushed some other stuff into it and that's what we use on our side."

"I see."

Jess looked up in amusement. "Doesn't make sense, right? But that's where some of the weird crap I say comes from. Old times."

"We only got taught to talk one way," Dev said. "Everyone talked the same up on station. I'm not sure why you would want to do it any other way, and not understand each other like I don't understand these notes." She pointed at the book.

"Ah, Dev. It's just how we were. It was more important to find ways we were different, because that meant we were better than the other guy. If we were all the same, no one wins." Jess saw that look of utter confusion come over Dev's face. "It's still like that. Look at what we're doing here. We're going over there to try and screw the other guys up because that takes away the chance that they'll do something better than us and get ahead."

"I don't really understand that. But I'll take your word for it."

Jess chuckled. "So anyway, this must be the old language of Sigurd's people. They've been doing this forever. Doesn't surprise me they still write in it. It's like a code, you know? This is probably where he puts down all his tricks about catching fish, and if it's in this language, only his family can read it."

"Oh." Dev nodded. "Okay, that I understand. Up in the crèche, sometimes, the scientists would do that, put their notes in code if they thought someone was trying to copy something they did. That's the same thing, right?"

"Exactly."

"Doctor Dan thought that was so silly."

"Bet he did. He seems like a pretty sharp guy," Jess said. "Wonder where he did his field training?"

Dev's head cocked to one side again. "His what?"

"C'mon. Didn't you see him with that blaster? He knew what to do with it as much as I did, and my bio bomb didn't scatter him to pieces. He's friends with Bain. He was one of us."

Dev shook her head. "He's been a scientist up on station his whole life practically. He told us so."

"Practically."

Dev stared at her, feeling anxious.

Jess seemed to sense that, because she pushed the log book away and put a hand on Dev's knee instead. "Sorry. Didn't mean to freak you out."

Had she been freaked out? Was she? Dev let out her held breath, and thought about that. What was it exactly that Doctor Dan had said once? That he'd spent his life in the crèche, except...now she remembered, for what he'd called a misspent youth. Had he misspent that time with Interforce? Really? Gentle Doctor Dan? She remembered how shocked she'd felt seeing him holding a gun, and holding it with...

Yes, he'd known well what to do with it. She remembered too, how he'd reacted when Bain had shot the man, coming between her and the rest of them, making sure she was safe. Had he been like Jess?

"Relax." Jess patted her knee. "It's a good thing. He knows and so he made sure you know. He was probably a kid, but you saw how he talked to Bain. He knew him."

"Yes," Dev finally said, in a soft voice. "He told me it was okay to trust him. Bain, I mean."

"He did?" Now it was Jess's turn to be surprised.

"Yes. Him, and you."

"And me? Damn man hardly knows me. And I don't know him at all."

Dev shrugged a little. "Well, he knows me. So maybe that's why," she said. "And also, he really understands people." She fell silent, a faint crease forming on her forehead. "He cares about what happens to us."

Jess wondered if that were really true. Certainly, watching Dev with Doctor Dan had given her the impression that the man was fond of her, but it was a business. Wasn't it? They had hundreds of bio alts doing all sorts of menial jobs around the place, after all.

"You're different." Jess spoke her thoughts aloud. "You're special. Not like the others. I've seen bios around for years. None of them are like you. He made you like us."

"What do you mean?"

Jess leaned on the console and regarded her. "He made you like us. He made you to pass as human, didn't he? Way before he was asked by us to."

"What?"

"All the other bios, they're like s...like machines," Jess said. "They can't think for themselves. That's the biggest problem in using them, but also the reason no one's killed them yet. No one cares about them. But you're different. Your brain's like mine." She studied Dev's face. "It always was."

Dev's eyes shifted and went unfocused for a long moment. Then she looked back at Jess. "Is it...am I...incorrect?" She asked, in a very soft, almost scared tone. "You think that's bad."

Jess felt her heart thump uncomfortably. She stared into Dev's eyes, seeing a deep emotion there that made her feel terrible. "N...no." She managed to get out. "I just wondered why." She reached out and touched the hand Dev had resting on the console. "How he knew."

"How he knew what?" Dev reached up and rubbed her eyes with her free hand. "I don't like how this feels."

Jess stood up, unsure of what to do. "Hey. I didn't mean to make you feel bad." She hesitantly clasped Dev's shoulders in both hands. "I like how you turned out. I like that you can talk to me, and think and all that stuff, whatever the hell his reasons were."

Dev exhaled, her shoulders relaxing under Jess's hands. "If there was a reason, he never told me," she finally said. "Maybe he just wanted to see if he could do it." She stared pensively at Jess. "He likes to do hard things."

Jess moved her hands and cupped Dev's face. "Fine by me. I like you just how you are."

Finally, that got a smile from Dev. "Well, I'm glad, since I don't really have much choice in it," Dev said. "Could we have more hot tea? This is a cold place."

"Sure." Jess released her and went for the thermal. "Some tea for the insides and I'll see what I can do for the outside"

Dev took a steadying breath and went back to the controls, staring quietly out over the waves.

DRIVING THE BOAT in the dark was hard. Dev kept one eye on the sonar and one on the dimly seen waves ahead of her as she concentrated on steering. The control room was dim, and behind her Jess was curled up in the hammock, getting some rest.

Her entire body was aching with the tension of doing this somewhat unfamiliar activity, and the uncertainty of piloting the boat through the night seas was wearing on her.

On the other hand, she was glad to be saving Jess from the effort. Jess had scrounged around and brought up enough odds and ends to feed them, and she was relatively full from it. She had a big, insulated cup in a clamp next to her, still with hot tea in it, and Jess had taken pains to try and make things as comfortable for her as she could.

That was gratifying. She'd even found a thick, soft blanket somewhere and now it was tucked around Dev's shoulders as she sat in the big pilot's seat.

It felt good, to have Jess be concerned about her. It made her warm inside, having nothing to do with the blanket. She had decided to see what she could do in return once they changed places. Surely there was something she could do for her partner.

Her partner. Dev risked a glance over her shoulder at the somnolent form in the hammock. Once Jess had conceded her that title, she hadn't looked back and then the rapidness of her acceptance of Dev had really surprised her. It felt good, and maybe that was why their discussion earlier about Doctor Dan had rattled her.

It had.

Dev didn't want to think about being different, or made a certain way or something that someone else shaped. It made her feel strange, but thinking about being a bio alt bothered her.

She knew that was incorrect. She knew she wasn't considered a person, not by anyone that was naturally born. And yet...

And yet. Just thinking about failure, about being sent back to the crèche and having to go back to being like she had been made Dev feel so bad she stopped it, just like that, because she didn't want to get that stomach ache again.

But it kept creeping back. Had Doctor Dan made her like a natural born? Dev caught sight of her profile in the reflection of the glass, a faint, ghostly figure outlined in the dim blue of the controls. She certainly looked like one. But then, they all did. You couldn't tell from the outside a bio from a natural.

What Jess had said was, it was something on her inside that he'd made the same.

The same as Jess. Dev considered that, soberly, acknowledging in her head that she had always felt a little different. Or had that been wishful thinking? Didn't they all want to think that? Dev exhaled a little, then she picked up her tea and sipped it, enjoying the mellow taste.

Didn't they all want to think they were special? Why else would they compete for the proctor's notice, and that rare, cherished good word from Doctor Dan?

And yet, Dev knew, that in certain ways she was in fact different. She was a dev unit. She was the only produced member of her set. That had given her status in the crèche, and she had begun to be aware of that, as she moved through the last of her classes and approached assignment.

Gigi had been so excited, when she'd gotten hers. To be given an assignment as the assistant to the director was about the best thing one of them could hope for, if you weren't specialized, and Dev well remembered how jealous the other bios in her class were when they heard about it.

What would they think about her assignment? Dev adjusted one of the throttles, and had to smile at her reflection. She had hoped for something interesting, and though she'd never mentioned it to him, remembered wishing for an assignment in the lab with Doctor Dan.

Being his assistant? Now that would have been something for them to be jealous of, if she'd stayed topside. Doss was the director, but everyone knew the most important person in the crèche was Doctor Dan.

Instead, here she was, down world, in a fish boat, driving across the water in the dark, in a storm, with a partner who liked killing people and enjoyed practicing sex in dangerous places.

Life could be quite unexpected. Dev smiled briefly. Now that she was here, though, she wouldn't trade this experience for all the status in the world, even for a place in Doctor Dan's lab. This was something none of them had ever even imagined.

She had done things already that no bio alt ever had, and experienced things she didn't think maybe a lot of natural born had. Though it had been so short a time, she absolutely knew she didn't want that to change. No matter how dangerous, no matter how scary and difficult, she wanted this.

Dev took another sip of her tea, and set the cup back in its swinging holder. A soft sound made her look around again, and she frowned, not entirely sure she'd heard it. As she cocked her ears though, it happened again. At first she thought it was maybe the hooks swinging, but then she saw Jess shift again, and cry out, her body and hands tensing visibly.

Dev's eyes widened, and she rapidly switched her attention back and forth between the window and the hammock. "Jess?" She called out softly.

Jess cried out again, twisting in the hammock.

Dev pulled the throttles back and slowed the ship, feeling the bow pitch down as it came off plane and they went with the motion of the waves. She glanced anxiously at the scanner and hoped there was enough free water around them as she left the controls and bolted back to where her partner was struggling and gasping. "Jess!"

She grabbed hold the hammock as they pitched and in the next instant found herself gripped in an iron hold around her neck as Jess sinuously twisted around and slammed them both to the ground.

Dev reacted instinctively. She got her hands around Jess's wrists and clamped down on them, tearing the hold off her and shoving herself and Jess off the deck, reversing their positions. She landed on Jess and held her down. "Jess!"

For a moment the staring blue eyes bored through her, then they blinked, and she felt the powerful form under her lose its tension.

Another long silence as they looked at each other. Dev was very surprised to see wetness around Jess's eyes and she shifted to one side and released her, afraid she'd done her some damage. "Are you all right?"

Jess lifted her hand and covered her eyes, breathing hard. "Fuck."

The hand, Dev noted, was shaking. She cautiously touched Jess's shoulder, feeling a shivering in it as well. "Jess? Are you in discomfort? Is there something I can do to help you?"

"No," Jess finally answered. "Get the boat moving again. I'm fine."

Dev didn't think that was true. But she understood that refusing to do what Jess asked would not make her be in less discomfort. She very gently squeezed the shoulder her hand was resting on, then she pushed herself to her feet and went back over to the controls.

She settled into the seat and started up the engines, applying power and steadying the boat's movement as they shifted forward and plowed back into the waves. She looked back over her shoulder, to see Jess sitting with her back braced against the cabinet, her head held in her hands.

Dev almost stopped the engines again, the urge to go do something to help overpowering her. "Jess?"

Jess's shoulders shifted and she straightened, resting her forearms on her knees before she slowly pulled herself up and walked over to the stool next to Dev, dropping onto it with a grunt. "Shit."

Her offers of help having been rejected, Dev sorted around to figure out what she should try next. "Would you like some tea?" She picked up her mug and moved it closer. "It's still hot."

Jess rested her hands on the console. "Soon as I think I won't throw it back up, sure," she said softly. "Crap I hate that."

"Throwing up?"

"Hallucinations. Dreams." She paused. "You know."

Hallucinations and dreams. Dev riffled through her programming quickly, then went over it again. "I'm sorry," she finally said. "I really don't know. What are they? They sound uncomfortable."

Jess looked at her. "You don't dream at night?" she asked. "See pictures in your head? Go to different places while you sleep?"

Pictures in her head. "Well," Dev mused. "Sometimes, when I got a lot of programming, I saw some pictures when I was waking up. But they weren't really different places. Just a flash or two, like a person's face, or a smell."

"Not the same thing," Jess said. "But if you don't have them you're damned lucky. Wish I was a bio in that case." She rested her forehead against her wrists.

Dev put a hand on her back, gently rubbing it. She wasn't really sure why she'd done that, or if it was helpful, but under her fingers she could feel, just a little, relaxation in the stiffness of Jess's body. "I was just thinking about how much I wished I wasn't one."

Jess reacted, lifting her head and looking back at her, the faint glow from the controls reflecting off her pale eyes.

"I mean, how much I'm really enjoying getting to do everything," Dev said. "And how much better it is than being in the crèche."

"Ah" Jess grimaced a little and rubbed her temples with her fingers. "Well, crap right now I'd trade ya. Thought I was past them."

"What does that mean?" Dev asked, softly. "Are you sure you don't want some tea?"

Jess sighed and straightened up a little. "Never mind. It's a stupid thing and I don't want to talk about it." She accepted the cup, though, and took a sip. "Show me how to drive this thing and you can go get some sleep." She got up and came close to Dev.

Then she stopped, and put the cup down and put her hands on her hips. "Wait a minute."

Dev glanced sideways at her.

Jess leaned on the console so she could see Dev's face. "Did you just pick me up and body slam me?" She watched as a flush of color darkened Dev's face, visible even in the dim light. "You did."

"I..." Dev felt nervous and suddenly very anxious. "I didn't mean to cause you discomfort," she said. "Did I hurt you?"

Jess was more than glad enough to let this distraction drive her recent nightmare out of her thoughts. To have had one at all infuriated her and she was embarrassed that Dev had witnessed it. "No," she said. "I just didn't think you were that strong. I'm bigger than you are."

Dev smiled briefly, relieved that Jess didn't seem upset. "Well, we did work out a lot in plus grav," she said. "So I guess that's why. I wasn't sure what was going on and I didn't want you to hurt yourself." She paused. "Or me."

"You?"

"You grabbed me by the neck."

Jess felt a shock go down her entire body. "I did?"

Dev glanced at her for a brief moment, her lips tensing into a faint smile. "I think you were sort of still asleep."

Well, that wasn't good. Jess frowned. "I..." She stopped speaking, and took a step back, half turning and folding her arms across her chest. Then she sat back down on the stool and studied the deck. "Sorry," she managed, after a moment. "When you've done all the..." She paused again. "Sometimes we relive stuff that's happened in our sleep. Agents. Like me."

"I see."

"I guess we don't have any really good things to relive," Jess said. "So we get all the bad things. All the attacks that went wrong, and the friend's we've seen die and—" She stared at the ground. "Anyway. I'm sorry. I don't want to do anything to hurt you."

"It's okay, you didn't," Dev said. "I just wanted to hold you still long enough for you to come back up." She adjusted a control, and glanced at the scanner. "Sometimes when we...when bio alts, that is, are down for programming they come up and if things aren't right security has to hold them until they integrate everything."

"I'm not a bio alt."

"No, I know," Dev said. "But it was the same sort of thing. You weren't really here."

"Oh." Jess sighed. "Thought I was past them from this last

clusterfuck." She rubbed her temples. "I had them after that one for weeks. Couldn't sleep worth a damn. Anyway, if you see me like that, just stay the hell away from me. Let me suffer."

Dev was silent for a long moment. "I don't think I can do that," she said in an apologetic tone. "Seeing you suffering causes me a lot of discomfort."

"Does it?" She watched Dev release one hand off the controls and extend it, and then felt the warmth of Dev's touch against her cheek. She was unable to look away from those eyes and there was something so compelling and intense in them, it made her a little short of breath.

"It does," Dev said. "So I'll try not to get my neck in the way of your hands, but don't ask me to not try and help you. Please."

The feeling of shortness of breath intensified. Jess felt a sense of almost lightheaded confusion as her cheek was gently stroked and she had the sudden suspicion that if she was standing her knees would have buckled under her and she had to wonder seriously what the hell was going on.

Why was she feeling like this? Her stomach felt strange, and she reached up to cover Dev's hand with her own as the memory of the nightmare rippled into shreds and released from her mind. It felt like getting a wash of seawater over her, and her body relaxed. "You're a funny old thing, Devvie," she finally said. "Just don't be afraid to pick my ass up and toss me if I turn crazy on ya, okay?"

Dev smiled faintly. "Okay," she said. "But you know, Jess, I really hope you get to see some happy pictures in your head sometime."

The sincerity of the tone got down into Jess's awareness and lightened her heart in a curious way. She got up and came closer, leaning forward and very gently kissing Dev on the lips. "Thank you," she said. "I appreciate that."

She draped her arm over Dev. "I never want anything bad to happen to you if I can help it." She added. "I...um..." She paused for a long moment. "That would make me nuts."

"What's a nut?" Dev asked, after a pause.

Jess pinched the bridge of her nose. "You know something? I don't have a fucking clue what a nut is. But I know what that means is, I'd be very upset."

It occurred to Dev that it wasn't really regular to have a natural born feel that way about a bio alt. It made her feel strange, though in a good way. "You would?"

"Yeah."

Maybe Jess really didn't think of her as just a bio after all. She hoped that was true. With a smile, she went back to the controls, finding a course through the waves as the weather came down harder, the rain going sideways in front of the console window. "Wow."

Jess leaned against her. "Show me how to run this thing," she said. "One of us should get some rest. Least the damn weather will keep me distracted."

"All right," Dev said. "These are the engine controls."

Jess rested her chin on Dev's shoulder. "Hey, you know something, Dev?"

It was all Dev could do to keep the boat going forward, her hands clenching lightly on the throttles as she felt Jess's cheek press against hers. "What?"

"Thanks for waking me up out of my nightmare, and for caring what happens to me."

The soft echo of plaintive wistfulness in that voice went right through Dev. She felt at once happy and at the same time sad. "I think you're my favorite person ever," she said. "Even more than Doctor Dan. Thanks for making me feel real, like a person."

"You are."

Dev tasted salt on her lips as she licked them. "Am I?"

"Oh yes. There's no going back for you now."

Chapter Twenty-four

IT TURNED OUT that driving the boat wasn't that difficult at all. Jess sat in the control chair, glad of the restraints as they crashed through the waves in the darkness of pre dawn. Behind her, tucked in the hammock and wrapped in her new sharkskin jacket Dev was sleeping peacefully undisturbed by the motion.

Jess envied her. Her own eyes felt red and sore, her body achy and tired, wanting to join Dev in the hammock in a huddle of warm comfort. But instead, she dutifully scanned the darkness, and worked to keep them on course as they followed a track through open seas now with no land in sight.

They were in no man's waters. Vast stretches of mostly dead ocean where the bottom was so far down, nothing they had left could plumb it. Far too deep for fishing, home to once again unknown life on this side of the mid Atlantic ridge. Left alone to repopulate after almost being fished to extinction.

Funny, how that was. Just before the change happened, they had come to a crisis point. The oceans had been raped to the extent that if the orbiting labs hadn't been functional, a huge human die off had been looming.

Chaos! Politics! Jess faintly shook her head, remembering the texts she'd scanned in school. They had been heading for a meltdown right up until the planet itself had taken control, wiping out ninety percent of its problems in one long, horrific descent into death and starvation.

She remembered films of the time, watching as cities drowned and the flood waters rose and rose and rose, eventually washing clean to rock everything it touched.

Only the tough and the lucky had survived. Jess remembered, vaguely, her father saying that the harrowing had helped the species in some ways, but narrowed their biological choices to almost disaster in other ways. They had to be careful now, who bred with who, since they'd seen what happened when the genes got too close.

Humans adapted at an almost frightening rate. Far more and far faster than the other species left on the planet, that being the one true advantage they'd had. Already the families who farmed the seas for a few generations, down by the shoreline had developed webbing between their fingers and toes, and oily skins to protect them against the seawater they spent so much time in.

Jess herself had some of it. She regarded her hand, and stretched the fingers out, then curled them into a light fist. She'd grown up with the sea wind in her face, and her body in the water for as long as she could remember and now that she was here, in this seat, her hands on the controls there was some ancient familiarity about it that echoed softly inside her.

She took a sip of tea and shifted a little. Soon they would be crossing over into enemy territory and she sorted through her memory of radio codes, planning out the ones she'd need to use once they caught her on scan and contacted them.

Always a danger. Always the chance that some bored controller would decide to hunt them through the comp, and realize something wasn't quite right about this incoming fisher with only two crew onboard.

If they got past that, to the fishery itself, they were home free.

A soft sound behind her made her turn her head, to see Dev stretching her body out and peering over the edge of the hammock at her. "Hey there."

"Hello." Dev rolled out of the hammock and stood up, keeping one hand on the edge of it to steady herself. "That was very nice."

"The hammock?"

"Yes. It felt like our sleep pods in the crèche," Dev said, coming over and peering out the window. She looked down at the nav console and raked the fingers of one hand through her hair. "It's darker."

"We're almost to the edge of their waters." Jess said. "Why don't you grab a cup of something downstairs, then let me get out of this chair for a while."

"Okay." Dev put her jacket hood up and bumped the outer hatch open, disappearing into the howling wind and shutting the door behind her.

The blast of cold air made Jess sit up straight, driving out the sleepiness that had started to overtake her. She could see ice lining the outside of the boat in the dim phosphorescence from the rail lights and briefly she felt homesick for the citadel and the warm blast of her own shower.

Ah well. She flexed her hands and leaned forward, watching the spray come up over the deck. Suck it up, Jesslyn. You're the one who told everyone how tough you were. Don't blow your rep now.

DEV LOOKED AROUND the gathering area, rubbing her hands together in the chill air. She was waiting for some water to heat up to make tea, having found a big carafe that would hold more than enough for both her and Jess. She'd gone inside and used the sanitary unit, and retrieved her kit and used that as well. Now she felt reasonably awake, though her body was craving food and she was still chilled.

While she waited, she decided to explore a little, and almost hesitantly started opening cabinets and peering at what was inside. Mostly supplies, all clamped down. Plates and things to prepare food with, none of which held any programming charge for her.

One cabinet had odd belts and closed containers, and she studied one for a while, then realized that it must be for the people who worked the fishing things when they were outside for a long time. Experimentally, she put one around her and studied the result in the piece of metal hammered to the wall nearby.

It was far too big for her, but she could see how useful it could be, having a cup to drink from that was sealed, and a container that could fit maybe a fish roll, or something like it. That way they could keep working outside and in fact it wasn't that different from the kit she had for the carrier.

With a grunt, she took it off and put it back away, closing the cabinet after it. Then she went over to the warming unit and removed the water, pouring it carefully over the pile of shredded seaweed in the big carafe. The steam came up at once, and she blinked as it bathed her face with faintly spicy heat.

She really liked the seaweed tea. It was less pungent than the real tea she'd had, and didn't have the sometimes bitter aftertaste. She glanced at the countertop while the tea steeped, cocking her head a little as she spotted a big, brown pot with a spoon sticking out of it.

Experimentally, she lifted the cover, and her nose twitched as she caught a sweet scent. She put the tip of her finger in the substance inside, and brought it back to her lips, cautiously tasting the gummy stuff on the tip of her tongue. "Oh." She went back for a second try and sucked the end of her thumb that came back covered in it.

It tasted like the mead. She wondered if this could be honey. It reminded her of the mead. The pot seemed to have a place there, and she remembered Jess saying that the honey came from the other side. So that fit with the notion her partner had that these fisher people would go wherever they needed to sell their catch.

She nodded, then she picked up the spoon and scooped up some of the substance, bringing it over and letting it drizzle into the still steeping tea. After it all went inside, she stirred it, then she put the top on the carafe and the spoon back where it belonged, picking up the tea and heading back to the control center with it.

JESS PAUSED IN mid sip, turning around to look at Dev who was taking over the control station. "What's in this?"

Dev smiled, as she tucked the comm bud from her scanner into her ear. "They have a big jar downstairs. I think it's honey," she said. "I thought you might like some in the tea. It tastes nice, doesn't it?"

"Big jar?" Jess savored the sweetness. "Those bastards."

"Well, if they could get it, why shouldn't they?" Dev asked. "You got that bottle, right?" She put her own cup in the holder, examining the board and pausing, then moving a switch into a new position.

Jess came over and leaned her back against the console, hooking one arm around a bracing bar and crossing her ankles. "Yeah I guess me taking that as a prize of war and then being pissed off at these guys for buying it legit is pretty hypocritical, huh?"

Dev gave her a sideways glance, then went back to her controls. "It looks like we're crossing into long range scan. I can see beams."

Jess turned and looked at the readout. "Yep." She sat down on the stool. "If they contact us, let me answer."

Dev nodded, tuning in the scanner a little more tightly and watching the screen. She could see the sine waves of the enemy scanners and the pattern they were running, a comprehensive sweep that would surely, eventually, go over them. She studied the scan output and typed in a request.

Jess stood up and went over to the grub she'd scrounged earlier, sorting amongst it and putting together a meal for them. She braced against the wall as the boat lunged and rocked, and managed to make it back over to where the big chair was with everything clutched in her arms.

Waves were coming up. She peered out the window, checking the chrono. "Should get a little lighter in a bit," Jess said as she handed over a packet of boiled fish. "Sounds like the weather's going to crap again though."

Dev pointed at the scanner. "That's the same kind of line we were avoiding the other day isn't it?"

Jess looked and exhaled. "Shit."

"I don't think it will affect the systems on this boat like it does the carrier," Dev said, placidly. She unwrapped her portion of fish and took a bite of it, surprised at the firm texture, and tasty flavor. Outside, as if in counterpoint, a blast of lightning showed in the distance, outlining the peaking waves in silver precision.

Jess got up and circled around her, putting her hands on the back of the control chair and looking past Dev, then moving over to the navigation station and studying the map. "Storm could help us."

"Keep them from seeing us you mean?" Dev noted the waves getting larger, and she brought the throttles down a little, easing into one of the larger ones.

"Uh huh. Fast learner." Jess glanced over her shoulder and gave her a rakish grin. "I do like that about you, Devvie.'

Dev finished her fish and neatly folded the bit of dried seaweed it had been wrapped in and put it back in the package. She could, she supposed, eat the covering, but she'd found them to be dry and somewhat bitter, and not really appealing.

There was another package though. She opened that one, then took a step back, leaving it on the console. "Jess?"

"Huh?"

"What is this?"

Jess craned her neck to look. "Crab."

Dev stared at the creature, a hard shelled animal the size of her hand. "Are we supposed to eat this?"

Jess snickered. "Yes. You wanna bet me you'll like it?"

Dev eyed her with what could only be described as excessively polite skepticism. "Would you like it? I'm going to finish my seaweed." She edged away from the crab and went back to her tea, sipping it and trying to ignore the mischievous grin she was getting from across the room.

"Nah, nah, none of that." Jess left the map and came over, removing the big, heavy knife from its sheath and reversing it. With a casual motion, she brought the hilt down on the crab and cracked it, then picked it up and wrenched its legs off, putting them down and smacking them as well.

Bits of shell went everywhere, nearly nailing Dev, who ducked at the last minute as one piece sailed past her ear.

Jess ignored the chaos she was causing. She pulled apart the shell and removed a chunk of white substance from it and handed it over to Dev. "Try it."

Dev regarded it for a moment, then she reached out and took the offering. It felt in her hand not that different from the fish, and she tentatively bit into it, extremely surprised at the rich taste. "Oh," she said, in a surprised tone. "That is good."

Jess took a piece for herself and popped it into her mouth. "Not too different from the shrimp at Quebec. Not as spicy though. These cost more creds than I have in the bank usually."

"Really."

"Really." Jess took a leg and went back to the weather map. "Damn these guys live good."

Dev investigated the shattered creature remains, pairing bits of the white flesh with her tea as she returned her concentration to the waves. "Jess?"

"Huh?"

"What's a bet?"

"Ahhh. I'll teach you all about that, my friend." Jess chuckled. "But first, let's find a way to drive through this mess and keep away from the bad guys. I don't think we'll stand up to a really decent scan."

DEV FINALLY SAT back and took a breath, her entire body stiff and aching from the tension caused by having to navigate the boat through the storm. The rough weather had kept them hidden, but the boat had almost rolled several times, and Jess had gone below deck to make sure nothing was broken.

For now, the rain had stopped and the winds had died down, and she was beginning to see structures on comp coming up that she understood were the enemy's. They were just wiremaps for now, but she set the scanner up to passive and turned up the volume on the old style radio, right now just issuing a soft, hissing static.

It seemed a moment of calm for them. The waves had settled, and the water had changed from a dark and angry black to a lighter color, her scanner confirming the depth decreasing as they continued on.

She heard the sound of boots on the stairs outside and glanced behind her as the hatch opened and Jess appeared, well wrapped and gloved. Jess swept the hood off her head and shook herself, rubbing her hands together as she crossed the deck.

"Looks good," Jess said. "I can hear those fish swimming around in there too. How far are we from...ah." She came to stand next to Dev, peering at the tracking map. "Nice. Good job." She touched her finger on the screen, pointing out a block on the wiremap. "There it is."

Dev stood by her chair and stretched her body out, pausing as she felt Jess's hands on her. They brought a warmth, and as she felt Jess's fingers kneading her back, a happy grin appeared on her face. "That really feels nice."

"I know." Jess smiled with her, moving her hands up Dev's spine as she rested her hands on the console, feeling the knots under her fingers. "Remind me to teach you this when we get back so you can return the favor."

"Absolutely," Dev said. "That seat is not really comfortable for a long time. Not like the carrier." She straightened and turned as Jess finished, looking up at her with a grateful expression. "Thank you."

Jess let her wrists rest on Dev's shoulders and met those eyes, letting herself get a little lost in that gentle regard.

Dev waited for a moment, then she cocked her head slightly. "Jess?"

"Yes?" Jess kept looking into her eyes, her face shifting to a mild introspection.

"Do we have to do something?"

"I'm sure we do."

Dev rested her hand on Jess's hip and in the next breath they were moving together, and kissing. Jess cupped her cheek and she wished that Jess didn't have her heavy jacket on as an intense craving erupted inside her.

It seemed crazy. They were in the middle of a mission.

Jess backed off a little, just enough to look at her. "Know something?" she said. "You're the first person who's made me want to forget about my job. Why is that, Devvie?"

Dev definitely wanted to go back to that whole kissing thing. "I don't know. But when you start doing that I don't really care about what's going on either."

"That bother you?"

"Does it bother you?"

Jess tilted her head and they kissed again, in a silence that lengthened quite a bit. Then she took a breath and let her head rest against Dev's. "Feels too good to bother me," she said. "That's never happened before."

Dev sighed. "Pretty much everything's never happened to me before so it's difficult to say."

Jess smiled. Then she looked past Dev to the comm console, which started crackling. "I think I hear my blaster calling my trigger finger."

Dev gave her a brief hug. "Did you want to talk to them?" She indicated the radio. "I'm going to take a walk downstairs."

"No I didn't." Jess returned the hug, startled by the jolt of positive emotion it gave her. "But I will." Reluctantly she released Dev, and eased into the chair. "I'm going to tell them we're pulling in with a full load, and bargain a little."

"Won't they know you're not the fisher people?" Dev asked, resting a hand on the chair arm. "You said they went to this place before."

"It's automated," Jess said. "We swing the boat in and they hook up to the back of it and the fish go out that way. Nothing face to face." A faint smile appeared. "Too dangerous for both sides. They don't want to be able to identify the fishermen, and the reverse is true too. Everyone knows trade crosses the lines."

"I see."

"Market's like that too. I've been there," Jess said. "It's all barter for weight chits, no record of anything. No one wants to know, they just want your money."

"Maybe they'll have that honey mead," Dev said, with a slight grin. "That happened up on station too. Sometimes a shuttle would...um...'get lost' or come in dock for repair from the other side. Doctor Dan has some things in his office that came that way. You weren't supposed to talk about it."

"We aren't either." Jess said. "It's against the rules. Everyone knows it. No one cares." She gave Dev's arm a squeeze. "G'wan and stretch your legs. Let me figure out what story I'm gonna tell them."

Dev tugged her hood up and trotted off, feeling oddly buoyant as she went out the hatch and rambled down the steps. Though it was cold outside, the spray had diminished and they were traveling relatively smoothly over the calming seas. Dev went over to the rail and looked out, sucking in a deep lungful of the salt misty air.

She felt a little strange. She felt like she wanted to jump up and down and laugh, which would be very inappropriate. It would also be very inappropriate for her to go back into the control center and pull Jess out of her chair and into the hammock.

She suspected, however, that Jess wouldn't mind it at all.

This was something she didn't have any programming for. Sex she understood, at least, she understood a lot more now than when she'd had classes about it. The class hadn't mentioned anything at all about this wild, warm, happy feeling that made her want to run around and laugh.

What did it mean? Was it correct?

Did she care?

Dev smiled into the wind, reveling in the rush as it pushed her hair back and moistened her skin. Then she turned and rambled toward the inner hatch, bouncing a little as she laughed, if only to herself.

"VESSEL NORTHERN STAR, come about to starboard, slip six Decca." The radio voice was rough, and harsh sounding. "Cut engines standby to offload."

"Check," Jess answered. "Put the chits on the deck when you're done. Crew's sleepin.''

"Got it," the voice said, then cut off with a burst of static.

The fishery was enormous. Dev was almost glued to the window as they approached, peering up and up and up at the structure that towered over the waves, almost as tall as the citadel.

This wasn't rock, however. This was steel, long and very heavy pylons going down into the ocean with spaces between them for boats, and huge hatches with solid doors just above the waves.

Above that was platform after platform, layered one atop the other with weather stained steel stretching up higher than she could see. "Wow."

"Big, huh?" Jess was standing next to her, hands tucked into her hip pockets. "Know what that used to be?"

"I have no idea." Dev trimmed the throttles, aiming for the slot they'd been directed to by the gruff voice on the radio.

"That used to be an oil rig, Devvie," Jess said. "Way way back in the day, when we pumped petroleum from everything we could to power combustion engines."

"Ah." Dev regarded the structure. "That really is old then."

"It is," Jess said. "Swing around and back us in. I'm going to watch the grapples." She moved to put her hood up, then frowned and carefully tucked her dark hair into it. "Hope no one's close enough to get a shot of my mug," she muttered.

There was an actual note of discomfort in her voice, Dev noticed. "Would you like to park this vessel?" she said. "I could go watch. If they see me, they'll think I belong to the boat."

Jess stopped in mid motion. "Are you reading my mind? Can they teach you to do that?"

Dev merely looked puzzled at the question.

"Never mind." Jess pushed the hood back. "Good idea. These guys are pretty well known here from the response I got on comms. You do look like them. More than I do anyway." She traded places with Dev and watched Dev shrug into her jacket and fasten it. "Be careful."

Dev cocked her head. "I'll try to," she said. "I'm going to go back in that area just behind where this is. It has that metal wall." She went to the hatch and ducked through it, moving quickly down the steps as she heard the engines change their timbre.

The fishery was in a calm area, and the winds had dropped to almost nothing, so the boat was comfortable to walk around as she went across the deck and squeezed back between the walls so she had a view of the back. Jess swung the bow around and then reversed the drive, moving them slowly back into their assigned dock.

It was still very cold, but not the bitter cold of the white. Dev pushed her hood down after a few minutes, and watched the approaching dock, seeing the worn chains and bumpers meant to cradle them as they moved in. The sense of the age of the structure increased as she got a better look, the metal stained with weather and age and dented in many places.

As the boat closed into its position, she saw the grapples start to move, and she watched in mild apprehension as they shifted around the boat, one of them with a big hook aiming for the hatch in the back.

"Station keeping," a loud, oddly accented voice sounded out suddenly. "Lock on."

Dev heard a set of thunks and then the grapples were all over the back of the boat, pulling open the hatch as a boom came sweeping down with scan on it and dove into the big tank where the animals were.

She watched it for a minute, before she realized there was another figure on the dockside, watching her.

What should she do? Dev looked at the figure, who was slowly walking down the edge of the platform, with an unhurried motion. He seemed to be searching for something, so she climbed casually up onto the platform where the fishing controls were and perched on the wood topped steel seat, letting her hands rest on the knobs.

He paused as the boat settled into idle, its back end fitting neatly between the bumpers as they came to a halt. He studied her intently. After a moment, he lifted a hand and waved.

Dev immediately waved back, leaning forward on her elbows after she let her hand drop. She was hoping that would be enough, but a moment later, the man made a motioning forward gesture to her, and seemed to expect that she'd obey it.

Well then. She got up and climbed down to the deck, moving out behind the wall and keeping near the rail to stay out of the way of all the grapples opening the hatches and starting to unload the fish, hooking up a chute to the rear of the ship making a path for them to swim out.

There was a space of water between the side of the ship and the dock, and Dev was glad of it as she came to the rail across from him. "Hello."

He leaned on the bumper. "Old man there?"

"He's sleeping." Dev said the first thing she could think of. "I could go wake him up if you want me to." She looked behind her.

He held a hand up. "No no." He shook his head to emphasize the thought. "Just wanted to know if you got any word about some renegades we heard about stealing fish."

"Yes," Dev said. "They tried that on us. They came over and dropped people on the deck and tried to take us over, but we fought them off."

"Yeah?" The man's brows lifted. "You got guns onboard?"

"Yes." Dev didn't see any point in denying it.

He shook his head. "Careful with that, lass. You get caught with them, you'll end up bait." He glanced at the chutes. "Nice catch."

"It was hard work." Dev felt an eerie sensation, as though someone were standing behind her watching her back. She kept herself from turning though, reasoning that with the water between them, and the steel wall of the ship she was relatively safe.

He nodded. "Betcha." He straightened up. "Thanks for the news."

Then he looked intently at her. "Know who they were?"

Dev shook her head.

He stared at her for a brief moment, then he merely nodded and turned and walked away. "Later." He lifted a hand, but didn't look back.

"Goodbye." Dev waved back even though he wasn't watching. Then she turned and crossed the deck, coming back inside the metal wall only to be startled nearly out of her wits when she came face to face with Jess, fully armed, with her big blaster in her hands and an extremely serious look on her face. "Oh."

"Nice," Jess said. "You have any idea who that was?"

Dev shook her head. "Um." She gently eased the muzzle of the blaster to one side. "Were you going to shoot him?"

"If he'd taken one step toward you, sure," Jess said. "And then since the back of this thing is hitched to the wall we'd have both died together in one big ass flame ball, but there you go." She put the blaster back into its side mount and sighed. "That was Davog Stern. He's one of the other side's big hot shot agents."

Dev sorted through all that. "Like you?"

Jess smiled briefly. "He's got ten years on me, but yeah, sort of. Maybe if I live that long I might get as nasty a rep as he has. Hard to tell." She edged over and peeked across the deck. Now that the other side's big bastard had left, the place was deserted again but that itch was surfacing between her shoulder blades and she wanted out of the shackles. "Good thing you were on deck. If he'd caught me he'd have probably gutted me with the laser knife he had in his right hand."

Dev blinked. "He did?"

Jess regarded her with a bemused expression. "Did they give you programming to fight?"

"You mean like you do?" Dev watched her nod. "Well, you sometimes don't know what you get but I don't think so. Is that incorrect?" She asked, hesitantly. "I remember in the hallway, when the base was attacked that Brent didn't have anything to fight with. Is that usual?"

Jess stepped back into the shadows. "Most of the time techs don't. That's not their gig. That's our job. But they know how."

"I see."

"Let's get under cover." Jess nudged her toward the stairs, tugging her hood up and tightening the catches so it hid her face. "Hope they hurry up."

"WHAT IN THE hell's taking them so long?" Jess growled. "How many damned fish were in that thing?"

Dev consulted her scan. "The tank is almost empty of animals," she said. "I don't think it can count them though."

Jess snorted softly. "What did you tell him when he first walked up?" She asked abruptly. "I missed that when I was falling down t...I mean, getting to the back of the deck."

"He asked for Sigurd. I told him he was sleeping," Dev said. "Then he asked me about the attack."

"And?"

"And I told him about the pirates. I said they tried to get our fish, but we fought them off, and they went away."

Jess had her arms folded over her chest, and she was thinking hard, her eyes slightly narrowed. "You tell them who they were?"

"No. I said I didn't know. He warned me not to get caught with weapons."

"That's where I came in," Jess said. "I heard the rest. Bastard." She paced across the deck again, her body language restless and almost jerky. "What's his angle. What's he looking for?"

Dev regarded her mildly, but didn't answer since she really didn't have anything to add.

"Now he's wondering if you knew who they were and didn't want to squeal, or what." Jess went to the vid and studied it. "What's he doing here, Dev? I didn't expect to see one of them out here. They usually steer clear of the fisheries. Too many uncertain loyalties for it to be safe for them."

"He didn't seem to be in any discomfort," Dev said. "He did seem very interested in who the attackers were, but..." She cocked her head. "It almost seemed like he was expecting me to say something different."

"He expected you to ID the bad guys as Interforce. Most any fisherman would have," Jess said, quietly. "So now he's wondering if it was because you didn't know, or because you didn't say that for a reason."

Dev frowned. "Is that a bad thing?"

"It could be." Jess leaned on the console. "C'mon, bastards. Get that tank empty before he decides to find out more about us."

Dev sat down in the control chair and let her hands rest on the throttles.

It seemed a way to get ready to do something since Jess was pretty sure that something was going to happen that would require her to do something.

"C'mon...c'mon." Jess was repeating behind her, shifting restlessly. She already had all her weapons on her, and her jacket was unfastened over her armored jumpsuit.

"Where do you want to go when they finish?" Dev asked, rubbing her thumb over one of the gauges, where the glass over it had gotten a bit cloudy.

"What?"

Dev half turned in the seat to face her. "When they're done. Which way do you want to go from here?" She was fascinated by the almost ceaseless motion of Jess's body, now channeled into a slightly rocking pacing stride. "Are you in distress? Should we do something?"

Jess went to the vid and stared at it. "I feel like a sitting duck."

Duck. Dev's brow furrowed. She'd heard people say that word but it had something to do with crouching down, which she supposed could be related to sitting. Was a sitting duck different than a standing one? "All right."

"I think they know something, Dev. I think they're planning on coming at us." She flexed her hands.

Dev got up and walked to where she was standing, looking up at the vid. It showed the back of the boat, where the grapples and arms were still busy, a heavy flow of water rushing down the chute and into the fishery's lower level. There didn't seem to be anything wrong, and yet, she could feel Jess twitching next to her.

It made her breathe a little faster. She wondered if she would be turning to the controls next, shoving the engines forward and trying to wrench them free of the fishery.

The radio crackled, making them both jump. "Northern Star, attention."

Jess went over and sat down, picking up the commset and slipping it onto her head. "Star," she said, in a brief, clipped voice.

Dev continued to watch the vid, seeing the water flow start to reduce.

Static sounded for a moment. Jess felt the tension in her ratchet up a few notches and she glanced quickly behind her. "Dev, you might want to come over here and hold onto something."

Dev obediently left the display and came over, settling next to Jess and wrapping her hands around Jess's arm.

"Okay."

It made Jess smile, despite everything, and after a moment her body relaxed a little. She clicked the comms a few times. "This is Star, who called?" She cocked her ears, and watched the vid, her body waiting for the sight of armored figures pouring down the dock.

Another crackle, then the voice came back. "Stand by for weighting. Check ninty-eight percent live. Good stock."

Jess stared at the speaker. "Thanks," she said, belatedly. "Two-hundred fathoms."

"Ice pack?"

"Not far." Jess kept to the clipped tone.

"Weighting 7.5K, 2.5 chits per. Stand by for delivery."

Wow. Jess did the math in her head and her eyes popped wide open. No wonder they had full jars of honey onboard. And that was for one load. "Holy shit." Her eyes tracked to the deck, seeing a grapple coming over with a large can dangling from it. "That's our payoff, Dev."

"Payoff?"

"That's what they get for delivering the fish. Trade spots. With any luck they'll let us loose and I won't have to start shooting."

Dev hopped into the seat Jess vacated, and got ready to start the engines up, not really understanding what was going on. Behind her, Jess went to the hatch and drew her blaster, inching the door open and watching the dock intently.

The grapple descended, and then they heard the loud, hollow sound as the can hit the deck. Then the grapple arm released and lifted clear, and the next moment the locks and shackles surged into motion, making Jess lurch against the door and start forward before she paused and relaxed. "Damn."

"Is there something wrong?" Dev asked.

"Plan worked," Jess said. "I wasn't really expecting that." She put her gun back in its holster and dogged the hatch shut, feeling the boat float free as the last of the grapples let loose of them.

"Northern Star, egress to starboard, keep to your lane," the voice warned. "Stay clear of station."

Jess got back to the console and grabbed the comms. "Acknowledged, out. Dev, take us out and to the right. Don't go anywhere outside those markers. They've got the waters mined."

"What does that mean?" Dev started the engines, and gently nudged the throttles forward. "What's a mine?"

"Big boom." Jess turned and watched the vid, her trigger finger still itchy. It didn't quite feel right, the normalness of the transaction. It was hard for her to believe that the fishery, greedy as it was for take, wouldn't question a thirty crew boat where only one crewmember was visible, and an unfamiliar voice on the comms.

Not after seeing Davog. Her guts clenched a little, thinking of him. Remembering the first few missions of her career, when she'd run full into him and nearly got her rookie head blown right off her body. She'd gotten lucky and gotten out, but she'd never forgotten his canny, icy precision and how his almost black eyes had bored through hers.

Davog there and they just let them go? A thought occurred to her, and she turned back to Dev. "Trade places for a minute. Run a scan on that barrel they dumped on the deck. See what's in there." She took over the throttles as Dev stepped to one side, feeling the vibration of the engines through the palms of her hands.

Dev turned and adjusted the scanner, opening up its field and walking to the back of the control room, watching the analyzer finish its sweep. The scanner focused in on the barrel, running first a bio sweep, which was negative. Then she went on for a threat portfolio, watching intently as it went through the various possibilities that included destructive things.

Also negative. "Clean so far," she called over her shoulder. "What am I supposed to see in there?"

"Gold."

"Ah." Dev nodded. "Atomic element seventy-nine, isn't it?"

Jess sighed, as she took the boat out and into the carefully lined lane. "I feel like such a dipshit around you sometimes."

Dev straightened. "What?"

"Never mind."

Dev came over and showed her the display. "The barrel is, in fact, filled with that element," she said. "So that is a good thing?"

"That's a freaking amazing thing," Jess said. "It makes me not trust it. Davog should have stopped us. We didn't look right." She increased speed a little and resisted the urge to look behind her, the spot between her shoulder blades itching fiercely. "We didn't look or act right and they should have held us."

"But they didn't."

"No."

"Do you think they will?"

"Damned if I know," Jess said. "I'd be very surprised if we weren't followed. Even though we turned over legit catch, and they paid us in legit chits. I know we were out of spec." She slid out of the way. "Here you take it."

Dev took the controls. "Maybe they didn't notice."

Jess went back to the hatch and opened it, keeping her hood up and tucked around her head in case long range scan was focusing on them. She watched the rapidly retreating docks, spotting another boat heading in behind them, but saw no sign of being chased.

Was Dev right? She scanned the huge structure, looking for a flash of motion or a reflection where there shouldn't be any. But the stained and battered metal remained just that, as they came around the side of the facility and went past the processing stations.

On this side, prepared product was loading onto trundles, the short haul delivery boats that would make the trip across the water to the isolated communities on the islands all around them.

As she watched, one of the trawlers started out from the bay, two men on the deck watching them idly. Was it really a trawler? Jess watched it closely, her fingers closing on the blaster at her side. But the other boat curved away to the south, while their route was north, and in a minute they had left them far behind.

So they were out. She had what she wanted, and they could head to the Highland Island market and pick up the tempting delicacies that would gain them entrance to the secure space they needed to get into.

It was all working great. Jess gazed unhappily at the empty sea. Wasn't it?

Chapter Twenty-five

DEV WATCHED THE approaching sea station with a sense of bemusement. It was a little like the fish place, but this was two of them, smaller, between a set of rocky escarpments so they formed a sort of gate. The boat would have to go between them, and she could see that there was something strung there blocking the way.

She was dressed in some of the fisher people's clothes that Jess had found below decks, a high necked thick fabric shirt and a pair of somewhat funny pants that had straps that went over her shoulders and held them up. It was all quite comfortable, and she had her sharkskin jacket to wear over it when they got to the market.

Dev slowed the engines as another boat ahead of her did the same, coming close enough now for her to see men on the little towers, holding guns.

That was confusing. She turned her head as Jess entered the control space, her partner's body also encased in borrowed clothing. "They seem in some discomfort ahead." She pointed at the gates.

"Nah." Jess came up to stand next to her. "That's normal. They don't like people to make trouble in the market." She rested her hands on the console. "I've been here about a dozen times. None of them as myself."

"I see."

Jess studied the boat ahead of them, which was longer but narrower than theirs, and had a haphazard pile of fishing equipment on the back of it. "Crabber." She indicated the boxes on the back, which were stacked up high all over. "Those guys make credit like crazy."

"That crab was good." Dev admitted. "Do you think they'll have some more of them here?"

Jess laughed. "That's the least of what they'll have here." She draped her arm over Dev's shoulder. "Market's sort of a no man's land in a way. The other side knows we come here, we know they come here, everyone pretends they don't know anyone but everyone's trying to get goodies to take home."

"It's something you have in common," Dev said.

Jess looked thoughtful, then she shrugged. "It's what all humans have in common I guess. We all like to get stuff. Get luxuries. Know that we can take a few chits and get some comfort."

"I like that too." Dev adjusted the throttles again, backing them down as the boat ahead of them went to idle speed. "So I guess you're right, if even bio alts do it."

"Even?" Jess bumped her. "You're a great barterer. I heard you in Quebec."

Dev smiled.

"Now. Keep it nice and steady as we're going through," Jess said as the boat ahead of them passed through the gates and they were coming up on them themselves. "This boat's known here."

Dev nodded, watching the men on the towers. They were examining them closely, but as Jess had said, they apparently knew the ship because the gate drifted open and the man on the right hand tower waved at them. She waved back, just as the radio crackled to life.

"Northern Star, over."

"Answer it," Jess said quietly.

Dev keyed comms. "This is Northern Star. Go ahead."

"Welcome. Third dock, inside jetty, first space, the usual. Compliments to Sig."

"Oh no. They really really do know them here," Jess murmured. "Bouncy little bastard. This could be trickier than I thought."

"Acknowledged," Dev said. "Sigurd sends his regards." She paused slightly then went on. "He says he hopes you have something worth buying this time."

Jess turned her head and stared, round eyed, at her.

The radio erupted in laughter. "Tell him I hope he's actually got chits this time not polished fish scales," the voice called back. "Over."

"I will, thank you." Dev unkeyed the comm. "I hope that was not really incorrect."

"How in the hell did you know to say that?" Jess said, after a long moment's silence. "Where did that all come from?"

How did she know? "I thought about what he might have said to that, and that's what it was," she finally answered. "Was it incorrect?"

"No," Jess said. "I think it's pretty much exactly what he would have said. But how did you know that? You only just met the guy."

"I don't know," Dev said. "Can we talk about this after I finish piloting? I don't want to hit anything."

Jess chuckled wryly. "That's the nicest way anyone's ever told me to shut the hell up." She gave Dev a light scratch on the back with her fingertips. "Sure. Third dock's that way, portside. One's up at the top, that's the ritzy harbor. Then three's on the east side."

Obediently, Dev steered toward the right, as the other boat puttered off to the left. She could see the many docks clustering around the edge of the island and it seemed rather busy with traffic. Very different. Very interesting.

Jess was watching everything with a look of intense alertness. Her eyes were sweeping all the other ships and searched diligently for outlines she might recognize, or people she knew. Highland Market was a fun but dangerous place, and having seen Davog at the fishery, she suspected she would find more of his ilk here.

It happened. Sometimes, between the escalations and insertions, she'd even shared a cup of grog with one or the other of them here, since it was recognized as a truce area. No nasty business allowed, or you ended up in the Highland lock down and what she'd heard of that wasn't something she wanted to experience. No one wanted to be outted, which they would be, and have their organization embarrassed, which they would be, and end up being punked and demoted which they definitely would be as she'd seen it happen to others including Jason.

So all of them kept up the facade and pretended not to be who they were, and ignored old grudges while they were there on the island. Jess, however, suspected that regardless of that, and of the unofficial rules, if she was spotted and recognized the rules would go out the window.

Not after blowing up half a damned mountain.

They motored around the edge of the island and Jess pointed at the entrance to the harbor they'd been assigned to. This one was about half full, and most of the boats were empty and bobbing quietly at rest. They passed between them and found the slip they were to park in, up near the front and handy to the long ramp leading up.

"Okay." Jess put her hands on her hips. "We're peace bonded here."

Dev's blonde eyebrow inched up.

"No weapons."

"I see."

"We're going to go out there and browse the market. You're gonna be the moneybags."

Dev's other eyebrow crept up to join its mate.

"You're the one who looks like Sigurd," Jess said. "So you'll carry the chit record. I'm just along to protect you. I'm not going to pretend to be someone else this time. I'm just gonna be an Interforce agent Sigurd hooked into protecting his patch."

"All right." Dev actually managed to follow that. "What about...I'm here by myself because I...um..." She frowned. "Remember that bet thing you mentioned? I looked it up in comp. What if I bet the rest of the fisher people that I couldn't take this boat here by myself?"

Jess grinned wholeheartedly. "Oh I like that."

"So he agreed but he sent you along to make sure I didn't get into trouble. Does that work?"

Jess leaned forward and gave her a lingering kiss on the lips. "You're the bomb."

"I am?" Dev was confused. "So that was incorrect?"

"No."

"I see. So in this case, bombs are good?"

"Yes." Jess wrapped her arms around Dev and hugged her. "I don't know what Bricker was thinking when he asked for you, but I'm damn glad he did."

Dev smiled in relief, returning the hug. "I'm glad too."

They shut down the control center and dogged the hatch, and Jess led the way down the steps to the side of the ship that was close to the walkway.

"Here." Jess handed Dev an embossed card. "That's the value of that can. They'll lift that up and bank it, see?" She pointed at the shore side grapple latching on to the can and picking it up. It was placed in a weatherworn casing right next to the dock marked with the same number as the ship had. "You can't carry all that around with you."

The container bong'd softly, and a number registered on the side of it. Jess grunted. "They also take a percent off for the service, but that's okay."

Dev merely nodded.

"So now you can use the card to get stuff. When they deliver it to the ship, they put their cards in that slot, and register chits to it. Then they pick up the chits before they leave," Jess said. "It's totally local to this island. Not worth anything anywhere else but it keeps people from being hit over the head in the market and getting their chits stolen."

"I see."

"It's anonymous in that, the card is only matched to that dock number," Jess concluded. "So let's go shop."

They crossed over onto the dock and walked up the ramp. It was late afternoon and the walkways were mostly empty, only two or three people strolling in the opposite direction.

It was cold, but not freezing, Dev noticed. Her jacket kept her reasonably warm, and she stuck her hands in her pockets as they reached a set of chiseled steps and started walking up them. There was some moss on the rocks, but otherwise it was clean, and as they got to the top she almost stopped at the view below them.

She had thought Quebec was chaotic? It had nothing on this place. The whole inside of the hill was full of stone shelters, lines and lines of them in concentric circles around a big tower in the center. Between the shelters were aisles full of people, and she could hear noise and the sound of people talking, brushing against her in waves that matched the confusion of smells and colors. "Wow."

Jess chuckled and led the way down the steps. "C'mon."

As they walked, the cold wind was cut off and it became a lot more comfortable. Dev pushed her hood back and drew in a breath full of strange scents and her ears caught the sound she now recognized as music somewhere in the mix. She followed Jess down the carved steps into one of the aisles, and as the stone walls rose up next to her she put her hand out and touched one. "Oh." She looked at it. "It's warm."

"Yeah." Jess paused to scan the aisle, and then moved forward again. "This is what's left of one of the smaller volcanoes that went off back in the day. That outside ring was the crater, and this island's what's left of the cone that got drowned when the seas all came up."

Dev wasn't sure she liked the idea of being inside a volcano, but she did enjoy the warmth and she was able to open up her jacket as they entered the area where all the stone shelters were.

Like in Quebec, there were people inside the shelters with all kinds of different things. It seemed more organized though, and the people around them were dressed both more richly and far more strangely to her eyes. Some had seashells decorating them, and others had colored marking on their skin that was a little like what Jess had.

"Hey there, kid! Whatcha looking for? Want some of this?" A male voice sounded just ahead of them. Dev realized belatedly he was addressing her, and she peered into his little shelter. It had some of the strange clothing, strips of one color intertwined with a second, looking more like undergarments than anything else.

"No, she doesn't," Jess said, steering her past. "She likes to wear things more than once."

Dev wasn't sure what that meant, but she saw the man glare at Jess until he saw the insignia she'd pinned to the collar of the fisherman's overall she was wearing and then he turned his back on them.

He was afraid. Dev saw it in his face before he turned. "What are those?" She whispered to Jess as they moved past. "I like the colors."

"Women wear them and dance in them to let people know they want sex," Jess said. "I'd rather we keep that private between us, if you don't mind."

Dev felt her face warm as the blood rose to her cheeks. "I see."

"Besides, that's not something the science boys would like. Now..." Jess led her down a cross alley and into the next ring. "This is more like it." She slowed down as they came even to a bigger shelter that was full of steel barrels and rows and rows of drink dispensers. "Ice wine."

Dev had absolutely no idea what that was, but she went with it and found herself face to face with a ginger haired woman in a deep purple one piece outfit that ended at her knees and left most of her arms exposed. Dev felt chilly just watching her. "Hello," she said, as the woman focused on her.

"Top of the day to ya," the woman amiably responded. "Looking for a bottle or two?"

Dev waited to see if Jess was going to intervene, but when she remained silent, she figured just being straightforward would be the best. "I don't know. What is it?"

"Ahhh." The woman didn't even look at Jess. She picked up a small glass and uncapped a bottle, pouring a bit into the glass and offering it to Dev. "Taste for yourself."

Dev took the glass and sipped it gingerly. It tasted like...well, nothing she'd ever tasted was like it. There was a clean sweetness to it that was very appealing, and it seemed to evaporate on the back of her tongue. "Oh. Wow."

The woman grinned.

"How do you make this?" Dev asked, curious. "It tastes excellent."

There were two other men in the shelter, and they were watching, but kept their distance. They looked for other people walking by to pitch their product to. Everyone ignored Jess.

"Family secret." The woman winked at her. "Let's just say we've got some family upside and we provide the ice. Like it?"

Dev nodded. She felt Jess lay her hand on her back, and her fingers tightened twice. "I think I would like two bottles. How much are they?"

The woman sat down on a box and they settled in to bargain.

Jess was content to listen. She was aware of all the eyeballs on them, but she'd put her insignia on for a reason and there was a bit of gratification on seeing the wariness. The crowd was light, she noted, far lighter than the last time she'd been on the island and the merchants around looked more than a little discouraged. Was it the weather?

The woman sighed. "You're a hard bargainer, shippy."

"We work very hard for our chits," Dev said. "So we don't like to give them up."

"And well you're known for it. All right." Two bottles were marked off, and Dev handed over the card. She waited for it to be recorded, and then she took it back. "Delivery's first bell."

"Thanks." Jess spoke for the first time. "We'll see you then."

The woman nodded briefly at her. "Agent."

Jess smiled at her, and they moved on. This ring seemed to be mostly edible and drinkable items, and they moved further in stopping here and there to taste. "Haven't seen most of this stuff in a long time," Jess said, after they tried some small crackers with fish eggs on them. "See that? It's made from octopus." She sampled a bit of the meat and watched Dev try some. "See if you can get a couple packages of that, and some of the snails."

Dev wasn't sure about the snails, but the octopus tasted nice, slightly briny with a chewy texture she liked. They had stacks of cryopacked product, and she met the eye of the man selling them, giving him a little smile that drew him over at once.

So far things seemed to be going well. She glanced up at Jess, who was searching for more things to nibble on. She was also sweeping the area every few steps looking for trouble. Her insignia flashed briefly in the light and Dev wished she'd been allowed to put hers on as well.

Octopus secured, they continued further on toward the center of the ring, where it seemed it was busier, the narrow path they were on crowded with other shoppers. These shelters were full of more exotic things, and Dev found herself pressing closer to Jess as they had to slow way down.

Jess put her hand on her shoulder, keeping herself between Dev and most of the crowd. So far she hadn't seen anyone she knew in a bad way, though she had spotted a few people who she had a slight acquaintance of and many more who recognized her collar bug and kept their distance.

That was fine. When she'd decided to wear it she knew she was going to be advertising what she was, and though they were peace bonded everyone knew that didn't make it safe. Didn't make them safe, either her, or her counterpoints on the other side.

"Oh, Jess." Dev stopped, and frowned. Her stomach turned at what she was looking at, and she felt a sense of muted horror fill her.

What? Jess peered around her and spotted a stall with furry animal skins on it. White fur, and big. Had to be bear. "Bear skins," she said, distracted by the distressed look on Dev's face. "We should get a few. Great for some bigwig's office."

Dev went over and peered at the skin, which had the bear's head attached with its glassy eyes and lurid, poking tongue. She turned back to Jess and put a hand on her arm. "Do we have to?" she asked. "I don't like this."

Jess studied her, intrigued by the fact that she had rolled over dead humans without a flinch but freaked out about a dead bear. "You're wearing a shark skin," Jess said.

"I know. But..." Dev looked behind her.

"But your jacket doesn't have eyes." Jess gave her a tolerant grin. "No problem. Let's move on." She guided Dev further, starting toward the stall she saw had golden jars prominently displayed.

Halfway there, they heard a loud commotion ahead, and Jess felt her instincts prickle. She immediately got ahead of Dev and looked quickly forward, where an open space between the ring made a crossroads. There were shouts and laughter, and she flexed her hands, wishing not for the first time that she'd chanced the peace bond.

They reached the edge of the crossroads and stopped, as the crowd closed in and made it impossible to go farther. Jess straightened to her full height and got a look at what the fuss was about, seeing two men in expensive looking clothing kicking a third man, who was dressed in a threadbare jumper.

The man sprawled on the ground, covering his head with both arms.

An older man, also in worn clothes darted into the opening, going over to the man on the floor and kneeling down next to him. "Leave him alone, you bastards," he yelled at the two attackers. "He didn't do nothing to you."

"Why are they harming that man?" Dev asked in a very low tone.

"People are assholes," Jess said. "They don't really need a reason."

"Yeah? Shut your mouth!" One of the men kicked the older man in the side. "Your kind should go back where you came from. We don't need you here."

"Are you going to assist him?" Dev asked

Jess sighed. "I shouldn't."

"I wish you would," she said mournfully. "Doctor Dan always would do that for us."

"That's not a bio alt. He's just a scrub."

"Would they treat one of us any different?"

Hm. Jess studied the two fancy pants, realizing why one of them seemed familiar to her.

He kicked the man again, and then in a quiet flicker of motion Jess moved, bumping her way through the crowd, getting across the open space before he could try a third time. "Stop," she said, in a quiet yet firm tone. "No place for this."

The man whirled and lifted a hand, then stopped, his eyes fastening on her neck, then darting away. "You've got no influence here," he said, as the second man came over, watching Jess warily.

"Neither do you." Jess had her hands clasped behind her back and she merely looked at him. "But making noise in the middle of the market is never a good idea." She stared him in the eye. "No one wants a bad rep, right?"

Both men glowered at her, then the shorter of the two slapped the other on the arm. "Let's go. It stinks around here."

Jess waited for them to leave, then she went over and extended a hand down to the older man. "I'd get out of here if I were you."

The man took her hand and let her pull him up. Then he squeezed her fingers. "Thanks, agent," he said. "My son didn't mean to cause trouble. He's just a little clumsy." He tapped the boy on the head. "Get up, Jeso."

The huddled figure got to his feet, blinking painfully. He kept his shoulders hunched, blood running from a cut on his head. The older man ducked his head in respect to Jess, then led the boy off down the crossroad away from the center as the crowd started milling around again, the entertainment seemingly over.

Dev ducked between them and arrived at her side. "That was excellent."

"That was idiotic, since everyone in the place now knows I'm here, especially the two agents I just pissed off. C'mon. Let's get some tea and honey and get out of here before someone decides to make trouble. She pulled Dev back into the side aisle in the direction they came from, aware now of all the whispers following her through the crowd.

THEY WERE HALFWAY around the ring before Jess sensed the presence and turned, tucking Dev behind her in a single fluid motion. Facing her were two men in plain woven clothes made of sea plants. The only sign on them was the metal bracelet on their right wrists. "What?"

"Man wants to see you," the one nearer her said. "Says with his compliments, would you please come up the hill."

Jess sorted through the invitation and relaxed a little, realizing it was an invitation and not an order. "Sure," she said. "Lead on." She motioned Dev to go ahead of her.

"Just you," the man said, not moving.

"No."

"The man just wants to see you," he replied, still in a quiet and calm voice.

"I don't leave my partner behind," Jess replied. "So you get us both, or neither, your choice."

The man reacted with some surprise, looking intently at Dev, and then tilting his head to one side. "Wasn't indentified. That's fine. Let's go." He turned and started down the aisle, turning at the next crossroads and heading up the hill with his companion and the two of them at his heels.

Jess remained silent as they walked, one hand resting lightly on Dev's shoulder. They quickly rose up out of the market and then were passing through the circles of stone houses that spread out right and left.

Dev wasn't sure what was going on, but she was sure it wasn't the time to ask about it. It was quieter up here, and she could hear the sound of the surf crashing gently up against the harbors down below.

There was a gate up at the top, and it swung open as they approached. Dev glanced up at Jess's face, but her expression was calm, so she walked obediently through it and only flinched a little as the gate closed behind them. They walked to a door, and paused.

Jess took advantage of the pause and fished something out of her pocket, reaching over and fastening it to Dev's high collar. "There."

Dev reached up and touched it, unsurprised to feel her tech's insignia there. It made her feel a lot better to have it and she suppressed a grin as the door opened and they moved through it. They walked down a long stone hallway, passing several roughly cut doorways leading to rooms with people in them doing various things.

They entered through a doorway and crossed a big, busy room until they came to a table that had a half dozen people around it, and one man sitting at the head.

"Drake." The man stood up and came around the table, extending his hand. "Good to see you."

Jess took his hand and exchanged grips. "Hello, Charles. Same back." She half turned. "This is my partner, Dev."

"Tech." The man ducked his head toward her in respect. "This was very unexpected." He returned his attention to Jess. "I sure didn't expect to see you in these parts after what we heard," he said. "Josan told me what happened down the hill. I'm glad you kept it quiet."

"They complain?" Jess asked, as they moved a few steps away from the group.

Charles shook his head. He was a tall man, with broad shoulders and tightly curled gray hair and a roughly weathered face. "And that in itself should be a warning."

Jess nodded. "I won't be here long," she said. "I don't want any trouble."

"Nor do I," Charles said. "So I would advise you to keep to your plan and leave as soon as possible. There are odd rumblings and I don't want anything to disrupt the market, Jess. Times are hard and as you know, we don't take sides."

"I know."

Charles turned and regarded Dev. "So this is your new partner," he said. "Somehow we heard it was one of Sigurd's pups."

"Intentionally since we borrowed his boat," Jess said, straightforwardly. "We're shopping."

"Using fisherman chits?" His eyebrows lifted. "Dangerous."

Jess shrugged lightly.

"No, that wouldn't matter to you would it." Charles smiled briefly. "Don't tell me anything. But I'm reasonably glad to see the rumors of your demise were somewhat exaggerated." He lifted a hand. "As long as you're spreading someone else's credit around, don't forget to stop at the spa. We've got some new treatments I think you'd like."

"Maybe we'll go there now," Jess said. "Seems like a good time for it."

"Excellent idea," Charles said. "Miklos, will you guide our friends here to the private door? Enjoy." He shook Jess's hand, nodded at Dev, and went back to the table where he sat down and picked up a pad he'd been looking at.

Miklos, the taller of the two men who had sought her out, gestured in a different direction than the one they'd entered from. "Please to come with me."

"Lead on." Jess put her hand on Dev's back and they followed Miklos. After a minute or two of even walking, they started downward again and passed dozens and dozens of closed doors on either side.

A door opened and a man started to emerge, then he spotted them and ducked back inside, shutting the portal as they came even with them. Miklos didn't say anything, and when Dev looked up at Jess, she put a finger up to her lips and then let it drop.

It was all very strange. Dev felt that there was danger there, and that Jess was unsettled, but she just kept walking with a calm look on her face.

They reached another door, and Miklos opened it, then stepped back and indicated they should go through. "Enjoy," he said, waiting for them to move past and then closing the door behind them.

They were in yet another hallway, but this one was round, and there was light coming in from the ceiling. Dev glanced up to see slanted holes going up through the rock. She looked at Jess, who was frowning.

Was it okay to talk? She watched her partner's face, and after a moment, Jess looked back at her.

"Okay," Jess said. "Let's go see what they have." She pointed toward an opening that showed a larger room behind it, and they walked through.

It was a big space, with a high, arched ceiling and there were quite a lot of people inside. Dev looked around and stuck close to Jess, following her across the space to a rock desk with three or four women behind it. She paused, and almost jerked when she saw the collars around their necks, not expecting at all to find fellow bio alts here.

"Good day," one of the women greeted them. "What do you wish?"

It wasn't a set she knew well, Dev realized. They were perhaps ten standard years older than she was, slim and tall with uniformly pretty faces. They reminded her just a little of Gigi.

"Private bath," Jess said. "With the works." She pulled out two big chits and set them down.

"This way." The girl picked up two large, folded pieces of fabric and bowed in their direction then walked behind the desk to one of a set of doors behind it. They followed her, and she opened the door to one of the rooms and offered them the fabric. "Enjoy."

"Thanks." Jess ducked inside, and waited for Dev to join her, then straightened up as the door closed behind them leaving them alone.

Dev wasn't sure where to look first. The initial thing she realized was that the air was very warm, and moist. It bathed her face and she blinked into it, smelling a rich, mineral scent as it entered her lungs. "Um."

"Um." Jess went over to one of the four stone beds and put the towel down on it. Across from them was a big misshapen pool with steps cut into it, full of water that had steam rising off the top. "Wasn't going to indulge in this, but what the hell."

"What is it?" Dev went over to a second couch and put her own wrap down, jerking back as she touched the top. "Oh. It's hot."

"Yeah." Jess sat down on hers, then lay back letting out a small groan as the heat penetrated her body. "Good a place as any to hide for a little while."

"Are we doing that?" Dev sat down on the stone, pleasantly surprised when the warmth penetrated the pants she was wearing.

"Uh huh. When Charles gives you advice, it's a good idea to take it," Jess said. "I'm not really sure what he was trying to tell me but it's clear he doesn't want trouble."

"I see." Dev got up and went to the pool, kneeling down and putting her hand in it. "This is really warm."

"I sure hope so, given what I just paid them for it," her partner remarked dryly. "At least we can enjoy ourselves before we go outside and probably have to fight our way to the boat and escape.

Dev came over and sat down on the edge of her stone bed. "Is that what's going to happen?"

"Probably." Jess let her hand rest on Dev's thigh. "Someone's hunting me. That's why Charles sent us down here. He doesn't want trouble and he knows if whoever's hunting me finds me, there'll be lots of that."

"I see."

"So he's got local info, but not current intel from our side, since he didn't know about you," Jess said. "So we'll get our splurge and then get back to the boat. With what you ordered so far, we can get into the science center." She studied Dev's concerned expression. "Don't worry, Dev. We'll get out of this."

"I didn't expect to find those of my kind here," Dev said. "Doctor Dan said the people over here didn't have them, but I know that set."

Jess looked at her. "This place is different. A lot of cred comes through here, most of it out of spec for both sides. You got enough cred, you can have anything you want." Her hand warmed suddenly as Dev's dropped on top of it. "It's the old story of humanity, Dev. The haves and the have nots. Charles and his family have plenty. They've run this place for generations."

"I don't think I understand."

"Your bio station is on our side," Jess said. "But Charles offered them enough to get them to give him what he wants."

"He's not on our side." Dev said.

"He's not really on any side. He's glad to suck in all of us ready to spend money on stuff we can't get anywhere but here, legally."

Dev frowned. "I don't think I really understand."

"Don't worry about it." Jess stretched herself out, savoring the feel of the heated stone leeching into her body. "Just enjoy yourself, Dev. We don't get this kind of treatment often. I'm going to warm these old bones and then we'll go in the pool. After that we can get some steam, and a rub and get our hair cut."

That all sounded very strange. Not unpleasant, but strange. Dev looked around. "It's nice to be warm. Is that why the walls were hot?"

"The walls are hot because we're in a volcanic cone. Charles's family led a bunch of renegades from the other side and found this place a long way back. They built it up. Word has it that they catered to pirates and outlaws first, then after the market built up, word got out and anyone with chits came here"

"I see."

"We always thought it was funny, on our side. Perfect capitalism." She patted the stone bench at her side. "Lay down. Enjoy the heat."

Dev did, settling on her back next to Jess, feeling the heat from the stone but also from Jess as her body relaxed. "That does feel good." She regarded the lamps in the ceiling, which had come on and were bathing them. "Is that sunlight replacement?"

"It is," Jess said. "One of the few places you can get it out here." Reluctantly, she sat up and started taking her clothes off. "Might as well take advantage of it."

"What do the fisher people do?" Dev undid the suspenders on her outfit and slipped out of the pants, then sat down to unlace her boots. "Scan didn't pick up anything on the boat that could do that."

"They don't." Jess left her borrowed clothing folded neatly on the couch and went to the pool, walking slowly in and then rolling over with a deep, heartfelt sigh. "Damn that feels good." She relaxed in the hot water, grimacing a little when it touched the puncture wound she'd paid scant attention to since their arrival. "Ow."

Dev joined her a minute later, holding her hand up over the pool's surface as steam gathered against her skin. Then she moved closer and examined the wound. "It seems to be all right."

Jess regarded her from half closed eyes. "Like the pool?"

Dev sat down next to her, thinking about that. The heat did feel good. She'd been so cold for so long on this mission, just sitting here in this hot water was letting her body fully relax for the first time in days. The rough rock felt a little abrasive against her bare skin, but the buoyancy of the water kept it from being uncomfortable. "So this is from the volcano?"

"The heat is." Jess let her head rest against the rock. "The water comes from the ocean."

"So, people come here, and they give them credits so they can sit in the water?"

"Yup."

Dev pondered that. "So all you get for that is feeling nice?"

"Yup."

"That seems odd."

Jess chuckled. "Yeah I guess it does. But I guess it's a little piece of how it used to be. Kind of like the stuff we do, the dinner thing in the citadel. Things people remember their grandparents remembering about the old days.

Like the place Doctor Dan had taken her, Dev realized. The place where they had eaten, up in the top of the station The scientists could easily have had that served in their offices, or in the natural born eating place but they chose to put a table and chairs up where you could see the stars and have it given to you that way. "I get it."

"You do?"

Dev nodded. She stretched her legs out and crossed them, leaning her elbows on the little shelf they were sitting against. "It's nice."

"It is nice." Jess picked up a piece of sea sponge resting on the shelf and half turned. "Here, see if you like this." She dunked the sponge and started rubbing it along Dev's arm, not missing the slight jerk as Dev reacted. "That's supposed to make your skin feel good. I never really was much for it myself since I always came here by myself and you can't reach everywhere."

"That feels very interesting," Dev said. "It reminds me of the flash rad cleaning we did in the mornings in the crèche. It took layers of skin off."

Jess stopped and eyed her. "Is that good or bad?"

Dev smiled and held her hand out. "Let me see if you like it." She moved around and got behind Jess, applying the sponge to her back. She could see the old injury there, still red and a little swollen and she carefully avoided the spot. There were other scars there too, one that went right across her spine from right to left, old and tense. "You were hurt a lot."

"Yes." Jess leaned against the wall, savoring the sensation of the sponge scouring her skin. "I take too many chances, they tell me."

"Why?" Dev was actually enjoying herself, exploring the storied skin in front of her.

"Why did they tell me that, or why do I do it?" Jess put her head down on her folded arms. "I don't know why I do it. I just get into things and what happens to me doesn't matter, I guess. Jason once told me that's why I was as successful as I've been because I always go all in. I don't hold back."

"But you get hurt." Dev started down the backs of her legs. "I hope that doesn't happen too much. I don't like to see you in discomfort."

Jess remained silent for a bit, the water of the pool lapping gently at her back. "You really care about what happens to me?" She asked suddenly, turning her head and looking back over her shoulder.

"Of course," Dev answered placidly, as she scrubbed her way back up Jess's back and over her the tops of her arms. "I've never cared about anyone as much as I do about you."

The matter of fact honesty of it surprised Jess. She had no doubt at all that what Dev was saying was true, or as true as she knew it to be but it touched her unexpectedly in a deep way. Did she feel the same way? She could scarcely remember what caring about someone meant, after that last visit home.

How did she feel about Dev?

"Does that cause you discomfort?" Dev asked. "I hope not."

"No," Jess finally answered, with a faint smile. "It makes me feel good because I think I care about you a lot too." She rolled over and put her hands on Dev's knees, studying the compact profile outlined in the dim golden light of rad. "I don't think I've ever felt like this about anyone else before."

Dev regarded her with a pleased, if puzzled expression. "Is that good or bad?" She reflected Jess's earlier question back at her.

"I don't know," Jess said in a soft voice. "I don't think I'm supposed to care about anyone. At least, that's what my mother told me." It still stung, that last meeting. That back turned, that door closed. There hadn't been any animosity in it, no dislike, just a kindly worded dismissal of her as something no longer part of the core of what was left of their family.

"We can't care about you, Jess. You're lost to us. You belong to them now."

Surprising, how much that had hurt. She remembered the tears, and the terrible constriction in her throat, as she'd turned and walked away, heading back to the transport center. Back to the citadel.

Her brothers had always kept in touch though. Paid to have an in with Interforce, after all.

"Well." Dev put her hands on Jess's shoulders. "They never told me that. So I do care about you. I want to care about you. It makes me feel really good."

Jess felt a smile forming on her face. She did want to care about Dev. Maybe it was wrong and maybe it was dangerous, like they'd told her, but she hadn't gotten to where she was by listening to anyone, now had she? "C'mere." She reached out and took hold of Dev's waist and pulled her forward.

Pressing body to body she wrapped her arms around Dev and hugged her wholeheartedly, letting herself indulge in a rare happiness. "It's good, Dev. It's very good."

Dev was aware of a pungent moment of delight. She returned the hug with enthusiasm, and then as Jess released her, she backed off so she could look at her face.

It was so nice to see that smile.

She felt like she could look at it for a long time and not get tired of seeing it. She smiled back and saw a distinct twinkle appear in Jess's pale eyes. She could sense a shift inside her, just a bit of settling that made her less of a stranger in a strange land and giving her a sense of belonging.

Strange and odd and endearing. The beginnings of a partnership in truth instead of just in a name.

Jess stood and held her hand out. "Let's go finish our pampering."

They moved into another chamber, this one with set of pipes in the ceiling. Jess waved her hand and a moment later they were drenched in cold water, making Dev inhale so sharply she nearly bit her tongue. "Yipes!" She got her hands up to protect her head just as the water turned off, and the sound of it was replaced by Jess's chuckling.

"Brr." Dev shook herself hard, spattering droplets from her body. "I didn't expect that!"

Jess started laughing. "It's supposed to be like that. You get hot, then you cool off." She regarded Dev, who was standing there next to her, dripping with cold seawater, drenched hair half in her eyes. She reached out and pushed the damp blonde locks back and watched an abashed grin appear.

So adorable.

Jess leaned forward and kissed her, tasting the saltwater on her lips. And she's all mine. She pulled back and lightly rubbed noses with Dev, then straightened up. "Okay, let's go dry off. Feel like getting your hair cut?"

Dev ran her hand through hers as she followed Jess through yet another hallway. "I don't know. In the crèche we just had to let the sets who were being trained for that work on us."

"Oh. That sounds like fun."

"Not really. There's not much programming for that they just have to figure it out."

"Oh."

"I don't really look that good with most of it shorn."

Jess put her arm around Dev and laughed. "Me either. But I don't have teaching to blame for it, we all got scalped for basic."

"Oh. Well."

"I'll show you pictures when we get home."

Chapter Twenty-six

"IS THIS LENGTH all right?" Jess glanced in the three part mirror in the tight alcove she was sitting in. Her hair tended to be unruly at the best of times. "Try and get it shorter here." She tugged the lengths near her ears, then leaned back and let the bio alt work, as she turned her attention back to Dev.

Dev was sitting quietly on a stool nearby, having finished with her turn under the scissors. Dressed in her fisherman's overalls and sweater, her burnished blonde hair neatly trimmed and layered, she was just so appealing to Jess's eyes it was hard to look away from her.

The overalls fit snugly around her slim form, and the sweater with its high collar framed her face neatly. The new cut seemed to lengthen her jaw a little and the light in the parlor they were in brought out the highlights in her hair and the intensity of the color of her eyes.

So damn cute. Jess watched her lift her head and meet her eyes, a grin appearing and compounding the adorable factor. She grinned back, idly wondering how Dev felt being here, being catered to by these other bio alts, who had fluttered around her so attentively.

Was it strange? Certainly Dev seemed relaxed, one boot hiked up on a brace of the stool, her elbow resting on her knee. She was watching the bio alt work on Jess, but every few seconds, her eyes would drift back to Jess's face, and that little twinkle would show, and damn it, she felt like melting into a puddle.

Weirdest ass feeling of her life. "What in the hell is wrong with me?"

"Ma'am?" The little bio alt snipping her hair paused and drew back. "Is it wrong?" She asked anxiously.

"Nah, fine. I'm just talking to myself." Jess waved her on, shifting a little in the chair. "G'wan."

The girl went back to her work. "Almost finished," she said, softly. "Soon, soon."

Soon, soon. Jess was getting restless, her instincts starting to drive her on from their hiding place and she had to force herself not to fidget when the old style, hammered scissors tickled her temple. Her mind started to shuffle through routes to the docks, wondering if they had any space at all to pick up anything else before they got off the island.

"Okay?" The bio alt asked, stepping back. "Good?"

Jess turned in the chair and studied her head, outlined in white lights. "What do you think, Dev?"

"I think you look beautiful," Dev responded straightforwardly. "Is that what you were asking?"

Jess blushed, the heat on her cheeks surprising her. She found she couldn't either meet her own eyes in the mirror, nor Dev's eyes in her reflection and so she just cleared her throat. "Something like that," she muttered. "Yeah, that's fine," she said, glancing at the bio alt. "It's good."

The girl looked relieved.

Dev regarded her reflection in the mirror thoughtfully, as she waited for Jess to get up from the low chair behind her. She rather liked the way the bio alt had trimmed her hair, neatly layering it back from her face and making it a bit shorter. It fell around the high collar of her sweater, and she found herself smiling a little as she watched the blush fade from Jess's cheeks.

She really was beautiful.

"Nice work," Jess said to the hair cutter. "Takes some talent to make this mop look like something."

Dev turned, watching the bio alt next to Jess blush and stammer. "It's very nice." She agreed. "I like it." Jess's long, dark hair was cut back off her face, the slight wave in it now framing her angular features and shortened to just past her shoulders.

Jess stood up and ran her fingers through her hair, then fished a chit from her pocket and handed it to the cutter. "Here. Go get you and your buddies a treat."

The cutter grinned, her hazel eyes lighting up as she tucked the chit away. "Agent." She bowed respectfully at Jess. "Tech, it was a great honor." She ducked her head at Dev. "Have a profitable day."

"We'll try." Jess put her hand on Dev's back and guided her toward a ramp leading to a large door. "I think we've wasted enough time to let the goons wander off. Let's try and get back to the boat."

"Okay." Dev willingly trailed along after her, fastening her jacket as the door slid open, bringing a gust of wet, cold air against them. They were let out into a small alleyway, which was lined with beautifully carved stone walls, stained with old green patches. "Did you want to say goodbye to your friend?"

Jess glanced at her. "Who? Oh, Charles you mean." She lifted a hand and let it drop. "He's not a friend. All he was doing was making sure I was out of the way for a while so the market didn't get messed up."

"I see."

Jess led the way to a small metal gate and paused, cocking her head and listening. Then she turned and lifted her hand to Dev's collar only to stop in mid motion.

"I took it off." Dev pulled her hand out of her pocket and displayed her insignia, then put it back in its hiding spot.

Jess patted her on the cheek, then she gently sorted Dev's newly cut hair. "I like this," she said. "What did you think of that place?"

Dev considered that briefly. "It was interesting."

"In a good or bad way?"

"I liked parts of it," Dev said, in a quiet voice. "Not the cold part so much."

Jess chuckled. "Sorry."

"The hot couch was nice, and the pool."

Jess in general agreed with that. Though she'd been known to plunge into the cold sea water under the citadel and never complained about it.

Jess went to the gate again, and cautiously examined the area. "Okay, now stick by me, Devvie. I've got a feeling we're not out of trouble yet." She eased the metal open and stepped down the stone stairwell to a lower alleyway that was equally empty and equally silent with Dev practically latched on to her coat. She felt more than a little conspicuous. A soft rumble of thunder sounded overhead, and she tugged her jacket neck a touch closer, very aware of the lack of weapons on her as the maze of stone passageways stretched out in front of them. She led the way down the aisle, her ears focused forward since the slot alleys were blind and she wasn't sure she wasn't going to be ambushed out here.

She knew if she continued down the ripples of lava lined with coral she would eventually get back to the market, but there was no easy way to run if a team came at them and it was easy to get lost in the maze.

She heard a buzz echo softly up to her, and slowed, coming to a crossroads and pausing before she went through it. She stood just shy of the opening, and went to tight focus, holding her hands out to stop Dev from passing her.

Dev had no intention of passing her, however. She tucked herself behind Jess and waited, watching in fascination as her partner's ears twitched and moved, the edges cupping a little as her eyes closed in concentration.

What was she listening to? Dev could hear the soft sound of voices down the way a little, but it was just a formless noise, without any distinguishing characteristics.

"Okay." Jess led them forward, through the crossroads and down a slanted pathway. "Careful." She indicated the path. "Gets slippery in the rain, and it's all downhill from here. You slide, you end up on your ass in the middle of the market."

"I see."

"Hope you don't," Jess said. "Not looking to be the life of the party this time around."

They neared the lower levels and the walls started to get wider. "Does that mean you experienced this ass thing?" Dev asked, as they went around a slight curve and could see the market below.

Jess cleared her throat. "Let's just say I'm glad I was undercover." She let her awareness sweep over the row they were exiting into, waiting to see if her senses picked up anything dangerous. Dangerous outside the obvious. But the row was clothing, not very exciting, and the straggle of people browsing didn't make her twitch.

She fastened her jacket up as the slight fog turned to a fine mist, blinking a little in reflex as the moisture impacted her eyeballs. The garment mostly covered her jumpsuit, and she attracted little attention as they moved through the stalls.

Dev looked at a stall as she passed, finding a booth full of colorful jumpsuits that had a soft plush lining to them. She slowed down and studied the nearest, imagining how it would feel to have that warmth next to her skin. "Ah."

Jess had gotten a few steps ahead, but apparently heard her soft grunt and stopped, turning to see what she was looking at, then retracing her path back. "Like those?" She glanced at the merchant, who was watching them with wary hopefulness. The jumpers were cute, not her style, but she could readily picture Dev's slight frame tucked into one.

She reached out and felt the sleeve, which was tough but soft to the touch. "What's this made of?" She asked the seller.

"Silk from topside," the man responded. "Inside's synth wool. Kelp mix."

Dev felt the garment, and gave the lining a wistful look. "It appears warm," she said. "Do you like this color?" She studied the fabric, which seemed to shimmer from red to purple as the light hit it.

"On you, absolutely." Jess removed a small, square piece of metal from her pocket and handed it to the vendor. "Wrap it up."

The man glanced at it, then at her. "Want to know the price?"

"No." Jess smiled faintly. "I don't."

"Wait." Dev held up her card. "What about this?"

"Put it away," Jess said in a quiet voice. "I'll explain later."

Obediently, Dev stuck the card back in her pocket, vaguely aware of discomfort she didn't quite know the source of.

The merchant touched his forehead and took the square, turning to put it into a battered old comp next to the back shelf. Then after it made a small booping sound, he handed it back to her. "Agent," he said. "Pleasure."

"All mine." Jess watched him fold the garment up and make a bundle of it, which he then handed to Dev with a slight bow. Then Jess clapped Dev on the back. "Let's go."

They got to the end of the row and turned right, going down the cross aisle until they reached the last row, the outer ring of the market that would bring them back to the docking area. Jess walked a little more slowly now, letting her senses extend out as they passed the ratty stalls at the shoreline, smaller and ruder, full of scroungers who were just trying to sell anything they found.

Hard life. Jess didn't pause at any of them. But not any harder than the seaweed harvesting that her family members did. She was just distracting Dev from seeing the seal skulls on sale when her warning senses tingled and she reacted instinctively, pulling Dev to one side and going flat against the wall between two stalls, half turning and putting her arms around her.

Dev found her view blocked but didn't mind. Jess's body blocked the misty rain, and it was nice to be pressed against her. "What's wrong?"

"Just hold still," Jess said, in a low mutter. "Some guys coming past us I don't want to see." She kept her back turned to the passing crowd, resting her head against Dev's as they regarded each other at close quarters. After a moment's pause, Jess ducked her head a little and they kissed.

It was like the whole damn island faded out for a minute. Jess felt her situational awareness slip, as her body reacted and Dev's hand slid up to gently touch her face. She literally forgot where she was, focusing intently on the tingle in her guts and how intoxicating it felt to hear the soft sound of passion that escaped her partner.

Then the wind picked up, and the surroundings faded back in and she lifted her head a little, rubbing noses with Dev as she gazed half lidded into her eyes. "Look behind me."

Dev shifted a little, and straightened enough to be able to see over Jess's shoulder.

"Anyone standing at those stalls, just browsing?"

Dev blinked a few times. "No. It's raining harder. People are going under shelter."

"No one sitting on a crate, just loitering?"

"No."

"Good." Jess leaned in and kissed her again, this time at least listening behind her. She heard only the faint scuff of seal hide boots and the low voices of the merchants, no hint of a government issued heel among them. "Okay," she finally said. "Let's move on."

"Do we have to?" Dev asked, in a straightforward way. "We have a covering over us."

Jess smiled. "Much as I'd love to just stand here and kiss you until dark, we need to get outta here. She casually put her arm over Dev's shoulders and made a natural turn to the left, her eyes flickering quickly over their surroundings but finding them as innocuous as Dev described them to be. With a faint sigh of relief, she started slowly down the path, keeping her arm around Dev.

She'd been damn sure she'd seen a pair of spooks. They'd popped into her peripheral vision a little behind them on the path, but now there was no sign of the bastards either before or behind them. Had she been mistaken?

Might have. Jess resisted the urge to reach up and rub her neck to ease the headache that had started to throb in her skull. She was looking forward to getting back on the boat, away from the island, and to the other side.

Just her and Dev for a while again.

Jess felt the slight jar through her boots and she paused, pulling Dev to a halt as well. She made a complete turn, then she started forward again, moving faster. "C'mon Devvie. Didn't like that noise."

"Was it a big boom?"

"Something like that." They reached the dock road and headed for their berth. The rain started coming down harder, almost seeming like it was chasing them as they moved quickly across the lava rock path.

Halfway across the dock, Jess felt the vibration under her feet again and she saw the chop in the harbor pick up. "Uh oh." She grabbed Dev's arm and sped up into a lope. "Move, move, move!"

Dev wasn't sure what was going on, but she heard the urgency in

Jess's voice and she picked up her pace, running next to Jess down the dock toward their boat just as the boom of footsteps behind them and a deep, rolling vibration rattled them both.

Jess risked a glance behind them as they reached the boat and she vaulted on board, snaking one foot out to kick the retaining clasp. The dock behind them was full of running figures, all heading for different boats as a long, low howl started to rise from the market.

"What is that?" Dev asked as she scrambled up the ladder to the control space.

"Warning." Jess ignored the stairs and jumped upward, grabbing the railing and pulling herself up and over it to trigger the hatch a hair before Dev got up to the top steps. She hauled ass inside and went to the comms unit, as Dev tossed her package onto the shelf near the door and slid into the captain's seat.

"Dock, dock," Jess barked into the comms.

Dev flipped the caps off the engine controls and started them, studying the readouts as she felt the rumble start underfoot. She scanned comp, reading the logs since they'd left. "The things arrived, Jess."

"Doesn't matter right now." Jess clicked the comms. "Dock!"

"Standby," the comms answered harshly. "All undock, standby for underway, release."

Dev felt the boat start to drift and she confirmed they were loose from the pier, as were lots of other boats around them. She could hear the alert going off louder now, and she sensed a vibration in the air that tickled her ears uncomfortably.

"Get us outta here, Dev. Get clear of the island north and go as far as you can without losing visual." Jess got away from the comms and headed for the door. "I'll secure the goodies. Try not to tilt up too much. I don't want to slide my ass into the water."

"Okay." Dev leaned forward a little as she started to take the engines online. "I would hate to be responsible for your ass getting wet," she added, as Jess left the room and headed down to the deck. "Except then you would probably take your clothes off, and that's always interesting."

She pointed the boat toward the entrance to the docks, trying hard to steer clear of the other boats doing likewise. It appeared everyone was trying hard to get away from the island but she had the advantage of bigger engines and she scooted the boat up to the front and headed for the gap.

A brief glance at the console showed her views of the back deck, and she spotted Jess working amongst the stacks of boxes that had appeared in the cleared area. She reassured herself that Jess was safe, then she focused on the route, giving the engines more power as she cleared the entrance and headed toward the two big gates.

The waves had come up and she fought the steering, trying to keep the bow on course as she felt the surge of the water. The rain was coming down even harder now. She heard a series of booms behind her and wondered if they were thunder.

It sounded too regular though, so she looked up at comp, searching for Jess and stopping in motion as she spotted a deep, black cloud rolling down from the island toward the water.

Toward them. Dev's eyebrows shot up, and she reacted instinctively, shoving the throttles to full forward and triggering the alarm for the deck. The boat dug through the water and picked up speed, coming up to plane just as they approached the gatehouse.

It was open, and the guards were nowhere in sight as she powered through, hearing the roar of engines behind her and then something else. It was a deep, uneven rumble, reminding her just a bit of the sound of the space shuttle's engines when it had landed her downside.

She didn't think it was a shuttle though. The gates flashed by her and she took the course Jess had told her to, north and as she curved that way, she saw other boats flashing by, and going the other direction.

A moment later the hatch burst open and Jess bounded inside, slamming the metal door behind her. "Son of a bitch!"

Dev evaluated the statement, and decided based on what she knew about the words, that it wasn't addressed to her. "Did you see that cloud."

"Did I see it?" Jess came into her field of vision, her skin smudged with black. "You got me out from under it just in time. Get to the outer buoy and slow down, then bring her around so we can see the show."

Dev had no idea what that meant. But she aimed for the buoy, the outer marker of the carefully drawn lanes and once they'd passed it she brought the nose around in a turn, facing back the way they'd come.

And then her jaw dropped in astonishment. The island was covered in a deep black cloud, and as she watched, it was bisected with a loud, sudden blast that shot debris far up into the air. "Oh!"

Jess came to stand next to her. "Look at that sucker go."

"What is that?" Dev asked, almost breathless. "It's amazing!"

"It's the volcano," Jess said. "Goes off sometimes. They never know when." She shook her head. "Hope they got everyone under cover. Let's get moving before that ejecta gets here." Jess pointed at the roiling cloud heading their way.

Dev gunned the engines and moved them into a turn, checking comp as she did so. "Jess? Should we move away from those too?"

Jess leaned over and saw what she was looking at. Three big boats were heading their way, making a beeline for them, and looking like the bad end of a piece of business. "Oh, yea," she said. "Finally figured out who I was, huh boys?"

"Are they bad?"

"Oh, yeah."

The cloud caught them, and Dev winced at the thunder of rattling crashes she heard all around her. "Wow."

"Faster."

"I don't think it goes any faster, Jess."

"Make it."

"Um."

"Or find someplace to hide us."

"THEY STILL THERE?" Jess stuck her head out of the hatch and felt the wind buffet her with startling impact. "Damn it." The three chasers were plowing through the mixed waves behind them, inching up closer from when she'd looked a minute or two before. "Dev, they're catching up to us."

Dev studied her console. The throttles were pushed as forward as they went. "The wind is too strong," she said. "It's making us slow."

"Yeah but they have the same problem."

"Not exactly," Dev said. "This vessel is higher than those are above the water."

"And?" Jess came to her side.

"It's a higher profile against the wind. More for it to push against."

Jess considered that, then made a face. "I don't see that changing anytime soon."

"No."

"Okay, let me get the guns out," Jess said. "Be right back."

Dev nodded, then she turned back to the controls, settling herself into the chair and searching the scan intently. There wasn't anything on the horizon for them to hide behind, and her portable comp showed very deep and very cold water beneath them.

The boat was performing as well as it could. It was a fishing boat, after all, and not something designed for running away from things. A glance at comp showed the three boats starting to split apart a little, two of them moving out and starting to aim on either side of them.

They would try to get around them, Dev thought, and maybe make them stop. She wished again that they were in the carrier, with its much greater abilities and she suspected probably Jess did as well. But the carrier was far behind them, so she had to find a way to make this thing work better.

Difficult, since she wasn't entirely sure of how it worked at all. The programming only went so far.

She went back to her scanner, setting it to search for obstructions. Then she curled her hands around the rudder controls and hunched forward a little, as though her posture could make the boat go faster. The waves were getting rougher, and she winced as the bow slammed into one, jarring her entire body.

Even her ears hurt. "Wow." Dev hoped Jess had been somewhere safe when that happened. She glanced in reflex at scan, but the back deck was empty. Frowning, she reset her scanner for internal and bio and relaxed a little once it showed Jess's wiremap in the common space.

Then she spotted a second wiremap in the hallway heading for her and her heart jumped into her throat as she scrambled for comms. "Jess! Someone is approaching you."

"Tac," Jess replied. "Secure."

Dev got up and went to the hatch, hesitating before she locked the wheel on it, shoving the metal bar Jess had left next to it into the mechanism. Then she bolted back to the controls and put her hands on them, giving a cursory glance at the waves as she focused on the scanner instead.

She could see Jess now in outline, the attitude on her body completely changed as she moved across the chamber and approached the inner door, the scanner picking up the weapons on her body and the big blaster she had in her hands. The other wiremap was approaching with equal caution, and...

"Tac." Dev triggered the comms. "Armed."

"Ack," Jess responded immediately. "Secure?"

"Ack." Dev confirmed. She wrenched her attention from scan and looked out at the water, noting a line of darker clouds on the horizon. It was already raining hard, but she reasoned maybe the storm front might afford some kind of distraction and she angled the bow slightly to the right and headed for it.

A quick look told her the other boats were now really gaining. She felt like she was being torn in pieces, one part of her demanding a tight focus on Jess, another part searching through the boat's controls to see if there was something she could do to speed it up.

It was uncomfortable. Dev watched anxiously as she saw Jess on scan take up a position behind the common room's table, then she saw the hatch opening and the intruder emerge. The scan picked up an energy flare then, and there was more motion than it could resolve.

Dev wanted to bolt for the door. Only the programming hammered into her kept her at the controls, and the knowledge that Jess knew far better how to handle the threat below than she had any hope to. She swept the console again, then focused on the small section that showed the condition of the big tanks as their readings were flashing.

Hm.

A shudder caught her attention, and she looked quickly outside to find the enemy boats even with them, and one of them shooting projectiles.

Oh, that was not good. She angled the rudders, sending the boat careening toward the boat shooting at them, feeling the stresses on her body as it listed over, blaster fire boiling the water just past her bow. She cut back in the other direction as the other boat moved to avoid them, wishing she had more speed to work with.

If only the boat were more agile. She paused, then her eyes tracked up to the console again. Without over thinking it too much she reached up and uncapped two switches, putting her fingers on them and then depressing them firmly.

At once, the boat nearly ripped itself out of her hands as she heard a rumbling sound that vibrated through the hull and nearly sent her vision blurry. The engines churned and she felt the boat buck under her as she tried to get it back under control.

On the bright side, the crazed motion made both sets of blasters misfire and the two chase boats closest to her peeled off, arcing around to try and come at them again. Dev didn't dare look at the scanner as she turned the boat in a tight circle, then powered the engines back up and put them into plane heading for the storm.

This time the boat surged forward with a good deal more speed, and rode higher on the waves, unburdened by the water in the fish tanks at the aft. The gauges showed them going faster, and after a few minutes, the other boats started to fall behind.

Dev made sure they were going to hold course, then she turned her attention to the scanner.

Both wire maps were gone. Her heart started pounding hard and she reset the scan, widening it out.

Nothing. She felt panic start to take her, and she got up from the chair, about to shut the engines down when she heard a knock at the hatch.

For a moment, she froze, then she responded to the drive of her programming and grabbed the scanner, tight focusing it and pointing it at the entrance, waiting for it to resolve.

"Hey. It's cold out here!" A voice penetrated the steel. "Open up!"

Dev put the scanner down and scooted over, pulling the bar out and working the latch. It popped open and Jess ducked inside, dripping wet and breathing hard.

She took a step back and cleared space, as Jess shut the door and leaned back against it, her face a little pale.

"Are you okay?" They both asked at the same time.

Jess smiled briefly. "Drive." She indicated the console.

Dev got back in the chair and put her hands back on the controls. "I let the water out of the animal tank," she said. "It seems to have made us faster."

"Oh." Jess trudged over and sat down on the stool next to her. "Is that what that was."

"Those other boats are behind us now," Dev said. "They were shooting at us. Trying to stop us I think."

"Yeah, they were," Jess said. "Not for the reason you'd think though." She flexed one hand, which now in the light showed dark bruises. "So you want the good news or the bad news?"

Dev eyed her doubtfully. "I don't know. The bad thing I guess, if we have to do something about it."

"Ah." Jess pushed her hood down and ruffled her hair. "Bad news is, I just offed one of the other side in a pretty ugly way."

"Oh."

"That's why those boats were chasing us," Jess said. "They were his buddies. Pain in the ass part is, I did it by accident. Boat tipped and I went flying into him and he went flying into the water outflow. Ripped him to pieces."

"Oh."

"Yeah. So that was a cock up. Didn't even get to ask him what he was looking for." Jess sighed. "On the other hand, he was about to blow my head off so I guess it worked out."

"You guess?"

Jess gave her a wry smile. "He was good. He was kicking my ass. I was flat on my back for too damn long after that last botched cluster." She rested her elbows on her thighs and rocked her head from side to side to loosen tense muscles there.

Dev glanced at scan, and sure enough the other boats were nothing more than a spot on the horizon, though they were still being chased. "I see. So what is the good part?"

Jess extended her hand and opened it. "Deck's full of black diamonds," she said.

Dev took the item and inspected it. A crystal the size of half her hand rested in her palm, glittering and reflecting the light in the control room inside it. "Wow. That is interesting. But why is it good?"

"It's good because I'm gonna have them cut something pretty from this one," Jess said. "And because we can use the rest to buy anything we want from those scientists. We're home free." She got up and stripped out of her drenched jacket, grimacing a little as it shed water everywhere. "So to speak."

Dev looked at the floor, then back at her. "I see."

"So that's the good thing." Jess came up next to her and leaned against the console, studying the view out the window. "Good idea to head for the storm line. Once we're up there, we'll see if we can find an ice field we can dodge around and maybe we'll lose 'em."

Dev put the pretty rock down and reached over to close her fingers around Jess's hand, feeling the chill in it. "Should you get dry?" she said. "It will be a while to get to the storm."

Jess straightened up and nodded. "Yeah and I need some kack. Want some?" She waited for Dev to nod, then stood up and patted her on the shoulder. "Good job, Dev. I wouldn't have thought to dump the water."

"Thank you."

Jess went to the back of the control area, where she'd stored their gear. She unsnapped the catches on her jumpsuit and stripped it down to her waist, picking up a piece of cloth from her pack and drying her skin with it. The rain hadn't penetrated the fabric, but the thunderous wash of tank water had, and she felt rubbed raw from the power of it.

Too damn close. She examined her shoulder, but it seemed to be healing and by some odd luck she hadn't taken any more serious damage to anything but her ego when by rights she should have been fish bait herself halfway down to the bottom by now.

She peeled off her jumpsuit and traded it for a dry one, very glad to get out of the half water filled boots she was squishing around in. It felt good to be dry, and the warmth of the control room was slowly seeping into her, their sojourn in the spa already just a half misty memory in her mind.

She went to the portable kack dispenser she'd brought up to the control room and started it brewing, resting her hands on the counter and listening to the drone of the engines. "They gaining on us?"

"No, it doesn't appear so."

"Good." Jess considered their options. They would have to lose the chase boats before she could even think about turning east, maybe in the ice pack. She'd make them think she was on a run home, and then maybe—

"Jess?" Dev called softly. "We're being hailed."

Jess rolled her eyes and walked over. "Assholes think we're going to answer? Give me a break."

"It's not them." Dev handed her the ear cup. "It's Base Ten. It's being relayed through the carrier."

Jess felt a shock jerk through her. She fumbled with the cup and got it set in her ear, then touched the receive node. "Copy. Copy Tac Base Ten?"

"Ops," the voice answered. "Recall. Urgent. Ack."

Jess blinked. "Repeat?"

The voice returned, with an edge. "Ack. Recall urgent. Copy acknowledge. Code twelve."

"Acknowledge, in work," Jess said, then she released the trigger. "Shit." She looked at Dev. "Something bad must have happened. They're recalling us." She removed the ear cup and handed it back. "Plot a course back to that iceberg, Dev. Looks like this mission's scrubbed."

That, at least was easy. Dev pulled the coordinates off her comp and plugged them in, not sure whether she should be disappointed or relieved.

Disappointed, she supposed, for not being able to finish the mission, but also relieved that with the enemy already chasing them that they would not get into more trouble trying to get into the enemy lab. There seemed to be a lot of opportunity for discomfort in that, and she didn't want to see Jess getting hurt.

Jess set a cup down for her and took her seat on the stool again. "So."

"What do you think happened?" Dev asked.

"No idea," Jess said. "Never been recalled like that before. I just know the codes." She cradled her cup between her hands and took a sip from it. "Now I wish we weren't so far. Bain wouldn't have pulled us for something trivial. When we get back to the carrier, you can do an encrypted session and maybe we'll find out what's going on."

The light was fading outside, and the rain was falling harder. Dev propped her scanner up and set it to probe their path, then she took a moment to take a drink from the cup, wishing they'd stopped for a day meal while they were on the island. "Okay, I'll remember to do that," she said. "But it's going to take a long time to get there."

Jess sighed. "I know." She put her cup down and got up. "Nothing we can do about that unless we pass those pirates again and steal their carrier." She rooted in the carry sack and pulled out some fish packets, bringing them back to the console and plopping them down. "Damn it."

Dev reviewed the rear scanner, noting the ships were still chasing them. But their speed now was enough to keep them ahead, and as they plowed into the increasing swells, she hoped it would stay that way.

So now things were changing again. The big question was, were they running away from trouble, or running to more of it?

To be continued...

OTHER MELISSA GOOD TITLES

Tropical Storm

From bestselling author Melissa Good comes a tale of heartache, longing, family strife, lust for love, and redemption. *Tropical Storm* took the lesbian reading world by storm when it was first written...now read this exciting revised "author's cut" edition.

Dar Roberts, corporate raider for a multi-national tech company is cold, practical, and merciless. She does her job with a razor-sharp accuracy. Friends are a luxury she cannot allow herself, and love is something she knows she'll never attain.

Kerry Stuart left Michigan for Florida in an attempt to get away from her domineering politician father and the constraints of the overly conservative life her family forced upon her. After college she worked her way into supervision at a small tech company, only to have it taken over by Dar Roberts' organization. Her association with Dar begins in disbelief, hatred, and disappointment, but when Dar unexpectedly hires Kerry as her work assistant, the dynamics of their relationship change. Over time, a bond begins to form.

But can Dar overcome years of habit and conditioning to open herself up to the uncertainty of love? And will Kerry escape from the clutches of her powerful father in order to live a better life?

ISBN 978-1-932300-60-4

Hurricane Watch

In this sequel to *Tropical Storm,* Dar and Kerry are back and making their relationship permanent. But an ambitious new colleague threatens to divide them—and out them. He wants Dar's head and her job, and he's willing to use Kerry to do it. Can their home life survive the office power play?

Dar and Kerry are redefining themselves and their priorities to build a life and a family together. But with the scheming colleagues and old flames trying to drive them apart and bring them down, the two women must overcome fear, prejudice, and their own pasts to protect the company and each other. Does their relationship have enough trust to survive the storm?

Enter the lives of two captivating characters and their world that Melissa Good's thousands of fans already know and love. Your heart will be touched by the poignant realism of the story. Your senses and emotions will be electrified by the intensity of their problems. You will care about these characters before you get very far into the story.

ISBN 978-1-935053-00

Eye of the Storm

Eye of the Storm picks up the story of Dar Roberts and Kerry Stuart a few months after *Hurricane Watch* ends. At first it looks like they are settling into their lives together but, as readers of this series have learned, life is never simple around Dar and Kerry. Surrounded by endless corporate intrigue, Dar experiences personal discoveries that force her to deal with issues that she had buried long ago and Kerry finally faces the consequences of her own actions. As always, they help each other through these personal challenges that, in the end, strengthen them as individuals and as a couple.

ISBN 978-1-932300-13-0

Red Sky At Morning

A connection others don't understand...

A love that won't be denied...

Danger they can sense but cannot see...

Dar Roberts was always ruthless and single-minded...until she met Kerry Stuart.

Kerry was oppressed by her family's wealth and politics. But Dar saved her from that.

Now new dangers confront them from all sides. While traveling to Chicago, Kerry's plane is struck by lightning. Dar, in New York for a stockholders' meeting, senses Kerry is in trouble. They simultaneously experience feelings that are new, sensations that both are reluctant to admit when they are finally back together. Back in Miami, a cover-up of the worst kind, problems with the military, and unexpected betrayals will cause more danger. Can Kerry help as Dar has to examine her life and loyalties and call into question all she's believed in since childhood? Will their relationship deepen through it all? Or will it be destroyed?

ISBN 978-1-932300-80-2

Thicker Than Water

This fifth entry in the continuing saga of Dar Roberts and Kerry Stuart starts off with Kerry involved in mentoring a church group of girls. Kerry is forced to acknowledge her own feelings toward and experiences with her parents as she and Dar assist a teenager from the group who gets jailed because her parents tossed her out onto the streets when they found out she is gay. While trying to help the teenagers adjust to real world situations, Kerry gets a call concerning her father's health. Kerry flies to her family's side as her father dies, putting the family in crisis. Caught up in an international problem, Dar abandons the issue to go to Michigan, determined to support Kerry in the face of grief and hatred. Dar and Kerry face down Kerry's extended family with a little help from their own, and return home, where they decide to leave work and the world behind for a while for some time to themselves.

ISBN 978-1-932300-24-6

Terrors of the High Seas

After the stress of a long Navy project and Kerry's father's death, Dar and Kerry decide to take their first long vacation together. A cruise in the eastern Caribbean is just the nice, peaceful time they need—until they get involved in a family feud, an old murder, and come face to face with pirates as their vacation turns into a race to find the key to a decades old puzzle.

ISBN 978-1-932300-45-1

Tropical Convergence

There's trouble on the horizon for ILS when a rival challenges them head on, and their best weapons, Dar and Kerry, are distracted by life instead of focusing on the business. Add to that an old flame, and an aggressive entreprenaur throwing down the gauntlet and Dar at least is ready to throw in the towel. Is Kerry ready to follow suit, or will she decide to step out from behind Dar's shadow and step up to the challenges they both face?

ISBN 978-1-935053-18-7

Stormy Waters

As Kerry begins work on the cruise ship project, Dar is attempting to produce a program to stop the hackers she has been chasing through cyberspace. When it appears that one of their cruise ship project rivals is behind the attempts to gain access to their system, things get more stressful than ever. Add in an unrelenting reporter who stalks them for her own agenda, an employee who is being paid to steal data for a competitor, and Army intelligence becoming involved and Dar and Kerry feel more off balance than ever. As the situation heats up, they consider again whether they want to stay with ILS or strike out on their own, but they know they must first finish the ship project.

ISBN 978-1-61929-082-2

Storm Surge

It's fall. Dar and Kerry are traveling—Dar overseas to clinch a deal with their new ship owner partners in England, and Kerry on a reluctant visit home for her high school reunion. In the midst of corporate deals and personal conflict, their world goes unexpectedly out of control when an early morning spurt of unusual alarms turns out to be the beginning of a shocking nightmare neither expected. Can they win the race against time to save their company and themselves?

Book One: ISBN 978-1-935053-28-6
Book Two: ISBN 978-1-935053-39-2

Othe titles you might enjoy:

Faultless

by Cleo Dare

How can enforced R&R turn so quickly into disaster? No sooner does Captain Dani Forrest try to relax at a desert resort than a murder takes place and reports are received that an entire village has been wiped out. Buxom, blonde and alluring mythologist Lindie Davis tries to keep matters in perspective for Dani through the telling of ancient hero tales but Dani's guilt over the recent suicide of her friend and fellow Minority Fleet Captain Sherri Wilmstead only escalates. Meanwhile, an entire rift valley is shaken by more than a natural earthquake and Dani must find out, before it is too late, who is at fault.

ISBN 978-1-61929-064-8

Universal Guardians: The Royal Descendant

by Michele Coffman

After the tragic death of her mother when she was eleven, Casey Malanight finds herself parentless, and left in the care of her grandmother and the house staff at the Malanight Castle. Raised with much love and guidance, she grows into a strong attractive woman, with a good heart and an intelligent mind. Able to choose any path that she wants, Casey finds her soul drawn toward a role as a protector, in the form of a police detective for the New York City Police Department. However, everything is not as it seems.

Elizabeth Malanight, a strong independent woman who has made many difficult decisions throughout her life, finds herself faced with the most challenging one yet...her Granddaughter Casey must die, and she must be the one who sees it through.

Casey quickly discovers that everything about her life is a lie. A fabrication designed to hide, not just the truth involving her life, but her Human heritage as well. Not only is there life out there, but she is more connected to it than she knows.

This is a unique sci-fi story shown through the eyes of the Malanight family. Their mission is to guard Earth from species millions of light-years away.

Take a journey around the cosmos in an adventure that will leave you wondering, if there really is life out there.?

ISBN 968-1-61929-074-7

OTHER REGAL CREST PUBLICATIONS

Brenda Adcock	Pipeline	978-1-932300-64-2
Brenda Adcock	Redress of Grievances	978-1-932300-86-4
Brenda Adcock	Tunnel Vision	978-1-935053-19-4
Brenda Adcock	The Chameleon	978-1-61929-102-7
Sharon G. Clark	Into the Mist	978-1-935053-34-7
Michele Coffman	Veiled Conspiracy	978-1-935053-38-5
Blayne Cooper	Cobb Island	978-1-932300-67-3
Blayne Cooper	Echoes From The Mist	978-1-932300-68-0
Cleo Dare	Cognate	978-1-935053-25-5
Cleo Dare	Faultless	978-1-61929-064-8
Cleo Dare	Hanging Offense	978-1-935053-11-8
Lori L. Lake	A Very Public Eye	978-1-61929-076-1
Lori L. Lake	Buyer's Remorse	978-1-61929-001-3
Lori L. Lake	Gun Shy	978-1-932300-56-7
Lori L. Lake	Have Gun We'll Travel	1-932300-33-3
Lori L. Lake	Jump the Gun	978-1-935053-50-7
Lori L. Lake	Under the Gun	978-1-932300-57-4
Helen M. Macpherson	Colder Than Ice	1-932300-29-5
Linda Morganstein	Harpies' Feast	978-1-935053-43-9
Linda Morganstein	On A Silver Platter	978-1-935053-51-4
Linda Morganstein	Ordinary Furies	978-1-935053-47-7
Andi Marquette	Land of Entrapment	978-1-935053-02-6
Andi Marquette	State of Denial	978-1-935053-09-5
Andi Marquette	The Ties That Bind	978-1-935053-23-1
Kate McLachlan	Hearts, Dead and Alive	978-1-61929-017-4
Kate McLachlan	Rescue At Inspiration Point	978-1-61929-005-1
Kate McLachlan	Rip Van Dyke	978-1-935053-29-3
Keith Pyeatt	Struck	978-1-935053-17-0
Rick R. Reed	Deadly Vision	978-1-932300-96-3
Rick R. Reed	IM	978-1-932300-79-6
Rick R. Reed	In the Blood	978-1-932300-90-1
Damian Serbu	Secrets In the Attic	978-1-935053-33-0
Damian Serbu	The Vampire's Angel	978-1-935053-22-4
Damian Serbu	The Vampire's Quest	978-1-61929-013-6
Damian Serbu	The Vampire's Witch	978-1-61929-104-1
S. Y. Thompson	Now You See Me	978-1-61929-112-6
Mary Vermillion	Death By Discount	978-1-61929-047-1
Mary Vermillion	Murder By Mascot	978-1-61929-048-8
Mary Vermillion	Seminal Murder	978-1-61929-049-5

About the author

Melissa Good is an IT professional and network engineer who works and lives in South Florida with a skillion lizards and Mocha the dog.

VISIT US ONLINE AT
www.regalcrest.biz

At the Regal Crest Website You'll Find

- The latest news about forthcoming titles and new releases
- Our complete backlist of romance, mystery, thriller and adventure titles
- Information about your favorite authors
- Current bestsellers
- Media tearsheets to print and take with you when you shop
- Which books are also available as eBooks.

Regal Crest print titles are available from all progressive booksellers including numerous sources online. Our distributors are Bella Distribution and Ingram.

CPSIA information can be obtained at www.ICGtesting.com
Printed in the USA
BVOW07s1904161213

339295BV00005B/476/P